SOHO NOIR

SERIES ONE

T.S. HUNTER

- TAINTED LOVE •
- WHO'S THAT GIRL? •
- CARELESS WHISPER •
- CRAZY FOR YOU •
- KILLER QUEEN •
- SMALLTOWN BOY •

RED DOG

Published by RED DOG PRESS 2019

Edited by Eleanor Abraham

ISBN 978-1-913331-28-3

www.reddogpress.co.uk

For all those who came before, who fought for us to have what we have now.

For all those who marched, shouted, suffered, and loved so that we could be just a little more free.

For the friends and allies loved and lost along the way.

For everyone who ever hesitated to love, to hold, to kiss.

For those who lived on the edges, who didn't conform.

And for everyone who stood up for their rights and ours, in the face of huge adversity and resistance.

Thank you.

TAINTED LOVE

SOHO NOIR #1

1.

SOHO, LONDON. 1985.

THE DANK WINTERY STREETS outside were a distant memory now. Tonight, this hot, sweaty, neon-lit club was Joe's whole universe. Music pulsed through his body like a brand new heartbeat. London was already changing him.

Sweat sticking his T-shirt to his ribs, arms raised high above his head, grinning wildly, hips pumping to Frankie's repetitive call to "Relax". Joe hardly recognised himself and he was happier than he'd ever been.

It had been a night of Bronski Beat, Sister Sledge, Culture Club and Madonna—the kind of upbeat pop Joe usually hated. He was into more brooding, melancholic stuff—*miserable shite*, according to his friend Chris—and yet these pulsing, happy beats felt like they defined him right now. The new him. His new start.

This whole weekend had been like none Joe had ever known. He'd always been the quiet one, never even daring to come down to London on his own. Not confident enough to admit who he really was. This year was different already.

His oldest friend from school, Chris Sexton, had called him out of the blue to invite Joe to join him in London for a long weekend. "A friend is having a party," he'd said. "It's going to be wild. You should come."

Chris had been the only person Joe had stayed in touch with from his school days. His first and only love, though he knew that particular accolade was one-sided, and Joe had long since given up hope of anything happening between them, even if he was still—and always would be—a little besotted with Chris.

Chris wasn't the kind of guy who went around falling in love, though. Handsome, confident, reckless, funny and the bravest man Joe knew—

Chris had left a trail of broken hearts behind him of those who'd fallen for him before they realised he'd never settle down.

So Joe and Chris had stayed friends, meeting up less frequently now that they had both left their respective universities, and Joe had secured a boring but well-paid job with the council back in their old home town.

Chris, on the other hand, had moved to London seven years ago to study fashion at St Martin's College. Two fingers up to his father, who'd wanted him to join the family accountancy firm. Maybe he'd go back to it when he'd settled down a bit. Though there was no sign of that happening any time soon.

After college, Chris had hooked himself up in a partnership with a couple of other young designers, and had been making a name for himself on the fashion scene ever since.

He was renting a flat in the heart of Soho and seemed to have a wide circle of friends of all shapes and ages. Joe wished he had Chris's life. Or his talent. Or his looks. Any one of those would do.

Joe laughed as his friend bounced across the floor in a series of typically ostentatious dance moves, deliberately bumping into a tall, skinny, blonde guy—exactly Chris's type—and planting a sly kiss on his cheek before sashaying away again. *Oh, for that confidence.*

Joe hadn't even come out to his family yet. In fact, Chris was the only person he'd ever confided in, though he was sure others knew.

His oldest sister suspected. She'd asked him outright once, but he'd just changed the subject. It was none of her business. She was like the mirror of their mother. She wouldn't understand. She would just worry.

All of that felt a lifetime away right now. Here in this club, Joe had found his spiritual home. This was living. This was who he really was. "Like a Virgin" by Madonna blasted out of the speakers, bodies bounced and writhed together—very few of them anything remotely like a virgin.

Joe leaned back against the bar, his sweaty T-shirt clinging to his skin where it pressed against the cold railing. The bass throbbed through his body, vibrating his core. He'd never danced like he had tonight.

He didn't even need Chris at his side, egging him on, and telling him not to worry about what people thought. He'd been right to come down to London. He should listen to his friend more often.

There was work for him here, surely. He didn't need the security, or oppression, of home any more. Chris had promised to help find him something, if he wanted to stay. Right now, he could think of nothing better.

Chris sauntered up and grabbed him by the arm, dragging him back towards the middle of the dance floor.

"I can't," Joe protested half-heartedly. "I need a break. I need a drink."

He didn't need any more to drink at all, he was already stumbling as Chris led him across the heaving floor.

The young French guys he'd been dancing with earlier caught his eye.

The sexy one was called Luc, but Joe couldn't remember the other guy's name. Something with a G. It didn't matter, "Mate" would do. He'd pretty much ignored Joe all night anyway, spending most of it leaning against the bar looking sultry.

Luc, on the other hand, had been flirting with Joe all night. And Joe wasn't really sure how to handle it. No one had ever hit on him before. Sure enough, Luc touched Joe's waist as he passed, and the look he gave him made Joe's stomach do somersaults. Joe let his own hand rest on Luc's for a moment. Holding back long enough for Luc to whisper in his ear.

"Come dance with me."

His breath smelled of beer and cigarettes. His accent was amazing. His lips close enough to kiss. And Joe knew he could, but still he hesitated. Apart from Chris, he'd never kissed anyone. Not like that. And that had only been the one time.

Chris always joked that just one kiss from him had spoiled Joe for other men. He may have been right once, but Joe had moved on. And no one—not even Chris—had ever looked at him the way Luc just had. For the first time in their friendship, Joe suddenly wanted Chris to just disappear.

"I'll be back," Joe called to Luc, as Chris dragged him on through the throng of dancers. Luc smiled as gyrating bodies closed the space between them. A squeal rose above the beat, and Joe turned to see Chris planting a full kiss on the lips of a tall woman in a tight red sequined dress which framed her stunning figure.

"Get off, you bugger! You'll smear my lippy."

Liverpudlian accent. Cheekbones to die for. Nails like knife blades. Red wig piled high, with a little curl teased down each temple. Six foot something in heels, and eye shadow that made Cindy Lauper look like she wasn't even trying.

The sequins glistened in the disco lights, making her look like she was made of glitter.

Up close, Joe could see make-up caking around a tiny missed patch of stubble. Barely noticeable, and it took nothing away from the overall effect. He was dumbstruck. *You're not in Kansas now.*

"Patty, darling," Chris gushed. "You look fabulous."

"All thanks to my gorgeous designer," Patty replied, eyes darting to Chris's hand, still clutching Joe's. The briefest frown, gone in an instant.

"Well hello, handsome," Patty smiled, red-nailed finger touching Joe's cheek. "Who've we got here?"

"Patty, this is Joe," said Chris. "The old school friend I told you about. He promised to come for the party. And here he is."

It almost broke Joe's heart that Chris seemed so happy to show him off to his friends. Joe had always thought he was the boring one, but Chris was nothing if not fiercely loyal.

"*This* is your school friend?" asked Patty incredulously. "God! I wish I'd gone to *your* school."

An over-dramatic eye roll had Chris laughing. Joe froze as Patty leaned in and kissed him on both cheeks. The smell of perfume and cigarettes, make-up and talc wafting around him.

"Enchanté," she purred. "God, he's so cute!"

Joe felt himself blushing. It would take a bit of getting used to, this new world he'd found himself in.

"You ready for the show then?" Patty asked.

"Wouldn't miss it for the world," Chris replied.

"Well come backstage and help me sort out this fucking corset, will you? It's tighter than my Nan's purse," Patty hissed, lips pouted. "You can come watch, if you want."

Joe wasn't sure that he did want. The song had changed to "Tainted Love". And all he wanted to do was find Luc.

JOE LEANED AGAINST the bar, out of breath and laughing. He felt euphoric. Luc was in the scrum, trying to get them both another drink.

Joe wasn't sure he had the energy to keep dancing like they had been for the last hour.

He was glad he'd overruled Chris on his outfit for the night. Not twelve hours earlier, the two of them had been crammed into Chris's small bedroom, with Joe awkwardly parading himself in one of Chris's new designs.

A brightly coloured suit, all big shoulders and sharp angles. It couldn't have been further from Joe's style if it had been a dress. He'd told Chris the suit was wonderful—it was—but Joe would never be able to carry it off.

He'd agreed to let his friend take a few snaps of him wearing it, for his collection, though he was sure they would only laugh at those images in years to come.

The afternoon had been one of the most relaxed, happy times they'd spent together since they were about thirteen. They had talked about life, about the future, being gay in the city, Chris's new friends. It felt like they had just rolled the years back to when they were two young boys, chatting about their hopes and dreams.

Chris had told him that the business was getting stronger and stronger. They'd signed a couple of celebrity clients and the new line was looking great, although his business partner wasn't so sure. Chris didn't care. The clients liked it and he'd worked really hard on it. He was sure it would see him hit the big time. Chris seemed so content in his new life here, and Joe envied him for it.

"You should move down here," Chris had insisted. "Come on, it'll be fun!"

Joe was sure it would be.

"What would I do for money?"

"You could come and work with me," Chris had enthused.

"I don't know anything about fashion."

"So what? Neither does my business partner, and it hasn't stopped him. Besides, you could answer phones or something. We could always do with a pretty receptionist."

That was Chris all over, as enthusiastic as a puppy, as practical as a chocolate teapot. He just wanted everyone to be happy and Joe loved him for it, even if he had just disregarded three years of a psychology degree and a decent enough job in social services.

As "Girls Just Wanna Have Fun" took over the speakers, Joe scanned the room, half-looking for Chris, but mostly taking in the strange mix of people: trendies and trannies, artists and arseholes.

Even the handful of self-conscious, floppy-haired New Romantics didn't look too far out of place, lounging on the raised sofas in the corner, scowling their disdain at the surrounding revellers. The club was a proper melting pot, and Joe was loving the easy anonymity of it all.

He looked over at Luc, who had reached the front of the bar queue, leaning in to get the barman's attention. His dark hair was a pile of soft curls with closely shaved sides. His pale brown eyes were almost golden and they danced when he spoke. Luc glanced over, caught Joe staring and winked. Joe's stomach did a flip. He was totally smitten already.

Luc turned his attention back to the bar, just as the barman began serving a tough-looking girl with pink tips to her bleach-blonde hair. Luc looked back at Joe and shrugged. Joe smiled.

"I'm going to the loo," Joe mouthed at him, pointing to the dark corner at the back of the club where the toilets were. Luc nodded.

Joe weaved his way through the crowd, smiling at the strange collection of dancers, not minding that they bumped and jostled him as he passed. Sticky floors and sticky skin. A slice of a strange new heaven.

He caught a glimpse of Chris, standing beside a concrete pillar with his back to the room, and headed over. He was about to pounce on him when he realised that Chris was not alone.

In the dark recess behind the pillar was an older man: heavy-set, broad-shouldered, tough-looking, with a black trilby hat pulled low over his eyes, and the collar of his thick, dark coat up, covering his chin. He must be boiling in here. Joe could tell by his body language that he was not happy with Chris.

Chris looked at the floor, cowed by this stranger. Joe took a few steps closer. The music was too loud to hear what the man was saying. Was Chris in some kind of trouble? Should he help?

He watched the man's fat finger pointing close to Chris's face, his other hand gripping Chris's wrist tightly. A warning, harshly issued. Chris looked as though he was trying to protest, but the man gave him one final word and Chris nodded a subdued, reluctant agreement.

The man bumped Chris's shoulder as he stalked off, parting a way through the crowded floor and pushing through a set of doors marked "private—staff only". Chris didn't move for a moment. His shoulders raised and slumped in a big sigh and he shook his head.

Joe slipped away quickly into the darker corridor leading towards the toilets. He didn't want Chris to know he'd seen the exchange. He'd only be more upset. Chris liked to maintain his reputation as a cool, controlled guy and he hated anyone seeing the cracks.

Joe glanced back and saw Chris coming right towards him. He ducked into the toilets quickly. Perhaps he'd catch Chris in there and make sure he was alright without letting him know he'd seen anything.

Inside, he kept his eye on the mirrors; watching the door as he stood at the urinal, but Chris didn't appear. Joe finished, washed his hands and splashed some cool water on his face, drying himself ineffectually with the bottom of his T-shirt, before pushing back through the door into the corridor.

"I can't believe you're doing this! You're such an arsehole."

Joe stopped in front of the door just as it swung shut. The voice was Patty's. Cracking with emotion. Angry and upset. Joe peered into the gloom at the end of the corridor, far from the bustle of the club, and saw Chris and Patty, face to face, mid-argument.

Chris muttered something urgent and placatory. It didn't work. Patty was trembling with rage.

"You promised, Chris."

"I know," Chris said, his voice tight, tense. "I'm sorry."

Patty raised a hand to slap him but Chris caught it. Patty's shoulders slumped, the personality stripped bare. With the glamour and vitality suddenly gone, Joe saw Patty now as nothing more than a nervous young man in a flamboyant outfit, not sure if he could carry it off.

"You just do whatever you want, all the time, and you don't care who you hurt."

"That's not fair," Chris snapped.

"It's true."

Joe tucked himself in against the wall, close enough to hear, but far enough away to remain discreet.

"You'll be great," Chris said, holding both Patty's hands in his. Even from this distance, Joe could see the tears welling in Patty's eyes.

"Oh, just fuck off, Chris," she snapped. "I could kill you sometimes."

The sound of the dressing room door slamming echoed up the corridor. Chris punched the wall with the side of his fist, swearing at the closed door.

Joe hurried back into the club before Chris could turn around and find him there. Whatever was going on with his friend, he was sure Chris wouldn't want him to know about either of the conversations he'd just witnessed.

CHRIS SHRUGGED OFF his annoyance, took a deep breath and headed back towards the dance floor. He still needed to find Joe and let him know he was leaving the club.

He lifted himself up to a small platform beside the bar to get a better view of the club floor, and finally spotted Joe in a dark corner, wrapped around Luc. He allowed himself a grin. It was good to see his old friend relaxing a bit. He'd missed having him around. Joe was the only link to his old life that Chris still enjoyed, and the only real friend he'd ever had.

He didn't feel too bad about ducking out early on their night out. Joe would be fine with his little Frenchman. Luc was a nice guy. Chris should know, he'd spent most of last week getting to know Luc's friend, Gabriel. And they'd had a lot of fun.

Besides, Chris hoped that a little fling with Luc would mean Joe would stop giving him those puppy-dog eyes. It was very sweet, but he didn't fancy Joe, and he never had. He loved him, but he didn't fancy him. He touched Joe's shoulder, not wanting to interrupt.

"I've got to head out for a bit," Chris whispered into his ear—the one that didn't have a hot Frenchman's tongue in it. "Don't do anything I wouldn't do."

"Where are you going?" Joe asked, frowning. Luc looked up and smiled at Chris before turning his attention back to Joe's neck.

"Something's come up. I need to go. I'll see you back at mine later."

He planted a kiss on Joe's cheek and pressed a door key into his hand.

"Don't wait up," Chris said, turning his back on Joe and Luc and twisting his way through the heaving dance floor before his friend could ask any more questions.

He hadn't lied, specifically. He definitely needed to get out of that club. Chris had learned the hard way that Tony Lagorio wasn't the kind of guy who took no for an answer. The Lizard, as he was known, was ruthless at the best of times, and Chris had just been given a very clear ultimatum. Unfortunately, it wasn't one he was able to deliver on yet. He had stuff to do, and quickly.

As he left the dance floor, Patty walked out onto the stage, beginning a smouldering rendition of "Fever" to cheers and whistles. Chris turned back, put his fingers at the sides of his mouth and issued a piercing wolf-whistle of his own to encourage her.

He knew the song had been chosen with him in mind, and he felt bad leaving now, but if he didn't, Patty would only insist on coming with him later, and he couldn't have that.

Patty—Paul as Chris knew him better—would forgive him, eventually, for walking out during her first ever public drag performance.

Chris burst through the club doors and the cold night air hit him like a wall. His thin jacket might have been stylish, but it was less than useless against the freezing drizzle. His breath fogged in front of him.

More out of habit than desire, he pulled a cigarette from the scrunched up pack in his pocket and cupped his hand around the end, protecting the flame as he lit up. The doors swung closed behind him, shutting out the sound of Patty's warbling.

The street was quiet. It was already late. Pink and red neon lights offering girls, sex and fun reflected off the oily, damp pavement. Chris blew out a thin line of smoke and shivered. He set off towards the all-night café on the corner. A strong coffee would clear his head, and he definitely needed a clear head tonight.

The café had large single-pane windows, looking out over the street. A couple of girls—punks in pink and black—sat at a table by the window, staring at him as he walked in, expressions barely shifting as he smiled at them. He turned his back on them and then blew a quick kiss over his shoulder. *Cheer up, love.* He grinned, but their aggressive snarls remained fixed.

He ordered a coffee to take away, loaded it with a couple of sachets of sugar, and topped it up with milk from an old jug by the till. Chris took another drag of his cigarette and stubbed it out in the ashtray on the counter. He blew on his coffee, took a sip, and headed for the door.

As he hit the road again, a dark car pulled up alongside him. He kept his head down and kept walking. He didn't have time for weirdos trying to pick him up. Not tonight. The car edged forward again, stopping just in front of him. The passenger door swung open. Chris bent down to tell the driver where to go.

"Oh, it's you," he said. "What do you want?"

"Get in. We need to talk."

He did.

2.

JOE FLOATED THROUGH the streets on his own little cloud of pure satisfaction. The hour before dawn in Soho was a strange time indeed. A pair of tired-looking prostitutes, still holding out hope for a last, late punter, cat-called to him, offering a good deal. *Not my type, love.*

He reached up to slap a street sign as he turned the corner into the square opposite Chris's flat, chirping a cheerful "alright?" as he dodged a council worker pushing a dustcart along the pavement. He got a sullen "piss off" in reply.

Joe grinned, shrugging. Nothing could shake his mood right now. Not a grumpy bugger in a miserable job. Not the icy morning air. Not even the fact that he'd spent most of his money for the weekend on one night out. *But what a night!*

His T-shirt was still damp under the jacket he'd borrowed from Luc, his sweat long since turned cold. His head buzzed with snatches of remembered conversation and his lips were swollen and tingling, the skin on his chin raw from stubble-burn. He had never kissed, or been kissed, like that before.

He and Luc had hung out together all night, moving on from the club to a little Italian coffee place on Frith Street which seemed to be open all hours—*Bar Italia.* It sounded so exotic and sophisticated, and in its own way, it was. Red and white formica tables, huge, gleaming silver machines spurting out delicious smelling coffee and whistling blasts of steam. A giant black-and-white poster of Rocky Marciano, gloved hands raised, about to unleash his might on a punchball.

The place had a vibrant energy far different to the club, but, like so much of Soho, everyone seemed welcome and the noise levels were high. They had perched in a corner, Joe and Luc, talking, laughing, and flirting as their coffees went cold.

Afterwards, they had gone back to the grotty little hotel Luc was staying in. There was still no sign of Luc's friend, and they had fallen straight into bed, tearing each other's clothes off, mouths locked, hearts pounding. Finally, he'd left Luc sleeping, with a scrawled note on the bedside table giving him Chris's address and an invitation to come find them later. He hoped he would.

Despite the early hour, there were a few people out—late night revellers, early starters, lost wanderers. They all shared the same pavements if not the same mood. A light frost glistened on the paving stones, reflecting the flickering signs from the sex shops which lurked behind every other doorway. Strings of fairy lights—leftover from Christmas—hung from lamp posts and gave the street an oddly innocent, magical feel.

Soho had a particular smell, he'd noticed—damp and slightly stale, coffee brewing, food frying, beer, cigarettes, old buildings breathing. He loved it. It made him feel alive. Such a stark difference to the quiet little town where he and Chris had grown up.

Joe realised it was the first time he'd thought about Chris for hours. He wondered whether he'd be back yet—he'd said he'd be home later, but now dawn was already creeping in. Joe hoped Chris wouldn't be too upset that he'd stayed out all night.

Chris had introduced Joe to the French boys in the first place, and he'd seemed quite happy when Joe had hooked up with Luc, but Chris's moods were notoriously volatile, and he'd grown used to being in control of Joe's feelings and actions. He demanded loyalty, and could sometimes fly into an irrational temper if he thought he was losing it.

Joe stopped at the edge of the square, momentarily unsure of which way to go. All the streets looked the same around here—narrow houses with small doors, set back from the street, with multiple doorbells up the walls of each.

He headed left, following his instincts, and quickly found the blue door beside the narrow alleyway which marked the top of Chris's road.

Turning into the road, he heard footsteps rushing up from behind him. Two skinhead lads, all bovver boots, bomber jackets and bad attitudes, were bearing down on him. He tried to dodge out of their way, but was just a little too slow. One of them shouldered him viciously into the wall.

"Watch it," the skinhead threatened. His friend laughed, and lunged at Joe, eyes wild and menacing, stopping just short of head-butting him as Joe flinched back into the wall.

Spitting at his feet, the skinhead backed off, and they moved on, shouting their goading taunts about poofs into the night air for all to hear. Pocket rebels, looking for a fight.

Joe's heart beat in his throat, and, as he took a deep breath to calm himself, he heard a stifled sob from the narrow alleyway he'd just passed. His stomach sank. What had those lads done?

Cautiously, he moved back to the alleyway. It was dark, with just one flickering lamp providing any light. Another sob in the shadows, and Joe saw a tall, thin woman in high heels, half bent over, leaning against the wall.

"Hey, are you okay? Do you need any help?" Joe asked.

The woman kept her head down, refusing to look up as Joe stepped into the alleyway, her hands covering her face.

"Just fuck off," she said, her voice low and cracking.

A voice Joe thought he recognised. Just like he recognised the tight red sequinned dress, sparkling in the dim light, and the killer heels kicked off on the ground.

"Patty?"

Patty looked up at him, pulling the wig off to reveal a stocking cap. The boy that looked back at him was scared, clutching the bright-red wig in hands streaked with what looked like dirt.

"What happened?" Joe asked, stepping forward. "Are you hurt?"

Without the wig, Joe could see the young man's features more clearly. His mascara had run, and clumps of black stuck to the puffy skin beneath his eyes. His lipstick was smudged across his cheek, and there was something else there. Not dirt, but blood.

Joe rushed forward to help, but got pushed back with surprising force as Patty barged past him and hurried away, barefoot into the night. Joe ran to the end of the alley, looking both ways, but Patty was already gone.

Joe turned back into the alley, collected both shoes from the ground, shocked and confused. Patty, or whatever his real name was, had obviously got into some kind of trouble. Had he come over to carry on the fight he and Chris had started earlier? Joe hoped not, or Chris would be in an unbearable mood, and Joe didn't want anything to ruin his buzz. He hurried towards Chris's flat, the heels dangling from his hand.

Reaching the door, he fished the key out of his pocket, his cold fingers scraping painfully on his tight jeans, but when he went to slip the key into the lock, he realised the door was unlocked. A streak of blood here too, just below the lock. He pushed on the door and, as it swung open, the smell hit him straight away—metallic and meaty.

The high heels fell from his hand and clattered on the doorstep as the reality of the scene in front of him hit home. A body lay on the floor in the hallway, in a pool of blood covering the black-and-white tiles. Legs bent awkwardly, head at an unnatural angle, face battered and bruised. Chris's face. Chris's head. Chris's legs. Joe stumbled into the hallway, his mouth open in a scream that was yet to erupt.

He wasn't aware when his screaming started, or that a door had opened further down the hallway, or that Chris's flatmate, Russell, had come hurtling down the stairs, dressing gown billowing out behind him, or that Chris's blood was seeping into the hem of Russell's gown as he bent beside Chris's body and checked his pulse.

Joe didn't flinch when Russell yelled at the downstairs neighbours to get back in their house and wait for the police. He didn't object when Russell wrapped his arms around him and guided him though his best friend's blood and up the stairs towards the flat.

Everything was happening in a bubble, removed from reality. Sounds, smells, thoughts were all far away and unreal. Their feet on the steps, the urgent voices from the neighbour's flat, the gentle wafting smell of old cigarette smoke from Chris's jacket, which Russell had scooped off the steps as they'd passed and now clutched in his hand, right beside Joe's face. There was a small spot of blood on the collar—nothing compared to the pool on the floor, but it drew Joe's attention like a beacon.

He let Russell guide him up the stairs and into the small kitchen where he slumped, numb and shaking, into one of the chairs at the tiny kitchen table. He heard Russell out in the hallway, calling the police. He heard the words "attacked" and "killed", but they weren't real. None of this was real. *Was it?*

Russell came back into the kitchen, muttering that the police were on their way, but Joe didn't respond. His hands were shaking, tears streaked his face. He finally became aware of the rumble of the kettle boiling and he looked up, half-expecting to see his friend leaning casually against the counter, smoking one of his trademark roll-ups.

But he wasn't there. Russell stood there instead, in his blood-stained gown, his hands pressed firmly on the counter to stop his own shoulders shaking, staring out of the window as the blue flashing lights pulled up outside.

JOE AND RUSSELL HAD been told to stay in the flat and wait while the police did their work downstairs. Neither spoke. Neither knew what to say. They barely even looked at each other. Russell had made them both several cups of sweet tea, which they had consumed in a fog of disbelief, anger and grief.

Joe felt numb. None of it made sense. Chris couldn't be dead. He just couldn't. But Joe knew it was true from the ashen look on Russell's face when he'd come back into the flat, when he'd uttered those fateful words that the police had confirmed—suspected murder. The two of them had collapsed into hard kitchen chairs and stared at each other in disbelief as the tears began to well again. It was true, but it just wouldn't sink in.

After a while sitting in silence, waiting for the police to come up and take their statements, Russell got up decisively, gathering his gown around him.

"I'm going for a shower," he said, and disappeared down the hallway. Joe heard the fan come on in the bathroom, and the sound of water splashing into the bath. He looked at his own hands, holding his fingers up to examine the smudges of Chris's blood. How had that got there? Had he touched Chris's body? Tried to help him? He couldn't remember.

He pushed the chair back and crossed to the sink, running the water over his hands and rubbing distractedly, continuously until there was no sign of blood any more. Washed away. Just like that.

Drying his hands on his jeans, Joe stared out of the window, watching the scene unfolding on the street below. A small crowd loitered in the square, craning their necks to see what all the fuss was about.

A single, uniformed officer stood on the road in front of their door, shepherding any passers-by off the pavement and out of the way. The official, dispassionate comings and goings that accompanied the discovery of a dead body on a London street.

He watched as the crowd of onlookers lost interest after Chris's body, safely wrapped in the black body bag, was loaded into the back of the wagon, already turning away to shrug at each other as the doors slammed.

He was rocked by a sudden urge to sprint down the stairs and stop them from taking his friend away, to hold him one last time. *How had this happened?*

The uniformed policeman stepped aside, disappearing from sight, and Joe shuddered as the first members of the public walked past the spot where his friend had laid, craning to see a glimpse of the horror through the open door. *What was wrong with people?* He wanted to shout at them to go away, to leave them alone.

But he didn't shout. He didn't do anything. All he could do was stare forlornly out of the window, slowly realising that he would never see Chris again. Russell came up and stood beside him, arm around his shoulder, and slowly turned him away from the window.

When Joe looked up at him, he realised that he, too, had been crying. Joe let his head rest on Russell's shoulder, feeling the weight of the awful truth they all now shared. Chris was gone.

A man knocked sharply on the open flat door. Russell looked up and pushed Joe away quickly. Too quickly.

The man—clearly police—hesitated at the door, saying nothing. His long, beige trench coat hung loosely around narrow shoulders. His ratty face pinched in distaste, his eyes darting between Russell and Joe, the judgement barely concealed.

"Come in if you have to," Russell said, bitterly, swiping the two empty tea cups from the table and putting them in the sink.

The man stepped in, his tongue flicking across thin lips as he cast his gaze around the kitchen. He kept his hands held tight in front of him as though scared of anything touching him, and yet there was an arrogance in his eyes—a gleam that made Joe feel he was enjoying this moment too much. The man cleared his throat, locking eyes with Russell.

"Mr Dixon," he said, emphasising the Mr. "I need to ask you a few questions about your... friend." The pause was loaded with inference, the word friend a sneering insinuation. "We can do it here, if you're more comfortable. I shouldn't think you'd want to come down to the station."

His smile was insincere. Joe hated him already.

"Take a seat, Detective Skinner," Russell said, pulling a chair back from the table and sitting down himself. Joe did the same, lining himself up between Russell and the visitor, feeling instinctively protective. *Detective Skinner.* Russell had been a detective too, Chris had told him. There was obviously history between Russell and this weasel-faced man.

"I'd rather stand," Skinner said.

"Suit yourself."

"What can you tell me about Christopher Sexton then? You two were obviously... close." No hint of sympathy.

"He was my tenant."

Skinner snorted.

"Paid you rent, did he? I'll bet."

The emphasis on the word rent was an obvious jibe and Russell rose to it immediately, lurching across the table and grabbing Skinner by the throat, squeezing until his face started to redden. Joe stood up and pulled him away.

"Don't, Russell. He's not worth it."

Skinner straightened himself up, shrugging his shoulders to readjust his shirt. He was trying to look unfazed, but Joe could see he'd been surprised by the ferocity of Russell's reaction. There was clearly no love lost here.

Russell turned to the sink, rinsing the cups as a distraction, trying to compose himself.

"What do you want to know, Detective?" Joe asked, sounding far more level-headed than he felt.

"And you are?"

"Joseph Stone. Joe. I've known Chris since we were four."

Skinner assessed him disdainfully. Joe refused to flinch under the scrutiny. He hadn't even changed his T-shirt from last night, his hair was a mess, his eyes probably puffy and red. He didn't care. *Judge all you like, you don't know me.*

"When did you last see the victim?" Skinner asked eventually, turning back to Russell.

The victim.

"At around eleven, eleven-thirty," Joe said.

"Well, which is it? Eleven or eleven-thirty?" Skinner sniffed.

"Closer to eleven-thirty, I suppose," Joe replied. "There was an act on. He left the club just as the performance started."

"The club?"

"Gossip's," Joe replied. "We'd been there most of the night. It was a friend's party."

Skinner raised an eyebrow.

"And Chris just left halfway through? Did he say where he was going?"

"No, he just said something had come up and he had to go. Said he'd see me back here later."

"Did he seem anxious? Nervous? Upset?"

"No…"

That wasn't true. Joe looked at Russell, who was leaning against the sink, staring at his hands, fingers fidgeting with one another. Russell glanced at him, the slightest frown on his brow. Had he noticed the slight hesitation in Joe's voice?

Joe hadn't had chance to get over the shock of finding Chris yet, let alone tell Russell what he'd seen in the club—the big man in the trilby hat, with hands like spades, telling Chris off. Or the fight Chris had with Patty. Or that Patty, or whoever he was really, had been in the alleyway, with blood on his hands and face. *Had Patty done this?*

Joe tensed, realising that he knew a lot more than he was saying. Something told him he should discuss it with Russell before he told Detective Skinner anything. He had a bad feeling about this policeman.

"And you can't think of anyone he may have fallen out with?" Skinner continued. "Anyone who would want to hurt him?"

"Hurt him?" Joe spluttered. "They didn't just hurt him, they bloody killed him!"

Russell caught Joe's eye and gave a barely perceptible shake of the head, the tiniest warning to keep his cool. Skinner clocked the glance between them and his eyes narrowed.

"He was a popular kid," Russell said quickly. "He had a lot of friends. I can't imagine anyone wanting to do… that. Not to him."

Skinner raised an eyebrow again, looking hard at both of them in turn before sighing.

"So, he left the club alone," Skinner summarised. "And you came home to find him in the hallway. What time was that?"

"I don't know," Joe stammered, reliving the moment he'd come through the door only too vividly.

"We called you straight away," Russell said, protectively. "Just before seven this morning."

"And where were you all night then, between eleven-thirty when you last saw him and seven this morning?"

Joe looked down, glanced at Russell, sighed.

"I met a guy, we went on for coffee when the club closed, and then we went back to his hotel."

"Did he have a name, this guy? Or was discretion part of the transaction?" Skinner didn't even try to hide his disgust.

"Luc," Joe muttered.

"Luke what?"

"I don't know. He's French."

What does it matter where he's from? Joe realised he was babbling. *Why should I feel embarrassed?* He raised his eyes to glare at Skinner.

"And he'll vouch for your movements, will he? This Frenchman?"

"Of course," Joe snapped. "Why wouldn't he?"

"You never know with you lot," Skinner muttered, almost inaudibly.

He sniffed again and turned to Russell.

"And you, Mr Dixon?" he asked, a sardonic note to his voice. "Where were *you* while all this was going on?"

"I was here all night," Russell said.

"You were upstairs all the time the attack was happening, were you?"

Russell looked up slowly, his eyes filled with hate.

"It would appear so," he said, flatly.

"And you didn't hear anything?"

"No."

"Because it was quite a brutal attack," Skinner seemed to be enjoying twisting the knife. "So I would imagine there would have been a fair bit of noise. You didn't hear anything at all?"

"I was asleep."

Russell sounded defensive. Joe frowned. Had Russell heard the attack and stayed upstairs, not wanting to get involved? Surely not. He was a former policeman, he wouldn't sit quietly by while someone was being attacked. Skinner folded his arms across his chest, recognising a stonewall when he saw one.

"I'll tell you what I know about your young tenant then, shall I?" he asked, leaning back in his chair. "Because I've met him a few times over the years. We've arrested him for being drunk and disorderly. We've arrested him for soliciting. We've had to caution him for assaulting a police officer during a protest. He's a known drug user. And we know only too well the kind of company he keeps. So, I'm afraid it's come as no surprise he's ended up how he has."

He stared at Russell coldly, willing him to challenge him again. Russell's jaw clenched, but he didn't move and said nothing. Silence hung in the room.

"Look," Skinner said, standing up and straightening his coat, "we've got nothing to go on here. As far as we're concerned, he hooked up with someone, brought them back here, things turned ugly, and he came out the worst for it. We've got no witnesses, you claim there's no motive, and I've got no reason to waste valuable police time on yet another dead rent boy. So, if either of you think of something else, let me know. Otherwise, I'm done here."

"He's a good kid," Russell protested.

"Was," corrected Skinner. "But I doubt that. I'll be in touch."

He walked out, leaving the door to the hallway ajar. His footsteps light and carefree on the stairs, the sound of whistling following him out.

Neither of them moved until the front door slammed and Russell picked up a glass from the draining rack and threw it at the wall, the crystal shards exploding into the hallway. Joe flinched. Silence flooded back into the room.

"He's not going to do anything, is he?" Joe said, eventually.

"No," Russell said, shaking his head.

Shards of broken glass crunched beneath his feet as he pulled a broom out of the hall cupboard and began sweeping. His hands were shaking.

"But don't they have to take it seriously?" Joe asked quietly. "It's murder."

"They should. But they won't. Believe me," Russell said, sweeping the glass into a dustpan. "As far as they're concerned, he's just another stupid little queer who fell foul on a bad hook up. They'll be glad to get him off the streets. And they're certainly not going to dedicate any resources to finding out what happened. Especially not Detective Skinner."

"You know him?" Joe asked, looking up at Russell.

Russell shrugged angrily, throwing the broken glass into the bin and slamming the lid.

"Yes," he said, finally. "I used to work with him. In fact, I used to be his boss. Which is exactly how I know he'll do nothing."

"Can't we file a complaint about him or something?" Joe asked.

"Oh grow up," Russell snapped. "They don't care about people like us. You heard him. He's already written Chris off as a rent boy who picked the wrong guy to bring home. The police don't care. Half the time, they're the ones attacking us."

Joe slumped, feeling suddenly childish. He had just assumed the police would want to prioritise catching Chris's killer. But why should they? They must see hundreds of crimes like this every year. There were always stories about gay-bashings, or random beatings, or unsolved murders. Chris would be just another statistic, not worth the manpower.

"I should have said something," Joe blurted.

"About what?"

"About last night. I saw Chris talking to someone in the club," Joe said.

Russell rolled his eyes.

"That doesn't mean anything," he sniffed.

"No, I mean, not just some guy. Not like that. He didn't look like he belonged there, you know? He was big. Huge hands. And he looked really angry, like he was telling Chris off."

Russell sat down opposite him and poured them both a hefty shot of brandy.

"What did he look like?" Russell asked.

"Big. Trilby hat. Heavy wool coat. And it was boiling in there."

"Oh shit," Russell said, downing his brandy and topping up the glass.

"You know who it was?"

"Tony Lagorio," Russell said, as though the name itself could conjure the devil. "People call him the Lizard."

"The Lizard?"

"You don't want to know," Russell replied. "Suffice to say, he's a nasty piece of work, and you don't want to end up on his bad side."

"You think he killed Chris?"

"No," Russell said. "When he hurts anyone, he makes damn sure people know it was him that did it. He likes his messages to be clear."

"How does he not get arrested?"

Russell smiled at his naivety.

"Believe me, I tried. I think you need to lower your opinion of the police a few notches, kid," he said. "Tony's a gangster, through and through. He's got most of the force in his pocket. Any time he needs a favour from the boys in blue, all he has to do is ask. I tried to bring him in a couple of times. Something always happened to the evidence, or to the bust itself. I probably know more about him now than his own mother does, and none of it would make her proud. Problem was, I could never make any of it stick."

"How did Chris know him?"

"Chris owed him money at one point," Russell replied. "But he told me he'd paid it off."

"Why would Chris owe someone like him money?" Joe asked.

"Tony stumped up Chris's half of the money to set up the fashion label," Russell said. "I told him it was a stupid idea, taking money from the Lizard, but Chris always knows best."

He paused, catching himself still using the present tense. It would take a while.

"I would have paid it off for him if I could," Russell continued. "But I couldn't afford it. And he wouldn't let me, anyway."

Joe frowned. The idea was preposterous—Chris's family were rich and, though they didn't approve of his lifestyle, Joe was sure they'd never let their boy go without. Would they?

At school, Chris had always been the kid with the best trainers, the nicest lunches, the newest toys. If he'd needed money, he could have just gone back to his dad and asked. Or had things really got that bad between them that Chris would rather get into debt with a gangster than see his father?

What the hell had Chris got himself into? Joe had thought that his friend had seemed far more relaxed and in control of his life than he'd ever seen before. With his nice flat, a good circle of friends, his fashion label growing stronger by the day—he'd seemed genuinely settled. Had that all just been a show?

"I also saw him arguing with Patty," Joe said. "His drag queen friend."

"He was arguing with Paul?"

"If that's his name," Joe shrugged. "They were in the corridor. Patty told him to fuck off."

"Well, if Chris was going to leave the club before Patty's show even started, Paul had every right to be pissed off. The whole performance was for Chris, after all. Poor old Paul is besotted with him."

Joe took a nerve-steadying sip of his own brandy. It burned, but it felt necessary.

"Just before I came back and found Chris, I saw him again. In the alley, at the end of the road. In a right state. I recognised the dress."

Russell scrutinised him—topped up both glasses.

"He had blood on his face," Joe blurted. "I thought he'd been attacked, but maybe he came back here to finish the argument with Chris, and it turned into a fight. Maybe he killed Chris. I should have told that detective what I saw."

Russell reached a hand out to hold Joe's.

"You need to calm down," he said. "I know this is a lot to take in, but they were friends. Paul would never hurt Chris. Not like that. He loved him more than anyone."

Joe could feel the anger boiling inside him. Chris was *his* friend. *He* loved him. More than Paul or Russell or any of his new friends ever could. And Paul had been right here, skulking in the alleyway with Chris's blood on his hands, and tears streaking his face. Either he killed him, or he knew something about what had happened last night. Joe stood up purposefully.

"Where are you going?" Russell asked.

"I'm going to find that detective and tell him what I saw."

Russell shot to his feet, blocking Joe's exit.

"Sit down," he said.

They stood face to face, neither backing off.

"Look," Russell said. "I know you're upset. Of course you are, you loved him and what's happened is terrible. But I can promise you that going back to that so-called detective with any of what you've just told me will end up with Paul being arrested and them throwing away the key. No questions asked."

"Good," Joe spat, but he already knew it would be wrong. He sat down heavily.

"The police aren't interested in the truth," Russell said. "Well, not that lot anyway. Not when it comes to our sort. If you give them a reason to arrest Paul, they'll take it and make the rest of the evidence fit. It won't help Paul, it won't help you, and it sure as hell won't help find who really did this to Chris."

"But we have to do something," Joe said.

"I know," Russell said. "And we will."

RUSSELL SAT ALONE at the kitchen table, his head reeling and his hands trembling gently. His old police instincts had kicked in the moment he'd heard the scream from downstairs and discovered poor Joe standing over his best friend's body. The kid would take a while to get over that.

Russell had slipped into autopilot as he'd cleared the scene, called the police, escorted Joe upstairs for sweet tea and brandy, and waited for the detectives to turn up and take statements.

Now that Skinner had gone, and Joe was in the shower cleaning himself up, Russell had a moment to think for the first time.

He had seen more than his fair share of corpses in his time on the force, and he'd watched enough of his friends die in recent years, but this was different. Chris had been such a dynamic force, a whirlwind of lively enthusiasm, constantly getting into scrapes, relentlessly moving, always on the go. Not any more. Just like that—a brilliant life snuffed out and all that potential, all that energy, just vanished into thin air.

He looked at Chris's jacket hanging over the back of the chair, one of Chris's new designs, the bright yellow collar now stained with his blood.

He'd gathered up Chris's wallet from the ground outside the flat, noticing straight away that it was empty of cash. Unusual for Chris on a big night out. He'd had money worries before, but recently Chris had been doing well, and was never short of a few bob. Perhaps there was something to Skinner's mugging theory after all.

He had also found Chris's small instamatic camera on the floor. Slim, silver and black, Chris always joked that it was his spy camera. Said it made him feel like James Bond. And he carried it everywhere, snapping inspirations for his shows, or quick camera tests for cute guys he promised could be his models.

And yet, when Russell had found it, the back was open and there was no film inside. If Chris had been mugged, surely the camera would have gone the same way as the money. So, whoever had killed Chris had taken the film and left the camera. But why?

Russell knew he should have mentioned it to Skinner, but his former colleague would have just buried both items in an evidence box and left them to gather dust. He'd already made his mind up about this case and had made it clear he wasn't planning on conducting much of an investigation. If there were clues to be found, Russell would have to find them himself.

He sat back in the chair, feeling the flimsy Formica seat back creak beneath his bulk. He'd let himself go since leaving the force. He needed to get back in shape.

He smiled sadly. Chris was always nagging him to get fitter, get back out there and start dating properly. He kept promising he would, knowing that he'd need some kind of catalyst to pull himself out of the depressive cloud that had threatened to swallow him up when he was forced from the job. And here it was.

Was he really going to do this? Was he actually going to investigate Chris's murder on his own? If he'd still been on the force, he would have been removed from the case for being too close to the victim.

But he wasn't on the force any more, was he? Skinner had made sure of that. And he was absolutely sure that Skinner would do nothing about Chris's murder. So unless Russell did something himself, his young flatmate—his friend—would never get justice.

3.

JOE HAD PERSUADED Russell to let him come along to talk to Paul, and was grateful he'd agreed. He'd felt better for a shower and a change of clothes, but he needed to be out of the flat and doing something or he would go mad.

The previous day had been spent in a fog of shock and sadness, drowned in brandy and revived by intermittent moments of anger and odd, uncomfortable levity.

Joe had talked fondly about memories of Chris from their school days. About his ridiculous teenage crush on his best friend. About the fact that Chris had always been so confident of who he was, and how his life would go. The memories had prompted both tears and laughter, each shrouded with the disbelief that Chris was no longer with them.

Russell for his part had shared stories of Chris's time in London, his celebrity friends, his wild parties. It was clear that Chris had been a tonic to Russell. He was so free. So open, while Russell admitted that he'd always struggled to admit his sexuality, not just because of the job. He felt like he'd been brought up in a different time. Chris had opened the door for him to admit who he was. Especially after Russell had been suspended from the force.

At some point in the afternoon, Joe had called his mother. His older sister, Deborah, came to the phone instead, her voice tinged with her usual judgement.

Apparently the police had already informed Chris's parents. Deborah said they were all shocked to hear about the life Chris had been leading. Joe could only imagine what Detective Skinner had told Chris's parents on the phone—their errant son, already known to the police for various petty crimes, had been murdered by some strange man he'd taken home for sex.

Deborah had told Joe to come home immediately. He'd refused. It was the first time in his life he'd properly stood up to her.

He'd never officially come out to his family, but Deborah had guessed years ago. Her disapproval was evident in all the little tuts and glances—the way she watched him, hawk-eyed, with her children. The way she quizzed him about any man he mentioned, from his boss to the kid in the corner shop. The way she tutted, from time to time, especially when he laughed. "So bloody camp," she'd muttered once. She didn't think he'd heard.

To let him know she knew and didn't approve, she'd taken to sending him articles in the post, studiously cut from the papers, espousing the dangers of the rising AIDS epidemic. *The Gay Plague*, according to the tabloids. A new omnipotent killer. Joe never mentioned the articles on the rare occasions they saw each other, and neither did she.

"Mum's very upset," Deborah had said.

"So am I," Joe had replied. He was sick of having to hide from his family, and he wasn't going to let Chris's memory be tarnished by their bigotry.

Russell had helped him handle the aftermath of the call, and by the end of the day, emboldened by booze, they'd agreed to do everything they could to find out what had happened to Chris. And so here they were, hitting the streets together, with no idea where to start.

The late-morning air was crisp and refreshing. The shock of Chris's death still chewed constantly at Joe's stomach, and he knew at some point it would overwhelm him again, but right now he was happy to keep moving. He wanted answers and he was sure Paul had a few of them.

Chris would have laughed at the thought of Joe and Russell as the caped crusaders, stepping in to defend his memory. For now, it was too painful to think of Chris laughing. It was too painful to think of Chris at all. Joe needed to be busy, and this was the perfect way to do that.

Soho was still alive and vibrant, getting on with the day as though nothing had happened. The air was filled with hollering market traders, angry car horns, music from windows above the shops and bars, leering calls from door girls tempting punters into the clubs that had seemed so exotic last night but seemed a little sad at lunchtime.

The streets felt different in the light of day—shabbier, seedier, less glamorous. Or perhaps it was the realisation that everything was different now and would never be the same again.

Russell strode purposefully along the busy pavement, weaving in and out of pedestrians, workers and tourists, managing to bend himself around them without ever touching—a practised Londoner. Joe struggled to keep up.

They finally stopped outside a corner pub called The Red Lion and Russell peered through the window.

"Come on," he said, opening the door and striding in.

The pub smelled of stale cigarettes, spilled beer, sweat and toilets. A couple of career drinkers at the bar looked up as they walked in, but turned quickly back to their pints. The barman stood up from his stool behind the bar as he saw Russell.

"Bit early for you, isn't it?" he asked, smiling.

"Hi Ron," Russell said. "Is Paul in?"

"He's upstairs," Ron confirmed. "He was in a right state when he got back. What's he gone and done now?"

"That's what I'm trying to find out," Russell said. "Mind if we go up?"

"Help yourself," Ron said, raising the bar flap so that they could step through. "Shouldn't think you'll get much out of him though."

Joe felt the barman watching him as he squeezed past. He was a big guy—tall, broad-shouldered, friendly face. Joe smiled, and quickly followed Russell up the narrow flight of stairs.

It was like walking into a different world. The décor here was fresher than downstairs—bright, primary colours covered the walls in bold blocks. The short corridor opened out into a large lounge room, full of modern, predominantly black furniture and clean lines. No sign of the seventies décor from downstairs, this room had embraced everything the eighties had to offer. It felt unnaturally cheerful.

"Paul?" Russell called.

No reply. Russell headed towards the first of three doors off the corridor, poked his head round and quickly turned away, heading to the next.

Joe peered through the half-open door to see the tidy bedroom behind it, all blacks, reds and whites—very modern. Very male. Very straight. Unlikely to be Paul's room.

Russell knocked gently on the next door.

"Paul?" he called again.

"Go away," came the reply. His voice sounded thick.

"Paul, love, we're all upset, but we really need to talk to you," Russell said.

"Leave me alone."

Russell turned the handle, and the door opened a crack. The look he gave Joe told him to stay where he was. Joe heard water splashing as Russell entered the room.

"Jesus. You can't just barge in," Paul shouted.

"I just did, petal. Here, cover yourself up," Russell replied. "We need to talk."

Through the open door, Joe caught a glimpse of Paul wrapping a towel around his waist. His face was clean of any make-up, his hair wet and tousled. He looked completely different out of drag. Smaller, skinnier, and much paler.

Russell put his arm around Paul's shoulder and led him out of the bathroom into the bedroom. He turned back to Joe.

"Kitchen's through there," he pointed. "Get the kettle on and see if you can rustle up some biscuits or something. Anything sweet."

By the time Joe brought three steaming mugs of tea and a half-empty packet of custard cremes back into the lounge, Russell and Paul were already sitting on the bright green sofa, deep in quiet conversation.

Russell held Paul's hands in his own. Paul looked up at Joe with red-rimmed eyes. Joe wanted to feel sorry for him, but he couldn't. Not yet. His own pain was still too raw, and he didn't trust him, even if Russell did.

"So," Joe said, putting all three mugs on the glass coffee table and sitting in an armchair facing the two of them. "Where have we got to? What happened to Chris?"

Paul stammered, unsure where to start. Joe couldn't help but chip in.

"I know you know something," Joe said, testily. "I saw you and Chris arguing in the club, just before he left. What was that about?"

Paul flinched, turning back to Russell, looking for support. Russell squeezed his hand.

"Take it easy, Joe," Russell warned, "we're all friends here."

Joe wasn't so sure about that. He wanted answers.

"I told him to fuck off," Paul blurted. "That was the last thing I said to him."

Russell glared at Joe as Paul dissolved into wracking sobs again.

"I'm sure you didn't mean it," Russell said gently.

"I did. I was so pissed off with him."

"Why?" Joe asked. "What were you fighting about?"

"He promised to stay and support me, and then just as I was about to go on, he said he had to leave. I couldn't believe he would do that to me. I was doing the whole bloody thing for him, and he wasn't even going to see it."

"Where was he going?" Russell asked.

"He wouldn't say," Paul said. "He just said it was important, and that it couldn't wait. He couldn't even look me in the eye. I was so angry with him."

Paul broke down again. Russell handed him one of the mugs of tea and rubbed his back, giving him time to gather himself again. He gave Joe another stern look, warning him to play nicely. Russell had only agreed to let Joe tag along if he sat quietly and let him do the talking. Joe hadn't managed that very well so far.

Paul sniffed, wiping his eyes with the back of his hand.

"Paul, love," Russell said gently. "I know it's hard. It is for all of us. But you have to be honest with me now. Was Chris in some kind of trouble?"

"What do you mean? What trouble?"

"Joe says he saw Chris talking to Tony Lagorio," Russell said.

"The Lizard?" Paul said, surprised. "Where?"

"In the club," Joe said. "I was heading to the toilets when I saw Chris. He was talking to this big guy and it looked like he was getting a right telling off. I went into the toilets, and when I came out, I saw the two of you arguing and I didn't want to interrupt because it looked quite heated. Then Chris found me at the bar, told me he had to go because something had come up, and that was the last I saw him."

Joe had intended the insinuation about Paul's argument to knock him, but the news about Tony seemed to unsettle him more.

"Tony was in the club?" Paul said, frowning. He looked from Joe to Russell in confusion.

"It's his club, isn't it?" Russell asked. "Why wouldn't he be there? I mean, he *is* one of the owners, right?"

"Yeah, but he never comes into the club. Not when it's open, anyway. He only ever comes when we're clearing up at the end of the night to make sure there's no cash left on the premises. I don't think I've ever seen him in there during opening hours, and I certainly didn't see him there the other night. Mind you, I wasn't working the bar that night, on account of my performance."

"Well, maybe it wasn't him," said Joe. "I mean, I don't know the man. I just saw Chris talking to a big guy in a trilby hat and a heavy, long coat."

"That's Tony," Russell and Paul said together.

"What was so important that Tony had to come down on a Friday night to see Chris? Did he still owe him?" Russell asked.

"No," Paul said. "Chris paid him back ages ago. He was fine financially."

Joe frowned. That didn't sound like the friend he knew. Chris had never been "fine" as far as money was concerned. His family were rich enough, but when he'd refused to join the family accountancy firm they'd as good as cut him off, probably in the hope it would force him to return when his fashion business failed.

Chris hadn't failed, but he *was* hopeless with money—spent it as soon as he got it, and not always on the most important things.

Joe had helped him out several times in the past, when he needed just enough to make his rent payments after he'd ploughed all his money into the business; or a couple of hundred quid to help with living expenses when he'd spent his last tenner on a present for a friend. He would always pay it back, eventually, but Joe had never got the impression that Chris was *fine financially*.

"I know," Russell agreed, "he's had no trouble with rent for the last few months and he's even bought some new things for the flat. He just said the business was doing well."

"Tell that to Gavin," Paul huffed.

Joe saw Russell's head tilt, a narrowing of the eyes. A small penny had just dropped for him. He made a mental note to ask him about it later.

"So," Russell said, "if it wasn't about money, why would Tony have come to find him last night?"

"I don't know," Paul said, desperately. "Honestly, if he was in any kind of trouble with Tony again, we'd have known about it, wouldn't we?"

Russell shrugged, frustrated. A dead end, for now.

"Why did you run away from me last night?" Joe asked, changing tack. "In the alleyway."

Paul got up quickly as though that flight instinct was kicking in again. He crossed to the window and looked out at the street below. So much for keeping quiet and letting Russell do the talking, but there was something going on with Paul, and Joe didn't like it. He hadn't studied psychology for three years to not recognise a guilty complex when he saw one—Paul was holding something back.

"I didn't know what to do," he said quietly, his back to them both. "I'd gone over to see Chris, to make him apologise for leaving me on my own up on the stage. The door was open, so I went in. He was just lying there..."

He turned back to face them, looking pale.

"He was already cold," he said, shuddering. "I tried to make him sit up. I thought there must be something I could do to help him, but he was gone. I panicked. I ran. I'm not proud of it."

"Why didn't you call up to me?"

Paul just shook his head.

"I couldn't..."

"So why were you hiding in the alley?" Joe cut across him.

"I didn't know what to do, I couldn't think. I wanted to get as far away as I could, but I couldn't leave him like that."

"So you hid in the alley?"

"There were these skinheads. They looked like trouble. I thought maybe they'd done it. I thought they'd come for me too if they saw me. I'd come straight from the club, I was still in drag."

"Yeah, I saw them too," Joe said. "Only, they didn't have Chris's blood on them, and you did."

Paul turned on him, lunging forward.

"Are you accusing me of killing Chris?"

Russell stood up between them.

"No one's accusing anyone," he said. "Sit down, both of you."

They both did. He might be short, and a little round in the middle, but when Russell told you to do something, he had an air of authority about him that made you do it without question.

"Why did you run away when I spoke to you?" Joe asked.

"Because I didn't want to talk to you, alright?" Paul said. "Because I didn't want to have to tell you that Chris was dead. I didn't want to say those words out loud because then it would be true."

They sat in silence for a moment, the sounds of the bar below travelling up through the floorboards. The unmistakable strains of "Love is a Stranger" on the jukebox. The clink of glasses. Mumbled chatter. A burst of raucous laughter. The lunchtime crowd was gathering.

"I know I should have done something," Paul said eventually. "I should've called the police, but I didn't know what to say. I should have called you, Russell, but I just couldn't speak. There was so much blood. I'm sorry. Who could do something like that to him?"

It was a question none of them could answer. For now. But at least Joe no longer thought Paul had murdered Chris.

4.

THE FLAT WAS SO QUIET. No noise from the street below. Monday in Soho was an altogether quieter affair, as though the streets and buildings needed time to recover from the weekend. Joe knew he did.

Russell had gone off on his own to try to speak to this Tony Lagorio character. When Joe had asked if that was a good idea, Russell assured him that he would be fine. He was going to Tony's restaurant, and was confident that there was enough of a lunchtime crowd around for him to feel relatively safe. Joe hoped he was right.

Tony had been one of the last people seen speaking to Chris, though, and whatever he'd said had made Chris change his plans quite suddenly. The next thing they knew, Chris was dead.

Given what Russell had told him about Tony Lagorio's history, Joe was glad he didn't have to meet him. He hoped Russell would be alright.

Despite his gruff exterior, Joe could see that Russell had a big heart. He'd obviously enjoyed having Chris share the flat, and he was clearly feeling the loss deeply too. Joe liked him and trusted his instincts. He must have been a good cop in his day.

Joe sat on the end of Chris's bed, feet tucked up under his knees, with echoes of their last moments in that room running through his mind. They'd been getting ready to go out to the club, laughing, messing around—Chris dancing around in front of the mirror, shirtless, lithe, alive. How could he be dead?

He looked at Chris's open wardrobe. Hanging on the inside of each door were two suits from Chris's newest fashion line, one of which Joe had tried on yesterday. He'd let Chris snap some photos of him in that suit, among the others of them both fooling around, full of laughter and enthusiasm for the night ahead.

They were photographs he would never see—Russell had already told him about finding Chris's camera in the hallway, the film removed.

Neither Joe nor Russell believed that Chris's death was a mugging gone bad. Somebody had wanted him dead, and that somebody had wanted whatever was on that camera.

What were you involved in, Chris?

Joe crossed to the wardrobes and stroked the soft, bright suit, holding the stitching between his fingers. Stitches that Chris had put there.

Joe ran his fingers over the label inside the suit jacket. The words SEXTON & JONES were picked out in gold thread, with a small crown embroidered over the letter "O" in each name.

What would happen to the company now? According to Chris, he had been the creative talent behind the duo, and his business partner, Gavin, dealt with the money. Would Gavin carry on without him? Had anyone even told him that Chris was dead yet?

Chris had confided in Joe that he and Gavin had been arguing about the new line, and about moving the studio. Chris was determined that they would stay in their original home, but Gavin wanted to move and expand.

Chris had said that Gavin was trying to push him out of the company, but he was resisting the split. "Over my dead body," he'd joked to Joe. There wouldn't be much of a company left anyway, without its star designer.

A fresh wave of sadness forced Joe across the room to the messy little desk in the corner. There was stuff everywhere. Little reminders of the life that had filled this room until so recently. Trinkets, treasures and mementos, suddenly reduced to little more than clutter to be swept away. Chris had been such a dynamic, focussed guy with a bright future ahead of him. How could this have happened?

Sitting at the desk, Joe opened the top drawer. Chris had never been particularly private or possessive of his things, never had any secrets from Joe. Or so he'd thought.

He hesitated before delving into the drawer. What would he find in here? Was he ready to unpack Chris's life like this? He had to if he was going to get to the truth of what had happened.

He removed a neatly stacked pile of photographs of young men wearing a range of Chris's outfits. He didn't recognise any of the models, but they all had that familiar look that Chris favoured: high cheekbones, angular chins, big hair, blue eyes. The opposite of Joe with his short, dark hair and brown eyes.

Beneath the photographs were a couple of dog-eared leaflets from a protest late last year about the threatened closure of the Campbell Centre, a charity-run clinic for people with HIV and AIDS.

Joe remembered Chris trying to get him to join them on that march, but he hadn't been able to get away from work, and if he was honest, he hadn't wanted to get in any trouble. He should have done it. Chris been so passionate about the charity, it would have meant the world to him if Joe had come. Too late for regrets now.

A copy of the front page of the newspaper from the day of the protest showed an image of Chris, front and centre in the line of protesters, hand reaching forward with middle finger raised, mouth open, shouting abuse at the police trying to protect some flustered looking MP. Joe smiled at the image. The world would be a lot smaller without Chris in it.

He absently opened drawer after drawer, pulling out the residual evidence of his friend's life. What would happen to all this stuff? Would Chris's parents want any of it? Would they come and pick over the remains of the young life they'd turned their backs on, tutting their disapproval as they discovered his darker secrets. Would they take any of the blame for how his life had ended, having cast him out instead of supporting him? Joe doubted it.

In the bottom of one drawer, he found a small diary, black and scuffed. "1984" embossed in gold on the front cover.

Flicking it open, he saw Chris's artistic scrawl on the first page: a list of initials with phone numbers beside them. A star system, scribbled beside their numbers, seemed to rate each between one and five stars.

Leafing through the pages, Joe noticed that at least one set of initials had been entered almost every week since September, sometimes two or three sets of initials per week, but never two on the same day.

Passing back and forth between the months, he discovered that some initials recurred regularly. Every other Tuesday afternoon: ECS. The first Friday of each month: LL.

On at least four occasions, there was simply the letter X written large. According to the ratings, X was a five star. Joe found a final reference in early December, where the X had been crossed out, and MJ scribbled in heavily and underlined, followed by an exclamation mark in brackets.

The exclamation mark was surprising. Who or what was MJ? Joe wished he could ask Chris what this little code was all about.

He laid the diary on the desk. He would show Russell later. Perhaps there was a simple explanation, but the way the book had been tucked in beneath the clothes at the bottom of the drawer and the secrecy of the initials made him suspicious.

A cork pin board above the desk was filled with all the photographs Chris *had* wanted the world to see. Him and his celebrity friends in clubs, in restaurants, in bars. Actors, musicians, socialites. So-called friends that had welcomed this dynamic and talented young designer into their social circle and made him feel special.

One image, partly concealed by newer ones, showed Chris, shirtless, lying with his head on a man's chest. The man's face was cut out of shot. Chris, as ever, the centre of his own universe. He looked content.

Joe felt angry, jealous tears pricking his eyes and grabbed at the images, tearing them off the board and throwing them in tatters on the floor. They didn't deserve to be part of his memories. They weren't Chris's real friends. Not like Joe was.

As the photographs fluttered to the ground, the realisation hit Joe suddenly, knocking the wind out of him—he hadn't known the real Chris any more than any of those celebrity friends had. And he'd let him down just as badly.

He slumped on the end of the bed, picking up Chris's jacket that Russell had neatly laid out on the covers. More than anything, he wanted to talk to Chris, and he knew he never would again.

He gathered the jacket tight, and curled up on the bed with it clutched to his chest, letting the tears flow.

RUSSELL TURNED INTO the narrow alleyway leading down the side of Tony Lagorio's restaurant—a dark building on the corner of the block, just off Dean Street. He knocked twice on the side door and waited.

There had been no point bringing Joe. It was going to be tough enough getting anything out of Tony without bringing a puppy into the dog pit. Besides, Russell was still reeling from what had happened to Chris, and needed a break from the relentless questions.

He knew his former colleagues on the force would let the case fade into obscurity as they had with so many similar attacks over the years. Gay-bashing wasn't exactly a high priority for any of them—quite often the police were the worst perpetrators of those kinds of attacks themselves. As Russell knew only too well, having been caught out in a sting set up by his own colleagues.

A young man, tight jeans, torn pocket, had approached him outside a club. They'd chatted briefly, and the guy had offered sex, saying they should go back to his place. Russell should have known it was a set up—no one ever propositioned him.

But booze and loneliness meant he'd fallen for it, and just around the corner they'd been surrounded by two other guys who identified themselves as coppers and arrested Russell on a charge of opportuning. An old, rarely used charge from the fifties which had been designed to stop men hanging round stage doors and harassing the showgirls.

Russell knew that Skinner had set it up. He was yet to prove it, but he knew. As far as detectives like Skinner were concerned, if you were gay and out, you brought any trouble you got on yourself. Skinner wouldn't break a sweat trying to solve Chris's murder.

He also knew that Skinner would blow a gasket if he knew Russell was looking into what had happened, which made him all the more determined to do something. If he found Chris's real killer, and proved it was more than just a random attack, it would make Skinner look bad. And nothing would make Russell happier than damaging Skinner's reputation.

One day, Russell would find a way to pay Skinner back properly. For now, he was more interested in what had happened to Chris.

He knocked again, harder this time, and finally heard the sound of bolts sliding back heavily on the inside of the door. The door opened a crack—chain still in place.

"What d'you want?"

"I'm here to see Tony," Russell said.

"Tony don't see no one without an appointment—least of all the pigs." His cockney accent was nasal and whiny, the voice of a natural-born scrapper.

"Tell him I'm here about Chris Sexton," said Russell, his foot stopping the door from closing. "The designer," he added.

"Remove your foot, or I will break your leg and remove it for you."

The way he pronounced every syllable of every word expressed such clear violent intent that Russell did as he was told. The door slammed shut, bolts sliding home again. He waited as footsteps thudded away.

A rusty fire escape ladder hung above his head, too far out of reach for him to grab. He would just have to wait, and hope Tony agreed to see him.

The door to the pub opposite opened, a burst of Jimmy Sommerville's distinctive falsetto following a couple of lads out onto the street—skinny boys in leather and denim, cropped T-shirts, shaved heads. They laughed, jostling each other as they passed the mouth of the alleyway, neither of them looking in.

Tony's building was three storeys high. The restaurant occupied all of the ground floor, and Russell could see lights burning on the second. He knew the place well—he'd tried to get a warrant to search it a number of times. Never succeeded.

There were two tables in the restaurant at which no one could eat without an invitation, and invitations were like hen's teeth. Both were empty today. The rest of the tables were open to anyone with enough cash to pay over-inflated prices for underwhelming food. The old-fashioned Italian was little more than a front for Tony's other interests, he didn't need it to turn a profit.

Try as he might during his time as a detective with the Metropolitan Police, Russell had never been able to make any charges stick to Tony Lagorio, and it still annoyed him. Probably almost as much as each of his attempts to do so had annoyed Tony.

There had been such bad blood between the two of them over the years that Russell felt uncharacteristically nervous about seeing him again.

The last time they'd seen each other, Tony had been striding out of a holding cell that Russell had put him in, with a smile on his lips, a threat in his eyes, and an expensive lawyer at his side.

Russell had always wondered if Tony hadn't deliberately sought Chris out and offered him a deal too good to be true on that loan, before turning the screws on him, simply to get back at Russell for one arrest too many.

He heard the footsteps returning. Not in any kind of hurry. Bolts shifted again. The chain was removed, and the door opened to reveal a short, broad man with one gold tooth in an otherwise solidly white, horribly chilling smile.

"You've got five minutes," he snarled.

Russell threw him a fake smile and headed up the stairs towards the rooms above. He followed the smell of cigar smoke down the dank corridor and into the large office overlooking the busy street below.

Tony Lagorio stood in front of one of the windows, gazing down at the street, his back to the room, confident to the point of arrogance.

A cigar smouldered in an ashtray on the desk in front of the window, and his chair was still gently swivelling—he'd only stood up for effect.

"So, the kid thinks he can send messengers now, does he?"

Russell stepped into the room and closed the door. He didn't want any of Tony's goons jumping him from behind.

"Chris is dead, Tony," he said. "That's why I'm here."

The Lizard turned around the moment Russell started talking. "You?"

Russell forced a smile, toothy and insincere. "Me."

"I thought you'd been... retired."

Russell sat down, uninvited, in one of the chairs facing Tony's oversized oak desk.

"Let's call this a personal visit," Russell said, forcing himself to speak slowly, play Tony at his own game. "Chris was a very dear friend, as you know."

Tony raised an eyebrow.

"I hear you went to find him in the club," Russell said. "On the night he died. Thought you might be able to tell me what was going on between you two?"

Russell may have arrested Tony Lagorio a handful of times in the past, but he'd never seen him look as shocked as he did right now.

The big man sat down, rubbed his spade-like palms over his face and stared at Russell for a moment.

"Dead?" he asked, finally.

"I'm afraid so," Russell replied. "We found him in the early hours of Saturday morning, in the doorway of our flat."

"I'm sorry," Tony said. "Truly."

And Russell felt that he meant it. He could see the big man's mind working, trying to process the information. The Lizard was no stranger to sudden deaths, but something about the news had shocked him.

"So," Russell pushed, not wanting to give Tony time to recover his composure. "You can imagine my surprise to hear that you, of all people, had gone to find him in the club that night. What did you have to say to him that couldn't wait for a phonecall in the morning?"

"That's none of your business," Tony said.

"I'm making it my business," Russell countered. "And you know how annoying I can be when I start doing that."

Tony smirked, relit the cigar and leaned back in his chair. He wasn't bothered. Was Russell losing his edge? Too long out of the job, and not even the leverage of the badge to force the pretence of respect. *Plough on, quickly.*

"From what I hear, you two had a bit of a disagreement. Made him change his plans for the night. And then he turns up dead. There are witnesses who saw you threaten him, Tony."

"Witnesses? What witnesses?"

"Not important. Just tell me what you said. Why did he leave the club in such a hurry?"

Tony leaned back in his chair, fingers steepled in front of his chest, cigar dangling from his fat lips. He sniffed. Blew out a cloud of smoke.

"I'll cut you some slack," he said quietly, "because, despite everything, I can see you were a good cop, and I don't agree with what they did to you on the force. What you do in your own life shouldn't hold any interest for anyone else. So long as you're not hurting anyone, right?"

An ironic sentiment from a man who'd spent most of his life having people hurt. Russell said nothing.

"And, regardless of what you think," Tony continued, "I liked the kid. I would have liked him a whole lot more if he'd paid his debts on time, and not made me chase him round the city, but them's the breaks. We got there in the end."

Russell sat forward. Tony stubbed out the cigar.

"So here's the deal," Tony said, leaning back in his chair. "We had an arrangement. A service arrangement, if you will."

"Meaning?"

"I have a couple of high-end clients who enjoy a discreet evening in the company of a nice, willing young man."

"You pimped him out?"

"Well, that makes it sound very crass. No. I made some introductions, and I let him take it from there. What he actually did with the guys was none of my business."

It was Russell's turn to get over the shock. He had no idea Chris had been working as an escort, but he supposed it made sense. He should have guessed when Chris suddenly seemed to be flush with cash all the time. He forced himself to keep listening to Tony's reply, he could ponder the rest later.

"Sometimes, I asked him to get me a little information while he was working. Pillow talk is a valuable commodity. And I paid him well for the information he got. It was a business arrangement. Purely financial. I knew he'd done worse before. Hell, he even offered to do me once, back in the day, if I let the debt slide. I told him no thanks." He laughed, as though the thought was ridiculous. "I was *helping* him," Tony protested, when he realised Russell didn't share the joke. "At first, he needed a way to pay back what he owed me. I just hooked him up with some clients who could pay properly for what he had to offer. He was a popular kid. We soon figured out that people would share secrets with him. But that was his idea. He came to me the first time, with information to sell."

"Okay," Russell said, "I get all that. I don't like it, but I get it. It doesn't explain why you were threatening him in the club on Friday though, does it?"

"I don't have to explain myself to you."

"Oh, come on, Tony," Russell said, leaning forward, elbows on knees. "I know you've probably got more friends on the force than I ever did, but you know what they think of kids like Chris. Do you really want to go through the hassle of having to explain what you were doing chasing him around a nightclub on a Friday night, making threats? On the same night he was brutally murdered in his own doorway? Even *your* friends might not be able to smooth that one over for you."

Tony held up his hands, the gesture more placatory than defensive.

"Hey, hold on there," he said. "I didn't hurt the kid. He was fine when I left him."

Russell stood up. He wasn't getting anywhere.

"You know what? The guy who's taken over from me on the force is eager to make a good impression. I'm sure he'll be very happy to claim a big scalp like yours on his first case. I don't know him well, but I'm sure he'll make time to listen to an old hand like me."

It was bullshit. Russell hadn't even been replaced on the force, and there was no way anyone in the department would bring in Tony Lagorio to answer for the death of a little gay boy. But, for now, Tony wasn't to know that, and Russell felt that he had just this one bluff to get closer to the truth.

"Fine. I'll level with you. I needed some information about a deal, and I needed it quick. Chris was supposed to be getting it for me, but he'd been avoiding me and I got tired of waiting, so I went down there to chivvy him along. He was a good kid, but he did get distracted easily."

"What information?"

"I'm not at liberty to say."

"He's dead, Tony," Russell said, exasperated. "Killed as he got home. If you know something, anything..."

"Whatever happened to him, I can tell you it was nothing to do with me. And that's the God's honest truth."

Tony's eyes flickered down to his watch. Whatever he knew, he wasn't about to share it with Russell. Tony shook his head, tired of this conversation, and pressed an intercom buzzer on his desk.

The door opened, and the gold-toothed man leered in.

"The gentleman is just leaving, Danny. Perhaps you could see him out."

Russell stood up to go. He wasn't going to get any more out of Tony today.

"I know you're a well-connected man," Russell said. "Ear to the ground and all that. So if you do hear anything, let me know, will you?"

"Oh, you'll be the first person I call."

He grinned at Russell, no humour there at all. As Russell headed through the door, Tony called after him.

"You know, this was probably all down to that fast mouth of his. Never could keep it shut. Looks like someone shut it for him. He was a good kid, but he was always going to end up on someone's bad side."

"I think you might be right, Tony," Russell said, an idea forming. "Chris knew a lot of secrets—but wasn't so great at keeping confidences.

Like you say, he did have a fast mouth. Never could keep it shut when he'd had a drink. The things he's told me…"

Russell raised his eyebrows, smiling knowingly, then turned and walked out, not waiting to let Tony respond. It was becoming clear that Chris had been killed because he knew something that someone else wanted to keep secret. Who and what were still to be discovered, but he guessed Tony wanted that information too. Not enough to kill Chris for it, but enough to chase him down to the club and hassle him for it. Playing Tony at his own game was a gamble. He only hoped it would pay off.

RUSSELL SAT IN THE WINDOW of the small pub opposite Tony Lagorio's restaurant, nursing a pint that was rapidly going flat, and monitoring the comings and goings down the side alley.

He had left Tony half an hour ago with the distinct feeling that the burly gangster knew more than he was telling. Russell didn't really know what or who he was waiting for, but he had a hunch he should watch the place for a while and see who showed up.

He was just beginning to doubt his instincts, when he spotted a young man he recognised hurrying down the street towards the restaurant. Gavin Jones—Chris's business partner in the fashion label. Sharp suit, high-waisted pants, nice brogues, hair slicked in an immaculately precise side-parting.

Russell sat up straight, suddenly intrigued as Gavin walked straight past the alley and pushed open the door of the restaurant. He disappeared from sight for a moment, and then reappeared at a table in the window. One of the two invitation-only tables. He said something to the waiter who scuttled off, leaving Gavin alone to settle down.

Russell hadn't spent much time with Gavin. Chris rarely socialised with his business partner outside of work. He had seemed charming enough on the few occasions that Russell had met him. A little awkward and uptight though that was probably more down to his family background and private education than his personality.

Gavin came from a very wealthy family and, from the sound of it, had spent most of his life not living up to his father's expectations. It was one of the few things Russell had thought Gavin and Chris had in common—disappointed fathers.

Gavin looked up from his menu as a Bentley pulled up alongside the kerb. Tinted rear windows, personalised plates. *Speak of the devil.*

The driver in the car behind hooted and swerved around them, waving an insult as he passed. No reaction from the chauffeur of the Bentley.

The rear passenger door opened and Gavin's father stepped out. Russell recognised him from the launch party for Gavin and Chris's label, not to mention the countless newspaper articles about his various deals and scandals. A businessman, multi-millionaire, and one of the most arrogant and dismissive men Russell had ever met.

He crossed the street quickly, entered the restaurant and joined his son at the table in the window. Gavin stood as his father arrived, but there was no embrace, not even a handshake. No wonder the kid was uptight.

The waiter arrived with a bottle of water and filled their glasses, took an instruction from Gavin's father and hurried off. The conversation was one-sided. Gavin's head nodding sullenly as his father spoke, fast and firm, hands gesticulating fluidly.

The conversation stopped abruptly as Tony appeared at the table and sat down between them, elbows on the table, fat fingers interlaced. He looked flustered and unhappy.

Gavin slid a folder across the table towards him, saying something as Tony opened it and read the contents. Tony closed the folder, looked up at Gavin who shut up quickly as Tony threw the folder back at him, scattering papers over the floor around the table.

Gavin fumbled the papers back into the folder while his father got to his feet. Tony did the same and the two men stood face to face for a moment before Tony snarled something and left.

The waiter stepped forward, offered Gavin's father his coat, and escorted him to the door. The millionaire turned back in the doorway, shouted something at his son, waved a warning finger, and strode out into the street, exuding rage and frustration.

In no time, the Bentley appeared again, and he slipped into the back, closing the door as the car pulled back into the stream of traffic.

What was that all about?

Russell tore his eyes off the retreating car just in time to see another familiar figure slip into the alleyway up the side of the restaurant. He'd almost missed it. He'd allowed himself to get distracted.

He watched as they approached the door and looked back over their shoulder before knocking. The door opened quickly, and they slipped inside without another backward glance.

That's interesting, Russell thought. *What are you doing here?*

5.

JOE WOKE TO FIND early dawn light creeping through the open window. He'd obviously slept through the night, though it had been a restless sleep, filled with half-forgotten dreams and disquieted voices.

Waking up on Chris's bed, he wondered if the whole thing had been a horrible nightmare, but when he saw Chris's jacket crumpled beneath him, that awful reality flooded back.

He walked into the kitchen to find Russell sitting at the small table, a sheet of paper in front of him, head bent and scribbling with a cigarette burning between his fingers. He looked up as Joe came in.

"Ah, you're up," Russell said.

"Yeah, sorry, I passed out. Must have slept through. Tea?"

"I've got one, thanks," Russell said, tapping his mug with the end of his pen.

Joe flicked the kettle on and craned over Russell's shoulder to see what he was writing. Meaningless doodling for the most part.

"Did you manage to get any sleep?" Joe asked.

"Enough."

Russell didn't look like he'd slept at all. His thinning hair was dishevelled, his eyes baggy and red, his shoulders slumped. Joe brought his mug back to the table and sat down heavily.

"Did you talk to him? This Lizard guy?" he asked.

"I did," Russell sighed, and took a drag of his cigarette, stubbing the half-smoked tab out in the ashtray and standing up to turn the radio off, drowning out yet another report of the miners' strike.

He placed the ashtray beside the sink, his movements precise and controlled. Russell liked things in the flat to be *just-so*, Chris had told Joe before he'd brought him home. "He's a neat freak," he'd said. "So don't move anything unless it's in my room. And don't leave your stuff lying around. He hates that."

Joe watched Russell pick up a dish cloth from the sink, wring it out, and wipe an already clean surface. Fast at first, gradually slowing until the cloth lay still beneath his clenched fist. Something was clearly bothering him.

"Well, what did he say?" Joe asked.

"Hmm?"

Russell turned from the sink and looked at Joe as though he'd almost forgotten he was there.

"It's what he didn't say that's more intriguing," he said, shaking his head.

He sounded distant, like he was trying to pull together a web of random, fleeting thoughts. Nodding to himself, he sat down again, lifted another cigarette from the packet and lit it, drawing the smoke in through tight lips. He offered the packet to Joe.

"No thanks," Joe said. "I don't really smoke."

"Well, aren't you the good boy?"

"Hardly," Joe said. But he was, if truth be told.

Russell blew a long stream of smoke out the side of his mouth, standing up again and pacing. Restless. Anxious. He stopped at the sink, staring out of the window, and seemed to freeze again.

"Did he say why he'd been to see Chris? Did he know where he went after he left the club?"

"Slow down," Russell said, tersely. "I'm trying to get everything straight in my head."

Joe took a sip of his tea and waited. He was beginning to figure out how Russell ticked, and too many questions when he was thinking definitely seemed to wind him up.

"He said he'd been paying Chris to get information for him," Russell said, eventually. "But apparently Chris was delaying, so he went to the club to chivvy him along."

"D'you think he killed Chris?"

Russell looked up at him.

"No. What happened to Chris was not Tony's style. But he knows where Chris went when he left the club."

"Where?"

"He wouldn't tell me."

"Great. So what now?"

"We go back over everything we know."

"Which is what?"

"Okay," Russell said, stretching. "Chris was struggling to make something of the business when Gavin stepped in. I saw Gavin, by the way, at Tony's restaurant, but we'll come back to that."

Joe leaned back, intrigued, as Russell continued.

"So Gavin stepped in as partner, with Daddy's money behind him and, like every other fool—present company included—promptly fell in love with him. But Chris refused to give him a managing share and, to keep his own half of the business, he decided to borrow the money from Tony."

"A known gangster," said Joe.

"Exactly. But then he struggled to pay it back, and Tony doesn't like waiting, so Tony offered him a different kind of opportunity."

"What?"

Russell hesitated to tell him.

"What?" Joe repeated.

"He said that he and had Chris had an arrangement," he sighed. "There were a couple of high-end clients, who apparently paid well for Chris's services."

"Services?" Joe spluttered. "You mean he was...?"

"Sleeping with guys for cash, yes," Russell confirmed.

"But—" Joe hesitated. "What, so this Lizard guy was his pimp?"

"I don't think he'd take kindly to that label. He says he just made a couple of introductions to clients who paid well for a high level of secrecy. It meant Chris could pay him back quicker. He doesn't know, or care, what they did together."

"So your detective friend was right," Joe said, feeling that another part of the friend he'd known had just been stripped away from his memory. "Chris *was* just a stupid rent boy."

He felt so angry with Chris. Had everything about him been a lie? Surely he hadn't needed to turn to prostitution to make money? He could have just asked. Joe would have helped him somehow. Then maybe he'd still be here.

Russell turned on him.

"No," he said. "Whatever he was doing, it wasn't as bad as you're imagining. You can't let this be how you remember him."

"But he could have asked if he needed money."

"He never would. You knew him. He had to be in control of everything. He always had a plan."

It was true. Chris would never have admitted to Joe that he was in trouble. He would never have asked for a handout. He would have been certain that he could solve his own problems without anyone else's help. He'd always been like that. It was one of the things Joe had loved so much about him.

"Besides, I think this was about more than just money," Russell said. "I should have known he was up to something, though."

"Why?"

"He came home this one time, about six months ago, really badly beaten—cracked ribs, broken jaw, the lot. He said he'd hooked up with some guy who'd turned nasty. I didn't press him for details. Maybe I should have."

"You think one of these clients beat him up?"

"I didn't know what he was doing at the time, obviously. But now... Well, maybe. You see, two days after he got beaten, a cheque turned up in the post for five hundred quid. He tore it up. Wouldn't talk about it. But the whole incident changed him. He seemed angrier after that, but also more driven."

"But if he was so desperate for money, why did he tear the cheque up?"

"He said it wasn't enough. Said he was going to make him pay properly."

"What did he mean? Make who pay?"

"No idea. Like I said, he wouldn't talk about it, and I didn't pry. The wounds healed, the bruises faded, and he seemed to be getting back on his feet."

"If he'd paid Tony off," Joe mused. "Why was he still seeing these guys?"

"Tony said they'd come to an arrangement where he would pay Chris for information he got from his clients. Pillow talk. Said Chris had a gift for getting people to share their secrets."

"So that's where all the money was coming from?"

"I'm not sure. It doesn't add up," Russell said, getting up again and pacing the floor. "I assumed the business was doing better, with all their new clients. But the amount he was spending—he paid back all the rent he'd missed in one hit, bought designer clothes, things for the flat. Unless the information he was getting was like gold dust, even Tony wouldn't be that generous. There's something we're missing."

"And Tony wouldn't tell you who Chris went to see the night he was killed?" Joe asked.

"Nope. There's bad blood between us. He's hardly likely to share his business secrets. All he said was that Chris was supposed to give him some important information, and he hadn't done it yet, so Tony went to hurry him up."

"So, where do we go from here?"

"Listen," Russell sighed, looking awkward. "I've been thinking about this, and… well, don't take it the wrong way, but I never was much of a team player, and I'm not looking for a new partner. I'm going to find out what happened to Chris, but I don't think you should get involved. It's just too dangerous."

Joe wasn't about to be shut out.

"Well, I *am* involved, whether you like it or not, and I'm not going anywhere until I find out what happened. He was my best friend. I loved him."

Joe saw a glimmer of resigned understanding cross Russell's face. A sudden thought struck him.

"Wait there," he said, excitedly, dashing off to Chris's room, and coming back with the little black diary.

"What's this?" Russell asked.

"I found it in one of Chris's drawers. It's a diary from last year, but look, it's a list of appointments or something. Some of them repeat regularly."

Russell flicked through the little book, back and forth through the pages.

"It's all just initials," he said. "It could be anything. Something to do with his label. His suppliers, maybe. Or new orders."

"I know, but it could also be a list of these clients Tony was talking about. The ones who didn't want their names used. When was it he got beaten up? Can you remember?"

Joe took the diary back, holding it eagerly. Russell bit his lip, thinking.

"It was just after my birthday. Must have been the Friday because we were all going to go out on the Saturday and he couldn't come. The cheque came on the Monday."

"So?" Joe prompted, ready.

"Friday the tenth of August."

Joe flicked through the pages until he found the right date.

"Huh," he said.

"What?"

Joe paged back through the diary to check. "MJ. Underlined twice. Hang on."

He turned back through the pages quickly, searching for the entry he'd seen earlier.

"See here?" he asked excitedly, holding the diary out to Russell. "He had this X marked in. And X was becoming more regular, see? And then, on this day, he's crossed out the X and put MJ instead. But look at that exclamation mark. Does that mean he figured out who X was? Because if so, then the next time he saw him was the night he got beaten up."

"Now that is interesting," said Russell, sounding more animated.

"But who the hell is MJ?" Joe asked.

"That's what we're going to find out."

They both stared at the diary. Was this a break, or another dead end?

AFTER A SOLID BREAKFAST, a couple of strong coffees, a shower and a change of clothes, Joe was ready to hit the streets.

The headlines on the stands outside the newsagent shouted that almost half of the striking miners had just gone back to work. It seemed the strike might finally be coming to an end.

Joe picked up a copy of one of the papers, determined to read it at some point in the day. He'd been following the miners' strike since the very beginning, and even more so since a small group of gays and lesbians from London had started going down to the picket lines with supplies and support.

It had been the only time he'd sent a newspaper cutting back to his sister, whose husband was a miner. *Stick that up your chuff, Deborah. Gays are good people too.* Unsurprisingly, she hadn't mentioned receiving it.

Joe and Russell had agreed to split forces, with Joe heading over to the fashion studio to have a chat with Chris's business partner, Gavin.

Chris had been so excited about a couple of big clients they had just secured, but he also mentioned that he and Gavin had been arguing a lot about the direction that their business should take.

If Chris's closest friends didn't know what had been going on in his life, did his business partner? How much of Chris's illicit income had gone back into the business? And did Gavin know about any of it?

At the moment it felt like they had lots of little leads, but nothing concrete. They had agreed to pull at every thread that was still hanging loose, and see what unravelled. One of them would lead to Chris's killer.

Joe remembered being particularly underwhelmed by Chris's business partner when he'd met him last year. In fact, he was struggling to remember what Gavin looked like. Still—hopefully he'd be able to tell them what Chris had been like to work with recently, and whether anyone had been bothering him at work.

"What are you going to do then?" Joe had asked. "While I'm talking to Gavin?"

"I have another couple of leads to follow up," Russell had said, dismissively. "Let's catch up at the Red Lion later, I want to talk to Paul again too."

Joe had a feeling that Russell had been trying to get him out the way. Russell had been distracted all morning, and Joe doubted he'd gone to bed at all. Something about that meeting with Tony Lagorio had disturbed him, and Joe had decided to engage in a little covert surveillance of his own, to see what was really going on.

He concealed himself in the alley where he'd found Patty hiding on the night Chris died. It was damp and smelled of piss, but it was dark and kept him hidden while he watched the front door of Russell's flat.

RUSSELL HAD A REASON for wanting Joe to go alone to see Gavin, but he didn't want to tell him about it yet. The figure he'd seen going into the alleyway had got him thinking and, slowly but surely, the old synapses were beginning to fire again.

With Joe safely out of the door and on his way, Russell sat down to wait—a fresh pot of coffee on the table, and a cigarette in hand. He'd deliberately planted a seed with Tony, suggesting that Chris might have shared a secret or two with him, hoping that the seed would take hold and Tony would scurry to get those secrets for himself.

The thing that had been disturbing him the most was the missing roll of film from Chris's camera. Whoever had come for him had wanted those photographs, and they'd been willing to kill for them.

While he didn't believe Tony had killed Chris, he did think that the big man knew exactly where Chris had been and what he'd been up to. Either way, he was sure Tony would act; and as soon as he'd seen the person entering the alleyway, he knew how it would play out.

He didn't have to wait long before there was a knock at the door, loud and official. Sure enough, when he opened the door, Detective Skinner was on the doorstep. Uncharacteristically, he'd come alone.

"I thought it'd be you he sent," Russell said, enjoying the frown that crossed Skinner's face. "Forget something, did you?"

Russell turned away from the door, heading back up the stairs, and felt Skinner hesitate for just a moment. He'd caught him off guard, and that made Russell happier than it should.

He'd known Skinner was corrupt for years, but he'd never been able to prove it. He was playing a dangerous game, given what had already happened to Chris, and knowing that Skinner was almost single-handedly responsible for him losing his job in the force, but he was onto something here, and if there was even the smallest chance he could find Chris's killer while exposing Skinner for the useless waste of skin he was, then he was going to grab it with both hands.

"Come on in, Detective," he said, lacing the man's job title with sarcasm.

Skinner followed him up the stairs and into the kitchen. Russell sat down, affecting the most relaxed pose he could muster.

"Coffee? I've just made a fresh pot," he offered, with obviously false bonhomie.

"No thanks, I'm not staying." Skinner said, standing in the doorway, as though entering the room would cause him to spontaneously combust.

"Found the killer yet?" Russell asked. "Got any promising leads?"

Russell was goading him and he was enjoying it. Skinner was not.

"I need to look through Mr Sexton's belongings," Skinner said.

"Sure," Russell said. "Show me your warrant and I'll take you through."

Skinner stood there, seething. Of course there was no warrant.

"I don't need a warrant."

"I'm afraid you do if you want to search my house," Russell smiled. "I'd have thought you'd know that. Man of your experience."

Skinner said nothing.

"What's the matter? Cat got your tongue?"

It was exactly the question Skinner had asked him the day Russell had been suspended—making sure he knew who had set him up for the fall.

"What did Tony send you back to look for, then?" Russell asked, cutting to the chase. "Documents? Lists? Photographs?"

"What?"

Too late. Russell had seen the flinch.

"The Lizard," Russell said. "That *was* you I saw visiting him yesterday, wasn't it? Funny, I thought, how you turned up just after I alerted him to the idea that Chris might have held some evidence back from him. Evidence that you didn't manage to take away when you examined the scene. Evidence that Tony clearly wanted."

"I don't know what you're talking about," Skinner stammered.

"Ah, it was ever thus," Russell teased.

Skinner stepped into the kitchen, jaw clenched, eyes black.

"Yes, I was there," he said. "I was simply pursuing a line of enquiry. Mr Lagorio was a known associate of the victim, and I had some questions for him."

"Oh, so you know he was one of the last people to see Chris alive, then? Arguing in the club, in front of all of those witnesses. Did he tell you how he'd been using Chris to steal information from his rivals?"

Each question was like a punch in the gut.

"That's always been your problem, Skinner," Russell tutted. "You've never asked the right questions. Never enjoyed the actual nitty gritty of detective work. It can be quite rewarding, you know? If done properly."

Skinner's lip curled. Russell stood up, sensing he might make a break for Chris's room. He leaned in the doorway to the corridor, coffee in hand.

"Unless you come back with a warrant, you're not coming in again."

"I could have you for obstructing an investigation."

"No, you couldn't," Russell replied. "We both know I'm right. So off you pop and do your paperwork like a good boy because you won't get anywhere in this house without it."

"I'll be back," Skinner said, realising he wasn't going to get past.

"Well you'd better be quick," Russell called, as Skinner stomped down the stairs. "Because my interest is already piqued, and you know what I'm like when I get my teeth into something. You wouldn't want me to beat you to it, would you?"

He didn't breathe until the door slammed and Skinner was gone. He still had so much to figure out. But it was all starting to take shape.

JOE DIDN'T LEAVE the alleyway until after Skinner stormed out of the flat, slamming the door. He'd half-debated nipping back up to the flat while Skinner was in there, just to make sure nothing bad was happening. He didn't trust that snivelling so-called detective, but he knew by now that Russell could handle himself. Still, he was surprised how protective he felt of Chris's former flatmate.

Having seen Russell come to the window to watch his old colleague leave, Joe slipped out of the alleyway and followed Skinner out of the square at a safe enough distance. When the detective ducked down into the underground station, Joe doubled back to get on with the task in hand—Gavin. He would talk to Russell about Skinner later.

CHRIS AND GAVIN'S STUDIO was, in fact, just a big-windowed room above a row of shops. An old lift ran a creaking service between the ground floor and the studio, but Joe took the stairs. He had never been good in confined spaces anyway, and the clunking and grinding of gears as the lift rolled up had given him palpitations the first and only time he'd used it.

As Joe approached the studio doors, a growing hum of animated conversation rose from within. It sounded like a party. He knocked, but there was no reply.

Joe pushed the door open, and the hum died quickly as everyone turned to look at him. His was not a face any of them recognised, so back to their conversations they went.

He scanned the room, noticing a few famous faces, people that he recognised from Chris's wall at the flat, or from recent episodes of Top of the Pops—clients, so-called friends, social vultures scavenging on the bones left behind.

Joe almost walked out again, but he had already spotted Gavin. As soon as Chris's business partner saw him, he waved, cutting his way through the room.

"It's you, isn't it?" he said, looking Joe up and down. "Chris's friend from..." he waved his hand, dismissively.

"School," Joe filled in. "Joe."

"Of course," Gavin said, with no hint of recognition.

Too distracted by all the celebrities in the room, Gavin waved casually at a mid-range pop star on the other side of the room that Joe vaguely recognised—eyeliner, earrings and a trademark quirky hat being the defining features.

"Is this a bad time?" Joe asked.

Gavin rolled his eyes dramatically, head tilted. Camper than Joe remembered him.

"People have just been turning up all day, darling. Apparently they all just want to feel closer to Chris. They're all putting their name down for the new line. Now they know it'll be his last."

Gavin didn't sound too put out by the new crowd of celebrity punters. He stared longingly at the gathered group, keen to get back to any potential orders.

"Vultures," Joe muttered.

"What?" Gavin snapped back into the conversation. "Don't knock it. Chris has finally managed to turn himself into the overnight success he always claimed to be."

"Is there somewhere more private we can talk?" Joe asked, feeling annoyed at Gavin's distracted nonchalance.

"Oh God, really? Right now?" Gavin huffed. "I mean, the studio is heaving. Can't it wait?"

"No. It can't bloody wait. This wasn't some publicity stunt. Chris was murdered. I'd have thought you'd be more upset." Joe snapped.

"I really haven't got time for this," Gavin said, trying to block Joe's entry to the room. "I've got clients to attend to."

"Chris told me you'd been arguing about the new line," Joe blurted. "He said you hated his designs. Thought they looked cheap and nasty."

Joe had said the last part in a loud enough voice for Gavin to suddenly decide that this conversation would be best pursued out of earshot of the eager fashionistas.

Gavin hurried them both into the small office, furnished simply with two uncluttered desks and a designer's easel covered in sketches and fabric samples. Chris's distinctive, artistic writing, sketches and colour swatches covered the board.

Joe felt immediately drawn to it, crossing the room to get a closer look, his hand hovering over the board.

"Right," Gavin said, closing the door. "Let's make this quick."

"What the hell is wrong with you?" Joe snapped, unable to bite his tongue any longer.

Gavin looked taken aback.

"Don't you care that Chris is dead?"

"Of course I care," Gavin said, "But, unlike Chris, I don't display my emotions in front of the clients. I still have a business to run."

"So, what's been going on?" Joe asked. "Why had you been fighting so much?"

"We didn't fight. I mean, of course we *argued* all the time—we're fiery, creative people, darling. We had creative differences."

"The way Chris told it, you could barely be in the same room as one another," Joe said.

"Well, he's always been prone to exaggeration," Gavin snapped. "We argued often, but only because we're both passionate about making the label a success. The problem was, Chris just wouldn't listen to anyone else. He had to be in control, he always knew best."

Joe was about to ask another question when he remembered Russell's advice—let the silence breathe. Don't lead him. Let him fill in the gaps for you.

Joe angled himself towards the design board and ran his fingers over the sketches there.

Chris had told him he thought Gavin was jealous. People in the industry had begun whispering that Chris was the real design genius behind the label. Gavin's lip curled ever so slightly as Joe's fingers traced the pencil lines.

"I mean, look at these new designs," Gavin said, bitterly. "They're just derivative crap. We're supposed to be throwing modern twists on classic styles, not pandering to the overnight whims of plastic pop stars."

"You seem quite happy to take their money though," Joe said, nodding towards those very pop stars outside the room.

"Well, that lot out there wouldn't know high fashion if it kicked them in the arse," Gavin snapped. "They're only here because Chris is dead and they all want a piece of him. It's like *The Emperor's New Clothes*."

"You don't seem that upset that your business partner was murdered," Joe said bitterly, stepping closer to Gavin.

"Of course I'm upset," Gavin spluttered. "But that doesn't mean I have to suddenly change my mind about the designs, does it? Or about the way he'd been behaving?"

"No," said Joe, picking up a pile of sketches from Gavin's desk and thumbing through them. "But I suppose it does mean you can take the credit for the success of the business without being challenged, doesn't it?"

Gavin snatched the sketches from him and placed them face down on his desk.

"I haven't got time for this," he said. "I'm truly sorry you've lost your friend. But I have to move on with my business. He caused me enough trouble when he was alive, and I'm damned if I'm going to let him keep doing it now he's dead."

He opened the door, waiting expectantly for Joe to file out. Joe didn't move.

"You also argued about money," Joe said.

"Always," Gavin said, dismissively. "Chris wasn't good with money."

That was an understatement.

"From what I heard," Joe said. "You had a huge fight on the morning he died. What about?"

"Who told you that?" Gavin asked, surprised. Joe had hit a nerve there.

"Chris did. He told me you were trying to kick him out of the company."

"Buy him out, not kick him out," Gavin said wearily. "It's simple enough. I didn't trust him. I couldn't be in business with him any more."

"But you wanted to keep the label? Trade on *his* name," Joe hadn't meant it to sound so spiteful.

"It's *my* name too."

Gavin shut the door again, a little too hard. Joe was getting to him. It must have been difficult being in the shadow of a tour de force like Chris. Gavin was probably the backbone of the business, which would have made him all but invisible compared to Chris.

"Chris was a liability. I just couldn't work with him. So I offered to buy him out. He said he'd see me in court."

Joe smiled to himself. It sounded just like Chris. Volatile, dramatic and unrealistic.

"It's not funny," Gavin snapped. Joe's smile dropped.

"So what will you do now?" Joe asked.

"I'll launch a new line in the spring," Gavin said. "I have a new investor wanting to buy into the business. I can finally move to a bigger studio and build the label properly."

"That was quick," Joe said.

"I've been working on the deal for months," Gavin replied. "That's what Chris and I fought about that morning. I had letters from the lawyers. They'd found a way that I could legally remove him from the business, but keep the name. Chris was livid, but it was the only condition my new investor had: the business had to come *without* Chris."

Joe was shocked. Chris had only hinted at a split with Gavin, he hadn't said anything about the relationship being this bad. Why hadn't Chris told him?

They had spent the whole evening getting ready to go out, chatting about work and the future, and Chris had been in great spirits. He'd had to go off and do some work earlier in the afternoon but, even then, he'd seemed pretty happy about it. And yet, he had been on the brink of losing his business—forced out by his partner and a bunch of lawyers. It would have destroyed him, and he didn't let on at all.

"But this was his passion," Joe said, indicating the studio. "His dream. He wouldn't just roll over and let you take it all away."

"Chris was obsessed with this grotty little attic, but it's hardly the image we... *I* want to project. I offered to buy him out. He could stay here and set up again on his own, with all this."

He waved his hand dismissively at the designs on the board.

Joe remembered coming to the studio on the day Chris had first signed the lease. Chris had been giddy with excitement. It was small and shabby, but it was perfect for the little collective he'd set up with a couple of college friends. There had been three designers crammed in here back then, and Gavin hadn't been one of them.

"What happened to the others?" Joe asked. "I thought the studio was supposed to be a collective."

Gavin laughed.

"That was all a load of hippy crap. Fashion is a cut-throat business, darling. Chris may have had the designs, but he had no idea how to sell them. He needed a business partner not a group of adoring fans and hangers-on."

Gavin fiddled with a sheaf of papers on the desk, absently tidying them into a neat pile.

"They all bailed quickly enough once SEXTON & JONES took off. Success breeds contempt, doesn't it? And Chris did like to shove his success in their faces a bit too often. I know he was your friend, but he was little more than a bully to most of us."

Much as he didn't want to admit it, Joe knew Gavin was right. Chris liked to be the centre of attention, adored by all, and he could be pretty bitchy if he felt threatened or unloved. Still, Joe didn't want to hear any of this from Gavin.

"But Chris seemed so excited about the new clients you had," Joe said.

"Yes, his new celebrity friends," Gavin sneered, rolling his eyes at the group outside the office. "I should have known he wouldn't be able to handle the success. Sure, he had talent and people liked his work, but in the end, he didn't really have what it took to run the business, and he hated the fact that I did."

Gavin looked at Joe, eyes hard. There was still so much anger and resentment about Chris. This must have been festering for a while.

"I think that's the real reason he wouldn't let me buy him out. Spite. He would rather ruin the label altogether than let me have it. That's why I had to go to the lawyers."

It was strange, Joe thought, how people's perceptions of Chris could be so wildly different. From Detective Skinner, to Paul, to Gavin—none of them saw Chris the way Joe had.

"In this game, your name—your reputation—is all there is," Gavin explained. "It doesn't matter how good the designs are if you can't deliver the product.

Gavin sighed, shoulders dropping.

"As soon as I offered to buy him out, Chris started doing everything he could to give the company a bad name: missing deadlines, showing up to meetings drunk, going off on protest marches when he should have been in here working. He was burning out. And he was pissing people off. I wasn't prepared to let him ruin the business."

"You seem awfully popular right now for a business on the brink of disaster," Joe said, indicating the throng outside the office window.

"They're shallow and vacuous," Gavin said. "Now that he's dead, he's some kind of saint. They can't order quickly enough. He'll become an overnight success."

"Or rather, you will," Joe sniped.

"Well, at least I earned it," Gavin replied. "I'm sorry, but dying is the best thing Chris has ever done for me, and I'm not going to pretend otherwise. Now, if you don't mind, I've got to get back to my clients."

JOE EMERGED ONTO the street from the side entrance, escaping the babble of voices and charged emotions. He should be shocked that Gavin was so vitriolic, but he could see that Chris had been putting his partner through the wringer recently.

There was obviously no love lost between Gavin and Chris towards the end of their relationship if Gavin had been forced to resort to lawyers and outside investors to get rid of a partner who seemed hell bent on running them both into the ground.

Yet again, Joe realised, this was just not the image he'd had of Chris. Had he really been so blinkered to his friend's true character? He hoped not.

Even in their last moments together, sitting in Chris's room, with Joe wearing one of his latest creations, Chris had been full of enthusiasm and excitement about his business. But thinking about it now, though, Chris had only ever referred to it as *his*. "My label. My designs. My customers." Joe hadn't once heard him mention Gavin.

It seemed like everyone Joe spoke to had some kind of axe to grind with his old friend. He'd always seemed so popular too. As the layers of Chris's life were being peeled away, Joe realised he was hanging on to an old impression of his dear friend, unwilling to believe that he had changed so much.

"Charming guy, huh?" Russell said, clapping a hand on Joe's shoulder. Joe jumped. "Sorry, didn't mean to scare you. How did it go with Gavin?"

"He'd obviously reached the end of his tether with Chris. And he didn't seem too upset about his death. He'd got the lawyers involved, apparently. He was going to force Chris out of the business. Did you know that?"

"Ouch. No, I didn't. There wouldn't have been much Chris could do to stop it, either, if he'd got the family lawyers involved."

Joe frowned.

"You know who his family is, right?" Russell asked.

"No," Joe replied. "Should I?"

"He's Gavin Melville-Jones. He dropped the Melville part to distance himself from the empire—make a name for himself. But he is happy to take Daddy's support when he needs it."

Joe looked blank.

"His dad's Nigel Melville-Jones. The property tycoon. Old money. Owns half of Mayfair. Always in the papers. Nasty piece of work."

"Don't think I've ever heard of him," Joe replied.

"The whole family are always in the news. The uncle's a Tory MP. There was a scandal a year or so ago to do with the two brothers colluding on something or other. Taxes, planning permissions... I can't remember now, but it was big at the time."

Joe shook his head. Obviously, he'd been too ensconced in his own provincial little life to notice.

"I just don't get it," Joe said. "How did someone like Gavin, from that kind of family, end up running a fashion label in a shitty Soho studio with Chris? I mean, I loved Chris, but he wasn't even the kind of person you'd trust with your beer, let alone your family money."

"You underestimate him," Russell smiled. "Chris was sharp. Canny. He knew what he was doing. And, my God, he could design clothes that people wanted to wear. And he could draw a crowd around him. Celebrities, musicians, all of them loved him."

"They're all up there now," Joe sneered, "fawning over the new collection. Gavin is seething that Chris is still managing to outshine him, even when he's dead."

They both walked on in silence, hit by another reminder of a fabulous life snuffed out too soon.

"So where do you think Chris was getting all this money from? Do you think he was still seeing these secret clients?" Joe asked.

"I think we should go and talk to Paul again," Russell said. "I got the feeling he's been doing a little more prying into Chris's secrets than he was letting on."

Joe agreed. He had sensed the jealous tone in Paul's voice too. And he still wasn't happy with Paul's explanation of why he'd been over at Chris's flat on the night he died, and why he'd run away when he'd seen Joe.

6.

THE RED LION WAS FULL, the windows steamed up. Smoke hung thick in the air. Clamouring voices vied for an audience.

"Blimey," Russell said, pushing the door open and squeezing his way through the bodies towards the bar with Joe following close behind. He hadn't seen the place this busy in years, not in the daytime, anyway.

"What's going on?" Russell asked the barman, finally reaching the front of the throng.

"They're all off on another protest in a while. Apparently the eviction notice has been served on the Campbell Centre. There's going to be a sit-in. It's a shame Chris isn't here, he'd have been the first to tie himself to the railings."

"You're not wrong there," Russell said. "Two pints please, Ron."

"Pride?"

"Sure."

"They'll be heading out in a few minutes," he said. "You'll be able to hear yourself think."

While Ron poured the pints, Russell scanned the bar, looking for Paul. He spotted him in a corner, laughing with a young guy in a fluorescent crop top. The laugh didn't reach his eyes though and, as though sensing he was being watched, Paul looked up and caught Russell's eye. The smile dropped away completely when he saw Joe there too.

Russell knew that Paul was smitten with Chris, and having Chris's oldest friend turn up on the scene, with all their easy camaraderie and long history, had been yet another challenge for Paul's already fragile ego.

Chris had always managed to surround himself with these adoring young men who would all end up vying with each other for his attention. He'd enjoyed the control of playing them off against each other, choosing his favourites like a general in Rome. Russell had pulled him up on it a couple of times, pointing out how hurtful it could be.

"Oh, come on, I'm just having fun," Chris had laughed. "They must all know they don't stand a chance. But it's so wonderful to be adored."

His flippant arrogance had been one of the only things that Russell hadn't liked about Chris. Though even that had begun to recede since that beating Chris had taken last year. Some of his cocky bravado had faded, and a more serious, pensive side had begun to show itself. He'd started to pay attention to the people around him, started having a conscience, socially and politically. Russell had felt he was actually starting to grow up.

Ron was right. Chris would have been leading the protest about the closure of the Campbell Centre. It had become a real mission of his to keep it open.

One of their close friends, Thomas Campbell—a former lecturer at the fashion school, and the guy who had introduced Chris to Russell when he found out his protégé had needed a room in London—had died of AIDS the previous year, and it had hit Chris a lot harder than Russell would have imagined.

Thomas wasn't the first of Russell's peers to fall victim to the awful illness, but he had been the first for Chris. When he died, he'd left his modest estate to the charity that had cared for him in his final year, and the charity had renamed themselves to the Campbell Centre in honour of his bequest.

Thomas's illness had brought out the side of Chris that others seldom saw. A kind, nurturing side; gentle and selfless. He had spent hours visiting Thomas as the disease stole more from him; and all the while, he had become more incensed that so little could be done for the victims of this terrible killer which hung over them all.

After Thomas had died, Chris had become a campaigner for better treatment of AIDS patients, and better care for the dying. It was a thankless task, and one that took a huge chunk of his physical and emotional strength.

So it was no wonder he had lost some of his passion for the fashion industry, or running the business, and even in his own welfare. He'd caught a glimpse of how unfair life could be, and it had eaten away at him almost as much as the disease had eaten away at Thomas.

Russell had sat up enough evenings listening to him rant about the Ministry of Health, the lack of care, the underlying homophobia which allowed so many to die unsupported. Chris had even taken to volunteering at the centre when he could, and he'd dragged Russell along a few times too.

He had changed in those last few months of his life. Russell wondered now if that change had been about more than Thomas's death alone. These secret clients, selling information to Tony, losing his business—it all must have weighed so heavy on him, and yet he said nothing.

"There you are, lads," Ron said, placing the beers on the bar and breaking into Russell's train of thought. "On the house. For Chris."

"Thanks, Ron," Russell said, and raised his glass to meet Joe's. "To Chris."

Joe smiled and clinked glasses with him.

"To Chris," he agreed.

Russell realised he was growing quite fond of Chris's friend. Despite the awful circumstances of the last few days, he saw that Joe was an intelligent, thoughtful young man, who could probably do with even the smallest bit of his old friend's self-confidence.

As they drank, a handsome, dark-haired young man, who looked like he needed both a good wash and a solid night's sleep, sidled up beside Joe and placed a kiss on his cheek. Joe turned quickly, and Russell saw him relax as soon as he recognised the lad.

"Luc," Joe said, sounding happy for the first time in days.

"I'm so sorry," Luc said. "I heard what happened to Chris. It's so terrible."

The guy's accent was as delightful as his face.

"Yes, it's been awful," Joe replied.

"I can't even imagine. Are you okay?"

Joe turned to look at Russell.

"Russell, this is Luc," he said, awkwardly. "I was with him on the night..." his voice faded.

"Nice to meet you, Luc," Russell said quickly. They all knew which night. "Excuse me a minute, will you? I'll be right back."

Russell headed through the now dissipating crowd, towards Paul and his friend. Having Joe suddenly distracted was a perfect excuse to talk to Paul alone. Given Paul's infatuation with Chris, and his obvious jealousy of the friendship Joe and Chris had shared, Russell guessed he'd get more out of him on his own.

"How're you holding up, Paul?" he asked, slipping himself into the corner between Paul and the guy in the neon crop top. The guy smiled a superficial, half-sneering smile, and slinked away, his style having been well and truly cramped.

"I'm okay," Paul replied, his voice heavy. "It's been a bit crazy, to be honest. I still can't believe it."

"Look," Russell said, guiding him further into the corner. "I've been asking around, trying to find out a bit more about what Chris had been up to. I wanted to run a few things by you?"

"Me?" He sounded defensive. "I thought you and the little school friend were the ones playing Cagney and Lacey."

"Nobody's playing anything, Paul." Russell snapped, voice louder than necessary. "We're just trying to find out what happened to our friend. It's not a competition. Chris is gone, and unless we do something, his killer will just walk away without ever being caught."

Paul leaned away from him nervously. Russell needed to calm down. These kids were so fragile. He took a deep breath.

"Now, I'm giving you the benefit of the doubt, because I know how much you loved Chris, but I'll tell you this for free: his mate over there was about to go to the police to tell them that he saw you running away from the scene with Chris's blood on your hands."

Paul looked shocked. His mouth goldfishing as he tried to come up with a reply.

"Do you think they'd give a shit about finding out the truth before charging you? Because, I can assure you, they wouldn't. They'd collar you without question and leave you in the slammer to take your chances with the rapists and the murderers."

Paul was trying to be strong, but Russell saw the tears welling in his eyes. They were all so young and naïve, he had to remind himself. He put his hand on Paul's arm.

"It's alright," he said. "I told him to hold off going to the police. I know you didn't hurt Chris."

He felt Paul's arm relax under his grip.

"But I also know there's something you're not telling me."

Paul shook his head in denial.

"I was a detective for ten years, Paul. And a cop on the beat for long enough before that. I heard what you said when we talked to you before, even if Joe didn't. You know something. You either tell me now, or we tell the police you were outside the house on the night he died and you can explain the whole lot to them. If they'll bother listening."

Paul sagged.

"Okay," he said, looking around the room as more people filed out of the door, the noise level diminishing by the minute. "He'd started being really distant and secretive. Not coming out when he said he was going to, lying about where he'd been. I guessed he was seeing someone, and I was jealous. I'm not proud of it, but I'd started following him."

Russell let him speak. He was fairly sure Paul hadn't hurt Chris, but the threat of telling the police he'd been there had been more than enough to open the floodgates of confession.

"Anyway, I followed him all the way to this big house up in Mayfair and I watched him go in. I waited outside. I wanted to know who he was visiting there because suddenly all the money he'd been throwing around recently started making sense. He'd got himself some kind of sugar daddy."

Or a rich client, Russell thought.

"I waited for about an hour, in the pissing rain, and when he came out, I saw the guy up at the window, watching him leave. I couldn't believe it."

"What? Who was it?"

"That MP. Robert Melville-Jones. The one they're all protesting about today. The one who's selling the house on the corner and closing down the Campbell Centre. He's Gavin's bloody uncle. And Chris said he hated them all. But I saw them kissing."

Russell's instincts began firing as more of the pieces slotted into place.

"Well, I ran after him," Paul continued. "Tackled him about it. I was raging. How could he even be in the same room as that prick? Eventually he told me what he'd been doing."

Russell took a swig of beer, letting Paul talk.

"Tony had got him into doing some high-end clients for money. He said it had helped him pay off his debt to Tony, but then he realised that it was easier than he thought. I think he had actually started enjoying it."

The bar was almost empty now, Russell leaned over to grab his beer and caught Joe's eye. Joe frowned, and Russell gave him a look which he hoped indicated that he should stay where he was and leave them to talk alone. A slight nod. Message understood. Joe turned back to his gorgeous Frenchman. Paul leaned back on the bar, in full flow.

"They were always these rich guys, who would pay extra for discretion," Paul said, unable to keep the sneer from his voice. "Like that bloody hypocrite MP. Chris said he didn't know who he was at first. It was only when he saw Melville-Jones at that first protest back in the summer that he figured it out. He challenged him the next time he saw him. Chris couldn't understand how he could be so duplicitous. Closing down that centre, stripping support from AIDS victims, and all the while he was gay himself. Anyway, Melville-Jones lost it. Beat him up really badly."

"Melville-Jones did that to him?"

Russell had seen the MP many times on the TV news. He didn't look like he could slap a backside with any kind of force, let alone break a young man's jaw.

"Apparently he was really scared that Chris would go to the papers about it. He totally flipped. But then he sent a cheque to say sorry."

"I remember," Russell said. "I didn't know it was from him though. Chris tore it up."

"Yes, because he said he didn't want his guilt money. But I got to thinking, well, just imagine how bad it would be for his career if it came out that he was gay, and that he was paying rent boys for sex."

Russell didn't need to imagine. That's exactly how his own career had been brought to an untimely end. Paul obviously realised what he'd just said.

"Oh Jesus, sorry," he said.

"Don't worry about it," Russell replied, downing another slug of his pint, putting the glass on the bar and wiping his mouth with the back of his hand.

He was trying to calm down, but he was furious. With Chris for being so stupid. With Paul for not saying anything sooner. And with himself for not guessing what had been going on right under his nose. He could have stopped Chris. Maybe he could even have saved him.

"Why didn't you say anything before?"

Paul looked down at his feet. There was something else he wasn't saying. Russell waited for it.

"Because I've been blackmailing Melville-Jones ever since I found out about the two of them," he mumbled. "And I think he killed Chris because of it."

"Oh Jesus Christ, Paul!"

Paul looked totally distraught. Russell could have swung for him.

"So, you decided to blackmail an MP," Russell sighed. "And not just any MP, one who's part of the wealthiest families in London, with power and control beyond your wildest dreams. And then, despite thinking that he'd killed Chris, you just sat on your hands and said nothing? Jesus Christ! Did Gavin know about any of this? His bloody uncle!"

"No," Paul said. "But Tony did. He's been trying to buy that corner plot on Frith Street from them. He's been paying Chris extra to get something on the family, looking for a way to drive the price down. But Chris wouldn't give him anything, because he didn't want him to buy the building and close the Campbell Centre. He said Robert had promised to block the deal, but then he'd gone back on his word. That's what Chris had gone to see him about that night. It's all my fault."

Paul broke down. Russell didn't console him. How could he have been so stupid? The Melville-Jones family had more influence and power than anyone could imagine. Why on earth did Paul think he'd be able to get one over on them? He took Paul's face and turned it to look at him.

"Have you told anyone else about this?"

"No," Paul replied.

"Good. Keep it that way."

"What are you going to do?" Paul asked, and Russell sensed he meant it as much about himself as about the information he'd just passed on.

"I'm going to get to the bottom of this whole mess," Russell said. "And put it right. You stay here. Don't go anywhere—and don't talk to anyone. Not even Ron. Okay?"

He turned back to the bar, drained his pint, and walked off, tapping Joe's shoulder on his way past.

"Come on," he said. "We've got to go."

Russell clocked Joe's wistful look as he walked away from Luc. Unsurprising, really—he *was* gorgeous.

"You going to see him again?"

"Would have been nice, but he's going back to France tomorrow. Everything okay?"

"Far from it—but hopefully it will be soon. I know where Chris went after the club."

JOE HAD LISTENED, RAPT, as Russell filled him in on the conversation with Paul. He'd found it hard enough to learn that Chris had been selling himself for cash, and sharing illicit information with a notorious gangster, but had Chris known that Paul was blackmailing the same politician he'd been seeing? Joe couldn't help feeling that Paul's jealousy might have cost his friend his life.

Russell had told him to go back to the flat and go through all of Chris's stuff again, looking for anything to do with the Campbell Centre or the Melville-Jones family. He promised to meet him back there shortly—he was going to call in a few favours from an old friend at the station and see if he could find Melville-Jones's address.

Joe opened the front door, and took a deep breath before stepping into the hallway. The memory of what he'd seen there was still too vivid and fresh and, despite Russell having paid for a team of professional cleaners to clear away all traces of Chris's blood, he couldn't help feeling uneasy as he stepped over the black-and-white tiles and headed up the stairs.

He paused on the landing outside the door to the flat. The door was open. Just a crack. Joe leaned in and saw that the lock had been forced. His heart jumped. Someone had broken in. What if they were still in there?

He held his breath for a moment, listening for sounds from within. Nothing. Slowly he stepped forward, pushing the door open gently, wincing at the soft creak from the old hinges.

Inside, the flat smelled different. Something sweet and musky. *Cologne.* And he recognised it. Joe stuck close to the wall and made his way up the corridor. The kitchen was empty, tidy, exactly the way they'd left it.

He froze as a floorboard creaked beneath his foot. He heard another noise too, a rustling noise, from further down the corridor. There *was* still somebody in the house. And they were in Chris's bedroom.

He approached Chris's door carefully, casting around for something within reach that he could use as a weapon. Of course there was nothing.

He held on to the door frame while he slipped his shoe off. It might be ridiculous, but at least it was something.

He pushed the door open quietly, seeing a slim, tall man in a dark hooded sweatshirt leaning over Chris's desk, turning out the drawers.

"Hey," Joe protested, stepping closer, shoe raised, heel first, ready to strike.

The man turned quickly, face still concealed by the hood on his sweatshirt, and charged at Joe, punching him quick and hard, right in the nose.

The pain was exceptional. His vision filled with a starburst of pinprick lights as the man shouldered him aside and sprinted away.

Joe held his nose, trying to stem the sudden flow of blood and ease the pain, willing it not to be broken.

"JOE? ARE YOU OKAY?" Russell asked, finding him lying on the couch with a cold compress on the bridge of his nose. "What happened?"

Joe peeled the compress away, blinking through the pain.

"There was someone in the flat when I got home," he said, his voice thickened by his damaged nose. "In Chris's room."

"Who was it?"

He swung his legs round, trying to lever himself off the sofa.

"I don't know. He did this before I got a chance to look at him."

"What happened to your shoe?"

"I thought I could use it to defend myself."

"Maybe you need to stop wearing pumps," Russell laughed. Poor kid. "Stay still a bit."

Russell headed to the sink and ran a tea towel under the tap. Joe had done a good job of cleaning up his face, but Russell noticed that he'd managed to drip blood all the way across the kitchen floor.

"Thanks," Joe said, taking the cool cloth from Russell and wincing as he pressed it to his nose.

"You okay?" Russell asked, peering at the cut.

"Yeah, I don't think it's broken, but it hurts."

"Makes you look ever so butch though. You'll live."

Russell left him nursing his bruises and went to check the damage to the flat. The lounge had been overturned, sofa cushions on the floor, his record collection spilled over the carpet, some of it smashed, pictures knocked from shelves. A mess, but it looked more like deliberate destruction rather than a search.

"I'll get you some pain killers," he said, passing Joe again on his way to Chris's room. Joe groaned, slowly standing up.

Unlike the lounge, Chris's room was completely destroyed—the contents of every drawer and shelf strewn across the floor, the mattress slewed off the bed, chair overturned, wardrobe emptied.

They wouldn't have found what they were looking for, but they'd had a good look. Had Skinner come back while they were out? Or was someone else also searching the evidence that Chris had gathered?

Stepping into the room, Russell took in the destruction. He picked up the small chair and righted it in front of Chris's desk. So much chaos. And for what?

He noticed the newspaper front page pinned to the board with Chris's face, front and centre, finger raised, screaming at Robert Melville-Jones. The image had almost captured the moment when Chris had discovered who his client was. The moment that would eventually lead to his death.

The jigsaw was coming together in Russell's mind. He knew why Chris had been killed, he just needed to figure out who of the potential suspects had done it.

Russell carefully took the page off the board and carried it back through to the kitchen. He handed Joe a couple of pain killers and poured him a glass of water.

"Is anything missing?" Joe asked. "What were they looking for?"

"Tony has been trying to force a quick sale of the Frith Street property. Chris was supposed to be getting him information that would help him get an advantage. But he died before he could give it to Tony, if he had it at all. Turns out Tony's also got Skinner in his pocket. Skinner came round earlier wanting to search Chris's room, but I'd already seen him at Tony's when I went in to rattle Tony's cage, so I knew what Skinner was after when he came back here. Naturally, I told him to piss off. He obviously waited for us to go out and he came back. Sadly for them, Skinner was too late. Whoever killed Chris, took the evidence with them. It was all on his camera."

"Who?"

Russell laid the newspaper article on the table.

"I think *he* may have an idea," he said, tapping the image of the MP. "Robert Melville-Jones."

"MJ," Joe said. "From the diary. Our mysterious Mr X."

"That's my guess."

"So what do we do? Tell Detective Skinner?"

"After what he just did to your face? No. Besides, the family has too much influence. Without the right evidence, they'll just shut any accusation down. I say we go and talk to him ourselves."

Joe's finger traced over the image of Chris in the newspaper. He obviously missed his friend. Russell missed him too.

They'd both been so caught up in finding out what had happened to Chris, neither of them had mourned the friend they'd lost. Perhaps that would come later.

"Come on," Russell said. "Let's have a drink, let those painkillers take effect, and in the morning, we'll go have a chat with our local MP."

7

RUSSELL AND JOE WAITED outside the expensive townhouse in Mayfair as the sound of the doorbell faded. There was a light on upstairs, so they knew someone was home.

Russell had been determined to get here early, to catch Melville-Jones before he left for work, and he had cajoled a reluctant Joe out of bed with strong coffee and more painkillers.

Joe kept his coat bundled up around him, standing just behind Russell. This place looked so grand and he felt suddenly scruffy in his old jeans and duffle coat, with a brawler's cut across his nose and two developing black eyes.

The light in the hallway came on and the door opened until the safety chain stopped it. A man peered out through the crack, eyeing them suspiciously.

"Mr Melville-Jones?" Russell asked, though it was unmistakably him.

"Can I help?" he asked nervously.

"Russell Dixon. I wonder if we might have a word. We have some questions for you regarding your relationship with a Mr Christopher Sexton."

He sounded so official, Joe thought. Years of practice door-stepping suspects would give you that confidence. Joe saw the look of panic flash across the man's face.

"I'm late for work," he stammered.

"I'm sure you'd rather we did this in private, Mr Melville-Jones. Rather than here on the doorstep."

"You'll have to come back another time," his voice was faltering. There would be no other time.

"We have some rather sensitive," Russell paused for effect, holding up a brown envelope, "matters to discuss."

A sigh. The door closed. Russell looked back at Joe and winked. The old empty envelope trick had worked. The chain slid back and the door opened fully.

"Come in then," Melville-Jones said reluctantly.

He peered up and down the street behind them as they shuffled in. It must be tough, Joe thought, living your life in the public eye like he did, terrified that one day someone would share your darkest secrets with the world, just like Paul had threatened to do.

"Follow me," Melville-Jones said, brusquely.

They did. He led them up a wide hallway and into a dark wood-panelled study. A heavy desk dominated the room, a green glass desk lamp casting a pool of light on ist crimson leather inlaid surface. The walls were lined with shelves of old books, neatly stacked in matching volumes.

"What do you want?" he asked, showing Russell and Joe to a pair of high-backed leather chairs in front of the desk as he took his own seat behind it.

"We're looking into the circumstances surrounding Chris Sexton's murder," Russell said, his voice calm and assured but careful not to give the wrong impression. They couldn't actually say they were the police, after all.

"And what does that have to do with me?" Melville-Jones asked. His accent was old money, public school, Oxbridge. A man used to commanding others, but his voice was thin and reedy, and wobbled a little as he asked. He knew damn well what it had to do with him.

"I'm going to cut to the chase," Russell said, tapping the envelope on his knee, letting the MP imagine the contents. "We know that you were, to put it delicately, seeing Chris occasionally. Paying for certain services."

He let it hang in the air. Melville-Jones began to stammer an objection but Russell cut across him.

"We also know that another party had threatened to expose your relationship, and had been using that threat to extort money from you."

Melville-Jones slumped back in his chair, realising that, in fact, they did know everything.

"You don't understand," Melville-Jones began. Russell wasn't going to give him any slack at this stage in the questioning.

"Where were you on the night of Friday the fifteenth of February?" Russell asked.

"I was here," Melville-Jones stuttered. "But you can't possibly think I killed Chris?"

He sounded so outraged and hurt by the suggestion that, for just a moment, Joe wondered whether they'd completely misjudged the situation. Russell clearly had no such doubt.

"That's exactly what we think," Russell said. "Was anyone with you? Can anyone confirm that you were here all night?"

"No, I was here alone," Melville-Jones said, but Joe heard the hitch in his voice.

"All night?" he asked.

Melville-Jones shot him an angry look.

"I had a visitor at around eleven," Melville-Jones admitted. "But he didn't stay long."

Russell stood up and paced slowly across the room, fingers running along the spines of books in the shelf. A bead of sweat broke out on Melville-Jones's forehead.

"This visitor," Russell said, "it wasn't Chris, by any chance? What happened? Did you catch him going through your files looking for more secrets to share? Is that why you killed him? Is that it?"

"I think you should leave now," Melville-Jones said, standing up angrily. "If you have any further questions, I'd like to call my lawyer."

"We're asking politely, there's no need to get agitated."

"I'll have you in front of the Commissioner of Police," Melville-Jones spluttered.

"Oh, that won't help. We're not police, Mr Melville-Jones. I'm sorry if we gave you the wrong impression."

Melville-Jones's mouth opened in protest and then shut, dumbfounded.

"We just want to know what happened to our friend," Joe said. "We know you were paying him..."

"It wasn't like that," Melville-Jones hissed, sitting back down. "I wasn't paying for sex. We were in a relationship. I was only too happy to give him money if he needed it, but it wasn't in exchange for sex. I loved him and he loved me. At least, he said he did."

Russell had been about to throw out the next question, confirming their assumption that Melville-Jones had killed Chris, but this confession knocked him off his stride.

"A relationship?" he questioned.

"Yes," Melville-Jones insisted. "Well, as much as our clandestine meetings could ever be called a relationship. It wasn't like you're suggesting though. I wasn't paying him for sex, and nor was I paying him to keep quiet. I was happy to help him. Especially if it was to help his business. He was such a talented young man."

He smiled sadly at them. Russell turned to look at Joe, frowning. Had they got this so wrong? Another creeping thought was beginning to form in Russell's mind.

"Did you ever talk to Chris about your business?" Russell asked.

"God no," Melville-Jones laughed. "It would be bad enough for the constituents to discover their MP liked boys, let alone find out I'd been sharing government secrets. Even I'm not that stupid."

"I don't mean your work," Russell clarified. "I was talking about the family business."

"Oh that," Melville-Jones said dismissively. "Sometimes. But it would always lead to quarrels, so I tried to avoid it. He was cross because my brother was selling the corner house on Frith."

"And evicting the Campbell Centre," Joe snapped.

"I tried to stop the deal, but I really don't have a lot of say in it. The purchaser wanted vacant possession. My brother had already agreed."

"The purchaser being Tony Lagorio?"

"How did you know that?"

"He told me," Russell said. "And he also told me he'd been paying Chris to get information from you so he could drive down the price."

"Oh," Melville-Jones said, deflating more as the realisation sank in. "Oh, well that does explain a few things."

"What do you mean?"

"Well, Chris was cross about the charity, so I promised I'd help them find a new home. Anonymously, of course."

"Of course," Russell said.

"And that seemed to satisfy him for a while, but then recently he started bringing it up again. He kept going on about the money and how my family were corrupt and selfish. I thought it was because he was annoyed with Gavin. They were always falling out, those two. Nothing I could do about it, of course."

Joe noticed Russell freeze—another piece had just slotted into place.

"I got quite annoyed with him, if I'm honest," Melville-Jones continued. "After all, I'd promised him that my share of the money from the sale was going to fund my contribution to the new Campbell Centre, and the rest was going to him, indirectly, anyway. Gavin's father, my brother, had agreed to invest in their label."

"Yes," said Joe, bitterly. "But only on the condition that Chris was no longer involved."

"What?"

"Gavin was forcing him out. The lawyers—your family lawyers—had already issued the paperwork."

Melville-Jones slumped in his seat.

"Oh dear," was all he said.

"Thanks for your time, Mr Melville-Jones," Russell said abruptly. "You've been very helpful."

He turned to a rather surprised Joe.

"Come on, we've wasted enough time."

"WHERE THE HELL are we going?" Joe demanded.

One minute they'd been grilling a suspect, and the next, Russell was out of the blocks like a hare on a dog track. It was all Joe could do to keep up as they dashed across another pedestrian crossing, heading back towards Soho.

"What's going on?"

"I can't believe I've been so stupid," Russell said. "It was staring me in the face the whole time."

"What?" Joe asked. "Slow down a minute!"

"I know who killed Chris," Russell shouted as they dashed over the pedestrian crossing, heading back towards Soho.

"Who?" Joe called again.

"No time, come on."

Joe had always considered himself quite fit, but Russell could move extraordinarily fast for a portly man. As they dashed through the streets, Joe tried to piece everything together. How did the conversation they'd just had tie in with everything they had learned so far?

On the way to see Melville-Jones, Russell had been convinced that he was the one who'd killed Chris. Now, something the MP had said had lit a fire under Russell, and Joe was damned if he could figure it out.

"Wait here," Russell said. "And cover the side door. If he comes out, tackle him to the ground."

"Who?"

"Who do you think?"

Russell dashed away leaving Joe standing in the street. He looked up at the building Russell had gone into, and everything started to make sense.

The door to the studio—Chris and Gavin's studio—swung shut with a bang.

RUSSELL TOOK THE STAIRS two at a time, annoyed that he had missed the clues until now and angry that he had wasted time. The studio doors bounced off the wall as he slammed them open and stormed through.

The main gallery room was empty, but there was a light on in the small internal office. Good.

Gavin jumped back from the desk as Russell barged into the office. He dropped the overnight bag he'd been busy stuffing with paperwork.

"Going somewhere?" Russell asked.

"What are you doing here?" Gavin stammered.

"Why did you do it?" Russell fumed. "You could have started again with your own business, with your own designs. Why did you have to try to take all this from Chris?"

Gavin backed up, trying to put some distance between himself and Russell.

"I don't know what you're talking about. Get out, or I'll call the police."

Russell stopped, effectively blocking the door in case Gavin tried to make a run for it.

"You do that. It'll save me the effort. I'm sure they'd be very interested to hear how you killed Chris," he said.

"What?" Gavin spluttered, but Russell could see he'd got it right. Gavin was already looking for a way to get out.

"You were jealous of his popularity," he continued. "Jealous of his talent. You wanted to crush his dreams because he was better than you."

"That's not true," Gavin said defiantly. "The company used both of our designs, not just his."

"But none of yours were in the new line, that's why you went running to Daddy to get his lawyers to help you buy Chris out."

"No, I…"

"But then you realised that it wouldn't work, because your father would never expose his company to the kind of scandal that Chris had uncovered in your family. And you couldn't handle the fact that Chris would get to keep the business. You couldn't cope with the idea that his designs would be the backbone of the new line. You could already see his popularity outshining yours."

Gavin looked down, his head sagged. Russell had seen it many times before; when the defiance leaves the suspect and the truth comes out.

"He always got everything he wanted," Gavin said quietly. "He was the handsome one, the talented one, the confident and funny one. He had everything, and he knew it. When I first met him, I was besotted. Did you know that?"

"No," Russell didn't want to interrupt the train of thought.

"Well, I was. I just wanted to be near him. I knew he needed money to make the business work. That whole cooperative thing was just more people hanging on his shirt tails. He almost bit my hand off when I suggested we partner up. I was so happy that I would be the one to make his dream a reality."

Russell relaxed his position slightly, feeling that Gavin was less likely to try running if he was talking like this.

"And we didn't just form a business partnership either," Gavin said. "We started sleeping together. And because of the fool I am, I thought it was because he liked me. I should have known he was just using me to cashflow the business while he paid Tony back his stake."

He shook his head at the memory.

"I was an idiot. It took me too long to see what he was really like. Then suddenly he had all this money, but he wouldn't tell me where it was coming from. And he kept lying about where he had been, and who he had been with. It was his friend Paul that let it slip in the end. He'd followed him."

"To your uncle's house?"

Gavin nodded.

"Uncle Robert wouldn't believe me that Chris was just using him too. He said they were in love, and he was happy to give Chris any money he needed. When I tackled Chris about it, he just laughed at me."

So it *was* Chris's arrogance that got him killed, Russell thought.

"I told him I would buy him out. Pay him to go away quietly and leave us alone. My father agreed to give me the money. I even got our lawyers to draw up the documents. He would get nothing but cash out of the deal. Everything else would be mine."

"So what happened?"

"Chris flipped out. He said he'd go to the press with what he had. Said he had enough evidence of corruption and fraud, and God knows what else to ruin my whole family if I carried on with the lawyers. He had photographs of him and my uncle in bed together. Photographs he said he would give to the papers."

Gavin shuddered.

"So you killed him?"

"I didn't know what else to do. He was serious. He was going to share everything: the business deals, the backhanders, my uncle's sexuality. He would have destroyed all of us."

Gavin looked up at him, his eyes red-rimmed and angry.

"I followed him to the club. I knew Tony was itching to find him, because he'd been by the studio earlier. I guessed why Tony wanted to find him, and when he left the club I picked him up. I was going to try and talk some sense into him, pay him off... I don't know."

Gavin shook his head. Russell said nothing.

"I drove him to the flat. I promised to pay him double what Tony was offering for whatever evidence he had. But when we got there, he started taking the piss. He said even my uncle was better in bed than me. I lost it. I was so angry. Before I knew it, I'd killed him."

"You took the film from his camera?" Russell asked.

Gavin nodded.

"I thought that it was the evidence I was after, but it was just some pictures of him and his little mate, pissing about like schoolboys, getting ready to go out."

"So you came back yesterday to get everything else before it got back to Tony?" Russell had been wrong thinking it was Skinner who'd trashed the flat and hit Joe.

"Or you. I'm sorry. I knew you were digging for answers, and I didn't want either of you to find whatever he had. He abused my trust. He abused my uncle's trust, and I stood to lose everything if he carried on. He had his little crusade about the charity. He wanted my father to just donate the building to them. He always thought he could just have whatever he wanted."

Gavin picked up the holdall, shoved another sheaf of papers inside, zipped it up and hefted it onto his shoulder.

"I didn't mean to kill him," he said, sadly. "I loved him, once."

He went to walk past, but Russell put an arm out and stopped him.

"I can't let you go," Russell said.

"You're not in the police any more," Gavin hissed, pushing his hand away.

Russell grabbed his arm to hold him back, but Gavin slammed his head forward, smashing his forehead into the bridge of Russell's nose. As Russell let go, Gavin dashed past.

By the time Russell had regrouped enough to follow, Gavin was already hurtling down the stairs.

"Shit," Russell said, sprinting after him.

JOE HEARD RUSSELL'S warning shouts just as the side door banged open and Gavin ran out. He barely had time to react, but got his leg out in time to send Gavin sprawling across the pavement.

Joe pounced on him, a knee in his back, and pulled his arm up behind him so he couldn't twist out of his grip. Gavin bucked and struggled, so Joe punched him once, hard and quick to the side of the head.

Gavin slumped as Russell arrived, panting, with blood dripping from his nose.

"Who'd have thought you'd end up being the brawn of the team?"

And Joe smiled, because they were a team.

"I didn't grow up as the weedy, unpopular gay kid in my school without learning a few killer moves," he said.

8.

THE RED LION WAS heaving again, filled to the rafters with Chris's friends, all gathered to celebrate him, mourn him, share stories about him.

Russell, Joe and Paul were crammed in at a corner table, and hadn't had to pay for a single drink yet.

"Chris would have loved this," Paul said, smiling sadly.

Russell punched his arm.

"I thought we had a deal," he teased. "No sad faces. Anyway, you said you were going to do a turn for us."

"Later," Paul said. "Patty needs a few stiffeners before she gets her frock on."

"I bet she does," Russell laughed.

Paul raised a glass.

"To Chris," he said. "And to you two for catching his killer."

He pressed his open palms to his cheeks, fingers splayed—the perfect impression of a helpless damsel from a vintage film. "My heroes..." he cooed.

"Give over," Russell laughed.

"It's got to feel good, though, hasn't it?" Paul asked. "Being back in the saddle."

"Not as good as seeing the look on Skinner's face when we hauled Gavin into the station. Skinner's going to have some questions to answer himself now."

"And Tony's going to have to find himself another bent cop," Joe said.

"I shouldn't think he'll have much trouble with that," Russell said.

He fixed Paul with his sternest look. "And you, young man, are going to promise me that you'll stop extorting money from that poor MP."

"He's hardly poor," Paul sulked.

"No, but it's his life, and his secret to keep. Not everyone has the kind of freedom you kids do. Besides, he loved Chris. He's suffered just as much as the rest of us."

"Okay, fine," Paul said, rolling his eyes, though they all knew his huff was just for show.

As three more pints were delivered to the table, Joe looked up to see Luc smiling down at him.

"I hear you're a hero now," Luc said, slipping onto the bench beside him, and handing out the drinks.

Joe felt himself blush as Luc squeezed his thigh.

"I thought you were going back to Paris?" Joe asked.

"Paris can wait," Luc replied.

As Bowie's "Modern Love" came on the jukebox, Joe took Luc's hand in his, lacing their fingers together. He would always miss Chris, but he had his own life to lead now too.

WHO'S THAT GIRL?

SOHO NOIR #2

WHO'S THAT GIRL?

1.

SOHO, LONDON. JUNE 1985.

IT WAS A LIGHT, bright summer's evening, but this seedy, low-ceilinged back room of the Red Lion felt as dark and exciting as he'd hoped. Almost nine o'clock, and the cabaret was just about to kick off.

Joe Stone settled into the high-backed chair as his friend and new flatmate, Russell Dixon, sauntered back from the bar with their drinks—two pints among the bright sea of cocktails that covered the other tables.

Russell was in his mid-forties, a former police detective, and one of the nicest, most honest men Joe had ever met. He and Joe had become close earlier in the year, when Joe's oldest friend—Russell's flatmate—Chris Sexton, had been murdered. Police apathy and a series of strange discoveries had led Joe and Russell to join forces and solve the case.

The whole affair had cemented their friendship and motivated Joe to move to the city and start a new life for himself among people more like him—the kind of people who were now crammed into this dark room, out the back of their favourite Soho pub, for an evening of pure camp.

This was what he loved about Soho: the strange, wonderful mix of people—artists and celebrities rubbing shoulders with gangsters and retired prostitutes. Everyone with a story to tell, everyone a friend, if only for the night. The smoke-filled basement bars, the all-night coffee shops, the revue bars and sex shops, all crowded together on these boisterous, vibrant streets—this was home.

There was a growing hum of excitement as people took their seats. A friendly crowd. Everyone there had come intent on making this the best ever fundraiser for the Campbell Centre—a charity close to both Joe and Russell's hearts—which took care of victims of HIV and AIDS.

Both of them quietly acknowledged that they were driven to help the charity by the memory of their mutual friend Chris. The Campbell Centre had been a passion of his, though his involvement had eventually turned out to be one of the reasons he was killed. But that was a different story.

After helping to solve his murder, Joe had decided to stay in Soho. He moved into Chris's old room in Russell's flat, and took a job as a runner in a small television production company.

He'd once held lofty aspirations for his psychology degree, but he'd quickly found that his job in the strange world of television production used every aspect of his training and more.

Besides, it was far more interesting than his previous, very junior role with social services, and it left him plenty of time to volunteer at the Campbell Centre whenever he could, helping to care for, but mostly entertain the patients there.

Funding for the centre was all privately raised, and though Chris had left some money behind by way of a small legacy from his fashion label, they always needed more. So, Joe and Russell had joined forces with some of Chris's other friends to put together this fundraiser in his honour.

Hopefully the first of many, *The Frock Show* was a celebration of the growing drag scene in Soho, and a safe stage for new acts to try out their routines alongside the seasoned veterans who'd been the mainstay of the scene since the seventies.

One of their other friends, Paul, was due to perform later in the evening as his alter ego, Patty Cakes. Still relatively new on the scene, Patty's was a sensual, breathy act, which Russell described as a poor man's Marilyn Monroe. Brutal as criticism went, but actually not that far off the mark.

Joe smiled his thanks as Russell delivered the drinks. He was so pleased Russell was there tonight given that he would usually shy away from big nights out on the scene. But Joe had been determined to get him out more.

A former detective with the Metropolitan Police, Russell had been run out of the job when some of his colleagues had discovered his sexuality and used it to entrap and arrest him, forcing a suspension and prompting a relatively well-paid, though not entirely welcome, early retirement.

Russell had gone into a bit of a depression afterwards, but helping to solve Chris's murder had reinvigorated him, giving him a new enthusiasm for life again. Just because he'd left the force, didn't mean he had to stop investigating.

Both Joe and Russell had changed irrevocably since Chris had died. He'd been such a fabulous, gregarious, wild young man, whose bright star had been snuffed out far too early. He had been widely loved by most, deeply resented by some, but definitely missed by all.

They had even taken to challenging each other to *Be More Chris*. Which was how Joe had persuaded Russell to come out tonight. Gone were the days of either of them hiding their sexuality or shying away from speaking out. Both had come to realise the value of being *Out and Proud*, despite the dangers that represented.

"When's it all kicking off then?" Russell asked, sitting down next to Joe and shaking the drips from his hands.

"Any minute now. But Patty's on second. At about quarter to ten."

Russell smiled and took a big swig of his beer.

"Plenty of time to get another couple of these down us then," he laughed.

Even though he'd helped to organise it, Russell never enjoyed being in this kind of crowd. He said it was all too extrovert. Maybe it was, but Joe thought it was good for him to get out every now and then. He was never going to meet anyone sitting around in their flat.

Besides, Joe liked the company. He was still not that keen on going home alone, even though they'd long since caught Chris's killer. Soho may be one of the more gay-friendly places in London, but it was far from safe.

"Here we go," Russell said, as a tall, elegant man stepped on to the stage and tapped the microphone. His tuxedo, frilled shirt, bowtie, top hat and cane were all bright white, glowing under the lights and contrasting his dark skin perfectly. Pure theatre. That was Danny Devraux.

"Ladies and gentlemen, boys and girls," Danny called, sounding like a circus ringmaster. "Welcome to *The Frock Show!*"

A light applause rippled across the room, a couple of whoops. The crowd wasn't warmed up yet, just how Danny liked them.

"Oh, come on now," he cajoled. "I've seen happier punters at a wake. Cheer up! I said: Welcome to *The Frock Show!*"

A cheer this time, still a little muted, but much better. Danny was a natural crowd-pleaser.

He stepped down off the front of the stage, slipping easily between the chairs and tables, greeting customers by name, a touch here, a kiss there, the consummate host and showman.

All the while, the microphone remained in his hand as he delivered the most intimate of public introductions for members of the audience he either recognised or liked the look of. Those he didn't know were treated to a joke or an invitation to introduce themselves.

Danny Devraux—Dan Carter to his friends—was the campest straight man Joe had ever met. Now in his late sixties, he was a jobbing actor with a passion for musicals and fond memories of a youth filled with sex, drugs, jazz and cabaret.

Joe had met him on the set of a television programme where Dan had been playing a tired, old ham of an actor. *"Not much acting required, really, darling,"* Dan had joked in the lunch queue. They'd hit it off immediately. Mainly because Dan did not take himself seriously at all, and was full of great tales which he told with contagious animation. Joe was in awe of anyone with that kind of confidence.

Dan and Joe had kept in touch after the shoot had ended, occasionally going to the theatre together, since Dan always seemed to have a ready supply of tickets to all the good shows.

Joe had even ventured up north to Camden a few times to see Danny Devraux in action as compere for the weekly revue shows and open mic nights in the Black Cap.

It hadn't taken much persuading to get Dan to wheel his Danny Devraux persona out to act as host for this evening's event. And Danny had even managed to pull in some of his Camden contacts—drag acts who'd been drawing in fans for years—to headline the show.

Danny Devraux knew people, and he had a way of getting them to do what he asked.

"Oh," he purred. "Who do we have here?"

He leaned in dramatically, lifting Joe's chin gently with the end of his cane.

"The inimitable Joe Stone," Danny announced. "Your host and organiser, ladies and gentlemen. This kid is going places, let me tell you."

Joe smiled and waved at the applause, embarrassed to be the one singled out. Though if he'd got the same look from Russell that Danny'd just got, he'd have gone for the easy target too. Russell did not do audience participation.

Another ripple of applause and a hearty wolf-whistle made Joe's smile a little wider. He'd worked hard to get this show together tonight, and he was looking forward to it. The whistle had come from Luc, Joe's boyfriend, who kissed him as he sat down.

"Am I late?"

"Just in time," Joe said, squeezing his hand, and then punching his arm as Luc stole a swig of his drink.

From the stage, a tinkling from the piano caught Danny's attention.

"Aha, Maestro," he cooed. "'Tis time, 'tis time!"

Trotting back onto the stage, lithe and athletic despite his advancing years, he struck a pose, leaning on his cane, top hat at a jaunty angle. The piano player began in earnest, and Danny launched into his well-rehearsed rendition of "Wilkommen".

By the time the song had ended and the first act had been introduced, the crowd were already whooping and cheering. Danny had done his job, and Joe could finally relax, knowing that tonight was going to go well.

Looking around the crowd, Joe recognised many of the faces. Who would have thought, when he'd arrived in London for the weekend four months ago, that this would be his life now?

It was such a far cry from the small village he and his late friend Chris had grown up in. Still, he wouldn't change it for the world. They may all be oddballs, weirdoes and freaks to the world outside, but they were his oddballs, weirdoes and freaks. He was one of them now.

"I'm just going to wish Patty luck," he told Luc and Russell, standing up and edging his way down the side of the room towards the makeshift backstage area.

He actually wanted to thank Danny again for hosting tonight, but he would also slip back and give Patty some encouragement before it was her turn to hit the stage.

There were already a few people leaning against the wall, now that all the tables were full, and Joe had to sidestep a drag queen he didn't recognise to get past.

She was tall, especially in those killer stilettos, with a straight, shoulder length wig in dark brown, with a sharp, unattractive fringe, badly cut in. Her whole outfit was strangely drab and old-fashioned, apart from the killer heels. High, sparkling blue stilettos. It was clear where the money for that outfit had been spent.

Joe was getting used to all sorts of strange quirks when it came to the Soho drag scene, but the spinster-aunt-in-kinky-boots look was a new one on him, and he wasn't sure it worked.

Joe smiled, squeezing past. She didn't smile back. In fact, she barely moved out of his way. Probably part of her drag persona—spinster aunts were notoriously grumpy, after all.

Joe shrugged and moved on. She'd paid to get in, so he couldn't really ask much more from her. He pushed through the swing doors and into the relative quiet of the backstage area.

IT WAS HARDLY BIG ENOUGH to swing a cat backstage, which wasn't surprising, given that the stage itself was just a section of the pub's old function room, separated from the so-called backstage area by some wonky theatrical flats.

Beyond, a narrow corridor led to a fire exit at the back of the pub. A small storeroom off that corridor had been commandeered as a dressing room and, other than that, there was nothing back here apart from a manky staff toilet, which bar owner, Ron, had promised to clean before tonight. Needless to say, he hadn't.

Joe found Danny Devraux standing in the wings, a tall glass of Cinzano in his hand. A favourite tipple, which added to his camp demeanour. The fact that he could happily sink six or more to start the night was neither here nor there.

"That was a great start, Danny," Joe said, shaking his hand. "Thanks again for doing this."

"Tough crowd," Danny smiled. "I thought I'd never get them warmed up."

"No fear of that with you," Joe said.

Danny peered back out through the wings, watching the performance. "She's good," he said. "I should try and get her up to the Cap."

Danny's regular night ran in a pub called The Black Cap in Camden, and part of the draw getting him down here tonight was that he may find some fresh faces to take back for his cabaret nights.

"You wait 'til you see the next one," Joe said. "Speaking of which, I'd better go find her, she'll need a little boost."

He noticed that Danny didn't respond. In fact, he was staring, wide-eyed, somewhere beyond the stage, his drink titled at a dangerous angle, a frown creasing his brow.

"Dan?" Joe asked. "You alright? You look like you've seen a ghost."

Danny snapped back into character almost immediately, taking a big gulp of his drink, shuddering at the strength of it as he swallowed. Breathing out slowly, he turned back to Joe.

"Are you still here?" he asked, the twinkle returning to his eye. "I thought you had a queen to attend to."

He clapped Joe on the shoulder and took another long swig of his drink. His hand shook a little, and Joe tried to recall if it usually did.

Danny was right though—there wasn't much time before Patty was due on stage and, right now, Joe's loyalty lay with his friend.

"See you for drinks after the show, Danny," he said, heading off.

Danny raised his glass, but something had slipped from his usual charming demeanour. Joe hoped it wasn't because he felt this was all too low rent for him. Still, Joe couldn't worry about it now. The show must go on.

He followed the sound of giggling laughter down the corridor to the former storeroom, its newly applied glittering cardboard star marking it out as the dressing room. Knocking gently, he opened the door without waiting, a tinny blast of Madonna's "Like a Virgin" greeting him. Nothing could be less appropriate for the occupants of this room.

"You decent, girls?"

"Oh, hardly, love."

"You wouldn't like us if we were."

This time last year Joe wouldn't have dreamed of walking into a room like this, and yet now he felt completely at home.

Inside, he found a handful of men in various states of undress: mid-tuck or full sequin, in skull caps waiting to be adorned with glamorous wigs, or peering into mirrors with tongs and combs already delicately teasing curls over foreheads. The smell of perfume and hairspray was almost overwhelming.

"Come in then," one of them called. "You're letting all the heat out."

Joe closed the door behind him, noticing that Patty instantly relaxed on seeing him. He could never refer to Patty as Paul when he was in drag. He became she straight away, and remained that way until the outfit—and the persona—came off.

They'd had a frosty start to their relationship—tinged with jealousy on Paul's part of Joe's long-standing relationship with Chris, and with suspicion on Joe's part because he'd seen Patty arguing with Chris on the night he'd died.

That had quickly become water under the bridge, and Joe thought they had quite a good friendship now. Which was how he knew that nerves almost always got the best of Patty before a performance. Paul made a beautiful showgirl, but Patty wasn't a natural performer.

"What's it like out there?" Patty asked.

"Lively," Joe said. "But very friendly. They've even given Belle an encore."

Belle—Maybelle Leen, to give her her full name—was notoriously polarising as an act. Crass, bawdy and acerbic, but with the voice of an angel. She was the cabaret version of the canary in the mineshaft—if the crowd liked her, the rest of the line up would have no problems.

"Oh, thank God. They're not going to kill me, then? How do I look?"

"Sensational, as always."

Joe brushed a fleck of dried mascara from her cheek and smiled reassuringly.

"You're too kind. I'm shitting myself."

The harsh Liverpudlian accent was an endearing part of the act, and the coarse language coming from such a pretty thing made it all the funnier.

"You'll be amazing."

Patty shuddered.

"Oh God, I can't stand the waiting around."

The words were barely said, when the temporary light they'd rigged up in the storeroom flashed red, calling her to the stage. Joe kissed the air either side of Patty's face, careful not to smudge any make-up.

"You can do this," he said.

Patty smiled. Joe turned her around and propelled her towards the door.

"Wait," she said, tottering back to the make-up table. "I need my feathers!"

And with that, Patty was gone in a chorus of support from the other acts, feather boa wafting behind her, one final "Ooh!" called over her shoulder in chorus with Madonna. Joe smiled at the retreating figure. Patty made a great woman. Ankles, cheekbones *and* an arse to die for.

"Everything alright back here then, ladies?" Joe asked. "Got everything you need?"

"Glorious," one of them said in a voice like gravel and honey. "Just like the fucking Palladium, love."

Reg Blakeley—or Mrs Saddlewick as her fans knew her—was one of the longest serving and most admired female impersonators on the scene. She spent so much of her time in drag that most people could be forgiven for thinking she *was* Mrs Saddlewick.

She was a great act, but, boy, did she like the sound of her own voice. With a sharp tongue, a keen mind and vocabulary that would make a navvy wince, she was never backward in coming forward.

As tonight's star turn, she'd kicked up a hell of a fuss when she'd realised she was going to have to share the cramped storeroom with the other performers, but fortunately Danny had quickly stepped in to smooth things over. He knew her well, and was able to talk down her tantrum with little more than the offer of free drinks all night. Joe didn't want to set her off again.

"Excellent," he said. "Well, good luck all, I'll be cheering you on from the wings."

As he stepped back into the corridor, he could hear Patty's opening number kicking off to rapturous applause. This was the closest to a home crowd she would probably ever see. Hopefully they'd be kind.

Joe intended to watch her from the sidelines, so that he could be there to support her when she came off. As he headed back towards the wings, he was barged aside by someone running away from the stage.

"Hey," he called, turning to see the same drag queen he'd had to navigate around earlier hurrying down the corridor. Dark wig, plain dress, blue heels clattering on the lino floor as she made off towards the dressing room. There was something wrong with the way she was running. Uneven. As though she was limping.

Joe didn't know who she was, but she wasn't on the line up and he didn't want any trouble tonight. He started back down the corridor after her.

"Hey! You can't be back here. This area is for performers only."

She didn't even turn at the sound of his voice. If anything, she seemed to move even faster, as though she knew where she was heading. But she ran straight past the dressing room, and Joe slowed. There was nothing down there apart from the emergency fire door.

Joe heard the metal door slam open and then bang closed again, the sound echoing angrily up the hall. The slam had barely faded when it was replaced by a piercing scream from the side of the stage.

RUSSELL SAW PATTY FALTER as the scream from offstage rose above her warbling performance. A terrible moment of hesitation as she tried to figure out whether it was a joke or if something awful had happened.

Russell knew from the hollow desperation in the scream that it was no joke. He was on his feet and hurtling towards the stage before he could think about what he was doing.

Among the theatrical flats that made up the temporary stage wings, Russell found the source of the scream: the first performer of the night, Maybelle Leen, was on her knees beside Danny's body.

Danny's once crisp white outfit was stained with a line of blood from a single stab wound to his chest. His hat had rolled across the floor when he fell, but his cane was still tightly gripped in his right hand. His glass lay broken beside his body, the contents staining the cuff of his jacket.

Russell gently lifted the traumatised performer away from the body and crouched down beside Danny, feeling for a pulse. There was nothing. Danny was dead.

Patty appeared in the wings, her fellow performer now whimpering at the sight of Danny's blood on her hands. Russell looked up at her.

"Call the police," he said, as pandemonium broke out front of stage. "There's a phone behind the bar. And try to keep people in the building until they get here. They'll want to talk to any witnesses."

For once, Patty didn't panic, but dashed back onto the stage and disappeared into the confused audience, heading straight for the bar.

Russell guessed by the noise levels out front that containing people until the police showed up would be a tough job. He could hear Ron, the barman, trying to tell people to stay put and calm down, his own voice filled with panic. No one was listening.

"What's going on?" Joe asked, arriving on the scene and stopping in his tracks as he saw Danny's prone body. "Oh God. What's happened? Is he alright?"

"Stay back," said Russell. "He's been stabbed."

"What? But I was just speaking to him not ten minutes ago."

Joe hovered behind him, trying to get a better look at the body to confirm what he'd just been told. Strange, thought Russell, the way we humans always have to see for ourselves.

Russell lifted Danny's suit jacket to reveal the stab wound—small, round, deep, straight into the chest.

"That's right in the heart, I'd hazard," Russell mused. „He would have died pretty quickly, if that's any mercy."

He let the suit jacket close again, and raised Danny's right hand, still clutching the cane. The rounded white handle had the smallest scuff of dirt on it. Looking closer, Russell realised it wasn't dirt, but make-up—foundation with a glittering hint of rouge. Whoever had attacked Danny would be sporting a nice bruise on her cheek for a few days.

"Looks like Danny tried to fight back," Russell said. "See?"

Joe crouched down beside him and looked closer.

"Make-up?" he asked.

"Exactly."

Russell picked up the bottom half of Danny's broken glass and sniffed it, wincing.

"What was he drinking?" Russell asked.

"Cinzano, as far as I know. That's what he usually drank."

"Smells disgusting," Russell said. "So sweet."

"Bloody rocket fuel, that. Especially the way Ron makes them," Joe replied, lifting Danny's left hand and peering at it closely. Several strands of dark hair were wrapped around his fingers. He picked one of the hairs free and examined it between his fingers.

"Look at this," he said.

"What is it?"

"Synthetic," he said. "A wig. And a pretty cheap one at that."

He held the hair up to the light for Russell to see.

"Dark brown," Russell said. "Which is neither Belle nor Patty. So who's the brunette?"

Joe let the hair drop, looking at Russell wild-eyed. And then he was on his feet and sprinting down the corridor towards the fire escape.

JOE BURST THROUGH the fire door, hearing it slam back against the wall just as it had before when he'd seen the dark-haired drag queen running away. He should have gone after her straight away.

He looked up and down the street. It was still surprisingly light outside—the sky only just beginning to fade into that late summer twilight.

Groups of drinkers—a heady mix of suited yuppies, flamboyant artists, tattooed punks and general layabouts—gathered around tables outside another bar further up the street, laughing and chatting, utterly oblivious to what had just happened inside the pub.

The pavement in the other direction was clear and empty. A streetlight flickered to life. A neon pink sign flashed on and off, advertising the live show on the corner. It would be dark soon.

There was no sign of the mysterious woman in either direction. Joe had wasted too much time coming after her. He turned back to the fire escape and stopped.

On the floor just outside the door was a single stiletto shoe. Dark-blue and glittering. Joe crouched down and picked it up, turning it over in his hands. The heel had snapped off at the base and was now dangling by a thin thread of overlapping fabric.

Danny's attacker would never have been able to run in this. No wonder she'd looked like she was limping.

He realised that the end of the heel had left a smear on the palm of his hand. It looked like blood. Joe almost dropped it.

Not wanting to get locked out, he eased the fire escape door back so it was almost closed but not locked from the outside, and set off along the pavement, still clutching the shoe. He was acting on instinct here, nothing more than a hunch. She couldn't have got far in one stiletto on these filthy Soho streets, could she?

Sure enough, he saw a black cab take a left turn out of the end of the street. In the back seat was the same drag queen he'd seen running from the club. The straight dark wig, the fine features, angled cheekbones, panicked eyes staring at Joe. She looked vaguely familiar. *Who was she?*

Just like that, the taxi turned the corner and she was gone. Joe looked down at the shoe dangling from his fingers. Not quite a Cinderella story, but at least it was a clue.

Russell arrived on the pavement outside the club, letting the fire door slam shut before Joe could stop him.

"Dammit," Russell said, realising what he'd done. "Sorry. What's going on, Joe?"

"Look at this," Joe said, holding the broken shoe out for Russell to see. "It's covered in blood. I think this might be what did for Danny."

"What?" Russell said, peering into his open hand. "Wow. Talk about a killer heel."

"There was this girl," Joe said. "I saw her in the club earlier, right by the stage. She didn't really seem to be that into the performance, but I didn't think that much of it because Belle was on, and she's not everyone's cup of tea, is she?"

Russell nodded an agreement as they headed off towards the corner of the block. They'd have to get back into the pub through the front door.

"Anyway, I went backstage, chatted to Danny, then went into the dressing room to see Patty. When I came out, the same girl ran past me and out of this fire door. And then, obviously, I found you with Danny."

"What did she look like?"

"Well, a bad drag, if I'm honest."

Russell looked at him sideways, seeking an explanation.

"Just a bit cheap," Joe clarified. "And plain. Like, her wig was this lanky, shoulder length bob. Cheap synthetic from the way the strands were all sticking to each other."

"She wasn't one of the acts then?"

"No, I've never seen her before," Joe said. "She was tall, though, especially in these." He held up the shoe. "But everything else was a bit plain. Apart from the heels, she looked more like she was going to a parents' evening than a drag night."

"Maybe she was trying to blend in? If she'd come with murder on her mind, she wouldn't want to stand out of the crowd too much, would she?"

"Well, if that was the case, she'd have been better off overdoing it a bit more, wouldn't she? She stood out like a sore thumb in that crowd."

They rounded the corner and Russell faltered.

"Oh great," he said.

Joe looked up to see what was troubling him, and spotted Detective Skinner—the nasty, homophobic cop, who had been instrumental in getting Russell removed from the force—climb out of an unmarked Ford Sierra and stride towards the pub.

Skinner had been the detective supposedly in charge of Chris's murder case, too, and his lack of interest in pursuing the case had been what had encouraged Russell and Joe to join forces and solve it themselves. When they'd handed the killer in at the station, Russell had hoped the complaint he'd made would result in some kind of disciplinary for Skinner. Obviously it hadn't been enough to remove him from the job.

"Come on," said Joe, taking Russell's arm and guiding him towards the door. "It's better we talk to him first, before he starts on any of that lot in there."

JOE WAS RIGHT, of course, but Russell still felt a sense of dread at the thought of having to deal with Skinner again. Whilst looking into Chris's murder, Russell had confirmed his suspicion that Skinner was a vicious, bent cop, who was on the payroll of some of Soho's shadier characters.

He had made no bones about his disgust at Russell's sexuality, and he had deliberately obstructed the investigation into Chris's death, simply because Chris was gay and Skinner thought that was a free pass to a short life.

His active hatred of the gay community would be a problem again with this case, Russell had no doubt. He would take one look at the clientele of the pub that evening, and deduce that Danny's death was just an inevitable outcome of the depravity that Skinner maintained went hand-in-glove with London's gay scene.

Nonetheless, Joe was right—it was better he spoke to Skinner himself, rather than leaving it to the shocked punters inside. So, Russell steeled himself and led the way back into the pub, with Joe hot on his heels.

Skinner was already on the stage, looking around at the assembled crowd of bedraggled queens. Mascara-smeared cheeks and lopsided wigs. No one here, apart from Skinner, cared. They had all just lost one of their own. A great supporter. A lovely man.

Russell hurried over to meet Skinner as the detective headed into the makeshift stage wings.

"Detective Skinner," he said, sounding a lot brighter than he felt. "I see you're back on the team."

Skinner turned, snarling with unconcealed distaste.

"You?"

"We've really must stop meeting like this," Russell said, smiling a false little flirtation. "Anyone would think you were stalking me."

He'd been Skinner's boss once. He wasn't going to let this weasel intimidate him. Joe caught up with them as both men squared up to each other. Skinner looked him up and down, lip curling again.

"I see you've still got Boy Wonder in tow," Skinner sneered.

"Detective," Joe said, flatly. He had no time for the man either.

"I do hope you weren't too inconvenienced by our last efforts," Russell said. "We didn't mean to get you into too much trouble. But it's always nice to see a crime properly solved, isn't it? Justice done, and all that."

Skinner took a deep breath. The reminder of his recent disciplinary would keep him vaguely civil for now.

"I don't have time to talk to you, right now," Skinner said. "I have a death to investigate."

"Oh, I think you could call it a murder," Russell said. "I've seen the body. In fact, I was one of the first on the scene, so I'm afraid you're going to have to talk to me anyway."

He smiled disingenuously. Skinner tried to mould his face into anything but a slapped-arse, and failed.

"I can wait while you get up to speed," Russell said. But I haven't got all night."

"Have a seat," Skinner said, head cocked to one side. "I'll be over to take your statements as soon as I'm ready."

Skinner turned and stormed off into the wings, where a uniformed officer was already standing over Danny's body.

Russell and Joe headed over to the bar to wait and found the barman, Ron—another friend of theirs—trying to reassure distressed punters that everything was okay, and they'd be allowed to leave soon. He looked ashen himself, so his reassurances were falling on deaf ears.

As soon as Russell and Joe sat down, the questions began flying from all sides.

"What happened?"

"Was he murdered?"

"Who killed him?"

"What if they come back?"

Most people there knew that Russell used to be in the police and, more importantly, everyone knew that Russell and Joe had been the ones to work out what had happened to Chris. Plus, they'd been the organisers of tonight's fundraiser. So it was only natural that people were turning to them for answers now.

"Hold on, all of you," Ron said, placing a full pint each on the bar in front of both Russell and Joe. "We've all had a shock. Let's just have a drink and see what the police want to do next."

Russell was grateful for Ron's stoic pragmatism, even if there was a hint that he was just trying to break even on the bar for tonight. Ron had been running The Red Lion in Soho for longer than Russell had lived and worked here, and he'd always been a friendly ear. He took in all sorts of waifs and strays and rented them rooms above the pub, often in return for glass collecting and dishwashing duties if they couldn't pay in cash. He was one of life's good sorts.

"But what's happened? He is dead, isn't he?" The questioner was a young man, wig and dress stripped off and tracksuit back on, but his face still caked with make-up.

Russell didn't recognise him, but then he had no reason to—Joe had been the one organising all the acts. Russell had been in charge of logistics—he was less likely to upset anyone that way.

"I hope we're still going to get paid," the rasping voice of Mrs Saddlewick enquired.

"Jesus, Reg," Ron said. "The man's dead."

"Look, I know you're all shocked," Russell said. "It's a terrible thing, but we really don't know much more than you."

Much tutting and muttering rippled around the room. They wanted more from him.

"All I know is that Danny was in the wings, having just introduced Patty, and he was stabbed."

"Stabbed?" Ron said. "Bloody hell."

"Looked like it, at least," Russell said, taking a much-needed drink of his pint. "The police will be able to tell us more."

"But when could it have happened?" Joe asked, as confused as the others. "Danny introduced Patty, right? And I left the dressing room moments after Patty went on stage. And Danny was already dead by the time I got back to the wings."

"More importantly, who would *want* to kill Danny?" Patty asked. "He's one of the most popular guys we know. Who's going to tell his poor wife?"

Skinner had sauntered over in their direction in time to hear the last comment.

"He had a *wife*?" Skinner asked, incredulously.

"Jean," Ron confirmed, shining a glass and putting it on the shelf. "She's sick enough as it is. This might just kill her."

"A word please, Mr Dixon," Skinner said to Russell. It was more of a command than a request. Russell's hackles rose immediately.

"Sure."

Russell gave Joe a subtle, warning wink as he got up. *Keep an eye on me.* Joe knew the background between the two men, and would step in to calm things down if he saw either of them looking tasty.

Skinner led the way back into the wings, where Danny's body had now at least been covered with a blanket.

"Well, you and your friends just can't seem to keep out of trouble, can you?" Skinner asked. "What exactly was going on here tonight? And you can spare me the seedier details."

Russell unclenched his fists. It would be so easy to swing for Skinner right now, but that would only land him in trouble. Skinner may be a hateful man, but he had friends in high places, and would certainly win any pissing contest Russell tried to start. That much had been proved already.

"Oh, don't worry. It was nothing to offend your delicate sensibilities," Russell said. "We'd organised a fundraiser for the Campbell Centre. Dan Carter was our compère for the evening."

"And how well did you know him?"

"Not that well, I'd seen him perform at one of his regular nights in Camden. It was Joe who knew him. Persuaded him to come down and help us out tonight."

"You say he was compère. What did that entail exactly?"

"He did a little opening spiel to get the audience warmed up, and then he was supposed to introduce each of the girls."

"*Girls?*"

"The acts," Russell emphasised, rolling his eyes.

Skinner's lip curled again.

"And people pay money to see this kind of thing?"

"I wouldn't expect you to understand."

"Good."

Skinner bent down and lifted the blanket enough to reveal the stab wound on Danny's chest.

"Stabbed, once, through the chest," Skinner said. "Would have been quick enough."

Russell peered at the wound again. It was quite wide, for a stab wound. Perfect size and shape for the stiletto heel Joe had found outside. Whoever had done this would have had to stamp pretty hard on Danny's chest to inflict the wound. And he'd have already had to be on the ground for it to work. It seemed an odd way to murder someone.

"Strange shape, isn't it?" Russell said.

"What's that?"

"The stab wound. It's an odd shape. More circular than you'd expect from a knife blade."

Russell was testing him, as he always had when they'd worked together. Not only was Skinner a vile person, he was also a lazy detective.

"Hmm," Skinner looked again, without much interest. "Blade probably twisted as he went down. Seen it before."

Russell doubted he had. He stood up, his feet crunching on a shard of broken glass from Danny's spilled drink.

"Perhaps," he muttered. "Or perhaps he was stabbed with something else altogether—not a blade at all."

"I don't recall asking for your contribution," Skinner snapped.

Fine. He knew he should mention the shoe Joe had found, and the drag act he'd seen running from the scene, but the look on Skinner's face stopped him. Even if that mysterious drag queen had killed Danny, Russell didn't want Skinner to be the one arresting or charging him—not with his reputation for violent homophobia. Russell decided to keep quiet for now.

Russell studied Danny's body again. *What happened to you, Dan?* Whatever it was it had obviously been quick and silent. Patty had started performing as Danny left the stage. The applause had died down, and she'd been singing a relatively quiet little number. If Danny had screamed when he'd been stabbed, everyone would have all heard him. So he must either have been silenced, or he was already unconscious when the fatal blow was struck.

"And where were you then, Mr Dixon? When all this was happening?"

There was something so disingenuous about the way Skinner used the "Mister" these days, now that he was no longer forced to respect Russell's position in the chain of authority.

"Hmm? Oh, I was out there with the rest of the audience," Russell pointed to the tables. "Watching the performance."

"And can you describe what happened, exactly, in the moments leading up to the discovery of the body."

"Danny had been out on the stage to introduce the next act, the lights went down as she came on, so it was just Patty in the spotlight. The audience clapped and she started singing."

Russell was making sure he referred to all of the performers in the feminine, knowing it would jar on Skinner's nerves every time.

"She'd barely got past the first chorus when there was a scream from backstage, and I ran through to find another of the performers standing over Danny's body. I moved her aside, checked for a pulse, found there to be none and had someone call the police."

"I see," Skinner said, casting his eye back to the small group gathered at the bar. "Are you able to identify that person for me?"

"What's that?"

"The person you saw crouching over the body when you got backstage. He is still here, I presume? Could you point *him* out?"

Skinner's turn to stress the pronoun. It was a cheap retort, but not unexpected. Russell signalled over to Joe, who was comforting the performer in question, Maybelle Leen.

Joe spoke quietly to the young man, and Russell saw him glance at Skinner and flinch—none of them liked talking to the police.

Joe followed the guy over, the blue stiletto still dangling from his hand. Russell sidled in front of him, blocking it from Skinner's sight.

"Detective Skinner," Joe said. "This is Matthew Dean. He was the one who found Dan."

Matthew said nothing, looking at the ground. He still had traces of mascara smeared under his eyes, and the thick line of foundation made it clear where his wig had been. Russell wished he would just look up and meet Skinner's eye, brave it out.

"Right," Skinner said, his usual, charmless self. "Maybe *you* can tell me what happened."

Matthew frowned.

"I don't know," he said, nervously. "I finished my set, left the stage. Danny went on as I came off, to introduce Patty Cakes. I wished her luck and went to the loo. When I came out, I thought I'd sneak a look at Patty's act from the wings…"

He was babbling. Nervous. Skinner pursed his lips sourly.

"Just stick to what happened to him, if you will," Skinner said, pointing to the covered body on the floor.

"Right, sorry," Matthew said. "Right. So I came out of the loo, walked back up the corridor and when I got to the wings, I saw Danny's feet sticking out of the shadows. I thought he was messing around, but then I came over and he was dead."

"And you saw no one else?" Skinner asked.

"Back here? No. It was just me."

Russell could see where Skinner was leading him, and Matthew really wasn't doing himself any favours.

"So you're telling me," Skinner said, the suspicion heavy in his tone, "that Mr Carter here introduced the previous act to the stage, retired to the wings, and mere moments later you turned up and he was already dead. And yet you saw nothing and no one?"

"Yes," said Matthew, for the first time not babbling.

"And you expect me to believe that you had nothing to do with his death? Despite his blood being on your hands, and you being the only one back here, by your own admission."

"I..." Matthew looked helplessly from Joe to Russell.

"If that's what the lad says happened," Russell began.

"When I want your opinion, Mr Dixon, I will ask for it," Skinner snapped. "Until then, keep your nose out."

Russell knew better than to push it. Skinner was just itching for a reason to come down on him.

"So, if your version of events is true," Skinner said to Matthew. "And you were the only one back here, then I have no choice but to arrest you on suspicion of the murder of Daniel Carter."

Matthew, Joe and Russell all began protesting at the same time, but Skinner heard none of it. He was too busy rushing through Matthew's rights and cuffing his hands behind his back.

"You can't do this," Joe protested. "Matthew didn't do anything."

"He can prove that to me down at the station then, can't he?" Skinner replied, caustically.

"Don't be so stupid, man," Russell stepped in, trying to stop Skinner from leading Matthew out. "There's no way he could have done this."

"Get out of the way, or I'll arrest you too. Do not test me."

Russell stepped aside. He'd be no help to Matthew in the cell beside him, and he didn't doubt Skinner's conviction.

As Matthew was led away, he looked back beseechingly at Russell.

"Help me," he mouthed, wide-eyed.

"It's okay," Russell called to Matthew, as Skinner shoved him towards the door. "We'll sort this out."

As the door to the pub swung shut again, the bar was silent for a second before erupting into a chorus of anger and disbelief.

"Shouldn't we tell him about this?" Joe said, holding up the shoe again. "And the woman I saw?"

"It won't stop him right now," said Russell. "Skinner's on a mission to get this wrapped up quickly, he'll just find a way to use them to convict Matthew."

"We've got to do something," Joe said to Russell. "Matthew didn't do this. We both know that."

"I know," Russell said, closing his eyes in frustration. "But if they're wasting time with him, it will buy us some time to figure out who did."

2.

RUSSELL HAD MANAGED to get hold of one of his less aggressive former colleagues—also working on the case—who had told him, reluctantly, where Danny's wife, Jean, was being looked after. He'd also warned Russell not to get involved. Apparently Skinner had made it clear he was still gunning for his former boss.

As Ron, the barman, had suggested, Jean's cancer was in its final stages and she was being cared for in a private hospice near Camden.

Ron and Danny had been close friends when they were younger, though Ron had told them he hadn't seen Danny much in the intervening years.

Still, he said he felt bad that he hadn't even been to visit Jean since her cancer diagnosis, and he'd insisted on coming down with Joe and Russell to smooth the way for any questions they may have, and figure out if she was even up to talking to strangers.

The hospice was an institutional building with very few frills. It reminded Joe of the place his grandmother had been in, though she had outwitted all of them and needed discharging again after she staged a miraculous fight back to her own cancer.

In the end she'd lived another year and died at home. *"Vitriol. That's what kept her alive so long,"* Joe's father had claimed of his mother-in-law.

The police had already been in earlier to deliver Jean the bad news of her husband's murder, and the nurses were worried more visitors might be too much for her to take. Ron had agreed, solemnly, but had played up their friendship and her dwindling time, and they'd finally let all three of them in, on the condition that they didn't distress Jean any further.

Joe sat on the plastic chair in the corridor, legs twitching as Russell paced the tiled floor. Ron had been in with Jean for a good ten minutes already, and Russell was terrible at waiting.

"Just sit down," Joe chided. "He'll be out in a minute."

Russell sighed and took the seat beside Joe's, leaping up again the second the door to Jean's room opened and Ron stuck his head out, his eyes looking bloodshot.

"She's up to seeing you, boys," he said. "But take it easy, alright?"

They agreed, filing into the room and standing awkwardly at the end of the bed.

"I would shake your hand," Jean said, her voice cracked and tired. "But they've got me wired up to all this gubbins. I can barely move for setting something off."

"Thanks for seeing us, Mrs Carter," Joe said.

She looked so small. Thin and frail, propped up on pillows and supported by wires, drips, and machines. Her skin was almost translucent, her hair gone, and the light blue bandana she wore had slipped slightly to one side.

"I'm so sorry for your loss," Russell said.

"It's just awful, isn't it," Jean replied, stoically. "Although, I suppose it stops me worrying about what he'll do after I'm gone."

Ron shuddered.

"I'm going to get us all some tea," he said, and shuffled out of the room.

Joe didn't blame him. The smell in here was antiseptic, chemical, deathly. He looked across at Russell, who was staring at his hands. He seemed strangely distracted by seeing her so reduced. Joe decided to take the lead.

"We were both with Danny on the night he died," he said, stepping forward. "He seemed happy. You know? Pleased to be there. Not worried about anything."

"He did love performing," Jean acknowledged. "And he was ever so fond of all the girls."

Jean said it with a fondness of her own, which surprised Joe. Her breath rattled in her chest as she spoke, prompting a huge paroxysm of coughing. She spat into an old, yellowing handkerchief and smiled at Joe—a surprisingly radiant smile, given her situation.

"Sorry," she said. "Disgusting isn't it? I'd be better off coughing the whole bloody lung up. At least it'd be out then."

"Was anything going on, Jean?" Joe said. "Only, I spent a fair bit of time with Danny in the last few months. And I know it was just in clubs and we didn't really talk properly, but I never got the sense he was in any kind of trouble or that he had any enemies."

He knew he was rushing, but he didn't know how much time the nurses would let them have with her, and he wanted to get any information he could. Russell put a hand on his arm.

"As far as we knew, Jean, he was well liked by everyone. I think that's the thing," Russell said. "We just can't imagine anyone wanting to kill Danny."

"I know," she said. "But don't kid yourselves. Everyone's got someone who'd be happy to see them six foot under, ain't they? We've all got our skeletons."

She was so cockney, it was almost stereotypical. But she was right. Joe hadn't thought his friend Chris had any enemies at all until they'd started digging into his life. *We've all got our skeletons.* But how many would go as far as murder? And in such a public place, too.

Joe was reminded of the dark-haired drag act he saw running away— the Cinderella with the broken shoe.

"Had he fallen out with any of the acts, do you know?"

"Danny? Nah. He loved them girls. He'd never hurt them. And they'd never hurt him."

"I know," Joe said. "That's what I told the police."

"Look, let the boys in blue deal with it, lads," Jean said wearily. "It'll no doubt end up just a case of him being in the wrong place at the wrong time. He always did have rotten luck, my Dan."

"Is there anything we can do for you, Jean? Anyone we can call?"

She collapsed in another coughing fit, and a flustered nurse bustled in, slipping a small tray beneath Jean's chin just in time to catch the phlegm that came up.

"I think that'll do for today, gentlemen," she said sternly. There would be no more questions for Jean.

"Wait," Jean said, her breath rattling. "Pass my bag a minute, will you?"

Joe lifted the small, burgundy handbag from the bedside cabinet and passed it to her. She fished around inside as the nurse fussed with her pillows. Finally, she pulled out a little plastic covered address book and opened it up. She held the page out for Joe to see.

"Could you call this number? Ask for Violet."

Joe jotted the number down on a piece of scrap paper.

"She's my sister," Jean said. "Tell her I'm really sorry, but I do need to see her again, after all."

"Of course," Joe said, patting her hand and tucking the slip of paper into his pocket.

He thanked her for seeing them as the nurse ushered them out of the room.

In the corridor, they found Ron edging his way through a set of double doors at the far end, three polystyrene cups of tea in his hands.

"Alright lads," he said. "I got us some tea. What'd she say then?"

"Exactly what we thought. That Danny didn't have any real enemies and she couldn't think who would want to hurt him," said Joe.

"You were in there a while to start with, Ron, what were you two talking about?"

Ron looked affronted.

"This and that," he said, obtusely. "Just old times. The truth is, we've all drifted apart over the years. I thought it would be a good idea to clear the air. I felt guilty, you know?"

"That was good of you," Joe said.

"Yeah, well..."

He handed out the teas, looking distracted. Regret and remorse were what inevitably remained after friends had died. Joe knew it only too well.

They all sipped their teas at the same time, both Joe and Russell burning their lips. Ron didn't seem to notice the heat.

"Jean asked me to call her sister," Joe said.

"Really?" Ron said, shocked. "Why she'd want you to do that?"

"Why not?"

"Hmm?" Ron sipped his tea, distracted and frowning. "Far as I know, no one's seen Vi for years, least of all Jean."

"Maybe Jean wants to put things right before it's too late," Russell said.

"Maybe. Yeah," Ron said, not sounding convinced. "Still, I don't know why she'd want to go raking all that up again now, after all this time."

Joe frowned. He'd got the sense from Jean that she'd seen Violet more recently than Ron was making out. Here in the hospital. Perhaps the sisters had reconciled their differences, once Jean knew her disease was terminal.

He caught Russell looking at Ron askance too.

"Raking what up?" Russell asked.

"Oh, I don't know. Don't matter," Ron said, quickly. "Sometimes history's best left in the past, innit?"

Joe wasn't at all convinced that bad blood should be left to fester. He would call Violet as soon as they got home and tell her to come back in to see her sister.

AS THE THREE OF THEM strode out of the hospice, a slim, mousy-haired man in a pin-stripe suit hurried after them.

"Excuse me, gentlemen," he called, his voice tight and nasal. "I wonder if I might have a word."

They all stopped and turned.

"Can we help?" Russell asked.

"I hope so, it's rather delicate, you see," he said. "You've just been visiting with Jean Carter?"

"Yeah, what of it?" Ron asked, stepping forward defensively.

"I'm sorry," the man said, sensing that he was putting his foot in it already. "I'm the manager here. Harry Underwood"

He extended a hand. None of them shook it. He tucked it back in his pocket.

"Are any of you, by any chance, her next of kin?" Underwood asked, wringing his hands.

"No, said Russell. "We're just friends. Her husband passed away, we came to share our condolences."

"Yes, terrible business," Underwood said. "The police informed us yesterday evening. She was very upset."

"Naturally," Ron said.

"And, do you happen to know who her next of kin would be now? Now that he's passed?"

Russell got the feeling there was something amiss here. He shot Joe a cautionary look, noticing him reaching for his wallet, and not wanting him to share the sister's name and number until they'd spoken to her. This guy could wait, or get it from Jean herself.

"What exactly is the problem?" Russell asked.

"Well, I'm not sure I can discuss it with you," Underwood said. "If you're not family."

"I'm family," Ron blurted. "I'm her brother-in-law."

Russell and Joe both stared at him incredulously, but he held firm.

"I may not directly be *next* of kin, but I'm as close to family as she's got left for the moment. What's the problem?"

"Ah," Underwood said, smiling weakly again. "It's just that there's been an issue with the payments for the last two months. I tried to speak to Mr Carter about it; he didn't want to worry Jean. He promised it would be sorted out, but, well, it hasn't and now… well, we may not be able to continue caring for Jean if there is no payment forthcoming."

He shuffled his feet. There, he'd said it.

"I'm sorry to have to bring it up, especially at a time like this, but I wonder if you'd be able to advise me on how we should proceed?"

Ron pulled a battered business card from his wallet and handed it to Underwood.

"Send any outstanding bills to me," he said. "Care of the Red Lion pub on Rupert Street. I'll make sure you get what's owed to you."

Underwood thanked him and turned away, back straight, adjusting his hair on the sides as he walked off, satisfied with himself.

Ron set off towards the underground station as Russell and Joe exchanged a confused glance and hurried after him.

"Brother-in-law?" Russell asked, catching up.

"It's a long story," said Ron. "And I don't want to talk about it right now. I've got to open the pub in less than an hour."

IT WAS STANDING-ROOM only on the tube, and Russell could tell that Ron was in no mood to be questioned. Joe, however, wasn't letting this go that easily.

"Of course I'm not legally her brother-in-law," he huffed. "But what does that matter?"

"Why did you say it then?" Joe asked.

"One," Ron said, between clenched teeth, "it's none of your business. And two, I was very close to Jean and Danny back in the day. Me and Dan were like brothers once, so that's that."

"But why did you agree to pay the bills?" Russell asked. "Surely Danny had enough money to pay for Jean's care? Why send her private if not?"

"Danny was an odd one," Ron said. "Didn't trust hospitals. Never has. When Jean got sick, he promised her she wouldn't die in one."

"But if he wasn't paying the bills, he obviously couldn't afford a private hospice," Joe said.

"Look, all I know is he was having a few money worries. I had no idea it was this bad." Ron said. "I should have helped him out earlier. But, well… look I barely saw the bloke any more and he's never been sharp with paying back his debts. He owed me too much already."

Russell got a sense he meant more than money.

"Yes, but…" Joe started.

"Just bloody leave it, will you?" Ron huffed.

"You spent more time with Danny recently than the rest of us," Russell directed his question at Joe, trying to stop his interrogation of Ron. "Did he ever let on to *you* that he was broke?"

"No," Joe said. "Look, he always got the drinks in, anyway. Didn't seem to be counting the pennies. I didn't really know him that well, though."

"Bloody idiot was always pretending to have more than he did," Ron muttered. "It was all Jean's though. She had the house, the career. And she earned well, too. They were pretty flush. He always liked to chuck it around. Showing off."

"Obviously he's been chucking it around a bit too much, because something stopped him paying those fees," Russell said.

The tube pulled into their station and they shoved their way through the crowd and took the stairs out of the underground, emerging at street level at the end of Tottenham Court Road.

"Where's their house then?" Russell asked.

"Cumberland Terrace. Number 4." Ron said, putting on his best fancy voice. "You know them ones looking over Regent's Park. Gorgeous, it is. Proper old townhouse."

"Bloody hell," Russell said.

31

It was a great postcode to own property in. An exclusive, expensive neighbourhood, right on the edge of the park. Far enough away from the seedier parts of London to be posh, but close enough to all of them to be relevant. Camden to the North, King's Cross to the East, and Soho to the South. All within walking distance, though Russell doubted whether many of the residents of Cumberland Terrace ever walked anywhere.

It seemed an incongruous place for Danny and Jean to live—too snobbish and gentrified for the likes of them. Russell could have better pictured them in some small flat in the heart of Soho.

"Yeah, they've lived there for ever. Jean was quite the celebrity in her time. Like I say, she was a big earner."

"What did she do?" Joe asked.

"She was a jazz singer," Ron replied. "Bloody brilliant she was. You wouldn't know it to look at her, but her voice could floor the toughest of men. Danny was lucky to win her heart when he did. Another year and she'd have been over in the States making millions, I reckon."

"Wow," Joe said. "I had no idea he was married to such a celebrity."

They'd reached the Red Lion by then, and Joe made his excuses and headed back to work, while Russell waited for Ron to wrestle with the lock before following him in.

Inside they found Paul already taking the chairs down from the tables and setting up to open. Russell was struck again by how much cuter Paul was out of drag and just being himself.

"You're going to need to change that barrel on the Pride," Paul said as Ron thanked him for setting up. "I still can't twist the thingy."

"Righto," Ron said, rolling his eyes and lifting the flap of the bar.

"I've cleaned out the dressing room, and all," Paul said. "What do you want me to do with this lot?"

"What's that?"

"All Danny's stuff he left back there. Keys, wallet, coat. I've also got his hat."

Russell cocked his head.

"Just shove it back in the storeroom for now," Ron said, dismissively.

"Shouldn't we hand it over to the police or something?"

"Well, they didn't ask for it, and I'm sure Danny wouldn't want that lot sniffing around his pad," Ron said.

"Mind if I use your loo?" Russell asked innocently.

"Help yourself," Ron said, heading down into the cellar behind the bar.

"I'll stick those in the storeroom for you on my way past, shall I?" Russell offered.

Paul smiled gratefully.

"Ta love."

"No problem."

Russell had hit upon an idea, but it was one he assumed Ron wouldn't be too happy with. He wanted to have a look around Danny's house.

Someone had deliberately killed him, and as yet he had no clue who or why. Hopefully he'd find some answers in Cumberland Terrace.

3

JOE WAS ON FAIRLY GOOD TERMS with his new boss at the production company—Paul "PJ" Davis was one of the nicer guys in the television industry, and had taken a chance hiring Joe without any training or experience.

Joe felt bad lying to him about where he'd been that morning, but he could hardly have asked for time off to go and see the ailing wife of a murdered acquaintance. So he'd lied and said he had an appointment of his own.

"How did it go at the doctors?" Paul asked, conspiratorially. "Everything okay?"

"Apparently so," Joe said. "I need to sleep more and worry less."

"Don't we all, love. Is that it though? He didn't give you any of the good stuff?"

"He gave me a prescription for something, I haven't picked it up yet."

"Oh, you should take everything you can get. Migraines are no joke. I should know."

Joe had deliberately chosen migraines, knowing that Paul was a sufferer and assuming that it would make him more sympathetic. Of course, it meant he was likely to ask far more questions, too.

"What have I missed?" Joe asked, changing the subject before Paul could grill him on his fictitious prescription.

"Well, the Beeb are asking for about a hundred changes to the voiceover script, as usual, and Jane's been locked in that room with the auditors since nine this morning. I don't think they've even let her out for a pee yet!"

"Better get on then," Joe said.

He sat at his desk and shoved the pile of release forms and other odd paperwork to one side. This afternoon's filing would have to wait. He took the slip of paper with Violet's number on it from his pocket and, smiling a hello at one of his colleagues, picked up the phone.

The call took a moment to connect, before the ringing began. No answer. He held on, letting it ring. Just as he was about to hang up, a woman answered.

"Hello?" She sounded annoyed already.

"Oh, hello there," Joe said, trying to sound official. "Is it possible to speak to Violet please?"

"Who's calling?" she asked, suspiciously.

"My name's Joe Stone."

"I've never heard of you. What do you want?"

Joe sighed.

"Violet? I'm actually a friend of your sister's. Jean? She asked me to call."

The line went dead. Violet had just hung up.

Joe dialled again. It rang out. No answer. He dialled again. Finally, she answered, her voice hard and bitter.

"You can tell my sister if she's got anything to say to me, she can do it to my bloody face."

"Good," Joe said, level and calm. "That's why I'm calling. She wants to see you."

"Oh yeah?" She sounded suspicious. "So, why isn't she calling herself then? Too scared to talk to me is she?"

Her tone was bitter and angry.

"She's not very well, Violet. And her husband has just passed away. I saw her today and she asked me to call you. She said to say she's sorry but she does need to see you again, after all."

There was silence on the line. Joe was worried that he'd lost the call again.

"Dan's dead?" Violet asked. Suddenly, all the fight had gone out of her voice.

"I'm afraid so," Joe replied.

A small silence. A shuddering breath. The smallest snort of a laugh. Joe waited.

"Huh. Heart attack was it? Or stroke? Never could keep off the booze, that one. Can't say I'm either shocked or sad to hear it." The hardness was already back.

"He was stabbed," Joe replied. He saw no reason to sugar-coat anything for this woman—she was harsh and abrasive. Especially compared to Jean.

"Jesus," she said. Flat disbelief. "Well I never. So, what's up with Jean then? Broken heart, is it? Am I supposed to feel sorry for her? Why didn't she call me herself?"

"Did you not know? I got the impression from Jean that she'd seen you recently."

"No love, haven't seen her for donkey's."

Joe frowned. He'd obviously got the wrong end of the stick from Jean. Or perhaps her mind was playing more tricks on her than they'd thought.

"She has cancer, Violet," Joe said. "It's gone too far, I'm afraid. She's in a hospice. End-of-life care."

"And she thinks by getting you to call me up out of the blue, I'll just come running to her bedside like the devoted sister? Well she can think again. Who are you, anyway?"

"I knew Danny," Joe said. "I was there when he died. I went to see Jean this morning and she asked me to call you. She said she needed to see you again."

Silence again. Finally, she cleared her throat.

"Where is she then?"

"You'll go and see her?" Joe asked.

"I'll think about it. Depends where she is."

"She's in a hospice, in London. I can give you the address."

"How long's she got?"

"I don't know," Joe said. "Not long. It's impossible to know, though. I think she wants to put whatever's happened between you to rest before she goes."

"I see."

"I'm sorry to be so morbid," Joe said.

"Don't worry, love. There's no love lost. What's the address then?"

Joe read it out for her, slowly, waiting until she prompted him for each next part. She read it back to confirm.

"Will you be there?"

"No," Joe said, momentarily confused. "I don't work there, I just told Jean I would call you. Pass on the message."

"Oh. It's just that I don't really want to see her on my own. Things haven't always been good between us. You said you were a friend."

"She's very frail," Joe said. "She just wants to see you. She can't hurt you."

The woman laughed.

"You have no idea how much that woman can hurt people," she replied. "If you don't come, I won't go and see her. Simple as that."

Joe sighed.

"Fine," he said. "When?"

"Tomorrow morning? Ten o'clock."

Joe looked at his boss furiously scribbling something on a whiteboard. He couldn't phone in sick again and hope to keep his job.

"Can we make it twelve-thirty? I have to work in the morning."

"Fine," she said. "I'll meet you outside the hospice. Don't go in without me. And don't be late. If you're not there, I'm walking away."

As he hung up, Joe already knew that Violet wouldn't be walking away at all. Her interest was piqued. And she had sounded genuinely surprised to hear that Danny was dead, so he guessed they could rule out the old family feud as a motive for his murder.

RUSSELL HAD BEEN RIGHT to be impressed by the address. Danny and Jean's house was a four-storey townhouse, overlooking Regent's Park, set back slightly from the road with ornate Georgian railings protecting it from any straying passers-by.

Compared to its neighbours, the whole place could do with a lick of paint and a general spruce up, but it was still a pretty nest egg to be sitting on.

Russell couldn't help feeling guilty that he was intruding without Jean's permission as he began testing the keys in the lock, but he hoped she'd understand. He was sure a neighbour would come out and challenge what he was doing, but no one did.

On the third key, he felt the lock give and the door swung open. He stepped inside and shut out the noise of London behind him.

A large, grand entrance hall led to a wide staircase, with a solid-looking balustrade, painted white but, like the outside, worn and chipped.

The carpet going up the stairs was deep red, held in place on each step by brass runners.

The decorative Georgian tiles on the hallway floor, some cracked and chipped, led down the side of the staircase along a narrow corridor, off which was a small sitting room.

Russell stepped inside to find the sitting room neat and ordered. The curtains were partly drawn, making the room feel dark and small.

He crossed to the window and opened the curtains slightly, letting the light seep in. There was a thick layer of dust on every surface, hanging in the air, illuminated by the sunlight streaming through the window.

The sitting room was quite old-fashioned. Two high-backed, deeply upholstered chairs sat either side of a small nest of tables, facing the window.

One wall was lined top to bottom with fitted shelves filled with books about singers, musicians, music and the arts. This was Jean's domain, Russell guessed.

An equally old-fashioned writing desk nestled in the corner, the kind with a lid that opened out to make the desk. It was closed, and when Russell tried it, he realised that the lid was locked. He scouted around for a key to fit the tiny lock. It wouldn't be very complex to pick, but he didn't want to damage anything at this stage.

In a handmade pot stuffed with pens, he found the tiny brass key he was looking for. Opening the desk, he found the contents to be just as neat as the rest of the room.

A pad of personalised notepaper, with Jean's name and address on top, sat squarely in the centre of the desk. An ornate fountain pen stood in a copper stand behind it. A neat stack of matching envelopes to the left. Russell could imagine Jean sitting here, writing her correspondence.

There were three small drawers on the right-hand side of the desk. Russell opened each one in turn finding nothing too interesting in the bottom two—some old paperclips, a few biro pens, an eraser.

In the top drawer he found a bundle of photographs, wrapped in a folded sheet of paper. He opened the little parcel up and looked at the photographs, laying each one down in turn.

The first few were of Jean as a younger woman, clearly professionally shot—a series of charming black and white headshots, each signed in her delicate hand, but never sent out to her adoring fans.

After the headshots came a collection of photographs from a performance in a club. Jean on stage in each, a full house in front of her, dancing, watching, applauding.

In one, she stood alone in the spotlight, in front of the microphone, eyes closed, singing her heart out. It was hard to reconcile this striking performer with the frail woman they had seen earlier that morning.

Russell turned the photograph over, reading the handwritten inscription on the back: *Ronnie Scott's Jazz Club, with Tubby Hayes. 1964.* Arguably London's most famous jazz venue, and Jean had been a star act.

Twenty-odd years later, and it wasn't just Jean's career that had faded. He wondered when she had stopped performing. Ron would know.

Russell tucked the photographs away in their paper cover, and was about to slide them back into the drawer when he noticed the corner of another photograph, shoved all the way to the back.

It had been pushed so far in that the edge had caught under the back panel, and Russell had to squeeze his hand into the drawer to get enough purchase to tease it out.

It was a picture of Jean from around the same time as the previous ones, but this time a snapshot, taken causally. Jean, Danny and another woman, smiling for the camera, Danny's arms draped around both of their shoulders, looking like the cat that got the cream. It had been taken on the steps outside this house, the colours all fading into dull, opaque versions of themselves.

Russell turned the photograph over. In faint pencil on the back it said: *Moving Day! Jean, Dan and Violet at Cumberland Terrace.*

So that was Jean's sister Violet? They didn't look much alike. Jean's lush golden curls, glamorous dress hugging her shapely figure, soft face, dancing eyes and warm smile were all entirely opposite to her sister's features.

Violet was at least a foot taller, with shoulder length brown hair, long slender arms and legs. No makeup, flat shoes, a brown A-line skirt and a baggy, pale yellow cardigan.

Russell held the photograph up to the light to study them all in turn. Danny was beaming directly at the camera, Jean looking up at him and grinning happily. Violet, on the other hand had a smile on her lips that went no further. Where Jean was held close against Danny's side, there was an awkward gap between him and Violet, though his hand still rested proprietorially on Violet's waist.

Russell tucked the photograph into his coat pocket. He wanted to talk to Ron a bit more about their relationship, find out what he knew about why the two sisters had fallen out. Russell sensed there was more to Ron's brother-in-law comment than he was letting on.

He tucked the rest of the photographs back in the drawer and locked the desk. Pulling the curtains closed again, he left the room almost as he'd found it.

Following the hallway further he found a huge kitchen and open-plan dining area. A high-ceilinged room, which extended directly onto a large glass atrium to the back, looking out onto a small, and now sadly overgrown, courtyard garden. In its day, this would have been beautiful. With a clean up, it could be again.

The whole room was full of clutter. Costumes, hats, wigs, flyers for concerts, posters half unfurled on the long kitchen table. A stack of dishes piled high in the sink. Empty takeaway cartons left to dry and grow mould on the work surfaces. Squalor.

This beautiful room had ceased to be place for entertaining a long time ago. It smelled of old food, mould and stale air. Russell crossed to the glass double doors leading to the atrium and flung them open, opening the door to the back garden as well. The cold blast of fresh air was a relief.

He walked back through the kitchen slowly, looking at the surface layer of mess. If anything had been troubling Danny recently, it would most likely be near the top of one of these piles. *But where to start?* He lifted up a pile of opened letters and began leafing through them.

Almost every one was a red bill, a final demand, or a threatening letter about foreclosure. Danny had been in a lot of trouble. Russell tidied the bills and put them to one side. He wondered what would happen with them now. Jean was in no fit state to deal with bills and payments, and now Danny was gone, the house would likely have to be sold to pay off their debts and her care bills. It felt like such a sad end for those happy faces in the photograph.

Russell found a pile of unopened letters from the Midland Bank. Some of the envelopes had coffee stains on them, some were wrinkled with age. Danny hadn't been opening his bank statements for quite a while.

Russell took the pile with him into the atrium and sat down in a rattan chair near the door, enjoying the breeze. He opened the letters one by one, knowing that technically it was illegal to open someone else's post, but figuring that no one would ever find out it was him who'd opened them.

The first few statements were perfectly normal. There were modest amounts in the account. What little money was going in more than covered the few bills the couple had going out. By the third statement he opened, Russell could see that the bills for the hospice were beginning to eat away into their balance, though.

He pulled the low coffee table closer to him and laid the statements all out side by side. Another couple of month's worth of slowly diminishing balances, and then came the statements for the last three months that each showed a huge drop in the total balance.

Russell scrutinised the bills, but there were no large individual sums that stood out, other than the hospice fees, and they weren't enough to reduce the balance as much as they had.

Running his finger down the transaction list, he realised that there had been a series of almost daily cash withdrawals of one hundred pounds a time, adding up to almost ten thousand pounds over the last three months. Why had Danny been withdrawing all that cash?

He folded the statements up and tucked them all back into their envelopes. The cash was untraceable, there was no point holding on to the statements.

At the bottom of the pile of bank letters was one envelope that had been opened. Russell took out the single page letter, also from the bank, rejecting Danny's application to remortgage the house—with no fixed income coming in, the bank wasn't willing to risk it.

Good job too, they were both too old to have got decent terms. Danny would have ended up losing the house if he hadn't lost his life first.

He put all the bank correspondence back on the table on his way through the kitchen and spent a few moments rifling through other bits of paper, documents, receipts and letters. There were no clues to what Danny had spent all that cash on.

His search of the rooms upstairs was just as fruitless. The master bedroom showed signs that Danny had been living in there, with a full laundry basket and a ruffled bed, but otherwise, the top two floors seemed as untouched as Jean's sitting room.

Russell wondered when the last time anyone had visited the couple was. Danny had seemed such a gregarious sort on the few occasions he'd seen him out and about, and Russell had never thought about the man behind the cabaret host's persona. With his wife terminally ill and the bills mounting, the house had become a kind of monument to the couple's decline.

On his way out, Russell spotted a sealed envelope on the telephone table by the front door, addressed to Crown Estate Agents. There was a stamp affixed, but it was obviously yet to be posted.

He eased the envelope open and pulled out the thin sheaf of papers inside. It was a contract from the local estate agent, agreeing to put the house on the market. Danny had signed it, but not sent it off.

So he was planning to sell the house to cover their debts. Russell guessed there hadn't been much choice if Jean needed on-going care at the rates they were paying. Danny's work at the revue bar in Camden would have earned him little more than pocket money. Nowhere near enough to cover the kind of bills he'd signed up to with putting Jean in that specialist hospice. So why had he been taking out their remaining savings as cash, and where had it all gone?

BY THE TIME RUSSELL got back to his flat just off Soho Square, he was starting to feel quite hungry. The smells coming from the kitchen as he walked in were amazing.

There was a lot to be said for Joe's new French boyfriend, Luc, staying over all the time, even if it meant they all had to share just the one bathroom.

Luc was an excellent chef, he had time on his hands while he looked for permanent work, and he was very easy on the eye.

When Russell had asked Joe to move in, it was because he recognised that they both missed their friend Chris, and with Chris gone, Russell needed to let the room out anyway, given his reduced income since leaving the force.

He hadn't really intended to take on two flatmates for the price of one, but Luc seemed to spend more time here than he ever did in his crappy little hotel near King's Cross.

Russell walked into the kitchen to find the boys sitting at the table, chatting away as usual, laughing together. He envied them their easy rapport. It was something he'd never been able to achieve.

He was only fifteen years older than either of them but he felt like they'd grown up in a different time. Somehow, it was easier for guys in their twenties these days to come out, and be proud of who they were. Not easy by any stretch of the imagination, but easier than it had been when he was their age. Or perhaps it was just that he'd always just been more uptight and less comfortable in himself than they were. Who knew?

He was truly happy for Joe, but seeing them so at ease together made him wish for something similar himself. *Maybe one day.*

Having been pushed from his job, Russell was finally able to be a little more open about his sexuality, but he still wondered whether he would ever find himself a partner, or if he was destined to just pick up casual lovers who ran off at the first sign of commitment.

"Evening lads," he said, interrupting their conversation.

Luc got to his feet and tinkered with a pan at the stove. Russell had tried to make him feel welcome, but he always felt that Luc was embarrassed every time Russell came home to find him here again.

"Something smells good, Luc. We might have to keep you."

Luc smiled. He really was a beautiful boy. Joe looked at Russell expectantly.

"Well? Where have you been? And, more importantly, what have you found out?" he asked.

"Give me a chance to take my coat off," Russell laughed. "Is there any wine going?"

Joe poured him a glass while Russell hung his coat in the hallway and flopped down in a chair at the kitchen table.

"I got hold of Violet, by the way," Joe said, sitting down again opposite him. "She wasn't particularly charitable about her sister."

"Did you tell her about Danny?"

"I did. She seemed shocked, but she didn't pretend to care too much."

"Nice," Russell said. "The rift lives on then. Will she go back to see Jean again?"

"Well, that's the weird thing," Joe said. "Violet says she hasn't seen her sister for years, but I got the impression Jean had seen her recently. Didn't you?"

"Yeah. She said something about seeing her one more time, didn't she? Maybe she meant after all these years."

"So it's not only me who finds your language confusing," Luc said, laying the table around them. Joe smiled at him.

"But she'll go then?" Russell asked.

"Only if I go with her, she says."

Russell frowned.

"Weird. Why would she want a complete stranger to go with her?"

"Moral support, I guess. Or maybe as a witness. I got the feeling she's frightened of Jean. I did reassure her that she was very frail and just wanted to make her peace, but I don't think she was convinced. Anyway, I agreed to meet her at the hospice tomorrow lunchtime. I can't really take any more time off work without them getting the hump."

"Fair enough, do you want me to come?"

"No, I'll be fine. I'm hoping I can just make the introduction and leave them to it."

"Voila," Luc said, presenting them with a delicious-looking bowl of pasta each. He settled down between them and topped up his own wine glass.

"Bon appetit," he said, smiling.

"Thanks Luc, this looks amazing," Russell said. And it did.

"So," Joe prompted. "Enough about that. What did you find out today?"

"Well," Russell swallowed his mouthful. "It turns out Danny left his keys and wallet in the dressing room at the Red Lion. Ron didn't seem that interested, so I may have liberated the keys while he wasn't looking and gone round to the house."

"You didn't," Joe laughed. "Breaking and entering. Tut tut."

Russell held his hands up, smiling too.

"Does Ron know?"

"No," Russell replied. "He seems quite protective of Danny and Jean. I didn't think he'd be that keen on me snooping around on my own, but I didn't really want him to come with me either."

He took another mouthful, rolling the flavours on his tongue. Simple and delicious. A lot of garlic.

"Anyway, I get the feeling that whatever happened between them all in the past, none of them really want to talk about it."

"No," said Joe, "I got that impression from Violet today too."

He looked at Russell while he ate another mouthful.

"Well, come on then," he said. "What did you find at the house, 'cause I can tell by your face you found something."

Russell smiled.

"Okay, so Danny was definitely in denial about their money troubles. I found about six months' worth of unopened bank statements, a rejection of an application to remortgage the house, and a mountain of final demands. He was right at the end of the line, financially."

"How, though? He always gave the impression he had cash to spend."

"Pride, perhaps," Russell said. "The hospice was certainly making a big dent in their balance, but Danny had also started withdrawing cash. About one hundred quid every day. Ten grand's worth in total."

"Jesus. Who needs that kind of cash in their pocket?"

"God knows. But he certainly wasn't using it to pay any of his bills, they were about to be cut off of most things."

"Do you think Jean knows?" Joe asked.

"I doubt it," Russell said. "I don't even think he was admitting it to himself."

"So what was he spending the cash on? You don't think he'd got into gambling, do you? Got himself into debt trying to win big enough to solve their problems?"

It wasn't a bad suggestion. Russell hadn't thought about gambling, but it would make sense. If there was nowhere else to turn for money to pay for Jean's care, and the bank had rejected their mortgage application, perhaps Danny had turned to gambling to solve their problems.

"I can ask around," Russell said. "See if he's been seen in any of the bookies, or down the track. He'd be pretty hard to miss, even in his regular clothes."

Danny had a reputation for always looking dapper. Crisp suits, smart shirts, good shoes. The perfect impression of a fine gentleman.

"Perhaps that's what got him killed," Joe said. "He got himself into debt and couldn't pay."

"Stop talking and eat," Luc said, tersely. "It'll get cold. You two are always so busy trying to solve your mysteries."

His French accent was adorable, but he had a tendency to boss Joe around. Still, the food was delicious and neither of them argued. They ate in silence for a while, but Russell couldn't stop his mind whirring.

"She was quite the celebrity in her time, you know, old Jean?" Russell said.

Luc sighed.

"She sang in Ronnie Scott's and everything. Seems to have performed with all the greats. There are some amazing photos of her in her heyday. It's such a shame they both ended up like this."

Remembering the other photograph he'd found, Russell stood up, heading to the hallway to retrieve it.

"I found this," he said. "Of the day Jean, Danny and Violet moved in to Cumberland Terrace together. They all look happy enough. I wonder what happened between Jean and Violet to end all that?"

Joe froze mid-mouthful, staring at the photo. He dropped his fork and picked the image up, studying it closer.

"When was this taken?"

"Sixties sometime," Russell said. "It says so on the back. Why?"

"This woman..."

"Violet? What about her?"

"This is the woman I saw in the club on the night Danny died," Joe said.

"What? It can't be. She'd be much older these days."

"No, that's just it," Joe said, looking at Russell, confused. "She looked pretty much exactly like this."

"What?"

"And I think Danny saw her too. There was a moment when I was talking to him before I went backstage to find Patty, and he looked out into the crowd and seemed to freeze. He looked really shocked. He must have seen her."

"But it can't be *her*," Russell said. "Violet would be twenty years older by now."

"I know that," Joe said, defensively. "But this is what she looked like."

"So who was she?" Russell asked. "Because it can't have been Violet. Look how much the other two have changed since this was taken."

Joe studied the photograph closely, shaking his head.

"I think we should see what Violet has to say tomorrow," Russell said. "I might come with you, after all."

4.

JOE STEPPED ONTO the escalator behind Russell, leaning his hip against the railing as they rode up out of the underground. He was glad Russell had decided to come along. He felt quite unsettled at the thought of meeting Violet on her own after seeing that photograph.

He knew it sounded crazy, but he was absolutely positive that the woman he'd seen in the club was the same woman in the picture. And if it wasn't Violet herself, it was someone who knew exactly how she'd looked back in the sixties and had deliberately dressed like her to kill Danny. But why? *Who was she?*

As they neared the top, Joe glanced across at the downward escalator and his heart skipped. There she was again. Was he going mad? It was the same person, dressed the same way. He was sure of it.

"Russell," he said, urgently. "Look. That's her!"

Russell looked where he was pointing. The girl noticed Joe pointing at exactly the same time and panicked, taking off down the escalator as fast as she could.

Joe and Russell ran up the last few treads, barged past the people coming in from outside as they rounded the top of the escalators, and followed her down as fast as they could, trying not to knock anyone flying.

Joe reached the bottom first and sprinted to the platform just in time to see the doors closing on a train leaving the station. The woman's face was framed in the window as the train pulled away. She looked frightened.

"Shit!" Joe shouted as Russell caught up with him on the platform. "We lost her."

Russell bent double, trying to get his breath back.

"You saw her though, right?" Joe asked. "She looks exactly the same, doesn't she?"

Russell leaned against the wall, still sucking in breath, but he nodded. He'd seen her. Joe wasn't going mad. Joe thumped the wall with the side of his fist.

"Dammit," he said. "What was she doing here?"

The realisation suddenly hit him.

"Jean."

And he was off again, sprinting towards the escalator back to the surface.

"Jesus. Wait," Russell called after him.

"I'll see you there," Joe shouted back.

There was no time to waste. Whoever that woman was, she had deliberately dressed like Jean's sister, Violet, in order to kill Danny and now she had been in to see Jean. There must be a reason, and whatever it was, it could only be malicious.

Joe pushed through the ticket barriers and out onto the street, his heart pounding. The only possible explanation for that woman being here was if she'd come to do the same to Jean as she had to Danny.

Joe ran faster towards the hospice, already convinced of the worst. He stopped at the front doors and looked behind him—there was no sign of Russell, but he couldn't wait. He had to check on Jean.

HE STRODE INTO RECEPTION to find it abandoned. *Strange*, he thought. He hovered nervously for a moment before looking around the corner to see if there was anyone there. Maybe the nurse was just away from her station. But no, the corridor was empty too.

Not willing to wait, Joe made his way quickly down the empty corridor towards Jean's room, feeling sick with worry. He knocked and, when there was no answer, pushed the door open.

Jean lay perfectly still on her back, mouth slightly open. He was too late. There were no alarms sounding, no rushing staff, but it looked like Jean was already dead.

He stepped into her room, letting the door swing closed behind him and stood for a moment, listening. Where was everybody?

Further up the hall he could hear voices, hurried and urgent, a trolley banging against a door. A shout. But inside this room, all was silent.

He stepped forward, his trainers squeaking on the linoleum floor, and cringed. The noise felt so wrong in this awful silence.

"Jesus, it's like Piccadilly-bloody-Circus in here this morning," Jean said, tilting her head and half-opening her eyes to look at him. "I'm supposed to be resting."

"Oh Jean," he said, the relief washing over him. "You're alive."

"Not for long at this rate," she tutted. "Can't a girl get any sleep? What do you want anyway?"

"I..." Joe didn't quite know what to say. "I spoke to Violet yesterday," he blurted out. "I said I'd meet her here, bring her in to see you."

"Yeah? Well, you just missed her," Jean said. "She didn't stay long. Always in a rush, that one."

Joe frowned. Jean coughed. Joe waited for the fit to pass. She spat her phlegm into her handkerchief and smiled weakly at him.

"Thanks for calling her," she said, her voice cracked and sore. "You didn't need to come all the way back down here though. We're big girls. We can sort out our own troubles. I'm glad she came back again."

There it was again—that lack of clarity.

"Jean?" Joe asked. "Has Violet been to see you here before? At the hospice, I mean."

"Of course she has. She came as soon as Danny told her I was sick. We may have had our differences over the years, but I'm still her little sister."

"It's just that when I spoke to her on the phone yesterday, it seemed like the first she'd heard of it."

Jean coughed violently again, collapsing back into her pillows. She was in no state to be having this conversation, but something strange was going on and Joe wasn't willing to leave without answers.

He edged closer to the bed, handing her the metal bowl by her bedside to spit in. When she had, she looked at him, eyes watering from the effort of coughing.

"I'm sorry, love. Disgusting. Just chuck that in the sink, will you? One of the nurses will deal with it."

Joe did as she said, but he rinsed the bowl under the tap before leaving it in the sink. His own Nan had died of lung cancer, he knew how it would be for Jean in the end, and he could tell she didn't have many more weeks, or maybe even days before her body just gave up.

"Jean," he began, tentatively. "You said Violet came in to see you this morning?"

"Of course she did," Jean sounded incredulous. "Just like you asked her to."

"What was she wearing? Can you remember?"

Jean looked confused, angry.

"What's all this? I'm not simple, you know? I haven't got memory problems," she said. "She wore what she always wears—plain dress, brown cardi. What do you care, anyway?"

Joe didn't really know how to answer. She'd just described the woman from the tube.

"It's just that..."

He didn't get the chance to finish the sentence before the door opened and Russell stuck his head round.

"Is she alright?" he asked.

Joe nodded, looking back to see that Jean had nestled back into her pillows, eyes closed. She was exhausted. This was all too much.

Russell opened the door and stepped in, looking flushed and flustered.

"Look who I found outside," he said, sounding falsely cheery.

Violet, the real Violet, stepped cautiously into the room. She looked nervous. Her hair was cropped short, dyed a deep, cheap red. She was wearing a uniform from a chain supermarket, obviously on her way to work.

"Is that her?" Violet whispered to Russell.

Russell nodded.

"Is she dead?" Violet asked, a little louder.

"No," Joe said. "She's just tired."

"Well, I haven't got long," Violet said, peering at her sister. "Can you wake her up?"

"Can I have a word?" Joe asked. "Outside."

He hustled the two of them back out into the corridor, with some tutting from Violet.

"Violet," he said, knowing that there wouldn't be much time to talk before the nurses found them all there. "Listen, Jean's had a bit of a strange morning."

"Well, what's that got to do with me? I came down here like you asked."

"The thing is," Joe said. "Jean believes you've been coming to see her for weeks."

"Well, she's lost her mind then, ain't she?" Violet said, ready to walk away. "Because I haven't seen her for best part of fifteen years."

"No. But someone *has* been visiting her," Joe persisted. "Pretending to be you. And we saw her here, just now, as we were coming off the tube. She was dressed just like you."

"What, she also works in Sainsbury's?"

"No, I don't mean like you *now*. I mean how you used to look."

Violet looked blank. Russell took her arm.

"I went to Danny and Jean's house," he said. "Looking for any kind of reason why he might have been killed. While I was there I found this photo of you all together, moving in to Cumberland Terrace."

He took the photograph out of his pocket and held it in front of her.

"So what? I lived with them for a while. It didn't work out."

"Why not?" Joe asked.

"None of your business," Violet said. "What *is* all this? Is this why you brought me down here? You think I had something to do with Dan dying? Is that it? What are you, coppers or something?"

"No," Russell said quickly. "No, we're not the police. And we're not accusing you of anything. We're just trying to understand what's been going on."

"On the night Danny died, I saw a woman in the club who looked exactly like you do in this photo," said Joe.

Violet frowned.

"Well, that don't make any sense. That was taken twenty years ago."

She took the photograph from him, looking at it for a moment before shoving it back in his hand angrily.

"It's nothing to do with me, alright?"

But Joe sensed some reluctance in her denial. What did she know?

"Can you think of anyone who would do this, Violet? Anyone who might dress up like you deliberately? To make a point to Danny, or to Jean?"

"No."

But she couldn't meet his eyes. So she *did* know something. He pushed her further.

"It's just that we saw this same woman again this morning. Right here. In the tube station. And we think she's visited Jean before, pretending to be you. So, who would do that, Violet? Who would know that she was here, and come to visit her, dressed like you used to look back in the sixties?"

"I don't know, alright?" Violet shouted.

She turned and started walking away, but stopped. She stepped right up to Joe, angry and upset.

"I told you I didn't want to come down here. I said I didn't want to go opening things up again. So you can tell Jean to shove it. I don't want anything to do with her, or her money, or that bloody house. She can keep it all."

Joe and Russell watched her stalk away.

"She knows something," Russell said.

"Shall I follow her?"

"No. Give her some space. We've got her number if we want to talk to her again. We need to figure out what we're missing first."

"Everything alright here?" A nurse had appeared behind them in the corridor.

"More or less," Russell smiled reassuringly. "We brought Jean's sister to see her, but she lost her nerve at the last minute."

The nurse frowned.

"I thought she only had the one sister," she said, questioningly. "Violet, isn't it?"

"That's right," Joe replied.

"Well, she's been in a handful of times now. She was in this morning, in fact."

"She told you her name was Violet?" Russell asked.

The nurse noticed his tone of voice and became anxious, feeling interrogated.

"Yes," she said cautiously. "And so did Jean. It really cheered her up that her sister had got back in touch. It's not good to let those old wounds fester."

"I hate to tell you this," Russell said, "but whoever has been visiting Jean is not the real Violet."

The nurse's face went ashen.

"The woman we were just talking to was Violet, and she hasn't seen her sister since the sixties. Not long after this picture was taken."

He showed her the photograph and watched her fear turn to shock and confusion.

"But..." she stammered. "That's her. That's the woman who's been visiting. She said she was Violet. What's going on? Who is she?"

"We're not sure," Russell said. "But we think it has something to do with Jean's husband's death, and we're trying to find out who she really is."

"You don't think she'd try to hurt Jean, do you?" the nurse asked.

"She hasn't yet," Russell said. "So that obviously isn't her intention."

He tucked the photograph away again.

"Look," he said. "If she turns up again, can you call me straight away? And don't leave her alone with Jean."

"Of course," she replied. "But, shouldn't we tell the police?"

"I will," Russell said. "I'm a retired officer, I know the detective in charge of Danny's case. I'll let him know. He may want to talk to you about it all."

"Right," she said. "I hope it doesn't get the staff into trouble."

"I'm sure it'll be fine," Joe said. "No harm done. Just keep an eye out in case she turns up again."

"Do you mind if we just have a quick word with Jean about it," Russell asked. "We won't be long."

"Please do," the nurse replied. "I'll just be at the desk there, if you need me."

She was obviously shocked to think that they'd been letting some potentially dangerous imposter into a patient's room. But at least she felt that Russell and Joe were trustworthy, which was good enough for now.

JEAN STIRRED AS THEY closed the door.

"You again?" she croaked.

"I'm sorry to keep disturbing you Jean," Joe said quietly. "I just wanted to ask you a couple of quick questions and then we'll be out of your hair."

"I don't know what else I can tell you," she replied. "But alright. Pass me some water first, will you?"

Joe filled her glass from the jug at her bedside and held it gently to her lips as she took a sip. Her hands were stick thin—papery skin over bone and vein. The disease had stripped away all of her vitality. She looked more tired, paler, and less present than she had done even fifteen minutes ago when Joe had first arrived.

"Fire away then," she said, smiling through thin lips.

"I was wondering how things were with Violet?" Russell asked, stepping closer to the bed. "I know you'd had a falling out, but you say she's been visiting you. Is that all settled now?"

"I think so, dear," Jean said. "I needed to apologise to her. I hurt her, you see? But I've said sorry now. So all is mended."

"I'm glad to hear it," Russell said. "You must have had a lot to catch up on, after all those years apart."

Jean frowned a little, blinked slowly. She was fading fast.

"She's hardly changed a bit, you know," Jean said. "Not like me. Mind you, she always *was* the strong one."

"What happened between you two, Jean?" Joe asked.

"It's not important any more," she said sadly. "I made a mistake. But it's all done and dusted now."

She broke into another coughing fit, and when it ended she closed her eyes, this time keeping them closed. Sleep taking her again.

Joe and Russell looked at each other and shrugged. *What now?* Joe lifted the empty water glass from her hands and placed it on the bedside cabinet. He noticed Jean's handbag on the floor, and crouched down beside it.

"What are you doing?" Russell hissed.

"Shh," Joe said. "Just looking."

He carefully opened the bag and looked inside, taking out the address book Jean had used before. He opened it up and found Violet's name.

"Violet Cole," he whispered. "Got an address in King's Cross."

"Good thinking," Russell said. "Now put it back."

Joe tucked the address book away, but noticed a folded brown envelope tucked in the bag. He took it out.

"Joe!" Russell warned. "That's private."

Joe unfolded the envelope and opened it up, lifting out the contents.

"This is a letter from her solicitors," Joe said quietly. "Acknowledging receipt of the changes to her will."

"What?"

"Dated last week."

"Does it say what changes?"

"No, it just says to find enclosed a revised copy of the will, duly notarised."

"Well? Is it there?"

"No," Joe said, putting the letter back in the envelope and tucking it into the bag. There was nothing else in there but some tissues, an old lipstick, a pen and some house keys.

"I wonder what she changed?" Russell asked.

"I suppose it's not that unusual to start putting things in order at this stage in a terminal illness."

"But to change it just before Danny was killed? Don't you think that's a bit of a coincidence?"

"You don't think she...?"

"No, that's not what I meant. I just wonder whether she is being manipulated."

"By our mystery woman?"

"Quite possibly."

"Do you think the solicitors would tell us?"

"Not while she's alive. But, given that Danny's is a murder case, they might be compelled to disclose something to the police."

"You're not thinking of digging out your old uniform are you?" Joe smiled.

"God no," Russell laughed. "There's no way it would fit me now, anyway. I was actually thinking I would share some of what we've learned with the lovely Detective Skinner. See if we can't cast some more doubt on his conviction that Matthew is guilty."

Joe looked at his watch.

"I've got to get back to work," he said. "I'll drop in and see Violet on my way home."

"And I'm going to go for a nice pint," Russell said. "I think it's time I talked to Ron properly about his so-called sister-in-law."

IT WASN'T THAT RUSSELL was particularly fond of lunchtime drinking, but he'd got the sense that Ron knew more than he was letting on when they'd been to see Jean, and he wanted to grill him a bit.

When he arrived at the pub, he found the place almost deserted, and his young friend Paul behind the bar, with no sign of Ron.

"He's got you doing shifts now, has he?"

Paul looked up from the glass he was polishing, smiling when he saw Russell.

"Oh, hey," he said. "I'm just covering while he's out the back talking to the police again. They've been in more times in the last couple of days than any of the regulars. What can I get you?"

"Pint of Pride, please," Russell said. "How're you doing Paul?"

Paul's Patty Cakes had been the act on stage when Danny's body had been discovered and Russell knew the kid was sensitive enough as it was without this happening to him. He probably should have checked in on him earlier.

"I feel like I'm some kind of jinx," he said. "Or at least Patty is. First Chris, now Danny. It's almost like every time I put a frock on, someone dies."

He was right of course. Soho wasn't exactly a country fair, but neither was it the hotbed of vice, murder and depravity the press made it out to be. Even though Paul had a tendency to think the world revolved around him, and Russell didn't have much time for that, the fact that they'd lost two friends in the space of six months was quite a big deal.

"Yes, we seem to be losing friends quicker than we can make them. But it's not your fault," he said, accepting his pint and sliding some coins across the bar. "Keep the change."

Paul raised a facetious eyebrow.

"Thanks, Big Spender."

"I'll take it back if you like."

Paul dropped the coins into a clear plastic jar nestled beneath the optics.

"Who's back there with him then?" Russell asked.

"That weasel-faced little one," Paul said. "Your mate."

"Skinner? Good. I wanted to talk to him anyway."

"Really? God, I can't think of anything worse."

Russell took a sip of his pint.

"Has Ron said anything to you about Danny?"

Paul pulled himself a half pint and sat on the stool behind the bar.

"Oh, you know Ron, he doesn't talk about much. I think it's freaked him out that it happened here. Maybe more for the reputation of the pub than anything else."

"But he hasn't talked about their past?"

"Not to me. Wait, they had a past?" Paul asked salaciously.

"Not that kind of past," Russell said, tutting. "They *were* friends though. Ron said they were like brothers at one point."

Paul looked surprised.

"That might account for the mood he's been in ever since."

"But he hasn't said anything?"

"I don't think I'm the kind of guy Ron is going to confide his deepest darkests to, do you?"

"Not if he was in his right mind, no."

"Oi!"

Russell took another sip of his drink.

"You know they're still holding Matthew, right?" Paul said. "It's outrageous. How long are they allowed to keep him without charging him?"

"Depends what evidence they have, and what Matthew's said to them. Has he got a lawyer?"

"Not unless he's found one who'll work in return for a hand-job. He's skint, that boy. He's more brassic than me. Did you see his wig? Cheap synthetic shit."

A small alarm sounded in the back of Russell's mind. Another piece had just slotted into place. He didn't know what it meant yet, but he would get there.

"You don't think Matthew actually did it, do you?" Russell asked.

"Oh, come on," Paul said. "Matthew can barely see a paper cut without retching, how would he have stabbed Danny?"

"Fair point."

"But then, they've kept him in, haven't they? And there's no smoke without fire, right? They must have something on him."

"I doubt it," Russell said. "Skinner's the kind of copper who makes the obvious arrest, not necessarily the right one. Matthew was just there.

He'll do everything he can to make it stick so that he can keep his quick solve rate. I'll have a word."

"Don't make it worse," Paul warned. Not without reason.

"Don't worry, I'll talk to his boss, not him. You know they've set up an independent panel now, to investigate anti-gay discrimination in the force? GALOP it's called. They're good guys."

"I didn't know that. Your mate Skinner should keep them in work for years."

"Unless we manage to put him *out* of work first, of course."

Paul was about to respond when the doors opened from the back room, and Ron led Skinner and a uniformed officer out into the main bar.

Skinner stopped when he saw Russell there, drink in hand.

"Bit early for a drink isn't it?" he sneered.

"Not if you don't have a job to uphold," Russell replied.

"If that'll be all, Detective," Ron muttered. "I need to get on."

"We'll be in touch," Skinner said. The threat hardly veiled. For some reason Skinner had his eye on Ron as well. Russell shook his head in frustration.

"Can I have a word?" Russell asked.

"I'm busy," Skinner said. "Why not call in at the station later, I'll see if I can get someone to talk to you."

"If I have to call in at the station, I'll be taking the information I have above your head," Russell threatened. "I'm sure you'd rather the glory lands on your shoulders than Earnshaw's?"

Skinner hesitated just long enough.

"Tell you what, I'll walk you out," Russell said. "Won't take long."

He winked at Ron on the way past, leaving him and Paul to exchange whatever glances they wanted to.

"I understand you're still holding Matthew Dean," Russell said, as they left the pub. "On what grounds?"

"That's a police matter," Skinner sneered. "I'm not at liberty to discuss the case with members of the public."

"Fair enough," Russell said, taking the wind out of his sails. "I thought I should let you know a few things I've discovered recently, which may help to inform your case."

"And why would I want any information from you?"

"Because, Detective, I understand this community and you do not. They trust me. Which means people tell me things."

Skinner's sneer didn't move from his face.

"And if you don't thoroughly investigate the information I am about to give you," Russell continued. "I will report you to the boys at GALOP and see what they think of the way you treat people in my community."

"You think I care about that lot?"

"You should, because I can promise you Earnshaw does, and thanks to how you treated me, and the appalling way you handled Chris Sexton's murder, you already have two strikes against your name. They need to be seen to be taking a stand, Skinner. Earnshaw wouldn't think twice about throwing you to the dogs for some good PR."

Skinner stepped forward, ready to swing for him but Russell stepped back calmly, smiling.

"You didn't think I'd take it lying down, did you?" he asked. "After what you did to me, I'm gunning for you, son."

Skinner settled, reluctantly.

"But whilst I would love to see you stripped of your badge," Russell said. "I'd far rather see justice done properly."

"This is just sour grapes," Skinner whined.

"On the contrary," Russell said. "You actually did me a favour getting me removed from the force. The pay-out was great, I no longer have to watch my back from the likes of you, and I don't have to get up early in the mornings. So I should thank you really."

"Fine," Skinner said. "Tell me what you know."

RUSSELL COULDN'T HIDE the strut as he walked back into the bar. He'd told Skinner what they'd found out about Jean, the will, the visits from the strange woman, and the fact that Joe had seen that same woman in the club on the night Danny had been killed, and again at Jean's hospice that morning. He'd even handed over the shoe Joe had found, claiming that they'd found it later that night, out the back, and had thought nothing of it.

Skinner hadn't wanted to hear any of it, especially not the suggestion that Danny had been stabbed with a drag-queen's high heel. As far as he was concerned, Matthew was as good a candidate as any for disgruntled degenerate turned murderer. All he had promised was to see whether the shoe fit.

Russell, in turn, had promised to come down to the station house later that evening to take Matthew home, and if he hadn't been released or charged, he would take the information he knew to the DCI, with a shiny new discrimination complaint attached.

"You didn't punch him, did you?" Ron asked, clocking his swagger.

"No," Russell said, smiling.

"Shame."

"I did point out how bad he was at his job, though."

"Nice one," Ron said, placing a pint on the bar in front of Russell. "On the house, that."

"Thanks Ron. Everything alright?"

"I could do without the hassle, to be honest, but it's fine."

"What did they want this time?"

"He's trying to fit young Matthew up. Wanted me to say I'd seen them arguing. I told him to sling his hook. He said something about Environmental Health. I swear, if he brings that lot in here, I'll swing for him."

"He should back off of Matthew now," Russell said. "I've just given him some real leads to follow. Should keep him busy, but I he'll get very far."

"Really?" Ron asked, suspiciously. "What kind of leads?"

Russell swigged his pint, he needed to talk to Ron about the past and it was going to be a difficult subject to broach. He was just going to have to get on with it.

"Ron," he started tentatively.

"What's up?"

"Look, I know you don't want to talk about the past, but there's something strange going on, and I think you can help me understand it."

Ron sighed heavily.

"I suppose it was all going to come out eventually anyway, wasn't it?" he said, sitting heavily on the stool behind the bar. "What do you want to know?"

"What was it that happened between Jean and Violet that meant they didn't talk for all those years?"

"Why's that important?" Ron frowned.

"It might not be, but can you just humour me?"

Ron shook his head.

"Jean and Violet were thick as thieves, growing up," he said. "They're not actually sisters, not by blood. Violet was adopted, see? And then Jean came along quite naturally. But you couldn't tell either of them that they weren't proper sisters. They always said it made their bond even stronger. They chose to be sisters—even though they weren't tied by blood."

Russell drank while Ron talked.

"Well, they were always together. Jean wouldn't have got anywhere near as famous without Violet pushing her, getting her auditions, hassling agents and producers. Violet was the older one, the confident one. She was such a strong character."

He smiled at the memory of her.

"Anyway, me and Danny met them around the time when Jean's career was just starting to take off. I don't mind telling you that we were both besotted with Jean at first, but she chose Danny. The girls always did."

He absently wiped at a watermark on the bar.

"Well, not long after that, their parents died, quite shortly, one after another. They were both devastated, of course, but they still had each other. Anyway, that's when they found out that the house at Cumberland Terrace had been left to Jean only."

Russell cocked his head. What a cruel thing for their parents to do. They must have known it would create a division between the girls.

"Well, Jean was having none of it. She insisted that it was both of theirs to share. But you could tell something had changed for Vi. They'd put her on the outside, and nothing Jean could do would put things back the way they were before."

"But they lived there together for a while?" Russell asked.

"Oh yeah. I mean, it wasn't like a huge crack appeared overnight. But it was definitely the beginning of the end."

"What do you mean?"

"I think Vi started seeing the differences between them more after that, that's all. I mean, Jean's career was taking off, everyone loved her, she was glamorous, she was beautiful, blonde, curves in all the right places."

"And then there was Violet," Russell said.

"Oi," Ron snapped, defensively. "Vi was a beautiful woman. Stunning, in fact. She just lost her confidence in Jean's shadow. Anyway, by the time they moved in to Cumberland Terrace, Jean and Danny were already engaged. And that was another wedge between the girls."

"She didn't like Danny?"

"I don't think it was that, as much as he was another reminder that she was on the outside. Jean and Danny were a unit, with their own jokes and their own secrets, and Violet was a bit of a third wheel."

"Why didn't she move out? Make her own life?"

"Because she had nowhere to go. Jean's wages supported all three of them, and obviously at the time she could live in the house rent free."

"So what changed?" Russell asked.

"I don't know what triggered it, but they started arguing all the time, usually in public too. Anyway, one night Violet turns up here at the bar, just as we were closing. Says they've had an almighty row, and Jean's thrown her out."

"Why did she come here?"

"Well, because I was mates with Danny, it had always been the four of us. Vi and me had been seeing each other, on and off. Nothing serious like, but still, I was fond of her. She had nowhere else to go. So, I said she could move in here, thinking it would all blow over in a week or so."

"So she moved in?"

"Yep. And then, of course, one thing led to another and we fell into a more, you know, permanent relationship. We didn't hear anything from Jean, and Danny barely spoke to me any more. We all just drifted apart. But the bar was getting up and running, and Vi was a brilliant landlady, and we got on alright, so things just muddled along like that for a while."

Ron stood and picked up Russell's empty glass, rinsing it in the sink. He took a clean one off the shelf and poured Russell another pint without asking. Russell would have to nurse this one, or he'd be too drunk to think straight.

"So you didn't really see Danny or Jean much after that?" Russell prompted.

"Danny would swing by every now and then," Ron said. "But it always upset Vi when he did, so even that tailed off. Jean never came. I always thought she'd got too high and mighty for the likes of us. But maybe she was just busy. Or maybe she still had the hump with her sister. Who knows?"

He had poured himself a drink too, and drained half the glass in one swig. Dutch courage.

"Anyway," he continued, wiping his mouth with the back of his hand. "After about three months living here, Violet announced she was pregnant."

"Wow," Russell hadn't been expecting that.

"Of course, I offered to marry her. She said no. Said we lived in different times now, we didn't need to get trapped in marriage just because of the baby. She said she didn't want to pressure me, or burden me. I can't quite remember which. Anyway, the kiddie's born. A lovely little boy."

Russell could see that the memory was full of mixed emotions.

"I was obviously pleased as punch. He was a little looker. And smart, too. So there I am, thinking I've won the jackpot. I've got this lovely woman, a beautiful baby boy. And we were happy. Well, I thought we were. Looking back, I should have seen how the pregnancy had changed her."

"What happened?"

"Vi had been acting funny pretty much since she found out she was pregnant. Like properly moody. I just thought it was the hormones, you know?"

Russell nodded.

"Anyway, one afternoon, when the nipper's only two or three months old, Jean turns up wanting to speak to Vi. Well, they'd only been upstairs for about five minutes, when all hell breaks loose. They start yelling at each other, chucking stuff, the baby's screaming. Bloody pandemonium. I had customers in and all."

"What were they fighting about?"

"I don't know. Everything and nothing. Jean had heard about the baby, and I think it had upset her. I don't suppose Vi was particularly sympathetic. Jean may have had all the celebrity and the pretty looks and the big house and the handsome husband, but Violet finally had one thing that Jean couldn't have—a baby."

"Jean and Danny couldn't have kids?"

"Jean had miscarried in the early days of their marriage, and then the doctors had found some problem with her downstairs, don't ask me what. And that was that. Danny hadn't been that bothered, either way, but he said it had broken Jean's heart."

"I can see how that would add to the tension," Russell said.

"Yeah, well, it was all obviously too much for Vi, 'cause the next night she sits me down and tells me she's leaving. That she can't do this any more. When I asked her why, she says she's sorry. That's all. It's just better for everyone if she goes. Well, I was gobsmacked, I don't mind telling you."

"Where did she go?"

"No idea," Ron said. "She wouldn't tell me, and I was that hurt by it all, I didn't even try to find her, I'm ashamed to say."

"I found out, a little while after, that Jean had given her a chunk of change if she promised to go away. They'd remortgaged the house to do it, but she gave Vi half the value of the place at the time, which was a lot of money, even in them days. But the deal was that she had to go away and never come back, and she took it."

"Wow," Russell said. "That's cold."

"Yeah, Jean could be like that," Ron said. "Danny was fuming about it, too. Kept coming round looking for Vi, shouting about her being a money grabber, saying she ripped Jean off."

"Charming," Russell said.

"Yeah, that's when we really fell out. He wanted to know where she'd gone. And I wouldn't tell him. Well, she never told me, but I wouldn't have told him anyway. She sent me a couple of cards over the years. I think she felt guilty. But I should have known from the start it was too good to last."

Russell felt really sorry for Ron. He was a big guy, with big features. Not at all your classic good-looking bloke, but he had a good heart and he'd obviously fallen for the wrong woman. Knowing him now, Russell would never have guessed that Ron had such self-confidence issues. *Just goes to show.*

"What about the boy?"

"I let him go too, I had to. I'd have done anything for Vi, but she was determined. And we weren't married, so that was that."

"He was still your son," Russell protested.

"Yeah well," Ron said, shutting the conversation down. "It's all in the past now. Better left there. But that's why I was surprised Jean wanted to see Vi."

"Well, she's the official next of kin, isn't she? Maybe Jean's trying to put things right with her, hand over the estate."

"What's left of it. Danny'd as good as run them into the ground with all his carrying on. You know he'd even asked me for a loan, to help him out. After everything they did to me."

"I had no idea," Russell said.

"No, well. And I wouldn't be surprised if Jean just wants to see her to tell her she'll never get her hands on anything. I wouldn't put it past her to have bequeathed the whole lot to the bloody Zoo or something daft."

With a bit of history now in place, Russell was beginning to see the bigger picture. A few more pieces of the puzzle had slotted into place in his mind.

"I saw Violet this morning," he admitted. "We went to the hospice with her to see Jean."

Ron froze, winded by the news.

"How was she?"

"Nervous," Russell said. "We didn't make it in to see Jean, though. It turns out someone else has been going to see her in the last couple of weeks, pretending to be Violet."

"What?" Ron looked totally baffled.

"Yes," Russell said. "But what's strange is that whoever it is, is going around dressed up as Violet from twenty years ago."

He put the photograph on the bar between them, and Ron picked it up, staring fondly at Violet's face.

"Huh," Ron said, distractedly, handing the photograph back to Russell.

"But she was alright though, Vi? In herself?"

"Yes," Russell said. "She seemed strong."

Ron smiled.

"And the boy? Did you see him?"

Russell froze mid-sip, the thought suddenly hitting him. He put the pint down and jumped to his feet, already heading for the door.

"You know what?" he called back, excitedly. "I think I actually might have."

JOE HAD FOUND RUSSELL waiting impatiently for him outside his office at the end of his shift. He'd been planning to go around to see Violet on his way home from work, but Russell had said he didn't want him going alone. So here they were, standing side by side at her front door, listening for sounds from inside. Joe knocked again.

"I don't think there's anyone home," he said. "Should we wait?"

Joe bent down and pushed the letterbox open, peering into the hallway beyond. The place was neat, but tired and old-fashioned.

A denim jacket hung over the post of the bannister, leading up stairs. Not Violet's. Russell had been right—Violet's son probably did still live here with her.

Russell stepped back off the doorstep and looked up at the windows above. No sign of life. Joe joined him on the pavement, looking down the alleyway at the side of the house.

Joe walked down the narrow alley, standing on tiptoes to peer over the wooden fence that surrounded a neat little courtyard garden. A metal and glass back door led into the kitchen, with a window in front of the sink looking out onto the garden. The window was open a fraction. Not enough to climb through, but enough to hear the faint crackle of the radio coming from within. The Eurythmics, "Who's That Girl?" Just finishing.

Joe turned back to Russell, smiling.

"Joe? What are you doing?"

"Wait here," Joe said. "He might try and do a bunk out the front."

Russell frowned, but Joe was already climbing over the rickety wooden fence, hoping it would hold his weight. He was pretty sure someone was hiding in the house.

Joe dropped down quietly into the back garden and sidled up to the back door. Waiting, he listened. The radio DJ was excitedly introducing "Karma Chameleon".

Above the sound of the radio, Joe heard a kettle clicking off as it reached boiling point, followed by the chink-chink of a teaspoon stirring against a china cup.

Taking a deep breath, Joe stepped out in front of the window, looking in, and came face to face with a young man in a loose white T-shirt, the word Relax printed in big bold letters on the front, a sharp bruise beginning to yellow on his cheekbone. The man yelled and dropped his mug into the sink, splashing tea everywhere.

The two of them froze for a second, staring at each other in surprise, before the young man inside made a break for the front door.

"Wait," Joe called out, but the kid was gone.

He dashed to the back door and, finding it unlocked, ran into the house. Another cry from the young man, and Russell's voice telling him to calm down and stay where he was—he just couldn't help sounding like a policeman.

Joe joined them in the hallway as the young man turned, looking for another way out.

"It's alright," Joe said, holding his hands up reassuringly. "We just want to talk."

"Who are you?" the young man asked, his voice trembling a little.

"We're friends of your mum's," Joe lied.

"Well, she's not here," the kid said.

"Great," Russell said, closing the front door behind him and guiding the kid back up the corridor. "We'll wait. Be good to have a chat with you in the meantime anyway."

The young man frowned, opened his mouth to say something and closed it again, lost for words.

"I'm Joe," Joe said, extending his hand.

"Scott," the kid replied, shaking Joe's hand automatically.

His hand was warm, the skin soft. Greenish brown eyes flicked over Joe's face, taking him in. He was young, not yet twenty, but taller than Joe. Slim shoulders, long legs, delicate features. Russell had been right. Throw on a plain dress and a cheap brown wig, and you'd have your mystery girl.

"We've met before," Joe said. "Well, not met, exactly. But then you already know that."

Scott's shoulders slumped, realising that they knew his secret.

"What do you want?" he asked.

"Why don't we all sit down," Russell said, guiding them to a small living room. "And you can tell us exactly what you've been up to."

THE THREE OF THEM sat awkwardly in the lounge, Joe and Russell on the small sofa, Scott in a tall-backed armchair, legs jittering, fingers fidgeting. The remaining blue shoe on the table in front of them.

Russell looked around, pretending to take in the surroundings. He was actually just letting Scott stew.

As soon as Ron had mentioned the son he'd had with Violet, Russell had known that, somehow, Scott was the mystery woman Joe had seen at the club, and the one that both of them had chased near Jean's hospice. What Russell didn't understand was why?

"So, you've been going to see Jean in the hospice?" Russell asked.

Scott nodded, looking guilty.

"How did you know where she was?"

"Her husband phoned," Scott said. "He left a message for my mum, saying she was ill and he thought she should go and see her."

"But when I spoke to Violet yesterday, she didn't even seem to know that her sister was ill," Joe said.

"I deleted the message," Scott replied. "Mum wouldn't have wanted to see her. She's said that for years. She's always said she doesn't want anything to do with her sister."

"So," Russell said, leaning forward, elbows on knees. "Why did you suddenly take it upon yourself to go and see her? And why dress like that?"

"Because he'd said in the message that she was sorry—they were both sorry—and Mum will never tell me what happened, and I thought if I could see her, I might be able to get Mum to go too, eventually."

"Why would you want her to do something she so clearly doesn't want to do?"

"Because they're rich, and we need the money. And if Jean is dying, then Mum might inherit something, if she played her cards right. She should get what's coming to her, shouldn't she?"

"So you thought you'd dress up to look like your mum did back in the sixties and go and see Jean. What were you hoping to achieve?"

"I didn't mean to dress like that, but I found the clothes in Mum's wardrobe, and it suddenly seemed like a good idea. I just wanted to give her a little scare. I wanted her to think about what she'd done, all them years ago. Kicking my mum out the house, cutting her off like that. I wasn't planning to talk to her dressed like that, just mess with her mind a bit."

"Did your mum ever tell you why they fought?"

"Nah, but now I wish she had. Would have saved a lot of bother," Scott said. "Anyway, Mum always said she'd never see her again unless she apologised, and I thought I could get her to do that much easier if I reminded her of the past."

Joe frowned at him.

"I know it sounds stupid," Scott continued. "But Danny had said in his message that she wasn't all there most of the time. I thought if I could just see her and trigger an old memory, then maybe she'd feel bad about what happened and apologise to Mum."

Russell leaned back again, inviting the story.

"Well, obviously, I looked younger than Mum would be, and nothing like her really, but the old bird is clearly losing it, because she took one look at me and started sobbing her eyes out, telling me how sorry she was for what had happened. How she should have believed me. How I wasn't the only one he'd done it to."

"Done what to?"

"She thought I was my mum, see? She told me how she knew that Danny had raped Mum, and how she knew that the baby was his. She told me she'd always known. But she'd thought Mum had asked for it, always flirting with him like that."

"Danny raped Violet?" Russell asked.

"Not just once, either," Violet said from the doorway.

All three of them stood up at the same time, talking over each other to explain what was going on.

"Mum, I…"

71

Violet held up a hand, silencing them all. She looked tired.

"I suppose I always knew you'd find out one day," she said, coming into the room and sitting on the arm of Scott's chair, resting her hand on his leg. "I should have told you. I know I always said you were never to talk to either of them, but I should have told you why."

"I'm sorry, Mum," Scott said. "I was just trying to help. I thought she owed you, you know?"

"What did you do, Scott?" Russell asked.

"After I'd seen Jean—after everything I found out—I was livid," Scott said, his voice thick with emotion. "I went to see him, to challenge him about what he'd done and he just laughed in my face. He said you'd asked for it. You'd enjoyed it really. And if I was after any money, I was out of luck 'cause they were stony broke, and he was going to have to sell the house just to cover their debts."

"You went to see Dan?" Violet asked.

"I had to. I had to see who he was. My dad."

"He is *not* your father," Violet said vehemently.

"Biologically he was, though, right?"

Violet let her head sag, shaking it sadly.

"Why didn't you tell me you'd been to see either of them?" she asked.

"Because I knew it would upset you, and I didn't want to do that unless I knew you were going to get what was owed to you," Scott said.

He took her hand in his, stroking her fingers with his own.

"So I went to see Jean again," Scott said. "I wasn't planning to, but when I found out that Dan was going to sell the house, I just wanted to make sure that if Jean died, you would get what was yours."

"You had no right," Violet said.

"I did it for you, Mum. They owe you."

Russell could see that Violet was suffering, but he didn't want to stop Scott's account of what had happened.

"So you went to see Jean," he prompted, "dressed as Violet again?"

"Yeah," Scott shook his head, embarrassed to admit it. "I told her I forgave her. I told I was happy in my life. That it was all okay. We talked for ages. She told me everything about her and Danny, all the girls she'd found out about, all the lies, the gambling."

"Oh Jeany," Violet said.

"I think it did her good, Mum," Scott said. "To get it all out. She said it was just her and I—well you—now. She said she was going to change her will, to make sure you got the house. Danny could have the scraps, she said."

"She said that?" Violet asked.

Scott nodded.

"But she didn't know he'd already tried to put the place on the market. And she didn't know he'd spent all their money. I was so angry with him. And with her. She knew that you weren't lying, Mum. She knew all along that he'd raped you, and she still chose him over you for all those years."

Violet got up suddenly, angrily wiping the tears from her eyes.

"Yeah, well, there you go," she said, turning away from them all and heading into the kitchen. "You can tell her I don't want that bloody house. I don't want her charity, and I don't want her apologies neither."

"I knew you'd say that," Scott said. "But you don't have any choice now. You're all she has left."

Violet stopped in the doorway and turned slowly.

"What did you do, Scott?" she asked.

Scott suddenly broke down.

"I'm sorry, Mum," he said, barely holding himself together. "I got it into my head that it was Danny who needed to apologise. To you, to Jean, to all of us."

He stopped, head bent, shoulders shaking as the tears began to flow.

"So you killed him?" Russell asked.

Scott nodded, sniffing loudly. He couldn't look at any of them.

"I didn't mean to kill him. I just wanted to scare him. I wanted to remind him of what he'd done. So I dressed like Mum again and confronted him with it. I thought I'd tackle him when he wasn't expecting it and he couldn't run away."

"At the club, between performances?"

"I thought I'd fit in, you know, among all the trannies."

"Careful…" Russell warned.

"Sorry," Scott said.

"You stabbed him, Scott," Joe said, incredulously. "That's pretty convincing for someone who wasn't intending to kill."

"I didn't stab him. Honest. He fell," Scott protested. He looked up at Joe, then at Russell, his bloodshot eyes beseeching them to understand.

"I started talking to him, but he just freaked out. He was so drunk. Slurring his words, couldn't even stand straight."

It was Joe's turn to frown.

"But I talked to him just minutes before. He seemed fine."

"Well, when I got to him, he was falling all over the place. I tried to talk to him, to get him to agree that he'd been in the wrong, but he went for me. Tried to punch me, but he was too drunk. He managed to hit me with the end of his cane." Scott touched the bruise on his cheek.

"I pushed him back and he stood there a moment, swaying, and then his eyes rolled back in his head, like he was struggling to breath, and I stepped away from him 'cause I thought he was going to puke or something, and he just fell forwards. Flat. Passed out cold. Didn't even put his hands out to break his fall."

"But when we found him," Russell said, confused. "And when the police examined him, he'd been stabbed in the chest."

"I didn't stab him. I swear," Scott said. "In the scuffle, my shoe had come off. When I turned him over, I realised he'd landed square on the heel of it. It had gone straight in between his ribs."

He mimed the action using the other shoe from the table.

"Well, I panicked. I mean, who would ever believe that? Especially given who he was. Who I am. So I grabbed the shoe and ran. I got out the fire exit, and I dropped it, but I was panicking too much to stop. I jumped in a cab and didn't look back."

Russell and Joe looked at each other, frowning. Something wasn't right here.

"You're sure he was drunk?" Joe asked.

"Yeah, I swear, I didn't mean to hurt him. He just fell."

Joe stood up quickly and Russell could see that the last penny had dropped. Joe looked at Russell, eyes wide with excitement.

"He was fine," he said. "I talked to him minutes before Scott did. He was fine. But he'd just got a new drink delivered. He said Ron always knew what he liked."

Russell looked at Joe, realising what he meant, and then at Scott.

"How did you find Danny?" Russell asked. "The first time you went to see him?"

"I followed him," Scott said. "He went straight to that pub, where the cabaret was. I saw him talking to you."

He looked at Joe as though he was somehow implicated.

"We were scheduling the gig," Joe said.

"Whatever," Scott said. "Anyway, I tackled him outside, as he was leaving. Like I say, he tried to give me the brush off, but I'd seen him having a bit of a barney with the barman, so I figured he'd be able to give me the skinny."

"Oh, Scott," Violet said, sitting down again. "You didn't?"

"What?" Scott asked. "I asked him about Danny. I told him I was his son, wanting a reconciliation. He clammed right up. Wouldn't say a word."

Violet looked at Russell, panic in her eyes.

"Ron's still there?" she asked. "At the Red Lion?"

"I'm afraid so," Joe said.

"And you told him?" she turned on Scott.

"What? Who? The barman? Who is he?"

"*He's* your father," Violet shouted.

"What? But Danny was the one who..."

"I know what Danny did," Violet spat. "I know what he kept doing, but you're not his. I mean, look at you, you're the spit of Ron. There's no question that Ron is your father. I just couldn't be there any more. Danny kept coming round, he wouldn't leave me alone. And I told Jean what he'd been doing, but she wouldn't believe me. She said I must have seduced him. She took his side. And she said she'd tell Ron that, unless I left. So I had to go. They would have destroyed Ron's life otherwise."

"Oh Jesus," Joe said. He shot out of his seat, as did Russell.

"Right you two," Russell said to Scott and Violet. "You're coming with us."

Both looked panicked.

"Where are we going?"

"Just get your things, and let's get this sorted out. Everything's going to be fine. I promise."

Scott and Violet both nodded. When Russell said something was going to be okay, people tended to believe him.

"Come on," Russell said turning to Joe.

6.

RUSSELL LED THEM ALL into the pub via the main doors, having sent Joe in first to secure any escape to the back. Ron looked up from the bar as he heard the bolt slide into place, locking the door from inside.

"What the..."

He stopped dead, realising who was in front of him.

"Vi?" he asked, his face breaking into a smile despite himself. "That you, girl?"

It almost broke Russell's heart. Ron had really loved her. He didn't really blame him for what he'd done. Danny had ruined his life, and when he'd finally found out what he thought was the truth, he wouldn't have been able to help himself—it was only natural he would have lashed out.

"Oh, Ronnie," she said, hurrying across the bar to meet him.

Russell let them have a moment together. Ron wouldn't be going anywhere, and he wasn't looking forward to having to level the charges at his old friend anyway.

Ron looked over Violet's shoulder at Russell.

"You figured it out then?" he asked, already knowing the answer. "I had a horrible feeling you would, in the end."

"What did you do, Ron?" Violet asked, holding his face in her hands.

"I did it for you, Vi," he said. "And for the boy. And for me, too, I guess. He ruined everything, for all of us."

She buried her face in his shoulder. Russell gave Scott a nod, and the young man stepped forward and took his mother's elbow, guiding her away from Ron.

"I'm sorry," she said to Ron as she broke their embrace.

He just smiled sadly.

"None of this was your fault," he said. And he was right.

Russell guided Ron towards to bar, poured them both a drink and sat down. It was time to have it out, properly.

"What happened, Ron?" he asked. "Did you spike his drink?"

"Yeah," Ron said, wearily. "I just wanted him to make a fool of himself for once. And I wanted the excuse to get him on my own. I'd thought if he'd passed out on stage, I'd be able to take him upstairs, wait until it wore off, and then get him to admit the truth."

"What truth?"

"The kid told me everything," Ron said, sadly. "How Danny had raped Vi. How Danny was actually his father. How Jean had found out and turned against Vi, claiming she'd tried to steal Danny from her. It all makes sense now, doesn't it?"

"Sure. Apart from Danny isn't Scott's father," Russell said. "I mean, look at him. Sure, he's a lanky streak of piss, but he's the image of you Ron, couldn't you see that?"

Ron looked across at Scott holding his mother's hand, both of them whispering earnestly to one another. His face went from anger, to sadness, to confusion. He looked back at Russell, the frown etched deep on his brow.

"What're you talking about?"

"Danny *did* rape her, Violet told me that. But the boy's not his, Ron. Scott is your son, always has been."

"You're kidding."

"No."

Ron slumped, the weight of the truth just too much for him.

"Why didn't she say?"

"Because Jean had promised to ruin your business and destroy both of your lives unless she moved away. She didn't want her around where Danny could find her, and Violet couldn't face seeing him again anyway."

"Why didn't she tell me?"

"You'll have to ask her, Ron, but I would imagine she was scared. Scared of what you'd do, scared of what Danny would do. What good would telling you have done? She had to go, and she knew you couldn't go with her. Not with the pub taking off like it was."

Ron sat quietly, watching the family he could have had.

"I would have given it all up for her," he said, sadly.

He took a long swig of his drink, wiped his mouth.

"I think she knew that. And she would never have asked that of you."

"What's going to happen now?" he asked, suddenly small.

"I have no idea, Ron," Russell admitted. "You say you spiked his drink?"

"Yeah, but I just meant for him to pass out, like he was drunk, so I could get him upstairs and tackle him for what he did. I didn't mean to kill him."

"You didn't kill him."

"No, no, I know. But if I hadn't have spiked him, he'd probably have been able to fend off his attacker. He was a strong guy. Oh God, I'm going down for this, ain't I?"

"You didn't kill him, Ron. There was no attacker. He just fell. It was an accident."

Ron look incredulous.

"Bollocks, he was stabbed."

Russell shook his head.

"No. He fell. Scott had gone backstage to tackle him about selling the house. You'd already spiked his drink. He was reeling all over the place. They got in a bit of a scuffle, Scott stepped out of the way, lost a shoe. Danny fell, impaled himself on the spike of the heel. Goodnight Vienna."

"That's ridiculous," Ron said.

"Neither of you killed him," Russell said, honestly.

"And yet both of us did."

"It was misadventure at best. Besides, who's going to miss him enough to push for charges?"

"What are you saying?"

"Don't you think everyone's suffered enough, thanks to Danny? Jean's not much longer for this world, and when she's gone, it's all over."

"You're saying you're just going to let this go?"

"You forget, Ron," Russell said. "I'm not a copper any more. It's got nothing to do with me, has it?"

"Yeah, but that Detective Skinner's already got his eye on me."

"Well, I wouldn't worry about that too much," Russell said. "His eye's not that good. Besides, if I have my way, he won't be in the job for much longer. How does your conscience feel?"

"Conflicted. Better now the truth is out. And at least I know it wasn't me that actually killed him."

"And it wasn't Scott either. It was just bad luck, like Jean said all along. So maybe he finally got what was coming to him."

Ron sat back, looking at Russell with a strange expression on his face. "You've changed."

Russell smiled. He had. Hopefully for the better.

RUSSELL MET YOUNG MATTHEW outside the police station. He'd thought he'd be happy enough to come down to his old workplace, but once they'd got here, he'd felt more reluctant to go inside. Joe had done the deed alone, bless him.

As it turned out, Skinner had just released Matthew anyway. The autopsy had shown that Danny had a cocktail of drink and drugs in his system, and though they hadn't been able to ascertain how he had been stabbed, they were calling the death an accident.

There were more than enough witnesses who had all confirmed that Matthew hadn't been alone with Danny long enough to stab him, dispose of the weapon and get back on scene before raising the alarm. Besides, Detective Skinner had found himself being stonewalled by the witnesses.

Everybody they had interviewed gave a different account of that night, a different description of the girl that had been seen running away, and a different set of timings for the events of the evening.

Nothing had made sense, and none of it would stand up in court. The only thing all witnesses were united on was that Matthew hadn't been alone with Danny for long enough to do the deed.

"Thanks for coming to get me," Matthew said as he bounced out of the station with Joe beside him. "What a shit hole. I thought they were never going to let me go."

"What happened to your face?" Russell asked, noticing a livid bruise across Matthew's cheekbone.

"Apparently, I was resisting arrest."

"Were you?"

"Of course not, they just wanted to show me how tough and manly they all are."

"Who hit you? Was it Skinner?" Russell was in the mood to bring the detective down if so.

"No, some nonce in a uniform. Don't worry about it Russ, it's not the first time, and I doubt it'll be the last. Besides, it'll earn me a free pint down at the Lion." He laughed, not seeing the injustice of it all.

"Come on then," Joe said. "First round's on me."

They turned their backs on the station and set off.

"Mr Dixon?" Skinner's unmistakable, nasal voice called across the street.

"Wait here," Russell said under his breath to Joe.

Turning around, he crossed the road to where Skinner was standing, hands on hips.

"Can I help, Detective?" He would never tire of making Skinner's job title sound like a piss-take.

"I know you know what really happened to Dan Carter," Skinner hissed. "And if I find one scrap of evidence that you've been tampering with my witnesses, I'll..."

"You'll what?" Russell snapped. "Have my job? Too late, pal."

"I'll arrest you for obstruction of justice," Skinner said, triumphantly.

"Save your breath, darling," Russell said. "If I were you, I'd chalk Dan Carter's death up to an accident. He was drunk, he was on something. He was always very accident prone, maybe he fell over, landed straight on that heel, you know? Stranger things have happened."

Skinner came right up close to him.

"I'm going to solve this case," he said. "And when I do, I'm taking you down too."

"Not if I take you down first," Russell said, turning his back on Skinner and crossing the road to join up with Joe and Matthew.

"I've got my eye on you," Skinner shouted.

"I'm flattered," Russell shouted back. "But you're not my type."

The look on Skinner's face made them all laugh.

"You shouldn't wind him up," Joe warned.

Russell grinned.

"I've got to have some fun in life," he said. "Come on, let's get that pint."

JEAN'S FUNERAL HAD GONE off without much drama. It was a bright, sunny morning, and just a handful of visitors had gathered at the graveside. Russell and Joe stood on one side, Violet and Scott on the other, with Ron just behind them. No tears, no wailing.

Violet stepped forward when the vicar ended his sermon and dropped a red rose into the grave. The others followed suit, a final encore for the once-celebrated jazz singer.

Ron put his arm around Violet's shoulder, and she in turn put one around Scott's waist—a family reunited. Russell and Joe smiled at each other.

"You alright?" Joe asked.

"I think so," he said. He knew what Joe was asking. *Are you really okay with Ron and Scott both getting away with Danny's death?* They had discussed it only once since finding out the truth, and whichever way they had looked at it, they couldn't see the value in either of them serving time for what had happened.

Neither of them had intended to kill Danny, though both had set out to frighten him. It was just dumb luck that they had both put their plans into action on the same night. Like father, like son.

Violet stopped in front of them, not letting go of either of her men.

"They'll put Danny beside her," Violet said. "She'll like that."

"So they've released the body then?"

"Yeah," Ron said. "Apparently they'll keep trying to solve the case."

"Yeah, right. Don't hold your breath," Russell said, patting Ron on the shoulder. "Drinks on you then?"

Violet linked her arm through Ron's.

"Technically, they're on me now," she said, smiling.

It was the first time that Russell had seen her looking genuinely happy. Ron closed his hand over hers.

"I want to thank you," she said. "For not giving up when I told you to. And for getting to the truth."

"It's in my nature, I'm afraid," Russell said. "I don't know anything else."

"Well, thanks," she said. "I owe you."

"Just look after each other," Russell said.

"Don't worry, we will," Violet said, squeezing Ron's arm.

"See you back at the pub, then," Ron said, leaning in. "And thanks, for everything."

Scott smiled shyly and thanked him too. Joe turned to face Russell, framing his face with upturned hands.

"My hero," he sighed.

"Piss off," Russell laughed.

The smile dropped from his face as he saw Skinner standing at the edge of the churchyard, watching them all. He'd hoped his old foe would have got bored with this case by now. Obviously, he still had an axe to grind with Russell. Joe followed his gaze.

"He's just trying to wind you up," Joe said. "Don't let him get to you."

He was right, of course. Russell set his shoulders as the two of them walked past Skinner.

"Detective," he nodded, sailing on past without a backward glance. Skinner may be coming for him, but he wasn't getting him today.

CARELESS WHISPER

SOHO NOIR #3

CARELESS WHIPSER

1.

SOHO, LONDON. 1986.

JOE STONE strode along Old Compton Street, the sun on his face, a skip in his step, and "Manic Monday" blasting out through the new Sony Walkman he'd bought himself with his last pay packet. A thoroughly appropriate soundtrack to the Monday morning he was having so far.

He was running late, juggling the three takeaway cups of coffee he'd just had to queue far too long for, feeling the minutes tick by, adding to his woes. He hated being late, but he'd woken this morning knowing that it would be his last with his boyfriend Luc, who was heading back to Paris at lunchtime.

Luc had finally run out of money and excuses to stay in London, and while Joe was sad to see him go, even he had to admit that their relationship hadn't developed the way either of them had hoped. Luc was gorgeous—a talented chef and an excellent lover, with an accent that still made Joe's stomach do flips, but he also wanted a lot more commitment than Joe was ready to give at this stage in his life.

Luc had been his first boyfriend, but this was Joe's first year as a proud, out, gay man in London. And while Joe wanted to be out there enjoying life, Luc was more of a homebody.

Joe would never have described himself—a year ago when he'd arrived in Soho—as a pop-loving club-bunny, and he wasn't sure he'd even go as far as to use the phrase now, but that was the way Luc had described him a couple of weeks ago, when they'd had yet another argument about staying in or going out. Ironic, given that they'd met in a club in the first place.

Joe's flatmate, Russell, thought he was mad to let Luc go, but Joe didn't like feeling as penned in as he had recently. Luc was jealous of everyone, reluctant to socialise, and unwilling to let Joe go out alone.

So, while Joe was sad to say goodbye, they had both agreed that a bit of space would be a good thing. They could always pick it up again in a few months, if they were missing each other too much.

So, after a slightly longer goodbye than he'd intended, Joe tenderly said "au revoir" to Luc and dashed to work, hoping that a peace offering from his boss's favourite coffee shop would appease him.

Joe had been working as a runner in a small television production company in the heart of Soho for almost a year now, and his boss, Paul James Davis—PJ, as he preferred to be known—had been promising him a step up the career ladder for most of that time. He'd said he was just waiting for the next big programme to get commissioned.

True to his word, when that moment had finally come, he'd called Joe into his office and told him that he was going to be working on the show.

Behind the Headlines was a new entertainment programme for Channel 4—one PJ had been pitching for several months before finally getting the green light. Featuring a different celebrity each week for a warts-and-all exposé, PJ was determined that this show would be the making of his company, and have good old Mary Whitehouse frothing at the mouth.

The first show in the line-up—the one Joe was currently assisting on—was following the multi-platinum selling pop group, Loose Lips, during the recording of what was looking increasingly likely to be their last studio album.

Adam Cave, the lead singer and arguably the main talent of the group, and twin brothers, Liam and Luke Millard, had been stuck in the studio for a couple of weeks now, and the lads could barely manage to be in a room together without all hell breaking loose.

All of which was fine for the purposes of PJ's behind-the-scenes documentary, but had made coming in to work something of a nightmare for Joe, who was no fan of conflict at the best of times.

Joe's principal role on set was to look after Adam Cave, which he'd been quite excited about until he'd met the guy and realised quite how off the rails he'd been driven by his life in the spotlight.

The last month had seen him splashed over the front pages of most of the tabloids several times for a series of drink- and drug-fuelled all-night benders, a very public meltdown in a shopping mall and, as of two days ago, the beginnings of a vicious legal battle with the record label the group were still attached to.

The other two band members, Liam and Luke, were doing their best to remain cleaner than clean, doing all the PR, signing autographs for their adoring fans, and smiling for the cameras. But behind the scenes they were all constantly at each other's throats, and footage for the documentary was increasingly becoming little more than a series of rows and silences, slammed doors and swear words.

Joe's boss, PJ, and Adam Cave had been friends for a couple of years—PJ had shot the band's first music video back in 1982—and he had pulled out all the stops to convince Loose Lips to come on board as the first celebrities in the line-up for the new series. PJ had confided in Joe that it had been the clincher for Channel 4 in securing the funding for the series. The world could sense a meltdown in the offing, and the group, but more specifically, Adam Cave, was a hot ticket right now— albeit for the wrong reasons.

Adam Cave was a narcissist, a diva, and a bit of a brat, but it hadn't taken Joe long to realise that those particular attributes were simply masking a much deeper anxiety gnawing away at the superstar.

Adam was a closeted gay man who had found himself trapped inside a teenage girl's wet dream. And not just one teenage girl either, given the crowd of mini-Madonnas that Joe was currently forcing his way through, trying not to spill his precious coffees all over their identikit white denim jackets and fluorescent T-shirts.

Joe had overheard enough conversations between Adam and his manager, Jack Eddy, to understand that the way Adam had been going off the rails lately was endangering his future career, with or without the band. Adam was sick of hiding, though, and Jack seemed to be running out of ways to persuade him to stay in the closet.

"Just finish the album," had become a bit of a mantra between the two of them.

The band's entire fan base thrived on the dream of one day being a girlfriend to one of the three of them and, judging by this crowd gathered outside, there wasn't a single young man in the throng harbouring the same dream for a life with Adam.

The band had been styled by their label and management to appeal to girls, and the difficulties Adam was having with his band mates had come in no small part from his desire to shed that persona and be himself.

The sad thing was that everyone around him who knew—Joe's boss, PJ, included—kept telling Adam to keep his sexuality a closely bound secret, if he wanted to maintain the level of stardom he had now. One more album, one more tour.

While Joe could see that the narcissist in Adam would love to hold on to his celebrity, the lonely young man in him just wanted to live his own life, out of the spotlight, before it was too late.

Joe finally cleared the squealing, shrieking crowd and pushed through the doors of the studio, nodding a flustered hello to the cute Australian guy on security.

After two weeks of daily visits, Joe no longer needed to flash his ID to get through the studio doors beyond reception. In fact, the security guard, Dustin, had even started holding the door open for him. Dustin couldn't have been much straighter, but he had a dazzling smile and arms like Rocky.

"Hey mate. How're you going?" Dustin asked in that broad Australian accent, leaping up from behind his desk, and heading towards the doors.

"Late," Joe said quickly. Dustin was always keen for a bit of a chat, and Joe usually obliged. The poor guy was probably bored to death on the front desk. No time today though. Despite Dustin's surf-bum good looks and tousled blond hair, Joe was in too much of a rush this morning to linger.

"You're not wrong there," Dustin agreed, holding the door open wide to let Joe through. "You've missed all sorts of dramas already."

"Why, what's been going on."

"Screaming and hollering," Dustin said. "You'll see for yourself."

Joe could feel his gaze lingering on those biceps just a little too long as he passed. He forced his eyes up to meet Dustin's.

"Thanks," Joe said.

Dustin beamed. *Such white teeth.*

The front door opened again and the sound of the crowd outside filled the entrance once more. The journalist from *Smash Hits* magazine who had been pestering the band for the past week, trying to get any kind of exclusive on the new album, burst through the door looking flustered but relieved to have made it through the crowd of half-crazed teenagers unscathed.

Joe paused in the doorway, Dustin stepped in front of him, blocking the journalist's passage.

"Can I help you, mate?" Dustin drawled.

"Hugh Brice," he said. "*Smash Hits* magazine."

He held out an ID card hanging on a lanyard around his neck, displaying his credentials for all to see. A tall, lanky guy with curly ginger hair, thinning slightly around the widow's peak, Hugh was no match for Dustin's bulk. He peered over the security guy's head at Joe, hoping for a pass in.

PJ had already warned everyone on set to keep Hugh Brice at arm's length. The journalist had a notion that Loose Lips's days were numbered, and he was desperate for the scoop. So far, the group's manager, Jack Eddy, had managed to keep Hugh at bay, knowing that any needling of the group members would probably make Hugh's notion a reality. Joe had to admire the journalist's tenacity, though. He'd been here every day so far and hadn't got more than a brief interview with the Millard twins.

"Why don't you get him signed in, Dustin," Joe said, still hovering in the doorway through to the studio. "Wait here, Mr Brice. I'll see if I can get someone to come out and help you."

Hugh Brice looked at him as though he were a stain on the rug.

"Go get Jack," he sneered. "Tell him I've got a deadline to meet and I am happy to go with what I've got and make up the rest, if he can't be bothered to line up any proper interviews. But tell him he won't like what comes out, though."

"I'll pass it on," Joe said, turning back to Dustin, with a raised eyebrow. That had sounded like a threat.

"Whatever you do, don't let him through unless either Jack or PJ specifically say it's okay," Joe whispered.

Dustin gave him a conspiratorial wink.

"Gotcha," he said.

Joe headed off down the corridor and hit the double doors at the far end with his hip, stepping through as they swung open. Unfortunately, someone else was coming the other way at speed, and Joe took the hit as they collided, coffee spilling all over him and the grey carpet tiles at his feet.

"Jesus," Joe said, looking at the mess of beige liquid staining his clothes and dripping onto his shoes. He looked up again into the livid face of his boss, PJ—his face almost as red as the shirt he was wearing.

"Where the hell have you been?" PJ demanded. His boss sounded more annoyed than Joe had ever heard him. Surely Joe's lateness couldn't be upsetting him that much?

"I stopped to get you a coffee," Joe said, feeling even guiltier now for his lateness.

"Where from, bloody Peru?" PJ snapped. "You should have been here half an hour ago."

"No, um..." Joe could already feel the warm liquid cooling as it soaked into his jeans.

"Doesn't matter," PJ tutted.

PJ looked Joe up and down, taking in the dripping coffee, the stained clothes, and Joe's flushed cheeks.

"Have you got something to change into?" he asked.

"No," Joe replied, glumly.

"There's a rack of stuff in the dressing room. You might find something in there that fits," PJ said, his anger already dissipating. Joe wondered what had happened this morning to make his boss this uncharacteristically stressed.

"And see if you can get Adam to calm down, while you're in there," he said. "He's in a right mood this morning. Jack Eddy is nowhere to be found, Adam's refusing to leave the dressing room, and the twins are waiting in the studio. We're already behind schedule, and the day's barely started."

"The *Smash Hits* guy is back," Joe said, not wishing to load more grief on his boss's shoulders, but keen to make sure he wasn't somehow held responsible for allowing the guy into the building. "I've told Dustin to keep him outside unless you or Jack says different."

"Christ, that's all I need."

PJ looked desperate. He had been trying to keep Hugh Brice at arm's length all week. If there was going to be an exclusive story about the break-up of Loose Lips, PJ was determined it would be in his film and not in bloody *Smash Hits*.

"He said to tell Jack he had enough of a story to run with, anyway. Said Jack wouldn't be happy with what came out."

"Oh Jesus," PJ said. "Do you think he's got his hands on a kiss-and-tell story on Adam? That will split the band for good. The only thing that's holding them together is the fans, and if they find out their sex symbol is a poof, they'll turn on them all."

After the spate of negative press Adam had been the subject of recently, painting him as a drink- and drug-addled pop star who was unravelling at the seams, it wouldn't take much to join the dots. Even without an interview, there was more than enough material in the public domain for Hugh Brice to create a juicy article about the real reasons behind the split of the most famous pop group of the decade. And, however it was framed, Adam Cave wouldn't come out of it well at all. Which was a shame, because Joe actually quite liked the guy.

In the rare glimpses he'd had of the real Adam, he saw a funny, intelligent young man, desperate to be himself, but being held in the closet by loyalty, money and fear. And not just his own fear, everyone around him was desperate to keep this pop bubble from bursting for as long as they could.

"Right," PJ said, suddenly moving with some urgency. "You go and get changed. And get Adam out of that dressing room and into the studio. He needs to at least look like he's working, or the twins will throw their toys out the pram again."

"How am I supposed to do that, if he's in one of his moods?"

"I don't care. Adam likes you. Use your charms, or… whatever else comes to mind."

Joe's only real job on set had been to make sure that Adam Cave had everything he wanted and that he felt safe and reassured. He had built a bit of a rapport with the pop star, but he wouldn't go so far as to say that Adam liked him. They had chatted a lot, and both had shared stories of their past, but he doubted if Adam even knew his last name. Still, he could tell his boss was panicking. He flashed PJ what he hoped was a reassuring smile.

"I'll do my best," Joe said.

"And find Jack. Christ knows where he's got to, but he needs to be here. I'm going to keep Hugh Brice sweet. What a shit storm."

Joe understood the pressure his boss was under, wanting to deliver the best programme he could about one of the biggest pop groups of the time, just as they were all falling apart. If Joe could help, he would. PJ had been good to him.

Sure, he was just a runner, but at least he was on set on an actual production—out of the office. So while he was still making tea and fetching coffee and sandwiches, he was also rubbing shoulders with the talent, and that was much more exciting than the endless photocopying and tape deliveries he had been doing until now. PJ had kept his word to give Joe a step up, and Joe was grateful, even if he had a creeping feeling that one day he would be asked to return the favour.

PJ was no soft touch—he'd certainly fired enough people in his time— but he had taken Joe on with no television experience and had shown him the ropes. At times he'd been a little too attentive with the younger, better-looking boys in his employ. Fortunately, he'd never tried anything too inappropriate with Joe, yet. Joe was fairly confident he could fend him off though.

As PJ hurried away to deal with Hugh Brice, Joe took a deep breath and turned back to the corridor.

RUSSELL DIXON STOOD on the pavement outside the health centre, not able to put off going in anymore. Having ended his third tour of the same block with some stern words to himself, he just needed to pull himself together and get on with it. It was just a test, after all. *Just a little prick.* He couldn't even make himself smile with that one.

He was already regretting not being brave enough to tell his flatmate, Joe, what he was doing today. Having thought he'd be fine alone, the reality of being here was all too much. When it had come to telling Joe, though, Russell had swallowed his words, hidden his fear behind a smile and a sip of coffee, and said nothing. It hadn't been the right time to tell Joe he was going for an HIV test. *When would it ever be the right time?*

Russell knew that half the reason he didn't want to tell Joe was because he hadn't wanted his friend to feel any pressure to be there to support him. And Joe would feel that pressure—it was how he was wired. He would definitely want to hold Russell's hand through this, even metaphorically. He would hate the idea of Russell being here alone and scared.

The other obstacle to telling Joe had been that his young flatmate was saying goodbye to his beautiful French boyfriend that morning—an act that Russell couldn't help but feel was a huge mistake. Joe had explained their decision, and it made a kind of sense, but Russell couldn't help feeling that Joe would regret it in years to come. Handsome men who were good in the bedroom *and* in the kitchen, *and* who wanted a monogamous relationship were as rare as hen's teeth.

Russell would have loved nothing more than a solid relationship with someone who wanted to stay in of an evening and hang out as a couple. He'd said that he understood why Joe didn't want it at this stage, but he actually didn't. In any case, it hadn't been the time to break the news of his test to Joe. Besides, if the result came back negative, he wouldn't have to tell anyone, would he? It could stay as his secret until there was something to tell.

Fiddling with the envelope in his hands, he checked the time again. He had three minutes to get inside and register his name at the desk. This wasn't his first time at the clinic—he'd been once before, when the virus first became prevalent.

At that time, he'd gone with an old friend, a one-time lover in fact—Thomas Campbell, lecturer in fashion at St Martin's college, lover of opera and theatre, aficionado of fine dining and fine wine. And one of the earliest victims of AIDS in the UK. His legacy had funded a charitable organisation in Soho which supported people with AIDS through a hospice now called the Campbell Centre. Joe often volunteered there, but Russell found it too difficult. He would go along, from time to time, knowing that he should offer more support, but his mind went into overdrive whenever he was there, and all he could do was imagine himself ending up in the same place.

On that previous occasion, Thomas's test had been Positive, and Russell's—done at Thomas's insistence—had come out Negative. How many times would he be as lucky? And it *was* all down to luck in the end, no matter how careful you were.

Russell had been safe. He was sure of it. But a recent casual fling had called him up to say he was Positive, and now Russell was panicking. Had he been safe enough? He was about to find out. Well, he was about to start the process. He wouldn't get the results for a tortuous few days.

11

When he and Thomas had been tested, it had been a two-week wait for results, and though the system had improved dramatically, they warned that it could still take up to a week. Russell already knew it would feel like a year.

He pushed the door open, immediately hit by the memories of his last visit here—the nerves, the fluttering panic, the desire to turn and run. Last time, at exactly this moment, Thomas had taken Russell's hand, defying any judgement that may come their way, and given him a firm, reassuring nod. *Come on.*

Channelling that memory, Russell let the door close behind him and approached the front desk. He gave his name, and took a form attached to a clipboard with a pen tucked into the clip.

"Take a seat, love," the woman behind the desk said. Kind eyes, practised smile. "You can fill that in while you wait. Won't be long."

Russell chose a seat as far from the desk and the main thoroughfare as he could find, but they were all fairly central. He felt exposed. Which was ridiculous, because everyone was here for the same thing and he also had nothing to hide anymore. He was no longer a policeman hiding his sexuality. Old habits die hard.

A man, somewhere in his early thirties, stepped out of the consultation room, his face barely able to contain the anguish and terror of the news he'd just received. He stood stock still outside the door for a moment, before taking a deep breath and beginning to walk away. He made it as far as the row of chairs against the wall before he collapsed, knees buckling.

He guided himself into the ugly plastic chair—expensive coat twisted around his body, his bright designer shirt looking incongruously cheerful. All the colour had drained from his face, and his shoulders shook. Russell felt moved to comfort him.

He crossed the waiting room and sat in the chair beside the young guy, who looked up at him with eyes full of confusion and anguish.

"You okay?"

He realised as soon as he'd asked it how stupid a question it was. It was clear that this young man had just been given the news that he was Positive, and he would feel that hanging over him like a death sentence. He was the furthest from "okay" that it was possible to be.

Russell reached out and took his hand, feeling there was at least some comfort to be had from company. The man resisted at first, and then slumped against him, letting out a short sob. Russell squeezed his hand. The man sighed—a deep, shuddering breath. This was too much for anyone to take in.

"It doesn't have to be a death sentence," Russell said, and the guy nodded through his tears.

The consultant poked her head out of the recently vacated room and looked up at the waiting area.

"Russell Dixon?"

The man lifted his head from Russell's shoulder and looked enquiringly at him. Russell nodded. This time, the man squeezed *his* hand instead.

"Good luck," he said, sadness catching his words in his throat.

Russell stood up. *Here goes nothing.*

THROWING THE EMPTY, crushed coffee cups into a bin as he passed, Joe made his way to the dressing room where Adam Cave had holed himself up.

This wouldn't be the first tantrum Joe had talked the pop star out of in the past two weeks. Even the band's long-suffering manager, Jack, had come in for a serious dressing down a couple of times, and he wasn't a guy to be trifled with.

Despite only being in his early thirties, Jack Eddy was one of the industry's real characters. He knew everyone, and most of them loved him. He could get you into any club or restaurant on a VIP list in the time it took you to get down there.

Joe was quite dumbstruck by his charisma most of the time. Which was probably why Jack had never really paid much attention to the stammering, gibbering runner in the corner.

Sure, Jack Eddy was overdramatic, overzealous, and sometimes overbearing, but he worked hard for the group, and doted on them all. Adam perhaps a little more than the twins, but then, Adam had the most talent and was the most damaged.

PJ had suggested—slightly bitterly, Joe thought—that their relationship went beyond just pop star and manager. Joe couldn't see it, though. Sure, they bickered like a married couple, but then Jack bickered with all three of the group members. If there was anything there, it was fairly one-sided.

Joe had instantly recognised the way Adam looked at Jack. It was the way Joe had looked at his old school friend, Chris, for so many years—hoping that one day he would notice him, *that way*. If there was any love there, it was unrequited.

"What the hell happened to you?" a voice asked behind him.

Jessica, one of the other runners, had come out of the small studio kitchen carrying two tall jugs of water. She was followed by her counterpart, Sarah, balancing a tray of glasses on one hand over her shoulder, waitress style.

Jessica and Sarah—the two of them could be twins themselves, with their almost identical outfits, crimped hair, and fluorescent headbands. *Desperately Seeking Something.* They could also fit in perfectly with the baying crowd of teenage girls outside, who were still managing to let out a piercing collective squeal every time the doors opened.

Jessica and Sarah were nice enough girls though, and they weren't shy of either working or partying hard. They'd taken a shine to Joe, and always invited him along if they were going out, which they usually were. They'd been given the slightly more enviable job of looking after the Millard twins while the filming was going on and seemed to be having an easy enough time of their task.

"Coffee incident," Joe shrugged.

"Has PJ found you yet? He's spitting feathers," Sarah said.

Joe pointed to his coffee-stained clothes.

"He more than found me."

"Oh, and your diva is throwing another strop," Jessica said. "Good luck."

Joe shook his head as they strolled on. *Manic Monday, indeed.* He knocked gently on the dressing room door. There was no reply. He waited. Knocked again, louder this time.

"Adam? It's Joe. Can I come in?"

Still no answer, so he turned the handle gently and let the door swing open. For a moment, he thought the room was empty; it was so quiet. But then he heard a sniff—short and quick—from the small bathroom on the far side of the dressing room. It wouldn't be the first time he'd caught

Adam Cave doing a line off the back of the loo, but this was a little early in the day, even for him.

The bathroom door opened and Adam spilled out, looking like a rabbit in the headlights. His eyes were red-rimmed. *Had he been crying?*

"What the fuck are you doing in here?" he asked, looking more surprised than angry, though he obviously didn't like being caught out.

"Looking for something to change into," Joe said, using both hands to show off his coffee-stained clothes.

"Well, don't let me stop you," Adam huffed, flopping down into a chair like a petulant child. He wiped the back of his hand roughly over his eyes. He'd definitely been crying.

Joe turned his back on Adam, rifling through the rail of clothes against the far wall of the dressing room. He could feel the star watching him and wondered if it would seem too strange for him to go into the toilet stall to change. Deciding it would, he plucked a pair of stonewashed jeans off the rail and held them against his waist. They'd do. A box of studio-branded T-shirts and sweatshirts in the corner provided the rest of the outfit.

With his back still to Adam, he peeled off his own jeans and T-shirt and dropped them in a pile on the floor.

"Are you okay?" Joe asked, tentatively.

"Hay fever," Adam said.

A likely story. Joe pulled the T-shirt over his head and turned around. Adam was sitting forward in his chair now, legs jittering. He looked nervous, or ill, or both.

"Are you sure you're okay? You don't look well."

"I'm fine," Adam lied.

Joe grabbed a small bottle of water from the fridge in the corner, cracked it open and handed it to Adam.

"Drink this."

Adam looked at the bottle as though he'd just been offered something entirely alien to try.

"It'll help settle your nerves," Joe said.

"I doubt it," Adam said, but he took a long gulp, anyway. "Where's Jack?"

"I don't know," Joe said. "I've just got here. There's a journalist here looking for him, though."

One thing Joe had realised very early on was that Adam relied on Jack for almost every part of his day. Everywhere they went, Jack had to get there first, making sure that the crowds of screaming teenage girls could be passed through safely, checking that the facilities were right, ensuring that every little detail had been considered. He formed the fragile barrier between Adam, the twins, and the rest of the world, who were all just looking for their piece of flesh.

Joe had never really thought before about how hard it must be for these huge pop stars. Having only accompanied Adam for a couple of weeks, Joe was already exhausted with the relentless badgering by adoring fans, the constant snapping from paparazzi, the cat calls and jeers from the public. He'd witnessed first hand how people were nauseatingly obsequious to Adam's face and then almost vitriolic behind his back. But not Jack. Jack was only ever supportive of Adam. So it was odd that he wasn't here now, especially with Adam so clearly in distress.

"A journalist?" Adam asked, standing up and pacing the room. "What did he say? What does he want?"

"To interview you," Joe said. "He's from *Smash Hits*."

Adam seemed to relax ever so slightly at that addition to the news, but not for long.

"Wait. Why only me? Why not all of us?"

"I think he's already spoken to the twins," Joe said. "That's what he said, anyway."

"Oh God."

Adam sank into the chair again, head in hands.

"What's going on?" Joe asked. "What's wrong?"

Adam sighed.

"You know, don't you?" Adam said. "About me?"

Joe nodded. They'd never actually said the words, but Joe had made enough cute comments about his own love life to let Adam know that he was among friends. It had helped the star relax around him.

"It's that obvious?" Adam stopped pacing, looking even more dejected, if that was possible.

"No," Joe said. "I'm just good at seeing things. Especially the things that other people don't. Look, I know it's hard, in your position..."

"There's this guy," Adam said quietly. "It was nothing. A drunken fumble. He's a friend of Liam's, or Luke's, I can't remember which. They said he was a good guy. That I could trust him. But he got pissed off when I wouldn't pay him to keep quiet. Said he was going to go to the press."

"When did this happen?"

"A couple of days ago. Jack's going to kill me."

So that's what was going on.

Joe crouched down on his haunches in front of Adam—which was no mean feat in the tight jeans he'd just procured from the rail. Adam's eyes, still glistening, searched Joe's face, confused by this sudden proximity.

"Listen," Joe said. "You barely know me. And I know I'm supposed to look up to you as the big pop star, but right now all I see is a lost guy, carrying around a secret he doesn't need to carry. Wouldn't it be better to just come out? Make a statement. Steal this guy's thunder."

"You don't understand," Adam said desperately. "I can't."

"Maybe not, but, I know you can't go on like this, either," Joe replied.

Adam sniffed.

"I was listening to some of the tracks you were playing yesterday evening," Joe said. "You sounded incredible. Your new stuff is amazing. I love it."

"You do?" Adam looked up at him, a small flicker of a smile on the corner of his lips, gone too quickly.

"Yes, it's much more gritty. Heartfelt." Joe wasn't making it up just to make Adam feel better, either. The new songs were such a departure from the bubblegum pop that Loose Lips had been famous for. He felt like they were finally about to see Adam's real talent.

"Jack and I wrote them together. He's much better at the lyrics than I am. But the twins hate the new stuff," Adam said, sadly.

"I'm sure they don't," Joe said.

"Well, that's what they said this morning. They've got their own songs they want us to record, but they're terrible."

He looked up at Joe, searching for answers.

"But maybe they're right," Adam continued. "Maybe we should do it their way, and then I can just leave as soon as it's done."

"That would be a crime," Joe said. "Your new songs are amazing."

"You're very kind," Adam said. "But they're probably right—the Loose Lips fans will hate them. They just want bouncy, happy pop."

17

He said the word with such clear distaste, that it was clear to Joe how far he'd already moved on from the group's trademark bubblegum sound.

"Come on," Joe said. "The stuff you've written for this album is amazing. It's raw, it's honest. The twins are just jealous."

"Well, either we do their songs, or we split up and they end up with nothing—the record label has already agreed that I take all the old song rights with me, since I wrote them. Jack thinks I owe it to the twins to do their songs for just this one album, so that they'll have some legacy. But it's my reputation on the line too. I just don't know what to do."

Adam shrugged, sighing.

"Would it be that bad if the group split now?" Joe asked. "You don't really owe the twins anything, do you? As you say, you wrote all the other songs. At least then you could relaunch your career, with the right kind of fans. You could let everyone see who you really are."

Adam slumped back into the chair, fiddling with his fingernails.

"I don't think I can."

"Why not?"

"What if no one comes with me?" he asked. "All those screaming fans out there—as soon as they find out the truth, it's all over."

And there it was. He was too scared to go it alone, too scared to come out.

"Well, then you'll have to make your own fans. New ones. You've already got one, right here."

Adam looked at him, a glimmer of resolve settling behind his eyes. A small smile lit on his lips. Joe's words had got through.

The door to the dressing room flew open suddenly, and Jack strode in, designer coat floating behind him, bright shirt hugging his neat frame. He looked stressed. He did a double take, finding Joe sitting beside Adam, one hand on his shoulder, the other clasped around Adam's own hand. They jumped apart.

"Oh for God's sake, Adam," Jack said, crossly. "Do you think you could keep your mind on the job for one minute?"

Joe stood quickly.

"We were just..."

"I can see just fine what *you* were doing," Jack said, bitterly. "Come on, out you go. I'm sure you've got work to do."

He put a hand on Joe's elbow, guiding him towards the door. Joe thought about protesting, but the look in Jack's eye told him he was not in any kind of mood for negotiation.

"Jesus, Jack. What's got into you?" Adam said, angrily. "He was just trying to help."

"We all are, Adam," Jack sniped. "That's all we ever do."

Joe saw any glimmer of confidence he'd just given the star drop away.

"PJ was looking for you, Jack," Joe blurted from the doorway, suddenly remembering. "That journalist from *Smash Hits* is back. Says he needs to talk to you now."

"Where is he?" Jack asked, looking worried.

"I left him in reception."

"Jack, I need to talk to you before…" Adam began, but Jack was already out the door and heading down the corridor. Joe looked back at Adam and nodded reassuringly.

"It's going to be okay," Joe said. "Maybe not at first. But in the end."

JOE HAD SPENT the majority of the day babysitting the three members of Loose Lips and trying to make sure that any arguments that did erupt happened out of earshot of the journalist, Hugh Brice, who had finally worked his way into the main studio, under PJ's close supervision, and had been making his presence—and his camera—felt throughout the afternoon.

The twins were lapping up the attention, larking around between takes, and making sure they were featured in any shots. It seemed they thrived on being in the limelight and were completely oblivious to their group mate's suffering.

Adam was doing his best to remain professional, but Joe kept spotting flickers of his annoyance and frustration with the twins, and he didn't blame him. They were behaving like children, making each other giggle during takes, pulling faces, and generally being annoying.

Despite having worked on the programme for the last couple of weeks, Joe hadn't had too many direct dealings with Liam and Luke Millard.

Before they'd started filming, he'd read up about them in magazine articles, and he'd seen pictures of the group, but even so, he hadn't quite been prepared for just how disconcertingly identical the twins were. Tight stonewashed jeans, torso-hugging T-shirts with BOY logos writ large across their chests, tans on the verge of unnatural. Blonde, close-cropped hair, poking out from beneath the upturned peaks of plain white baseballs caps. And if it weren't for the fact that the L on Liam's baseball cap faced the correct way, and Luke's faced backward, there would be no way to tell them apart. The two Ls, back to back, formed the Loose Lips logo, in which, Joe realised, Adam played no part.

Not only did the twins look and dress identically, but their movements and gestures were almost synchronised. If one looked up, the other did so too. When one crossed his legs, so did his twin. And both sneered, perpetually, as though there was some stench beneath their noses that couldn't be placed.

Right now, they were standing behind Adam in the studio, while he was singing a particularly tricky note, high and sustained. Liam was doing a snide, mimed impression of Adam's singing behind his back, and Luke was trying, and failing, to suppress a giggle.

Outside the booth, listening through headphones, Jack watched the recording through the large window above the mixing desk. He looked sad, Joe thought. And far away.

Adam's note finished, and Jack shook his head, bringing himself back into the present. There was definitely something else going on with him today.

Joe's attention was drawn back to the recording booth by a sudden eruption of swearing from within. The twins stormed out in quick succession, leaving Adam looking furious. The doors out into the corridor slammed behind them and, in the silence that descended, the only sound was of the automatic winder on Hugh Brice's camera, snapping the whole altercation.

Hugh lowered the camera, looked around the studio and, sensing blood in the water, hastened after the twins. PJ, who had been lounging on the sofas along the back of the studio wall, moved as though to follow him, but suddenly realised that Carl, the director of the documentary, had refocused the cameras on the recording booth, where Adam and Jack were now in the midst of a conversation that no one could hear, since the recording engineer had flipped the sound off. PJ hurried to the desk and slipped the headphones on, listening in to the last of their conversation.

Joe looked across at Carl, and the look on the director's face made him spin back to see what Adam and Jack were doing now.

They were right up in each other's faces, in a way Joe had not seen them do before. Confrontational. Angry. Adam gestured angrily with both hands in a picture of abject frustration, following up with an irate point at the door that the twins had just stormed through, and a finger wagged in Jack's face. The briefest pause, where Jack's face went through a range of emotions from confusion, to surprise, to anger, to cold stone. And then he slapped Adam, hard and fast, right across the cheek.

A sharp intake of breath rippled around the studio, Carl's eye was fixed on the monitor, making sure he was getting the shots, while PJ's hand pressed the headphones to his ear, listening to every word. Only there were no more words to be spoken. All that would be said, had been said. Adam looked shocked. Jack started crying. Adam tried to apologise, went to hug him. But Jack ran out, leaving Adam alone in the studio.

All eyes and one camera, followed Jack across the room. As the sound of the door slamming behind him rattled around the studio, and the director cut the camera, PJ took the headphones off and called Joe over.

"Get Adam, and take him back to the hotel," he whispered. "Go out the back way. Wait for me in the bar, I'll try to bring this lot back over. We need to sort this out. Fast. Or we're not going to have a film to present."

"What's going on?" Joe asked.

"I think the group have just split up."

JACK OPENED HIS EYES, feeling disorientated and sick. It took him a moment to figure out where he was. This wasn't his room. He struggled to lift his head, as though the muscles didn't want to respond to the instruction his brain was trying to give. He gave up—breathing heavily. He was so hot.

Lying on his back, the room spinning overhead, he let his head roll to the side, realising, as he did, that he was in Adam's room. He had a flash of memory of the two of them coming up here after leaving the others in the bar. They'd been talking all afternoon, the group and associated hangers-on. Some of them drinking, some—like Jack and the twins—doing a couple of lines of cocaine to get them through. He'd had heavier afternoons, that was certain. So what had happened? Why did he feel so bad? Why was he in Adam's room? And where was Adam?

"Adam?" he croaked, his tongue feeling fat and chalky.

There was no reply. He looked at the gilt-armed Georgian armchairs, and the low coffee table with a wine cooler in the middle, bottle upturned inside it. Empty. They'd sat there for a while, he remembered now. Adam crying. Both of them crying. Staring out of the huge windows at the street below. He'd had a drink. "Fuck it," he'd said. "What harm can it do now?"

How long had he blacked out for? It was dark outside. Jack could see himself reflected in the window, and it was only then that he realised he was naked. But he didn't remember getting undressed. What the hell had gone on? He hoped to God he hadn't done anything with Adam. The guy was besotted enough without encouraging him.

He tried to sit up, but found he couldn't even lift his head. He closed his eyes as the nausea crept up on him again. His head felt thick, black dots and light flares popped inside his eyelids, his breathing became shallower, more laboured. Maybe he could just lie here for a moment until the feeling passed. The sheets were damp with his sweat, but even that felt distant, he realised, as though he was one step removed from his sensations. *What was happening to him?*

He barely heard the lock on the hotel room door click open. He tried to raise his head to see, but could barely open his eyes to see the figure stepping into the room.

"Adam?" the sound barely a crackle.

"Oh dear, Jack. Not feeling so good?"

There was something different about Adam's voice, or maybe he just wasn't hearing right. It was all Jack could do to move his head to watch him walk across the room. He reached up and closed the curtains, turning to look at Jack. Jack's vision swam—he couldn't focus on the face.

"Adam?"

He blinked and by the time he opened his eyes again, Adam was already on the other side of the bed again. Jack still couldn't focus on him enough to see his face.

"What's happening?" Jack tried to ask, but the words slurred into one incomprehensible noise, his tongue too thick to form the shapes required for speech.

"Let's get you more comfy, shall we?"

Jack felt himself being rolled onto his stomach. His face pressed into the soft pillows briefly before his head was pulled back up to let him breathe. *Not now, Adam. Not like this,* he thought, trying to shake his head, desperate to force his lips to say the words out loud. A face swam into his vision—too close to focus—breath hot on his cheek. And a smile, so sinister, so full of menace, it really didn't suit its wearer.

You're not Adam, was the last thing Jack thought.

2.

RUSSELL HAD THE RADIO on, as ever, while he was making breakfast. It wasn't that he particularly enjoyed the relentless upbeat banter of Mike Read's Breakfast Show, but he needed something to give him a bit of a boost.

Joe strolled into the kitchen, his hair still tousled from sleep and his skin still marked with creases from his pillow. He turned the volume down as he passed the radio.

"Ugh," he grumbled. "Do you honestly enjoy this shit?"

"Morning, sunshine," Russell said, cheerfully.

"How can it be morning already?" Joe complained, draining the remains of a cafetière into a clean mug and then wincing as he discovered it was already cold.

"I'll have another, if you're making a fresh pot," Russell said, smiling. Joe was universally terrible in the mornings, but even more so when he'd been out the night before.

"I didn't hear you get home last night," Russell said. "Go anywhere fun?"

"I wish," Joe said. "We had a shitty day in the studio yesterday. I ended up babysitting Adam in the hotel until PJ could get the others to agree to a reconciliation meeting, and then I escaped to the Red Lion—where you were missed."

"What was going on?"

"Nothing particularly exciting. Too much drinking, too much moaning. Same old, same old. Speaking of which, Patty is organising a debut show for Scott—or Miss Terri as he will henceforth be known. It's on Friday. I said we'd go."

He swilled the dregs of the old coffee out in the sink and poured a fresh pot, breathing the flavour in deeply and sighing. Russell stood up and shepherded Joe into a chair.

"Sit down," he said. "Breakfast won't be long. It may not be up to your usual standards, but then neither are you this morning."

Joe smiled, looking both weary and a little sad. Despite the split with Luc being mostly Joe's choice, Russell knew these first few days of waking up alone would be tough on the kid.

Luc had taken to staying over most nights, and while Joe had come to find that a little claustrophobic, Russell had to admit that he was going to miss the young Frenchman's cooking.

"What time have you got to be in this morning?" Russell asked.

"Normal time," Joe said, rubbing his face in his hands. "I don't even know what we're going to be filming. I think the band split up yesterday. It was crazy. Unless PJ's managed to get them all back in the studio, we won't have much of a programme."

"Welcome to the world of celebrity television, dear."

"What are you up to today?" Joe asked, as Russell sat down at the table with two plates of scrambled egg on toast.

"There's a guy over in D'Arblay Street, runs a little café. Thinks his night team are lifting some of the takings. Asked me to have a look."

"Ooh, aren't you a proper Miss Marple these days?" Joe teased.

"Less of the Miss, thank you," Russell said, punching his shoulder playfully.

Since being forced out of his job as a detective with the Metropolitan police by a homophobic colleague, he had found a role for himself as a kind of unofficial private detective, often with Joe's help.

He and Joe had even solved two murder cases together now, both of which the police had turned their backs on—mostly because the cases had involved someone from Soho's queer scene.

Active discrimination against the gay community from the boys in blue was a huge problem, especially in Soho. It was an issue that the police authorities had only just begun trying to address, but their attempts were reliant on victims filing complaints, and that rarely happened. So Russell had found himself being both sympathetic ear and incidental detective for members of Soho's gay community who needed something solving and had nowhere else to turn. Russell didn't mind—it paid the bills and kept him busy. He was only in his mid-forties, so he was far too young to retire, anyway.

He was far too young to die, too. But he had to stop thinking like that. The wait for his test results would be interminable. He looked at Joe, wanting to tell him what was going on, but not being able to find the words. Besides, it may be nothing. He may be clear. What was the point of both of them worrying?

"I was thinking of going away for a couple of days," Russell said. "Go out to the country, perhaps. Get some fresh air."

Joe paused, a forkful of breakfast hovering between plate and lip, head cocked curiously to one side.

"You feeling alright?"

He looked across at Joe. *Tell him.* Joe's face waiting expectantly. *Just say it. He'll be fine. He'll know what to say. He's your friend.* But now that it came to it, he couldn't quite bring himself to say anything. This was the problem. The stigma, the shame, the fear. This was what stopped men getting tested, and what helped the disease to rampage through them all.

"I just fancy getting away," Russell said.

"Now, come on, love," Joe smiled patronisingly. "You wouldn't last five minutes in the country. You won't get a Piña Colada out there, for a start."

"Oh, piss off," Russell said, knowing he was right. He didn't want to go to the country at all. He just didn't want to sit around in the flat all week, waiting for news either.

They both ate in silence as the beeps from the radio signalled the beginning of the nine o'clock news. Joe would have to go soon to get to work on time.

"This is the nine o'clock news, from the BBC," the announcer declared. "Adam Cave, the lead singer of pop group Loose Lips, has been arrested at his hotel in London's Soho district, following the death of another man last night. Early reports from police say that the body of a man was found in Mr Cave's hotel room by cleaning staff early this morning. A spokesman for Mr Cave has told us he is helping police with their enquiries. More to follow on that story as it breaks. Meanwhile, Buckingham Palace have officially announced the engagement of Prince Andrew to Sarah Ferguson..."

Joe had leapt out of his seat at the mention of Adam Cave's arrest.

"What the hell?" he said, rushing from the room and coming back moments later, still pulling on his T-shirt and zipping up his jeans.

"I've got to go. Shit."

He stumbled as he pulled his plimsoles on, and then turned back to Russell, a look of near panic on his face.

"I've got a terrible feeling about this," he said, and the wobble in his voice confirmed it. "Do you think you could come with me?"

"Where are we going?"

"To the hotel."

RUSSELL AND JOE STOOD on the pavement facing the hotel, at the back of a growing crowd. The front of the old luxury hotel was swamped by police cars, a coroner's van, and some harassed-looking uniformed officers trying to hold a sea of reporters at bay. Off to one side, behind a flimsy cordon, a mob of identical gum-chewing, backcombed-haired girls consoled each other as they waited for news of their hero, or a glimpse of his bandmates. That fan grapevine worked quickly.

"Uh-oh, arsehole alert," Joe said, nodding towards a tall, rat-faced man in a beige mac, striding out of the hotel entrance in a blizzard of camera flashes. "Keep your head down."

Russell was already hiding his face beneath the peak of one of Joe's borrowed baseball caps, hoping that none of his former colleagues in the police force would spot him. He was on reasonable terms with some of them, but he had clocked his old subordinate, Detective Simon Skinner, at the same time as Joe had, and dipped his head further, stepping in behind Joe for extra protection.

Smiling smugly, taking the pats on the back from colleagues as he threw out a couple of instructions, Skinner piled into a waiting police car, which pulled away with sirens blasting unnecessarily. A staged exit for the arrogant detective.

Skinner would be loving the high-profile nature of the arrest he'd just made, and would have deliberately hung around the scene, making sure that enough journalists got his photograph to go alongside those that his pet hack would have got of the arrest itself—having been tipped off just in time to get there, no doubt. It never changed with Skinner.

The detective had been the man responsible for the sting that had seen Russell entrapped, charged with so-called importuning, and forced into an unwanted early retirement from the job he loved. Needless to say, there was no love lost between the two men.

Skinner was a homophobe, which was annoying enough, but what really made Russell's blood boil was that he was a lazy detective and, worse still, a bent cop. Russell and Joe had already gone over Skinner's head twice since Russell had left the force, solving two murders that Skinner had shown no interest in.

In both cases the victims had been people they'd known, but the first had been, quite literally, on Russell's doorstep, when his flatmate—and Joe's best friend from school—had been murdered.

Skinner had made it clear on both occasions that he would not be putting too much effort into finding out what had really happened. He was a huge proponent of the idea that if you were gay and bad things happened to you, you'd obviously asked for it.

Russell was determined to see the detective stripped of his badge, if it was the last thing he did. But he knew he had to be smart about it.

Skinner wasn't the only bent cop in the department, nor was he the only one who had taken against Russell once they'd all found out his sexuality.

He couldn't afford to make any mistakes. Even being here was a big risk, but he had promised Joe that he'd come down to the hotel and see if he could find out a little more about what had happened, and whether Adam Cave's sudden arrest had been justified.

"Oh my God, have you heard?" a nasal whine of a voice asked. "Jack's dead."

Russell looked up, relieved to see that it was Joe's boss, PJ, asking the question. Short, round, and balding, he reminded Russell of a poor man's Danny DeVito—his Hawaiian shirts seemed to get louder every time Russell saw him. This beacon of flapping panic would certainly get him noticed.

While Joe greeted his boss with similar expressions of disbelief, Russell leaned forward and whispered in Joe's ear:

"I'm going to try to get inside, see what I can find out. I'll see you in the Red Lion in an hour."

Joe nodded, turning back to PJ as Russell slipped into the crowd. He'd seen a possible chance to get into the hotel and, though it would be a huge risk, it would be worth it if it paid off.

Russell headed slowly but purposefully through the crowd, head still down, cap pulled low, and only looked up when he reached the forensic team, unloading paper suits and evidence kits from the back of their van, led by their boss, Harry Palin.

Russell had a lot of time for Harry—he was intelligent, honest and fiercely passionate about justice, and had always been very supportive of Russell while he'd been on the force. They had often promised to meet up for a drink outside of work, but both knew it would likely never happen.

When Russell had been drummed out of the job, he'd had a message from Harry, expressing concern. He'd never him called back, which he was now regretting.

"Have you got a spare one for me?" Russell said brightly. "I've been caught somewhat on the hop this morning. Wasn't expecting to be needed at all."

Harry's face broke into a broad smile when he saw Russell.

"Oh, hello Russ, long time no see," he said, then suddenly frowned. "I thought you'd left the force."

"You thought right," Russell said. He liked Harry, and he knew he wouldn't get away with any kind of outright lie. This guy could see through anything. "I sometimes come in if they're struggling with the finer detail. An old set of eyes, and all that."

In a roundabout way, it was the truth. Skinner had no eye for detail, and Russell was happy to undermine him at any turn if it meant getting to the truth of a case.

"Sounds like a full-time job, then," Harry said, handing him a package of paper suit and shoe covers. "I was truly sorry to hear what happened to you, you know? I tried to get in touch."

"Don't worry," Russell said, feeling more embarrassed than he should to be having this conversation. "It was bound to come out at some point."

"Or *you* were," Harry smiled, his eyes twinkling. "I'm glad it hasn't put you off working though. Although I have to say I'm surprised you'd want to be anywhere near Detective Skinner again."

"Trust me, I don't. But I do like to see justice done, and we both know Skinner is a big fan of the easiest route to any conviction, rightful or otherwise."

"You're not wrong there. The man's barely better than a trained chimp."

Russell smiled. *Harsh, but true.*

"So while he's off taking the glory for arresting a celebrity suspect, I get pulled out of my bed to come down here and do the dirty work. Let's hope he's got it right this time. He can't afford another disciplinary hearing."

Russell desperately hoped Skinner hadn't got it right at all, not just for the fact that he'd love to stick another nail in the coffin of Skinner's career.

Joe had told him that Adam Cave's sexuality was a barely concealed secret, and that the star was struggling to keep up the pretence of being the good, clean boy next door and idol of a million screaming teenage girls.

If Skinner got a whiff of it, he'd make damn sure it was front page news.

Russell followed Harry and his team through the revolving doors, noting the look of distress on the manager's face as yet more police officials flooded his upmarket hotel.

The grand lobby was in barely controlled chaos, with concerned and frustrated guests wanting more information, and trying to find out when they could get back to their rooms. The staff looked both shellshocked and flustered as the police moved about efficiently between them all, taking names, asking questions, gathering statements.

Harry didn't waste any time finding out where they needed to go, and Russell hung back until he moved towards the lift.

"They'll be having kittens about all the bad publicity," Harry commented as the lift doors closed and they began to ascend. "Though I'm sure they'll realise quite quickly how well scandal sells. They'll be inundated with people wanting to stay here as soon as the full story gets out."

"Who's the victim?" Russell asked.

"A Mr Jack Eddy," Harry replied. "Manager of the band, Loose Lips."

The doors opened with a ping, and the team sidled out, Russell in tow. There were two uniformed officers standing either side of a door halfway down the corridor.

Fortunately he didn't recognise either of them from his old station, which meant it wasn't likely they'd recognise him either—he'd always made an effort to get to know his colleagues. Still, he let Harry take the lead.

"Harry Palin, forensics," he said dismissively, as he approached the two officers on guard. Both nodded.

"Right," Harry said to his team. "Let's get kitted up and get this over with."

The two officers said nothing, remaining unmoved at their posts as the team slipped paper suits over their work clothes and gathered their kit.

Channelling his former role, Russell stepped forward authoritatively and followed Harry into the crime scene, with no ID, no right to be there, and not a backward glance from the pair of chumps guarding the door from civilian access.

WHAT GREETED THEM INSIDE was as strange a crime scene as Russell had ever been to. Jack Eddy lay face down on the bed, naked, with his hands trussed behind his back with a long, colourful scarf that was also tied around his neck.

His face was turned slightly toward the door, eyes staring blankly, tongue lolling. Russell stood and stared, open-mouthed at the body on the bed. It wasn't the nature of his death that was so shocking, it was the fact that this was the same guy that Russell had consoled yesterday morning in the health clinic. The guy who'd just been given a terminal diagnosis. *Did he do this to himself?* Had he taken the news so badly that he'd committed suicide?

Surely not? Not like this. Far from a suicide, this looked like a sex game gone wrong. Russell had heard of people using asphyxia for sexual gratification. Had that been the case here? A panicked lover suddenly realising that the game had gone too far and fleeing the scene?

Russell stared at the body for a moment, realising that his mind was throwing up the same question he'd been asking himself all night: "What will you do if you are Positive?" He bent down to look at Jack Eddy's face a little closer. *Not this, that's for sure.* It was a small blessing, perhaps, that Jack had died before the disease could take him. Russell shook his head. This was no blessing. This was almost certainly murder.

As Harry and his team unpacked, Russell crouched down by the bedside, studying the colourful cotton scarf that had been fastened around Jack's neck, tied tight and looped back around his wrists—so tight, it was pulling his shoulder back awkwardly, making his back arch and his head hang forward so that only the top of his forehead was touching the bed.

Jack's mouth was open, and his tongue was blue and swollen. White powder stuck to the edge of his right nostril, presumably from the line still partly evident on the bedside table. What kind of party had been happening here last night? And how had it all ended so badly?

Russell stood up and turned slowly, taking in the rest of the room as Harry's team began marking and photographing the scene. A pair of expensive-looking leather shoes sat neatly by the side of the desk, but the rest of Jack's clothes were strewn around the floor, discarded where they fell. He felt bad for Jack. Skinner would have been quick to jump to conclusions about what had happened in this room, and Russell had no doubt the corrupt detective would be quick to leak the juicier details to the press for the right price. It wouldn't be the first time he'd taken a bung in exchange for case details.

Still, no point worrying about that now. At least the scene was still intact, which gave Russell a good chance of finding out what really happened. Turning his back on the body, he looked around for any other clue as to who else had been here last night. The room was clean and tidy. A suite—so all the luxuries one would expect for a star of Adam's status—which had afforded him a lounge area as well as the huge bed, an ostentatious bathroom, a pair of elaborate armchairs around a low coffee table looking out on the street below through floor-to-ceiling windows.

Russell wandered around the room slowly, studying everything, listening to Harry's running commentary noting everything he'd already spotted. An empty wine bottle, upside down in the cooler, an empty glass—just the one—beside it. Cocaine on the nightstand, three cigarettes in the ashtray—all the same brand, one butt longer than others, barely smoked. Only Jack's clothes left strewn about. All of Adam's items were either clean and hanging neatly in the wardrobe, or tucked into the hotel laundry bag. Harry instructed the team to pack up all the clothing and start checking for fingerprints.

Russell bent down and lifted a wine cork out of the dustbin under the desk, sniffing it. It smelled fine. The labelling branded into the body of the cork told him that the wine was a Chablis—there were worse last drinks to have. He tossed the cork back into the bin and turned back to the body.

A discarded magazine on the floor beside the bed caught Russell's eye. *The Face*—a kind of grown up *Smash Hits*, all fashion, music, beautiful youth.

On the cover, a sultry image of Nick Kamen—he of the nearly naked man in the laundrette advert currently titillating everyone on the telly. Down one side, a list of the featured celebrities to be found within mentioned Adam Cave.

Russell crouched down again, and using the tip of a pencil he'd pulled from his pocket, turned to the page in question and saw something that made his heart sink. In the photograph which accompanied the interview, Adam was wearing very same scarf that was now tied around his manager's neck.

"Harry," he said, still crouched by the magazine. "Take a look at this."

Harry joined him beside the bed, looking from the image on the page to the scene on the bed.

"Huh," Harry said, standing up but looking perplexed. "Fancy that."

He peered closer at the scarf around Jack's neck again, the turned to Russell.

"So, tell me what we have here then?" Harry asked.

"Looks like the boys were having a private party, things got a little out of control, and Adam did a runner when he realised what had happened."

Harry said nothing. From experience, Russell knew Harry always enjoyed hearing other people hypothesise while he examined his scenes. And he'd learned the hard way not to ask too many questions. Just say what you think and wait for Harry to unpick your logic.

"And you think this..." Harry indicated vaguely at the way Jack was tied, "...was consensual?"

33

"To begin with, at least. I mean, he's not a small guy, and it doesn't look like there was much of a struggle. No scratch marks, no blood, no bruising."

"Aha," Harry said. "Exactly."

He bent down on his haunches, using a gloved finger to move the scarf away from the skin on Jack's neck.

"Let's get him untied, then, shall we?" he said to one of his forensic officers.

The young man stepped forward, took a series of photographs of all the details, and then carefully placed the camera on the floor and began loosening the knots around Jack's wrists. As the scarf came away, Harry and Russell both peered at Jack's neck together.

"Just as I thought," Harry said.

Russell frowned, not understanding what Harry had just found confirmation of. Jack's neck had a single red welt in a straight line where the scarf had cut into the skin. Bruising flushed on either side, which Russell knew meant that Jack must have at least been alive when the scarf was tied. Harry stood up, decisively.

"Get some more shots of that for me, will you?" Harry said to his colleague, pointing to Jack's neck. Once again the room flared with the camera's flash.

"So, what do you see now?" Harry asked Russell, testing him.

"Bruising around the neck, so he was strangled..." Russell began, not really knowing where he was going with this.

Harry held up a hand to stop him. He hated wasting time.

"You're seeing exactly what the killer wanted you to see."

"What?" Russell looked from Harry, to the body, to Harry again.

"Take another look at that mark."

Russell did, waiting for elucidation. Harry tutted.

"When we're strangled—even if we're enjoying it—there comes a moment when our body's fight-or-flight response kicks in. That awful moment when we realise we are going to die, and the body fights back. In every other strangulation case I've seen, there has been evidence of that struggle. The marks of strangulation are deep and brutal. This? This is almost civilised."

Russell looked again. He was right—the line was clean. Yes, there was bruising, but it seemed to be more from the pressure of the scarf than from a fight for life.

"He wasn't exactly in a position to try to free himself, was he?" Russell reminded him.

"No, but in that moment when the pleasure ended, and the fear kicked in, he would have thrashed about, trying to alert his lover—*if* this was a game, that is. He would have tried to free himself. But this bruising doesn't say that. This says he just lay here, still and silent, while his last breath was choked out of him."

They stood in silence for a moment staring at Jack's naked corpse.

"So he was already incapacitated by the time he was killed?" Russell asked.

Harry stood up, stretched his back and looked at Russell.

"Looks highly likely," he said. "And judging by his eyes, and the colouring around his mouth, I would say that he took, or was given, something which meant he couldn't defend himself. And I'm not talking about the Happy Powder on the nightstand over there."

"Well that doesn't make any sense," Russell said. "Why would Adam murder him in his own room, with his own scarf, and then leave him here to be found?"

Harry beamed and clapped him on the back.

"Now you're seeing things clearly. He wouldn't. I think your old friend has arrested the wrong man. But look, I'll know more when I've run all the tests. I'll let you know what I find, shall I? Or should I go through Skinner?"

"I'd love to say you can come straight to me," Russell admitted. "But you'd better go through the official channels first."

Harry smiled sadly.

"Well, either way, I hope you get to the truth before he does," Harry said. "Maybe we can get that drink soon."

"I'd like that," Russell replied, taking his cue to leave. He turned back in the doorway. "Oh, and Harry..." he began.

"Don't worry. Pleasant as it's been, I won't mention I saw you here," Harry said, with a wink. "Good luck, Russ."

"BUT NONE OF US really know what he's capable of, do we? What if he *did* do it?" PJ asked, for the third time in the space of ten minutes. Joe and he stood side by side on the pavement, with PJ's constant nervous pacing having created a decent amount of space around them, giving them a clear view of the comings and goings at the hotel.

"There is no way Adam would kill Jack, PJ. Think about it. This will all turn out to be some tragic accident. Besides, we shouldn't speculate. We don't even know what happened yet."

"You're probably right," PJ conceded. "But..."

"No, come on," Joe said. "You know Adam. This is ridiculous. He's your friend."

PJ stopped pacing and turned to frown at Joe.

"Well, he's not really a *friend*," PJ said. "I mean, I barely know him."

You've changed your tune, Joe thought. When Joe had first started on the production, the pop star's name might as well have been "My Friend Adam" where PJ was concerned—he wanted everyone to know he was in the inner circle. And yet, at the first sniff of trouble, here he was, denying all knowledge. *Judas.* Maybe PJ wasn't such a nice guy after all.

"I mean, I know he's got a temper, and he doesn't like being ignored. And they did have a big fight yesterday, remember?"

"It looked like they made up as well, I mean, you were with them in the bar after I left. How were they then?"

"Frosty," PJ said, eyes wide, scandalised. "There was definitely something going on. Oh God, this is such a mess. We're never going to finish the film now."

Joe had wondered, briefly, if PJ was in such a state because he somehow blamed himself for this situation. Had the filming driven them all to argue the way they had yesterday? Had that led to whatever had happened to poor Jack?

"I mean, we've only got half the break-up on tape at best. What are we going to do with half a bloody film?" PJ asked, revealing the real reason he was so anxious.

"I don't know," Joe said. He didn't care either. Jack had been a nice guy. A little standoffish at times, but he'd never been rude or demanding, even to Joe. He didn't deserve to die, and he certainly didn't deserve for his death to be part of the media circus this would become.

Speaking of a media circus. Joe's heart sank as he saw Hugh Brice approaching them, a broad grin on his face. *Here comes the clown.*

"Oh hey," Hugh said, directing his greeting at PJ and steadfastly ignoring Joe.

"Hugh," PJ said, suddenly looking like he wanted to escape.

"Incredible, isn't it? I mean awful, but God—who knew Adam had it in him?" Hugh said, eyes wide, almost rubbing his hands in glee.

Hugh Brice was giddy with excitement. Joe felt his bile rising. Jack was dead, and Adam had just been hauled off by the police, and this guy was getting off on it.

Before PJ could respond, the hubbub from the crowd out front boiled up again, and both Joe and PJ were carried forward as the tide of journalists, Hugh Brice included, rushed towards the entrance. The Millard twins had just walked out into the sunlight, not bothering to shield their faces from the cameras. Their identical expressions of sombre grief were absolutely on point. They were flanked by two members of the record label's management team that Joe had only seen once before at one of the production meetings. Their dark suits and stern faces stood in bold contrast to the twins' bright orange, big-shouldered suits, white T-shirts, white high-top trainers and trademark white baseball caps with their peaks up high, the mirrored Ls of their logo dictating the position they always stood in.

The twins turned their heads in unison to every call from a new photographer—pouts at the ready, making sure to milk their time in the limelight.

Joe saw his fellow runners from the documentary shoot, Jessica and Sarah, step out of the hotel behind the twins, and sidle off to the side of the throng, deliberately removing themselves from the centre of attention. They both looked like they'd had a pretty rough night.

As Joe moved through the crowd to join them on the fringes, one of the record label guys held up his hand for silence and began delivering a rehearsed statement, expressing his sadness to hear of the death of Loose Lips's manager, Jack Eddy, and asking for the press to respect his friends and family at this time.

"Bloody vultures," Jessica muttered as Joe reached them.

"It's crazy," Joe said. "What happened, do you know?"

"We'd all been partying together," Sarah said. "Last night. The twins invited us back here, and we ran into PJ with Jack and Adam in the bar, so we all hung out for a while."

"Thanks for the invite," Joe said.

"PJ said you'd already gone home," Sarah said.

"Don't sweat it, Babyface, it wasn't as much fun as it sounded," Jessica added. "The group were splitting up. It was all pretty tense. Underneath, like. On the surface everyone was all fake smiles and falseness, but you could tell it was over. They'd all admitted it, by the end of the night."

"PJ was trying to persuade them all to come back in to the studio and let him film it," Sarah said. "To tell the full story of the break-up. He promised to make them all look good."

"Always hustling," Joe commented.

"He's just panicking cause he's already spent the budget and now he's got no film to show for it." Jessica said. "Anyway, then PJ just got drunk and started getting handsy, as usual, and that sort of cleared the room."

"Apparently, Jack and Adam took the party on up to Adam's room, and in the morning, Jack was found dead in Adam's bed, all trussed up like a Christmas turkey." Sarah said.

"Oh God," Joe said again. "And where was Adam?"

The statement from the record label spokesman over, the twins were ushered back into the hotel and the crowd of reporters—sensing the fun was now over—began to filter away.

"He'd gone off clubbing with the barman," Jessica said. "He just left Jack there, dead in his bed. Can you imagine?"

"That's cold, man," said Sarah.

Joe couldn't imagine for one minute. The way Adam always looked at Jack, the way he worried about upsetting him. Joe couldn't imagine Adam hurting a single hair on Jack's head. Something wasn't right.

JOE HAD WALKED ALONG the pavement to the corner of the hotel to get away from the chaos of the departing crowd—he'd decided to take the long way back to the Red Lion and wait for Russell there.

As he reached the corner, he spotted a young man in hotel uniform leaning against the wall, smoking a cigarette, jacket unbuttoned, shirt half untucked.

Joe recognised him immediately as the barman who'd come on shift last night, just as Joe had left PJ trying to talk Adam and Jack back into the studio and in front of the cameras.

The guy looked exhausted now, which would make sense if he was the same barman who'd been out with Adam all night.

"Can I buy one of those off you?" Joe asked, pointing at the cigarette hanging from his mouth as he approached.

"Nah, you're alright," the barman said, reaching into his pocket and holding out the packet for Joe to take one. "Help yourself."

Joe took a cigarette and leaned in to the lighter the guy held out, taking a deep drag. He had only started smoking a few months ago, mainly because both Luc and Russell always did. He fought the urge to cough and won. *Act cool.* The barman's name badge, attached to his jacket, said Cameron. No surname.

"Thanks, Cameron," Joe said, leaning against the wall beside him.

The guy frowned, and Joe pointed to the name badge, eliciting an eye-roll from Cameron.

They smoked in silence for a moment, Joe stealing a glance at the young man as he exhaled. His eyes were red-rimmed, and dark smudges in the sockets spoke of too many heavy nights. His hand shook, ever so slightly as he raised the cigarette to his lips.

"Do you mind if ask you something?" Joe asked.

Cameron looked at him quizzically, frowning.

"About Adam Cave," Joe said, noticing Cameron's face twitch with the slightest hint of distaste.

"You with the papers?" he asked. "Because I already told that other guy, I don't know nothing."

"I'm not a journalist," Joe said.

"Well, you're not police, are you?" It was a statement of fact rather than a question. Joe wondered what gave it away.

"No. I'm a friend of his. I'm just trying to help," Joe said.

"Sounds like he's beyond help now, doesn't it?" Cameron sniped.

"Not if he's innocent," Joe said, and Cameron sneered, taking another drag of his cigarette and blowing the smoke out of the side of his mouth.

"You think he is?"

"Yes," Joe said. "I think. But that's why I wanted to talk to you about what happened last night. It *was* you he spent the night with, wasn't it?"

39

Cameron looked panicked.

"How d'you know that?" he asked, looking around surreptitiously.

"Like I said, I just want to help," Joe replied, realising that Cameron obviously hadn't told anyone about his night on the town with a potential murderer.

"Yeah, but how did you know? Did Adam tell you?"

"My colleagues saw you leave with him at the end of your shift. They were still in the bar."

Cameron nodded. That made sense.

"Look, we just went out clubbing, alright? Nothing happened. I thought it might, I invited him back to mine, but nothing happened."

"I don't really care, either way," Joe said. "I'm only interested in figuring out a timeline of events."

"I don't want any trouble."

"Is that why you haven't told the police you were with him?" Joe asked.

"No. Yes. I don't know. Do you think I should?"

"I don't know yet. It may do more harm than good at this stage. The guy in charge hates our sort."

"Typical," Cameron sniffed.

"Look, why don't you just tell me what happened?" Joe said. "If Adam's innocent, I'm not going to let them air his dirty laundry for no reason."

Cameron pursed his lips for a moment, blowing on the tip of his cigarette, and then turned side on to face Joe.

"Okay," he said, sucking in a final drag and throwing the butt on the floor, crushing it beneath his shoe. "He's been at the hotel a couple of weeks now, Adam. He comes to the bar most nights, usually with Mr Eddy, the guy who... well, anyway. We'd chatted a couple of times, nothing important, but he seemed like a nice enough guy. Shit at flirting, mind, but then when you're as famous as him, you probably don't need to be much cop at that, do you?"

Joe took a drag, saying nothing.

"Yesterday, he was already here when I started shift at three in the afternoon. He was at a table round the corner, so I almost didn't see him. He was already several vodkas in.

Oliver, the guy I took over shift from, said he'd been there for a couple of hours. So I took him a jug of water, asked if he was alright, but he didn't want to talk to me. He looked like he'd been crying."

Joe nodded. He remembered that a jug of water had appeared while he'd been in reception on the phone to PJ. As soon as he'd got the all clear to leave Adam in the bar, on the promise of PJ's imminent arrival with the rest of the crew, Joe had gone back to the table, said his goodbyes and scarpered. He wished he'd stayed now.

"They'd had a bit of a bust up in the studio," Joe confirmed.

"Right. Yeah, so I left him to it, got on with prepping the bar for the night shift. Twenty minutes later, this guy comes in and goes straight over to Adam's table and sits down. He waves me over like I'm some skivvy and orders two more shots. Anyway, I make them and take them over, and I hear Adam saying that he'll sue if this guy prints it. Prints what, I don't know, but the guy's not taking no for an answer. He had a right smug look on his gob and all."

"Did you recognise this other guy?"

"Nah, I'd not seen him before. Tall fella. Ginger. Cocky sort."

Hugh Brice.

"So they're sitting there, all sullen like. It's obvious Adam doesn't want to talk, and I'm about to offer to remove him, when Mr Eddy comes in, and goes over to join them. And if it was tense before, it went up a notch when he got there."

"How so?"

"He's not even there for a minute before old Ginger stands up, tells them both to sling their hook, only not so polite, like, and storms off. But before he gets to the door, he turns back and says: 'The truth will come out someday, Jack.' And then he's gone, but he still had that smug look he'd come in with, plastered all over his chops."

"Right," Joe said, prompting for more.

"Well, those two sit for a bit longer, deep in conversation, lots of hand-holding. Then the older bloke that's always hanging around them in the evenings—short guy, flouncy, always in the Hawaiian shirts..."

PJ, thought Joe, not interrupting Cameron's flow.

"He comes in, all serious like, sits with Adam a while, patting his hand, giving him a pep talk. Nodding all round. And that seems to do the trick, 'cause after that, he's back to his normal self. Life and soul of the party.

Then the twins joined them, with a couple of girls in tow, and the party moved into one of our private bar rooms. Champagne, shots, charlie, all sorts. Not my place to comment, but they were properly on it, you know?"

"And they all seemed happy enough?"

"Totally," Cameron said. "It was one of the only nights since they've been here when there wasn't some kind of drama with that lot."

"So how did you end up spending the night with Adam?"

"Well, at about ten o'clock, Adam and Mr Eddy come through the bar, bottle of wine in hand. They asked for an ice bucket and some glasses, and they went off together."

"Back to Adam's room?"

"Can't tell you that, mate. I dunno. But that was pretty much the end of the party. They left in dribs and drabs after that. The twins hung around for a while, with their girls, I kept seeing them all in and out of the loos.

"Anyway, not long before my shift finishes, Adam comes back down. He's totally wired. A bit pissed. And he wants another drink. I offer him a bottle of the same wine they took up before, but he goes for a Negroni. Tells me his mate's passed out, and he's up for some fun. He asks where I'm going next and if I want to carry on the party upstairs, but I tell him I can't—not in the hotel. So I invite him to come out with me. I was going for a few drinks in a club down the road, and I could see he wanted the company."

Or the alibi, Joe thought.

"We had a couple more drinks, and he started getting a bit frisky, so I invited him back to mine but, when we got there, he got all teary again, and kept going on about keeping quiet, and how he'd ruined everything. Wouldn't stop snivelling. Put me right off, if I'm honest. So I gave him another drink and eventually he passed out and slept through. He was even worse in the morning though, so I said I had to come into work early, and he came in with me and that's when the police arrested him."

"D'you think he did it?" Joe asked. "I mean, you spent the night with him. Surely you'd have been able to tell if he killed his best friend before he came back downstairs?"

"Well, I don't know, do I?" Cameron said, defensively. "Like I said, he was acting pretty strange, really down in the dumps. But all these celebrities are the same, ain't they? Whether they're flying high or down in the dumps, it don't matter, as long as it's all about them. He was a bit odd, but I thought he was just coming down off a high, you know? I mean, who kills their mate and then pisses off out for the night, and comes back to the scene of the crime the next day? Bold as brass. Doesn't make sense, does it?"

Joe thanked Cameron and made his excuses. Cameron was right— none of it made any sense, but he was even more convinced now that Adam was being framed for Jack's murder. It was time to catch up with Russell and see what he'd found out.

RUSSELL HAD ALREADY TAKEN up residence at what had now become their usual table, in the window of the Red Lion pub.

Neither he nor Joe ever had to pay for their drinks here after helping the barman, Ron, to solve the murder of a drag show cabaret host found dead in the pub's function room last year.

The Red Lion was close enough to their home and Joe's work that they could easily meet for a quick catch up, and often came here for lunch. The small table in the window had become their unofficial office.

Russell was halfway through his first pint, waiting for Joe to turn up. "West End Girls" by the Pet Shop Boys playing on the jukebox providing the perfect syncopated soundtrack to the bustle on the street outside.

He'd found a new passion for people-watching, enjoying the wonderful mix of self-proclaimed weirdos that Soho always seemed to attract. He'd even come to recognise his own place in that strange melting pot.

Since Joe's arrival in his life, Russell had become increasingly content with who he was and how at home he felt in this odd little quarter of London.

Seedy and loud, at almost all times of day or night, Soho was a place where sex shops and coffee shops sat side by side. Populated by celebrities, gangsters, drunks, poets, actors and prostitutes—the smoke-filled bars, clubs and streets all now felt like his domain.

This afternoon, though, the lively hustle out there only seemed to enhance his melancholy. He was worried about his test results, of course, but ever since seeing Jack Eddy's body in that hotel room this morning, he'd realised that he had no choice but to tell Joe about seeing Jack at the clinic, and the thought filled him with dread.

He had a feeling that whatever had happened between Jack and Adam in the studio yesterday—whatever harsh words had been spoken—had been down, in large part, to Jack's diagnosis.

Russell knew that it was likely to come out once Harry Palin had finished all of his tests on the body, and it was only right that Joe found out from him, before the papers spread it.

His conversation with Harry Palin had also been swirling around his mind ever since he'd left the hotel room. Harry was convinced that someone had drugged Jack prior to killing him, which made sense of Jack's injuries, but threw up so many more questions.

Why stage it like that, rather than a straightforward suicide? Why make it look like a sex game gone wrong, unless it was to expose Jack's sexuality? And why frame Adam Cave unless you wanted to out him at the same time as getting him charged for murder?

Surely it would have been easier to just go to the papers with a story, if outing them both was the end goal. Why stoop to murder?

Russell hoped that Harry could get someone on the police force—obviously not Skinner—to ask the same questions, rather than just jumping to conclusions. After all, if you were going to drug and kill your manager, you sure as hell wouldn't do it in your own room, with your own scarf, and then leave the body there to be discovered by a maid while you went out partying.

Unfortunately, the one thing Russell was absolutely certain of was that Skinner would use those exact arguments to suggest Adam's guilt. Either way, the pop star would be outed by the press now, whether he liked it or not. There was no way the full details of Jack's death would stay out of the papers if Skinner had anything to do with the case.

A car horn blared outside, and Russell looked up to see Joe leap out of the way of a black cab as the driver waved an irate gesture. Russell had warned him about wandering around with that bloody Walkman on. Joe waved at him as he passed the window, and Russell smiled.

He had grown to love Joe very easily, and he knew the nervousness he was feeling right now was because he was scared of how Joe would react to the news of his test. Maybe he *should* wait until he knew the results. He couldn't. Not really.

"Ready for another?" Joe asked as he plonked himself down at the table, skin glowing, the tips of his hair newly bleached. He looked great. Alive.

"Why not?" Russell said, forcing a smile.

Joe bounced over to the bar, joked with Ron while he poured the pints, and came back smiling.

"What's up with him?" Russell asked, reading Joe's smile.

"He's got the hump 'cause Patty's upstairs helping his son perfect his drag act."

Russell laughed. Patty—or Paul as they knew him when he wasn't in drag—was a good friend to both Russell and Joe, a part-time barman in the Red Lion, and no doubt a terrible influence on Ron's twenty-something son, Scott.

Scott had only recently moved in, and had been embracing the Soho lifestyle in full, including trying out his own drag persona. Ron blustered about it, but they all knew he wouldn't mind really—he was a big-hearted guy, and he judged no one. He just liked to complain about all the make-up now cluttering the upstairs bathroom in what had once been his perfect bachelor pad.

All puff and bravado—it was Ron's way of saying he was proud of his son. He was the kind of Dad any one of his regular clientele would have loved to have, and he often stepped in as a reluctant surrogate.

It was why he ran one of the most successful and popular gay bars in Soho—everyone was welcome, and anyone caught throwing shade was kicked out.

"So, what did you find out?" Joe asked, clearly eager to hear the details. "Did you get into the hotel?"

"Better than that," Russell said. "I got into the room."

"That is impressive work, Mr Dixon," Joe said, tipping his glass to Russell.

Russell told him everything he'd seen in Adam's room and filled him on his—and Harry's—belief that Adam was being set up. What they couldn't figure out was why? It was too elaborate a scheme just to out them. Joe agreed.

"That's exactly what I thought, after talking to the barman that Adam spent the rest of the night with," Joe said. "I mean, you'd have to be a bona fide psychopath to kill someone you loved the way I'm sure Adam loved Jack, and then go out clubbing for the rest of the night with a relative stranger."

"So the question is, who is setting him up? Who has anything to gain from either killing Jack, or destroying Adam's career?"

"Jealous fans, an ex-lover, celebrity stalker?" Joe said, "I mean, it could be anyone, couldn't it?"

"What about the people closest to him? You said he and the Millard twins had been at each other's throats. If the group was splitting up, would they have motive?"

"Not from what I can see. The twins are a pair of jokers, but they're harmless," Joe said. "Adam was the real talent of the outfit. But setting him up like this stops the whole party, and I can't see the twins wanting to lose their time in the spotlight. They need him around—at least until this album is finished. That's why they've been covering for him all this time—they have as much to lose by him being outed as he does."

"You said there was a fight at the studio yesterday, though," Russell said. "What about?"

"The twins were mucking around, as usual. Adam lost it with them, and they stormed out. It happens almost every day. The only difference this time, was that Jack also lost it with Adam."

"Why?"

"I didn't hear it, but PJ was listening in," Joe said. "He told me that Jack had said he was tired of it all. He couldn't do it anymore. He told Adam that he was quitting as their manager. Adam didn't take it well. Jack lashed out, slapped Adam, and walked off before any apologies could be made."

Joe took a long swig of his beer, puzzling things over.

"The thing I don't understand is why Jack quit right at that moment? I'd seen them have far worse arguments, and no one threw in the towel. Why would Jack quit like that, in the middle of recording the album? When he knew the group was already on the verge of splitting, and he was pretty much all that was holding them together?"

Russell took a long drink. *Now or never.*

"Maybe because he just found out that he was HIV Positive."

Joe put his drink down, and stared at Russell, head cocked to one side. "What?"

"He was Positive, Joe. He found out yesterday morning."

"Oh God. That's terrible," Joe said, as a deeper frown wrinkled his brow. "Wait, how do you know that?"

Russell felt sick. He considered making something up, pretending he'd found it out this morning somehow, at the hotel. But Joe wasn't stupid. *Just tell him.*

"Because I bumped into him at the clinic yesterday morning. He was there on his own and he'd just had the worst news, and there was no one there to comfort him. So I did. I didn't know who he was, until I recognised him in the hotel this morning."

"You were at the test clinic?" Joe said, sounding nervous.

Russell nodded. He couldn't look at him. He was too scared of what he would see in his young friend's eyes. Too scared that the fear he was feeling would finally have a face.

"Being tested?"

He nodded again. He could feel the tears brimming his eyes. He wasn't strong enough for this.

"And?"

He looked up, blinking the tears away. He shrugged, tried to say he didn't know, but stumbled. Joe looked so concerned.

"I have to wait for the results," Russell finally blurted. "I don't know yet. That's why I didn't say anything."

Joe shook his head, lips tight. His concern slipped to anger. Disappointment. Then back to concern. And then he stood up, and came around the table and wrapped his arms silently around Russell, kissed his cheek and held him tight.

"You're going to be fine," he said eventually. "Only the good die young, remember?"

Russell smiled through a deep, relieved sigh. He should have known Joe would support him.

"Come on," Joe said. "Let's have another drink."

3.

JOE WAS HUNGOVER, yet again—the result of a long night with Russell in the Red Lion, which had carried on once they'd got home and opened an expensive bottle of brandy that Russell had been given when he left the force. Neither of them had been sober enough to appreciate it.

He was still shocked that Russell had gone to be tested without saying anything. They had become such close friends, and Joe was sad to think that he'd been worrying about it alone.

Joe had spent a large part of the evening admonishing him for not mentioning it, and the other half reassuring him that he would be fine. In the end, they'd agreed not to talk about it again until the results were back.

At least he wasn't late for work, this time. PJ had already decided that they should reframe the documentary to focus on this one awful incident, and be the first to break any shocking story that was going to come out of it. Adam's life was about to be scrutinised by the nation, and PJ was determined not to let everything he'd filmed so far go to waste.

"It's our responsibility," PJ had said on the voice message Joe'd found on his answering machine last night, "to tell the full story, from all sides."

Whatever way he justified it, PJ just wanted the fame of having the inside scoop. And so this morning, they would be going through all the footage from the shoot so far, and reframing the documentary to tell a different story instead—the build up to, and aftermath of, a murder.

With that in mind, PJ had called a production meeting with the whole crew, and Joe had been ordered to bring the breakfast. He was considering handing in his notice at the same time. Everything about what PJ was doing to Adam now felt calculating and manipulative. He'd always thought PJ was better than that. Clearly he'd been wrong.

Joe had phoned André at La Maison before he'd left home and ordered a few rounds of homemade baguettes, some croissants and pastries, and as he scooped in to pick them up, he had the briefest flash of a memory of Luc introducing him to the little delicatessen last summer, in the early days of their romance. He'd been so smitten at the time.

Not for the first time, Joe questioned why exactly he'd let his lovely Frenchman go. But he'd reasoned it out with himself enough times to know that it had been the right decision—he needed a bit of freedom, to be himself. Even if he'd never look at a French stick the same way again.

Joe left La Maison clutching three paper bags of warm bread and pastries and crossed the road towards the office. Passing the newsagent on the corner, he stopped, staring at the image repeated on almost every tabloid paper on the display stand—a photograph of Adam Cave being led out of the hotel in handcuffs, with a beaming Detective Skinner beside him.

Troubled Pop Star Arrested for Murder, screamed the headlines, supplemented with phrases like *sex game gone wrong*, and *drug-fuelled orgy*. Adam's trial by media had started already. No wonder PJ had been so keen to recut what they'd filmed so far. The story was hot right now, and he had the inside track on the exclusive.

Joe quickly bought a copy of each of the papers and headed to the office. Using his back to push through the revolving doors, he arrived in reception to find Jessica and Sarah loading a drinks trolley—laden with everything from coffee and tea, to beers and spirits—into the lift.

"Alright ladies?" he called. "I got breakfast."

"Who's a clever boy then?" Jessica said playfully. She always accused him of being like an enthusiastic puppy and had taken to speaking to him like one from time to time.

He stuck his tongue out at her as he crowded into the lift with them both. As they waited for the doors to close, a tall, dark-haired man in an expensive-looking designer suit marched into reception, dripping power and importance. Strikingly attractive, if the open-mouthed gapes of the girls on reception were anything to go by.

"I'm looking for a Joe Stone. I believe he works here?" he said, his voice smooth and confident.

"Oh, hello sailor," Jessica said cheekily, lifting the bags of baked goods from Joe's hands and gently pushing him out of the lift.

"That's me," Joe raised his hand as the lift doors closed.

The man turned and looked him up and down. Strong jaw, green eyes, blue button-down shirt.

"Freddie Gillespie," he said, striding towards Joe. "Of Gates, Randall and Gillespie. Thanks for seeing me."

Dark, neat hair, no sign of stubble, broad shoulders. Joe took in his features, and struggled to keep the collection of tabloid newspapers tucked under his arm, so vigorous was Gillespie's handshake.

"Uh, no problem," he said, guiding Gillespie towards the sofa area of the foyer and away from the prying eyes and ears of the two gossip queens on reception. "How can I help?"

"I represent Adam Cave," Gillespie said. "I'm his lawyer. He said you were the guy who could prove his innocence."

No preamble, no pleasantries. This was a guy who got stuff done. He looked Joe straight in the eye. Up close, his eyes were piercing—pale green, strong dark brows, long lashes. Joe felt thoroughly scrutinised.

He saw the faintest hint of a smile pass over Gillespie's lips at Joe's confusion. And then the seriousness returned.

"Look," Gillespie said, his deep voice had a slight midlands accent, long since trained out. "I'm assuming you're a 'friend' of sorts, but before we start, I need to know what else you are to him."

The inference was clear. Was Joe a lover? Was he an alibi? And would he be willing to talk, to help, to hide as requested?

"I just work for the production company here. We've been filming a behind-the-scenes thing. I'm a runner."

Gillespie looked almost annoyed by the response.

"Yes, I know that," he said. "It's just that he was quite insistent that it was you I called. So, whatever the thing is between you two, I want you to do me a favour—or not me—him. I want you to try to remember he's just a man, like you and me, and any secrets you think you may have would be better used helping prove his innocence, rather than earning yourself a few quid from the red tops, okay?"

Joe got the sense that this was not the first time Gillespie had needed to intervene in a liaison of Adam's for the good of his client.

"Oh God, no, we've never done anything like that. I just make his tea."

He realised quite how lame it sounded. Gillespie couldn't be much more than ten years older than Joe, and he was already a named partner in a law firm big enough to have a client like Adam Cave. Joe felt his face flush. Gillespie nodded.

"Okay, good. That's good. Listen, if we can do anything to keep his...personal life...out of the spotlight, that would be great. But if you aren't um… Why is he asking for you?"

"Because he knows I'll listen," Joe said. "And, if he's innocent, he knows I'll be able to prove it."

Gillespie frowned.

"You?"

"You'd be surprised," Joe said, feeling a sudden flush of defiant confidence. *Think what you like, but I'm more than just a runner.* "Let's just say, I have a reputation for solving problems like this."

It was Gillespie's turn to frown; this was obviously not what he'd been expecting to hear.

"Shall we?" Joe said, heading back towards the revolving doors, turning as he reached them to find a baffled looking Freddie Gillespie still standing in reception.

"I assume you'd rather talk in private?" Joe said, and Gillespie nodded, following him back out of the building and onto the street.

"Where are we going?" Gillespie asked.

"Somewhere safe," Joe replied. "Not far."

JOE LED HIM STRAIGHT to the Red Lion, even though he knew the bar would be closed at this time of day.

He knocked on the door, loud and hard, and then stood back on the pavement and whistled up to the half-open window above.

His friend, Paul, stuck his head out the window, face full of make-up but wig not in evidence.

"Alright love," Paul called down, his Liverpudlian accent always seemed to grate against his soft, aquiline features, especially when he was in drag. "Hang on, I'll be down in a tick."

"What are we doing here?" Gillespie asked, inadvertently looking over his shoulder.

"This," said Joe, "is my other office. And the safest place in London to have the conversation we're about to have."

Joe quite enjoyed the look of surprise on Gillespie's face as Paul opened the door. Silk nightie with a feather hem that hung just below sea-level, no shoes, exquisite make-up under his usual close-cropped, pale-brown hair.

Joe was quite used to finding Paul halfway into the transition as his drag alter ego, Patty.

"'Excuse the ensemble," Paul said, smiling coquettishly at Gillespie. "I'm just trying out a new look."

"Eyes look good," Joe said, smiling. "Green suits you."

Paul air-kissed him and guided them through to the bar.

"Coffee machine's not primed yet, but you can help yourselves to anything else," Paul said, and leaned in closer to Joe, whispering. "Jesus, Joe, he's gorgeous."

Joe shook his head and gently pushed Paul away.

"Thanks, we don't need anything, just a bit of privacy."

He led Gillespie to the window seat, feeling a moment of swagger as the lawyer still looked entirely out of his comfort zone. This was Joe's manor.

"Right," Joe said, sitting down. "Let's cut through any crap. I know he's gay. I know he loved Jack. And I know he didn't do this. So you tell me what he's told you, and I'll tell you what I know. Everything will be okay."

RUSSELL HURRIED OUT of the flat and onto the busy street below. Joe had called minutes earlier to say that he was sitting in the Red Lion with Adam Cave's solicitor and they both wanted Russell to join them. He hadn't needed to be asked twice.

The summer heat made the streets feel sticky and close. The smell of coffee, beer, cigarettes and food all sat heavily in the air—the smells of Soho.

As he crossed the square, heading towards the pub, he smiled at the couples lying intertwined on the grass, stretched out with picnics, or sleeping off the previous night's excesses. Languorous, hot, carefree. He wanted to join them, soaking in the sunshine and feeling the heat on his skin. He wanted to feel alive and not scared.

Walking into the Red Lion, he took a moment to let his eyes adjust to the gloom. The bar was empty, apart from Joe and a ridiculously handsome man that Russell assumed must be Adam Cave's lawyer.

Paul had taken up a perch at the bar, face made up, but dressed in a baggy tracksuit, trouser legs rolled up enough to show off his fluorescent yellow leg warmers. He was staring at the lawyer with undisguised lust.

"Who is *he*?" Paul asked, full wide-eyed gossip-face in place.

"None of your business," Russell said. "And way out of your league. Get us a coffee, will you?"

Paul tutted, but slipped off his stool and began priming the old coffee machine on the corner of the bar.

"The machine's not ready yet," he said. "I'll bring it over, if you like."

A likely excuse, Russell thought, but agreed and headed over to the table himself. The lawyer stood up as he approached. Tall, broad-shoulders, kind eyes.

"Russell Dixon," Joe said. "This is Mr Gillespie, Adam Cave's solicitor."

"Freddie," Gillespie said, shaking Russell's hand for just a little too long. "Thanks for coming over."

His voice was smooth, reassuring. They all sat, Paul clattered away banging coffee grounds out of the hopper over at the bar.

"My pleasure," said Russell. "I'm sure we can help."

"I hope so," Gillespie said. "The more time he spends in that place, the worse this whole thing gets for him."

"So they're still holding him, then?" Russell asked.

"You know how it is," Gillespie replied. "They just love having a big fish on the line."

"Don't they just," Russell agreed, a little bitterly. *Not they*, he thought. *Mostly Detective Skinner.*

"I'm sorry," Gillespie said, picking up on his tone. "Joe mentioned you used to be in the force. I didn't mean any offence."

"None taken. I didn't really fit in well there, anyway," he said, sadly.

"I'm not surprised," Gillespie said. "They're not good people."

On the table in front of them were a collection of the day's tabloids, and there was Skinner's smug face beaming back at him. Russell couldn't stop his lip from curling in a snarl.

"Have they charged him yet?" Russell asked, pulling one of the papers closer to him and leafing through to the full article on Adam's arrest inside.

"No," said Gillespie, firmly. "But he…" he tapped the photograph of Skinner on one of the tabloids, "he's doing everything he can to get over the threshold of proof."

"So you've met Detective Skinner, then?" Russell asked.

"Unfortunately," Gillespie confirmed. "He seems convinced Adam is guilty."

"He does tend to favour the line of least resistance," Russell said. "And Adam denies it, obviously?"

"Of course."

"So, what have they got on him?"

"It was his room they found Jack in, and his scarf Jack was strangled with. There were witnesses to a number of arguments across the days, weeks and months before. It was Adam carrying the wine they took back to their room, which they suspect is how Jack was drugged."

"So how come Adam wasn't drugged, too?" Joe asked.

"He was drinking whisky," Gillespie said. "He said he never touched the wine. Which, of course, makes them think he knew it was spiked."

Russell spread the pages of the newspaper flat, looking at the images contained in the two-page spread. Crime scene photographs, showing Jack's body, still tied up. Russell frowned, peering closer to the images.

"It's incredible they're allowed to get away with printing those," Joe said, noticing that Russell was distracted by the photographs. "How did they get hold of them? I bet that bloody Skinner handed them over. Anything to fan the flames of scandal."

Russell opened a couple of the other papers to check, but the first, *The Sun*, was the only one which had any pictures of the scene, and Russell had just spotted something disturbing.

He looked to the byline to find the credit for the article.

"Who is Hugh Brice?" he asked.

Joe cocked his head quizzically.

"He's a journalist from *Smash Hits*," Joe said. "Why?"

"Because he wrote this feature for *The Sun*," Russell said, turning the paper round to face Joe. "And those photographs were taken from outside the room, on a long lens, sometime in the night. But before the body was found, and I'd hazard before the police were called."

"What?" Joe asked, scanning the pictures.

"When I went in with the forensics team, the curtains were already closed. So, how did Hugh Brice get these photographs?"

The three of them exchanged an excited glance, and Russell and Joe stood up.

"I know where to find him," Joe said.

Russell turned to face Gillespie.

"We'll get to the truth, I promise," he said.

JOE AND RUSSELL STOOD outside the *Smash Hits* offices down a side street just off Oxford Circus. They'd been staking out the entrance for an hour or so, having been denied entry by the security guard on the front desk.

They'd been assured that Hugh Brice was in the building, but had refused to see them. Joe could tell that Russell, who was never patient at the best of times, was already considering other ways to get inside to confront the journalist.

Joe lit his third cigarette of the hour, offering one to Russell who turned it down with a shake of the head, nudging his arm as another limo pulled up to the kerb outside the *Smash Hits* office.

There had been a fairly steady stream of celebrities heading in and out of the building all morning, but so far neither Joe nor Russell had recognised many of them.

The moment the limo door opened and those trademark white trainers hit the pavement, Joe recognised the Millard twins. For once, they weren't surrounded by screaming teenagers. Heads down, they dashed into the reception and were whisked away to the lifts.

"They're not wasting much time getting their side across, are they?" Russell muttered.

"They're desperate for the publicity," Joe sniffed. "Good or bad. It's probably killing them that Adam is getting all this media coverage.

Besides, Hugh Brice has been desperate to get the scoop on the Loose Lips split. He'll have offered them the world to get their side of this story."

Russell looked across at Joe, a flicker of a frown on his face.

"What?" Joe asked.

"You don't think this Brice fella set all this up, do you? For the story?"

"What, you mean did he kill Jack and frame Adam just to have a good story to sell?"

"He did have photographs of Jack's body that were taken before the body was examined by forensics, and he obviously wasn't the one who eventually called the police."

Joe frowned, chewing his lip. It wasn't beyond the realm of possibility that a journalist could cross the line in an attempt to get the biggest story.

Jack had been blocking Hugh's access to Adam all week, and Joe had already got the idea that Hugh was threatening to out Adam in his article, anyway. What if he'd set this up as a sure fire way to expose Adam's secret and pay Jack back for blocking him?

"It's too extreme though," Joe said, shaking his head. "I'm pretty sure he had enough on Adam to print a story about his sexuality without killing Jack. I think there is something far more personal about what happened in that room. Somebody wanted Jack dead, and they wanted Adam to suffer for it."

Russell nodded.

It took another hour-and-a-half before Hugh Brice finally showed his face outside the building. He had come down to escort the twins back to their limo, all smiles and glad-handing. Joe and Russell were quick to block his path before he got back into the building.

"Hugh Brice?" Russell said, in his best police voice.

"Who's asking?" Hugh replied, looking them both up and down with a sneer. There was a glimmer of recognition when his eyes rested on Joe, but it didn't last. Hugh had looked straight through him every day he'd been on set, he was unlikely to recognise him out in the real world. It was the downside of being in such a lowly position on the celebrity food chain, but it did mean you often got to go around unnoticed.

"We're friends of Adam Cave's," Russell said, stopping Hugh's attempt to pass them and escape back inside the building. "We just want a minute of your time, it's important."

"I've got nothing to say," Hugh said. "I'm not interested."

"I think the police would be very interested," Russell said, his low voice threatening, "in how you came to have a series of photographs of Jack Eddy's body, taken from across the street, before the police themselves had even been called."

Hugh froze for a moment, a worried frown creeping over his face.

"I don't know what you're talking about," he said, trying to move past them again.

Russell shoved the newspaper against his chest.

"The photographs you printed alongside your article in here," Russell said. "They're taken before the body was discovered."

"How can you possibly know that?" Hugh asked, incredulously, a nervous laugh escaping his lips.

"Because the maid who found Jack's body told the police she'd shut the curtains after she found him to stop anyone being able to see into the room from the buildings across the road. She said there were always paparazzi hanging out in the offices opposite, trying to get snaps of famous guests. I guess she was right. Only she was already too late to stop you."

Joe could have sworn that the colour had drained from Hugh's cheeks.

"That's ridiculous," he said. But he didn't sound so sure. "That can't be right."

"So the question is," Russell continued. "How did you get these photos? Did you take them yourself? Did you set all this up to get a story that would finally sink Adam's career?"

The panic hit Hugh like a tidal wave. He stepped back involuntarily, his body recognising the need for flight.

"What?" he spluttered. "No. What?"

"What happened, Mr Brice?" Russell asked, stepping up close to Hugh, who was casting about for a way to get out of this conversation. "You got so desperate to tell the world that Adam was gay that you decided to make the proof yourself? Wasn't it enough just to print your speculations?"

"No," Hugh said. "You've got this all wrong."

Joe put a hand on Russell's arm. His shoulders had dropped into a fighter's stance, his neck extended bullishly. Joe wasn't sure he would control his temper if Hugh said the wrong thing at this stage.

"Those photographs arrived on my desk by courier the morning after Jack was found. I had nothing to do with them."

"But you were still happy to print them," Joe said.

"I don't dictate the news, kiddo," Hugh said.

He was barely into his thirties himself, so the smug use of "kiddo" grated on Joe's nerves. Letting go of Russell's shoulder, he watched his friend's punch hit Hugh squarely on the jaw. Joe stepped back between them, smiling, before Hugh could retaliate.

"I'll sue you," Hugh said, spitting a little blood onto the pavement and testing his teeth.

"Yeah, and I'll tell the cops what you've done, son," Russell replied. "Let's see who comes off worst, shall we?"

"Look, I don't know where the photos came from, I knew they were authentic, and I assumed that they'd come from one of my sources. Maybe I should have checked, but this story is moving too quickly to hang around. If I hadn't printed them, someone else would have."

"But it looks like you were the only one who got them," Russell said. "No one else has any images other than those they took outside the hotel. Somebody wanted you to have the scoop."

"What can I say?" Hugh said, smugly. "I have friends in high places."

Russell looked like he was going to swing for him again.

"Look," Hugh said. "I'm sorry I can't help you. I genuinely don't know who sent them to me, and I didn't realise they were so dodgy. If anything else comes up, I'll tell the police straight away."

It was a dig, and they both knew it. Hugh knew Russell and Joe couldn't do anything about it themselves, and he wasn't about to give up the source of his lucky break.

Before either of them could say anything else, a young woman in big, round, bright yellow glasses with a matching Alice band stuck her head out of the office door—the harried looking receptionist who had been greeting people all morning. She cleared her throat nervously.

"I'm sorry to interrupt, Mr Brice," she said, looking flustered. "There's a call for you. It's urgent."

Joe watched through the darkened windows as Hugh leaned over the reception desk to take the call. It lasted under a minute, before he was dashing back out of the door. As he stood on the street, trying to hail a black cab, Joe pestered him.

"What's going on?"

A taxi swerved across the road to collect him. Just before he closed the door, Hugh leaned back out.

"Your friend Adam Cave just tried to kill himself," he said. "He's being taken to hospital now."

Joe heard him give the name of the hospital to the taxi driver as the door closed and the cab pulled away.

4.

JOE HAD BEEN SITTING outside the private room on the top floor of the hospital for an hour already this morning.

He'd called Freddie Gillespie straight away when they heard the news, and Gillespie had confirmed that Adam had been taken to hospital after being found unconscious in his cell. But he'd also said there was no point in either of them going straight over, since Adam had been sedated and wasn't allowed any visitors. He wouldn't be able to see anyone until morning.

Joe had got there at eight to find an exhausted looking Gillespie sitting alone in the corridor, and they'd been taking it in turns to sit outside the ward and wait for news ever since.

There was a young-looking policeman outside the hospital room door, who had only come on shift just after Joe had arrived. Satisfied that Joe could handle him if anything kicked off, Gillespie had gone to fine some refreshments.

Joe still couldn't believe what they'd been told. Adam had apparently tried to hang himself but had actually just managed to damage his throat before passing out. He'd been found unconscious by the duty officer when they'd gone to take his lunch in. They'd found a pulse and Adam had been rushed to hospital.

Russell had got the name of the duty officer and had arranged to meet him when his shift ended, to try to find a little more about what had actually happened.

Since Gillespie was certain that he'd left Adam in a bullish and defensive state of mind that morning, he wasn't convinced that Adam would try to take his own life by lunchtime, which Joe had felt inclined to agree with.

The duty officer had given little away, apparently, but he *had* admitted that he'd had to go and help settle an altercation between a younger policeman and some aggressive prostitute he'd brought in, and so had missed the mid-morning checks.

Adam had apparently been interviewed a couple of times in his cell by Skinner and the other detective on the case, Alan Greenslade, which Gillespie was still spitting feathers about. They weren't supposed to talk to him without his lawyer present.

Russell had told Joe that Greenslade was a nasty little thug, who wouldn't hesitate to turn the screws to get the confession they needed.

He also reminded Joe that the police would be running out of time to hold Adam unless they could come up with enough evidence to charge him, which Gillespie was fairly confident they didn't have.

Gillespie walked back from the vending machine with two cans of Diet Coke and a couple of chocolate bars, offering Joe the choice of a Marathon or a Yorkie. Joe took the Marathon and smiled gratefully—he hadn't had breakfast yet and his stomach was making itself heard.

"Any movement?" Gillespie asked.

He'd left Joe on watch while he went to make a few calls, freshen up and get sustenance. He'd said that he didn't trust the police to keep Adam safe, and half-suspected that they had inflicted these injuries on him themselves. He wasn't going to risk letting either Skinner or Greenslade in to the room to talk to Adam without him present again.

Once Joe had reported back what Russell had found out, they'd agreed to split forces keeping their own watch on his room to make sure no one tried to hurt him.

"Nothing," Joe said. "All quiet."

The doctors had sedated Adam to let him sleep through the night. Gillespie was waiting until he came round again to be able to talk to him properly, and Joe was keen to join him. As they tucked into their chocolates, Gillespie looked across at Joe, watching him chew.

"So you enjoy all this then?" he asked. "Being a private detective?"

Joe smiled.

"I wouldn't call it that, so much," he said. "It's not a job or anything. But I guess I do enjoy it, yes. I don't like seeing people getting into trouble for things they didn't do, especially not friends."

"Very noble," Gillespie said.

"And I also hate the fact that coppers like Skinner and his mates have it in for innocent people, just because they happen to be gay."

Gillespie smiled a little sadly.

"Oh, but that's fairly universal, isn't it?" he said.

It was true. Joe had been reasonably well protected from that kind of prejudice, living in Soho and working with PJ, but even so, he'd seen his fair share of gay bashings and abuse.

Luc had been so open about his sexuality, and he'd tried to encourage Joe to be confident holding hands in the street, or kissing in bars, but they'd had enough awful comments hurled at them, even in supposed safe places in Soho, that Joe never really felt comfortable with any public displays of affection.

"Most of the people I work with are just the same," Gillespie continued. "I can't stand it."

It was the first time that Joe had even considered that Gillespie may also be gay. He had appeared so straightlaced, in his sharp suit and neat tie, but those, of course, were just trappings of the job.

"Yes, I imagine it must all be a bit macho," Joe said.

"It is. Even I have my moments," Gillespie said, with a small chortle.

The door to the hospital room opened and the kindly nurse who'd kept Joe informed of progress walked over to them. Lydia—according to her name badge—was a short, wiry, red-haired Irish woman, with an infectious grin and a compelling turn of phrase.

"Well," she said. "He's awake, and he said he's up to visitors. But I'm only going to give you a few minutes with him for now. He's very tired, and he's been a bit battered, poor boy."

Her comment was pointed, loud enough for the young police officer to hear. It was clear that she blamed the police for Adam's condition.

"We'll go easy on him," Gillespie said.

"I'm just glad he's alright," Joe agreed, and Lydia patted his arm with a soft smile on her lips.

"Try not to get him too worked up, alright my love?" she said, scuttling off down the corridor to her next patient.

Joe nodded to the young policeman as they passed him, but he continued to stare straight ahead, making no eye contact. *Suit yourself.*

ADAM CAVE LAY ON his back in the bed, propped up on his pillows, with the covers tucked under his armpits. His pale green hospital gown made him look unwell, highlighting the bruises on his face and neck. His hair was flat and lank and, for probably the first time since he'd met him, Joe saw the human Adam Cave. He looked so sad and alone.

"How're you holding up?" Gillespie asked, pulling up a chair next to Adam's bed.

"Feel like I've gone ten rounds with Chris Eubank," Adam said. "Am I still under arrest?"

"Afraid so, there's a goon outside the door, in case you try to make a run for it."

This elicited a small chuckle from Adam. Short-lived and hollow.

"What happened, Adam?" Gillespie asked, taking his client's hand in his.

"Oh, apparently, I tried to hang myself," Adam said bitterly.

Joe poured a glass of water from the jug and handed it to Adam.

"You haven't got anything stronger, have you?" he asked.

Gillespie slipped a hip flask from his inside pocket, opened it and passed it over. Adam took a grateful swig, coughed at the burn and took another.

"Thanks," he said, as Gillespie screwed the lid back on and tucked the flask away.

"So, what really happened?" Gillespie asked.

"Those two detectives were questioning me about Jack," Adam said, and a shudder ran over him as he said Jack's name. "I had nothing more to tell them, but they wouldn't believe me. The fat one got really uptight about it. Got me in a headlock. Wanted to see how I liked being strangled."

"Jesus," Joe muttered.

"I tried to fight him off, but he had me so tight around the neck I could barely breathe. Next thing I know I'm being loaded into the back of an ambulance and I arrive here. Doctors have been talking to me like I'm some kind of basket case since I woke up."

"We're going to sue them," Gillespie said. "Don't you worry."

Adam shrugged. A broken man compared to the one Joe had been working with the last few weeks.

"Maybe I should just have told them," Adam said. "Come clean."

Joe froze. He had spent all this time convinced that Adam was innocent of Jack's death. Was he about to find out that he'd been wrong?

"Adam, we talked about this," Gillespie said. "You don't say anything without me in the room, and you don't tell them anything that isn't relevant to the case. You didn't do it. You don't know who did, and no amount of beating is going to make you confess."

"It doesn't matter, anyway," Adam said.

He was a man defeated. Nobody had stopped to consider that he had just lost the one person he relied on to do everything for him. The friend he trusted with his deepest secrets. The man he loved. How was he supposed to cope alone?

"Should have told them what, Adam?" Joe asked, and Gillespie frowned at him.

"It's alright," Adam said to his lawyer, giving his hand a squeeze. "I should have told them that I actually spent most of that night with someone else, but I didn't want to drag him into it."

"The barman?" Joe asked. Gillespie's jaw dropped. Adam nodded. Head cast down, embarrassed.

"What?" Gillespie spluttered. "You've had an alibi all this time?"

"Not necessarily," Joe said quickly. "I spoke to the guy, and he seemed to think there was over an hour between you and Jack leaving the bar to go to your room, and you coming back down alone. He's also none too polite about your mood on the night."

"I don't blame him," Adam said. "I thought I wanted to let off some steam. But when I got out there, I realised I just wanted to be with Jack and I knew it would never happen. I'd already lost him."

"Come on Adam," Gillespie said. "He'd quit as your manager, but you hadn't lost him."

"You don't understand," Adam said. "He was dying."

So he did know.

"You *knew*?" Joe asked.

Adam looked up at him with a mix of confusion and anger.

"*You* knew?" Adam replied incredulously.

"A friend saw him in the clinic," Joe clarified. "He'd just had the diagnosis."

"That's why he was leaving," Adam said sadly. "He didn't want to spend any more time on the group. He said he needed to live for himself for a while. He told us all that morning. That's why the bloody twins stormed out."

"What diagnosis?" Gillespie asked, still trying to catch up.

"He was HIV Positive," Adam said. "That's why I knew I'd already lost him. Not just as a manager. He needed to go and do his own thing."

"I thought you two were...together." Gillespie began.

Adam smiled.

"No," Adam said. "Oh, I loved him alright, enough for both of us. But I wasn't his type. He liked them a bit older, and a lot freakier. But I did love him."

"So that's what the fight was about in the studio?" Joe asked.

"I can't believe all three of us made it about ourselves, when poor Jack had just had such bad news. You expect the twins to be selfish, but I behaved no better. And I owed him so much more."

A fat tear brimmed over onto his cheek. A little thought was brewing in Joe's mind.

"If he told all three of you," Joe said, thinking aloud. "Do you think he told anyone else? A lover perhaps, a former partner. Maybe that's who did this?"

Adam shook his head.

"There wasn't anyone," he said. "Not anyone serious. He'd had a partner, on and off for the last few years. Crazy guy. Sound engineer. We met him at Live Aid. Anyway, they'd have these huge fights, and then get back together. A real rollercoaster.

It was only when he died—of AIDS, of course—that I realised how much Jack had loved him. He just wasn't the same after that. He said he was fine, but something had changed. I made him go and get tested. I mean, the risk for him was high, anyway, but he was still sleeping around, you know? It was really destructive."

"So, there was no one who could have found out, who would have been angry enough about it to kill him?"

"Sure. I don't know. Maybe. Perhaps he called someone over after I'd left him, but he was completely out of it. I've been running over it in my mind ever since I got arrested. We'd all spent the night putting the world straight, you know. It was tense, with the twins, but PJ had forced us all to sit down together and talk it through. He'd bought all the wine, he kept us all in the room until we agreed that going our separate ways would be the best thing all round. For all of us, as people, not as the group. I could tell the twins were still pissy about it, but they could get someone to pick them up as a duo, no problem. Stock, Aitken and Waterman have been banging on their door for months now. It'd be right up their street."

Adam sighed again, readjusted himself on the pillows and winced as another bruise got pressed awkwardly.

"Anyway, when Jack said he wanted to head off to bed, I couldn't see much point staying, so I suggested we have a nightcap together, just the two of us. I was worried about him—I didn't want him to be alone. He can be quite self-destructive when he'd down."

"So you took a bottle of wine up to your room," Joe said.

"Yes," Adam replied. "We took one from the table—PJ had ordered another couple of bottles, but I could tell Jack wanted to go. Bless him, PJ was also worried about Jack. He told me to take care of him."

Adam laughed sadly, remembering.

"He even took me aside and told me to tell Jack how I felt about him. Before it was too late. As though Jack would suddenly realise that he loved me too."

He shook his head.

"Did you tell him?" Joe asked.

"What? That I was in love with him?" Adam smiled. "No. What would have been the point? I wasn't his type, and he certainly wasn't about to start a new relationship, given the news he'd just had. He just wanted to go away, crawl into a hole, and not have to worry about anything."

"So what happened?" Joe asked.

"We left the table, took one of PJ's bottles with us, and picked up an ice bucket from the bar on the way. I should have just left the wine behind. I'd already had more than enough. But PJ insisted we take one up with us."

"Was the bottle already open when you picked it up?" Joe asked.

Adam frowned, trying to remember, but shook his head.

"I don't know," he admitted. "They think I drugged him, don't they? Because I didn't drink any of it myself?"

Gillespie nodded.

"Why didn't you?" Joe asked.

"Like I said, I'd had enough wine," Adam said. "I moved on to whisky. I just took it in case Jack felt like more. I mean, Jack doesn't usually even drink." Adam flinched. "Didn't," he corrected himself, and his voice caught.

"But he had been drinking that night?"

"Yes. I should have stopped him, but it wasn't the time to judge him. He was properly tying one on, and I didn't blame him. He'd even done a couple of lines down in the bar."

"Oh, you didn't…?" Gillespie asked, sounding annoyed. Adam had not long been out of his last stint in rehab and was supposed to be sworn off the hard stuff.

"No," Adam reassured him. "I wanted to, though. But I could tell they were all watching me. I didn't want to give any of them the power."

He shook his head.

"Anyway, me and Jack sat up in my room and talked for a bit. He was so scared of what was going to happen. I noticed him getting slurry, but it was to be expected, really, given everything he'd had. I mean, it was his first drink for well over a year. I thought it was better if he drank enough to pass out and not have to think anymore. Just for that night. Maybe if I'd drunk some of the wine too, it wouldn't have hit him so hard. Maybe I would have noticed there was something wrong with it."

"Yeah," said Gillespie. "And maybe you'd be dead too."

Adam frowned, looking from Joe to Gillespie and back again.

"This is all my fault, isn't it?" he asked. "Whoever did this to Jack, did it to get to me, to ruin my life, to set me up. But why? Why *kill* him?"

Another cog clicked into place for Joe. He got the sudden feeling that he'd been looking at the motivation for Jack's death from the wrong angle all along.

JOE HAD CALLED RUSSELL from the payphone in the hospital and told him what he thought. Russell had agreed to meet him in the Red Lion at lunchtime, but Joe had to go into the recording studio first. There were a few loose ends he wanted to tie up.

PJ had been scheduled to interview the twins that morning—getting his new film on track. He'd asked Joe to be there, but Joe had made up yet another excuse, not wanting to tell PJ that he was in the hospital with Adam.

He understood that his boss needed to make something out of the footage they'd already captured, and he knew that an exclusive on one of the hottest stories of the year was too much to pass up, but he hated the way PJ had just changed his tune on Adam, dropping any pretence of friendship so that he could hang Adam out to dry with a clear conscience. Joe wanted no part of it.

He planned to tell PJ to his face that he was resigning his position, and he also wanted to double-check something that had been bothering him since talking to Adam. Why had PJ been so intent on Adam telling Jack how he felt that night? Why had he insisted they take a bottle of wine up with them? Had he been the one to spike their drink?

Joe was finding it hard to believe that PJ would go as far as to kill Jack in order to get something out of the footage they'd filmed before the big bust up, but he couldn't think of any other explanation. He had to ask him what he'd done, and for a moment, he wished he had got Russell to come and meet him at the studio instead. What if this turned nasty? Could he take PJ in a fight? He reckoned he could.

He walked through the quiet studio, wondering how the morning's interview had gone. What kind of mood would he find his boss in? Joe spotted movement in the recording booth, and crossed to the window to see PJ sitting inside alone, watching a monitor.

From this angle, Joe could see that it was a recording of the conversation they'd filmed through that same window between Jack and Adam, before Jack had slapped him and walked out. PJ stopped the footage and spooled it back, watching it again. What was he doing?

PJ looked up as Joe stepped into the room.

"Ah, Joe, you're here," PJ said. "Look at this."

Again, he wound the tape back and, looking up expectantly at Joe, he pressed play. The scene came to life, this time with sound they had recorded directly from the mixing desk. Adam's voice was the louder of the two, because he was directly in front of the microphone, but Jack could be heard clearly enough.

"You three should keep going, Adam," Jack said. He sounded exhausted. "Finish the album. Give them what they want and part company nicely. Life's too short."

"I can't," Adam said.

"You don't need me to hold your hand. There are good guys on at the label that can manage you all better than I can right now."

"You can't leave me," Adam said. "I won't let you do this."

"You don't have any choice, Adam. I'm sorry. I have to go. Just do this album with the boys, sing their stuff. I know you hate it, but then you'll be free."

"I can't do it. I won't."

"You have to. There's a contract, remember. The label needs its pound of flesh."

"But their songs are terrible, I can't even sing them."

Jack stepped closer to him, speaking quietly.

"Look. Everything we did, all the new songs? They're yours, okay? Don't waste them on the group. They're what will make you great, on your own."

Adam grabbed the handful of music scores from the stand in front of him and threw them at Jack, papers floating ineffectually to the ground.

"After everything I've done for you? How can you do this to me?"

Jack actually laughed. The last of the papers wafted down to the floor. He stared defiantly at Adam.

"Don't you see?" Jack asked. "I'm dying here. None of it means anything anymore. Not the money, not the songs, not the awards. Not even you."

"Fine," Adam bellowed, causing the sound to distort slightly. "Go then! But don't come crying to me when you need someone to hold your hand. You made this bed."

Jack lingered for the slightest moment as the expression on his face turned from anxious guilt to cold stone. The slap came out of nowhere, hard and fast. Adam's hand shot to his cheek, shocked. Jack stood still, breathing hard, but he couldn't stop the tears from coming. Adam tried to apologise, but he turned and walked away. Adam's face was dark and brooding. PJ stopped the tape and looked up at Joe.

"Well?" he asked.

"Well what?"

"Don't you see?" PJ said. "That's the moment. Look at his face. If that doesn't say cold-blooded killer, I don't know what does."

He waved his hand towards the monitor, as though questioning why Joe couldn't see the obvious conclusion.

"You think Adam killed Jack—like that—because he threatened to stop being his manager?"

"They were lovers, Joe," he said, sotto voce, as though sharing some great secret. "Jack was ending it with him in more ways than one."

"No, PJ," he said, trying to keep hold of his rising temper. "They were *not* lovers. Adam loved Jack, but they were never lovers, and they were never going to be."

"But the twins said..." PJ stammered. "They said the band was splitting up because it was always them against Adam and Jack."

"But not like that," Joe said. "There was never anything like that between Adam and Jack. You've got it all wrong."

"But I..." PJ looked nervously back at the monitor. Adam's angry face frozen in time, Jack on his way out of the room.

Those synapses that had already been firing in Joe's brain sparked again.

"Jesus," Joe said. "What did you do, PJ?"

"What? Nothing." But he didn't sound so sure. "What are you saying?"

"You encouraged Adam to go upstairs with Jack. You told him to tell him how he felt—to tell Jack that he was in love with him."

"That was just advice from a friend. It was obvious he wanted to be with him."

"But you had already made sure that Jack had done a few lines of coke. You'd made sure the wine was flowing, even though Jack didn't drink. You insisted they take a bottle up with them."

"He looked like he might need to let his hair down," PJ said. "What exactly are you accusing me of?"

PJ stood up, trying to look intimidating but was thwarted by both his height and weight. Joe stood still, unflinching.

"You knew that if the group didn't get back in the studio, you would only have half a film. That's why you went over to the hotel, and got them all together, to agree to use the film to tell the full story of the break-up instead, like you'd always planned."

"So? Where's the harm in that? I have a company to run. We made a commitment to deliver a film. I couldn't just let it fizzle out halfway through, could I?"

"But Adam didn't want to play ball, did he? He was sick of it all."

"He said that, yes. And so did Jack. Can you imagine? The manager of one of the country's biggest pop groups and you're sick of it?"

"He was," Joe said, "But not in the way you think."

"I know," PJ said. "He was tired of all the bickering. He was tired of having to cover for Adam, and keep his secret. Look, the twins knew they'd done the wrong thing, telling Hugh Brice about Adam's sexuality, but they only wanted to use the threat to make sure the group stayed together long enough to finish the album. Hugh wasn't going to publish the story. Unless he had to."

PJ relaxed again, just a little, leaning against the sound desk. He was settling into his story.

"After you took Adam back to the hotel, I spoke to the twins. They were desperate. They've spent all their money. They needed this album to happen."

"So you thought you'd help them—and yourself—out by getting something on Adam that would force him to see the album through? Knowing that you would get great footage of a group in tatters trying to hold it together for that last album. But you took it too far, as usual."

"What?"

But Joe could see by PJ's flustered expression that he'd got it right. He was only annoyed that he hadn't spotted it before.

"You bought the wine, you made sure that Jack had a little more cocaine to take back to the room to ease any tension, you told Adam it was now or never, sold him the big love story, encouraged him to confess his love. Why?"

"All I wanted was for them to be caught in bed together. I'd arranged for a photographer to be in the office block on the other side of the street. He was supposed to get the photos to go with Brice's story. I just thought that if we had the story waiting to happen, we could persuade Adam to stay on in the group, at least until the album was done. And the film, of course. I didn't mean for any of this to happen."

"So what happened?" Joe asked, his heart racing. "How did Jack end up dead? What did you do, PJ?"

"I don't know," PJ said, slumping back into the chair, facing the monitor again. "The photographer said they just sat there talking and drinking. At one point Jack started stripping off, and he thought we were about to get the money shot, but then Adam just put him in bed, and Jack tried to sit up, but then slumped again and then, after a while, Adam got his coat and left him there."

"Why didn't you tell the police?"

"There was nothing to tell, was there?"

"What did you spike the wine with?"

"I didn't spike the wine," PJ said defensively.

He looked at Joe, studying his face to see if he could get away with any more covering up, and obviously deciding he couldn't.

"I mixed some Mandrax with the cocaine," he said, reluctantly. "Just a little. I guessed he needed something to make him more susceptible to Adam's advances."

Mandrax was the official name of a drug known as Quaaludes on the street. It gave a powerful high, but also had a reputation for making people relaxed enough to have free sex, with no inhibitions. There had been a number of high-profile cases of Mandrax being used as a date rape drug. It was also widely known to have fatal consequences if taken in high enough doses when mixed with alcohol. People would just lie down and go to sleep and never wake up. *Was that what had happened to Jack?*

"But you sent them up with a bottle of wine," Joe said. "You know you shouldn't mix Ludes with booze. You killed him, PJ."

"But he didn't drink," PJ insisted, confused. "Adam had been drinking all afternoon, but Jack was teetotal. He always took his escape in powder form."

"So why insist they take a bottle with them?"

"I thought Adam needed some Dutch courage, too. Why on earth would Jack suddenly start drinking after all this time? He wasn't supposed to be drinking."

And Joe had the answer.

"Because he knew he was already dying," he said. PJ looked confused.

"He had HIV, PJ. He'd found out that morning. That's why he was quitting the group. Not so that he and Adam could set up home together, not to hurt the twins, and not to ruin your film. He thought he was dying, and when he went back to the room with his best friend, and they talked things through, and he started relaxing, he let himself have a drink. Because how could it possibly hurt now?"

"So I did kill him?" PJ asked, in disbelief.

"Yes," said Joe. "I think you did."

JOE WALKED INTO the function room out the back of the Red Lion to find Paul in tracksuit bottoms and a crop top, walking Ron's son, Scott, through a step-sequence for a dance routine.

Scott tottered along behind him in a pair of unfeasibly high heels, wobbling like a newborn foal, with his own tracksuit rolled up to mid-calf and his tongue sticking out of the corner of his mouth. Paul looked round at the interruption.

"Hiya love," Paul said. "Can't stop—Miss Terri over here is on stage on Friday, and right now she's more *What the Fuck* than *What a Feeling*, if you get my drift?"

"You seen Russell?" Joe asked, smiling. "Ron said he came out this way."

"Gone to the bog, love. He'll be out in a jiffy." Paul said, turning back to Scott and clapping his hands. "Right, come on. And five, six, seven, eight..."

Joe left them bickering about which of Scott's left feet Paul was going to shove up Scott's arse, and went back into the bar. Russell had joined him by the time he'd got the pints in and they retired to their usual table.

"You seen those two back there?" Russell asked, still chortling.

"Flashdance eat your heart out," Joe replied. "How are you?"

Russell raised a warning eyebrow—he'd made Joe promise not to keep asking how he was.

"I've had a quiet morning," Russell said. "What about you? How was Adam? Did you get to speak to him?"

"Yeah. Sounds like it was one of Skinner's guys who got a little heavy handed with the questioning. They tried to make it look like he'd tried to hang himself. Gillespie's going to sue."

"I hope he gets their badges," Russell said.

"I wouldn't like to go up against him, that's for sure," Joe agreed.

"Where've you been, then?" Russell asked. "You called ages ago. I'm already two pints in."

Joe sat back, a little smugly.

"I think I've solved the mystery," he said, smiling.

Russell looked confused.

"And," Joe continued. "The killer is on his way down to the police station now to confess all."

Russell's confusion turned to incredulousness.

"And you're here having a drink and gloating about it instead of getting down there and making sure that goes to plan."

"You worry too much," Joe said.

Russell leaned back, rocking on the short stool he was perched on.

"Pray, tell then, Sherlock. Whodunnit?"

Joe grinned, took a drink of his pint, eyes glistening over the rim of his glass.

"PJ," he said triumphantly, smiling at Russell's frown.

"PJ?"

"Yes," Joe said. "Only he didn't mean to kill him."

"Right?" Russell prompted.

Joe filled him in on his conversation with Adam, and his follow-up with PJ, including his boss's confession.

"He'd spiked the cocaine Jack had been taking with a little Mandrax. He knew the group was splitting up, and he thought if he could catch Adam and Jack in bed together, he could use it to blackmail them all into sticking around until the album—or at least his film—was finished. He didn't know Jack would start drinking as well though."

"Well, at least it explains how Hugh Brice got those photographs," Russell said. "But I'm afraid I'm going to have to disagree with your detective work there, Joe."

"What?" Joe asked, the smug grin falling from his face. "Why?"

"Because, if you remember, Jack died by being strangled, not from an overdose," Russell said. "Sure, the drugs put him in a catatonic state, so he couldn't fight back, but someone still went in there and tied him up the way they did, and left all those handy clues that helped to frame Adam, and unless PJ is admitting to all that, then I'm afraid you've got the wrong man."

"Oh," Joe said, feeling deflated. "You're right. Dammit."

CARELESS WHIPSER

Russell smiled kindly as Joe took another sip of his pint, mentally running over everything he'd heard. It had all made so much sense, thinking that PJ had done it, but of course Russell was right. They were back to square one, though it felt like they were just going round and round in circles.

They both looked up as Freddie Gillespie walked into the bar.

"Ah," he said. "I thought I'd find you here."

"Charming," Russell said, smiling. "Bunch of soaks that we are."

Joe looked at Russell askance. *Are you flirting with him?* Russell pulled a face at Joe, quick and playful, as Gillespie arrived at their table.

"How's Adam?" Joe asked.

"Getting there," Gillespie said. "They've agreed to keep him in the hospital though and not put him back into custody. So I've taken a break. The twins wanted to go in and see him now that he's feeling stronger, so I thought I'd give them some space. I've left them with strict instructions to call me if the police show up, and good old nurse Lydia is on red alert for any funny business."

Joe smiled. He wouldn't want to try to cross nurse Lydia.

"I've just been down at the police station filing a long list of complaints against the officers who hurt him," Gillespie continued. "If I get it right, that Detective Greenslade will be on traffic duty for the rest of his working life. He's been suspended, pending an inquiry. Now I'm gunning for Skinner."

"Well done, you," Russell said. "Greenslade will take the fall, for sure. But Skinner's like Teflon—you'll be lucky to get anything to stick to him."

"You leave it with me," Gillespie said. "If I set my mind to something, I usually get it."

His tone of voice, and the way the lawyer held Russell's eye on that statement, Joe got the distinct feeling he was flirting back.

"Anyway, I hear someone else has just turned themselves in," Gillespie said, brightly.

"Ah, yes," Joe replied. "That'd be my fault. I encouraged my former boss, PJ, to go down and admit his part in supplying the drugs that helped to knock poor Jack out. I thought I'd solved the case for a moment there."

"PJ?" Gillespie asked. "The TV programme guy? Why would he do that?"

"Long story," Joe said. "Basically, he had a film to deliver. And he'd promised the twins he'd come up with a way to get everyone back in the studio to finish the album, and the film."

Russell slammed his pint down on the table, making both Joe and Gillespie jump.

"Oh, for fuck's sake," he said, suddenly standing up.

"What?" Joe asked, also standing.

"The twins," Russell exclaimed, turning to Gillespie, who obviously clocked his meaning immediately.

"Shit, I left them going up to see Adam," Gillespie exclaimed.

Russell was already running for the door, with a shouted instruction for Gillespie to call the hospital and make sure they were detained.

BY THE TIME Russell and Joe sprinted into the private wing of the hospital, they were expecting the worst. The twins had gone to see Adam just as Gillespie had left the hospital over an hour ago. If they'd had malicious intent, Adam would have stood no chance.

Nurse Lydia met them as they ran up the corridor.

"Calm down, you lads," she said, her Irish accent both maternal and authoritative. "We'll have no running in my corridors. Anyway, he's fine. No thanks to you lot."

Russell stopped, chest heaving as he tried to catch his breath.

"Are they still here?" Joe asked, seemingly unperturbed by the high-speed dash across Soho.

"Oh, yes," the nurse smiled. "They should have known better than to try to trick a good Catholic girl with a basic twin routine."

They both obviously looked bemused enough to elicit a clarification from her.

"This one boy arrived, asking if he could go in and visit his friend. Obviously, I recognised him as one of the twins, and Mr Gillespie had said it was fine, so I let him through. And then, only minutes later I get a call from one of the patients down the far end of the corridor, so I go all the way down, but when I get there, the poor woman's fast asleep, so I know someone's playing silly buggers. Anyway, when I get back to the desk, the young fella is just leaving. "Thanks he says, he's sleeping, so." Makes a big thing of his goodbye, and off he goes. Only he must think I'm born yesterday, because he's wearing the other hat, isn't he? The one with the L backwards. As if I didn't know there were two of them. I may be old, but I don't live under a rock. My girls have got those boys plastered all over their bedroom walls. The feckin' eejits."

Russell laughed.

"So I send your little work experience police chappy running after that one, and I go into Mr Cave's room to find the other bugger still in there. But he obviously hadn't counted on Mr Cave being almost right as rain again—thanks to some extra TLC from his aunty Lydia," she pointed both thumbs proudly at her robust chest. "Because he seemed more than a little surprised to be pinned to the bed with his arm half-breaking up behind his scrawny little back, and Mr Cave sitting on him, riding him like a bronco."

She chortled at the memory.

"But Adam's okay?" Joe asked.

"Absolutely," she beamed. "Sure, I don't know why everyone's got it in for that poor soul. He's such a nice lad. Did you know he bought his mum a house? A house!"

"Where are the twins now?" Russell asked. "Have they been arrested?"

"Oh no," Lydia smiled. "Your lovely lawyer friend called to warn me they were up to no good. A bit late, mind, but he said to hold off calling the police for a while, until you two got here. Butch and Sundance."

She took a moment to look them both over, as though checking the description.

"Took a little persuading to get the young plod to calm down, but I told him to keep guard while I called the boys in blue. I suppose they're all still holed up in room four over there."

She beamed at them and led the way.

"He really is lovely looking, isn't he? That lawyer," she said, and then nudged Joe's arm conspiratorially, leaning in to whisper. "Though I suppose he's more your type than mine, isn't that so?"

"Something like that," Joe laughed.

"Always the way," she sighed. "They're in there, lads."

"You'd better go and call the police now, Lydia," Russell said. "And thank you."

Lydia smiled and patted his arm, wandering off towards her desk muttering about "such a waste" and "charming young men".

Russell opened the door and Joe followed him in to find the twins squatting, back to back on the floor, hands cuffed together, and a nervous looking officer—who made even Joe look old—watching over them from a plastic chair on the other side of the room.

"You?" Luke spat, staring angrily at Joe as he came in.

"Thanks, officer. We'll take it from here," Russell said, sounding official.

"But," the young policeman stammered. "I'm supposed to wait for my senior officer."

"And here I am, lad," Russell said. "Detective Skinner's been held up."

The policeman looked dubious, but stood up.

"Just wait outside the door, there's a good boy," Russell said. "In case I need any assistance."

Still looking dubious, the officer complied. Joe shook his head in amused disbelief as Russell scraped the chair across the tiled floor and straddled it, facing the twins on the floor.

"Lads, lads, lads," he tutted. "You didn't really think you'd get away with it, did you?"

"No comment," Liam said, sullenly.

"No problem," Russell replied, casually. "Good old PJ's already down at the station spilling his guts. Poor bugger thinks it's his fault. But we all know different, don't we?"

Neither twin could even look up anymore.

"PJ tells us he'd hatched a plan," Joe said. "To catch Adam and Jack together and use the photographs to blackmail them into finishing the album."

"Did you really think that was going to work out in the long run?" Russell chimed in, in his best disappointed voice.

"How are we supposed to know what PJ was up to?" Luke asked. "He just wanted a story—any story—for his stupid film."

"But you needed more than that, didn't you?" Joe asked. "Adam was going to leave and, since he'd written all of the songs on the last three albums, he'd be taking any future royalties too. You two would get, what? Five percent? Little more than backing singers, really."

"We weren't going to let him drop us," Liam said, and his brother flinched, before both of their petulant lips curled into a snarl.

"He always thought he could just do what he liked and Jack would clear it up," said Luke. "And Jack always did."

"So it seemed only right that PJ try to stitch them both up, so that Jack couldn't help him this time," Liam completed. "They would have no choice but to do the album, with our songs. So that we could have the credit we deserve."

"Only, the new album wouldn't be enough, would it?" Joe asked. "Adam was right. Your songs are terrible, and the album would tank. And take your reputation with it."

"They were *all* our songs, too," Liam whined. "Those first albums. We were part of those hits."

"No," Joe said. "They were his. And you knew that. You needed to do something drastic to get anything from those early albums."

Liam sighed. Luke hung his head. They weren't going to be able to talk their way out of this.

"We thought we could go along with PJ's plan, and catch them together, and blackmail them to get our names on the credits too. To get listed. Then the back catalogue would be our songs too, see?" Luke said.

"Adam was so scared of everyone finding out about him," Liam joined in. "But the way they were talking, down in the bar, we thought they were just going to come straight out and tell everyone. They kept going on about telling the truth. And if they'd done that, there'd be nothing at all. We'd look like idiots."

Russell raised an eyebrow.

"So we added a few more 'Ludes to the cocaine that we gave Jack to take upstairs with them, and smiled and said we wished them well," Liam continued.

"We reckoned, once they got upstairs, Adam would be straight on it too. He always liked to pretend he was clean, but we knew he would succumb. They were as bad as each other."

"So you planned to kill them both?" Joe asked.

The twins shook their heads in unison.

"Just Adam," Luke said quietly. "He'd been drinking, see? A lot. We thought, with the mix, it would do for him."

"I mean, Jack didn't drink," Liam protested. "How were we supposed to know?"

"But when we saw Adam come back down and go off with that

barman, we knew it wasn't going to work how we'd planned. We heard Adam say that Jack had passed out, so we had to come up with something else," Luke said.

"It was so quick," said Liam. "It was perfect."

"Shame it didn't work out for you boys," Russell said, smiling. "You'll have plenty of time to think of a better plan next time. The police will be along shortly to take your statements. We'll be sure to tell them everything you've just told us."

The looks on the twins' faces were priceless as Russell and Joe strode back out of the room, just in time to see Detective Skinner arrive at the end of the corridor. The officer guarding the door looked panicked.

"Don't worry, son," Russell said. "I'll handle him."

"What are you doing here," Skinner demanded, his nasal, weaselly voice grating on Russell's nerves immediately.

"Your job, by all accounts," Russell replied. "Two men, the Millard twins—band mates of Adam Cave—just made a second attempt on his life. The first having resulted in the death of his friend and their manager, Mr Jack Eddy. They've admitted it all to me. I'll be happy to give you a statement. They're handcuffed in that room there, thanks to the quick thinking of your young officer here, who managed to apprehend both suspects single-handedly."

Skinner's mouth opened and closed again quickly.

"Looks like you arrested the wrong guy yet again, Detective," Joe sneered. "It's becoming a bit of a habit. Anyone would think you had some kind of prejudice."

Gillespie arrived, looking calm and collected, though he, too, must have sprinted through the summer streets in that fine suit.

"Detective Skinner," he said. "Good of you to show up. I assume my client can now be released, with a fulsome apology from you and your colleagues."

"We haven't finished our investigation," Skinner whined.

"Oh, you're finished alright," Gillespie replied, the threat clear for Skinner to hear.

Russell smiled, turning away, so that only Joe could see him pretending to fan his face with his hand.

"Not to worry," Skinner said, false charm restored. "I'm sure we'll be seeing your client again very soon. He can't seem to keep himself out of trouble, can he?"

Gillespie stepped up so close to Skinner that their noses were almost touching.

"Your days are numbered, son," said Gillespie, close and threatening. "Us lot? We're *all* coming for you."

5.

THE RED LION WAS crammed for Cabaret Night. It wasn't a full Frock Show, but the debut act on the glamour stage tonight was Ron's son, Scott, and, according to Patty, the poor queen was like jelly back stage.

The twins had been arrested, and were now answering questions of their own, and with PJ's full statement in the bag, the three of them were in a lot of trouble.

Joe almost felt sorry for PJ, but then remembered what he'd tried to do to someone who'd apparently been a friend, and the feeling faded.

He had no doubt that the police would be giving all three of them a good grilling in the cells, but at least Skinner and Greenslade had now been removed from the case—both temporarily suspended, pending an inquiry, according to Gillespie.

Russell still claimed that Skinner would get away with it, and Greenslade would take the fall, but they important thing was that they had been challenged.

As yet, no apology had been issued, but Gillespie said that suited him just fine. He was taking this very personally.

Adam Cave had declined the invitation to join them tonight, despite having come out in what had turned out to be a gentle and compassionate interview with Hugh Brice.

The journalist had obviously felt bad for his part in the whole sordid affair, and had actually done right by Adam, and still managed to get his story.

Adam was taking some time off before heading back into the studio, to record the solo album he wrote with Jack.

The bar throbbed and hummed with a lively buzz. The people here happy and at home, if not a little pissed. Just as Patty called an intermission, demanded "a Manhattan, darling" and swanned off the stage, Joe saw Russell push through the doors.

"You're late," Joe said. "Where have you been?"

"The clinic called," Russell said, his face glum. "I've just come from there."

"And?" Joe asked, quietly, trying not to draw anyone else's attention to their tense conversation.

Russell shook his head.

"What does that mean?" Joe asked, panic in his voice.

"I'm Negative," he said, breaking into a smile.

Joe launched himself into a bear hug, showering Russell in kisses.

"Get a room," Patty said, and Joe laughed.

"Oh, please," Joe laughed.

He turned to see Freddie Gillespie standing just behind them.

"What's he doing here?" Joe asked.

"I invited him," Russell said. "He seemed like he could do with letting his hair down a bit."

Patty was already rounding everyone back up to the stage as Freddie Gillespie offered to buy both Russell and Joe a drink.

As she took to the stage, belting out "I'm Every Woman" to a chorus of cheers, Joe stepped up to help Gillespie with the drinks.

"You should ask him out, you know," Joe said.

"Who's that?" Gillespie asked, innocently.

"Russell," Joe said, eyebrow arched.

Gillespie laughed quietly, looking across at Russell holding court among the random group of drag queens, queers, poofs and weirdos that had become their friends over the past year.

"I don't think he'd be interested in a boring old lawyer like me," he said. "Not when he's got you lot."

"You'd be surprised," Joe said. "What have you got to lose?"

Patty finished her number, thanked everyone for their enthusiastic applause and introduced Scott and his backing dancers to the stage as Miss Terri and the Lady Killers.

Joe grinned as the look of concentration on Miss Terri's face dissolved into one of unadulterated happiness at having made it to the microphone without falling off her heels.

As the number began—"Papa Don't Preach"—Joe turned to see Gillespie ask Russell something. And then he saw the blush creep across Russell's face as he agreed.

CRAZY FOR YOU

SOHO NOIR #4

CRAZY FOR YOU

1.

SOHO, LONDON. 1987

CHARLOTTE FENWICK JUMPED off the bed at the sound of her father's footsteps approaching on the stairs. Not the sound so much—that couldn't be heard over the strains of Madonna's latest album—but the heavy-footed thumping was unmistakable. And if he caught Kieran in here, he would go mad.

"Get up," she said, hurriedly slipping the ashtray out of the window and onto the gutter above. "He can't find you here."

"Where am I supposed to go?" Kieran asked, pulling on his T-shirt and grabbing his shoes, while Charlotte misted the air with a burst of body spray—Impulse. Girls loved it.

"Quickly," Charlotte said, bundling him towards a huge pile of stuffed animals in the corner of her bedroom.

"I'm not hiding in that lot. I'm not bloody ET."

"Shut up," she hissed, clearing a space behind an oversized teddy and pushing Kieran into it. He wasn't a big lad—so long as he didn't move, they'd get away with it. "Just get down and stay still."

He was still muttering as she loaded the toys up on top of him—her childhood collection of Care Bears and other cuddlies that she just hadn't been able to bring herself to part with. Not because she had any sentimental attachment to them, but because they helped her keep up the pretence of being Daddy's little girl, which was essential. Especially right now.

She was still clutching a small pink pony when her father opened the door, his tanned face red from the exertion of stomping up the stairs. Charles Fenwick was not a man accustomed to having to do things himself.

"Will you turn that racket down? Right now! You're upsetting your mother."

Charlotte looked down at the soft toy still clutched in her hand and gently placed it on the pile. A risk, of course, but that was half the fun, wasn't it?

Ironically, Madonna had started beseeching her own Papa not to preach on the stereo, and Charlotte sang the line at her father as she crossed the room to lower the volume. As it turned out, she was in trouble, deep. If only she could tell him. Would facing his rage be better than the alternative she now faced?

"Sorry," she said, sullenly. *Not sorry.*

"Have you been smoking in here?" he asked, stepping into the room, nose aloft like a gun dog on point.

"No, Daddy," she said innocently, grateful for the Polo Mints she always ate after each cigarette. "You know I hate smoking. It must be coming from Mummy's room."

She was nineteen, nearly twenty. An adult, for God's sake. Why did she still have to bow to his stupid rules? If she wanted to smoke, why shouldn't she?

She had asked, countless times now, for her allowance to be extended so that she could move out, get a small flat in Soho, where all her friends were. But Daddy Dearest wasn't having any of it.

She would get access to her trust fund when she turned twenty-one and not a day before. Unless, of course, she agreed to marry whichever dull but eligible bachelor her father managed to line up, in which case she would get it straight away.

Even the promise of an instant fortune hadn't ever been worth tying herself into a lie of a marriage like her parents had. Although, right now, she was almost desperate enough to go along with the idea.

What her father didn't know was that she had already spent quite a lot of her trust fund before she'd even got it and, having taken loans against it from some very dodgy guys, she knew there was no way they would wait a year and a half for her to pay them back.

"What are you doing up here, anyway?" he asked, looking around suspiciously. Charlotte tried not to look at the pile of toys in the corner. Her father wasn't a stupid man but, where his little girl was concerned, he didn't always *want* to see the truth.

"Just having some quiet time," she said, smiling as sweetly as she could at him.

"Not with that racket on," he pointed at the stereo, where the graphic equaliser still flashed and bounced in time to the now barely audible track.

"It's not a racket, Daddy," she said, plonking herself down on the bed. "It's Madonna. Besides, I don't feel well."

He turned from the window, suddenly concerned. It worked every time.

"What's the matter? Shall I call a doctor?"

"No, silly," she said, hugging a cushion across her stomach and looking up at him with big eyes. "It's girl trouble."

She saw his face flush. This would surely get rid of him now. If there was one thing her father absolutely couldn't talk about with her, it was her periods.

"I'll get your mother, shall I?"

"Don't be daft, I'm fine. It just hurts, that's all. I was just lying here and listening to some music to cheer myself up. I'm so bored, and everything hurts, and I feel fat and icky."

She could hear her own voice, sickly sweet and sing-song. The childish tone she reserved for wrapping her father round her little finger.

He sat gently on the edge of the bed and took her hand, looking at her with such love in his eyes. It was cruel to play him like this, but needs must. And, right now, she needed a bit of a fighting fund.

"How about," he said, reaching into his pocket and pulling out his wallet. "You go and get yourself something nice to wear for Saturday night?"

So predictable.

"You know we've got the Ramplings coming for dinner. Their son Edward is back from University. They're very keen for you two to meet again."

"Oh, I don't know, Daddy," she said, still laying it on thick. "I'm not sure I feel like shopping today."

5

She watched him peel a few notes from the stack in his wallet. It worked every time—but that wouldn't be anywhere near enough.

"Although," she continued. "I suppose it wouldn't hurt to make a good first impression on Edward. Maybe I could go to Sergio's and get my hair done nicely too. He does half-price on Wednesdays."

His eyes rolled, but his fingers barely hesitated. Nodding, he peeled off another couple of fifties and handed the folded notes to her. Holding her hand in his for just a moment.

"That should be enough," he said. "But you've got your credit card too, haven't you?"

"Of course," she beamed. "But I know you don't like me using it. This will be fine. I can economise."

The truth was, her credit card was already maxed out and if her father found *that* out, he would probably cut her off altogether.

He sighed heavily, opened his wallet again and took out the rest of the notes.

"Look, that's all I've got in cash," he said, handing it over with the resignation of a man who knew he'd been played but didn't know what to do about it. "And I expect some change out of that, young lady."

His tone was soft though—he never expected change. She reached up and kissed his cheek.

"Thank you, Daddy," she said, saccharine rather than sugar.

He smiled, standing up.

"And if I catch you smoking in here again, I'll take your allowance away altogether," he said, turning his back on her and walking out of the room.

He was definitely not a stupid man, but she was his Achilles' heel—he just didn't know how to tell her off. And she knew it.

He turned in the doorway, hand on the door knob.

"And make sure you get something appropriate this time, alright?" he said. "These are important people, and I want them to see you at your best. Edward is a good man. Excellent prospects."

Her best, in his eyes, would be something demure and pretty. Something feminine. Frumpy. She knew he was hoping that there would be some convenient match with Edward Rampling. But that was never going to happen, no matter what she wore. He was not her type. He was a boy, for a start.

"Of course," she replied. "I love you."

He had already turned away, letting the door swing closed behind him. He didn't reply. She did love him, though.

For all his controlling, pompous, pseudo-aristocratic behaviour, he was a good man who loved his daughter. He just had no idea who she really was.

He would probably be devastated if he found out the half of it, but he'd get over it because he loved her. What he wouldn't get over, and Charlotte knew that with unerring certainty, was finding out that she'd spent all of her trust fund on partying and drugs for herself and her friends, and now had nothing to show for it.

Charles Fenwick had worked hard for his money and he had tried to raise his daughter to be as cautious and prudent as he was. He had failed. Life was just too exciting, and excitement cost money. Besides, she had a reputation to uphold.

She felt the notes burning in her palm. Seven hundred pounds should be enough. Just about. It would have to be.

"Jesus, you've got some nerve," Kieran tutted, extricating himself from the pile of cuddly toys. "What was all that 'love you, Daddy' crap?"

His impersonation of her little girl voice was spot on.

"Well, it got me this, didn't it?"

She waved the sheaf of notes at him and saw his eyes light up.

"Sure, that's grand," he said, eyes glinting greedily.

"Yes, and it's mine," she said, tucking the notes into the pocket of her jeans.

Kieran was a good friend but, admittedly, a bad influence. He was like that little devil on her shoulder that kept telling her to have fun. She knew she shouldn't listen to him, but she didn't want people to think she was boring. That's what had got her in this mess in the first place.

"Come on, let's go," she said, hurrying him towards the bedroom door.

"Shall I not go out the window?" he asked, nervously.

"You're not the bloody Milk Tray Man," she sneered. "Besides, he'll be back in his office with the door closed now. He's done his parenting for the day."

She led Kieran down the long, sweeping staircase and, having checked that her father's study door was indeed closed, she took his hand and they

7

dashed across the wide entrance hall, giggling as they let the front door swing closed behind them.

Had she looked back over her shoulder, she would have noticed that they were being followed. And had she noticed, perhaps everything would have been different.

Instead, Charlotte linked her arm through Kieran's, laughing, and they set off without a backward glance.

2.

JOE STONE STOOD behind the bar in the Red Lion, polishing glasses and hanging them on the rack above his head while trying, and failing to reach the same high notes as Jimmy Somerville.

The bar was strangely quiet for a Friday lunchtime and the summer songs blasting out of the jukebox had been keeping Joe entertained.

The landlord of the Red Lion, Ron, had become a firm friend of Joe's ever since Joe and his flatmate Russell had helped him figure out who had murdered the compere of a cabaret night being held in the back room of the pub.

When Joe had suddenly found himself out of work, Ron had stepped up and offered him some shifts behind the bar despite both of them knowing Ron didn't really need the help.

"Just while you get yourself back on your feet," Ron had said, kindly.

Joe was having no success getting himself back on his feet yet, though. He really should have been focussing on the job hunt, but it was too hot, and the work in the bar was too easy.

The television production company that Joe had been working for since moving to London had closed its doors after failing to deliver their last programme, and he'd not found another position.

They had been filming a warts-and-all documentary about a pop band, but when the manager of that band had turned up dead in the lead singer's hotel room, the singer had been arrested, and somehow Joe and Russell had found themselves charged with figuring out what had really happened.

By the time the murder had been solved, the programme was in the bin and the company in tatters. If he was honest, though, Joe had already known his days at the company were limited. He loved working in television production, but that company had been a bit of a one-man ego trip for his boss PJ. He'd find something else, eventually.

Every morning he promised himself that he'd get out there and look for another television job, and by lunchtime every day, when the regulars started filing into the Red Lion, he found himself transfixed by their lives, their crazy tales, their dramas.

They laughed so much in that pub. It felt like family. And that was the real reason he hadn't put too much effort into finding anything else, yet. He was happy here. Sure the money was terrible, and the prospects non-existent, but it was more like home than home had ever been.

So far, the only customer at the bar was George Jensen. Betting pages spread in front of him, pen and pad to his right filled with barely legible scratchings.

George was one of the regulars and his face told the tale of every afternoon he'd spent in the Red Lion; the whites of his eyes yellowed, the veins in his nose broken. He was always there. Part of the furniture. And everyone knew not to sit on his stool.

George had once been a journalist, before the drink had ruined both his ability to string a sentence together and file copy on time. But, for all his booze-fuelled rants, he still had his finger on the pulse as far as current affairs were concerned, both on the global stage and in the very close confines of the strange little village that was Soho.

If you wanted to know any gossip, you only had to sit beside George for an hour and you'd be all caught up. Depending on his mood, that hour could cost you anything between one and three drinks.

George had not long since arrived in the bar, and was working his way steadily through his first pint—tending to nurse the ones he had to pay for himself. He kept looking up and scowling at Joe's singing, issuing a cross tut every now and then. Joe didn't care, it was part of George's schtick to be grumpy.

"Any hot tips for today then, George?" Joe asked, nodding at the racing pages.

"Yeah," George grumbled. "Stop trying to hit those high notes or you'll do yourself a mischief."

His rattling laugh turned into a phlegmy cough, washed down eventually by a good gulp of ale. They both looked up as the door swung open and a woman walked into the bar. Early twenties. Short cropped hair, dark and neatly combed. Trilby hat in hand. A full three-piece suit in dark brown, tie precisely knotted, shoes gleaming, watch chain in evidence. Antonia Lagorio: "the Gecko"—as she was known behind her back, on account of being a smaller, but arguably more ruthless, version of her father, Tony "the Lizard" Lagorio.

Recognising her immediately, George swore under his breath and began folding up his papers.

Antonia Lagorio styled herself on the villainous gangsters of the 1920s, and traded largely off the terrifying reputation for violence her father had built over his years controlling the drugs, prostitutes and gangs of Soho. She had grown to be feared in her own right, though, as a sadist with a penchant for torturing confessions, cash and confidences out of her victims.

Joe gave her a cautious smile. He had nothing to fear from either Antonia or her father. Ron didn't pay protection money to anyone—he'd been the landlord of the Red Lion for too long for that. Ron was a kind man with a big heart, he didn't bow down to anyone, especially not gangsters who'd blown in to his little corner of the world. As a result, they had come to an early agreement.

If the Lizard wanted information from Ron, he had to come over and buy a drink, just like everyone else. And if Ron needed the kind of help that Tony could offer, he had to pay for it, just like everyone else.

Antonia had tried to exert a little authority of her own when she'd first started out in her father's business, but both Ron and the Lizard had quickly put her right—Ron was not to be messed with.

George Jensen had slid off his stool with uncharacteristic speed and, with his racing papers under his arm, was looking to make a quick escape.

"Hold your horses, Georgey-boy," she said, her voice low and threatening as always. "Where's the fire?"

"Oh hello, Ms Lagorio," he flustered. "I didn't see you come in. I was just off to see a man about..."

"Save it," she replied. "I'm not here to see you anyway. Though Sticky Vicky says I should be having a word."

Sticky Vicky's name, apparently, came from the fact that she needed a walking stick to get around. But Joe knew that was the polite version of the story. An ageing prostitute and an all round hustler, Sticky Vicky was lucky that there was still a polite version of any story relating to her.

"Now hang on," George said, looking both concerned and annoyed. "Whatever she's told you..."

"I said save it, George," Antonia said. "I told her, and I'll tell you, I'm not bloody marriage guidance, alright? Now piss off out of my sight, I want a word with dancing boy here. In private."

Grumbling, George huffed away, plonking himself at a table in the corner usually reserved for the rabble of journalists that enjoyed their extended lunch there. They wouldn't be in for half an hour yet.

Joe raised an eyebrow at Antonia.

"What can I do for you?" he asked, feeling slightly nervous, despite knowing that he had no beef with her.

"Vodka. Straight. Please."

Something was wrong. She never said please. Close up, he could see that her eyes were red-rimmed, and her shoulders slumped uncharacteristically as she leaned on the bar.

Joe poured her a shot and placed it on a coaster in front of her.

"Are you alright?" he asked.

She downed the shot in one. Tapped the glass. Joe refilled.

"I've got a spot of bother," she said, eventually. "I was told you might be the man to help me."

Joe frowned, not quite sure how to respond. One thing was certain, regardless of his current boss's relationship with Antonia's father, refusing to help her when she'd asked him directly would be a mistake.

"What kind of bother?" he asked, cautiously keeping any fear from his voice.

"It's personal," she replied, sipping her second shot more delicately this time. "Sensitive."

At least it wasn't business. The last thing Joe wanted to be doing was getting involved in anything illegal. And pretty much everything the Lagorios touched was illegal. Joe noticed that she kept looking around, surreptitiously, as though not wanting to be overheard.

"Go on," Joe prompted.

"There's this girl," she said. "Posh piece. A bit younger than me. We've been... well..."

"I see," Joe said, realising that she was hesitant to come out to him, despite her sexual proclivities being worn on every inch of her finely tailored suit.

She finished the second shot. Joe went to refill the glass, but she put out her hand to stop him.

"She's gone."

"What do you mean, gone?"

This had not been the kind of problem Joe had been expecting Antonia to present him with. A missing girlfriend.

"What do you think I mean? She's disappeared."

"What? How long..."

"Look, something's happened to her and you have to help me find her."

Beneath the hard glare, he saw a glimpse of a softer side to the Gecko. She really was asking for his help.

"Are you sure she hasn't run away?"

"She wouldn't. Not on her own. And not without me knowing."

"Okay. Well, when did you last see her?"

Antonia looked at her hands, fingers fidgeting nervously with the edge of the towelling mat on the bar.

"Two days ago. On Wednesday. I went over to her house. I shouldn't have done it. She doesn't like me going there—doesn't want her old man to see me. But she'd been hanging around with that little scrote Kieran Doherty, and I wanted to make sure she was okay. I saw them leaving her house together. And I haven't seen her since."

Joe frowned. Kieran Doherty wasn't a name he knew.

"Who is he?"

"He's bad news, that's who he is. Kieran Doherty. Ma Doherty's youngest..."

She said it expectantly, as though that should clarify everything. Joe still looked blank. Antonia tutted.

"Look, doesn't matter," she said, crossly. "The point is, he's trouble and his brothers are even worse—they're trying to muscle in on our action."

They're either very brave or very stupid, Joe thought.

"Anyway, this Kieran's latched on to my girl, Charlotte. Keeps getting her to buy him stuff. Drugs. Drink. You know? I told her she'd end up in trouble. And now I reckon I was right."

"It's only been a day and a half," Joe said. "Isn't it a bit early to be…"

"You don't understand," she cut him off. "I *always* know where she is and what she's doing. Always. She's missing. I'm telling you."

"And is he missing too? This Kieran?" Joe asked, not really wanting to suggest that Antonia's girlfriend may have done a bunk with the young man, but seeing it as the most likely scenario. Especially if Antonia was as controlling as she sounded.

"No, he's still swanning around the gaff. Says he hasn't seen her. Which I know is a lie because I saw them leaving her house with my own eyes. I'll kill him if he's done anything to her."

Joe didn't doubt her for a minute.

"Do you think he has?"

"I don't know. I told her a hundred times to drop him. He's only after her for her money."

Joe frowned, realising he didn't even know who this girl was that they'd been talking about.

"She's Charlotte Fenwick," Antonia said, seeing his confusion. "The heiress to the Fenwick millions. Eventually. Unless she gets cut off before that happens. That's what Kieran wants to get his mitts on. I told her to stop letting him hang around with her, but she's too soft."

"Right," Joe said, trying to stop her descending into self-pity. "So, you want me to talk to this Kieran guy?"

"Well, it's either him and his brothers," she said, "or her father's found out what she's been up to and has finally lost it properly with her."

"You think her father would hurt her?" Joe asked. He didn't know much about the multi-millionaire Charles Fenwick as a person. There had been articles in the papers over the years, detailing his success. But given that his money had all been self-made through his various entrepreneurial ventures, Joe'd always had the impression he was pretty cool. Still, you never knew what went on behind closed doors.

"He's got a temper on him, alright," Antonia said. "And he is pretty strict with his 'little girl'."

"Is there anyone else she hangs around with? Anyone who might know if she'd gone to ground for a bit, or if she'd got into trouble with her father? What about her friends?"

Antonia sighed.

"I don't really know any of them," she said. "It's not my scene, see? Sitting around in bars with a bunch of airheads. She has a group of friends that she meets up with, some of them posh totty like her, but most of the others just hang around her because she always picks up the tab."

"Any names at all?" Russell asked.

"Amelia something, North London girl. I can barely understand her she speaks so posh. Never has any cash on her either. She says it's 'cause she's like the Queen. She doesn't come out much though, only to the champagne bars, you know?"

Joe made a note of the name, looking expectantly at Antonia for more. She shook her head. He could tell she was frustrated about not knowing enough about Charlotte's friend group.

"She hangs out with her friends from school a lot. But I couldn't tell you their names. I didn't really meet any of them properly. They're all the same, though, you know? All look the same, sound the same, act the same. But they won't have anything to do with her going missing, I can tell you that much."

"She could have gone away with one of them, perhaps? For the weekend? She hasn't really been gone long, has she?"

"Long enough. Look, she would have told me. She knows I worry. Anyway, she doesn't really like any of them enough, really. It's just a part she has to play until her trust money comes through."

"Which is when?" Joe asked.

"At twenty-one. So just over a year's time. But she gets a pretty healthy allowance in the meantime, she just has to toe the line at home to keep her daddy sweet, and she can have pretty much what she wants."

"Lucky girl," Joe said. He would have loved a trust fund, but the only cash his parents had managed to scrape into any savings had been spent on his two sisters' weddings.

"Not really," Antonia said. "Her father's a controlling bastard. She's terrified of him. Petrified he'll find out."

"Find out what? That she's a lesbian?"

"No, you clown. That she's not the sweet, innocent little girl he thinks. Or that she's been spending all his money—even the trust fund she doesn't have yet—partying with her mates."

She thought for a moment.

"Mind you," she continued. "I doubt he'd be too chuffed about the other, either. He's been looking to marry her off since she turned eighteen. Keeps promising to hand over her fund early if she agrees to one of his matches. So far, she's been having none of it."

"I'm not surprised," Joe said.

"So, are you going to help, or not?"

The way she asked didn't really suggest he had too much choice.

"I'll try," Joe said.

By the time Antonia got up to leave, she'd had another shot of vodka and filled Joe in on the wonderful, beautiful, wild creature that was Charlotte Fenwick—Charlie.

It was clear that Antonia was smitten and—given the tale of wild parties, drink and drugs, growing debts, the dodgy Irish friend and his even dodgier brothers, coupled with having to hide it all from a fiercely controlling and powerful father—Joe felt there may be some substance to Antonia's fears that Charlotte had come to some harm.

Though it was equally likely that she had been sent away to some kind of finishing school by her father, and hadn't had the heart or guts to tell her gangster girlfriend before she went.

As cut up as Antonia clearly was, Joe had to question how likely the relationship would have been to last, anyway. The daughter of a notorious gangster and the heiress to a multimillion-pound empire was hardly a coupling likely to make either of their over-controlling Daddies happy.

As Antonia left the pub, she almost walked into Joe's flatmate, and good friend, Russell.

"Alright, Antonia?" Russell said, cheerfully. "What are you doing here?"

"Fuck off, pig." Antonia replied, barging past him and the incredibly handsome Freddie Gillespie, Russell's new boyfriend, who had followed him in through the door and now had to make way for an angry lesbian in a great suit.

"Charming," Freddie said. "Friend of yours?"

"We have history," Russell said, smiling. "I arrested her father on an almost monthly basis for a while. Until he found some friends on the force to cover his back."

"Looks like she's close to forgiving you," Freddie joked.

Joe was already part-way through pouring Russell's usual pint by the time they reached the bar.

"You not working today, Freddie?" Joe asked. "What can I get you?"

"Sparkling water please, love," Freddie said. "I'm actually here for work, sort of. You got a minute to join us?"

Joe looked around the bar, which—apart from George—was empty.

"Sure, I think I can fit you in."

Freddie Gillespie was in his late thirties. Not that much younger than Russell, though his full head of hair was showing no signs of grey yet, which made him look about ten years younger.

A hugely successful lawyer with a client list bursting with celebrities and hotshots, Freddie was a named partner in his own law firm, and fulfilled every one of the four S-words—the criteria Joe and Russell had laid out as a benchmark for a potential lover: single, solvent, sane and sexy. Russell had hit the jackpot, and Joe was delighted for him.

Russell had struggled with his sexuality for most of his twenties and thirties, being forced to hide it for all of the years he had served in the police force. And he'd been right to do so.

When one of his particularly nasty colleagues had finally found out Russell was gay, he'd mounted a sting that had seen Russell arrested and retired from the force, with a good pay-out but a horrible taste in his mouth.

Detective Simon Skinner had been on Russell's hit list ever since, and Freddie was also now keen to help see the corrupt cop brought low.

The delightful Freddie Gillespie had come into Russell and Joe's lives only a few months before. His client had been that same lead singer of the pop sensation, Loose Lips, who had been accused of murdering the band's manager.

The pop star, Adam Cave, had sent Freddie to Joe for help, knowing that Joe and Russell had a reputation for helping gay men in trouble.

Adam Cave had, at the time, still been trying to keep his sexuality under wraps, and the scandal around the death of his manager—and best friend—had threatened to expose everything.

Of course, it had been Detective Skinner at the helm of that investigation too, trying to incriminate and expose Adam Cave to further his own celebrity on the force. He hadn't expected to be up against a lawyer quite as formidable or dedicated as Freddie Gillespie.

By the time the case was over, Skinner was in Freddie's sights too, and his bosses were under pressure to discipline him, thanks to Freddie's reports to GALOP—the independent organisation set up to investigate discrimination by the police force. It wasn't Skinner's first strike with the watchdog either—his name was already high on their list. But without any legal powers, they could only harass his superiors to bring him into line.

Joe took the drinks over with him as he joined Freddie and Russell at their usual table in the window.

"What's going on?" he asked.

Russell took a long drink of his pint, smiled and signalled to Freddie. He was happy. In love. Relieved to be able to be himself. And busy using his finely honed detective skills to help people in his own community. Joe grinned at him and turned to Freddie, who looked less happy.

"I've got this client," he began. "Insanely rich."

"Aren't they all?" Joe said, smiling.

"Anyway," Freddie continued, in no mood for banter. "His daughter's gone missing, and he's very worried about her."

Joe sat forward. This couldn't be a coincidence.

"Has he gone to the police?"

"No," Freddie said. "He would rather that it was handled privately for now."

Joe frowned.

"He doesn't want a scandal. Her reputation... He's worried that she'll come out of this badly. If the police get involved, inevitably the press will find out, and he's worried that some of the stuff they'll dig up on her may not be so great for her future eligibility."

"Charlotte Fenwick? Right?"

Freddie's jaw dropped. Even Russell cocked his head in surprise.

"How did you know that?" Freddie asked.

Joe smiled cockily, letting them ponder his powers of deduction for a moment. Then he laughed.

"Antonia Lagorio was just in asking me to help her find out what's happened to her girlfriend Charlie," he said.

"Her girlfriend?" Freddie spluttered.

"Apparently so," Joe said. "She seems quite in love, and terribly worried that something awful has happened. In fact, she suggested I should even be looking at the father for it."

Freddie reached over and picked up Russell's pint, almost draining it in one.

"Oi," Russell complained.

"Why would she say that?" Freddie asked, though his expression suggested he knew what his client was capable of.

"Apparently he is pretty controlling, and wouldn't take too well to the idea that his daughter was dating a gangster, let alone that the gangster in question was a woman."

"She said that?" Freddie asked. "She actually said she thought Charles Fenwick had done something to his daughter?"

"Well, I assumed she meant he'd sent her away. Although she did paint a picture of a pretty wild child, spending all of Daddy's money on drink, drugs and dancing. Antonia said Charlie was terrified that her father would disown her if he found out. Maybe his temper got the better of him. Maybe that's why he doesn't want the police involved."

"Wait. You don't think the Lizard's got anything to do with it, do you?" Russell asked, looking to Joe.

"The Lizard?" Freddie asked, nervously. There were so many strange characters in Russell's life he hadn't met yet.

"Tony 'the Lizard' Lagorio," Russell clarified. "Antonia's father."

"I didn't get that impression," Joe said. "Apparently there's some dodgy Irish kid who's been hanging around, helping her spend her money. Kieran somebody-or-other. He might be worth talking to."

"Do you think Charles Fenwick knew about Charlotte's lifestyle? Or about her relationship with Antonia?" Joe asked. "If he found out, would he punish her? How well do you know him?"

"He's a client," Freddie said. "He's a ruthless businessman and a hard negotiator. I've seen him lose his temper in the boardroom, but if you're asking whether I think he's capable of hurting his own daughter, I'd have to say no. He seemed genuinely distressed that she hadn't come home since Wednesday afternoon. I'm not sure he's that good an actor."

"Right," Russell said. "Well, we'd better get out there and do some digging."

THE BIG HOUSE on York Terrace was impressive, even from the outside. Only a twenty-minute walk from the Red Lion—but a million miles away from the seedy grime of their beloved corner of Soho.

Houses this size in the centre of London didn't come cheap, and the convertible Bentley Continental that Russell and Joe had just watched pull into the garage down the side of the house only confirmed what they already knew. They were dealing with serious money here.

Even the doorbell's chime was ostentatious and grand. Russell raised an eyebrow as they waited on the doorstep. Joe self-consciously straightened his shirt—a ridiculous gesture given that it hadn't seen an iron since it had left the shop.

The door was opened by a tall, slim man in a black suit. Crisp white shirt. Thin black tie. Hair scraped to one side, thinning slightly, but he could still just about get away with the style.

"Russell Dixon and Joe Stone," Russell said. "Mr Fenwick is expecting us."

"Very good," the man said, tersely. "Follow me."

They both shared a wide-eyed exchange as they followed him into an entrance hall that was larger than their entire flat.

A huge, sweeping staircase rose off to the right—the kind of stairs you could imagine high-kicking down in a pair of killer heels. Russell caught Joe's grin and knew he was thinking the same thing.

They had grown to know each other well over the past year and a bit. It hadn't been a long time, really, in the bigger picture of close friendships, but they had both been through some terrible times together, and it had brought them so much closer.

They had become friends when it had been left to them to figure out who had killed Russell's flatmate, and Joe's best friend, Chris Sexton. After they'd put his killer behind bars, Joe had taken on Chris's old room in Russell's flat.

Just over a year later they had solved another two murders, both of which had also involved someone from their local community.

Boyfriends had been lost and gained, AIDS scares had haunted them, all supported by drag nights and endless pints in the Red Lion. Their relationship had cemented into a solid and unshakeable friendship, and gave them an unspoken shorthand, which came in incredibly useful when looking into the kinds of cases that kept landing in their laps.

Since being forced to leave his job as a detective in the police force—thanks to that rat, Detective Skinner—Russell had become something of a private detective to Soho's strange mix of residents.

He had known that homophobic discrimination was rife in the police while he'd been there—it was the main reason he'd kept his own sexuality hidden. What he hadn't realised—until it happened on his own doorstep—was that the police, especially Skinner, would actively refuse to take cases seriously if there was a hint that anyone involved was gay. The eighties might be a world away from the fifties, but they weren't even close to equality yet.

As far as Skinner was concerned, if you were gay and bad things happened to you, you'd as good as asked for it.

In fact, as Russell had found out to his own detriment, the police would actively target gay men coming out of clubs, trapping them in a sting with a hot young undercover cop, and boosting their arrest rates by charging the unsuspecting men, Russell included, with the outdated crime of importuning.

It had hurt at the time—the police force had been Russell's whole life—but meeting Joe, and solving Chris's murder had started Russell on a path to a better, more honest, life.

He wouldn't have believed, even a couple of years ago, that he would have such a close circle of friends who were all just like him *and* a gorgeous boyfriend who made him happy just to be alive.

"Jesus," Joe whispered. "Look at that. Do you think it's an original?"

He was pointing discreetly to a painting on the wall of the large sitting room they'd just walked into. A Mondrian. Russell pulled a low whistle over his teeth. That painting would be worth a fortune on its own. And it wasn't the only thing in this room worth stealing.

"I hope they've got good insurance," Russell said.

"Please sit down," the tall man said, waving his hand towards a pair of armchairs. "I'll let Mr Fenwick know you're here."

Joe sat, as he was told, but Russell couldn't help strolling around the room, looking at the perfectly placed knick-knacks.

There was a collection of framed photographs on the coffee table, stiff and formal: mother seated with her daughter on the floor at her feet, skirt spread on the floor around her. Father stood proprietorially behind them both, hand on his wife's shoulder. All in their Sunday best. A snapshot of a different time. The girl couldn't have been more than seven or eight in that picture. An only child. Destined to go off the rails.

Russell picked up a picture of the same girl, now in her teens. Braces on her teeth, wide cloth band holding her blonde hair back from her face. School uniform in pristine order. A strange half-smile that gave the smallest hint of her personality. Charlotte Fenwick. *Where have you gone?*

"Thank you for coming," a deep baritone said from behind him.

Russell turned to find a tall, broad-shouldered man standing in the wide doorway. Hair peppered with grey, cut close on the sides. Jacketless, tailored shirt, tie pulled loose. The kind of natural tan that is only achieved by extended breaks in a Tuscan villa or the slopes of Val-d'Isère. Charles Fenwick exuded wealth.

He pulled the doors closed behind him, as though wanting to keep their conversation private even from the other occupants of the house.

He indicated for Russell to sit beside Joe with that casual confidence of a man seldom questioned.

"Gillespie tells me I can trust you two?"

"Absolutely," Russell said. Joe just nodded.

"Good," Fenwick said. "Because this matter needs to be handled very discreetly. I don't want to risk any harm to my daughter's reputation."

Or to your own, thought Russell.

"We're here to help," Joe said.

Russell noticed that Joe'd put his posh voice on. The one he used when he phoned home and got his father on the other end of the line. The one that slipped as soon as his mother took over the call.

"Good, okay. I'm putting my trust in Gillespie's word."

Russell felt Joe glance at him. He ignored it. Freddie was a big boy, he wouldn't have asked them to get involved if he didn't think they could help.

"We'll help you find your daughter," Russell said. "I'm sure of it. We'll have her home safe in no time. Why don't you tell us everything? From the start. How long has she been gone?"

"Since Wednesday afternoon," he said despondently. "She said she was feeling low. I gave her some money to go shopping, get her hair done. We have guests coming tomorrow, and I wanted her to make a bit of an effort."

"And how did she seem?"

"I just told you," he said. "She seemed low. A little morose. Distracted. She cheered up when I gave her some cash though. She's just like her mother, that girl. Loves her shopping. I try to limit her ability to spend, but she can wind me round her little finger."

"Can't they all," Russell said. It was a blank statement of agreement. He'd met enough spoilt little rich girls in his time.

Although, whenever he'd been dealing with them, they were usually shouting the odds about how awful it was that they were being treated like common criminals when they had, indeed, been caught doing something commonly criminal.

"Did she say where she was going?" Joe asked. "Perhaps we can check with the shop assistants? See if they saw anything."

"No. Look, I don't know where they go for these things. I just pay for them. My wife might have a better idea."

Joe and Russell exchanged another glance at that. This guy was not the most charming man they'd ever interviewed.

"Is she here?" Joe asked. "Your wife? Would we be able to talk to her too?"

"Oh, she's here alright. Whether you'll be able to get any sense out of her is a different story. She's usually pissed by lunchtime. She'll probably be passed out in her room."

There was clearly no love lost there. Russell wasn't surprised. The expression on the woman's face in that photograph from about ten years ago already spoke of depression and disillusionment. He doubted the relationship would have got better with time.

"What about friends? Is there anyone she sees regularly that she could have gone to stay with?"

"Do you think I haven't checked?" Fenwick snapped. "I've had poor Mills running around London looking under every rock since yesterday morning. No one has seen her."

"Perhaps they're covering for her," Joe suggested. "They might be more inclined to talk to me."

Fenwick looked him up and down, the faintest hint of a sneer on his lips.

"Maybe you're right. I'll get Mills to give you a list of establishments he's been to so far."

He paused again, assessing them both.

"You understand that this is all very sensitive," he said. "To be handled in the strictest confidence."

"Of course," Joe said.

Russell wondered exactly how much of Charlotte's lifestyle Fenwick already knew about. He assumed that if old Mills had been able to go asking questions at her usual haunts, he must have followed her once or twice before to know where they were. Fenwick sighed, obviously realising that he would have to give them more than he had.

"I've tried," he said, sadly. "I've really tried to let her have her freedom, but she's too naïve and too reckless. She thinks I don't know what she gets up to, but I'm always watching her. I have to."

Russell nodded. Just as he'd assumed.

"You have her followed when she goes out?"

"That makes it sound too controlling. I have Mills drive her where she wants to go, so that we always know where she is. He often waits for her to come out. Makes sure she gets home safe."

"Lucky girl," Joe said.

"Are there any friends in particular that you think we should talk to?" Russell asked, noticing the small wrinkle deepen on Fenwick's forehead.

"There was a boy here on Wednesday. She thought I didn't know he was here, up in her room, but I'm not as green as I am cabbage looking. I saw them leave. I was going to tackle her about it when she got back. But then she didn't come home."

"You know the lad?" Russell asked.

"Mills is trying to find out who he is," Fenwick said. "No luck yet."

So they were already a step ahead of Charles Fenwick and his man, Mills. That gave Russell a little confidence.

"Had she mentioned anything unusual, anything that had upset her recently?" Joe asked.

"No," Fenwick said. "Although another young man came to the door a few days ago. Smart-looking. Suited and booted. *He* seemed to upset her a bit."

"Did you get a look at him?" Russell asked.

"No, I caught a glimpse out of the window there as he walked away. Slight fellow. Dapper. Trilby hat."

Antonia Lagorio, Russell thought, not disavowing Fenwick of the notion that the caller had been a young man for now. Joe clocked it as well.

"And Charlotte didn't say who it was?"

"No, she just ran up to her room. But I heard her crying," Fenwick said. "She wouldn't let me in. She can be terribly emotional, you see. Just like her mother."

"Do you think I'd be able to have a look at her room?" Joe asked.

Fenwick frowned slightly, but nodded. He reached over and rang a small, silver bell on the side table. A moment later, the doors opened, and the tall man—who they now knew to be called Mills—stepped in.

"Sir?"

"Take this young man up to Charlotte's room please," Fenwick said. "And then pop back down here. I'd like you to fill Mr Dixon in on your… enquiries."

Russell caught Joe's eye and nodded. He still had some questions to ask of Mr Fenwick, ones that the multimillionaire might be happier to discuss one-on-one, and he was keen to find out what Mills had been doing since Charlotte had disappeared.

Besides, Joe had a keen eye. If there was anything to be found in Charlotte's room, his young friend would find it.

MILLS LED THE WAY up the stairs in silence. Joe ran his hand along the wide banister. At the top, a wide corridor stretched away from them. White painted doors, mostly closed, led to six or so rooms.

The cream carpet was thick and lush, small occasional tables dotted between the doorways—doubtless worth a fortune themselves—held antique busts in marble and bronze.

Joe trailed a finger over one as he passed.

"Don't touch," Mills admonished, without even looking back.

Joe curled his lips like a petulant child, mimicking the man's instruction silently.

They passed a series of closed doors, before arriving at one that stood partly ajar.

Mills stopped on the far side of the door and turned to face Joe, pushing it open further. He smiled, a curt, polite, meaningless smile. Joe could have sworn he heard the man click his heels as he passed him.

"Thank you," he said, wondering if Mills would hang around to watch him. He didn't really mind, though he would prefer to have the room to himself for a while.

Unlike the rest of the house, this room at least looked as though it was properly lived in, although by a far younger girl than Joe knew Charlotte to be.

An avalanche of soft toys in the corner spoke of a girl unable to part with her childhood, but from what Antonia had told him about Charlotte, she was a bit of a wild child. The teenage stylings here all felt at odds with the girl Antonia had described. From the floral bedspread to the Hollywood lights around the mirror on her dressing table.

Joe glanced back at the door to see that Mills had, in fact, left him to it. He took a deep breath, smelling sweet body spray, a hint of old tobacco smoke, bubblegum. Girl smells, just like the bedroom his sisters had shared when they were all growing up. *Where to begin?*

He crossed to the dressing table, lifting her hairbrush and inspecting it. Long blonde hair trapped between the bristles didn't tell him anything he didn't already know. Stuck into the edge of the mirror was a strip of four photobooth images, all of Charlotte on her own, pulling a different face in each, none genuine. Usually the kind of thing you'd do with a best friend, faces pressed together. *Who puts up photographs of themselves on their own mirror?*

It made Joe wonder if Charlotte actually had any real friends, or whether, as Antonia had said, they were all just after her money.

Joe opened a drawer that ran the length of the dresser, finding half-used make-up and bits of ribbon, hair grips and other beauty paraphernalia. He moved the detritus around a little, but saw nothing of special interest there either.

In the bedside cabinet, he found a diary that hadn't been filled in since last year. It held the musings of a young woman with too much time and money on her hands. No great secrets or confessions and certainly no clues. It felt, if anything, almost too stereotypically girly. Not what he would have expected from a young woman who was in a relationship with Antonia Lagorio.

Joe wondered if it had been left there as a decoy to avert attention from her real secrets.

Where was the stash of booze? Where was the half-empty pack of cigarettes, badly hidden from prying eyes? Joe sat on the bed, flicking through the pages of the diary briefly. It was all the same nonsense, written in a large, looping, childish hand. Almost definitely a decoy.

He leaned forward to replace the diary in the drawer and spotted a small black box hidden beneath the bed—a pair of pink and white hi-top trainers half-hiding it from sight.

Joe reached down and pulled the box out, lifting it onto his lap. Black cardboard, with a loosely fitting lid—this looked like a box for secrets. Peering inside he found another small book, the same style as the diary but its address book partner.

Joe lifted the address book out and opened it up. Names, addresses and phone numbers, all written in that same looping handwriting. Nothing particularly significant that he could see. No special symbols, no mystery initials—nothing to pick out one address in particular.

Below that was the half-empty packet of cigarettes that he'd been expecting to find somewhere in the room, and an opened tube of Polo Mints—the standard trick set of any teenager who didn't want their parents to know they smoked. Utterly ineffective, and yet all the kids did it.

He laid the book and the cigarettes aside and lifted a collection of Polaroid photographs from the box. This was more like it—images of Charlotte that revealed more of her wild side and gave a hint of the friends that her father would doubtless not want her hanging around with.

The first showed Charlotte lounging on a big red sofa, hand-rolled cigarette in hand, hair teased and backcombed into a blonde mane, eye make-up electric pink and yellow. Beside her was a skinny young man, his fiery red hair, tightly curled, standing out against his pale skin.

He looked about the same age as Charlotte, perhaps a couple of years older, but still waiting to fill out into his adult shape. He also looked completely wasted—head lolling to one side, eyes glazed, jaw slack. Joe could almost smell the weed through the photograph.

The next photo showed the same boy, shirtless and dancing, in the middle of some club Joe vaguely recognised. The hair was the same but he was moving so fast, most of him was just a blur of pale skin and red hair.

The next was him again, still shirtless, but this time lounging on Charlotte's bed in this very room. Joe wondered if he should ask Charles Fenwick about the boy. Was this the kid he'd seen her with yesterday? There was no way of asking without revealing Charlotte's secrets though, and Joe felt bad about that. Better to look into it himself first.

He flicked through to the next image, which showed Charlotte glammed up again, arms draped around Antonia Lagorio's shoulders this time. Again, her eyes had that distant, glazed look, though it wasn't helped by the glare of the flash bouncing off her retinas either.

Their body language was interesting, Joe thought. Antonia looked proud, almost defensive. Her hand extended, palm out, trying to stop the photographer from capturing the image. Was it herself she was trying to protect, or Charlotte?

Charlotte herself seemed oblivious to the photographer, to whatever threat Antonia saw in the image being taken. She was having fun, and no one was going to stop her.

Joe thought it was mean to judge her, given that he'd never even met her, but the images she had chosen to keep of herself and her friends all pointed to a selfish little rich girl, who was used to getting her way, acting out in secret and probably walking on a lot of feelings along the way.

The contrast between the girl in these photographs and the smart young woman shown in the family portraits downstairs was marked. Joe assumed this version of her was closer to the truth.

Had she been taken because of her father's money? Or had she done a runner to get away from his controlling nature. Or had she just gone off on some wild bender, with no regard for the worry it would cause her family and friends?

He tucked the photographs into his back pocket as he stood up, deciding he would ask Antonia about the boy in the images. Was this her young Irish friend—the bad influence that Antonia had warned her away from?

With nothing else of interest in the box, he replaced the little address book and the cigarettes, closed the lid and tucked the box back under the bed. He would give Charlotte her photos back when—if—they found her.

Her father obviously knew something of her lifestyle outside of the house, but Joe still wasn't sure how much. The least he could do for now was keep her secrets safe.

"Who are you? What are you doing here?"

Joe turned to find a woman in a deep blue silk dressing gown standing in the doorway, hands held up in some crazed kung-fu pose, though her obvious swaying did little to support the threat.

Joe recognised her immediately as Charlotte's mother. She hadn't changed much since those family photographs. Her shoulder-length hair was neat and perfectly set, dyed identically to how it had been ten years ago.

Her make-up was pristine, though her eyes gave away the fact that she'd been crying, and her unsteady lean on the doorframe told tales on her drinking.

"Mrs Fenwick," Joe said. "My name is Joe Stone. Your husband asked me here to help find your daughter."

She made a good effort of trying to look sober as she tottered into the room, but Joe felt compelled to reach out and guide her to sit on the end of the bed. The smell of alcohol on her breath was potent. Perhaps Charles Fenwick wasn't being quite so harsh after all.

"You a friend of hers, then?" she slurred. "I don't know you. Do I?"

"No," Joe said, seeing the confusion in her eyes. He wondered how often she found herself staring at a blank memory bank, hoping for a light to come on. "I'm just here to help find Charlotte."

She laughed. A mean, short, angry laugh.

"Is it not enough to drive her away from us? Now he has to hunt her down, too? Admit it, you're just here to snoop for him, aren't you? He's always spying on her."

Joe stood awkwardly opposite her, not wanting to get into a domestic dispute with her when she was clearly upset and not fully in control of her faculties.

"No," he said. "Honestly, I'm just here to help. Your husband didn't want to bring the police in at this stage. He's worried that a scandal may damage Charlotte's reputation."

She laughed again. The same mean little snort.

"*Her* reputation?" she snorted. "It's *his* reputation he's worried about."

Joe felt inclined to agree. The multi-millionaire had been concerned for his daughter, but not for her safety as much as for her social standing if any scandal came out.

"He knows where she is," Mrs Fenwick continued. "I can see it in his eyes. I know when he's lying. He's always lying."

Joe sat beside her—keeping a safe enough distance between them—and looked at her. Up close, the cracks were easier to see. Small clumps of mascara stuck to the edges of her eyelids, expertly applied, cried off and then shakily reapplied. Her floral perfume did nothing to mask the smell of gin, and her hands shook even as she held them in her lap, fussing at the edge of a tattered tissue.

"What do you mean?" Joe asked, gently.

"He's been threatening to send her away for ages. And he knew I would never agree, so he's done all this to make it look like she's run away. But I know my girl. She wouldn't leave without saying goodbye. She wouldn't leave me here alone with him."

The tears brimmed again, fat and true. This was exactly the kind of concern that had been lacking in Charles Fenwick's response. Joe reached out and patted her hand, and she looked at him with such sadness that he felt inclined to believe her, for just a moment.

Was Charles Fenwick really just using them to cover up for the fact that he'd sent his daughter away?

"Where do you think he's sent her?" he asked.

"To Switzerland," she replied. "He's been on about sending her to this finishing school there for over a year, and I won't let him do it. I know what those places are like. They break your spirit. They turn you into another good little wife to be farmed off to some rich bastard."

Joe assumed from the way she spoke that this was exactly how she had found herself married to Charles in the first place.

"I refused to let him send her. The first time he tried it, I even went and got her back," she said, smiling at the memory. "I made quite a scene.

He was so angry, but he couldn't do anything about it. He can't bear to be embarrassed, you see. It's the only weapon I have."

She dabbed at her eyes with the corner of the tissue. Willing the tears to stay in. It worked. She gave Joe a weak smile.

"You don't think she's run away of her own accord, then?" Joe asked. "Your husband seems to think she has."

"If she has, it's because he forced her to," she said, but she was already shaking her head. She didn't believe it. "He keeps her locked up here. Daddy's little girl in her ivory tower. But I know what she's really been getting up to. She needs her freedom. To become a woman."

She emphasised the word woman by cupping her own breasts and squeezing them together. Joe did a slow blink, trying to erase the image from his mind.

"He just wants to control everyone and everything. Did he tell you he was trying to marry her off to some awful computer scientist? Like there's any future in that!"

"Computer science?" Joe asked. As far as he knew, there was likely to be a good future in that. Joe just wished he understood them better.

"Yes, he'd arranged a dinner for tomorrow night. They were supposed to meet each other then and agree to his little merger. Nothing to do with love, or lust."

Joe looked away quickly before she could demonstrate lust.

"Did Charlotte know that was the plan?" he asked, standing up again and crossing to the dresser, looking at the strip of photos of a young woman with a shallow, fake smile.

Had he judged her too harshly? Was that fakeness he saw just her putting on a brave face, realising that her whole life had already been mapped out for her, and that she was destined to do nothing but toe the line and end up drinking gin for breakfast like her poor mother?

"She'd be an idiot not to," Mrs Fenwick snapped. "And *she* is no idiot."

"So it's possible she's run away to get out of whatever arrangement her father had in mind?"

Mrs Fenwick seemed to consider this for a moment, and then she shook her head again.

"She wouldn't risk it," she said. "Look, I love my daughter more than life itself, but she is more like her father than she cares to admit. There is no way she would turn her back on her fortune. She knows that her trust fund, which is sizeable, is dependent on her doing as she is told. She is mercenary enough to go along with any hideous plan of his, just to get her hands on that money. It's all she ever talks about. The day her fortune will be hers to manage."

"When she turns twenty-one?"

"Or gets married. Whichever comes sooner."

"But only if she marries someone her father approves of, I assume."

"Bingo," Mrs Fenwick replied, bitterly.

Joe left Mrs Fenwick sitting on the end of her daughter's bed with a promise that he would do his best to find out what had happened to her. The woman may be being paranoid about her husband's involvement in Charlotte's disappearance, but Joe had at least managed to learn of another couple of potential reasons why the young heiress might have gone missing.

If her father had sent her away, that would be easy enough to figure out, but if Charlotte had run away to escape what was effectively an arranged marriage, that was a different story altogether, and he wasn't sure he would be happy handing her back to her father if that was the case.

Joe headed back downstairs to find Russell thanking Charles Fenwick for being so candid, and assuring him that they would do everything they could to find his daughter.

RUSSELL JOINED JOE at their table in the window of the Red Lion, handing him a pint as he sat down.

Their friend Paul—another one of owner Ron's waifs and strays—was working at the bar, regaling a handful of regulars with some tale of two hapless young policemen who had tried to raid George's illicit betting book, and been thwarted by Sticky Vicky, the now strictly part-time prostitute.

Apparently, the quick thinking Sticky Vicky had shoved all of the ill-gotten gains in her underwear to stop the cops getting it and George was now refusing to touch the cash until she changed it for clean notes.

The dispute about money laundering between the two drunken regulars had been raging for days now, with Sticky Vicky all the while using George's sullied cash to generously get the rounds in for all and sundry.

"So Charles Fenwick didn't mention he was planning to marry her off then?" Joe asked, as his friend sat down.

"No," Russell replied. "Not explicitly. He mentioned that he had arranged a dinner with some friends, who were bringing their son. He said it was why he had given Charlotte some cash to go and treat herself to an outfit, get her hair done. Apparently she seemed quite excited to meet the young man. According to Charles, anyway."

"I get the feeling that Charlotte is quite a convincing little actress when she needs to be. The Charlotte her parents know almost certainly isn't the one her friends see. If these are anything to go by."

He pulled the handful of Polaroids out of his pocket and handed them to Russell.

"Interesting," Russell said, flicking through the images. "Who's the redhead?"

"No idea," Joe replied. "I'm guessing it's the same kid Antonia was talking about."

"He looks like our next port of call, then."

"Antonia's given me the address. A bar on Shaftesbury Street. I'll go check him out later," Joe said.

"What about the mother?" Russell asked. "You spoke to her, right?"

"She's a ball of resentment and frustration, pickled in gin. But she's clearly worried about her daughter."

"So she didn't think Charlotte has run off to get away from her controlling father?"

"Apparently she wouldn't risk losing the cash. *She* thinks Charles has sent Charlotte off to some finishing school in Switzerland without telling her, and is trying to cover it up by bringing us in to look into her disappearance."

"You think there's anything in that?"

"Well, you spoke to him more than I did. Did you feel like it was all a bluff?"

Russell took a long swig of his pint, thinking.

"No. I mean, he seemed more worried about a scandal than the thought that something bad had happened to his daughter, but I didn't get the feeling he was hiding anything. He told me that he knew she could be wild, and that she would sneak out when she thought he was locked in his office and wouldn't notice."

"So he's more aware of what she's been up to than she thought?"

"Seems so. He was worried that she was hanging out with the wrong sorts. That was why he was withholding her money until she was older. He thought she'd just waste it all on being rebellious for the sake of it."

"What if this party lifestyle has exposed her to the kinds of people who would take her hostage to get their hands on some real money?"

"You really think she's been kidnapped?"

"Well, Antonia does. And she's convinced it's something to do with this Kieran kid. Perhaps he, or someone else she'd been hanging around with, saw a chance to make some quick quids."

"But then, surely there would have been a ransom demand by now," Russell said.

Joe nodded. That was true.

"I bet she's just gone off on a bender and now she's too scared to go home and face the music," Russell said.

"Probably," Joe agreed. "Did the old bloke—the butler, Mills—did he give you any more?"

"Not really. A better description of Antonia, though he still thought she was a lad. But I guess we can count her out. He's talked to all her friends though. None of them are saying anything."

The pub fell quiet, as it always did when the doors opened. The briefest moment while everyone scoped out whether to hide what they were doing or welcome a friend. Russell smiled as Freddie Gillespie walked in and headed straight for them.

"You alright?" he asked, as Freddie reached the table and slumped down on the bench, rubbing his face in his hands. "What's the matter?"

"I've just come from the Fenwicks'. Charles called," Freddie said. "He's had this."

Freddie wiped the pint rings from the table with his sleeve before spreading a roughly folded piece of paper in front of them.

It was a crudely collated ransom note, made of cut-out magazine headlines. Just like in old TV shows. Both childish and sinister at the same time.

"One million pounds if you want to see your daughter alive," Joe read, disbelievingly. "Is this a joke?"

"No," Russell said, lifting the note to look at it closer. "But it's a signature. And it's one I've seen a few times before."

3.

JOE AND RUSSELL stood across the road from the quiet little restaurant that formed the legitimate front for Tony "the Lizard" Lagorio's less legal business ventures.

Given that Charlotte's disappearance had now escalated to kidnap and extortion, Russell was keen to see if Tony knew anything about it, and Joe wanted to make sure they saw Antonia before they tackled Tony about any of it.

Russell was convinced they should jump straight in with Tony, before he got wind of anything, just in case he had a hand in Charlotte's kidnapping himself. But Joe didn't agree.

"It's only fair that I talk to her first," Joe protested. "She was the one who brought the case to me in the first place. If there was any way she thought her father was involved, she wouldn't have done that, would she?"

It wasn't the first time they'd gone over this argument since leaving the Red Lion, but Joe was sure that Antonia would know if her father was involved. She knew everything about their business.

Russell, however, was insistent that Tony delighted in sending ransom and extortion notes exactly like the one Charles Fenwick had received. Apparently, it had become something of a trademark—some kind of homage to an old show he used to watch on TV.

Of course, Joe trusted Russell's instincts, but the last thing he wanted to do was out Antonia to her father by blundering in there with a bunch of accusations that would inevitably link her to the missing heiress.

"Fine," Russell said. "But if she takes much longer, I'm going in anyway."

"Fine. Now will you just leave me to it? She's not going to talk if you're here. She hates you."

While Tony Lagorio may have forgiven Russell his previous role as an incorruptible detective, Antonia was finding it harder to be so gracious. Joe guessed it was because she had been the little girl left at home each time her beloved father had been hauled into the cells.

Tony was a more calculating fellow—he was able to reassess relationships based on how much they could help him on any given day. Antonia, on the other hand, held grudges.

"Right. I'll be in there," Russell said, pointing to the pub over the road. "Watching. Give me the nod when it's all agreed."

Joe realised that Russell was going to talk to Tony anyway, regardless of what Antonia said—even more reason to warn her.

Russell had barely gone inside the small pub facing the restaurant when Joe felt a tap on his shoulder and turned to find Antonia Lagorio standing far too close to him. He jumped.

"What you doing talking to that pig?" she asked.

"Hello, Antonia," Joe said, calming himself. "Firstly, he is no longer on the force, and secondly he is my... partner."

Joe hesitated to describe the relationship. Of course they were great friends, but he wanted Antonia to know that Russell was trying to help her too.

"What?" she spluttered. "You two are..."

He realised she'd misinterpreted the partner comment.

"No, we're friends. He's *got* a boyfriend. But we work together. To solve things. Like your missing girlfriend."

Antonia raised an eyebrow appreciatively.

"I had no idea he was a poof. Good man."

She turned sharply and headed across the road towards the restaurant.

"Well come on then," she called without looking back. "I haven't got all day."

"Antonia, wait." Joe said, before she could open the door.

"What?" She turned.

"Look, there's been a ransom demand. For Charlotte."

"See? I bloody told you? Who's it from?" She stopped, hand on the door handle, eyes glancing back inside.

"Russell thought he recognised the style," Joe stammered, suddenly not sure he wanted to be the one breaking the news to her.

"What style? What are you going on about?"

"Antonia," Joe sighed. "How much did your father know of your relationship with Charlotte Fenwick?"

When she turned to face him, Joe took a step back, feeling her animosity rising. She was like a viper, quick to anger, quick to strike.

"Oh, wait," Antonia said, suddenly piecing things together. "Is that cop friend of yours trying to pin this on my dad? He's always had it in for us."

"No, not at all," Joe said. "But he *is* going to talk to Tony. I just wanted you to know first. In case you wanted us to keep any confidences… you know? Confidential."

Antonia looked at him for a moment, and then smiled, clapping him hard on the shoulder.

"You're alright," she laughed. "You know that? But you don't have to worry about me. Pop's my biggest fan."

She turned to the door of the restaurant, looking back at Joe.

"Well, come on then," she said. "I assume there's some kind of time limit on this ransom offer. So let's get on with it, shall we?"

Joe looked back at the pub opposite to see Russell in the window, half pint untouched in front of him. He waved him over, and saw his friend neck most of it before Joe turned and followed Antonia into the restaurant.

RUSSELL NOTICED the strange, almost appreciative, look Antonia Lagorio gave him as he walked into the restaurant.

She and Joe were already sitting at a table in the window, facing each other, but as he approached he was sure he saw a little knowing smile cross her lips. Not something she'd ever graced him with before. He found it strangely disconcerting.

Before he reached the table, the swing doors to the kitchen burst open, the space filled with the huge, advancing frame of Tony "the Lizard" Lagorio. His face like thunder, brow lined with beads of sweat, shirt sticking to him where it touched, which was almost everywhere.

"What's so urgent you've got to make me come all the way down the stairs?" he grumbled, his Italian accent making him sound even more petulant than he was behaving. "And what are these clowns doing here?"

"Pop, sit down will you?" Antonia said, springing to her feet. "I'll get you a drink. This is important. Okay?"

Russell and Tony exchanged a terse greeting.

"And you are?" Tony snapped, as Joe jumped to his feet.

"Joe. Joe Stone," he said, and Russell saw him try not to flinch as Tony's oversized grip crushed his hand.

"Joe is a friend of mine," Russell said, quickly.

"Huh," said Tony, lumbering his great frame into a chair seemingly ill-equipped to take the weight, as Antonia came back with a glass of red wine and another of water. Both for her father. Nothing for the rest of them. They all noticed. Only Tony smiled.

"So," he said, leaning back as Joe and Russell both sat down together on the other side of the table. "What's all this about."

Antonia sat too, placing her trilby carefully on the table, ignoring her father's admonishing glance.

"You remember I told you that Charlie'd gone missing?" she began.

"Sure, and I said I'd get some of the boys to look out for her. Nothing to report."

Russell was intrigued to see the dynamic between them. Less father-daughter and more Chairman and CEO. This was a business partnership based on trust.

"Well," Antonia said, her voice showing the first wobble of concern. "There *is* something to report, because it turns out she's been kidnapped."

She looked at Russell expectantly, and he pulled the note from his inside pocket and spread it on the table.

Both Antonia and Tony looked disturbed to read it in person. Russell studied Tony's reaction to see if there was any hint that he had either commissioned the note, or sent it himself. Nothing but shock and anger registered.

"What is this?" he thundered, turning to his daughter. "Did you know about this?"

"I just found out now," Antonia said, quickly. "I hadn't seen it."

Tony picked up the note and held it up towards the window, turning it this way and that to get a better look, like an art dealer trying to expose a forgery.

"And you think *I* did this, do you?" he asked, addressing Russell.

"You've got to admit it looks familiar, right?" Russell said.

Tony put the letter down, took another sip of his wine, picked up the water glass and drained it in one hit and arranged both glasses beside the note with studied precision.

"To a dull mind like yours," he said, with a wry grin. "I suppose it does."

He turned the note round in its place to face Russell.

"But, if you remember, all the ransom notes you ever accused me of writing—which I still strenuously deny, by the way—were all made from clippings of *The Sun* and the *Daily Star*. Or so I was told, of course."

"Of course," Russell said. They both knew he was no longer in any position to pursue Tony for old crimes.

"But this," Tony said, tapping the brightly coloured letters, "this is some girly magazine or other. See? Too much pink."

Russell nodded. It hadn't struck him before, but Tony's notes—and they all knew they were Tony's—had only ever been black, white and red. The red usually only coming in when a specific threat to life had been carried out and the victim, or at least part of them, had been sent back along with the note.

"Okay," Antonia said. "So, let's drop the shit, shall we?"

It was only Joe who didn't look surprised by her comment.

"This wasn't us, right?" She turned to her father, more to confirm she could continue rather than to question him. He nodded.

"But it's similar enough," Antonia continued, "that it could be someone trying to drop us in the frame for it."

Tony slammed his hands on the table, making all of them jump.

"God damn them," he growled.

"Who?" Russell asked.

"Doesn't matter," Tony snapped. "I'll deal with it."

Russell noticed a smile cross Antonia's face, which dropped again as soon as she saw him looking. He looked back at Tony, face like thunder, neck flushing red as his blood pressure rose.

Russell had spent enough years trying to bring Tony to justice to know that when he said he'd deal with something, someone would end up getting hurt.

His empire spanned every nefarious pastime that Soho had to offer, and more beyond. From girls, to drugs, to kink, to extortion, Tony was the guy in charge. Although, the way he looked right now, he didn't look like he could be in charge of his own restaurant's lunch menu, let alone a criminal gang.

"What if they hurt her, Pop?" Antonia asked in a timid little voice Russell had never heard her use before.

Tony squeezed her hand, gently reassuring her.

"Then I will kill them with my bare hands, my treasure. I will kill them with my bare hands. They're not playing me for a patsy."

"You think someone kidnapped this girl just to set you up?" Russell asked.

Tony's shoulders slumped slightly. Antonia still sat like a coiled spring, violence just below her surface at all times.

"That would be my first guess," Tony replied.

"So who is it?"

"Brendan Doherty," Tony said, looking expectantly at Russell. "Ma Doherty's boy."

Oh. Shit. Ma Doherty had not been on Russell's radar for a long time, but the name was as familiar as his own.

Ma Doherty was a violent and psychopathic Irish woman who had set up shop on the other side of Shaftesbury Avenue and had gone about systematically terrorising the southern part of Soho. The same Ma Doherty who had made Tony "the Lizard" Lagorio look like a puppy.

"I thought we'd put them out of action back in eighty-one," Russell said.

"You did," Tony said, sadly. "And I was very grateful for it. We never quite saw eye to eye, Ma and me. She wasn't a fan of pasta."

Russell knew that when Ma Doherty had gone down, a number of her guys had moved across to work for Tony, and brought their rackets with them. It was how Russell had first come to know Tony Lagorio—by continuing to pursue the men who had once worked for Ma Doherty.

Her sons had just been teenagers back then. But that was six years ago. Brendan would be in his early twenties by now. The same kind of age as Antonia. The new generation was coming up fast.

"And you're saying Ma's back?" Russell asked. "But we put her away for fifteen years. She won't have even done half that yet. There's no way she could have got out on good behaviour. She wouldn't even know what that was."

"You really are out of the loop, aren't you?" Tony said. "Ma's dead. She died about a year ago. Terrible accident, apparently. In her cell. Dangerous places, modern prisons. You never know who to trust, do you?"

The way Tony said it told Russell that he knew exactly what had happened to Ma Doherty.

"The trouble is," Tony continued, "her boy Brendan is just like Ma, but smarter. *And* he's got a point to prove, and a mother to avenge."

"He's trying to restart her business?"

"Not trying," Tony said. "He's done it. I thought I could ride it out, you know? I thought I had their loyalty. Turns out, a lot of my boys had never stopped being Ma's boys at heart."

That explained the haunted look Tony had these days, the face that said he hadn't had a decent night's sleep for months. The Lizard was losing his grip on his empire.

"And now you think they've got something to do with Charlotte's disappearance?"

"It's obvious isn't it?" Antonia snapped. "The youngest of the brothers, Kieran, has been hanging around her like a bad smell. He's the one who got her into buying the drugs in the first place—mostly for him, I might add. And it's their boys she's been buying from. So it's them she owes all the money to."

"But she didn't even have the money to pay with in the first place, right? Even with a healthy allowance."

"Exactly," Antonia said. "Kieran hangs around with all the pretty, rich girls that come into the club, charms and cheeks them, gives them little tasters of the good life, and then gets them spending. Once they're hooked on the party lifestyle, they're like a walking cash machine for the brothers."

"Only this time," Joe said, "the pretty rich girl didn't actually have her hands on the kind of cash Kieran thought."

"I swear to God I'll kill that little runt if he's touched her," Antonia said.

Tony put a heavy hand over Antonia's, holding her back.

"That's exactly what they want, kid," Tony said, and Russell saw Antonia bristle at the diminutive. "Don't you see? They're trying to get a rise out of us. They want to pull us into a war."

"Well I say we give it to them," Antonia snapped, banging the table. "They can learn the hard way that they don't try to take what's mine."

Tony's grumbling moan was alarming. A low bass rumble that erupted into an animal roar.

"How many times?" he shouted, face red, spittle flying from his lips. Even Antonia recoiled. "We are not getting into a war with these boys. Not now. Not ever."

"But, Pop. We have to do something. They're calling me out."

"No, Antonia," Tony said. "This is not the way we do things."

Antonia stood up, clearly not willing to be reprimanded in front of two relative strangers.

"Yeah? Well, maybe it's the way *I* do things," she shouted, picking up her trilby, jamming it on her head and storming out.

"Antonia!" Tony shouted after her. "Toni! Stop."

But she was gone.

"Damned kid," he said. "She'll ruin me with this. We can't afford a war."

"I'll go after her," Joe said, and before Russell could stop him, he was gone too.

The two older men sat in silence for a moment, Tony's heavy breathing wheezing out through puffed cheeks. He really didn't look well. His hands were shaking. Beads of sweat had broken out on his forehead, and he dabbed at them with a folded handkerchief.

"Is everything okay?" Russell asked. "You don't look well."

"I'm not," Tony replied, looking him straight in the eye. "I'm not okay."

"Do you need a doctor?" Russell asked, suddenly worrying that the big man would pass out and he'd be left trying to wrestle his bulk into some kind of rescue position.

"No, I don't need a doctor," he huffed, panting now. "It's just stress. It will pass."

"You're having a panic attack?"

"You tell anyone and I will kill you. I promise you that."

Russell held his hands up as though the thought had never crossed his mind.

"What's going on, Tony?" he asked, softly. "This is not like you."

"Have you got kids?" Tony asked, then corrected himself immediately. "No of course not, sorry. Well, you should count yourself lucky."

"I do," Russell said.

Tony smiled.

"Don't get me wrong," he said. "I love my daughter."

"She's a chip off the old block, alright," Russell said, and Tony gave him a sideways look, eyes narrowing.

"She's a good kid."

"I sense a 'but' there," Russell commented.

"It's this girl she's got you chasing after," Tony said.

"Charlotte? What about her?"

"She's bad news," Tony said.

"Surely no one approves of the people their kids want to date," Russell said.

"The thing is," Tony said, shaking his head, draining the wine glass, and looking forlornly at it. "And I hate to say this, because I do love my daughter. But I think their whole relationship may have been a little... one-sided."

He held his glass out to Russell—an unspoken request for a top up.

Russell got up, grabbed a glass for himself and brought the bottle to the table. This was surreal. He had never expected to be having a heart-to-heart with Tony Lagorio about his daughter's love life.

"Antonia can be a little... full on, you know? She's got a lot of love to give."

"And you don't think Charlotte is that into her?"

"I know she isn't. And I'm pretty sure that Doherty boy is more than just a friend."

"Ah, I see."

"But here's the problem," Tony said. "If Antonia finds out, she will kill him. For real."

"Let's hope Joe can talk her down then," Russell said, suddenly worried for his friend who might find himself unwittingly caught up in a love triangle with two very sharp points. "You think he deliberately went for Charlotte to goad Antonia?"

"Yes," Tony said. "Well, that and the chance to get his grubby little hands on her millions. There's not as much money in this racket as there once was, you know?"

Russell laughed. Tony still had plenty.

"So poor Charlotte's just been a pawn in Kieran's game?" Russell asked.

"You remember what Ma was like?" Tony asked. "She loved the idea of stealing from the rich. And she had no qualms about destroying innocent people to get what she wanted."

Rich coming from you, Tony, Russell thought, but again he kept quiet.

"And her son—this Brendan—you think he's the same?"

"He's worse," Tony said. "The next generation always strives to exceed the previous one, isn't that so?"

Russell had to agree. Tony's own daughter had a far worse reputation for violence than her father, it was just that he kept her on a tight rein. Without Ma Doherty to keep her sons in check, they would almost certainly be running wild.

"So what are you going to do?" Russell asked.

Inter-gang rivalries never ended well, but this one seemed particularly personal, and, for all his flaws, Tony clearly loved his daughter and wanted to protect her.

"They've taken so much already. I can't let them take Antonia too. But that's what they're trying to do. They want her to get into it with them, so they can destroy her. Destroy us. We just can't afford it. So I want you to find this girl, and stop the Doherty brothers, before they destroy me and my girl."

No big deal.

"I can give you some muscle, if you need it," Tony said. "But I need you to keep our name out of it? Okay? I *cannot* afford to start a war with these boys."

Russell couldn't quite believe he was agreeing to help a man he'd tried to put away for so long, but he was only too aware how ruthless Ma Doherty had been. If her sons were anything like her, he'd be doing all of Soho a favour by stopping a potential turf war between their two gangs. But first, he just had to hope that Joe could stop Antonia.

"ANTONIA, JUST WAIT, will you?" Joe called as he tried to catch up with her.

"Go away." She was marching down Frith Street, in the direction of Shaftesbury Avenue and the Palace nightclub, main haunt of the Doherty brothers.

"What are you going to do?" Joe asked, finally reaching her side, still trotting to keep up.

"I'm going to do what my father is obviously too scared to," she said. "I'm going to get her back."

"Just you? All on your own?" Joe asked, hoping the sarcasm in his voice hit the mark.

"I don't need anyone else," she said. "besides, you're here now."

"Antonia, think about it a second, will you? This isn't a good idea."

"What do you know?"

Her obstinacy was incredible. She was walking into a gun fight with little more than a bad temper and some fast fists. If the Doherty brothers were trying to start a war, Antonia was about to lose the first battle before any declarations had even been made.

"What I *know*," Joe said, "is that you need to do this properly. You don't even know if they have her, let alone where she is. What do you think you're going to do, just walk in there, bat them all out of the way and get the girl? One against many. On their home turf? Come on."

He'd noticed her slowing her pace as he talked, which he was grateful for, not least for his ability to keep up while trying to talk her down.

"Why don't you let me talk to Kieran, sound him out a bit. And, if they really have taken her, we can make a proper plan to get her back. Without a fight."

"And what if I want a fight?" Antonia said. "If he's touched her..."

Aha, Joe thought. *She's jealous.* Worried that there may be something going on between Charlotte and Kieran. He thought of the Polaroid, currently tucked into his pocket, showing a bare-chested Kieran lounging casually on Charlotte's bed.

They had just crossed Shaftesbury Avenue. The Palace was in sight from here, and Joe had a feeling Antonia would find out more than she'd bargained for if she barged in there now and started asking questions.

The mood she was in, if she found out that her so-called girlfriend had also been playing around with Kieran Doherty, there would be no telling the damage she could do.

"Just let me talk to them," Joe said again.

Antonia finally stopped walking and turned to face Joe.

"Fine, but I'm waiting right here for you to get out," she said, crossing her arms and leaning against the wall of the building opposite the Palace.

Joe turned to look at the nightclub, willing it to be locked up so that he would have a bit of time to consider how to approach this madness. Unfortunately, the double fire doors at the side of the building opened up with a clatter and Kieran Doherty came out carrying a bucket of dirty water, which he sloshed into the gutter.

He looked up, as though sensing he was being watched and spotted Joe and Antonia on the other side of the street. Antonia stepped forward. Joe held her back. Kieran looked like a rabbit in the headlights.

Empty bucket in hand, Kieran turned and ran back through the double doors.

"Stay here," Joe said, dashing after him.

The doors had slammed but hadn't closed properly and, with a glance over his shoulder to check that Antonia had listened to his instruction, Joe pulled them open again and went in.

INSIDE, THE CLUB WAS DARK—just a working light on over the bar area. It had a musty smell of smoke and sweat and spilled drinks, and the carpet surrounding the dance floor was stained and sticky.

Joe had made it inside just in time to see Kieran scarper through a back door marked Staff Only. Did he risk following? What if the other brothers were back there and caught him trespassing? Kieran was obviously scared of Antonia, but had he been he running away or running for help?

Joe hovered in the entrance, trying to figure out what to do for the best. Another door slammed, further away this time, and he guessed that Kieran had chosen to run away. *What was he so scared of?*

The place was silent apart from the tinny sound of the radio behind the bar playing Lionel Richie at low volume. To be honest, "Dancing on the Ceiling" was probably a much safer bet, given the stickiness of the floor.

The echo of the slamming door faded into nothingness. Joe strained to hear anything over the radio, but just got a hum of activity from the street outside. It seemed he was alone in here for now.

Cautiously, he stepped into the room. The dance floor creaked underfoot. The bar in front of him wasn't set up yet—the optics hung empty, the till drawer open. A cleaning cloth and bottle of disinfectant spray were left abandoned beside a tray of dirty glasses. He'd obviously caught Kieran early in the clean-up operation from last night.

Joe crossed the room to the Staff Only section and gently pushed the door open. It squeaked on old hinges, sucking stale air from the bar behind him into the narrow corridor beyond.

Three plain doors stood closed along the corridor. Any one of them could be harbouring young Charlotte Fenwick. Or the Doherty brothers, come to think of it. Maybe not such a good idea to go sneaking around back here, after all.

The door at the very end of the corridor was another fire exit, presumably leading to the streets. Kieran's escape route.

Joe guessed there was more value in waiting for him to return than trying to follow him now.

He turned back to the bar to find Antonia standing there. He jumped.

"Look at this," she said, waving something soft, pale and furry at him.

"What is it?"

"A glove," Antonia said. "It's Charlie's."

"How do you know?"

She chucked it at him. Soft, pale leather, trimmed with even softer fur, the back of the hand embossed with the initials CJF.

"It's hers," Antonia said, flatly. She was behind the bar now, rummaging beneath the shelves.

"And look at this," she said, standing up triumphantly. "I bloody knew it."

She thrust a magazine into Joe's hands, all tattered where the letters had been cut out. Antonia stormed past him towards the Staff Only area.

"Antonia, wait," Joe called.

He was getting tired of her impetuous stubbornness. But she wasn't about to listen to him. She pushed the door open, already calling out into the quiet corridor beyond.

"Charlie? Charlotte, you in here?"

Joe set off after her, and then froze. Just as the staff door started to swing shut with Antonia on the other side, he caught a glimpse of a taller, broader, tougher looking version of Kieran stepping out of one of the other rooms in the corridor, baseball bat hefted over his shoulder.

Brendan Doherty looked exactly as ruthless and violent as his reputation made him out to be.

The door had barely swung shut when Antonia came backpeddling through it again, reaching into her jacket to pull out a metal baton which, with one deft flick, became three times as long.

Of course she'd have come tooled up and ready. She set her stance, ready to meet Brendan when he barged through the door.

"You!" Brendan shouted as the door clattered shut behind him. His baseball bat was held in both hands now. Batter ready. "You come into my house? Into *my* house?"

His face burned red beneath that ginger hair, his eyes wide like a wolf zeroing in for attack. His fists clenched and unclenched around the handle of the bat. Antonia stood her ground, legs slightly bent, letting him come to her.

"What about it?" she replied, fierce and cold. "Your house is in *my* town. We run this patch. Now where is she?"

She looked entirely unfazed by the huge man coming at her with both pace and intent. She was ready. Joe was not. He started backing away towards the door he'd come in through.

"Going somewhere?" a voice behind him asked.

He turned to find Kieran standing in the doorway, his own baseball bat slung casually on his shoulder. He must have alerted his brother and then circled round the building.

Joe had nothing to defend himself with. A bar stool nearby looked the most likely option, but before Joe could move, all hell broke loose.

With an animal roar, Brendan threw himself at Antonia, bat swinging. She dodged left and snapped her own metal baton across the back of his shoulders. Brendan howled, rounding on Antonia, bat still raised and ready to swing.

Kieran took the distraction as an opportunity to launch his own attack on Joe. Fortunately, Joe had a height and agility advantage—he'd spent more than enough of his childhood fending off bullies to know how to feign a move and sneak out of it at the last second.

Kieran rattled past him, all shouts and brandished weapon, but no impact.

Joe spun quickly and drove his elbow into Kieran's shoulder, sending the baseball bat clattering to the floor and forcing a cry out of his attacker.

Meanwhile, Antonia was going for Brendan again, dropping low and swiping her baton across his shins. Joe was sure she had broken at least one of his bones with that last drive.

Kieran turned back to Joe, fists raised and circling like a 1950s boxer. He managed to land one punch, almost square, just below Joe's eye, before Joe fired off a quick one-two and Kieran went down crying about his nose being broken.

While Brendan rolled on the floor clutching his shins, Antonia moved to stand over him, kicking him flat on his back and pressing her foot over his throat.

"Where is she?" she snarled.

Joe saw it coming before it happened. Brendan still had hold of his bat, and he swung it round firmly, smashing it into the back of the knee that was controlling the foot on his throat. He was back up on his feet in an instant as Antonia hopped away, swearing like a trooper, with a hobbling, furious Brendan bearing down on her.

Joe grabbed her arm and pulled her out through the door, not looking back. He could still hear Kieran whining about his nose as he slammed the door closed behind them. He shoved his hand out, brought a black cab to a rapid halt, and bundled the furious Antonia in.

"Frith Street, mate," he instructed. "And not a bloody word out of you," he said to Antonia.

FREDDIE GILLESPIE HAD LEFT the restaurant straight after the dinner and well before the drinking got serious.

He'd made it something of a tradition at work that he never stayed out with the clients. Unlike his partners who all had wives at home they were trying to avoid and kids they didn't want to see.

In the beginning he'd enforced the rule because he didn't want to let his guard down in front of them. These days it was because he had somewhere better to be.

His law firm was home to a number of yuppie alpha males and, though no one had ever explicitly said so, Freddie was sure that none of them would be too happy that one of their own was gay.

There was still a stigma, no matter how far the equal rights movement had got since the start of the eighties.

So he had always avoided getting drunk with them, partly to keep his secret, but mostly because he didn't want to join in the pissing contest that inevitably followed, judging by the stories they told the morning after. The call girls, the drugs, the fast cars and cell phones—it was all just dick swinging. It had never been his scene anyway, but having reconciled himself to his own sexuality, he despised it even more now.

Still, it seemed to work for the kind of clients their firm tended to attract—themselves rich businessmen, with points to prove and inadequacies to compensate for.

Freddie usually ended up with the celebrities and the fashion designers on his client list, so perhaps his partners did suspect something anyway.

Recently, though, he'd been leaving dinners even earlier, because now he had a life to go to outside of work. For the first time in his life he had a proper boyfriend and, though they hadn't been together very long, it was already starting to feel serious.

He and Russell had talked about him coming out to his partners. And Russell had understood entirely why Freddie didn't want to, having been on the receiving end of a targeted sting by his own colleagues.

Russell had come out better for it all in the end, but he knew how much it had hurt, and he would never put any pressure on Freddie to risk his own career.

So for now, Freddie lived two separate lives—work-Freddie and Russell's-boyfriend-Freddie. And he knew which one he preferred.

He let the door to the restaurant swing shut behind him and stood for a moment to soak up the atmosphere on the street outside.

Soho was just starting to come to life, but it would be hours yet before it showed its true face. The post-work, pre-theatre rush had abated, and now the restaurants and bars were starting to come alive with vibrant young things, chatting loudly, laughing explosively.

Music blared from different locations—Bronski Beat wrestling with Duran Duran, drowned out by the odd burst of Freddie Mercury's effortless brilliance. The place felt vibrant. Sweaty in the late summer heat. The evening had grown humid as the sun faded.

Freddie smiled as a young man approached him on the pavement. Tight denim shorts hugging his thighs and a loose fitting, bright orange T-shirt. Baseball cap at a slight angle. He looked the picture of summer.

"Alright, love?" the young man said, slowing as he saw Freddie smiling.

"Evening," Freddie replied with a nod, still smiling. Life felt good.

He set off along the pavement, intending to cut up through Soho Square and head over to the Red Lion.

It was only when he looked back over his shoulder to check for traffic before crossing the road that he realised the young man had turned back and was following him.

"Hey," the guy called. "Hey wait!"

Freddie didn't want to wait. He was still too close to the restaurant and his colleagues for any kind of scene with this guy. *What does he want?*

The guy caught up with him and grabbed his arm.

"Wait up," he said again. "Where you going?"

Freddie stopped and turned to him, shoulders set defensively.

"What do you want?" he asked.

"Oh, don't be like that, mate. I'm just being friendly. You have a lovely smile."

"I'm late," Freddie said, starting off again.

"We can be quick," the guy said, keeping just ahead of him. He crossed in front of Freddie, blocking his path. "Come on, how about it? Just a quickie?"

Freddie had only ever been approached like this by young men in pubs, never on the street before. But he guessed that's what summer did to the young and carefree. The guy was good-looking enough, and clearly up for it.

"See," he teased. "You're thinking about it, aren't you?"

Suddenly he reached down and put his hand on Freddie's crotch, his other hand snaking itself around his neck, pulling him in. Freddie pulled away, but not before the guy landed a kiss, full on his lips.

Freddie pushed him off, harder than he meant to, and the guy sprawled across the pavement. It was only then that Freddie saw how many people were watching.

"Leave me alone," Freddie said, harshly. He didn't want to shout, didn't want to make even more of a scene. But he had to make sure that people knew he wasn't complicit in the spectacle.

The guy picked himself up and dusted himself off, looking more upset than angry.

"You shouldn't have led me on then," he shouted in Freddie's face. "You shouldn't have said you wanted it."

Freddie watched as the guy stormed away, muttering to anyone that would listen. *What the hell just happened?* Had that simple smile really given the impression he was up for sex? He'd have to be more careful who he smiled at.

A young couple walking past leered at him as he turned to head off, the man muttering something about queers before spitting at Freddie's feet.

As Freddie turned the corner, heading for Soho Square and the safety of the Red Lion, he saw a familiar figure cross the road. Long beige coat. Face in shadow, but the stoop of his shoulders was unmistakable. Detective Simon Skinner. And Freddie was pretty sure it was no coincidence that he'd been there to witness that little altercation.

THE RED LION WAS FULL, loud and sweaty. "Radio Ga Ga" was already on its third repeat on the jukebox. Joe and Russell were on their second pint.

They were sharing their usual table with their friend Paul—Patty when he was in drag, which was at least half of the time—and Ron the barman's son, Scott.

Scott and Paul had struck up a firm friendship since Scott had been reunited with his father and moved back into the rooms above the Red Lion, where Paul also lived.

Paul, or rather Patty, had been helping Scott to hone his own drag routine, and it was coming along as well as could be expected from a tall, lanky kid without much coordination.

Joe was in a bit of a grump, having gotten into a scrap with the Doherty brothers thanks to Antonia, and it was only now that he was on his second pint that he had stopped fuming about her reckless bravado.

Having fled the club, he'd dropped Antonia back at her father's restaurant and left her getting a stern talking to from Tony about starting trouble she couldn't finish.

Now they were all pondering the single glove they had found in the nightclub, which Antonia had insisted was Charlotte's, and the cut-up magazine that seemed to match the note the kidnappers had sent.

The problem was that Joe had now been seen with Antonia, and Russell had been the cop who put the boys' mother in prison, so neither of them were likely to be able to get close enough to the brothers again to find out what was going on.

And while Paul was coming up with all sorts of hair-brained schemes involving him and Joe in drag, none of them would work to get the boys into the Palace to see if Charlotte was even there in the first place.

As they considered their next move, Russell spotted Freddie arriving and waved. Freddie's expression was thunderous, scowling over the heads of the other punters. He saw Russell's wave, but acknowledged it only with a nod as he headed straight towards the bar.

"Wait there," Russell said to Joe, standing up quickly. Joe frowned, followed Russell's eye line and his frown deepened.

Freddie was usually such a happy guy, especially after work when he could be himself. Russell had never seen him look this angry.

"What's up?" Russell asked, as he reached him through the throng of punters. He noticed that Freddie flinched away when he went to touch his arm.

"I need a drink," Freddie said, gruffly.

"What's happened, Fred?" Russell asked, feeling nervous as he followed Freddie through the tight, hot bodies to the bar.

Freddie called his order over the head of another young man, who looked up angrily, saw the big lawyer's expression and decided to let him cut in.

Neat vodka in hand, Freddie stood where he was and downed it in one. Signalling to Ron behind the bar that he would have another right away. Ron glanced at Russell, but poured the drink anyway. None of them had ever seen Freddie look this angry before. Only with his second vodka down and a pint in his hand, did he turn back to Russell.

He already looked a little calmer, though Russell could see that there was something behind his eyes.

"What's happened?" he asked again, and Freddie's face relaxed more.

"Nothing," he replied. "Bad day in the office, that's all. Come on."

He turned his back, heading over to their table. Russell didn't know what to think. Freddie had always been quite honest about his situation at work. He'd shared any frustrations about his partners, any horror stories of nightmare clients. Very little about his job seemed to faze him. But the expression he'd been wearing when he came in, the way he'd flinched from Russell's touch, the way he'd downed that first drink as though it was some kind of lifeblood—it all said Freddie was hiding something from him.

He watched his boyfriend sit down among his friends, the smile on his face still not his usual warm one. As Russell joined them, just the slightest narrowing of Joe's eyes asked if everything was alright. He had seen it too, then.

Freddie reached over and squeezed his hand as Russell sat down. Feeling only a little more reassured that they were still okay, he couldn't help studying Freddie's body language as he let yet another of Paul's tall tales about the Red Lion regulars wash over him.

Whatever had been troubling him seemed to have passed for now. Perhaps they would talk about it later.

Russell had been so preoccupied by Freddie's odd behaviour he hadn't noticed the young redhead approaching their table. Kieran Doherty, sporting a bigger bruise around his eye than the one that graced Joe's cheek.

Joe jumped to his feet as he saw the kid approaching.

"Take it easy, Joe," Russell warned.

Kieran stopped just short of the table as soon as Joe stood up. He looked nervous. The Red Lion's punters—misfits, reprobates, queers and queens—closed around him. Joe was one of theirs. This kid was a stranger.

Kieran looked around skittishly, sensing he was out of his depth. He held his hands up, palms out—a conciliatory gesture.

"I just want to talk," he said, though his body language already said he'd have a go at anyone who tried to jump him.

"I'm listening," Joe said. Russell thought he sounded tougher than he was.

"Is there not somewhere more private? I don't want to be shouting any of this. Not here."

"Follow me," Joe said, standing up with a slight nod to Russell. "Follow me."

Russell wondered whether he should go with them. Ma Doherty had been a nasty piece of work and he was sure her sons were all capable of equally heinous acts of violence. They certainly had Tony running scared, and that wasn't something Russell had ever thought he'd see.

Joe glanced back once, just as he led Kieran to the back room of the pub. "Five minutes," he mouthed, letting Kieran pass through the door in front of him. Russell nodded, and they were gone.

THE BACK ROOM of the Red Lion served as a function room, rehearsal space, and stage for the regular cabaret nights Ron's son, Scott, now hosted here as an excuse to exercise his alter ego, Miss Terri and her support act, the Lady Killers.

Right now, the room stood empty, mercifully sealed off from the dull roar of the pub beyond.

Kieran paced nervously on the parquet floor which doubled as the stage, while Joe pulled two chairs off one of the stacks against the wall and brought them over.

"Take a seat," he said, doing the same himself.

Kieran hesitated, moved the empty chair back a bit as though Joe was somehow contagious, and sat down, hands fidgeting, lip biting.

"So," Joe said, seizing the initiative. "Talk."

"Who are you?"

"I'm a friend of Charlotte Fenwick's," Joe lied, looking for a tell on Kieran's face as he mentioned her name. A slight narrowing of the eyes.

"I've never seen you," Kieran said, petulantly. "And I know most of her friends."

"Well, I've been away for a while," Joe said. "Anyway, that doesn't matter. All I want to know is where she is."

Kieran tilted his head to the side, assessing him.

"So, you work for *her* then, do you? The *Gecko*?" He sneered her nickname.

"What? No. Well. She asked me to help her find her girlfriend. She thinks you might know where she is."

"Her girlfriend?" Kieran's laughter was explosive. "Sure, that crazy bitch is no more her girlfriend than I'm the bleeding Pope. She's a bloody stalker is what she is. The woman's crazy."

He circled his finger beside his temple to elucidate, in case there was any confusion. Joe couldn't argue—Antonia Lagorio had a crazy streak a mile wide, but she had definitely told him that she and Charlotte had been seeing each other romantically. *Hadn't she?*

"She's always hanging round Charlotte," Kieran continued. "Trying to get her away from the rest of us. She's mad, man. She follows her everywhere."

"You don't think she's just trying to look out for her?" Joe asked. "I mean, look at all the trouble you've managed to get her into. Don't you think she needs a friend looking out for her?"

"Sure she's got one," he said. "And it's not Antonia Lagorio, that's a fact."

He slumped back down in the chair, head hanging between his knees. Joe felt confused. *What was really going on here?* Obviously, Kieran and Antonia were rivals for Charlotte's affections. Perhaps she was playing them both off against each other.

"Are you and Charlotte...?" Joe began.

Kieran looked up.

"An item? God no. I wish. But she's into the ladies, you know?"

Kieran wiped his nose on the back of his hand, looking a little more resolute.

"Look," he said. "Charlotte's got a lot of stuff going on. You know? She's a free spirit. She's probably gone off to see her aunt in the country."

Joe inclined his head, trying to make sense of this new suggestion.

"Without telling anyone?" he asked.

"Well," Kieran backtracked. "She might had said something about it. I probably just wasn't listening. So. Right. Well."

He stood up, as though he'd said all he'd come to say.

"Antonia reckons she owed you—or rather your brothers—money for all the drugs she'd been buying. You sure they didn't just get tired of waiting for her to pay up and go straight to the source?"

Kieran sat back down with a sigh.

"Sure that's mad," he said. "If she owed us anything, my brothers would just get it out of me, wouldn't they? I mean, she's my friend. I introduced her. I *vouched* for her. Besides, they may do some bad shit— I'm not denying that. But kidnap… That's not our style." He stood up again, straightening his shoulders. "So, I suggest you stay away from me and my family now. We don't take kindly to fighting talk. And tell that Antonia bitch that if it's a fight she's after, she better be ready to lose everything."

He stomped towards the door, muttering.

"Kieran, wait," Joe said, but he didn't turn back.

Fortunately, Russell came in before the kid made it back through the door.

"Going somewhere?" Russell asked, his best detective voice sending a visible chill down Kieran's spine. "Sit down, sunshine. We're not finished with you."

"Ah, come on..." Kieran moaned.

"Sit down," Russell shouted. They wouldn't be heard in here, and Joe was impressed at the volume he managed to create. Kieran sat.

"Let's start again, shall we?" Joe said, as Russell brought his own chair over and placed it backwards, straddling it with his arms crossed over the top.

"We know you've been hanging around with Charlotte, cadging off her."

"No, come on, now..." Kieran began. Joe didn't pause.

"We know you've been selling her drugs."

"I don't sell anyone anything," Kieran spluttered.

"Well, you've been getting her to buy them from your brother's guys," Russell snapped. "Same thing."

"Ah, hold on there," he said. His Irish accent became stronger when he was nervous, Joe noticed. *Good.*

"How much does she owe you, Kieran?" Joe asked. "I bet it's a damned sight less than the million quid you'd trying to stiff her dad for."

Kieran looked utterly dumbfounded.

"Are you drunk?" he asked.

Joe didn't answer. He hadn't expected Kieran to just roll over and admit everything, but he also hadn't expected him to be this good at hiding their involvement. He glanced nervously at Russell. Had they got this all wrong?

Russell rolled up his sleeves, slowly, deliberately threatening. Filling the silence with menacing action. He'd done this a few times before.

"Listen," Russell said quietly. "This all still has a chance of resolving itself without anyone getting into any trouble."

Kieran was still shaking his head in confusion. Russell leaned further forward over the back of his chair, going for full intimidation.

"I'll tell you what I think, shall I?" he said. "I think you trapped a young, rich girl into a debt with your family that she couldn't pay. And now you've taken her hostage so that you can extract even more money out of her father."

The brief silence that followed was broken by Kieran's strangled laughter. He had genuinely found that funny.

"What?" he asked, when he'd finally half-composed himself again.

"Don't play dumb with me, son," Russell said, standing up now. "You know where she is, and you're going to tell us. Her family is worried sick."

"I told you," he said. "I don't know where she is. Like I said, she's probably off visiting her aunt in the country. Sure, have you thought of that?"

He sounded so cocky Joe could have swung for him.

"So, what? You think her aunt sent this, do you?" Joe said, standing up and reaching into his back pocket. Kieran flinched as Joe shoved the ransom note against his chest.

Kieran peeled the sheet of paper off his chest and opened it, reading the words. Joe studied his expression but the look he saw was of genuine confusion. He looked up at Joe, across at Russell, back to the sheet of paper in his hand.

"Wait? That's not... Where did you get this?"

"Don't play dumb with me, son," Russell said. "We know you delivered this note to her father's address. You were seen doing it."

"Seen?" Kieran looked even more confused. "This is a stitch up. Seen by who?"

"Whom," Russell corrected. "It doesn't matter. Now tell us where she is, and we can end this now."

You really think *this* was us?" Kieran asked, head cocked to one side, scowl deeply set. He tossed the note back at Joe.

"We found the magazine in your club, all cut up," Joe said, with a strange feeling that he wasn't actually winning this battle despite the evidence they had. "We found one of her gloves."

"Ah, Jesus," Kieran said. "That girl leaves her stuff everywhere. I'm always picking up after her. That means nothing. And I've never seen this note."

"Just tell us where she is, Kieran," said Joe. "And we can get all this sorted out without calling the police."

Kieran laughed again.

"You can call the bloody Queen for all I care," Kieran said. "You're barking up the wrong tree here, lads. You won't find her anywhere near our place. And we didn't send this note."

Kieran's confidence seemed to have returned a little, though Joe could see that his mind was still whirring. Kieran Doherty was hiding something.

Before any more could be said, Kieran stood up.

"I don't know where she is, lads, and that's the truth, but I don't want any bother, so I'll tell you this: Charlotte told me she was in trouble, but she said she was going to sort it out. She'll be fine. I swear on me Ma's honour."

And the look he gave Russell told them both that the kid knew who he was.

With that, Kieran walked out, leaving Joe and Russell staring after him, more than slightly confused.

JOE STOOD IN the shadows on the corner of Shaftesbury Avenue, peering at the windows of the Palace nightclub, trying to see inside.

He felt ridiculous in the white baseball cap and pink sweatshirt he'd borrowed from Paul back in the bar.

The sweatshirt was far too small for him, for a start, and he never wore pink. But then that was entirely the point. It may not be much of a disguise, but it was better than nothing.

It was swaying room only on the dancefloor, bodies pressed close together, feeling the beat and the heat. The place was packed, but noticeably straighter than any clubs Joe ever found himself in.

For years, the sight of men and women dancing together had been the norm for Joe, but since moving to London he'd found his own crowd and they had their own—safe—places to hang out. Sadly the Palace wasn't one of them. *So why have I sent my friends in there?*

Joe could just about make out the back of Patty's red wig in one of the booth seats in the window. Scott was beside her as a pared down version of his own drag character, Miss Terri and they'd even managed to rope in a couple of Miss Terri's more feminine backing singers—The Lady Killers—to go with them.

They had all toned down the high camp and, for the most part—from a distance—they passed for a group of young women out on the town. Which was exactly what Joe needed them to look like.

After Kieran had left the Red Lion, Joe'd gone back to their table and cooked up this odd little plan to get inside the Palace and see if he could find any clues as to where the Doherty brothers might be keeping Charlotte.

He had seen something in the way Kieran had reacted to their questions and was sure that the kid was lying to them.

Kieran's shock at seeing the note had seemed genuine, though, and Joe wondered whether his brothers had gone behind his back once they realised who Charlotte was and how much she was worth.

Paul and Scott had both jumped at the chance of being involved in a stakeout, and neither of them needed much persuading to get frocked up and hit the club, despite the fact that they knew they were walking into a lion's den.

Joe couldn't help feeling nervous for them. Though it was only a few roads down from their beloved Soho, the Palace was not known as a particularly gay-friendly place.

But Patty was tougher than she looked and, so long as they kept their wits about them and stuck together, they would be okay.

Joe, on the other hand, knew that what he was about to do was plain foolhardy.

He had asked the girls to create enough of a distraction downstairs that he could slip in unnoticed and make his way up to those private rooms upstairs.

Russell had told him that, back when Ma Doherty ran the show, those upstairs rooms housed illicit gambling dens, prostitutes, dealers, you name it.

Joe didn't doubt that the same was true now. He also wondered if one of those rooms may be harbouring a missing heiress as well.

The fire escape doors on the side of the building opened quietly, and Miss Terri slipped out onto the pavement followed by a burst of Bon Jovi's "Livin' on a Prayer". Her neat, angular bob suited those high cheekbones, giving her the look of a slightly dowdy Annie Lennox.

Joe dipped his head and crossed the road to join her.

"Alright?" he asked.

"Christ, it's like a meat market in there," Miss Terri said. "Have you heard the bloody music? Cock Rock! How is anyone supposed to dance to that?"

"Are they all in there, though? The brothers?"

The idea was that the girls would make sure that any Doherty brothers that were in the club were all downstairs before they created their distraction, thus making sure they would all get involved.

"Yes." She exhaled smoke in a thin plume from tightly pursed lips. "But I wish I'd worn more sensible shoes. I've got a feeling we might need to run."

Joe looked down. The killer heels Miss Terri had become famous for were going to make for a tough getaway if things turned sour.

"Ditch them if you have to, I'll buy you a new pair," Joe said.

"On your wage?" she sneered, laughing. "I don't think so, love. Speaking of which, the drinks in here are crazy prices. You got a float for this operation of yours?"

Joe fished a tenner out of his pocket and handed it to her.

"That's all I've got."

She rolled her eyes beneath long lashes, taking another deep drag on her cigarette.

"Big spender," she muttered. "Right, hang tight. You'll know when it's time."

With that, she squashed the cigarette under one of those killer heels and turned back to the door.

"Be careful," Joe said.

"You too."

She blew him a kiss and pulled the door shut, but didn't close it fully—this would be Joe's route into the building when it all kicked off.

He leaned back against the wall, waiting for his moment and half-wishing he'd never roped his friends into this kind of madness. *Too late now.*

He didn't have to wait long. The first sound of smashing glass was followed by a scream and then a cacophony of shouted swearing.

If the girls followed the plan, they'd get everyone tussled up in the middle of that heaving dance floor and leave Joe a route around the periphery while they were all distracted.

He sneaked a look through the door. The girls had done exactly what he'd asked of them. The centre of the dance floor was a scrum of arms, legs and raised bottles. Drinks flew into the air and screams descended.

Three shocks of ginger hair skirted the edge of the fray, baseball bats raised higher than their voices—the Doherty brothers were going in.

But as his brothers dived in, young Kieran stayed back behind the bar, a bat in his hand and a nervous expression on his face. He wasn't like the other two. Yet.

Joe slipped through the fire escape doors, keeping himself pressed against the wall. All attention was focussed on the dance floor, though he could already see that both Patty and Miss Terri had managed to retreat to the side lines as the latent testosterone in the room fuelled whatever fire they'd ignited. *Now or never.*

Joe slinked along the wall, heading towards the doors marked Staff Only and those stairs he's seen heading up to the floors above. He glanced back once, leaned against the Staff Only door and disappeared through it. He had to be quick.

The corridor was much cooler than the club but still had that stale, musty smell about it.

Joe took the stairs to the first floor two at a time, not sure how long he would have to search the rooms for any hint that Charlotte was, or had been, there.

He listened patiently outside each door before cautiously opening them.

There was no sign of life in any of the rooms. No illicit card games, no brothels, drinking dens or gambling rings, and certainly no damsels in distress. Just boxes of stock for the bar, chairs and tables in neat stacks, mountains of rolls of toilet paper bought in bulk. It was hardly the den of iniquity he'd been led to believe.

At the end of the corridor, though, he found a room with a heavy padlock on a bolt locking the door. He pressed his ear to the thin panel, willing his thumping heart to quieten. *Was Charlotte locked inside?*

He wondered whether he would get away with the noise of breaking the lock.

There was no sound from inside, and when he stooped to peer through the keyhole, he half-expected to see the missing heiress.

Instead he saw a table laden with plastic wrapped bundles. Packages he could only assume were cocaine.

With that much marching powder in their hands, the Dohertys wouldn't need to stoop to anything as crass as kidnap, would they?

Tony Lagorio must be right, after all. If they *had* taken Charlotte, it could only be to pick a fight with Antonia. *What a mess.*

Joe turned to the next door along the corridor and found the first of three bedrooms, side by side, with a bathroom separating the second and third. All messy. All a little funky smelling. All definitely male. No sign of Charlotte at all.

That was the last of the rooms. If they *had* taken Charlotte, they weren't keeping her here.

Hearing the kerfuffle below beginning to abate, Joe realised he was on a hiding to nothing with his search and headed back towards the stairs. He should get out of here while he still could.

Passing back along the corridor, he stopped at one of the first rooms again. He could have sworn he'd heard a faint cry from within. Little more than a whimper. There! He'd heard it again. *Charlotte?*

He flung the door open, already chiding himself for missing her the first time round. As the door swung open, he failed to suppress a small scream as a tiny black creature leapt up at his knees.

The first of two small, yapping puppies hurled itself at him, before slithering past his feet and out into the corridor. He scooped the first pup up, just as the second wriggled past, making its own bid for freedom towards the stairs.

"Shit," Joe hissed. "Come here."

Needless to say, the puppy paid him no attention and kept bounding for the stairs with Joe in hot pursuit.

He bent to scoop the pup up in his free hand, just as it reached the top step.

Joe straightened up to find Brendan Doherty striding up the stairs towards him. Joe was relieved to see he no longer had his baseball bat in hand, but his stomach flipped nonetheless.

"What are you doing to Reggie and Ronnie?" he snarled.

Of course you have puppies named after the Kray twins.

With no time to think and a silent apology to the small dogs, Joe thrust them at Brendan, pushing his way past and relying on Brendan's instinct to protect his pups to buy him enough time to leg it.

"I know who you work for!" Brendan shouted after him. "I'm coming for you!"

Joe piled out of the fire escape door and onto the street to find Patty and Miss Terri leaning on a lamppost sharing a cigarette, seemingly untouched by the scuffle they'd caused earlier.

"You took your time," Miss Terri said. "The Lady Killers have gone for chips."

"Come on!" Joe called, sprinting off.

"Not in these heels," Patty called. "We'll see you back at the Lion later."

4.

RUSSELL WOKE TO FIND the other side of the bed empty. It was still early—way before Freddie usually had to get up for work, but the sheets were already cool. He'd obviously got up a while ago.

It had been a rough night in Soho, with police sirens and shouted brawls running into the early hours. Perhaps Freddie hadn't been able to get to back sleep.

Not for the first time in twenty-four hours, Russell wondered what was going on with his boyfriend to make him so edgy?

Russell had tried to talk to him when they'd got home, but Freddie had just said he was tired and rolled over as though to go to sleep. Russell had laid there for ages, listening to his breathing, knowing he wasn't asleep at all, but not wanting to ask the question again in case the answer was the one he was dreading: Freddie was having second thoughts about their relationship.

Every time the niggling doubt raised its head, Russell reassured himself that if that was the case, he would've gone home to his far more tasteful apartment in Clapham, rather than stay over. So what was going on? There was clearly something he was hiding, and that was never a good thing.

With a big sigh and a knot in his stomach, Russell slid out of bed, pulled his dressing gown on, and wandered through to the kitchen.

Before he'd even got through the door, he could hear voices, hushed but casual. Joe and Freddie.

"Well, he probably just doesn't want to see the truth," Joe said, in the middle of a conversation. "Even if it's staring him in the face."

Russell's paranoia radar flared. He stopped walking and held his breath. *Were they talking about him? Was Freddie trying to justify wanting to break up with him?* How dare he discuss it with Joe first?

"Maybe," Freddie replied, sounding tired. "But you'd think you'd be able to tell if someone just wasn't that into you, wouldn't you?"

Russell's heart sank. He knew Freddie had been struggling to keep a balance between his private and professional lives, and he understood it completely, having fought the same battle for long enough himself. Was all this just too much for Freddie?

Steadying himself, he walked into the kitchen. If this was going to happen, he was damned if he was going to let them sit there and pick over it behind his back. He deserved better than that.

"Morning sleepyhead," Freddie said, standing up quickly as Russell walked in. *Was that guilt?*

Russell shrugged out of his embrace, and crossed to the sink, busying himself with making coffee. He realised his hands were trembling.

"What's up with you?" Freddie asked, sliding up behind him and putting his arms around his waist.

"He's pre-caffeinated," Joe said. "You should know not to try get any sense out of him before his first cuppa."

"I would have brought one in," Freddie said. "But you looked so peaceful."

"We were just talking about young Kieran," Joe said, and Russell felt his face flush. He kept his back to them both, hiding his embarrassment, but leaned into Freddie a little more now. They hadn't been talking about him after all.

"Oh yeah?" he said, moving over to the kettle as Freddie retook his seat.

"Yeah," Freddie replied. "Joe here thinks he's in love with the girl and doesn't want to admit she's got a thing with Antonia."

"Really?" Russell asked, carrying the coffee pot to the table and sitting down. "Well, Joe doesn't know the kind of family that boy comes from. Trust me. Love's got nothing to do with it. He would have looked at her and just seen pound notes. He already admitted he's been using her to pay for the party lifestyle."

"He didn't really say he'd been using her, did he?" Joe said. "He said he'd assumed she could pay, that was all."

"Pretty much the same thing, if you ask me. Doesn't count as love, in my book."

He couldn't help but look at Freddie when he made that last comment. He just couldn't shake this feeling of paranoia. Freddie, however, didn't even raise an eyebrow.

It was only when he looked back at Joe that he noticed how red Joe's eyes were. He didn't look like he'd slept much, either.

"What did you find at the club? Anything?" he asked. He'd been so preoccupied with his worries about Freddie that he hadn't even thought to ask Joe how their reconnaissance mission had gone last night.

"Nothing. Apart from a mountain of coke and a cute pair of puppies," Joe said. "I tell you what though, if the Lizard wants rid of the Doherty brothers, a quiet word to one of his old mates on the force would probably do the job. They've got half of the Bolivian supply up there."

"Hold that thought," Freddie said, with a strange expression on his face. "So you still honestly think the Doherty brothers have got Charlotte even though you found nothing?"

"I still think it makes the most sense," Joe said. "But, from the way Kieran reacted to that note, I don't think he knew about it until we brought it up. It's more likely that his brothers realised who she was and what they could get out of her father. The chance to set Tony Lagorio up for it was probably too good to be true. They probably guessed he'd assume they were going after his daughter's girlfriend deliberately and come looking for a fight."

"So do you think they'll come good on their threat?" Freddie asked. "If the money's not forthcoming?"

"That and worse," Russell said. "If they're anything like their mum, they won't think twice. It's not like they need the money."

"We really *should* go to the police," he said.

"There are so many things wrong with that suggestion," Russell said. "Firstly, they probably have most of the squad on the payroll anyway— these guys make Tony Lagorio look like a lightweight. Secondly, they explicitly said no police in the note, and I wouldn't like to test them on that."

Freddie nodded, but looked as though he was about to protest.

"Thirdly," Russell continued. "Charles Fenwick doesn't want his daughter's reputation damaged by any of her secrets coming out, and, if she has had been sleeping with either Kieran Doherty or Antonia Lagorio, or both, he won't want that getting out. Let alone the fact that she's been buying drugs for half the socialites in London."

"That's true," Joe said.

"And finally, it would mean having to spend time in a room with that weasel, Skinner."

Russell saw a look pass across Freddie's face that was somewhere between panic and anger. He knew Freddie had inherited Russell's hatred of the corrupt detective as soon as he'd met him, so the anger was understandable, but that look of panic was strange. Fleeting, too.

"Well, that's a very compelling argument," Freddie said, realising that Russell was looking at him and forcing a smile.

"So where do we go from here?" Joe asked.

"Well, I suppose we do what they ask," Russell said. "Pay the ransom, get the girl back, and see if we can catch them out somehow in the process."

"You're still thinking of helping Tony bring them down?" Joe asked.

"That's a bit overdramatic," Russell replied. "But look, the last thing Soho needs right now is a turf war, and it does seem as though the Doherty brothers are gunning for Tony. If we can come up with a way to stop them, we'll have a powerful friend for life, and keep some of the trouble off the streets for a bit longer. It's a win-win."

"Uh-huh," Joe said. "And how are we going to do that?"

"No idea," Russell said, smiling. "But I'm sure I'll come up with something. First things first, though, let's get the girl back safely."

"I'll go see Charles Fenwick. Tell him what we know. Try to convince him to pay up," Freddie said. "But it's not going to be easy. He's as tight as they come."

"I'll come with you," Russell said. "Maybe once I explain the kind of guys we're really dealing with here, he won't think a million is too much of a sacrifice to get his daughter back in one piece."

Freddie nodded his assent. Russell was sure he could scare Charles Fenwick into agreeing to pay up, but that wasn't his only motivation for volunteering to go along. There was something going on with Freddie, and he wanted to keep a closer eye on him to see if he could figure out what it was.

RUSSELL AND FREDDIE sat in awkward silence in the drawing room of Charles Fenwick's London mansion.

They had barely spoken on the way over, sharing a cab from Shaftesbury Avenue instead of walking the twenty minutes together.

Freddie had said it was too hot to walk, but Russell had a feeling that it was because he wanted to get there quickly, rather than risk any questions about what was going on with him on the way.

Russell had desperately wanted to ask why had he been acting so strangely last night, but he couldn't bring himself to do it because he was terrified of the answer.

Every time he plucked up the courage to start the question, he looked at his beautiful boyfriend and lost his conviction.

A little voice inside his head constantly reasoned with him: Freddie wouldn't have hugged him like that this morning unless he still loved him. *Unless it's guilt, and he just can't bring himself to do the deed yet*, the other voice countered.

In the end, Russell had settled for a simple "You okay?" to which Freddie had just nodded, with a tight smile. But Russell could tell his mind was working on something and the longer it went on, the more convinced he was that it was something Freddie couldn't bring himself to confess.

They had been waiting in the drawing room for ten minutes already, and there was no sign of either Charles Fenwick, or his man, Mills.

The door had been opened by a maid with a heavy Russian accent, who had shown them into the drawing room and disappeared.

The house was silent. Even the sounds of the city didn't permeate these walls. Freddie glanced over at Russell and smiled, his leg jittering. Russell smiled back but his heart wasn't in it. He felt disturbed. Disquieted.

They both stood as the doors opened, like schoolboys waiting on the headmaster. Charles Fenwick walked in, hair a little wilder, clothes a little scruffier. He was clutching a large padded envelope, which he thrust at Freddie without so much as a hello.

"This came this morning," he said, his voice tremulous and cracking. "It's hers. Mills saw the young lad deliver it. He's set off after him. Not back yet. Unlikely to catch the bugger though. The man's too slow."

Freddie opened the top of the envelope and peered in, frowning. Russell waited expectantly. Freddie cleared a space on the small glass coffee table and carefully tipped the contents of the envelope out onto it.

There was what looked like another ransom note, folded in quarters. And a glove. Soft leather, fur cuff. The initials CJF monogrammed on the back. Exactly the same as the one Joe had found in the Palace.

The pale fur cuff was matted and stained with something dark and sticky. Russell crouched down to take a closer look and realised it was blood.

"It's definitely hers?" Freddie asked.

"Of course it is," Fenwick snapped. "I had them handmade for her birthday. There's not another pair like them in the world."

"This looks like blood," Russell said to Freddie, voice low, though Charles had clearly already come to the same conclusion.

Freddie picked up the folded note and straightened it out, reading aloud.

"Time's up. One million tomorrow or we send her back in pieces. Phone box on the corner of Greek Street and Romilly Street at eleven am. No police."

"I'm not paying," Fenwick said. "This is robbery."

"This is serious, Charles," Freddie said, holding the note up to him. "You don't want her hurt, do you?"

"Of course not, but... a million pounds? I won't do it."

"You don't know these people," Russell said. "If they don't get what they're asking for, they could kill her."

Charles Fenwick turned on Russell with an expression of such anger on his face that Russell took a step back, hands up.

"Wait. You *know* who has my daughter?"

"We don't *know*," Russell said quickly. "We *think* she's been taken by a gang in Soho. But if it *is* them, they don't mess around."

"A gang?" Fenwick asked incredulously. "What kind of gang? Who are they?"

Freddie shot Russell a warning look. They had agreed not to reveal too much about the Doherty brothers in case Charles Fenwick decided to take matters into his own hands. He had a hot temper, and wouldn't hesitate to go round there making demands. Which would probably only get him killed.

"It's better that you don't know too much at this stage," Freddie said. His voice was quiet and authoritative. Fenwick looked as though he wanted to argue but thought better of it. Freddie had talked him out of a number of rash decisions in the past. He would trust him.

"Well, we should go to the police then, shouldn't we?" Fenwick asked.

"That's not a good idea," Russell said. "Trust me."

Should he tell Charles Fenwick about his daughter's drug habit? About the party lifestyle, the drugs, the boyfriend, the girlfriend, the debt?

The threat in the note was clear—the blood on the glove underlined it. He had a right to know, surely? But maybe not all of it.

"You said at the beginning that you wanted to protect your daughter's reputation. If the police get involved in investigating this, you won't be able to do that."

"What do you mean?"

"She's been living quite a risky lifestyle for the past year," Russell said. "Drinking, partying, hanging around with some dodgy sorts."

Charles laughed insincerely.

"We all go through a wild stage. It's not the end of the world. She'll come right."

"She's in trouble, Charles," Freddie interjected. "She's been buying drugs for her friends on tic from some pretty nasty guys, and she's run out of time to pay them back. It looks like they got tired of waiting."

"I see," he said, sitting down. "Right."

They watched him in silence, waiting for him to concede that stumping up the cash was the only sensible thing to do.

"Okay," he said, finally. "Here's what we're going to do."

He indicated for them to both sit, too. They did.

"You know these people, right?" he asked Russell.

"Yes, but..."

"Good, so you will go and make them the following offer: I will pay them what she owes them, and not a penny more. And in return, they will release her unharmed. Or I will go to the police and have them arrested, and let the chips for her fall where they may. There is only so much I can do to protect her reputation if she is determined to ruin it."

"They will never agree to that," Russell said. "It's already gone too far."

"Then they can keep her," Charles Fenwick said.

"What?" Freddie spluttered. "Charles..."

"If what you say is true—drugs, debts, drinking—if that is the level of deception she's capable of, then she is no daughter of mine. Make them the offer. If they don't accept. Walk away. That's final."

He rung the little hand bell on his desk. Nothing. He'd obviously forgotten that poor Mills was still chasing down whoever had dropped the package off.

He rang again, longer this time. Russell and Freddie both stood up, ready to show themselves out, when a panting, dishevelled Mills burst through the door.

"He got away, Sir," he said. "I'm sorry. Blasted fast, the bugger."

But Fenwick wasn't listening. He quieted the bell, replacing it on the table.

"No matter, Mills," he said. "These men know where she is, they're on their way there not to make an offer. See them out, will you?"

"Sir."

RUSSELL AND FREDDIE stood on the street as the door shut behind them, knocked by how quick Charles Fenwick had been to disown his daughter.

Perhaps they shouldn't have told him everything after all, but there was no other way to make him see that bringing the police in would expose his family to a huge scandal.

As the door closed, leaving them on the street outside, Russell looked at Freddie.

"What the hell?" he said.

Freddie shook his head sadly, lips tight.

"I should have remembered," he said. "Fenwick's older brother overdosed. He'd been bailing him out for years."

"And you just forgot to mention it?" Russell hadn't meant to sound so angry, but he was still suspicious of what was going on with Freddie and, had he known about the family history, he might not have mentioned her involvement in drugs at all.

Freddie looked a little hurt by his tone.

"Yes," he said defensively. "It was a long time ago. I didn't have any dealings with him at the time and I only knew about it because I read it in his file. It's not something we ever spoke about."

"You know they're not going to go for this offer, right?" Russell said. "Especially not if it's me making it. I put their mother in prison. Where she died. I probably won't even come out of there alive."

"It's fine," Freddie said, "I'll do it. I have to go into the office first, though. I'll meet you back at the flat at lunchtime."

HAVING LEFT FREDDIE on the pavement outside Charles Fenwick's house, Russell had walked back to the flat slowly, taking his time but not really noticing the world around him.

As he reached the flat, he told himself to buck up. If something was going on with Freddie, he would find out one way or another and, until then, all he could do to protect himself was start putting that wall back up. The one he felt he'd only just begun dismantling.

With a heavy heart, Russell turned away and headed back towards Soho and the sanctuary of his flat. He wanted to see how Joe had got on with Antonia anyway.

He opened the door to the communal lobby that led up to his flat— the site of the murder of his former flatmate and friend Chris—and stooped to pick up the mail from the black-and-white tiles.

He sorted everything that wasn't for him and Joe into a pile, put it on the shelf for the other tenants in the building, and made his way upstairs.

An intriguing envelope caught Russell's eye. A4 with his full name handwritten on it in thick marker pen, but no address.

Dropping the rest of the mail on his kitchen table, he carefully opened the envelope and reached inside.

What he pulled out made his heart stop and his stomach sink. A series of black-and-white photos, blown up large, of Freddie kissing a young man. *Out on the street.* The guy's hand on his crotch, his arm around Freddie's neck. *His Freddie.* Who wouldn't even hold hands in public because he was too afraid of his work partners finding out he was gay. *What had he done?*

Russell felt sick. He slumped down into a chair at the kitchen table, not wanting to look at the images any more, but not able to tear his eyes away. He felt hot and cold at the same time.

The door closed downstairs. Footsteps approached.

"You here?" Joe called out as he came in to the flat.

Russell couldn't answer. He couldn't move.

"Hey," Joe said, walking into the kitchen. "What's news?"

He walked behind Russell towards the sink, and stopped when he noticed that Russell hadn't moved.

"Russell? You okay?" he asked. But he had already spotted the photographs on the kitchen table. "Is that...? Oh, God. Russell."

As Joe put his hand on Russell's shoulder, the dam broke and the tears started.

THE RED LION was the last place Russell wanted to be right now. He wanted to be curled up in his bed, crying into his pillow. *How could Freddie have done this to him? And so publicly, too?*

Joe had insisted he come out, though, refusing to leave him to wallow at home.

Every time the door opened, Russell looked up nervously, wishing that it would be Freddie and at the same time hoping it wouldn't. What would he say to him, anyway?

Joe had assured him that there was probably some perfectly innocent explanation—he couldn't believe Freddie would do something like that. And Russell wanted to believe him, but the photographs didn't lie.

Still, Joe had forced him to put his emotions aside for the time being and focus on finding Charlotte. He could deal with Freddie when, and if, he showed his face.

Having put his melancholy aside temporarily, Russell had told Joe about the meeting with Charles Fenwick, and how he had shut down as soon as he'd heard about Charlotte's drug debts.

They'd both agreed that the bloodied glove—a match for the one Joe and Antonia had found in the Palace—was as much confirmation as they needed that the Doherty brothers had taken Charlotte.

"Perhaps I should go and help Freddie," Joe had said. "Although I don't fancy seeing Brendan Doherty again while he thinks I was trying to nick the Kray twins."

"Let him go alone," Russell had said, knowing he was being spiteful. He didn't care. He was hurt.

There was so much about the case that seemed off to Russell, but he was aware that his brain wasn't clear enough right now to see through the mist.

Young Charlotte Fenwick, in debt up to her eyeballs thanks to her extravagant lifestyle and naïve personality, finds herself in debt to a bunch of ruthless crooks. When they find out she can't pay, they kidnap her and issue a ransom note. So far, so straightforward.

But why issue a note clearly incriminating a rival gang? Why start a turf war you're not yet in a position to win, against a ruthless villain like Tony Lagorio and his psychopath daughter?

Was Tony right? Had they targeted Charlotte in the first place just to get to Antonia? It seemed like quite a long game to Russell, and that was where things started falling apart in the chain.

If all of this was a way of targeting Antonia, it was too longwinded and with far too many risks for failure. If you wanted to pull the Lagorios into a war, why not try something more direct? Like lobbing a Molotov cocktail though the restaurant door. That would have been Ma's style.

And then there was the fact that Kieran didn't even think that Antonia and Charlotte were an item. Fair enough, he had admitted *he* wanted Charlotte for himself, but his description of Antonia as an over-possessive stalker seemed to ring truer to the character that Russell had come to know over the years, rather than the concerned girlfriend she'd managed to convince Joe she was.

Russell only realised he'd tuned out Joe's own questioning of the same issues when his flatmate nudged his arm.

"Shall I leave you two to it?" Joe asked, and Russell looked up to see Freddie approaching the table.

"Thanks," Russell said, taking a steadying breath. Joe squeezed his hand.

"I'll be at the bar."

Russell noticed the look of confusion on Freddie's face as Joe walked past with the tersest of greetings.

"What's up with him?" Freddie asked, sitting down.

"I wasn't expecting to see you tonight," Russell said, not quite managing to keep his voice level.

Freddie leaned back in his chair, frowning. "Look, Russell, there's something I need to tell you. You're not going to like it."

Even though he'd been expecting it, Russell still felt his stomach sink again. They'd only just begun their relationship and already it was ending. Was this what he was doomed to experience for the rest of his life? He'd genuinely thought Freddie was different.

"I already know," Russell said.

"What?"

"I already know."

Freddie looked completely confused. Russell lifted the envelope from the seat beside him and threw it across the table at Freddie. Frowning, Freddie opened it and took the photographs out. His face paled.

"He sent them to you too?"

"Who is this? Who is he?" Russell asked, trying not to get hysterical. "How could you do that? Out in the street like that, as well?"

"It's not what you think."

"It bloody well looks like what I think," Russell spat, bitterly. "I hope he was worth it."

He went to stand up, no longer able to face his soon-to-be ex-boyfriend.

"It was Skinner," Freddie said, grabbing his wrist and holding him back.

"What?" Russell asked, the wind taken out of his sails by the mention of his nemesis.

"Just hear me out, okay?" Freddie asked, holding Russell's arm until he sat down, and then moving his grip to rest his hand on top of Russell's.

Russell nodded, still feeling furious. But also a little confused.

"I'd just come out of the restaurant after that work dinner, I was on my way over here. This guy approached me out of nowhere, offering sex. I refused, obviously. But he threw himself at me, landed a kiss. I pushed him off, and he started making a real scene in the street. Everyone was watching. It was awful."

Russell frowned, saying nothing. The photographs still lay between them, but looking at them with this version of the story ringing in his ears, he could see that Freddie was not enjoying the kiss. His eyes were wide open, shocked, not the sensual half-closed flutter Russell had seen when *they* kissed. Why hadn't he noticed it before?

"Then the guy walks off and, as I'm crossing the road, I see Skinner stepping out of the shadows," Freddie continued. "I knew exactly what he'd done, and then I guessed what he was going to do."

"Why didn't you say anything?" Russell asked,

"Because you would blame yourself," Freddie said. "He wouldn't be doing any of this to me if I wasn't seeing you, would he?"

"What did he do?" Russell asked, already suspecting.

"He sent the same pictures to both my partners at the firm," Freddie said.

Russell felt like his world had just shifted. Here he was thinking that Freddie had been cheating on him and was about to break up with him, when he was actually having his career ruined because of their relationship and Russell's ongoing feud with Skinner.

"Oh my God, Freddie, I'm so sorry."

"It's okay," Freddie said. "It was all going to come out at some point soon anyway. I was just hoping I could leave it until I introduced you at the Christmas lunch. The partners get to bring their wives, you know?"

Russell smiled, punching his arm. He would have protested more at being lumped in with the wives, but he could see now that Freddie'd had a terrible afternoon.

"What happened?"

"I managed to get our PA to hold back all our mail until I got to the office, so I managed to intercept it. But I told them anyway. Just on my terms. Not Skinner's."

"And?"

"And, they were surprised. Or, at least, they pretended to be. But they were fine. And then, when I told them what had prompted me to tell them now, they got angry."

"With you?"

"No, no. With our friend Detective Skinner," Freddie smiled. "I hope you don't mind, but I told them what he did to you."

Russell sighed. Freddie had put everything on the line this afternoon, and he had doubted him.

"I don't mind," he said. "It just makes me mad that he's still pulling the same trick."

"Ah, well," Freddie said, smiling genuinely for the first time since he'd sat down. "The good thing about my business partners, is that they know their way around the law. They're busy working on a plan to see Skinner hoisted by his own petard. And I, for one, can't wait."

He sat back and looked at Russell quizzically.

"Did you really think I would do something like that? In the street?"

"No," Russell said. "I don't know. I was so angry."

"You need to learn to trust me."

He was right, of course. Russell should have known better. Freddie leaned across and kissed him, and the world of noise and life flooded back in. They were going to be okay.

"So how did it go with the Doherty brothers?" Russell asked, waving Joe back over.

"Very confusing," Freddie said, smiling at Joe as he sat down with fresh pints for all of them. "Thanks."

"You two alright?" Joe asked, cautiously.

"Skinner up to his old tricks," Russell said, clearing the photographs from the table and winking at Joe's smile.

"Bastard," Joe said.

"So, I went to see the Dohertys," Freddie said. "Sat down with Brendan who was actually quite charming, for a psychopath. Anyway, they claim to have nothing to do with Charlotte's disappearance."

"Well, they *would* say that, wouldn't they?" Russell said.

"Yes, but Brendan seemed genuinely confused," Freddie said. "They'd seen her in the club a couple of times, apparently. Brendan thought that she and Kieran were friends, but laughed when I suggested there might be more to it."

"Really?" Russell asked.

"Yes. Apparently, she's made it quite clear where her enthusiasm lies and it's not with boys. Especially not—and these are his brother's words—scrawny gingers like Kieran."

"So, you told them the offer," Joe said. "And, rather than getting angry, they denied any knowledge? That seems very odd."

"That's what I thought," Freddie agreed. "Though Brendan did say he wouldn't put it past Tony to be going all out for a war. They don't want it though. I can tell you, he was none too happy that Antonia had told us it was them who'd taken the girl. He thinks she needs bringing down a peg or two. We might need to warn her to keep her head down for a bit."

"So we're back to square one then?" Russell said. "If they didn't take her to frame the Lagorios and start a war, who the hell has her?"

Joe took a sip of his pint. Paused midway. Swallowed deep. Closed his eyes and shook his head slowly.

"Oh, for God's sake," he said.

"What?" Russell asked.

"We've been looking at this all wrong," Joe said, standing up urgently.

Before they could ask him what he meant, all hell broke loose on the street outside. Fire engines whipped past the window, panicked voices shouted, glass shattered. A scream.

Russell leaned close to the window to see what was going on.

"Oh shit," he said. "It's Tony's place!"

5.

"WHAT IS IT, JOE?" Russell asked as they hurried towards the corner of Frith Street, where a crowd had already gathered to watch the flames licking at the windows of Tony Lagorio's restaurant.

Two fire engines had blocked the street and the firemen were hurriedly unfurling hoses and trying to keep the crowds back.

"We've been looking at this all the wrong way round," Joe said.

"Yeah, you said that," Russell said, panting as he tried to keep up. "What do you mean?"

"The Doherty brothers didn't take her," Joe said. "They've never had her. Kieran told us that. He said she'd gone to see an aunt, remember? I thought it was a strange thing to say at the time."

"But..." Freddie began, trying to keep up in both senses.

"I think he was telling the truth. Or at least, he was telling the story he'd been told to tell."

"Slow down, Joe," Russell said, but his friend was already carving his way through the crowd towards the burning building.

"Only she didn't make it to the aunt," Joe continued, "but Kieran didn't know that. Until we showed him that note."

Joe disappeared into the crowd, leaving Russell's way blocked by a nosey passer-by. Freddie held Russell's arm to stop him getting any closer to the flaming wreckage himself.

"They won't let him through, anyway" he said. "He'll be back."

Sure enough, a frustrated looking Joe came back through the gawking crowd to meet them. He'd almost reached them when he was intercepted by Kieran, barging his way through.

"I didn't know they were going to do this, I swear," he said, his eyes pleading with Russell to believe him. "I came as soon as I heard."

He looked at Joe, tears brimming. "She's in there, isn't she? Charlotte?"

"I think so," Joe said.

"Ah, Jaysus," Kieran wailed, watching the firemen anchoring themselves and beginning to blast water into the restaurant. "I should have known as soon as you showed me that note. I should have known what that mad bitch had done. It wasn't meant to be like this. It wasn't."

"Help me get her out," Joe said.

A police siren rang out above the hubbub and Kieran looked panicked.

"I can't," he replied. "They'll kill me."

And before anyone could stop him, he bolted.

"You two stay here," Joe said to Russell and Freddie. "Keep your eyes on the door and the alleyway. If she comes out, grab her."

"Who?"

"Antonia, of course."

"What are you going to do?" Russell asked, feeling nervous.

"I'm going to get the girl back," Joe said, and dashed off around the side of the building before either of them could stop him.

JOE HAD TO PULL a dustbin over and up-end it to be able to reach the ladder of the old metal fire escape hanging from the building.

He gave it a hard tug, and swore when it didn't move. Realising that there was a catch holding it in place, he stretched up and flicked it with his fingertips and the ladder rattled down with a clang.

Joe took a deep breath, shook his head and started to climb. *Better be right about this.*

It made perfect sense, now that he thought about it, but he had been wrong before, as Russell was only too keen to point out. *This time though...*

He pulled himself onto the narrow platform outside the window on the first floor, and peered in. Tony Lagorio's office had a low cloud of smoke filtering up from the flames from the floor below.

For now, the fire was being contained on the ground floor, but this was an old building and Joe knew those Victorian floorboards would take the flames like kindling.

What if I'm wrong? He hesitated at the window. A piercing scream from inside told him he wasn't.

Without another thought, Joe smashed the window with his elbow, knocked the glass out as best he could, and climbed in.

The heat coming up through the floor was intense, and the smoke wafted higher as the fresh oxygen in the room gave it wings. Joe took his denim jacket off and wrapped it around his mouth and nose as best he could.

The door to Tony's office was open and the corridor beyond was filled with more smoke. He could hear muttered swearing and, as he arrived in the corridor, he was nearly bowled over by Antonia rushing past with a bucket full of water.

"You?" she spluttered.

"You have to get out, Antonia," Joe said. "These floors could collapse any time now."

"Shut up," she said. "Take this. I've got it covered."

She thrust the bucket into his hand and dashed back to what must be a bathroom further along the corridor, reappearing seconds later with another bucket of water.

"Well don't just stand there," she shouted. Get these floors covered, stop the flames taking hold. She threw her bucket down the corridor towards him, and the water sloshed around his feet, hissing gently as it hit the heat. Joe did the same.

"The fire brigade are already here," Joe said. "Let them do this and let's get out."

"I'm not leaving," Antonia said, grabbing his bucket and turning back to the bathroom. Joe could hear a continuous flow of water there, she must be filling the buckets from the bath.

"Where is she?" Joe asked. Antonia stopped dead, turning slowly.

"You know?" she asked.

"It's over, Antonia," he said. "You've got to get her out of here before something terrible happens."

He could see she knew it was true, but she couldn't bring herself to admit it.

"I can't…"

"It's over," he said again.

Another scream from behind them, and Joe didn't wait to find out where Charlotte was. He followed the sound, kicking the door open as he reached it.

He found the stricken young woman tied to a chair in the corner of the room with smoke rising around her.

He wrestled with the knots, quietly reassuring her that everything was going to be alright, but not feeling so sure as he heard the awful groaning and creaking of the floorboards below their feet.

With Charlotte finally free, he threw her onto his shoulder and headed for the steps. Antonia was still frozen in the corridor, empty bucket in hand.

"Antonia! Come on," Joe called.

Charlotte coughed again, squirming wildly on his shoulder.

"Let me go," Charlotte yelled. "I'll kill you for this, Toni! You've ruined everything."

Joe held Charlotte tighter, stepped back into the corridor and grabbed Antonia's arm, freeing her from her trance.

"Move," he yelled, pushing her in front of him towards the stairs.

The heat coming through the wall of the restaurant as they reached the bottom of the stairs was incredible. Fortunately, Antonia didn't hesitate to open the door out onto the alley around the side of the restaurant and they all piled out, coughing and spluttering, sucking smoke out behind them.

"I swear to God," Charlotte yelled. "I'm going to kill you!"

Antonia turned with a look of pure desperation on her face.

"But I did it for you," Antonia said. "For us."

"There is no us! There was never any *us*," Charlotte yelled. "Put me down," she shouted at Joe, who was still carrying her as he tried to usher them all up the alleyway and away from the burning building.

Joe reluctantly put her down and she launched herself at Antonia, fingers extended like claws.

"You've ruined everything!" she screamed. "I had a plan. Everything was going to work out perfectly, and you *had* to get involved. You had to ruin it, didn't you?"

Joe held her back and saw Antonia crumble before him.

"I'm sorry, Charlie," she said quietly. "I thought my way would be better. You were going to give it all to him. I thought you were going to run away with him. I'm sorry. I love you."

"And I hate you! You're crazy!" Charlotte shouted, dissolving into wracking coughs again.

"I love you," Joe heard Antonia whisper again, before a fireman came running down the alleyway yelling at them all to get away from the building.

Joe followed the two young women as they were dragged out of the alleyway. Russell and Freddie were both waiting for him. It was only as Russell hugged him that he realised he was going to pass out.

JOE SAT IN THE open door of the back of the ambulance, sipping water from a polystyrene cup. Russell was trying not to fuss around him, but was loitering anxiously, having in turns both admonished Joe and smothered him in concerned affection.

"If you ever do something that stupid again, I will kill you," he'd said, before pulling his young friend into a massive bear hug which had almost squeezed the life out of him anyway.

The paramedics had signed Joe off, but told him to rest there until he was ready to move. They were still busy treating both Antonia and Charlotte for smoke inhalation and, in Charlotte's case, shock.

The young heiress had not stopped bickering with her former captor since she'd got out of the building, so Russell was sure that the effects of any smoke damage were not too serious.

Freddie leaned against the ambulance door, looking at Joe.

"So how did you figure it out, then?" he asked.

"I don't know," Joe admitted. "It was when you said that Brendan Doherty had denied all knowledge of the kidnap or the ransom note. It all just kind of came into focus. But, really, both Antonia and Kieran had been saying it all along."

"How so?" Russell asked. He couldn't help but be impressed by Joe. Had he been so distracted by his own life that he had missed something obvious?

"Well," Joe said. "When Antonia first came to me, she said her girlfriend was in trouble. She told me that she had seen Charlotte leaving her house with Kieran on the day she went missing. When Mills told us he'd seen a young man running away after the note was delivered—we all just assumed he meant Kieran. But we both knew he had mistaken Antonia for a boy several times before."

"True," Russell said, following so far.

"Then, when we asked Kieran where Charlotte was, he said she'd probably gone to her aunt's in the country. Don't you think that was such a strangely specific comment?"

Joe saw Russell's confused expression, and continued.

"The kind of thing you would only say if you'd been told to say it. It's too random otherwise."

"They all planned this together?" Russell asked.

"Not all of them," Joe said. "Judging by Charlotte's reaction when I cut her free, Antonia seems to have taken things into her own hands. And not for the better, either. Come on, let's go and talk to them."

Russell looked across at the two girls, sitting side by side—but a world apart—on the bench in the back of the ambulance.

Joe stood up and headed over. Russell was about to follow when he felt Freddie take his hand. He looked back and Freddie nodded at the officer climbing out of the police car that had just carved its way through the throng. Detective Skinner.

"Well, well. Look who's here," Freddie said.

"What will you do?" Russell asked, suddenly feeling that he should do something to stop Skinner hurting his boyfriend any further.

"Oh, I'm just going to give him a little tip," Freddie said. "If we're going to bring him down, we're going to do it properly. And it's going to take some time."

He leaned down and kissed Russell full on the lips. On the street. In front of everyone. And then he smiled and headed over to where Skinner was standing.

"ALRIGHT ANTONIA?" Joe asked, walking up to the back of the ambulance where they were being treated.

She scowled at him. "Just fuck off."

"Don't be like that, darling. You were the one who asked me to get involved in the first place."

Charlotte looked at Antonia with even more incredulity than she'd already been giving out.

"Just leave us alone," Antonia said.

"I *told* you," Charlotte shrieked. "There *is* no us!" She batted the paramedic out of the way and tried to do the same to Joe.

"Not so fast," Joe said, taking her wrist.

"Let go of me," she said, spitefully.

"I saved your life, princess. I think I deserve a little explanation. Because you can't blame Antonia for everything that's gone on here, can you?"

Russell stood back and watched his friend read the girls the riot act. He couldn't help but feel a small welling of pride—he was only just beginning to catch up with everything Joe had already figured out.

Head bowed and voice low, Charlotte admitted that yes, she had cooked up a plan to disappear for a few days, and have her loyal—but dim—friend Kieran deliver a ransom note to her father demanding enough to pay off her debts and a little more for a good night out.

"And it would have worked, too," Charlotte said. "Until *she* got involved."

Antonia looked up defiantly.

"I did it for you," she said. "You said how you needed to clear your debts without your dad finding out. How you wanted your own place. You said how you wanted enough money to be free of your father. So I thought..."

"So you thought you'd tie me to a chair in your back room until he paid up?" Charlotte said. "Half starve me. Sit there reading me your shit love stories. Did you really think that would make me love you?"

Antonia looked at the floor. Charlotte laughed.

"You did, didn't you?" Charlotte said. "You honestly thought I would be so happy with the money that I would forget what you did to get it. That I'd think you were some kind of hero?"

"Your way wouldn't have worked. He wouldn't have paid. It wasn't enough," Antonia protested. "It was the only way to stop you messing it up."

"Huh," Charlotte said, bitterly. "Looks like you managed to do that yourself, anyway."

Russell saw how the comment cut Antonia. He cast a glance at Joe. *Do something.* Much as she had caused them all a lot of trouble, he hated seeing someone being humiliated like this.

"Don't forget you were the one who started this, Charlotte," Joe said, and the slightest glimmer of a thankful expression passed Antonia's eyes. Charlotte, on the other hand, looked like thunder.

"You'd got yourself into trouble," Joe continued. "You were terrified your father would find out, so you roped poor Kieran into your scheme to fake your own kidnap."

"Yeah, but *she* just had to stick her nose in," Charlotte muttered. "It was just meant to be a couple of days. He would have paid. It wasn't even that much money. But you had to make it bigger, didn't you? A million pounds? What were you thinking?"

Antonia stared steadfastly at the ground. She had no comeback.

"She was trying to help you," Joe said. Flat and quiet. He didn't agree with what Antonia had done, but this whole situation was Charlotte's fault for leading both Antonia and Kieran on in the first place.

Russell felt a heavy hand on his shoulder and turned to see Tony Lagorio lumbering past. He approached his daughter, lifted her chin, kissed her forehead and took her arm, leading her away. Soundless, sympathetic, supportive.

As he passed Russell, he whispered: "Thank you." It wasn't the time to tell him it had all been Joe's work. They were a team now anyway.

When they reached Tony's car, Russell saw him pull his daughter into a hug that looked like it would never end. It would probably be the only time anyone ever saw Antonia Lagorio cry.

At the same time, there was a murmur in the crowd behind him. They parted, having already lost interest slightly after the fire had been quelled, to let Charles Fenwick be ushered through by his man, Mills.

Fenwick reached his daughter—who immediately began apologising. He slapped her face once, silencing her. She hung her head. It was only when her mother tottered through that Charlotte got a hug of her own. Russell could see from the way she fought back the tears that it wasn't the hug she wanted.

"What did she do to you? My precious baby," her mother fawned. Charlotte finally pushed her away.

"You're going to that finishing school, young lady," Russell heard Fenwick say. "And that's an end to it. And if I hear any more about drugs or parties you will be out on your ear and I'll have nothing more to do with you. Do you hear me?"

"Yes Daddy," she replied. There would be no more arguments from her. The worst had finally happened. She'd lost her father's devotion.

6.

"SO, CHARLOTTE AND KIERAN cooked up a plan for her to disappear for a few days and for him to deliver a ransom note so that they could get enough money to pay off her debts and have a little more to party on the side?" Freddie asked, as Joe brought the pints to their table back at the Red Lion.

"Foolproof, right?" Joe said, rolling his eyes and sitting down.

"Apart from the part where Antonia found out about it and decided to improve on the plan," Russell said.

"She swapped out the notes before Kieran made the delivery, raised the price to a million and nabbed Charlotte before she could get on the train." Joe said.

"But why?" Freddie asked. "Surely she knew this wouldn't end well for her and Charlotte?"

"I'm guessing she thought Charlotte would be grateful that her debts were paid off and that she had money to spend without her father ever finding out what she had been doing." Joe said.

"But surely she can't have imagined that holding the girl hostage would make her agree to go out with her?" Russell took a large sip of his drink, shaking his head.

"She was blinded by love and jealousy," Joe said. "She'd been stalking her for months. I should have spotted it when she first came to see me. She was jealous that Kieran was spending time with Charlotte. But she was also angry with his brothers for trying to muscle in on their territory. Tony himself said they couldn't afford a fight. He said business was bad. I guess Antonia thought a million quid would solve their financial problems, and leave plenty to get Charlotte out of her own troubles."

"And blaming the Dohertys for the kidnap, suggesting they were coming for her directly?"

"I guess she hoped her father would leap to her defence and run them out of town," Joe said. "She probably hoped it would get rid of Kieran once and for all."

"Except neither Tony nor Brendan wanted a war," said Russell.

"Exactly."

"And Charlotte didn't want saving."

They all drank in silence. None of them could blame Antonia for wanting to fix everything when the opportunity arose, but she had been incredibly naïve.

"Poor kid," Russell said.

Nods all round. Antonia had got it badly wrong.

"What did you say to Skinner, by the way?" Russell asked Freddie.

"Oh, I just wanted to tell him a little tip I'd had for him."

Russell frowned. Freddie smiled.

"He's not the only one that can set up a photoshoot. As soon as Joe told me about that drugs haul sitting in the Palace, I figured the one cop who wouldn't be able to resist trying to get in on the action would be Skinner. It turns out that Skinner is not one of the cops on Brendan Doherty's payroll, and he was only too happy to set up little trap for him. We may not need to use it, but it's always handy to have some dirt in your back pocket."

Freddie took Russell's hand.

"Meanwhile, he's got nothing over us anymore. And we've got everything on him."

Russell wanted to feel reassured, but he knew Skinner had a habit of wriggling out of any trouble. At least neither he nor Freddie had to live in fear of their secret being exposed any longer.

"I'll get him," Freddie said. "I promise."

They all looked up as a shadow fell on the table. Tony Lagorio stood, slightly awkwardly, in front of them, his daughter at his side.

"Antonia has something to say to you all," he said, steely faced. When she kept her own face fixed steadfastly on the floor, he nudged her.

"I'm sorry I wasted everyone's time," she muttered. "I was stupid and selfish and it won't happen again."

The line sounded rehearsed. This was what Tony had told her she was going to say to everyone. His way of making things right, restoring her honour.

"The things we do for love, eh?" Joe said, jogging her elbow.

She didn't respond. This was total humiliation—being walked around the village, apologising to everyone for your mistakes. Despite everything, Joe felt sorry for her.

"Is Charles Fenwick going to go to the police?" Freddie asked.

"No," Tony said. "We've both agreed that it's better for the girls if we all just forget it ever happened."

"And what about the Dohertys?" Russell asked.

"Seems they had a visit in the early hours last night," Tony said. "Lost a lot of their supply. Not sure of the details, but they won't be troubling our patch for a little while."

He smiled. There was a tiredness in his eyes which brightened as Ron, the barman, appeared beside them all with a tray of vodka shots. He'd been in a similar situation before. Parenthood was never easy, but in Soho it took on a different shape all together.

"To love. And family," Ron said, handing out the drinks. They all toasted. And they all meant it.

KILLER QUEEN

SOHO NOIR #5

KILLER QUEEN

1

SOHO, LONDON. 1988

AS THE CURTAIN FELL, the audience erupted in rapturous applause. Lexi Goode lay in the exact spot where she had died only minutes before, savouring the moment.

As the other cast members filed back onto the stage around her, she resisted getting up, feeling the thunderous applause echoing through the hollow boards of the stage. Cheers and whistles. Whoops and hollers. For her.

Of course, she knew the plaudits weren't *all* for her, but she could definitely hear her father's distinctive whistle, loud and piercing, not a theatre-goers whistle.

"Come on Lexi," her co-star, Samuel Hobson, said. "The curtain's about to go up again."

Lexi jumped to her feet. A thin stream of artificial blood trickled down her stomach from the small bag that had been attached to her chest, burst by the knife she had plunged into her breast. Only, this time, she almost stabbed herself for real—the blade of the prop knife had got stuck and when she realised it wasn't slipping into the handle as it should, she'd been forced to cover the error with her hands. She thought she'd got away with making it look fairly realistic, but she would be having stern words with the young prop guy after the show. She could feel a sting where the tip of the blade had actually pierced her skin through the costume bodice. It was a good job the knife had failed on her and not the usual lead, or there would have been hell to pay.

Grabbing Samuel's hand, Lexi grinned at him as they stepped forward in line with the rest of the cast.

"That was brilliant," he said. "You were fantastic."

And she could see he meant it.

3

The curtain rose and the full cast stepped forward for the first of their joint curtain calls. Arms up together and then a bow led by Samuel and Lexi. The applause continued undiminished. A group of raucous young men in the front row threw single red roses onto the stage.

Lexi lapped it all up, rolling smoothly into the second bow and feeling Samuel let go of her hand on the way up so that each of the main performers could take their turn in the limelight.

She couldn't keep the smile from her face. Even though she had heard the grumble of dissatisfaction and disappointment before the show had started when it had been announced to the audience that their beloved star of the show, Ms Hattie Duval, would not be playing the role of Lady Fenella Earnshaw tonight, and that her understudy Lexi Goode would be standing in for her.

Lexi knew that it was Hattie Duval's name that had sold most of the tickets for the show, and she very rarely missed a performance. Hattie had become something of a mentor to Lexi—an old hand in the theatre, despite only being in her early fifties herself, Hattie had started out as a child star, aged just eleven. A consummate professional—a perfectionist, even—she made their director's life hell, and Cameron Beattie was no pushover.

As Lexi stepped forward to take her bow, she saw Cameron standing in the wings, clapping as enthusiastically for her as any of the audience out front. She was glad. He was a hard man to please, but if he thought she'd played the role well, she might get more opportunities with him. Perhaps even a lead of her own.

The lights shone bright in her eyes, obliterating all but the front few rows of the theatre. Up in one of the boxes—where Cameron had kindly put them—were her parents. Denzil and Patricia. Cameron had insisted they sat in his private box, instead of the cheap seats Lexi had managed to get for them at the last minute when she'd found out she was playing the lead tonight.

Her father whistled again, letting her know that he was still her biggest fan, and Lexi beamed and waved at them as she took her final bow.

As the curtain fell, the applause began to die down and that post-performance sadness descended upon them all. Quietly, the cast filed from the stage, the odd murmured conversation passing between the actors as they made their way to the dressing rooms.

"You were brilliant tonight, Lexi," Samuel said, catching up with her. "So much better than that tremulous old ham."

"Shh," said Lexi, smiling at his very accurate impression of the little wobble of the voice Hattie Duval affected when she was playing Lady Earnshaw. Lexi couldn't ever bring herself to emulate it offstage, let alone in front of an audience—it sounded even more old-fashioned on her young tongue.

Still, Cameron didn't seem to mind that Lexi gave the part her own voice, though he had directed her to deliver it in received pronunciation, rather than letting her slight Caribbean lilt come through.

Samuel had made no bones about his feelings for Ms Hattie Duval, insisting always on using her stage name as though it was somehow a reflection of her character that she didn't use her married name.

Lexi found it all a bit too bitchy. What did it matter which name she used? She'd been an actress since her teens, why change her name? But then Lexi didn't have the history that the two older actors shared, and the ill feeling was obviously mutual. Still, it made her uncomfortable if Samuel was mean about Hattie when she wasn't around to defend herself.

"Oh, don't worry," Samuel said. "She's not here, is she? She's not going to hear me."

"No, but the wings have ears, and she has a lot of friends," said Lexi, the slight Caribbean lilt returning to her voice now that she was offstage.

"Ha!" Samuel replied. "With those kind of friends, who needs enemies, huh?"

He took her arm and held her a moment, looking at her sincerely.

"Well, anyway," he said, "I thought you were great and I hope you get to do it again before the run ends."

She liked Samuel. He was a kind man, with a dry sense of humour and a sharp wit. She had wondered at first whether he was just trying it on with her, but he had confided in her early on that he had a long-term partner called Steve and, since then, she'd relaxed, finding him easy company and a supportive friend. There was no denying their chemistry as Lord and Lady Earnshaw sparked well on stage, making far more of the comedy in their dialogue than when he played opposite Hattie.

"Thanks," she said. "Me too. Goodnight, then."

Kind as his words were, she doubted she would get to play the lead again. Whatever illness had kept Hattie Duval away this evening would

5

doubtless be cleared up by the morning and she would be back in her role, and in the large, main dressing room. But for tonight, Lexi had that all to herself.

Before she could push the door to the dressing room open, Cameron Beattie appeared in the corridor. Tall, broad-shouldered, masculine. He turned heads, and he knew it, which brought him down just on the wrong side of arrogant. But he was an excellent director, and Lexi had been so proud when he'd offered her a minor role in his new play, let alone promoting her to understudy for the lead just a week into rehearsals.

"I know you've got it in you," he'd said to her, taking her aside after one of their longer days.

Lexi hadn't been so sure herself, but he'd assured her that it was unlikely that Hattie would miss a single performance, and it would be a great opportunity to learn from a seasoned pro. As it had turned out, Hattie had missed three so far, and while she always called in with some illness, Lexi knew that in truth her marriage was struggling, her career was faltering and her anxiety about both would often get the better of her.

Hattie Duval had once had a reputation for being reliable. Or stubborn. Lexi had heard both terms used in equal measure to describe the star. But recently, she had become distracted, often late, sometimes drunk.

"Hang on, Lexi," Cameron called, slowing as he reached her and bending to kiss her on both cheeks. "Fabulous, darling, just sublime."

She felt herself blushing. Even though he was at least ten years older than her, she couldn't help having a crush on Cameron. He was even better looking up close, and the twinkle in his eye right now told her he found her as attractive too. Besides, he'd said as much many times over the past few weeks.

Every time she saw him it made her stomach hitch, but only partly in a good way. Guilt and fear needled at her. It had been a mistake to sleep with him. It had only been once, but she had crossed the line. It wasn't like she had even needed to do it to secure the role. It had happened once, late in the rehearsal process, when he had kept her behind to run her understudy part through without Hattie adding her own criticisms.

He had been playing Lord Earnshaw and the stage kiss had turned into a real kiss, and before they knew it they'd been tearing each other's clothes off. They'd both agreed that it had been a mistake, but it hadn't stopped either of them feeling that it could happen again at any point.

She had tried to keep him at arm's length ever since, just in case. At least until the run was over, but he was becoming more persistent as they reached the final couple of weeks in the show's run. Only ten more performances to go. And then what?

"How about I take you for dinner," he said. "To celebrate."

The blush deepened, her light brown skin doing little to hide the rising heat. She would love to go out with him, but she had already promised her parents that she would take them out after the show, since they had cancelled their plans to get there at such short notice to come and see her.

"I can't tonight," she said. "My parents are here. I promised them I'd have drinks with them."

"Even better," he said, a lascivious smile played on his lips as he slid his arm around her waist and pulled her against him. "It's about time I met your parents."

"Don't," she said, pushing him away gently. "Not here."

The last thing she wanted was for any of the other cast members to think she was getting any special favours because she was sleeping with the director. She was building a good reputation, and something like that would ruin it straight away.

"Such a tease," he said, smiling, as he let her go. "You can't blame a man for trying."

She pushed the door open a crack, stepping away from him.

"Oh, and Lexi," he said.

She turned back.

"I've just been offered a new play at the Lyric. Starting in the summer. I want you to be my lead. I'll tell you all about it tomorrow, okay?"

This time, it was her turn to kiss him—a happy peck on the cheek. No more. But she felt his hand linger on her hip, briefly.

"Thank you," she said, and felt his gaze fall on her as she disappeared into her dressing room.

As the door closed, she leaned back on it, enjoying the moment of solitude and letting the strange mix of feelings wash over her. She'd just delivered one of the best performances of her career and, regardless of any feelings Cameron may have for her, he had just offered her the lead in his next play. This was everything she'd ever dreamed of and it was really happening. Maybe she could make it, after all. Give up the other work, forget she'd ever had to struggle, turn her back on her past—her secrets—and become the woman she'd always wanted to be. An actress.

"You were very good, dear."

The dry, crackling voice surprised her. *Hattie Duval.* Lexi's eyes shot open and only now did she see the actress sitting at the mirror, in the half-darkness, looking back at her in the reflection. She looked tired. A little sad.

"Hattie!" she said, not bothering to hide her surprise. "What are you doing here? I thought…"

"Oh, I snuck in, darling. I'd left some things behind yesterday. Mind like a sieve these days. I thought I'd just pop in and collect them. I didn't want to make a scene."

"How are you feeling? Are you okay? You should have said. We could have sent anything you needed over in a taxi," Lexi said, walking across to the clothes rail perched in the corner of the room and unbuttoning the tight, bright-red hunting jacket she'd so enjoyed wearing tonight. If she was honest, wearing it had made her feel as though a little of Hattie Duval's greatness was rubbing off on her.

She knew the others laughed at Hattie's portrayal of the Lady of the Manor, but Lexi found it charming. Exactly right for the part. She knew, despite Cameron's praise, that her own Lady Fenella Earnshaw was no comparison. Still, she could dream.

"I'm not myself, I'll be honest," Hattie sighed. "Must be this bloody menopause, darling. I don't know whether I'm coming or going. I can't even think straight half the time. One minute I'm laughing and the next I'm sobbing my eyes out. It's a living hell. Speaking of which, with these bloody hot flushes, I may as well be down there already."

"I'm sorry to hear that," Lexi said. "It must be hard." She found herself hovering beside the rail, not really wanting to get undressed in front of the older actress, but equally not wanting to throw her out of what was her own dressing room. Maybe she should excuse herself and go and change in the toilets instead.

She noticed that Hattie had dropped her head again, looking down at the framed photograph of her and her husband, both much younger, laughing happily, sitting on the edge of a stage, the spotlights creating a halo around their heads. It was a great photo, but Lexi had laid it face down earlier, not wanting to look at it while she dressed.

"Oh, don't worry, dear. It happens to us all, eventually," Hattie sighed again. "Where does it all go, eh? All that youth and mellow fruitfulness." She put the photograph back in its place, looking up at Lexi in the reflection in the mirror. "It will happen to you too, no doubt, my dear. Besides, maybe it's nature's way of telling me to step aside for a younger talent."

"Nonsense," said Lexi, unaccustomed to hearing Hattie sound so downhearted. "You're not even old."

Hattie—who had only recently sailed past her fiftieth milestone—was a legend of stage and screen. Sure, she could be bitchy, scathing, hilarious, sometimes naughty and often downright disgraceful, but Lexi had never seen her express the slightest hint of self-pity or despondency. The woman was a diva, for God's sake—she wouldn't know what insecurity was if it slapped her face.

"You're just feeling under the weather," Lexi continued, looking at the pair of them—two Lady Earnshaws, with and without the make-up— side by side in the mirror. Hattie's Lady Earnshaw was naturally middle aged, and no matter how much make up Lexi used to age herself and hide her darker skin tone, she felt fake and ridiculous under these harsh lights.

But Hattie looked even older tonight. A little more drawn, perhaps. Maybe it was just because Lexi was so used to seeing *her* as Lady Earnshaw that it was strange to see their two faces together in the mirror. She took the blonde bouffant wig off her head, running a hand over her tight, dark curls as they bounced free of the skullcap.

There was something else about Hattie's expression though, which made her seem older, smaller even. Lexi couldn't put her finger on it, but she felt compelled to touch the woman's shoulder sympathetically.

Hattie smiled thinly, with no real conviction and patted her hand in reply. "Anyway," she said, sniffing and hauling herself up out of the chair, "I thought you were very good. Gave her a real passion."

"You saw me?"

"Just the last scene, darling. Fabulous death. I almost believed it for a moment. Though, just a smidge over-the-top right at the end, I thought," she said, a little too patronisingly.

"The bloody knife failed," said Lexi. "Did you see? I nearly stabbed myself to death for real!"

"I'm sure no one noticed. You'll get better with practice," Hattie said.

Not quite sure how to respond, Lexi sat down in the now-vacant chair and leaned across to pick up the make-up remover and cotton wool. At least she could make a start on her face until Hattie left her alone to change. Hattie frowned, lingering for a moment as though she was about to tell Lexi off for using her things, but then obviously thought better of it.

"I don't mean to be critical, my dear," she said. "Just being honest. You were really very good up there tonight."

Before Lexi could respond, there was a hurried knock at the door.

"Who is it?" Hattie called out. It was her dressing room, after all.

"Miss Goode?" a male voice came through the door, sounding uncertain. "It's Joe. I've got your parents here to see you."

Joe Stone was Cameron Beattie's assistant. A sweet guy, keen to help, and definitely more interested in the stable boy than Lexi, from what she could tell. Lexi didn't care. Each to their own. Besides, she had to fend off more than her fair share of unwanted attention most of the time anyway, so it was nice to have a young man talk to her as though she was a person rather than just a pair of boobs.

"Come in, Joe," Lexi called, over a tut from Hattie.

Joe opened the door and guided her parents into the room. Squeals of delight from her mother and a booming celebratory round of congratulations from her father bore them in like a tidal wave of happiness and support.

Lexi smiled as Hattie graciously air-kissed both parents—Patricia Goode would dine out on that one—and kindly agreed that their daughter had done a fabulous job. Lexi felt bad. They shouldn't really be celebrating an understudy stepping into a role for the evening, should they? Still, it made her so happy that her parents had seen her in the lead role. And that they were so proud of her.

Her father had always been concerned that her choice of career would leave her desperate or destitute. And if that was all she did for money, he would probably be right. But they didn't talk about her other job, not any more.

"You were fantastic," he bellowed, his deep bass voice tremulous with pride and his heavy Caribbean accent stressing the syllables perfectly. "My daughter, the superstar."

He expanded his hands as though framing her name in lights. She grinned.

"Oh, and these came too," Joe said, holding out a huge bunch of flowers.

Lexi took a look at them and frowned.

Before she Lexi could do anything, Hattie lifted the flowers from Joe's hand. "These must be for me," she said. "My regular delivery. How sweet."

Of course, Lexi thought. Hattie Duval received a regular bunch of flowers each week, all tied with the same distinctive ribbon. The card always simply read *From an Admirer. X.* Samuel had often joked that Hattie sent them to herself, but he would never say it to her face.

"Huh," said Hattie. "Not for me after all."

She thrust the flowers back into Joe's hands, roughly shoving the note card back between the blooms.

"I'd better be going," she said, to no one in particular, and Lexi saw a look of sadness and confusion cross her face beneath her tight smile.

"Nice to see you, Ms Duval," Lexi's mother called after the actress as she left the room. There was no reply.

Joe filled an old jug with water and stood the flowers in it on the long dresser. Lexi saw him lift the card and read the message before shrugging, and leaning the card against the vase. He turned back to Lexi and her family.

"I'll leave you to it. Unless there's anything else you need?"

"No. Thank you, Joe," Lexi replied.

Joe said his goodbyes to Lexi's parents, wishing them a pleasant evening and then left, doubtless overhearing Lexi's mother's gushing assertion that he was "such a charming young man".

"So, are we going out for some drinks now, then?" Lexi's father asked. "How about someplace fancy?"

"Of course," she said. "Why don't you two wait in the bar downstairs while I get changed, and then I'll take you out for a real treat."

Her mother clapped her hands in delight as they both shuffled out of the dressing room, bickering gently about which one of them had given her the looks and which the talent. They never talked about how Lexi could afford to take them to the kind of places she did—on the rare occasions they did come to a show, she always took them to a high-end bar for champagne or cocktails afterwards.

She had told her mother about her other job, and she often wondered whether Patricia had shared that with her husband. *Don't ask, don't tell.* Perhaps he just assumed she was successful enough as an actress, and all the fancy bars and restaurants, the help with their bills at home, and the expensive gifts, were all part and parcel of her success.

It made her feel guilty whenever she saw them so proud and happy. Still, it wouldn't be for much longer, would it? Cameron Beattie had just offered Lexi her first lead. She could finally say she'd made it.

LEXI MADE sure the door was shut tight behind her, the deadlock engaged, before she let herself breathe. Even here, in the safety of her gorgeous flat, she couldn't relax until she knew she was safely indoors. She should get out of this game, it was setting her nerves on edge. At least, after tonight, she was now one step closer to getting out.

She was exhausted. Aftershow drinks with her parents had been quick but enjoyable, and she had lapped up their praise and delight in her performance that evening. But she had been watching the clock the whole time they were together, knowing that she had another performance to deliver before she could call it a night. In the end, her father had noticed her check the time once too often and had declared, none too subtly, that it was time for them to get home.

"You can't have us tiring you out with all this praise," he'd laughed. "Your head will be too big to fit back on that stage!"

She loved her father. He was a good man. Unlike so many others she met. He adored his wife, enjoyed the simple things in life, like a win in the cricket with a cold beer in hand, and he was nothing but supportive to both of his daughters.

Having packed her parents into a cab, fully paid, she'd waited until they were well out of sight before slipping out of the bar and across the road to the hotel where her late-night appointment was waiting. A quick change in the downstairs loo and she was ready for her next performance. Far harder than the one she'd given on stage earlier.

Eyes shut now, she stripped off her coat and leaned against the closed door of her apartment. The cold wood veneer cooled the skin on her back, making her shiver. She sighed heavily and reached up to pull the long, straight wig of glossy, red hair from her head, revealing her natural, short Afro beneath. Stretching out her neck she felt her pulse begin to slow. She was home.

Her top floor apartment was undeniably beautiful—more beautiful than anything she could ever have dreamed of owning as a girl growing up in Brixton, and far more than she should have been able to afford as the bit-part actress she was.

She hadn't ever meant to fall into her other profession, but once she'd seen how easy it was to earn big, she'd felt compelled to carry on. First to pay off her own debts, and then to help her parents, and finally, now, because she'd grown used to having the income and was terrified of losing it.

Besides, it wasn't like she was a prostitute. Nothing that cheap. She was a high-class escort, playing a different role—a different persona— every time. A demure housewife-to-be, or a savvy business woman. You name it, she could play it. It was all acting, at the end of the day. And it's not like she actually had sex with any of them. Not real sex. Sure, they got off, but she hardly ever let them even touch her, that was part of the thrill for them.

The guys who hired her weren't just interested in sex from her. They wanted a different experience. One that their wives knew nothing about, and which, she always argued, probably helped keep their marriages together in the longer term.

Her client tonight, though, had taken it all too far, and that's why she'd had to end it. The previous appointment she'd had with him—two weeks ago—he'd told her that he'd fallen in love with her. That he was going to leave his wife. That he wanted to be with her.

When Lexi had explained that would never happen, he got angry. He'd hit her. A slap maybe, but it had hurt and she'd struggled to hide the bruise on her cheek from Cameron. She'd passed it off to him as the result of her clumsiness, but the incident had really shaken her— reminding her that what she was doing was *not* just another acting role. It was sordid and dangerous.

It had got worse after that night too. Over the last two weeks, he'd turned up at the theatre, almost exposing their secret. He said he didn't care who knew. And then he'd turned up at her flat, making a scene on the street, late at night. No wonder her neighbour was annoyed with her.

She'd told him to leave, or she'd call the police, and the threat had seemed to make him see sense. But then she'd got the message in the flowers, suggesting one last meeting tonight. So she'd gone and, when she was about to leave, they'd agreed that it would be the last time. She hoped it would.

She shuddered, leaving the doorway and walking into the kitchen. Ever since he'd turned up on her doorstep that night, she'd lived in fear that he would come back. Hence the deadlock. Hence the paranoia.

Lexi often found herself wishing she'd never left that seedy little flat she'd shared with Sarah and Cassie. She'd been ashamed to take her parents back there when she'd moved in because it was above a live revue bar and she'd been worried that they would think she was slumming it. The small kitchen where they had spent most of their time—since the lounge had been converted into the third bedroom when Lexi had moved in—was illuminated at night by a neon pink sign outside the window that screamed "Girls! Girls! Girls!".

The three of them had taken a Polaroid of themselves leaning out the window in front of the sign. Three girls, not for sale. If they could see her now.

But Sarah and Cassie were probably the only people she knew who wouldn't care. It was what they did, anyway. Only, they did it the hard way, on street corners and in dive bars, in alleyways and dodgy cars.

When she'd started getting regular acting work, she'd suggested moving out—only because they would come in at all hours, and she couldn't keep turning up for auditions or performances looking tired.

Of course, they assumed she thought she was better than them. She didn't. She wasn't. By then, she'd already started taking on escort clients. But she couldn't tell them that. Even that would have made her seem snooty and elite. So she'd paid them an extra month's rent and taken out the lease on this place. This beautiful, big, glamorous, lonely place. They may have been a pair of street-corner prostitutes, but they had been her friends once, and she still missed them every day.

Lexi placed the wig on the kitchen counter and opened the fridge. A cold glass of champagne would help settle her uneasiness right now—decadent, but it was the only drink she actually enjoyed. She knew she was being paranoid, but all the way home she'd felt as though she was being watched. She'd asked her taxi driver to change the route a little, telling him she didn't mind that it would cost more, but there had been no one behind them but other cabs and the odd night bus.

Champagne in hand, she crossed to the large windows overlooking the street four floors below. She'd taken the flat for the view. She would probably have been more sensible taking a cheaper flat and saving her hard-earned money so that she could stop all this, but she had convinced herself that if she was going to be a star, she needed to act like a star, live like a star, *be* a star. Besides, this view was about the only thing that kept her sane.

London's Soho. Bustling, vibrant, alive. And if she pressed her face to the window and peered down at the corner below, she could just see the reflection of that pink glowing "Girls! Girls! Girls!" sign that had lit up her old kitchen.

She took a long sip of her champagne, enjoying the taste on her tongue. She hadn't had a drink with her parents, even though she'd ordered a bottle for them all to share. She didn't like to drink if she was going to be working later. She liked to keep her wits about her.

With the window slightly open, she listened to the distant murmur of the street below, traffic, shouts, music. A neighbour in the flat several floors below was entertaining friends on his balcony—the strains of Whitney Houston floated up to her over their drunken voices.

Saturday night had long since slipped into Sunday morning, but in Soho things were still pumping.

A sharp knock at the door made Lexi jump. Who on earth would be knocking on her door at this time of night? Maybe the strange French woman who lived in the other top floor flat opposite hers.

Constance, or Clarice, Lexi couldn't remember now—they didn't really speak much. The woman had knocked on her door late at night when she'd first moved in. She'd said she'd heard raised voices and wondered if everything was okay. Lexi had already been in bed at the time—alone—but with the radio on. Although her neighbour had apologised for the misunderstanding, Lexi had been left with no doubt that she thought Lexi was too loud.

Since that first time, she had often heard her muttering behind her closed door when Lexi came home late—which she invariably did in her line of work.

Again, as she had slid the deadbolt into place this evening, she had heard her neighbour cursing her through her own doorway. She knew the woman often spied on her when she came home. Sometimes, she opened her overcoat before closing the door, giving the nosey cow something to gawp at.

She put her glass down and walked back to the door, in no mood for a confrontation tonight. Peering through the spyglass, though, she was relieved to see it wasn't her neighbour at all. *A bit late for a visit*, she thought as she unlocked the deadbolt. *Had something happened?*

"Hi," she said, opening the door fully. "Is everything okay?"

It was only after she closed the door again that Lexi Goode realised nothing would ever be okay again.

2

Joe Stone tried not to giggle as he shut the door behind them. He'd gone out with a few of the actors from the show after they had all finished up for the night, and he had finally found his chance to try it on with the slightly gangly but surprisingly cute actor, Ben Higson, who played—in order of appearance—the stable boy, the second farmhand, and the errant son and heir to the Earnshaw estate.

None of Ben's parts had more than a handful of lines each, which meant that he'd spent plenty of time hanging around backstage, where he'd caught Joe's eye.

Despite a few flings, and one more serious relationship with a gorgeous Frenchman called Luc, Joe was still quite shy about approaching guys. Tonight, with a few drinks inside him and enough encouragement from a few of the other actors, he'd made his move, and Ben, though taken aback to be propositioned in the first place, had been delighted.

Having decided that Ben's Vauxhall flat was far too distant to get to on the night bus, they had opted to head back to the flat Joe shared with his friend Russell.

More often than not, recently, Russell had been staying over at his boyfriend Freddie Gillespie's place. Their relationship had faced a slight challenge from homophobic police detective, Simon Skinner, who had a personal vendetta against Russell and was determined to destroy anything that made him happy.

Unfortunately for Skinner, Russell and Freddie were made of stronger—and considerably more intelligent—stuff, and after the very briefest of wobbles, they had come out of it stronger than ever. The incident had forced Freddie to come out to his partners in the law firm he jointly ran, and ever since then, he and Russell had been acting like an old married couple.

Joe put a finger to his lips, still giggling and silenced Ben's ridiculously loud shushing. Perhaps bringing a thespian home in the dead of night wasn't his brightest idea after all. He was sure they'd wake the house if Russell and Freddie were in.

Ben leaned in and moved Joe's finger away, replacing it with his lips. It was the first time they'd actually kissed. Having known it was going to happen before they'd even left the club, Joe felt his stomach hitch.

He pulled away gently, took Ben's hand and led him quietly along the hallway towards his bedroom. He could hear the faint sound of Russell's snoring from his room. Good. They hadn't been that loud, after all.

Russell wouldn't mind him bringing a guy back. It wasn't that. There had never been anything between them, and they were very close friends.

What Joe was trying to avoid was his gregarious flatmate getting up and inviting them to join him for a nightcap, which he had done a couple of times when Freddie hadn't been staying over.

While it was lovely to chat, Joe had other plans for tonight and, as he pulled the door safely behind them, closing them into his small bedroom, he realised that Ben more than shared his intentions.

"LATE NIGHT?" Russell asked, with a cheeky grin.

"I don't know what you mean," Joe grinned back, pouring out a coffee for both of them.

"So come on, spill the beans," Russell said, tapping the table with his hands like an overexcited schoolgirl. "Who was he? Where did you meet him?"

"I don't kiss and tell," Joe said, head raised haughtily.

"Bullshit." Russell laughed.

"Fine," said Joe, sitting down opposite him, savouring that first, hot sip of strong coffee. "He's an actor from the show."

"Ooh, fancy," Russell teased.

"Bit parts, love," Joe replied, smirking. "He plays the stable hand."

"Oh my," Russell said in his best Kenneth Williams voice. "Did he bring his costume home?"

"Give over," Joe said, sipping again. "He's nice. You'd like him."

"Is he staying for breakfast?"

"No, he left first thing."

"Shame," Russell said. "Do you think you'll see him again?"

"Hard not to when we work together."

"You know what I mean," Russell said.

Joe smiled contentedly.

"I might do," he said. "He *is* very cute. And he seemed keen."

Russell knew that his young flatmate wanted to play the field a bit before settling down and he didn't blame him. Things were different now than when Russell had been Joe's age. For good and for bad.

It was far easier in many ways to be out and proud these days, especially in Soho, where everyone was welcome. But there was a growing discontent again, following last year's general election, and the toxic campaigns that Margaret Thatcher's Tories had posted suggesting that to vote Labour was basically tantamount to turning gay.

The predominant media position during the election had been that anything to do with gay rights was just an irrelevant drum being beaten by the "Loony Left". The divisive rhetoric that framed the politics reopened the door for persecution, hatred and distrust of the gay community. Not to mention fear at the rising spectre of HIV and AIDS.

A few years ago, in eighty-four and eighty-five—when all around him had been calling for gay rights to be acknowledged—Russell had stayed in the closet, fearful that he would lose his job as a detective with the Metropolitan Police. Now that he had come out and was in a happy, settled relationship, it seemed that everything was going backward again.

Russell had been devastated to see the hugely contentious Section 28 bill to amend the Local Government Act being passed into law. The vile bill stopped schools from allegedly promoting homosexuality by mentioning same-sex relationships in lessons. Despite all the protests—tens of thousands of people marching, even the four angry lesbians who abseiled into the chamber of the House of Lords on the day the debate ended—the bill became law on the 24th of May.

As a result, Russell couldn't help feeling that they had an even bigger fight on their hands now, to reclaim some of that lost ground.

Sitting in his little bubble in Soho, though, it was easy to believe he wasn't in the minority where attitudes and opinions were concerned, but then every newspaper, every report and every comment seemed to chip further away at any progress the gay rights movement had made.

"What are you up to today then?" Joe asked.

Since being forcibly retired from the police force after his colleagues outed him—in a cruel sting involving an undercover officer pretending to be gay to lure Russell into a compromising position—Russell had found himself increasingly involved in helping his local community. Often with Joe's help.

The pair had developed something of a reputation for solving crimes in their community that the police—thanks to their blatant homophobia and inherent laziness—had no interest in looking into. So far, Russell and Joe had solved three murders and a kidnapping together and, in-between times, Russell was constantly being asked to look into small crimes and odd disputes that beleaguered the random mix of gays, lesbians, queers, prostitutes, gangsters, actors and celebrities who shared the streets, bars and flats of Soho.

Joe often teased him that he should grow a moustache like Tom Selleck's Magnum P.I. and wander the streets with his shirt open to the waist. Russell thought not.

"I said I'd pop into the Campbell Centre this morning," Russell said. "Scott's doing a lunchtime show and needs help to set up. Other than that, I'm free."

The Campbell Centre was a charity close to both Russell and Joe's hearts. A place of support and treatment for those with HIV and AIDS, which was a cross between a hospice and a community centre. Everyone was welcome, everyone was safe and everyone was a friend. The pair had taken to volunteering at the clinic when they could, filling the void that had been left by their mutual friend, Chris, who had been a staunch supporter of the place before he'd been killed.

"Are you staying for the show?" Joe asked.

"Might as well," Russell replied. "Patty tells me Scott's hilarious."

Scott was the son of Ron, the barman at Russell and Joe's informal office, the Red Lion pub on the corner of Rupert Street. He had recently been reunited with his father, thanks to Joe and Russell, and had been taken under the wing of Ron's tenant and rising star on the drag scene, Patty Cakes—or Paul, as he was known when not in drag. Scott and

Paul—Miss Terri and Patty—now hosted a regular drag night in the back room of the Red Lion, with Ron's blessing.

Scott's act, Miss Terri and the Ladykillers, involved Scott and a trio of incredibly effeminate queens doing a pure cabaret turn, packed with comedy, improbably good dance routines and some impressive vocal work. If anything, Patty had already been eclipsed by her protégée, but she didn't mind that one bit.

"Shame I'm working, or I'd meet you there," Joe said.

"Why are you working on a Sunday?"

"The lead's sick, so all the understudies have had to shuffle up a part. The prompt was working overtime last night. It was chaos. Cameron has called them all in for a run through."

"So why do you have to be there?"

"God forbid he should have to write any notes on his own, or move any furniture himself."

"You're wasted in that job," Russell said.

"It's better than pulling pints in the Red Lion," Joe replied. "And besides, the colleagues are cuter."

"I'll tell Ron you said that," Russell laughed.

"I'm sure he'll be devastated," said Joe, grabbing the slice of toast that had just popped out of the toaster. "Right, I'd better go."

Russell watched his flatmate dash out of the door, jacket half on and toast hanging out of his mouth. It was hard to believe they'd been friends for almost two years already, and yet so much had happened in that time.

Russell sat back and sipped his coffee. Life was pretty good right now.

JOE HAD barely arrived at the theatre, already running late, when Cameron turned him straight back round again and told him to get over to Lexi Goode's flat and bring her in himself.

It was unlike the young actress not to show up when called for extra rehearsals, even though she was the only one of the understudies who genuinely didn't need any more rehearsal. She was dedicated and talented, and Joe had a lot of time for her. She was understudying a role far older than she would ever have been cast to play but, when she was in that costume, in that wig and make-up, she was transformed.

Joe could tell—despite his bluster and feigned annoyance—that Cameron was worried about her too. Joe had seen the way they looked at each other. He'd clocked the same kind of lingering touches, the secret smiles and shy blushes between them that he had shared with Ben. If they weren't already sleeping together, it was certainly on the cards.

He'd decided to walk instead of getting a cab. Lexi didn't live that far away, and Joe thought it would be a good idea to walk off some of the late-night hangover before he arrived at her door.

He had no idea how an up-and-coming actress could afford a place on the fringes of Soho, but he'd learned several years ago not to judge on that score. She could have inherited a load of cash or she could be sharing with ten other actors in a bunk room. After all, he would never have been able to afford a flat off Old Compton Street if Russell hadn't offered him the room for the tiny sum he'd been charging Chris.

At first he'd thought it was a sympathy thing, and then he'd assumed that it was because Russell didn't want to live there alone. But since his flatmate had found love with Freddie Gillespie, Joe had realised that he was able to stay and pay such a low rent simply because Russell was a true friend, and he didn't really need the money from renting out a room, he just liked knowing there was someone there.

They both still missed Chris, though they only ever spoke about it on the day that would have been their old friend's birthday. Both had refused to acknowledge the anniversary of his death, though they had shared a Negroni, in silence, on that day for the last two years, and probably would do the same again this year.

Turning into Lexington Street, Joe checked the address that Cameron had jotted down and looked up at the impressive building in front of him. A Georgian mansion, converted into stylish apartments. This place was chic. Even if she *was* sharing, it was gorgeous.

Just around the corner from the bustling heart of Soho, you could still hear that particular sound of local chaos that seemed to ooze from the streets themselves, but somehow—here—there was a level of sophistication. Peace. As much as there was ever peace in Central London.

Joe stepped into the entrance porch and looked at the neat strip of buzzers on the central intercom system. No higgledy-piggledy stickers and peeling bits of tape here to show who lived in each flat.

When he realised that Lexi Goode's name was against one of the two top-floor flats he gave a canny smile. She was doing something right, for a girl from Brixton. Though, if she could afford this, Joe had no idea what she was doing playing bit parts in the theatre.

He pressed the buzzer and waited, wondering what had happened to stop her coming into rehearsals today. She hadn't phoned in with any kind of excuse, and she hadn't answered her phone when Cameron had tried to call several times. When Joe had suggested she may not have got the message about rehearsals, Cameron insisted that he come and get her.

As he waited for a reply, he stepped back and looked up at the building. If her flat was the one overlooking the street, then it was her window that was open, curtain billowing out through the gap.

Joe stepped forward, about to press the buzzer again, when a flustered-looking woman opened the front door from inside and clutched her bag closer to her chest when she saw Joe standing in the entrance porch.

Her eyes narrowed, looking at him suspiciously, following the line of his finger to see who he was trying to reach.

"Huh," she said, dismissively. "She doesn't answer, as usual."

Her French accent laid a different intonation on the words so that Joe wasn't sure if that was a simple observation, or a warning that Lexi never answered her buzzer.

"Is she in, do you know?"

"Yes, she's at home. I saw her door is open. People coming and going all night and day. I will tell the landlord."

She held the door for him, indicating that he could go on through.

"Thank you," Joe said.

"Tell her I heard her last night," the woman said miserably. "Again. So noisy."

Obviously, this was an ongoing complaint. Joe had grown used to the noise of his neighbours coming through the walls of their flat. It was part and parcel of city life. But, he guessed, if you're paying these kinds of prices, you had a right to expect a little privacy.

He let the door swing shut behind him and stood in the small lobby. A neat block of letter boxes lined the wall, all locked. He could see some flyers and junk mail sticking out of one on the far end, but the others were all neat and uniform.

A faint smell of pine-scented bleach hung beneath a more fruity smell of polish. A far cry from the communal entrance to his own flat, which was old and tired, usually home to at least one bicycle belonging to the downstairs neighbours and a sliding avalanche of free papers, old telephone directories and mail for tenants who had long since moved on.

Joe walked across to the lift and pressed the button to call it, hearing the mechanism clunk into life as soon as the light lit.

The doors opened with a gentle ping and Joe stepped in, looking at himself in the mirrored panel that lined the back of the lift. He looked tired, unsurprisingly. It had been a late night. But a fun one. He grinned. Look at you, Joe Stone.

It wasn't that he'd changed that much physically since leaving his small home town several years ago to follow his best friend Chris to London. Sure he'd filled out a bit, cut his hair and changed his style. But the difference he saw in that mirror was deeper than that. He had grown into himself. Become confident with who he was. He was smiling more these days, and when he did, it was genuine. He was happy.

The lift juddered to a halt, and the doors slid open to reveal a short corridor with two doors facing each other. Each flat occupied exactly half of the top floor, bisected by this corridor.

Joe stepped out and approached the doors, seeing that the one on the right was slightly ajar, just as Lexi's neighbour had said it would be. The sound of Tracy Chapman's sultry voice tempting us to drive away in our "Fast Car" carried through the open door.

It was hardly intrusively loud, but Joe could imagine that if the door was always open and the radio always on, it could become annoying for Lexi's neighbour. It struck him as odd though, because Lexi had never come across as either selfish or loud at work.

Joe knocked at the door and waited.

"Lexi?"

Nothing.

"Miss Goode? It's Joe Stone. Cameron sent me over to check if you were coming in to rehearsals today. He wasn't sure you got the message."

He waited again, listening for sounds of movement from within the apartment. Nothing, apart from the radio DJ cheerfully confirming that Tracy Chapman was still driving up the charts.

Joe pushed the door open gently, calling out again, in case she hadn't heard him over the radio. Stepping into the apartment, he noticed an empty champagne glass lying discarded beside the cream sofa—the damp stain of spilled champagne barely darkening the plush, pale carpet. A hand, palm up, protruded around the side of the sofa. Joe stepped closer and froze.

Lexi Goode lay on her back between the sofa and the coffee table, her arm extended away from her as though reaching for something. A bloom of dark blood spread beneath her shoulder, almost joining up with the stain of her spilled champagne. Her eyes were open, glassy, staring at the ceiling.

Joe stepped closer, crouching beside her. A single, small but deep stab wound on her chest, just to the left of centre, was the source of all that blood. Straight through her heart. She wouldn't have stood a chance.

"Lexi?" he said quietly, knowing already that there was no point. Lexi Goode was dead. Murdered in her own home. With a shaking hand, Joe closed her eyes.

JOE KNEW he should probably be waiting for the police outside the apartment, but it was so clear that Lexi had been murdered, and once he'd made the emergency call and got over his initial shock, he'd had a moment to think more clearly. He'd used Lexi's telephone to call both Russell—who had said he was on his way—and Cameron Beattie, the director, to let him know what had happened and that he would be waiting at Lexi's apartment for the police to arrive.

Having steadied himself, he returned his attention to the dead actress. She looked so young. He couldn't believe she was gone. Her face looked peaceful, if you were able to focus your gaze above the chest area where the deep stab wound marred her otherwise flawless skin. Peering closer, Joe realised there was another small cut near the stab wound, almost as though the killer had hesitated the first time.

She looked as though she had been in the process of undressing when the incident had happened, and Joe felt uncomfortable looking at her lying there in her suspenders and fancy underwear—a matching lacy lingerie set that seemed out of character for the relaxed young woman Joe'd thought he knew from the show.

He wondered whether he should cover her up, but didn't want to disturb any evidence the police may find. Instead, he walked away from the body to look around the room. His natural curiosity, and the fact that he and Russell had already solved a couple of murders that the police had shown no interest in solving, meant that he felt automatically obliged to look for clues as to what might have happened.

The door had been open when he arrived, so the murderer had either wanted the body discovered relatively easily, or had simply not cared if it was.

Joe checked the door again. There was no sign that it had been forced open, so Lexi must have let her killer in. Either she knew the person, or they were let in, like he had just been, by another resident in the building. He made a note to talk to Lexi's strange French neighbour again and see what it was she had heard last night.

She'd said there'd been a disturbance from Lexi's apartment in the night. She'd been angry about the noise. But had she actually heard the poor young actress being murdered and not realised?

Only in Soho, Joe thought, pushing the door closed slightly with his foot. He was fairly sure no one, apart from the neighbour, would come up to the top floor, but he felt he should try to preserve some kind of privacy for poor Lexi until the police got here.

He turned back to look at the flat. Neat, organised, and everything in its place. That's what struck him first. Lexi liked things tidy.

The kitchen housed a good-quality coffee machine, an expensive-looking toaster and kettle set, and a hob and cooker that looked too clean to have been used much. A corkboard on the wall held a calendar that reminded her she was due in for rehearsals this morning.

Joe stepped closer to look at the other dates marked on the calendar and realised that there were a series of marks on regular days every couple of weeks. Every other Tuesday she'd written the word "Ritz". Alternate Wednesdays: "Savoy". And the second Saturday of every month: "Langham". Last night, then, was the Langham.

It struck him as odd that she would put the location in but not the name of the person she was meeting. Perhaps she was running shifts as a cleaner. The Savoy. The Ritz. The Langham. All classy hotels.

Joe noticed that the word Langham written against yesterday's date had a question mark beside it in a different colour pen. As though she'd added it later. Looking back through the calendar, none of the others entries had a question mark. He wondered if she'd made it to this one.

He turned back to the kitchen, looking closer at a deep-red wig—long and straight—abandoned on the counter. A pair of strappy high heels discarded on the floor below. A long coat, pale beige with a tie belt, was draped over one of the two high stools pushed up against the counter.

If she'd taken these items off when she got home, where were the rest of Lexi's clothes. Surely she hadn't come home with nothing but a coat over some skimpy lingerie? Had she?

Perhaps she'd come home and got dressed up. Maybe she'd been expecting a lover and had gone all out on the sex appeal. It didn't feel like the Lexi he knew, but he reminded himself that he barely knew her at all. On balance, it looked as though she'd taken the wig, shoes and coat off after getting home. But it didn't make much sense. *Each to their own.*

On the far wall in the kitchen, beside an oversized fridge, was a small cabinet. It looked like an old French birdcage, also oversized, with the base on the floor and the top reaching Joe's chest; the thing was filled with bottles of Moet & Chandon.

Joe crouched to look at it, trying to work out how many hundreds of pounds worth of champagne Lexi had. He opened the fridge to find another four bottles lying on the top shelf, and an open bottle in the door—half-empty.

He tried to imagine Lexi coming home last night, shedding the wig and heels, dropping the coat on the stool and opening the fridge in her lingerie to pluck out a bottle of expensive champagne. None of these were the actions of a young woman alone. None of them were actions he could imagine Lexi doing.

He turned back to the sofa which was fortunately shielding her body from his sight. Casting his eyes around the rest of the room, he noticed that there was no sign of another champagne glass, and no sign of any clothes shed in the haste of passion either. It really didn't make sense.

A small canvas bag lay beside the front door too, dropped as she'd come in. Joe cautiously opened the zip to see the olive green, thick-knit jumper Lexi had been wearing when she'd left the theatre. Joe frowned, wondering why the clothes would be in a bag when she'd obviously worn them to go out with her parents. Had she changed while she was out? Or was she planning to go somewhere, with her bag all packed and ready.

"Don't let the police catch you rifling through her goodies," Russell's voice said behind him.

Joe stood quickly, relieved that his friend was here to share the responsibility.

"Come on," Russell said, scooping his arm through Joe's, "let's wait in the corridor. Don't want to rub any detectives up the wrong way, do we?"

He allowed himself to be guided out of the apartment, unable to help himself from taking one last look at Lexi's body on the floor beside the sofa, the champagne glass on its side, and the blood soaked carpet.

Joe shuddered. Something very strange had happened here last night. And something even stranger was going on with the girl he had only known as an up-and-coming young actress.

JOE SAT ON the floor in the corridor outside the apartment, only half-conscious of the bustle of bodies around him. The police had arrived just minutes after Russell had taken him out of the flat.

Russell handed him a steaming cup of sweet tea in the plastic lid of a Thermos flask.

"Thanks," Joe said, looking across at Russell as his friend joined him on the floor, patting his arm. The policeman hovering in the doorway gave them a sideways glance but said nothing.

"How're you doing?" Russell asked, quietly.

Joe just shook his head. The last thing he'd been expecting was to find the young actress murdered in her apartment and he didn't know how to feel about it. He closed his eyes as the sweet tea made its way to his stomach, making his gut bounce with an automatic reflux.

He couldn't shake the image of the deep hole in Lexi's chest. A single, fatal stab wound. But what had caused it? And who? The small pendant Lexi wore around her neck had become stuck in the congealing blood. It was strange that the pendant was the thing that had disturbed him most. A solitary diamond, bound in a silver teardrop shape.

It wasn't the first time he'd seen a dead body—he'd been the one who had found his best friend Chris murdered too. But there was something so neat, precise, unreal about the small hole that had ended Lexi's life. It looked too small to have caused so much damage.

His mind kept flashing back to Lexi's smile yesterday evening as he'd guided her parents into the dressing room. She had looked so alive, so happy. And yet, here she was dead.

"Have you given a statement yet?" Russell asked.

"No," Joe said. "They're still waiting for the right team to arrive."

"Typical," said Russell. He had very little time for his former colleagues these days.

"I'm sure they won't be long," said Joe, taking another sip of his tea and swallowing hard.

If he was honest, he wasn't sure he was ready to give a statement, anyway. He seemed to be struggling to keep his mind in check. He kept hearing Lexi's father's happy celebrations as he'd embraced his daughter—already a superstar in his eyes. They had seemed so sweet. This would be devastating for them.

"I hope it's not Skinner," Russell said.

"I thought you and Freddie were in the process of getting him suspended," Joe said. The last thing he wanted was to see that rat of a man.

Not only had Detective Simon Skinner been responsible for the sting that lost Russell his job, but he had also been the detective in charge of at least two cases now that Joe and Russell had been left to solve.

Skinner was an unreconstructed homophobe, and firmly believed that if you were gay, and anything bad happened to you, you had somehow asked for it by choosing a gay lifestyle. Russell and Freddie had both reported him on numerous occasions to the independent body that monitored police discrimination, but they were virtually powerless to do anything unless Skinner's bosses felt it was time to act.

For now, the insidious little rat was still one of the more senior detectives and was always likely to turn up on a high profile case like this.

"We're working on it," Russell said. "But he has always been Teflon coated, that guy. He's got enough support from on high to keep himself out of trouble, unless we can get something more concrete on him than just a few complaints from the gays."

"I just don't understand who would do this to her," Joe said, glumly. "She seemed like such a nice girl."

"She was the lead in the play?" Russell asked.

"No, the understudy," Joe said. "She usually plays a couple of smaller parts, but last night she was in the main role. The lead actress was off sick."

"Hell of a pad for a young actress," Russell said, leaning aside to look into the flat that he'd only briefly seen in the moments before the police had arrived. "Rich family?"

"Not from what I saw," Joe said. "I met her parents yesterday. They'd come to see her on her big night. Her dad said they'd got all dressed up. They'd come up from Brixton on the Tube."

"Well, she must be doing something right to afford this place," Russell said.

"What are you doing here?"

Joe and Russell turned their heads at the sound of Skinner's whiney voice, both wore similar expressions of disappointment. So he *was* going to lead this case after all.

"At least she wasn't gay," Russell muttered under his breath, standing up. "Joe was the one who found the body," he said to Skinner.

Joe noticed that Russell had positioned himself defensively between him and Skinner. Joe stood up too, resigned to talking to the detective and not wanting Russell to make the situation worse.

"Joe Stone," he said, subtly nudging Russell out of the way. "I work with Lexi."

"Lexi?" Skinner said, unable to keep the sneer from his lip as he tore his eyes from Russell to look at Joe.

"Alexandra Goode," Joe said. "The victim."

"I see," said Skinner. "Well, I'll need a statement from you. Wait here."

"What did you think I was doing," Joe whispered as Skinner strode past them.

Russell flashed two raised fingers behind the detective's back and caught a small smirk from the uniformed officer keeping guard on the door. Without saying a word, both Joe and Russell sidled along the corridor to watch Skinner's work in the room.

"Did she share this place with anyone?" Russell asked, keeping his voice low so that only Joe could hear him.

"Not that I could I see," Joe said. "I didn't really look around much though."

"Of course not," Russell said. "I guess I'm just wondering how she paid for it."

Joe shrugged. Russell had a point. Joe'd thought the same when he arrived. Perhaps whatever Lexi was doing on the side is what got her killed.

Joe's eyes wandered to the long, red synthetic wig lying abandoned on the kitchen worktop, and the killer heels kicked off underneath. The name of a swanky hotel written on her calendar. A thought was beginning to form of how Lexi could afford all this, but he wasn't sure he was ready to give it a name yet. Although, if he was right, her poor parents would be in for a shock.

Her parents. They had seemed so proud of her, so ecstatic that their little girl had made it to the big time—a West End star. Even if she was just the understudy for now. The way they had reacted to her last night she may as well have been handed the lead. Joe hoped it wouldn't be Skinner breaking the news to them of their daughter's death.

He wondered if there was a way he could get in touch with them. Perhaps he could drop the flowers round that had been delivered for Lexi last night and were still sitting in a makeshift vase in the dressing room. Anything to be able to express his sadness, maybe soften the blow.

"Sir, look at this," a uniformed officer said, handing Skinner a padded envelope. Russell jostled Joe closer to the door so that he could see what it was they had found.

Skinner opened the envelope, peering in cautiously before reaching a hand inside and pulling out a neat pile of twenty-pound notes. Even assessing from this distance, Joe guessed there must be over a thousand pounds in there. Seeing Skinner's eyes light up, Joe felt compelled to do something—anything to let the bent cop know that he and Russell had seen the cash too.

"Will you be much longer, Detective?" Joe asked in a loud voice, smiling inside as Skinner flinched and dropped the cash back into the envelope. "Only I have to get off."

Skinner laid the envelope on the kitchen counter beside the red wig and sauntered back towards the open door.

"Why? You finally got a job, have you?" he sneered.

"As a matter of fact…" Joe began.

"Save it, Sunshine," Skinner said. "You're not going anywhere until I've talked to you, and I'll talk to you when I'm finished assessing the scene."

He turned his back on Joe, thought about it and turned back to the uniformed officer guarding the door.

"You. Keep an eye on this man, and if he tries to leave, arrest him."

Joe saw the slight clench of the policeman's strong jaw as he agreed with a staccato "Sir."

Russell had pointed out to Joe previously how Skinner never bothered learning any of the lower-ranked officers' names. How he never showed them any respect.

"He's not going anywhere, Mike," Russell said, addressing the officer as though reading Joe's mind.

Joe saw the man's face soften.

"I didn't think you'd remember me, Sir," the officer said.

"Of course," Russell said, stepping closer. "Though there's no need for 'Sir' these days, is there? Russell will do. Mr Dixon if you're feeling particularly formal."

The cop smiled. Joe admired the way Russell was always able to put people at ease while still commanding authority.

"It's good to see you," the officer said. "It's not the same without you down at the station."

"No one to bring in the biscuits any more?"

Joe was sure he saw the officer blush. In his uniform, of course, he looked like any other policeman, but Joe saw a few hints now of secrets the young man may be keeping. The shaved head, the cheeky smile he gave Russell—put him in a white T-shirt and some tight jeans, and you'd have yourself a contender in any of the clubs in Soho.

"I'm surprised to see you here, though," Russell said. "I thought you'd gone for a transfer."

"He blocked it," the officer said, nodding his head in Skinner's direction.

"Does he know?" Russell asked. "About you?"

The officer shook his head with an almost guilty expression.

"No," he said, looking nervously over his shoulder. "After what happened to you…"

"I know," Russell said. "I get it. Listen, we're working on getting him sacked. If there's anything you know that you think can help us, you'll always find me in the Red Lion on Rupert Street."

"Always?" he asked, with a quizzical grin.

Russell smirked back. "More or less."

"I may pop down then," the officer said. "One evening after work. It would be good to catch up."

The look he shot Joe over Russell's shoulder gave away more than he intended, and when Joe smiled, he blushed again.

"Oh, and don't turn your back on either of those two, mate," Skinner called to the officer from inside the apartment. "They'll do more than lift your shirt, I can tell you."

Some officers inside laughed, but the majority kept their heads down and carried on with their tasks.

"Just ignore him," Russell said. "It makes life a lot easier. He'll get what's coming to him."

"I hope you're right," the officer said. "He's insufferable."

They all turned as the lift gently pinged and the doors opened. Cameron Beattie hurried out of the lift and, seeing Joe, made a beeline for him.

"My God," the director said. "I can't believe it. Are you sure?"

He caught sight of the police officers buzzing around the apartment through the open door and almost staggered backward.

"I'm sure," Joe said, supporting the director's arm. "The door was open when I got here. I found her myself."

"Lexi?" Cameron asked.

Joe nodded.

"Why?" Cameron asked. "Who would do this?"

Joe took him by the elbow, gently but firmly, and guided him down the corridor, away from police ears. Russell took the hint, and began asking Mike, the uniformed officer, about some of their other colleagues, creating enough of a distraction for Joe to have some privacy with the director.

"Cameron," Joe said, his voice calm and low. "You knew Lexi better than most of us, this must be a huge shock."

Cameron gulped in a breath of air, sighing it back out again.

"I just can't believe it," he said, shaking his head. "I mean, yesterday she was out there in front of a full house, putting in the performance of a lifetime, and today she's gone. It doesn't make sense."

"I know," Joe said. It didn't make sense at all, but then the fragility of life never did. "Did you know if she was going on anywhere last night? After the show?"

"No," Cameron said. "I asked her if she wanted to have dinner to celebrate playing the lead so well, and she declined. She was going out with her parents, she said."

"Right," said Joe. "That's what I thought. Well, maybe she went on somewhere else afterwards."

"What do you mean?" Cameron asked.

"Well," Joe said. "It's just that when I found her, she was all dolled up. Like she'd been out to a party, but when I saw her leave with her parents she was dressed casually."

"Huh," Cameron said, seeming lost and deflated.

"Did you know she lived here?" Joe asked.

"I got her address from the files," Cameron said, a little too defensively.

Joe had suspected that Cameron and Lexi'd had a bit of a fling. Was that why he was being defensive, or was there something else Joe should know?

"I'm only asking because it seems a pricey place for a young actress to rent alone at the start of her career," Joe said.

"How is this important, Joe?" Cameron snapped. "The girl's dead. Who cares how she paid her rent?"

As Joe saw the tears welling in the director's eyes, he decided not to explain why it was important—how it could hold a clue as to who had killed her. Instead, he patted the man on the shoulder.

"This must be a terrible shock," he said. "I know you two were... close."

Cameron's eyes narrowed. His face paled.

"I can't do this," Cameron spluttered, already heading for the lift at the far end of the corridor. "I've got to go."

Joe let him go, knowing he'd catch up with him later.

JOE TOOK the pint gratefully as Russell sat down. Sure, it was only just past twelve, but the events of the morning so far had more than justified an early pint for the poor lad. He looked done in.

"Thanks," he said.

"How're you coping?" Russell asked.

Joe shrugged. "I'm okay I guess," he said. "I didn't really know her that well."

"Sure, but it's not easy being the first on the scene."

Russell knew only too well how shocking it was to be the one to find a dead body—he'd dealt with more than enough shocked witnesses in his time on the force. And this was not Joe's first body either. He would doubtless be flashing back to the time he found his friend, Chris, or even to the murdered cabaret host, Danny. Both of those cases had been solved a while ago now, but the shock of discovery could bring back all sorts of memories to haunt you.

Joe simply nodded, taking a sip of his drink.

"What did Skinner ask you?" Russell asked.

Joe rolled his eyes, swallowing his sip. "Obviously, where I was last night, what I was doing and who with. Naturally, I didn't tell him the whole truth."

"Nothing to do with the case then?"

"Well, he asked me how I knew her and why I'd come calling, and whether I knew of anyone who would want to hurt her."

"Wow," Russell said. "Almost sounding like an actual detective there."

Joe smiled, but it was weak. He wasn't in the mood to be cheered up.

"And?" Russell asked. "What did you say? Could you think of anyone?"

Joe cocked his head, smiling gently, acknowledging that Russell would never leave the detective in him behind.

"Well, no," Joe said. "As I said. I didn't really know her that well. I know she had a bit of a fling with the director, Cameron, at one point.

Or, at least, I guessed they had from the way they acted around each other, but that seemed to have tapered off."

"He disappeared pretty sharpish," Russell said. "What's his story?"

"I don't know," Joe said. "He also seemed a little defensive when I asked him if he'd known she lived in a place like that. It could have just been the shock, but it's a little odd."

"You think there might have been a lovers tiff?" Russell asked. "Could he have done that to her if she'd turned him down? I mean, you saw how she was dressed."

"Maybe," Joe replied. "But then why would Cameron come over to her flat again, knowing that the police would be there. He seemed pretty shocked when I called him to tell him I'd found her dead."

"He is a director, though," Russell said. "If he *had* done something to her, he'd be expecting the call as soon as he sent you to get her, wouldn't he? Surely he'd be able to pull off a performance of his own, and know how to deliver it convincingly."

"Maybe," Joe mused. "But I'm not so sure. I think he might have been more worried how it would look, if it got out that there'd been a relationship going on and she had got the lead understudy role as a result."

"Wouldn't be the first time," Russell said.

"No," said Joe, "But it still doesn't explain the expensive flat, the designer clothes, the champagne on tap."

"Maybe she had a sugar daddy," Russell said. "How well off is that Cameron?"

"As far as I can tell, not very. I mean, he dresses well, but it's all a little faded, you know? He makes a living from the theatre work, but not enough of a one to support a flat like that."

"Maybe someone else then," Russell said. "Some rich benefactor?"

"Hmm," Joe mused, taking another sip of his beer.

Russell could see his mind working. "What is it, Joe?" he asked.

"Well, there *was* a huge bunch of flowers delivered to the theatre for her yesterday. The note on the card said something about a final curtain call. It's probably still in the dressing room."

"What does that mean? A final curtain call?"

"I don't know," Joe said. "We thought they were for Hattie."

"Hattie?"

"Hattie Duval, the regular lead. She gets a bunch from an admirer every week."

"How sweet."

"But Hattie said they weren't for her."

"I thought she was off sick," Russell said, looking confused.

"She often comes in to watch, even if she can't perform. She says it helps her understand her craft."

"It's a bit of an ominous message, isn't it? Given what's happened."

"Hmm," Joe agreed. "Maybe we should try to find out who sent them."

"It'd be a start."

Joe looked up at Russell over the rim of his pint. "You think we should look into this ourselves, don't you?"

"Well, you don't think Skinner's going to suddenly do a good job, do you?" Russell said.

"I figured, because she's not gay he might be more inclined to help."

Russell laughed.

"Homophobia is not the only string to his intolerant bow, dear boy. He's no race relations ambassador either."

Joe sighed.

"Anyway, what harm can it do to lend a hand?" Russell said. "I'll come with you, if you like."

JOE LED the way down the dark backstage passage towards the suite of dressing rooms. A large, communal one housed long benches with wooden pegs above and tall lockers for the main bulk of the cast. A couple of smaller, individual dressing rooms had been set aside further down the corridor for the leads.

"Ordinarily, Lexi would have been in there with the rest of the cast," Joe said as they passed the communal changing area. "It's usually buzzing during show time."

"But not last night?" Russell asked.

"No. As Hattie was off sick, Lexi got her dressing room."

"Talk about filling her shoes," Russell commented, as they reached a door with Hattie Duval's name written on the sign outside.

"It's just practical, really," Joe said. "It's where all the costume and make-up for the role is anyway, so it's easier to move the actress than the wardrobe. Besides, Hattie didn't seem to mind. Like I said, she was here last night, and very supportive."

"But she was sick?"

"Not sick so much as not able to perform."

"What was wrong?"

"Apparently, she struggles with depression a bit," Joe said. "She's very private about it, and I gather that she and Cameron have an understanding. She has a specific phrase that she says when she phones in, so that he knows what's going on but no one else does."

"What's the phrase?"

"She says she's got to take the dog to the vet."

Russell chortled.

"The old black dog, huh? Good one."

Joe opened the door to the dressing room, and they both stepped in, smelling the musty scent of old greasepaint, hired costumes and powdered wigs.

"But she still came in yesterday," Russell asked. "Despite the depression kicking in?"

"Yeah, she does that sometimes. Prefers the company," Joe said. "Hattie was in here when I brought Lexi's parents along to see her. She left almost as soon as we got here, but she seemed friendly enough. I know it seems strange, but she does come in, when she's not well, and hangs around in the wings to watch. Cameron tries to stop it. He says she's just doing it to torture herself."

"How so?" Russell asked.

"Well, watching someone else play her role. Sometimes it sends her further down her spiral. She convinces herself that everything will go on much better without her."

"Wow," Russell said. "That's so sad. I've seen her tread the boards a few times and she is quite mesmerising. It's hard to think that someone so famous could suffer from such anxiety."

"You'd be surprised."

Having worked in a television production company, and now in the theatre, Joe was convinced it was almost the other way around. The more famous you became, the more the self-doubt and anxiety gnawed away at you, convincing you that you were little more than a puppet. He'd seen it several times already.

Joe crossed to the long make-up table that spanned the length of the far wall, facing a huge mirror with lights all around it. The large bouquet still stood in the jug he'd used as a makeshift vase. Wrapped in paper and cellophane and tied in that distinctive ribbon. The card was still exactly where he'd left it, propped against the jug.

He picked it up and pulled the card from the envelope.

"One final curtain call," he read. "With a question mark."

"That's it?" Russell asked.

"And the initials TG."

"Rather odd message," Russell replied. "Usually you'd go with 'Break a Leg' or something. Given what happened to Lexi later, do you think this was a warning?"

"It's a line from the play," Joe said. "Well, without the question mark, but still—it's what Lady Earnshaw says to the maid, just before she dies. 'It was to be my final curtain call...' and then she stabs herself."

"And this was the character Lexi stepped up to play last night?" Russell frowned, trying to work out the logic of the message.

"Yes," Joe clarified. "It's how the play ends."

"That is very strange," Russell said, plucking the card from Joe's hand and reading it himself. "And who is TG?"

"No idea," Joe said.

Russell turned the card over to look at the back.

"It's from Betty's," he said, almost triumphantly.

The little florist was a small, independent affair on Poland Street. Joe had used them often while he was still working with the television company. Flowers were the kind of gift that no one could really object to, and Anton the owner was a real character.

"Makes sense, I guess, it's only a couple of blocks away," Joe said.

"I'll pop in there on my way home if you like," Russell said. "Ask old Anton if he remembers who made the order. I don't suppose they were dropped off in person?"

"No idea," Joe said. "I can ask the box office girls once they get in."

Russell lifted one of the wigs from the wooden head it was resting on and raised it over his own head as though about to slip it on.

"Ah, you're here."

Cameron's voice made both of them jump and Russell quickly put the wig down.

"Where the hell have you been? I need you out front, now."

Joe and Russell exchanged a concerned look as Cameron turned to go.

"I had to stay to give a statement to the police," Joe said incredulously. "I didn't think we'd be working today. Not after…"

"The show must go on, dear boy. The show must go on."

"But…"

Joe didn't know what to say. Surely they weren't going to continue with the rehearsal now? How could they?

"Come on, Joe. I need all hands to the mast here," Cameron insisted. "Even Hattie has come back in, the poor love. We're all shocked. But we have a full house tonight, and only two weeks left on the run. So like I said, the show must go on."

Joe shook his head in disbelief as Cameron turned and marched away. Russell patted him on the shoulder.

"Might be a good opportunity for you to talk to the other cast members," he said. "See if they know who this TG person is, or if there was anything else going on with Lexi that we should know about."

Joe nodded.

"I can't believe he's just getting on with things," Joe said.

"Grief can make us act strangely," Russell said. "Don't judge him too soon."

Joe shrugged. "I guess."

"I'll go and see Anton at Betty's and find out what he knows. See you at the Red Lion later? Patty's big night tonight."

Joe nodded. He wasn't sure he'd be in the mood for a drag show tonight, but Patty—or Paul as he was known out of costume—was a good friend, and worked hard to make these Frock Show nights spectacular.

"I'll be there," Joe said, heading off towards the stage.

RUSSELL LEFT the theatre via the stage door at the back, having realised that the front doors were all closed up and there was no one in the box office yet to let him out.

He slipped his jacket off and slung it over his shoulder, enjoying the summer heat on his arms and face. He checked his watch. Nearly four o'clock already. Freddie had agreed to meet him for an early supper before they both went along to Patty's Frock Show. Plenty of time for him to get to the florist and see if Anton was there, and still get home in time to change into something a little more flamboyant.

Russell had never been particularly into the so-called "gay scene", despite living in Soho for so many years, he'd always found himself shying away from the more "out-there" side of the community. Clubbing hadn't been his thing and, probably because he had been so fearful of his secret coming out at work, he had kept a low profile around even the quieter gay bars in the area.

The Red Lion had always been gay friendly—the place was *everything* friendly. An old favourite of all of Soho's strange mix of characters: gangsters, prostitutes, drag queens and queers, actors, celebrities, journalists and even minor royals could rub shoulders with relative anonymity within the sticky, nicotine encrusted walls of the old boozer. No tabs. No favours. No problems.

Since leaving the police force, Russell had been far more comfortable embracing the more flamboyant side of his odd little village. The worst had happened—his secret had been exposed—and it actually hadn't been that bad. Once the shock wore off, and the fury at being forced to retire from his beloved role as a detective, Russell realised that he actually, finally, had a place to call home, and people to call family.

Joe had been instrumental in that change, and so had Freddie Gillespie—his boyfriend and the love of his life. What would he think of the fact that Russell and Joe were looking into another murder in Soho?

Freddie seemed happy to support Russell's new career as a kind of unofficial private detective for the Soho residents. There was certainly enough work around to keep him busier than he had expected.

Soho wasn't exactly a safe place, but the local residents had a way of looking out for each other that gave the area the feel of a small village. Sure, people knew your business, but it meant that when trouble arose, you had friends around you, closing ranks and offering support.

Given that Russell's old colleagues on the police force had more than a passing disdain for anyone outside a mainstream walk of life, it was little surprise that people turned to him when they needed help.

Joe had proved himself to be a quick learner and an intuitive detective in his own right too. Russell knew that he was wasted in the run of junior jobs he'd had since moving to London, but at least he got to use some of that psychology degree of his, working out what had happened in the trickier cases they'd had to solve.

Joe had a way of getting people to share their secrets with him that Russell envied. Perhaps it was his youthful good looks that caught them off guard, underestimating how much information Joe could surmise from the most innocent of questions.

Coming to a stop outside Betty's florist, Russell found it closed, with a dainty little sign hanging in the door to confirm such, though the light inside was on. He smiled at the sound of Anton's voice carrying loudly through the closed door.

Anton was a small barrel of a man—camp as Christmas, with his lurid shirts always open one button more than necessary and topped off with a silk cravat in a vain attempt to hide his loosening jowls. He had a sharp tongue, a comic turn of phrase, and couldn't speak without using his hands.

Russell had found Anton to be a font of useful information when it came to knowing who was seeing whom, behind whose back. Flowers, after all, were often the sign of a guilty conscience.

The little old-fashioned little bell jingled as Russell pushed the door open and stepped in. Anton was there, talking to a glamorous woman in a large red hat and matching knee-length red dress. She looked like a model.

"Sorry love, we're closed," he said without looking up. "So, I said to him, look darling, this is Betty's, not a bloody petrol station. You pay for what you get here. Class. Am I right?" He touched her arm, as was his wont when talking to anyone.

The bell rang again as the door swung shut and Anton finally looked over.

"Oh, look," he cooed, shuffling the woman aside to embrace Russell like an old friend. "If it isn't my favourite detective. Have you come to take me away?" He held out his wrists as though waiting for the handcuffs to be slapped on.

Russell saw the woman's eyes widen for a moment and he smiled.

"Not this time, Anton. I'm here for some advice, actually."

Anton patted his arm understandingly and turned back to the woman.

"You can tell Her Majesty that everything will be ready, exactly as promised, on Friday night. And if she checks up on me one more time, I will make sure to include something to set off her allergies."

Without giving her time to reply, he shepherded the woman towards the door and closed it behind her, rolling his eyes.

"Isabella Latour's assistant, or one of them," he said, as though Russell should know who that was. "The woman is such a control freak. Fancy bringing me in on a Sunday. I swear every time it will be the last, but I just can't resist the glamour."

He drew the last word out, framing his face with his hands like a 1920s flapper. Russell chuckled.

"I'm sure the pay's alright too, right?" he said.

"We get by, darling. Now, what can I do for you?"

"I'm looking for some information about a bouquet bought yesterday," Russell said. "Big, blousey, purples, reds and pinks."

"Cheeky bitch, we don't do blousey," Anton said, already stepping behind the counter and pulling out the tatty handwritten ledger that was his accounting system. "Right, let's see. Yesterday you say?"

"It was delivered to the Palace Theatre last night. I don't suppose you made the delivery?"

"No dear, sorry. That level of personal service costs a little extra," he smiled coquettishly at Russell, and returned his gaze to the ledger.

"I'm guessing it would have been a man doing the purchasing. They were for a young actress in the West End."

"Aha!" Anton said, spinning the ledger around and tapping the page for Russell to see the entry. "One large exotic bouquet. Cash paid. Buyer collects."

"No name?"

"Please, darling, as if we would be so crass. A good florist must be the height of discretion at all times. And I am an excellent florist."

Russell rolled his eyes.

"I don't suppose you remember what the guy looked like then, do you? It's important."

"Pray tell," Anton said, rubbing his hands together in anticipation. Russell knew he would get nothing more without a little quid pro quo.

"The young woman they were delivered to was killed last night. Murdered."

Anton's hands shot to his face covering his mouth in exaggerated shock. "No!"

Russell nodded. "So if you can remember anything about the person who bought the flowers, I'd be very grateful."

"Of course. Well, let's see now," Anton began, suddenly serious. "He was a tall man, but then, most are compared to me, aren't they darling? About your height, I'd say, maybe a little taller. Slim. Wiry even. Nice suit. Posh accent. Couldn't crack a smile."

"And he paid cash, you say?"

"Yes. And there was plenty more in that wallet of his too."

"Anything else?"

"He was wearing a wedding ring," Anton said. "I tend to notice these things. And let me tell you something, that was not a bouquet you'd buy for your wife, if you get my drift?"

"What time did he come in?"

"Just before closing—seven-ish. He seemed in a bit of a rush, I thought. He had a car waiting for him outside."

"You didn't spot the make, did you?"

Anton flapped his hand as though Russell had said something hilarious.

"Well, it was black."

"Great," Russell said sarcastically, shaking his head. "Thanks."

"He did have a driver though," Anton said, "so he must be high up somewhere. Seemed strange that he'd be coming in himself to buy flowers, but I suppose he wants his secret kept safe."

"Okay, well, thanks a lot," Russell said, starting to go.

"Wait," said Anton. "You're not going to buy anything? We've got some lovely roses, fresh in this morning. For your beau."

"You know you're supposed to ask for the bribe before you give out the information, right?" Russell said.

"The cheek," Anton pretended to be affronted.

"I'll take one rose," Russell said, smiling.

"Oh, come on, I've got cats to feed," Anton protested.

"You hate cats," Russell replied. "One rose. That's it."

"You'll be the death of me," Anton sighed.

"You're doing alright. And thanks. I appreciate it."

Russell took his single red rose and headed for the door before Anton could try to sell him anything else.

THE MOOD in the rehearsal room was flat and sombre. Joe was on prompt, which meant he was basically reading out most of the lines to each of the players who had been forced to step up into new roles. None of them could concentrate and Joe wasn't surprised.

He still couldn't believe that Cameron was ploughing ahead with the rehearsal. The public would understand, surely? I mean, who would expect a show to still be raising the curtain the night after one of their rising stars had been murdered.

Joe looked up as Cameron let forth another frustrated tirade on young Ben Higson for not knowing his lines. Joe had been trying to give him encouragement, but Ben seemed unable to meet his eye today. Perhaps he was feeling strange that they had been fooling around at exactly the time when Lexi was being murdered. The thought had certainly crossed Joe's mind as soon as he'd seen Ben.

"Why don't we all take a break for half an hour," Joe said quietly to Cameron. "No one's getting anything right any more. They're too upset."

Joe couldn't hide the inference in his voice that he felt Cameron should be upset too. He looked across to see the muscles in Cameron's jaw flex. His eyes were steely cold. He blinked, long and slow and then stood up.

"Alright everyone," he said, "we've done our best. Let's call it a day."

There was relief all round.

"But I want you in early tomorrow. We are putting this play on tomorrow, and, for Lexi's sake, I want it to be perfect."

Joe heard the hint of a crack in his voice as Cameron said her name. Cameron turned away before anyone could see the tears beginning to well in his eyes. Joe noticed, but did nothing to comfort the director.

"Bring the folder backstage when everyone's gone, will you, Joe? I want to go over my notes."

Joe nodded his agreement as Cameron marched off into the wings. Joe turned, looking to have a quick word with Ben, and was disappointed to see the young actor hurrying out of the door with a couple of colleagues, without so much as a backward glance.

Oh well, Joe thought. *Must have been more casual than I realised.*

"It's hit him hard," the voice beside him made him jump. *Hattie Duval.* "Cameron, I mean. You mustn't judge him. He's under enough pressure as it is. You can see how upset he is."

Joe turned to find her staring, almost wistfully, into the wings where Cameron had disappeared.

"Don't you think it was a bit odd carrying on with the rehearsal today?" Joe protested. "I mean, we're all in shock."

"It's never straightforward is it?" the veteran actress said. "He's got financiers to please, ticket sales to honour, wages to pay. It's terribly sad, of course. But show business is more business than show, these days."

Joe couldn't tell whether she was referring to Lexi's death as sad, or the decline of show business. Either way, he wasn't much in the mood for Hattie Duval today. She always needed so much reassurance. Joe began to pack away the folder of notes he'd been taking as Cameron shouted directions.

"I can't help feeling this is somehow my fault," Hattie continued, sighing and sitting heavily in the seat that Cameron had vacated. Joe looked over, and she patted the seat beside her, inviting him to sit. There was no way he'd get out of this now.

Taking a reluctant breath that he disguised as a sigh of his own, Joe sat, folder clasped in his lap, ready to make an escape at the earliest convenience.

"You mustn't blame yourself," Joe said, not seeing any reason at all why the woman could believe it was anything to do with her. Mind you, that was Hattie Duval all over—had to be at centre of everything, whether she had any business there or not.

"*Au contraire,* dear boy," she said, voice wavering. "If I had been able to perform last night, perhaps she wouldn't have been thrust into the limelight."

"I don't think her death had anything to do with her performing the lead last night," Joe said.

Hattie's eyes narrowed. Her lips pursed. She didn't like being contradicted, especially when she was placing herself at the heart of a drama.

"Oh, you don't?" she said. "And pray tell, what do you know of it?"

"Nothing," Joe said, quickly. "I just mean that I can't see why anyone would want to hurt her because she had played the role for one night, that's all."

"Well," Hattie said, straightening her back, about to explain just how. "That just shows how little you understand the demands on a young leading lady stepping into the shoes of a national treasure."

Joe rolled his eyes mentally, a rictus grin on his face. Hattie may be a household name within theatre circles, but she was hardly a national treasure. She was not to be dissuaded, however.

"The fans get jealous," she continued. "They can be fiercely loyal."

"You think one of your fans hurt her?"

"Not a fan, darling, one of the others." She shuddered. "The stalkers, the obsessives, the freaks. They get carried away, you see. Think they know you. You can never be too careful."

It hadn't struck Joe before that Lexi may have been hurt by someone angry that she had taken Hattie's role. Surely people understood the concept of an understudy enough to know that she was not stealing any limelight.

"I mean, she did get a wondrous reception last night," Hattie continued. "Three encores. I ask you. And did you see the roses they threw for her? Anyone would think it was opening night. Bound to have raised a few eyebrows, that."

She smiled sadly, as though remembering a fond moment from long ago. It was true, there had been a group of young men in the front seat who had all thrown single roses onto the stage during Lexi's curtain call. Joe wondered what had happened to those flowers. Probably scooped up by the other performers.

"Is there someone in particular," Joe asked, assessing the idea. "That you think might be upset enough on your behalf to do this?"

"Oh no, dear," Hattie said. "I try not to have much contact with them. It's not good for my sanity. Too much pressure, you see. No, I'm just thinking aloud, that's all. It has been known that an overzealous fan can take things too far. That's all."

Joe made a mental note to look into the idea further.

"So, will you be alright to step back into the role, then?" he asked, trying to steer her away from maudlin thoughts of vengeful fans.

"Oh," Hattie smiled, patting his hand. "You are kind to worry. I'll be fine. I was just having a little wobble. I'm better now. All sorted."

But the look on her face said that was a lie. Whatever demons she was fighting with roiled just below the surface. The poor woman should be resting, not pressed back into a stressful performance just days after a colleague had died. Perhaps he should have another word with Cameron about Hattie's state of mind.

Joe made his excuses and left Hattie sitting alone in the auditorium. He knew that Cameron liked him to make sure everyone had left, but he figured Hattie was fine to see herself out when she was ready.

RUSSELL squeezed in beside Freddie on the bench at their regular table in the window of the Red Lion. The place was already buzzing. The Pet Shop Boys were blaring out of the jukebox and there was standing room only at the bar.

"It's going to be busy tonight," Freddie commented, accepting his drink from Russell. "They're going to have to start thinking about a bigger venue soon."

"I know," Russell said. "God forbid anything goes wrong out the back tonight, there'll be no getting out in this crowd."

"Great for the charity though, isn't it?"

They were both shouting above the hum of music and conversation in the bar. Russell settled for nodding his reply instead. Since they had started hosting the Frock Show drag nights here at the Red Lion, both Ron, the landlord, and Patty, the organiser, had decided that all proceeds should go to the Campbell Centre. Ron kept half the takings from the bar and the rest went straight back into helping the community.

The deal made people generous with both time and money, and it meant that the turnout for the monthly events had grown each time as word spread. And the show was great too. Patty had become a seasoned drag queen—funny, talented and strikingly beautiful. She had even roped in Ron's son, Scott as the other main act—Miss Terri and her support dancers, The Ladykillers. Miss Terri was a real crowd pleaser and was rising up the rankings quickly.

Between them, they'd pulled in ladies from Camden and King's Cross, and even had guest acts from Wales and Manchester. The event usually ran to a couple of hours of entertainment. And, judging by the crowds gathering already, tonight was going to be another stormer.

Russell waved as he saw Joe pass the window, showing him that they already had a drink for him. Joe gave him a double thumbs up.

"Poor kid," Russell said,

Freddie looked at him askew.

"Oh God, I haven't told you the news," Russell blurted. "Joe found one of his colleagues from the play this morning. Dead."

"What?" Freddie said.

"Murdered, by the look of things."

"Jesus, it just keeps happening, doesn't it?" Freddie said, shaking his head.

It was a fair point. They had seen more than their fair share of murder in the past few years.

"Who was it?" Freddie asked.

"A young actress," Russell replied. "Lexi Goode. On her way up too."

"Poor kid."

Joe arrived at the table, squeezing past a pair of hot guys and grinning cheekily at Russell as he lingered between them for a moment.

"He let you out then?" Russell asked.

Joe nodded, taking a deep draught from the pint in front of him. Russell could almost see his friend relax as the beer hit the spot. Tonight would be a great way to take his mind off the trauma of this morning, and if there was one thing Russell knew, it was that you needed to find ways to shut off after finding something like that.

"Nobody was into it," Joe said. "Not surprising. No one could remember their lines. People were crying. It was crazy to think they could all just carry on."

"The director had called all the understudies in to rehearse this morning," Russell explained to Freddie. "And when one of them didn't show up, old Joe here was sent to find her."

"I'm sorry, Joe," Freddie said.

Joe shrugged.

A burst of laughter from the bar accompanied a ridiculous attempt by a small group to dance to "Walk Like an Egyptian". They glanced over at the disruption before coming back to the conversation, half-smiles on their faces.

"I can't believe the director thought anyone would be able to rehearse today, though," said Russell.

"To be honest," Joe said. "I don't think it was about that. I think he just needed to be with people who knew her. He was pretty broken up by it. We all are."

"I'm sure," Freddie said.

"So you don't think he did it?" Russell asked.

Joe shook his head. "It doesn't really sit right," he said. "But something's up with him."

"I popped by Betty's, by the way," Russell said. "Anton ended up being reasonably useful. Said the flowers had been bought by a tall, skinny man in a good suit. Wedding ring. Private car—with driver—waiting outside."

"Did he get a name?"

"No," Russell shook his head. "Cash buyer. Didn't seem accustomed to buying flowers himself, though. Anton got the feeling he'd had a falling out with his mistress and was looking for a way to make it up."

"His mistress? Not his wife? You said he wore a wedding ring."

"He insisted they weren't the kind of flowers people buy for their wives."

Joe nodded, drinking more of his pint.

"Does that sound familiar?" Russell asked. "Tall, skinny, rich? Over middle-aged. Anyone like that been hanging round the theatre recently?"

"Not really," Joe said. "But then most of our clientele are rich and old. The thing is, we never really hung around together. Lexi would always head off pretty much straight after the show. There were only a couple of times she ever came out with the rest of us and, even then, she never stayed long. I never saw her with anyone. Apart from Cameron."

"So," Freddie said, collecting the empty glasses as he stood up. "Do I gather from the way you're both talking that you may be 'helping' the police on this one? Who's in charge?"

"Skinner," Joe and Russell said at the same time, in the same world-weary tone.

"God help us." Freddie rolled his eyes and headed for the bar. "Same again?" he called, but didn't wait for their replies.

"Are you okay?" Russell asked.

Joe may not have known Lexi Goode very well, but it must still have been a hard day, first finding her, then dealing with the police—especially Skinner—and then going back to work as though nothing had happened, when in fact everything had.

Joe nodded. "I'll be fine. Just a bit much, that's all. Brings it all back."

They both stayed quiet. There was no need to say any more.

"I keep feeling like I should go and talk to her parents," Joe said. "See if they're okay?"

"It's a good idea," Russell said. "And I'm sure they'd appreciate it. But not tonight, okay? Just try to give yourself a little time and space."

"Hullo, Sir—uh, Russell," a deep voice interrupted them, and they both looked up to find Mike, the young policeman from outside Lexi's door standing beside their table.

"Mike?" Russell asked, surprised to find his former colleague in the bar, but even more surprised to find him barely recognisable. "Nice to see you."

Out of uniform, Mike's thick, dark curls had been backcombed and piled up high on his head, leaving the shaved sides exposed. His eyes had a soft-punk sheen of make-up and he was wearing two earrings in his left ear. His leather jacket was layered with silver studs, stars and spikes, and his tight black T-shirt showed off how fit he was beneath it. He was clutching a full pint. Russell saw Joe's jaw drop as the young cop blushed.

"Sorry," Mike said. "You said to come along sometime, and I thought, well, why not now?"

"Marvellous," Russell said. "You look great. Not at all what I was expecting. Why don't you join us?"

Mike blushed again.

"I wouldn't want to intrude."

"Nonsense, budge up, Joe," Russell said, touching his finger below his chin to indicate that Joe should close his mouth.

Joe shuffled along to make room just as Freddie arrived back with the next round.

"Mike," Russell said, "this is my partner, Freddie. Freddie, this is Mike. We used to work together."

"Well," said Mike, as Freddie said his hellos. "I wouldn't have said we worked together. I'm just a grunt in uniform. Doc was always very kind."

"Doc?" Freddie asked, looking perplexed.

"On account of his name is Dixon," Mike explained, and when they all still looked confused, "Dixon of Dock Green. It became Doc."

"Oh," said Russell. "I thought it was because I always asked 'What's Up?'"

Mike laughed, then cast a quick glance at Joe. "I'm sorry about your friend… this morning," he said.

"That's okay," Joe said. "She wasn't a friend, really. I worked with her."

"Real shame," Mike said.

"You got any leads yet, Mike?" Russell asked.

Mike shook his head. "If Skinner's onto anything, he wouldn't tell me. But I doubt he is. He couldn't find his arse with his hands, that one. All I know is what we found in the flat."

"Have her parents been told?" Joe asked. "They'll be devastated."

"Yes," said Mike. "I was one of the officers Skinner sent to do it. He never does the hard stuff himself. But you're right. It broke them. Especially when we told them about the money. Well, they just couldn't understand it."

"The money in that envelope?" Joe asked.

Mike hesitated.

"It's alright, Mike," Russell said. "You're among friends here. It'll go no further."

"Well," said Mike, leaning in and gathering them all closer to him at the centre of the table. "There was at least a grand in notes in that envelope, and then we found another two grand in her knicker drawer in her bedroom."

"Where the hell was that kind of money coming from?" Russell asked. "She was just an actress."

Mike laughed, mirthlessly.

"Judging from what else we found in her knicker drawer, I'd hazard she was working a few shifts on the side, if you get my meaning."

They didn't.

"In the sex trade," he explained.

"Bloody hell," Joe said.

"I mean, she'd had to have been either very good or very busy to be earning that kind of cash, but she had a fantastic collection of saucy stuff. Fetish. You know?"

"I think we can imagine," Russell said.

"Huh," Joe said, as though a penny had just dropped.

"You suspected it?" Russell asked, and all eyes turned to Joe.

"No," he said. "Yes. I don't know. It's just that she had the names of hotels and rooms marked fairly regularly on her calendar, but never any names of who she was meeting. And that seemed a bit strange to me. That, and what she was wearing when I found her, as though she'd come home in just a coat and her underwear."

"I guess it explains how she could afford the nice flat," Russell said.

"And," Mike continued, "it looks like she'd been entertaining on the night she died."

"Really?" Joe asked. "But there was only one champagne glass. I checked."

"We found another one in the bin in the corridor," Mike said. "Looks like she knew her killer well enough to share a drink with them."

"Laydeees and Gentlemen!"

The loud call came from Patty Cakes, dressed to the nines in a powder blue wig, a shimmering sequined dress that hugged tight around her perfect frame, and a pair of three-inch stilettos that Russell knew she could barely stand, let alone walk in. "Please make your way to the performance area and prepare to be bedazzled, bewitched and, frankly, bewildered."

Freddie and Russell stood up straight away. They had a seat on a front table.

"Are you staying for the show?" Joe asked Mike.

Mike looked from Joe to Patty, to Russell and back to Joe again.

"Why not?" Mike said.

Joe shuffled another pace forward in the queue, waiting to be served the coffee he desperately needed. He had left a still-blushing Mike having breakfast with Russell and Freddie.

It may have been the booze talking, or it may have been his fresh bravado at being out and about on the scene with his former colleague, but Mike had made it clear that he had his eye on Joe before they even left the pub. Joe had been enjoying his company too, and when they'd all decided to carry on the party back at their flat, they'd invited Mike to join them.

As it had turned out, the young policeman had fallen asleep on the sofa and, aside from putting a blanket over him, Joe had left him to it. His head had been in a whirl about poor Lexi, and he was still regretting the one-night stand with Ben. The last thing he needed right now was a fling with one of Russell's former colleagues.

"What can I get you?" the harassed girl behind the counter asked as Joe reached the front of the queue.

"A double espresso, please."

The girl shouted the order across to her colleague behind the steaming coffee machine, took Joe's money and turned immediately to the next person in the queue. The steam, shouting and clattering of crockery all hurt Joe's head.

Stepping back out onto the pavement with his shot of coffee in a small cardboard cup, Joe looked at the polished entrance of the Langham hotel. A glorified security guard in footman's livery greeted guests as they flowed out of taxis or private cars and sidled into the hotel, or issued a piercing whistle to stop a passing cab in its tracks if a guest wanted one.

This was the place that Lexi had marked on her calendar for last night. Joe wondered if he would be able to find out who she had been meeting. Probably not, looking the way he did right now.

He turned back and appraised himself in the window of the coffee shop, tucking his shirt into his trousers while clasping the rim of the cardboard cup between his teeth. He used one hand to smooth his hair where his cows lick insisted on sticking straight up and sighed. It wasn't going to get much better than that.

He downed his coffee, winced at the bitterness, took a deep breath and strode across the street, not pausing to greet the doorman. He pushed through the revolving door, shuffling at its slow pace until he emerged into the lobby of the hotel.

It was so glamorous in here. Everything chic, stylish, not too traditional. It looked like something out of the movies. Black-and-white tiles on the floor, worn by years of footfall, but still polished to within an inch of their lives. A long, sleek bar, all black glass and mirrors, lined the far wall. Plush red velvet furniture positioned around matching black glass coffee tables created a kind of lounge area in front of the bar. Even at this early hour, there were a couple of guests making use of the facilities.

Joe turned to the reception desk—chest height to the two staff members standing behind it—with more gleaming black glass as its surface. A padded, studded black leather front gave it a softer, more welcoming look than the bar.

A stocky businessman in a mid-range suit was in the process of checking out, shuffling in embarrassment as the receptionist went through the items on his room bill. He'd obviously not realised that he'd be picked up on his viewing habits when he came to pay.

Joe smiled.

When the man had moved off, Joe approached the reception desk.

"Can I help you?" asked a tight-lipped woman in an ill-fitting uniform jacket. Her tone of voice suggested she had no interest in helping Joe. Her badge read "Jeanette".

"Yes, thank you, Jeanette." Joe said, all charm. "I'm looking for a friend of mine." He produced a headshot of Lexi clipped from the programme of the play in the theatre and slid it towards Jeanette. "I wondered if you'd seen her in the last few days."

He saw Jeanette's face sour immediately. She'd seen her alright, and she wasn't happy about being asked. She looked Joe up and down with a curl on her lip and turned to her colleague.

"Martin," she called. "I think you'd better deal with this one."

She forced her lips into a smile that was more of a grimace and stepped back.

"My colleague will deal with you," she said.

As she swapped places with an annoyed looking Martin, a glamorous woman sailed up to the desk, and Jeanette turned on the full, fawning charm for her.

"Yes?" Martin said, casting his eyes across the photograph on the desk before looking up at Joe with a look of bored annoyance.

"Hello... Martin," Joe said, pointedly reading his badge even though he didn't need to. "I'm looking for my friend. Lexi. I believe she was here last night, and I wondered if you'd seen her."

Joe saw no reason to beat around the bush. From the way Jeanette had reacted, it was clear that they knew Lexi's face and they knew what she did in their hotel. Joe just wanted to know who she'd been with. Martin drew himself up to his full height, head cocked to one side.

"She's a friend, you say?" Martin said, suspiciously.

"Well, no. I'll be honest with you. She's not a friend. But I would like to know if you saw her last night."

"Who are you?"

"Does it matter?" Joe asked. "It's a simple question."

"Of course it matters," Martin said. "We're not in the habit of giving out information about our guests to anyone that walks in off the street."

"Listen," Joe said, leaning in. "This is a young actress called Lexi Goode. She was killed two nights ago, and I have reason to believe she was in this hotel, however briefly, on the night she was killed."

Martin's eyes opened wide.

"Killed?" he asked.

"Yes," Joe said, as matter-of-factly as he could manage. "Murdered in fact. I just want to know if she was here on Saturday night. Did you see her?"

"Are you the police?" Martin asked, looking nervous. "You don't look like police."

Joe looked around conspiratorially.

"Well, it wouldn't do to have a bunch of men in uniforms stride in here asking questions and making a scene now, would it?" he said. Technically it wasn't a lie. He hadn't said he was the police. "But, if that's what it would take to get the job done…"

"No, no, no," Martin said, suddenly all smiles. "I know her. She's something of a regular. Nice enough girl, although strictly we don't approve of what she does…"

"Meaning?"

"Well," Martin said conspiratorially. "This is not the kind of establishment that rents rooms by the hour, if you catch my meaning."

"You're saying she's a known prostitute?" Joe asked.

"Well, we wouldn't want people to think we were that sort of establishment," Martin said. "Escort, I would say, would probably be a better word. She's a very glamorous girl. She was. Sorry."

"I see. And was she here on Saturday night?" Joe asked, more insistent now.

"Yes," Martin said. "She came in at about ten-thirty. It was a quiet enough night. I was going off shift at midnight. But I saw her come in, use the bathroom to change and head upstairs."

"Did you see who she was with?"

Martin smiled patronisingly.

"Oh, she never arrives with him," he said. "She just comes in and goes to his room."

"I see," said Joe. "Wait, is it always the same man?"

"Well, yes," Martin said as though Joe was stupid.

"And who is he?" Joe asked.

"I'm afraid I…" Martin began to bluster.

"Don't worry," Joe said, holding up his hands. "I don't want to get you into trouble. I can send someone down to seize the records. Shouldn't cause too much disruption to you."

Martin had started moving on the word seize. He pulled open a drawer and flicked through a long Rolodex inside.

"Aha!" he said triumphantly. "Room 617. Mr Theodore Goldman. Checked in yesterday evening."

TG. The phantom flower sender.

"And I assume he's already checked out?"

Martin checked the record and nodded. "Paid in cash," he said.

The name meant nothing to Joe, but he thanked Martin anyway and left the hotel. Who the hell was Theodore Goldman?

RUSSELL WAS waiting for Joe outside the theatre when he finally got to work, leaning against the wall, head resting on the bricks, soaking in the sunshine.

"What are you doing here?" Joe asked.

"I had a thought," Russell said. "Or rather, Mike did."

Joe cocked his head.

"You left early, by the way. He was worried he'd made you feel uncomfortable."

"Who, Mike? Nah. I woke up early and I wanted to pop into the hotel I'd seen on Lexi's calendar to see if she'd been there on Saturday night."

"And?"

"She had," Joe said, strolling down the small side street that led to the stage door and the keypad that would grant him access. Cameron had called the cast in early to finish the rehearsals they'd aborted yesterday, and Joe was already running late.

"Did they say who she was with?"

"Someone called Theodore Goldman, apparently," Joe said. "Which explains the initials on the flowers. But they couldn't tell me anything more about him."

"Not heard the name," Russell said. "What did they say about Lexi? I assume you were right in thinking the hotel rooms added up to her being on the game?"

"The guy on reception called her a high-class escort," Joe said. "Made a distinction between that and a prostitute. He said they didn't condone it, but they obviously didn't try to stop her either. Apparently, she never arrived with the client, but would come in and head straight up to his room. Everyone on the desk knew what she was up to."

"So, she's doing high-class tricks on the side to earn some proper cash," Russell said. "Could well have been what got her killed."

Joe tapped in the access code on the small, steel keypad and the door buzzed quietly. He pushed it open.

"I wondered that," he said, holding the door ajar. "But if it was the guy she'd seen last night, why not just kill her after she left the hotel?"

"I suppose," Russell said. "Whoever this Goldman chap is, he's unlikely to have followed her all the way home and killed her there."

"So who did?" said Joe.

"Maybe we're back to the jealous lover theory," Russell said. "In fact, that's what I'm here about. There's something else you should know about your director."

"Cameron? What about him?"

"You know how Mike said he'd recognised him yesterday?"

"Yeah?"

"Well, this morning he remembered where he'd seen him before. He's got a good memory that boy."

"Well?" Joe asked, getting increasingly frustrated.

"He arrested Cameron Beattie, back in eighty-three for assault."

Joe stopped.

"Assault?" he asked incredulously. "Cameron? On who?"

"Some young actress brought the charge," Russell replied. "Apparently, Cameron had tried to use his position to get her into bed, and she refused. He didn't like the rejection. Gave her a slap."

"Really?" Joe asked, unable to believe it. "Cameron?"

"Yeah, why? Doesn't seem the type?" Russell asked, raising an eyebrow.

"Well, no," said Joe.

"Well, guess what? There are no types when it comes to hitting women."

"No, I know," Joe said. "But, wow."

"See if you can find out a bit more about it? Unless you want me to talk to him?"

"No," Joe said. "I'll do it. Has Mike told Skinner yet?"

"Not yet," Russell replied. "But he said he would have to as soon as he got to work. It puts Cameron right in the frame, and if Skinner gets a sniff at a suspect, he'll be straight down here with his cuffs. See what you can find out, but make it quick."

"Okay."

"And meanwhile, I'm going to have a chat with Lexi's parents. See if they know anything about this Theodore Goldman chap. Mike was going to see what he could find out too."

"He's very keen," Joe said, raising an eyebrow.

"Not on *me*." Russell smiled. "You should have stuck around for breakfast. He was very disappointed not to see you."

"I've got to go," Joe said, smiling as he let the door swing shut between them.

How was he going to get Cameron to talk to him today? He was already late and, if he was unlucky, they'd be into the rehearsal already and there would be no separating him until it was over.

He didn't know why it felt so unlikely that Cameron had been arrested for assault before. After all, he'd seen the size of the man's ego, and ego usually went hand in hand with temper. There was every chance that Cameron could have lost it if he'd been rejected. He did walk around with an air of invincibility about him. But would he have gone so far as to kill Lexi? In her own flat?

Perhaps if he'd found out what she'd been doing that night, his jealousy could have bubbled over. He had invited her to dinner, after all. She'd refused, saying she was out with her parents, but what if he'd seen her going into that hotel, or worse—leaving it?

Cameron may not like it, but Joe was going to have to question him about his past, and about his relationship with Lexi, before Skinner turned up and arrested him. If there was even the slightest chance that Cameron was innocent—and Joe still hoped he was—Skinner wouldn't be the man to listen to any arguments. But if he *was* guilty, Joe wanted to know why he'd done it.

He headed off along the corridor, past the dressing rooms and towards the backstage area. He could hear voices coming from the main auditorium, but it wasn't until he passed Hattie Duval's dressing room that he heard the actress shouting from within.

Joe froze outside the door, knowing he shouldn't really be listening in, but unable to help himself.

"She was just a child," Hattie shouted. "She was too young for it. What were you thinking?"

Joe sidled closer to the door as silently as he could. Who was she talking to?

"She was no child," Cameron's voice said. "She was a bright young woman. She had a future."

"Ha!" Hattie's laugh was bitter and explosive. "We all have a future, darling. Until we become the past."

"Hattie," Cameron's voice pleaded. "You weren't well. I had no choice."

"And now you come crawling back," Hattie spat, "wanting me to jump back in?"

"She's dead," Cameron shouted.

"And who's fault is that?" Hattie screeched back.

Something smashed. A scream. And Joe was through the door before he could think any further.

He found Hattie and Cameron on opposite sides of the room, both staring at the smashed vase of broken flowers—the flowers that had been left for Lexi on Saturday night. They both looked up at Joe. Cameron's glare was full of rage. Hattie's full of sadness.

"Sorry," Joe said. "I thought I heard…"

"Get this cleaned up," Cameron ordered and pushed past Joe to get out of the room.

"Cameron, wait—" Joe called, following him into the corridor. "I need to speak to you before…"

"I don't have time," Cameron snapped. "I've got a rehearsal to run"

"The police are on their way," Joe blurted.

He had no idea if they actually were, but he needed to get the director's attention.

Cameron stopped and glanced sideways at Joe.

"What do you mean, the police are on their way? Here? What for?"

Joe took his elbow, already leading him away from the dressing room.

"It's better if we go somewhere private," Joe said, nodding over his shoulder to where Hattie was pretending to pick up the broken glass, but actually just earwigging on their conversation.

Cameron followed him into the communal dressing room and, as Joe closed the door, he saw how nervous the director looked.

"What's going on, Joe?" Cameron asked. "Is this about Lexi?"

"Of course it is," Joe said. *What else would it be about?* "Sit down."

Cameron did as he was told, suddenly subdued.

"They're going to arrest me for it, aren't they?" he asked.

"Why do you say that?" Joe asked, sitting beside him on the narrow bench, their backs against a wooden locker.

"You know I'd been seeing her, right?" Cameron asked, head hung low.

"I guessed," Joe said.

The director looked at him, eyes narrowing slightly.

"Well, I wanted to make it more, you know, official," Cameron said. "I watched her on that stage on Saturday, and I knew, I just knew, she was the girl for me."

"Cameron," Joe began.

"Oh, I know what you're thinking," Cameron said bitterly. "She'd only be doing it for her career, right? What would she see in an old fart like me?"

"That's not what I was thinking, at all. You're not even old."

"Older than Lexi," Cameron said, putting his head in his hands.

Joe waited, knowing he just had to give the director time to spit out whatever was troubling him. "I shouldn't have gone to see her, but I needed to know if she felt the same."

"You followed her home?" Joe asked.

Cameron lifted his head, confused.

"No," he said. "I'd gone out with some friends, had a few glasses of wine with dinner. After I couldn't stop going on about it, they convinced me to go to her house and declare my love. It was a stupid idea."

"Why was it a stupid idea?"

"Because when I got there, she wouldn't let me in anyway."

"You're sure she was there?"

"Of course. The light was on. I rang the buzzer, and she answered, but when she heard it was me, she wouldn't say any more. She wouldn't even let me in to talk to her. She left the buzzer open though, so—" he shook his head, full of regrets, "so I told her how I felt over the bloody speaker. Imagine that, declaring your undying love for someone through an intercom."

Joe felt a sinking feeling in his stomach.

"What time did you go over?" he asked.

Cameron looked back at him, frowning as though this was the least important detail to be asking.

"God, I don't know, late," he said. "Well after midnight, probably closer to two in the morning, I guess. I just keep thinking, what if she was there with someone, a boyfriend that I didn't know about? What if he heard what I said and got so angry he killed her? It's all my fault isn't it?"

Joe patted Cameron's shoulder. Parts of this strange puzzle were starting to come together, but there were still more questions than answers. So it was Cameron that the neighbour had been complaining about, ringing the buzzer and shouting through the speaker in the early hours. But that still didn't explain who had been in the flat with Lexi, and why Lexi didn't try to warn Cameron that she was in some kind of danger when he turned up.

Either way, given Cameron's history, and the fact that enough of the cast and crew would be able to testify that he and Lexi had been having an affair, it would be enough for old Skinner to put two and two together and make five.

"The police know about your... previous charge," Joe said, feeling that it was only fair to warn the director what was coming.

The colour drained from his face.

"What?" he asked, whispering.

"The actress. The assault charge. The young officer at the door recognised you from your previous arrest."

"But those charges were dropped," Cameron said. "It was all a lie. I didn't attack her at all, she got a friend to hit her to try to set me up. The woman was obsessed. I'd rejected her for a role, and then she'd tried to come on to me—offering to sleep with me if I gave her the part. I knocked that back as well, so she decided to ruin my reputation. But she dropped the charges when her story started unravelling."

His eyes implored Joe to believe him. Joe felt inclined to. It had struck him as odd from the moment he'd heard it. Cameron could get frustrated with actors not hitting their lines, but Joe had never seen a hint of aggression in him.

"Well, you'll be fine then," Joe said. "Even if the police do try to suggest some kind of pattern, you have the evidence to deny it."

"Not really," Cameron said. "Not long after she dropped the charges, she was found dead in an alleyway. She'd been beaten to death."

"What?" Joe spluttered.

"Yes, the police took me in for questioning, but I had an alibi—my show was opening that night. But I could tell they still thought I had done it. I didn't, obviously. But they had the idea in their heads, and even when some other guy confessed, the detective in charge still said he knew it was me. Like it was some kind of personal vendetta."

Joe had a horrible feeling he knew exactly who that detective was, and if it was Skinner, Cameron was in more trouble than he thought. He could hear raised voices in the corridor outside, loud, sharp knocks on doors.

"They're here," Joe said.

Cameron stood up, as though ready to make a run for it.

"I didn't do this, Joe," he said desperately.

"Okay," Joe said. "Don't worry, I'll—" but before he could promise anything, the door to the communal changing room flew open and Skinner marched in, flanked by two officers in uniform. One of them was Mike. He couldn't meet Joe's eye, and his face flushed bright red.

"Cameron Beattie," Skinner asked, already knowing the answer. "I'm arresting you on suspicion of the murder of Alexandra Goode."

Cameron tried to protest his innocence, but Skinner spoke over him, reading him his rights as the other officer cuffed Cameron's hands roughly behind his back and marched him out of the door.

Skinner turned to Joe, a nasty sneer on his face.

"And if I catch you sticking your nose in any of this, I'll have you arrested for obstructing the course of justice. Do you understand?"

Joe didn't even answer. He just stared back at Skinner, eyebrow raised defiantly until the corrupt cop turned and walked out. Mike watched him go and then hurried over to Joe.

"He didn't do it, you know?" Joe said.

"You sure of that?" Mike asked, checking that Skinner wasn't looking back.

"Pretty sure," Joe replied.

"Skinner's properly got it in for him," Mike said. "Says he's killed a girl before."

"That wasn't him either," Joe replied.

"PC Duggan," Skinner yelled. "Get moving."

"I've got to go," Mike said. "I'll try to make sure he gets a fair go at it, but I can't promise. You know what Skinner's like. If he didn't do it, you two had better figure out who did, and quick, because Skinner's not going to stop until this guy's behind bars." And with that, he scuttled off.

Joe followed them out into the corridor, and Cameron looked back beseechingly one last time before they herded him out of the stage door.

Joe turned to find Hattie standing in the doorway of her own dressing room. She looked at him and pursed her lips.

"Terrible business," she said, and shut the door.

RUSSELL STOOD on the doorstep of the ground-floor Brixton flat where Lexi Goode's parents lived, listening to the fading chime of the doorbell. He'd always hated having to question grieving families when he was in the force, but he had grown adept at easing his way into the conversation slowly, with empathy and compassion.

This time, of course, he wasn't here as an officer of the law, but to offer condolences and possibly help. He had brought a small bunch of flowers that Anton had put together for him, with the trademark Betty's ribbon tied around their stems. Not much of a gesture, really, but enough, hopefully, to encourage Lexi's parents to talk to him.

He could hear shuffling from inside, a shadow moved behind the glass, a throat cleared and Lexi Goode's father opened the door, just a crack—the security chain holding it in place.

"Mr Goode?" Russell said, trying to keep his voice gentle. He had such a habit of sounding like a policeman, even now. "My name is Russell Dixon. I was a friend of Lexi's. I wanted to pay my condolences."

He held out the flowers, as though to prove the point. The door closed, but only for long enough for the chain to be removed. When Mr Goode opened the door fully, Russell could see the fresh tears in his eyes, the shake of his lip.

"That's very kind of you," Mr Goode said. "My wife will be very moved."

His voice broke as he came to the end of the sentence. He reached out for the flowers, and Russell wondered for a moment whether he should just leave them to their grief. But he reminded himself that he was here to make sure they got justice for their daughter. If Mike was right, and Skinner was going over to arrest Cameron, then that would draw a line under any further investigation, whether the director was guilty or not.

"I wondered if I might come in," Russell said kindly. "I wanted to talk to you, to ask you a couple of questions about Lexi."

Mr Goode's eyes narrowed suspiciously.

"Who are you?" he asked. "Are you with the papers, because I told those bastards I do not want any stories about my beautiful girl."

He was at breaking point. Russell could tell. Time to come clean.

"No," Russell said. "I'm not a journalist. I used to be a police detective. My friend worked with Lexi."

"Police, huh?" Mr Goode said, his suspicious glare deepening. Russell saw his way in. It wasn't only the gay community that got a rough ride from the police. Russell had been in the force long enough to have seen the deep seam of racism that ran through the boys in blue.

"I used to be," Russell said. "I quit. I couldn't stand the corruption."

He saw Mr Goode's demeanour change immediately.

"The thing is," Russell continued, "I know the man in charge of the investigation into Lexi's murder, and I don't think he'll do his job properly."

"Oh yes?" Mr Goode said.

He was softening, but he wasn't there yet.

"Since I left the force, I've been working as a private investigator," Russell said.

"We haven't got any money," Mr Goode replied quickly, as though suddenly seeing what this was all about.

"And I don't want any," Russell said, just as quickly. "I just want to make sure that justice is done. I think they are about to arrest the wrong man for this, and if they do, you may never find out who killed your daughter."

They both stood in silence on the doorstep, the small bunch of flowers between them. After a moment, Mr Goode nodded.

"You'd better come in then," he said.

JOE STOOD outside the building on Lexington Street again, looking up at the window of Lexi's top-floor flat. There had been no point everyone hanging around the theatre after Cameron had been arrested, so Joe had left Hattie describing the shame of it to the rest of the cast in lurid detail, and made his exit. There would be no performance tonight.

He needed to get a few things straight in his head and, for some reason, he'd decided that the best way to do that was to come back to the scene and get a better feel for what had happened.

This time, he selected the buzzer for the other top-floor apartment. A Constance Bouchard. The angry neighbour. He didn't have to wait long before her heavily accented voice replied over the intercom.

"Hello?" she said, swallowing her aitch.

"Miss Bouchard. My name is Joe Stone. I spoke to you briefly yesterday morning. Outside the building here. I wonder if I can have a quick word with you again. About your neighbour?"

"I have already given my statement," she said, sounding annoyed that Lexi was still managing to disrupt her so much, even after death.

"Oh, I'm not police," Joe said. "I'm just a friend. I just wanted to ask you a couple of questions."

Silence.

"Her parents are very distressed," Joe said. "They have a lot of questions about her life. I said I would ask. But if you're too busy…"

He heard her sigh, and then the intercom buzzed and he pushed the door open.

She was waiting for him in her doorway as the lift doors opened, and they both glanced briefly at the police tape covering Lexi's still open door.

"Thanks for seeing me, Miss Bouchard," Joe said, extending his hand. She didn't take it, staying half-hidden behind her front door and peering out at him around the edge.

"Constance," she said, dismissing the formality. "What do you want to know?"

She looked at him suspiciously, obviously not planning on letting him into her apartment.

"When I saw you the other day, you said you'd heard voices," Joe said. "On Saturday night. You told me that you had been disturbed by voices from Lexi's apartment."

The woman cast her eyes down.

"Yes," she said. "But I didn't know then what was happening."

"Of course not," Joe said, sensing her reaction was more defensive than guilty.

"She is always making too much noise, that girl. She comes home late. She leaves early. Plays her music too loud. Always slamming on her door."

Joe smiled at the slight error in her speech. It reminded him of his ex-boyfriend Luc. That lovely French accent had been part of the attraction in the first place and his small errors of translation had only ever been endearing. He missed Luc.

"But for the last week it's been terrible," Constance continued. "People ringing on the button all the time. And when she doesn't answer, they ring on mine. She has too many boyfriends, always men shouting in the street. I told her. It will end in trouble. And it did, you see?"

"Did you see anyone," Joe asked. "On Saturday night. Did you see who she was with?"

Joe could imagine the neighbour pressing her eye to the spy hole in the door, watching the comings and goings from Lexi's apartment. Had she seen the killer?

"No," she replied. "I already told the police. I heard shouting. Screaming. But I couldn't see. The door was closed. Then the music started. And I thumped on the wall, and she made it softer. But I could still hear it. I couldn't sleep——"

She trailed off. Perhaps realising that her own woes were far fewer than Lexi's.

"It went on all night," she said. "And the button kept buzzing. There was a man in the street, I saw him. Shouting through the speaker."

Cameron, Joe thought.

"Do you remember what time it started?" He asked, trying to get a timeline of the evening straight in his head. If, as he suspected, Cameron had arrived at the apartment while Lexi's killer was still with her, had his confession of love really been the catalyst for her murder. Constance had heard shouting and screaming, so it made sense that there had been some kind of argument that had ended in Lexi's murder.

"I heard her come home at about twelve-thirty," she said. "Too late. Banging her door. She was dressed like a whore. I told her. She's too pretty to dress like that. Men will get the wrong idea. But she doesn't listen."

Joe remembered the red wig on the counter, the high heels kicked off. The sensible clothes tucked into her holdall by the front door, and the sight of Lexi in her underwear, lying dead on the floor. He shuddered.

"But she was on her own, when she got home?" Joe asked, frowning.

"Yes," Constance replied. "But not long after—maybe ten minutes—I heard the lift come up. It rattles in my kitchen."

"And you didn't see who arrived?"

"I don't spend the night spying on my neighbour," she snapped.

"I'm sure you don't," Joe placated her. "So, when did the shouting start?"

"Straight away," she sighed. "I always tell her, no noise after midnight. I have to work. I need to sleep."

"Did you hear what they were shouting about?"

"Not so much. It wasn't long. There was swearing. And she was shouting that she knew and she would tell everyone. And then there was screaming, but that has happened before. She's got a bad temper. And a high voice." She stopped herself again. "But I didn't know what was happening."

This time, Joe *did* sense a hint of guilt. Despite the frustration Constance had clearly had with Lexi's night-time routines, nobody wants to think that they just sat by while their neighbour was being murdered. Something else had occurred to Joe, though.

"And you're sure this was just after twelve-thirty?" he asked.

"Yes, I'm sure," Constance said, the defiance back. He had no reason to doubt her.

"And then the radio started, and you banged on the wall?"

"Yes, I told you."

"What time did the man come to the buzzer?" Joe asked. "The man you saw in the street."

"Much later. I was already asleep. He woke me up again. It was after two in the morning. I could hear him talking through the button—the buzzer, you call it—but he didn't come up."

"And did you hear anything else?"

"Yes, about half an hour later, the lift went down again."

"Thank you," said Joe, already turning to get back in the lift himself. "You've been very helpful."

She watched him as he waited for the lift to arrive, making sure he left. He suddenly turned back.

"Just one more thing," he said. "The man you saw in the street on Saturday. Was he the same man who had come calling previously? The one you saw shouting?"

"Oh no," she said. "That was an older man. A businessman. This one was younger. Wore a coat with the buttons like Paddington the Bear. And a soft hat."

The second description was definitely Cameron.

"And the businessman?" Joe asked. "Can you describe him?"

"Yes, he came a few times. She got cross with him. Told him not to come to her home. Tall. Very tall. And thin. Like a stick. Grey hair. Baldy." She indicated where his hair had been thinning on top, and where the grey had remained on the sides.

"Thank you," Joe said again, as the lift doors opened with a ping.

RUSSELL accepted the cup of tea graciously. He had refused the offer, but Lexi's mother had insisted. Tea was, after all, the great salve for all broken things. He noticed the little nod of encouragement and strength that Mr Goode gave his wife as she sat down again. They would get through this together.

"I'm so sorry for your loss," Russell said. "And I'm sorry to disturb you at a time like this. I can assure you, I only want to help."

"This man used to be with the police," Mr Goode informed his wife. "And he don't trust them to do right by our girl."

His Caribbean accent added a surprisingly melancholy tone to his voice. Mrs Goode looked up. Her eyes were red-rimmed from crying, and her pale skin was blotchy, but Russell could see immediately where Lexi got her fine features from. Her mother could have been a model, in her time. Perhaps she had been.

"What do you mean, you don't trust them?" she asked.

Her accent was hard South London. No nonsense. She, too, would have a deep distrust of the police.

"Why not?"

"What have they said to you, so far?" Russell asked. "About Lexi's death."

"Not much," Mrs Goode said. "The older fella—weaselly little face on him—he stopped by this morning to ask about her friendship with that director fella. Said they had reason to believe he was the one who'd hurt her. But I told him it couldn't have been him, could it love? He was only ever good to her. He was going to put her as the lead in his next play. Full lead, that is, not this understudy business. He wouldn't hurt her."

"You could see just by the way he looked at her that the poor guy was in love," Mr Goode added. "We told that detective it wouldn't be him that hurt her."

"I take it he didn't believe you?" Russell asked.

"Who knows what he think," Mr Goode said, his accent cutting off the end of the word. "He just came to tell us what he knew."

Russell noticed Mrs Goode hitch back a sob.

"You mustn't believe everything he says," Russell said, fearing that Skinner had already told Lexi's parents about her other income stream.

"Oh, don't worry, love," Mrs Goode said. "We knew what she was up to." She dabbed her eyes with a crumpled tissue and half-smiled. "She thought we didn't, but you don't get the champagne lifestyle on an actresses wage, do you? We didn't come in on the last boat. We know she'd been turning tricks."

Mr Goode stood up, pacing. He may have known what his daughter had been up to, but he wasn't happy about it.

"I told her it would end in tears," Mrs Goode continued. "But she promised me it was just a couple of fellas, and it wasn't even sex, she said. They liked a bit of the other, you know? Role play? Spanking."

"Alright, Patricia," Mr Goode said, sitting down again. "He gets the picture. She promised us there was no sex. She got paid well for her company. Very well. She said it was just like another acting job."

"Do you know anything about her clients?" Russell asked, choosing his words carefully.

"There were only two or three, she said. Older businessmen. She said they were harmless. And rich." Mrs Goode's tone was matter-of-fact. She believed her daughter.

Mr Goode humphed.

"We didn't need the money," he said. "We were alright. We got by."

"No, but you didn't turn it down, did you, love? When she paid off our bills. Neither of us turned it down."

Mr Goode shook his head sadly. Russell hated that they felt guilty for this too, on top of their grief.

"Did she ever have any trouble with any of them?" he asked.

"Only one," Mrs Goode said. "He showed up at her work, apparently. She said it was proper awkward."

"Did he make a scene?"

"No. No, it wasn't that. I think he was there with his missus. He tried to come and see her afterwards, to explain himself. Said he was proper upset."

"I suppose he was scared of being caught out," Russell mused.

"Apparently he turned up at her house later in the week, shouting about how much he loved her and how he wanted to leave his wife for her. She put him right, though. Said she couldn't see him any more."

"And that was an end to it?"

"She didn't mention it again."

The tears welled once more, and she apologised as her voice cracked. She dabbed at her eyes, sniffing. Her husband reached over and took her hand.

"Did she mention a name for this man, at all?" Russell asked. It was a long shot, but if she'd been that open with her parents, perhaps she'd had the precaution of making sure they knew his name, just in case things turned nasty.

"Yes," Mrs Goode said. "Langley, wasn't it, Denzil?"

"Langham," he replied.

JOE WAS already at the bar when Russell arrived, talking to Scott about the performance the night before. Apparently they had made a record amount, and Scott was nervous about walking it over to the Chapman Centre on his own.

"I'm sure Russell would be happy to escort you," Joe said as Russell joined them.

"What's this?" Russell asked.

"Scott needs a big, strong man to hold his hand while he crosses the road."

"Piss off," Scott said, slapping his shoulder. "You'll be sorry if I get mugged."

"You're right," Joe said. "I would."

Scott handed them both a pint, and they headed over to their regular table.

"So, what did Cameron say? Do you still think he's innocent?"

"Yes," Joe said. "I'm sure of it. Apparently all that stuff with the other actress was just a set up. He turned her down for a part, then turned down her kind offer to sleep with him to get it, and she went mental. The charges were dropped, but she turned up dead not long after."

"Oh," Russell said, wincing.

"Apparently, the detective in charge was certain Cameron had killed her, even though he had a solid alibi. Still tried to pin it on him."

"Skinner, by any chance?"

"Bingo," Joe said. "You should have seen the smug look on his face when he turned up to arrest Cameron."

"So they took him in?"

"Yes. But it wasn't him. I'm sure of it. He did admit that he'd been round to her apartment on Saturday. Or rather, in the early hours of Sunday morning. He was drunk and had plucked up the courage to go over and tell her he was in love with her."

"And how did that turn out?"

"Apparently, she didn't let him in," Joe replied. "But it doesn't make any sense, because when I spoke to the neighbour, she said that she'd heard screaming and shouting from the flat just after Lexi got home, around twelve-thirty."

"So someone else was already up there with her?"

"Hmm," said Joe. The hint of a thought forming in his head.

"What is it?"

"Well, Cameron thought that Lexi had answered the intercom when he buzzed, and then when she heard it was him, didn't say any more, but wouldn't let him up."

"Yes?" Russell wasn't following.

"Well, what if it wasn't Lexi who answered the intercom? What if she was already dead, and the killer was in the flat when he called by."

"Why would the killer answer the intercom though?"

"To stop him drawing attention to the flat," Joe said. "Cameron said she left the buzzer open, which meant he could talk through it, but he couldn't buzz any more."

Russell raised an eyebrow, intrigued with the line of thinking.

"Alright Doc?"

The voice was Mike's. Neither of them had even noticed him coming in.

"Sorry, force of habit."

"Hi Mike," Russell said, and nudged Joe's knee under the table. Joe smiled.

"I just wanted to let you know that Skinner has just officially charged Cameron Beattie with Lexi's murder."

"He didn't waste any time," said Joe.

"He sent me to find you," Mike said. "He needs a statement from you. He's already interviewed most of the cast."

"Really," Russell said. "He's not usually that efficient."

"He's really got it in for this guy," Mike said.

"Hmm," Russell replied. "I know how that feels."

"I hope the cast backed him up," Joe said. "I'm pretty sure he didn't do this."

"Most of them said there was no way he would have done anything to hurt her," Mike said. "Seems like everyone thinks he's a pretty nice guy. Well, everyone apart from Hattie. She said it was pathetic that a man his age had been trying to pursue a woman Lexi's age."

"Why?" Russell asked. "How old is Cameron?"

"He's in his thirties," Joe replied. "He's hardly old."

"Well," said Mike, "Mrs Goldman didn't have too many good words to say about him, either way."

"Mrs Goldman?" Joe asked.

Mike frowned. Reached into his pocket and drew out a notebook, checking his facts.

"Yep, Hattie Goldman," he confirmed. "Acts under her stage name. Duval."

"Oh God," Joe said.

"What?" asked Mike.

"Theodore Goldman," said Joe. "TG. He's Hattie's husband."

"You think Hattie's husband killed Lexi?" Russell asked, trying to catch up.

"No," Joe said, "I don't."

And he left the pub with half of his pint still sitting on the table, and Russell and Mike debating whether to follow him.

BACKSTAGE at the theatre was dead quiet and, for a moment, Joe wondered whether he'd got it wrong. He'd been sure that he would find

Hattie here anyway, regardless of the fact that there would be no show tonight. Where else would she go?

As he'd hurried over from the Red Lion, it had all started falling into place and he was annoyed he hadn't seen it before—it felt so obvious now.

He checked the dressing rooms, but they were all empty—no sign of the rest of the cast having been there. He walked into Hattie's dressing room and found it empty too, with fragments of glass still on the floor where the flower jug had broken earlier.

Of course, now, her strange reaction to reading the note on the flowers made perfect sense. Had she suspected that her husband was seeing a prostitute? Had she known that the woman he'd been seeing was Lexi? Or had she found out for definite on Saturday?

Closing the door on the dressing room, Joe headed through to the stage. He could hear a voice, low and quiet, echoing in the empty auditorium. He'd been right, after all.

He found Hattie standing centre stage, just a single light illuminating her position, which she must have switched on herself, since there was no one else there. She was quietly running through a speech from the play—the scene after she discovers that Lord Earnshaw had been sleeping with the maid. Right after she kills the maid, and the Lord, and just before she kills herself.

Joe stood silently in the wings, watching her. There was none of her usual over-the-top performance here. None of the wavering voice or dramatic gestures. Just a woman, alone on the stage, unravelling the lies that had made up her life, in a low monotone to an empty auditorium.

She slipped straight into the final scene, not pausing for change, delivering the whole scene as a single monologue. Her voice began to crack and waver, moving into the final speech of the play.

Joe figured he'd let her finish her strange, lonely performance before interrupting her flow. It was only when she raised the blade above her chest that he suddenly realised that all may not be well.

Hattie delivered the line about the final curtain call, her hand trembling even more than her voice. She held the blade over her chest, not able, yet, to bring herself to finish the scene.

"Hattie?" Joe said quietly, stepping onto the stage, still in relative darkness. "Don't do it."

Hattie spun to face him, the knife still firmly in her grasp and the light blinding her to who she was looking at.

"Who's there?" she asked, startled.

"It's me, Joe." He stepped into the light, both hands half-raised in front of him, making sure he didn't look like he was presenting a threat.

"What do you want? What are you doing here?"

"Just put the knife down, Hattie. We need to talk."

"I don't *need* to do anything," she spat, knife still firmly clasped in her hands, blade pointing towards her chest.

Joe eased forward another step.

"Hattie," he said, a little more insistently now. "I know what happened. I know what you did."

She looked for a moment like she was going to drop the knife and collapse, but instead she dropped her hands to her sides, knife still held firmly in the right.

"You don't know anything," she said, and, for the first time, Joe saw real spite in her face. Gone was the bumbling matriarch he'd grown to know and tried to avoid. In her place was a woman scorned, with venom in her blood and a blade in her hands.

"I know you knew what she did to earn money. I know you found out that your husband had been seeing her. I know he had threatened to leave you for her." Joe said. *How's that for an opener?*

She looked at him in disbelief, mouthing hanging open slightly, lips trembling, eyes fierce.

"That bitch thought she could take everything that was mine," she said. "My husband, my life, my role."

"Cameron had offered her the lead in his new play," Joe said, still piecing bits together.

"She was too young for it," Hattie spat. "She was just a child."

So that's what they had been arguing about in the dressing room.

"She was too young for all of it. I saw the way he looked at her. He only offered her the part so that she would sleep with him. They're all the same."

Joe saw it clearly now, how the older actress had seen Lexi playing her part to rapturous applause, and then learned that she'd been offered the lead in Cameron's new play—a role that Hattie clearly felt should have been hers. Not to mention Lexi's relationship with her husband. And with

Cameron. She must have felt as though she was being replaced in all aspects.

"When did you find out about Theodore?" Joe asked and saw her fist tighten around the knife handle.

"I knew he'd been up to something," she said, bitterly. "A woman can tell. But it was only when I saw those flowers that I knew what he'd been doing. Or who."

"How did you know they weren't meant for you?" Joe asked. The note hadn't been addressed to Lexi, after all.

"Because he wrote it himself," Hattie said and, when she saw Joe's frown, she continued. "We have a tradition. He always sends a bunch of flowers from 'an Admirer', and he never writes the card himself. From the first bunch he sent, when he was too shy to tell me how he felt."

Tears glistened in her eyes, and she wiped them away angrily with the back of her hand, the knife blade glinting ominously.

"I followed her. To the hotel. When she left, I confronted him. He confessed everything. Said it was all over."

"Hattie," Joe said, stepping forward slowly. "Why don't you give me the knife?"

She laughed—a tight, bitter snort of a laugh.

"No," she said, firmly. "No, it's no good. I can't live with people knowing."

"Hattie, please," Joe said, fearing that she meant it. "We can work this out. You don't have to do this. It was a crime of passion. You were driven to it. They may go easy on you, if you just explain—"

"Oh, it's far too late for all that, young man," she said.

Joe saw her cast a glance into the shadows behind her again, and when he followed her eyeline, he saw a pair of feet. Good shoes. Toes pointing skywards. It took a moment longer to register that they belonged to Theodore Goldman, Hattie's husband. And a moment more to determine that he was dead.

"You killed him too?" Joe blurted.

"Of course," Hattie replied. "He had it coming. They both did."

"Put the knife down, Hattie."

Joe moved closer to her still, knowing that he had to disarm her before she either took her own life or did a runner. He couldn't tell which it would be.

77

"Don't come any closer," she shouted, pointing the blade at Joe.

"Just calm down, Hattie," he said, voice low and even. "It's over."

He took another step forward, hand out—palm up, asking for the knife. He was close enough to see the tremble in her hand, the blood on her fingers where she'd stabbed her husband. When he looked into her eyes, Joe was surprised how hard her gaze was. A woman scorned.

"It's over," Joe said again.

"No," Hattie roared and lunged at him. Joe danced to the side, but not quickly enough. He felt the blade pierce his side, just below his ribs.

Hattie turned to look at Joe, who was examining the blood on his hands, looking in disbelief at the handle of the knife sticking out of his side.

"I'm sorry," Hattie said and disappeared into the darkness in the wings.

Joe felt his head spinning. Shock and panic rocked him, and he dropped to his knees, feeling as though he may pass out.

Voices, shouting in the darkness, but the ringing in his ears meant he couldn't hear what they were saying.

Hands reached under his arms and lifted him up, squeezing a grunt of pain from his lungs. A voice in his ear, firm and solid. "You're going to be alright." And then he was being carried, like a baby, and he let himself go.

4.

Joe woke to find Russell sitting anxiously beside his bed. Not *his* bed, he realised, but a hospital bed. Beeps and whirrs echoed around the space. Voices, hurrying feet, bustling activity behind the pale-green curtains that shielded him from the rest of the ward.

Russell squeezed his hand.

"Hello," he said quietly.

"What happened?" Joe asked, his voice dry and raspy.

"Well, you managed to get yourself stabbed," Russell said. "And scared the bejeezus out of me."

Russell stood up and poured some water from a jug into a plastic cup and handed it to Joe, who drank gratefully.

"Did you get her?" Joe asked, remembering the pain he'd felt as Hattie Duval had stabbed him.

"I did," said Russell. "And our not-so-friendly detective was very unhappy about it, I can tell you."

"She killed her husband too," Joe said.

"I know," Russell said. "We found him. She's going to be spending a fair while at Her Majesty's pleasure."

"What a mess," Joe said, finishing the water.

The curtain opened and Mike Duggan stuck his head round.

"Is he awake?" he asked, and then grinned broadly when he saw that Joe was, indeed, awake.

"Here he is," Russell said. "The hero of the hour."

Mike came in and closed the curtain behind him, a blush spreading up his cheeks.

"Give over," he said.

"It was Mike who scooped you up and carried you out," Russell said.

"Yeah, while you chased down a killer," Mike countered. "I think we all know who the hero is. How are you feeling?"

"Fine, I guess," Joe said. "Thanks."

"Doctor says you'll be fine," Russell said. "She didn't hit anything major, and they've patched you up and topped up all that blood you left on poor Mike's uniform."

"Sorry," Joe said.

Mike smiled, shuffling a little awkwardly from foot to foot.

"Right," Russell said, sensing something. "I'm going to pop to the loo and get us all a cup of something."

Joe noticed the wink Russell gave Mike as he left. Mike sat in the chair Russell had just vacated, looking into Joe's eyes. His own blue eyes sparkled under his dark brows.

"I'm glad you're okay," he said.

"Me too," said Joe. "Although I'll be happier when I get out of here. I hate hospitals."

"Me too," Mike agreed.

Joe was surprised when Mike reached out and took his hand.

"Listen," he said. "I'm no good at this kind of thing, so I'm just going to come out and say it. When you're out, and feeling better, would you come for a drink with me? Just the two of us."

"What, like a date?" Joe asked, still a little taken aback.

"Yes," Mike said. "Like a date."

Joe looked at Mike's half smile, the ways his eyes searched Joe's face nervously for some kind of hint. Joe smiled back.

"I'd love that," he said.

Mike broke into a huge grin, leaned forward and kissed him, quickly, on the lips.

"Good," he said. "That's settled then."

5.

The Red Lion was relatively quiet, which Joe was grateful for. He'd been out of hospital for a couple of days, but this was his first outing in the big wide world and he was feeling a little overwhelmed. Lucky to be alive, they'd told him.

Hattie's blade had fortunately missed any vital organs, but the surgeon had told him that if she'd been an inch higher, it would have been a very different story. The news had given him pause for thought.

Scott was behind the bar, polishing glasses and humming tunelessly to Bananarama, while Ron handed Russell and Freddie their drinks.

Russell set Joe's down in front of him and they both sat opposite, glasses raised for a toast.

"To a speedy recovery, and a long life," Russell said.

"Hear! Hear!" Freddie cheered.

Joe clunked his pint glass against theirs and smiled. "Thanks, guys."

"So when's your hot date then?" Russell asked.

"Tonight," Joe said, still smiling. "After Mike finishes his shift. Although it feels like we've got a bit beyond first date already."

Mike had been to see him every day, and by the time Joe left the hospital after his short stay, they had already got through most of the awkward small talk and embarrassing confessions.

They all looked up as the pub doors opened. Cameron walked in, peering into the gloom and, as his eyes adjusted, he spotted Joe, waved, and headed over.

"How are you feeling?" Cameron asked.

"Much better," Joe said.

"I can't thank you enough," Cameron said. "I thought I was getting done for that, regardless."

"I knew you didn't have it in you." Joe smiled. "Mind you, I didn't think Hattie did either and look where that almost got me."

"I'm gobsmacked. I still can't quite believe it. I mean, I knew she'd been struggling with her confidence. I knew she resented Lexi's youth and talent. But to kill her like that?"

"I think it was finding out that her husband had been meeting Lexi for a different kind of role play that sent her over the edge. She must have felt Lexi had replaced her in all aspects. It was too much to take."

"Well, thank you, Joe—and you both," he said hurriedly to Russell and Freddie, who both nodded. "I'm in your debt."

"It's a pleasure," Joe said.

"Okay, so I'll see you back at work," Cameron said. "When you feel up to it. No rush."

Joe smiled. "Thanks, Cameron. I'll keep you posted."

He wasn't sure that he would go back to being the director's assistant, but he wasn't going to make any decisions like that right now.

As Cameron left, Mike arrived, squeezing onto the bench beside Joe and planting a peck on his cheek.

"You're early," Russell said. "Everything okay?"

"Uh-huh," Mike said, smiling lopsidedly. "I just finished filing my report with the PCA, so the boss sent me home early. They're going to need a bit of time to wade through the list of complaints against old Skinner."

Now it was Russell's turn to smile. The PCA was another independent authority that reviewed police misconduct and, with Russell's help and encouragement, Mike had just given them a long list to look into for Detective Simon Skinner. And they carried a little more weight coming from a serving officer of the law.

"We'll get him, boys," Russell said, holding his glass up in a toast. "We'll get him."

KILLER QUEEN

SMALLTOWN BOY

SOHO NOIR #6

SMALLTOWN BOY

1.

SOHO, LONDON. 1988

RUSSELL DIXON CAME OUT of Liberty—the department store off Regent Street—laden down with bags and boxes. Why he always left his Christmas shopping until the last minute he didn't know. Every year he promised himself he'd be more organised, and every year he'd find himself wading through denuded shelves, looking for some kind of inspiration on a budget whilst trying not to be driven mad by the incessant loop of repetitive Christmas songs. This year's nauseating earworm was Cliff Richard bleating on about Mistletoe and Wine.

The shock of the cold air hit Russell like a wall, and he shrugged his shoulders to try to get his jacket collar a little closer to his neck.

"Here, let me help." It was Freddie, his boyfriend, who had refused point blank to go into another shop with Russell until they'd had a pint and a sit down. Freddie put his own scarf around Russell's neck and gave him a quick kiss.

"Fucking poofs," said a belligerent young skinhead on his way past.

"Happy Christmas to you, too," Freddie shouted back at him.

Both Russell and Freddie had already spent far too many years in the closet to hide what they had now. Besides, they'd got used to the odd hateful comment called at them in the street. It didn't happen too often in Soho, where the strange mix of oddballs, queers, criminals and celebrities gave the place the feel of a small village. But they had to remember that—though they were just a short walk away from the middle of Soho—Regent Street was miles away from its heart.

As the young man walked off with his middle finger held aloft, a mother guided her young son around them with a loud tut, and Russell raised his eyebrows and sighed.

"You had enough yet?"

Freddie asked.

"God yes," Russell replied. "I think I've got everyone covered."

"You're mad, you know that?" Freddie laughed. "But I love you."

"They're only little things," Russell said. "But most of the guys are on their own in there. It's important."

For the third Christmas in a row, Russell had bought a small gift for each of the patients in the Campbell Centre, an HIV and AIDS hospice that was close to all of their hearts.

Usually Russell and Joe would go in on Christmas morning and deliver their gifts by hand, specifically chosen with the recipients in mind, but this year they all had other plans.

"Besides, I feel bad that I'm going to have to drop them in early. Are you sure we're all invited to this shindig?"

"I'm more than sure," Freddie reassured him for the umpteenth time. "Nathan's already threatened to sack me as his lawyer if I didn't come bearing gays."

"And you're sure he meant to bring everyone?"

"Yes, I've given him the numbers," Freddie insisted. "It's a banquet, not a sit-down dinner!"

They had been invited by one of Freddie's celebrity clients to spend Christmas Eve at his Soho mansion, and Russell was resisting going. As far as he was concerned, Nathan Bentley was a flamboyant queen: bitchy, self-opinionated, arrogant and nowhere near the catch he used to be.

A well-known television presenter with a formidable reputation, his parties were legendary—with drink flowing, wall-to-wall celebrities, drugs, dancing, ill-tempered Cordon-Bleu chefs providing the catering and world famous musicians providing the entertainment.

Russell and Freddie had been to one for Nathan's fortieth birthday in the summer and it had taken them both about a week to recover, and they hadn't even touched any of the really hard stuff.

"Come on, it'll be a laugh," Freddie said. "The more the merrier, and all that. Besides, it's better than us sitting in the Red Lion drowning our sorrows and bemoaning the lack of a family Christmas that none of us have ever enjoyed anyway."

"I don't know," Russell said. "Now that you've invited everyone, it'll probably end up feeling just the same, but with better food."

"Anyway, I thought you were glad Joe was coming?"

"I am, but why did you invite the rest of them?"

"Because, my darling," Freddie said, guiding them around the corner into Carnaby Street. "Nathan likes to pretend that he has a wide circle of gorgeous, interesting friends of all ages. You know what he's like when he's showing off a new beau."

"God help us," Russell said. "Don't tell me, Gayzilla's back."

"Stop it. Look, it'll be fun," Freddie said. "Besides, it's only round the corner, so if it's really hideous, we can just leave."

Russell knew that the likelihood of them being able to get away once the doors to the townhouse were closed was slim to none. He sighed. *The things we do for love.*

"Anyway," Freddie said. "Nathan wants us to meet this new squeeze and there's no way I'm going alone."

The revolving door of Nathan Bentley's love life was busier than the turnstile at Piccadilly Circus Tube station.

"What poor sap is it this time?" Russell asked.

"I haven't met him yet, but Armand tells me he was a waiter at The Ivy, and is about half Nathan's age."

Armand was Nathan's long-suffering assistant and erstwhile lover. Everyone knew he was still in love with Nathan. It was written through his very core. Why else would he put up with the bitching, sniping, demanding prima donna for as long as he had? Nathan made sure to throw him just enough crumbs to keep him there, and to keep his hopes alive. It was like a form of exquisite torture.

"I don't know why he puts up with it," Russell said. "I'd have ditched the old queen years ago."

"On that payroll?" Freddie said, raising an eyebrow. "And don't let him catch you calling him old. Hitting the big four-oh has made him neurotic enough."

"Well, you couldn't pay me enough to put up with that," Russell said.

"Ah, he's not that bad," Freddie said. "Most of it's just an act. Armand knows him better than anyone. Besides, Nathan needs him just as much as he needs Nathan."

"Well, I hope you've warned the boys what they're letting themselves in for," Russell said, pausing outside the door to the Red Lion pub on Rupert Street. "You know how handsy he gets when he's showing off."

"They can handle it," Freddie smirked as he sidled past Russell and pushed the door open, holding it for him to go through, carried in on a wave of Wham's "Last Christmas".

RUSSELL'S FLATMATE AND best friend, Joe Stone waved as Russell and Freddie walked in. He was at their usual table in the window, which was currently serving as a wrapping station for Joe's own pile of gifts.

"Good job I wrapped yours before you got here," Joe said, greeting them both.

"You shouldn't have," Freddie said.

"Oh damn," Russell said. "I knew there was someone else I needed to buy for."

Joe grinned. "Looks like you bought the whole shop, anyway," he said. "I thought you said you were going to take it easy this year."

"This *is* him taking it easy," Freddie laughed as he headed off to get the drinks.

"Have you managed to talk him out of it yet?"

"No chance," Russell said, dumping his multiple bags on the floor beside the table. "But you still have a chance to cry off. You could feign illness. Or tell him that your mum has insisted you go home for the holidays."

"Like he'd believe that," Joe laughed. "Besides, Mike is so excited it would break his heart."

Mike Duggan had rapidly become a fixture in Joe's life. He hadn't been looking for a full time boyfriend, but Mike had come out of the blue and they'd clicked straight away. A former colleague of Russell's on the police force, Mike was still serving as a uniformed officer and, since he and Joe had become an item, he'd put up with more truncheon jokes from the regulars in the Red Lion than was necessary.

A kind man, a great dancer, and a surprisingly good kisser, what Mike lacked in the kitchen he more than made up for in the bedroom. And he was funny, especially when he was drunk. Which, now that he was hanging around with Joe and Russell a lot more, was quite often.

"When's he getting here?" Russell asked.

"In about an hour," Joe said, looking at his watch. "Apparently a few of the lads from work are going for a drink when their shift ends and he's joining them."

Russell raised an eyebrow. "I don't miss those days," he said.

"Tell me about it," Joe said. "They sound like a bunch of neanderthals."

"Some of them were alright, individually," Russell said. "But when they all get together it's like a pissing contest for who can be the most macho. It's pathetic."

Russell had been forced to take a very early retirement after one of his colleagues had learned of his sexuality and organised a sting outside a nightclub to catch Russell out. He'd been approached by a hot young guy offering sex, and Russell had been drunk enough and desperate enough to agree. The young guy had turned out to be an undercover cop, and the rest was history. Russell still hadn't forgiven his old subordinate, Simon Skinner, for setting it up and—between him and Freddie—they'd made it their life's mission to see Skinner relieved of his badge too.

It wouldn't be easy though—the detective had somehow managed to get away with every form of terrible miscarriage of justice so far, from wrongful arrests to falsification of evidence and beating up innocent witnesses. Somehow, he'd wriggled out of all blame each time.

But Russell and Freddie were gunning for him and, now that they had a man in the inside in the form of Mike, they were closing the net on Skinner once and for all.

The police force was changing, slowly but surely, and Detective Skinner's particularly insidious brand of homophobia and racism had started to land him in hot water. Not enough to see him out on his ear yet, but it hopefully wouldn't be long.

They both looked up as Mike knocked on the window and waved.

"Quick, hide this," Joe said, shoving a half-wrapped gift box into Russell's hands. "I got him that watch he wanted, because he's usually late! Bloody typical that he turns up early just as I'm wrapping it."

Russell tucked the box into one of his bags and promised to finish wrapping it for him later.

"You're early," Joe said, as Mike arrived at the table having stopped at the bar to help Freddie with the drinks.

"Skinner turned up," Mike said. "Put me right off my beer. Besides, I figured you lot would be having lots more fun."

"Yeah, it's a laugh a minute," Freddie said, pushing the gifts and wrapping paper out of the way so that he could put the pints down.

"Alright Scrooge," Russell said. "You better get into the Christmas spirit a bit more before we get to Nathan's tomorrow. I'm not putting up with your moaning as well as all of his madness."

Freddie just rolled his eyes.

"I can't believe we're going to be spending Christmas Eve at Nathan Bentley's house," Mike said with a tone of genuine bewilderment. "If you'd told me that last year, I'd have laughed you out of the room."

"Me too," said Russell, "but probably for very different reasons."

"It's going to be amazing," Mike continued. "What did you buy him in the end?"

"A Rubik's cube," Joe said, holding up the brightly coloured cube in its plastic box and waving it happily.

"What?" Mike spluttered. "You bought Nathan Bentley a Rubik's cube? What the hell did you do that for?"

"So that he could make *that* joke," Russell said, shaking his head and twisting his lip in mock disappointment.

"What joke?" Mike asked, innocently.

"The more you play with it, the harder it gets," Joe and Russell chimed together.

"Jesus," Freddie said, hanging his head. "You two really need to get out more."

The door to the pub swung open and both Paul and Scott—or rather Patty and Miss Terri—came tottering in on impossibly high heels. Patty was dressed as a young Mrs Claus, with a low-cut red top and a tiny red mini-skirt, both trimmed with white fur. Miss Terri, on the other hand, looked more like an out-of-work bridal model, though Joe guessed from the wings hanging limply from her shoulders that she was supposed to be the Christmas Fairy.

Both squealed as they tottered over to the table to greet the boys.

"Bugger me, it's cold out there," said Patty, her rough Liverpudlian accent at odds with her fine features. "I'm freezing my chuff off in this! Oh God, look at me arms! They look like bloody Spam."

"I told you you should have gone as Rudolph," Miss Terri sniped, pulling the wings off awkwardly and almost knocking over Joe's pint as she did.

"Bugger off, you," Patty said.

"Right, well, we've got the last of everything," said Miss Terri, holding up the shopping bags. "So let's get all of this wrapped and get over to the Campbell Centre for this party. Brace yourself boys, Christmas season is officially open."

2.

THE STREETS OF SOHO were strangely quiet for a Saturday. It was Christmas Eve, and it seemed that everyone had finally left the capital for the festive season. Everyone, that is apart from the last-minute shoppers, the early revellers, and those who'd drawn the short straw and were still stuck working.

Russell, Joe, Freddie and Mike turned the corner, chatting as they walked from the Red Lion to Dean street, and Nathan's luxurious townhouse. Mike was excited, Russell resigned, and Freddie and Joe had both already sunk a couple of pints and were in buoyant spirits.

It was cold, but not cold enough for snow, though Freddie had assured them that Nathan had said something about a winter wonderland theme, which would doubtless involved vodka luges and fake snow anyway. Russell was only grateful that tonight's feast was not one of Nathan's notorious fancy dress parties.

"It's going to be fun," Freddie said again, squeezing Russell's hand.

Russell smiled. "I know. I'm fine. I'm looking forward to it, honestly."

"You look amazing," Freddie said with a small wink. It wasn't fancy dress, but they had all made an effort to dress up, and Russell had ducked into the barbers for a last-minute trim and shave, dropping off a Christmas tip as he left.

Even though they hadn't gone far, it felt like they'd entered another world. The houses on Dean street were tall and grand—four storey townhouses, many of which had already been divided into flats or maisonettes.

Nathan's was one of the few that remained unconverted. Towards the top of the street, with a navy blue door that looked both wider and grander than those of his neighbours—the place looked stylish and exclusive, even from the outside.

The curtains in the upper windows were all drawn, and the lower windows were shielded by plantation shutters, partly-open, but not enough to allow prying eyes to peer inside. Nathan Bentley was fastidious about his privacy. Probably, Russell thought, because he had so much to hide.

He was a notorious party boy, and had no qualms about everyone in the world knowing he was bi-sexual—God knows he would shout about it every time he was interviewed. Despite the fact that he'd only ever had one relationship with a woman—his now ex-wife, Grace—Nathan loved to crow about his open sexuality as though it was somehow more shocking that everyone was at risk from his advances.

Strangely, it hadn't seemed to harm his career, either. People seemed to accept unconventional sexuality more from their stars and celebrities than from your average man in the street or local bobby.

Nathan had somehow managed to become the face of dawning tolerance, with constant work in entertainment television during those early evening family slots. He loved to shock, loved to tease, and loved the sound of his own voice, and it was a constant surprise to Russell that the nation seemed to have taken him into their hearts so fully.

Perhaps, as Freddie had pointed out, it helped that he had been able to line any pockets that needed lining on the way to keep the wheels of his career greased. His assistant, Armand, certainly spent a lot of time clearing up after his boss, paying for silence and discretion, apologising for offence, and repairing any collateral damage.

The four of them huddled together on the steps leading up to the grand front door as Freddie rung the bell. The distant hum of music— Erasure's "A Little Respect"—grew louder as the internal door opened. A gentle buzz of laughter and conversation carried on the air as the door swung open and a flustered looking Armand greeted Freddie first.

"Thank God you're here, darling, it's absolute chaos." His German accent gave his camp pronunciation a clipped edge. Tall, with his head shaved clean, thick-rimmed round-lensed glasses framed his eyes beneath pale brows. He air kissed Freddie as he guided him inside with one flapping hand. "Come, come."

Russell, Joe and Mike all exchanged a glance as they were left standing on the doorstep. Armand turned back and waved them all in too. "Come on, all of you. Yes, yes. Welcome, welcome. Shut the door behind you."

Inside the townhouse was like something out of a film set. The hallway decorated ostentatiously with red, gold and green tinsel and baubles, a huge Christmas tree almost filled the space inside the front door, presents spilling out from underneath and scattering across the tiles. The hallway was big by London standards, but the oversized tree meant they had to sidle past in single file.

Russell nudged Joe and pointed to the almost life-size reindeer ornament in the front room off to their left. It had been mounted on small wheels with a silver platter attached to its back and was acting as a drinks trolley, adorned with bottles of spirits and champagne in a cooler. A young man, scantily clad in dangerously short shorts, was waiting to serve anyone who wanted to sample his wares.

"Thank God Nathan's got the heating on," Russell whispered, making Joe giggle. "Poor lad could catch a death otherwise."

"Leave your coats in the corner here. Lewis will help you to a drink," Armand said, guiding them all into the front room, and showing them a corner where small collection of coats and jackets had already been stashed.

"Is everybody here already," Freddie asked, nodding towards the burble of chatter and laughter from the kitchen.

"Don't worry, darling," Armand purred, patting Freddie's chest. "You're fashionably late, but you're not the last."

"This place is *amazing*," Mike mouthed to Russell, wide eyed. Russell nodded.

"Right," Armand said, breezing back out into the corridor. "Take a drink and make yourself at home. But be careful, the old bitch is in the kitchen."

"Grace is here?" Freddie asked.

"She tagged along with Serge and Simon, cheeky bitch. And you know Nathan—he never says no to her."

Russell smiled, he actually quite liked Nathan's ex-wife, from the one time he'd met her before. Though the marriage had been little more than a show, their relationship was probably one of the only genuine ones Nathan had.

Grace Bentley—of course she'd kept the name—always came in for flak from Nathan's new partners, and she and Armand absolutely hated each other, but she was loyal to Nathan and his fiercest defender. She was also riotously funny and a caustic bitch. Russell found he was suddenly looking forward to seeing her again.

Grabbing a drink from the festive trolley, they followed the sound of chat, laughter and music into the kitchen. The room had been recently extended to incorporate a modern-looking conservatory at the back, making a huge open-plan area downstairs with arches and open doorways into other smaller rooms.

Russell remembered how stressed Nathan had been about the forthcoming building work when they had come to the house in the summer for his last party. It had been worth it, though, the place looked incredible.

The equally elaborate decorations in here were all shades of blue and silver, and the windows of the conservatory had been misted with fake snow spray, giving the whole space a winter wonderland feel. Sure enough, a huge ice sculpture took pride of place—a vodka luge in the form of a little pissing cherub—and Patty was already crouching provocatively in front of it, enjoying a shot.

"For God's sake," Russell said, with a wry smile, as Patty wiped the corner of her mouth delicately with the back of her hand and adjusted a boob with her elbow.

She had swapped her red Mrs Claus outfit of yesterday for an equally skimpy pale blue version, with white trim, and an ice white wig piled high on her head like Marie Antoinette. Her make up was all pale blues and silvers. She looked spectacular. Russell always thought that their rather plain friend Paul was far more beautiful as his alter-ego, Patty.

"Look out," Freddie warned as Patty spotted them and waved. "The ice queen cometh."

"You lot took your time," Patty said, gliding over and air kissing all of them in turn. "You should have a go on the little fella."

She waved her hand towards the ice sculpture, before tucking her hand through Mike's arm and dragging him over to the luge. Mike turned back to Joe, mouthing "Help" but clearly not meaning it. Russell shook his head as Mike positioned himself to accept the shot, mouth open like a cheap porn star.

"He's a keeper," Patty cooed as Mike half-choked on the shot. "Doesn't the place look fab? I did most of it, of course. Poor old Armand has been having kittens all day. The bloody caterers have only just turned up and all. We thought we were going to be feasting on Mother's Pride and fish paste, for a moment there, didn't we?"

She dipped a knuckle into something pink and mousse-like that the chef had just set aside, and tasted it delicately, wrinkling her nose.

"Will you get out of this kitchen," yelled an already stressed-looking chef with the faintest hint of an Italian accent. "And I am *not* a caterer."

"Well, until you start cooking something decent, love, you're hardly a chef either. Chop chop." Patty clicked her fingers, her nail extensions looking fierce.

Armand shook his head. "Leave Giuseppe to work," he said through clenched teeth.

Giuseppe Bianchi was a rising star in the London restaurant scene. His own restaurant had a waiting list of around six months. Nathan was partly responsible for him getting his big break, but he still must be paying a fortune to get him doing a private banquet on Christmas Eve.

"Will you go and see Nathan, Freddie? Please." Armand asked, turning away from the flustered chef. "Let him know you're here. He's in the study. He wanted to discuss something with you before the party begins."

"Of course, Freddie said, and took Russell's hand, guiding him away from the hubbub in the kitchen, while Joe and Mike sidled in and started chatting to some of the other guests.

"Why don't you go," Russell said, hanging back. "I'll wait down here."

"Stop being a baby," Freddie said. "You're my boyfriend. He'll be happy to see you. Besides, I don't want to get stuck in a long session talking work with him. Which is exactly what will happen if I go in there alone."

Russell smiled. Nathan Bentley had been one of Freddie's clients for over five years and, though Nathan had tried both approaches on many occasions, he had discovered that his lawyer had no interest in either sleeping with him or pandering to his whims. Freddie had a soft spot for the man beneath the persona, but he wasn't about to let him take advantage.

"You're a big boy," Russell said. "Besides, you can use the fact that you've left me downstairs with all these hot young things as an excuse to come back quickly."

He planted a kiss on Freddie's cheek and ushered him off towards the stairs. But Freddie wasn't taking no for an answer. He grabbed Russell's hand firmly.

"Just come and say hello," he said. "If it looks like it'll drag on, you can leave us to it."

RUSSELL FOLLOWED FREDDIE along the plush, carpeted hallway, admiring the collection of original pop art prints by Andy Warhol and personally signed celebrity photographs by Annie Leibovitz.

A series of awards for various television shows that Nathan had presented lined a long, high shelf, just at the right height to allow anyone passing to read Nathan's name on most of them.

Freddie stopped in front of a wide set of french doors, solid oak, which had been left just slightly ajar. The smell of cigar smoke carried on the air. Stepping in beside him, Russell could hear voices from within.

"Are you sure? It makes me look like I'm due in court." The Estuary accent wasn't familiar, but Russell guessed it must belong to Nathan's new boyfriend, Archie.

"Rubbish," Nathan replied. "You look gorgeous, darling. Very dapper."

Freddie looked across at Russell, fist poised to knock. Russell raised an eyebrow, wanting to wait a moment longer before revealing their presence. The sounds from inside suggested that there was more undressing than dressing going on in the master bedroom and Russell wasn't sure he could handle the embarrassment of finding them in the middle of something.

"Ahem," Freddie said loudly, grinning as he knocked on the door. "Nate, it's Freddie. You better be decent, because I'm coming in."

Russell looked at him aghast, but Freddie just shrugged and pulled the door open.

The bedroom was a monument to opulence—all gold and marble, with black silk sheets and a four-poster bed with deep crimson drapes. A young man, somewhere in his late twenties, stood at the end of the bed, rapidly zipping up his trousers as Nathan used one of the bed posts to haul himself back to his feet.

"Trying to get a free show, were you, you dirty bugger?" Nathan said, and Russell noticed the young man's face flush to match the curtains. He clearly hadn't been expecting any intruders.

"Hardly," said Freddie. "I just wasn't going to stand out in the hallway waiting for you to finish. Armand said you wanted to see me."

"Yes," Nathan said, straightening his bowtie. "Archie, darling, this is Freddie Gillespie, my incredible lawyer and good friend. And this," he gestured towards Russell, "is his lovely partner..."

"Russell," he filled in himself, knowing that Nathan never remembered his name—he wasn't one to bother with the details. Archie smiled at Russell, eyes narrowing slightly as Freddie stepped forward and shook his hand.

"Nice to meet you."

He was about the same height as Freddie, but slim shouldered, with that aquiline look that was favoured by the modelling agencies. And he was immaculately dressed enough to be a model, too.

What on earth does this beautiful young man see in Nathan Bentley? Russell chided himself for such a mean-spirited thought. Freddie had reassured him plenty of times that what most people saw was not the real Nathan Bentley, and that there was actually a kind and loving man beneath the showy exterior. Russell was yet to see it, though.

Archie held up two ties, either side of his face. A deep red one and a blue one.

"You gents can help us decide," he said. "Red or blue?"

"Definitely red," Russell said. "Don't want anyone thinking you're a Tory."

Archie laughed. And it was a joyful, genuine laugh. From downstairs came the sound of a glass smashing and a sarcastic cheer from the growing party.

"Oh, for God's sake," Nathan tutted.

"You can't be regretting inviting everyone already, can you?"

Nathan smiled ruefully.

"Regret doesn't even come close, dear," he said. "I don't know why I do it. It always seems such a good idea until it's actually happening."

"Oh, come on," Freddie said, cheerfully. "It's going to be great. It's a lovely thing to do—taking in all of us waifs and strays for the festive season. We're looking forward to it, aren't we Russ? And the house looks amazing, as usual."

"Well, it does for now," Nathan said. "It'll probably be trashed by the time everyone goes home."

"Sign of a great party," Russell commented.

The sound of the doorbell ringing below chimed up the corridor and Nathan crossed to the window and peered down to catch a glimpse of who was arriving.

"Oh good," he said. "Debbie's made it too. That's everyone. Archie, why don't you and Russell go and get us some drinks lined up—mines a champagne—and Freddie and I will join you in a moment."

Archie hesitated, doubtless nervous about hitting the party alone.

"Come on," Russell said, giving him a reassuring smile. "I'll introduce you to some of the nicer ones."

Freddie gave him the slightest of nods, and Archie followed him out of the room.

"What are they going to be talking about in there?" Archie continued.

"Oh, God knows," Russell said, draining the last of his champagne glass. "But believe me, you do not want to hang around and listen to those two talking business."

"Probably marginally better than listening to Grace go on about herself," Archie sniped.

"You've met her then?"

"Oh God, the woman practically lives here."

"They've got a long history," Russell agreed. "She's been through a lot with him."

"I know," Archie said wearily. "I just wish she could be a bit more history and a bit less present..."

Russell smiled at the wordplay. It must be hard, Russell thought, having to share your partner with so many other needy people who he once had history with. Russell wasn't sure he'd cope, especially having most of them in the house on one night.

"Do you know everyone here then?" Archie asked.

"Most of them," Russell replied, sensing the young man's nervousness to be introduced. "They're all nice enough. Besides, if you've survived meeting Grace, you'll be fine."

"It's weird, though, isn't it? Having all your exes round for Christmas Eve. Wait," he stopped, looking at Russell. "You two weren't..."

Russell laughed.

"God no," and then he checked himself. "No offence, I'm sure he's lovely. But no, I only know him because my boyfriend is his lawyer. And, before you ask, no they have never, either. Not everyone here tonight is an ex."

"Thank God," Archie said.

Although most of them are. Russell had already seen Serge and Simon downstairs, both of whom had previously been Nathan's lovers and both of whom looked disconcertingly like an older version of Archie.

Then there was Grace, his ex-wife, and of course Armand. Doubtless there were others on the guest list who'd slept with Nathan. And Archie was right—it was strange to keep them hanging around all the time, but then Nathan was a bit weird.

Russell guessed he enjoyed feeling like they were all fighting over him, but it must be very uncomfortable for the new love interest, and there was always a party of sorts, every time a new love had to be introduced. Like a baptism of fire. *Poor kid.*

"Stick with me," Russell said. "I'll keep the more bitter ones at bay." He grinned at Archie, feeling sorry for the kid.

"You know no-one back home would believe this," Archie said, his half-smile growing.

"What's that? That you could actually pull off a suit and tie for dinner?" Russell teased.

Archie laughed.

"No. That *this* would be my life. That I'd be the one here in the big house with the celebrity boyfriend. When I think of all those lads who used to chase me down the road with their bats and blades..."

"Yeah, well, hopefully they're all either in dead-end jobs or at her Majesty's pleasure by now. They can't hurt you now."

"They wouldn't recognise me now anyway," Archie said. "I'm a new man."

"Glad to hear it," Russell said. "So where's back home?"

"A shit hole in the arse end of Essex," Archie said. "Small town, small minds, small everything. I couldn't wait to get out. That's why Nathan and I get on so well—he also came from a small place and had to get out. No going back, huh?"

Russell knew what he meant. They'd all had to run from something.

"Well. You're here now," he said. "And there's champagne calling. Come on."

He waved his glass and headed for the party.

THE LONG TABLE in the open-plan kitchen diner was groaning under the weight of a huge spread. Platters of the most delicious food, all lovingly presented, filled every inch of the surface, and a team of waiters flitted among the gathered revellers, filling glasses, taking empty plates and offering more tasty morsels from expertly handled trays. All of them dressed in tight white shirts and red bowties, gliding easily among the guests.

Joe thanked the young guy who topped up his glass. He was already feeling a little tipsy thanks to his tendency to drink everything at the same speed as he drank beer. The three glasses of champagne he'd sunk in quick succession had gone straight to his head, and the young waiter gave him a knowing smile as he topped up his glass for the fourth time, before moving on to refresh Archie's.

Nathan had made a grand entrance, sweeping in like royalty. He'd made a show of kissing Archie, and Joe had noticed how it had embarrassed the young guy. He'd been talking to Joe and Mike when Nathan had come in, and Joe could have sworn he saw Archie steel himself. Perhaps he was just shy. Not surprising, in front of an audience made up of a series of ex-lovers.

With champagne aloft, Nathan raised a toast to love and friendship, which they all supported, and the banquet was officially open.

Now—plate in hand—poor Archie had been abandoned by Nathan and was getting a grilling from two almost identical-looking guys in their early forties, Simon and Serge—Joe couldn't remember which was whom since they both dressed the same, had the same hairstyle and both wore similar glasses. They reminded him of Thomson and Thompson from the Tintin comics, especially with their neatly combed dark hair and full

19

moustaches. All he'd figured out so far was that they had both been in a relationship with Nathan at one time or another, and while they both obviously still craved his attention, there was a simmering resentment of the way he flaunted his new boyfriends in front of them.

As the waiter poured his wine, Archie turned his face away, as though he was too good to be associating with any of the waiting staff. Ironic, Joe thought, since Archie had been a waiter himself in Giuseppe's restaurant when he and Nathan had met, and had probably worked alongside some of these young men. Maybe he was trying to make a point that he had moved on now.

The waiter serving him frowned, waiting for some kind of acknowledgement and when none came, he sniffed haughtily.

"You're welcome," he said, sarcastically, and Joe was sure he deliberately spilled that glug of red wine that covered Archie's sleeve.

"Jesus, watch it," Archie exclaimed, angrily.

"Oh, I'm *so* sorry," the waiter replied, head tilted to one side. He wasn't sorry at all.

Archie put his glass back on the reindeer drinks trolley and dabbed at the wine, huffing to himself as the waiter moved on with a snide grin on his face. Joe didn't blame him, really. Just because Archie had landed on his feet here, didn't mean he had to drop his old friends, did it?

With a mountain of delicious-looking food piled on their plates, Joe and Mike leaned against the wall, shoulders pressed against each other, watching the guests mingle.

On the other side of the room, Joe caught Russell's eye and grinned. He was laughing as Grace—Nathan's larger-than-life ex-wife—regaled her end of the room with some story about a film producer friend of hers who had accidentally ended up winning a tiger in a poker game in LA. The group burst out laughing as she got to the part where the truck had arrived at their apartment with an angry tiger trying to claw its way out. "And to top it all, he's allergic to cats, darling," she finished.

Joe had heard a lot about Grace Bentley, but he'd never met her until tonight. She'd been pouting around in the corner of the kitchen when they'd arrived, and had immediately latched on to Mike, incessantly touching him and telling him what lovely strong arms he had, and how handsome he was.

"Is he good in bed?" she'd asked Joe. "I bet he is."

Freddie had once described her as the ultimate Fag Hag, and Joe was beginning to think he was right. Russell had said he found her quite funny, but Joe didn't see it. He just saw a desperate hanger-on trying to seem accepting, but actually only managing to be offensive.

Everyone knew that her marriage to Nathan had been a farce, anyway, and yet she swanned about the place proprietorially, always by his side, as though they were still together. And why wouldn't she? Being associated with Nathan Bentley was how she'd made her name—and her money.

The only time Grace had left Mike alone until now had been when Armand had come over to talk to them—her residual hatred for the man who stole her husband was obviously still strong, and Joe had thought it surprising she hadn't soured her Snowball with the expression she'd pulled as he'd approached.

Fortunately, Russell had stepped in to talk to her, and they were now in a friendly enough gaggle along with Patty and a handful of people Joe hadn't met yet.

"Isn't this beef sensational?" cooed a wild-haired woman called Debbie, grinning at them both before flitting on to join Serge and Simon in their interrogation of Archie. She looked familiar, but Joe couldn't place where from.

She was trying hard to look like a punk version of Madonna, and had the craziest high-pitched laugh, which pierced the air again as Serge leaned in to whisper something in her ear—doubtless something disparaging about Archie, given the black look that crossed the young man's face as he excused himself from their company.

"Who's that?" he asked, knowing that Mike had been talking to her earlier.

"Debbie something," Mike said. "She's some kind of pop star, apparently, but I can't tell you what band she said she was with. I'd never heard of them."

Realising that Archie had escaped their clutches, Serge and Simon turned back to Joe and Nathan, bitchy sneers on their faces.

"Well, I wonder what it was that attracted the gorgeous young man cub to the millionaire Nathan Bentley," one of either Serge or Simon said, bitterly.

"Oh Serge, you're such a bitch," Debbie said, gleefully, play-slapping his arm and finally answering Joe's question as to who was who.

"And you love it," said Simon.

Debbie laughed again, making Joe clench his teeth and down another glug of champagne.

"I give it a month at the outside," Serge said with a sneer. "There's not exactly much going on behind that pretty face."

"Excuse me," Joe said, giving Mike a sideways nod to tell him to come with, before following after Archie. He felt bad for the guy. It was difficult enough meeting a new partners oldest friends, but when half of them still felt more entitled to his affections and the other half still carried their residual bitterness about being replaced, Archie didn't really stand a chance. Besides, Joe didn't want to hang around with those three any longer—their cynicism and negativity was too grating.

Before they caught up with him, Nathan tapped his glass and silence descended apart from the buzz and clatter from the chef in the kitchen. All eyes swivelled to face him and he tilted his head in exasperation, but stopped work for long enough to let Nathan enjoy the rapt silence.

"Gentlemen. And *ladies*," his stress on the word 'ladies' made both pop-star Debbie and drag queen Patty giggle. Grace not so much. "Thank you for coming to my humble little soiree."

Humble it was not. They all tittered politely.

"Oh please, queen," Simon muttered under his breath. "Like we had a choice."

"Delighting us in the kitchen tonight is my good friend Giuseppe Bianchi and his team of minions."

A ripple of polite applause, accompanied by a bow from the chef and weak smiles from the waiting staff. Many eyes turned to Archie—most of the group knew he'd been one of Giuseppe's waiters when he'd met Nathan. Archie's face remained impassive.

"It means the world to me and Archie that you have chosen to spend Christmas Eve with us. We couldn't think of anyone we'd rather pass our festive season with. So, make yourselves comfortable, and help yourselves to anything you need, want or desire."

A crude murmur greeted this suggestion.

"Within reason, of course. And I'll be counting the silverware before you go," Nathan joked.

With the scantily clad waiters, the hot tub in the courtyard garden, the small piles of cocaine on black slate tiles in every downstairs room, and the rumour of poppers too, Joe realised that Russell hadn't been lying when he said Nathan liked to make sure all tastes were catered for at his parties.

"Now," Nathan continued. "Enjoy the evening, enjoy the food, and save a little of yourself for the entertainment later!"

With that, he raised his glass in a toast.

"To wonderful friends, to fine wine, to great food. And... to love. Merry Christmas!"

"Merry Christmas," they all echoed. The toast was raucous and cheerful. Joe caught Russell's eye and raised his glass again. To wonderful friends, indeed. And those no longer with us.

The room filled once more with the convivial hum of chat and laughter, clinking glasses and calls of "cheers" and one "up your bum" from Patty.

Joe crossed the room to join Russell and Freddie, who were both looking a little serious.

"What's up?" he asked.

"Nathan is brewing up for a big announcement," Freddie said. "And I don't think it's going to go down too well with the old guard."

THE CONSTANT LOOP of tedious Christmas songs playing on the stereo finally took a turn for the better as The Pogues and Kirsty MacColl began calling each other some rather unpleasant names. "A Fairytale of New York" was about the only Christmas song Russell could stand, given that he'd spent many Christmas evenings in the 'drunk tank' himself. Though at least he'd been on the outside of the bars.

"Happy Christmas, you arseholes," said Patty, quoting the song as she arrived at their little group with a plate of vol-au-vents expertly balanced on one hand. "Help yourself," she said.

"They've got you working now?" Russell asked.

"Those boys Giuseppe brought are doing a line a minute back there. Be a miracle if they can still stand by the end of the night."

Russell had grown used to turning a blind eye to the consumption of class-A drugs within their strange little community these days. Now that he was no longer legally obliged to do anything about it, he was happy enough for people to do what they wanted to their own bodies, just so long as none of his close friends got into it.

He gave Mike a knowing smile. As a serving policeman, he shouldn't be anywhere near illegal substances but, just as Russell had done for all those years before he was outed and ousted from the force, Mike had to learn to draw a line between his professional and personal lives. Mike raised his glass in recognition of their shared understanding.

Noticing that Archie was standing alone, Russell left Patty detailing exactly how much of Nathan's cocaine supply was currently being inhaled by the waiting staff and headed over.

As he squeezed past a few people to get to Archie, he thought the guy looked like he was brooding on something. Russell felt sorry for him as the new face in this difficult crowd. *Typical of Nathan to leave him to fend for himself,* he thought.

Before Russell could reach him, though, he saw one of the waiters sidle up to Archie and offer him a top up. Russell was close enough to see Archie grab the guy's wrist, though not close enough to hear the angry words he hissed into the young man's ear.

Whatever he said hit the spot though, because the waiter recoiled with an angry smirk on his face. By this point, Russell was close enough to hear his reply.

"We had a deal, Arch," the waiter said.

"Yeah, well things have changed," Archie replied. "You keep your mouth shut and your hands to yourself. D'you hear?"

The waiter snatched his wrist out of Archie's grasp and stalked away, sniffing hard. From the way he was chomping his jaw, Russell guessed he was one of those Patty had been talking about—helping himself to the produce.

"Everything alright?" Russell asked, noticing that Archie jumped as he spoke.

Archie's smile didn't quite reach his eyes.

"Fine," he said, and tentatively took a sip of wine. "Just a bit overwhelming, all this."

"I bet," Russell said, thinking that Archie was about to be even more overwhelmed when Nathan made his announcement.

Nathan hadn't told Freddie what tonight's announcement was about, just that he wanted him to be there to witness it, and that had made Freddie suspect that the crazy queen was about to make another one of his over-the-top proclamations of love again.

Russell assumed it would be Nathan's usual stunt of presenting his new lover with a key to the house—as though it were some sign of commitment. He certainly reclaimed them quickly enough when he got tired of them. Even Grace had moved out. Only Armand had ever kept a key.

On cue, Nathan tapped his glass and silence once again descended, interrupted only by Madonna singing "Santa Baby" in her best faux Marilyn. Armand walked over and turned her down, hovering by the stereo to restart the music after Nathan's little speech.

"Now," said Nathan, sounding a little nervous. "I know tonight is all about the joy of Christmas, and being together, love and friendship, and all that."

A clatter in the kitchen and they all looked around at one of the waiters, his white shirt now covered in red wine from the tray of glassed he'd just spilled and shattered. Swearing in Italian, Giuseppe waved him away to clean himself up. It was the same waiter that Archie'd just had his altercation with, Russell noticed. The guy was clearly losing it.

"Sorry, Nathan," Giuseppe said, looking like he would happily kill any of his so-called helpers. Nathan nodded, lips pursed as another couple of waiters began clearing the mess. After enough of a disapproving pause, Nathan fixed his smile again and continued.

"But I also wanted all of you to be here tonight to be my witnesses."
Confused glances all round.

"Witnesses to what, darling? Your undoing?" Grace heckled.

"Or yours. If you play your cards right," Armand sniped.

"As my closest *friends*," Nathan continued over their bitching, stressing the word friends. "And trusted confidantes," Russell wasn't so sure he, Mike or Joe fell into either category. "I wanted you to all be part of what, I hope, will be a very special moment for me."

With a nod to Freddie, Nathan reached into his pocket and pulled out an envelope.

"Archie, my darling," Nathan said, taking the papers and clasping them over his chest, and stepping out to walk around the pissing cherub towards Archie.

Simon and Serge both groaned in unison. Armand rolled his eyes and sighed. Archie looked nervous.

"I know we've only been together for the shortest time, but," and he looked excitedly at the gathered guests as he dropped to one knee. "I've got a surprise for you."

This was not the usual key giving ceremony that Russell had seen before, and clearly the other guests were intrigued too—moving quickly from resigned tutting to excited whispers.

Archie carefully laid his plate on the counter, taking the smallest of steps backward. Russell thought he looked almost as though he was going to make a run for it, but Nathan took his free hand and held on to him.

"This," he said, holding up the envelope as though it was a prize in one of his game shows, "is your Christmas present."

"What? Nathan I..." stammered Archie.

"Shh," Nathan said, pressing his finger to Archie's lips. "Let me say this."

Archie nodded, the finger still there and obviously making him feel a little awkward.

"I want to spend my life with you. I want it to be official. And since we can't ever get married, I thought I'd give you the next best thing."

"What is this?" Archie asked.

"It's a contract," Nathan said. "No. It's a proposal. This gives you everything you would have if you were my husband. Everything."

"Nathan, I don't know what to say," Archie said.

"Say yes."

There was a long, awkward pause as Nathan waited for the affirmation he needed. Archie flicked open the front page of the document, shaking his head as though he couldn't take any of this in. He looked back at Nathan, mouth open.

"Don't do it love," called Simon, to a small bitchy flurry of high-pitched laughter from Debbie.

"Run for your life," Serge quipped.

Archie looked across at them, scowling, and then back at Nathan.

"Nathan, I... This is so unexpected."

"Well?" asked Nathan, taking a pen from his pocket and waving it in the air. "What do you say?"

But, before Archie could answer, all hell broke loose.

Grace started shouting about her own claims as Nathan's wife—"*Ex-wife!*" Armand yelled over her, before trying to remind Nathan that he barely knew the boy, and that Archie was probably just in it for the money.

Archie, in turn, started screaming at Armand, calling him a jealous old bitch, while Grace called Archie a money-grabbing brat before storming out of the room, telling Nathan he could come and apologise to her.

"Haggard old cow," Archie shouted after her. Armand stepped forward and tried to grab the papers, but got shoved away roughly by Archie.

Russell grabbed Archie's arm to hold him back, and Archie managed to swing a wild elbow into his face in his attempt to shake himself free as Armand lunged at him, trying to claw at Archie's face.

Freddie grabbed Armand, while shouting at Archie for hitting Russell, while Russell tried to stop the blood pouring from his nose.

"I can't take this anymore," Armand announced, breaking free of Freddie's grasp. "I won't! I deserve better than this."

"Armie, please," Nathan pleaded. "I thought you'd be happy for me. It doesn't change anything for us, does it? This is your home. It will always be your home."

"Not while that little gold digger is here," Armand said, bitterly.

"Fuck you," Archie shouted.

"This is a huge mistake," Armand protested to Nathan. "You're acting like an old fool."

The slap that Nathan gave him was hard and shocked them all.

"And to think I felt sorry for you," Nathan spat. "Fine, go on then. Pack your things and get out."

"Good. I will." And Armand stormed out of the room too.

Nathan stood still for a moment, looking perplexed, before heading out of the room after Armand and Grace, muttering something about "nobody bloody leaves me until I say so."

Archie slumped back into a chair in the corner, envelope in hand, unopened, and a bewildered expression on his face. As the door swung shut behind Nathan, Patty clapped her hands excitedly.

"Well, it wouldn't be Christmas without a blow out, now would it? Cheers everyone!"

Raising her wine glass to the room in general, she downed it without waiting for a response and immediately poured a fresh glass, keeping the bottle.

Debbie, Simon and Serge all looked confused and shocked, Mike bemused. A ripple of dramatic reaction ran around the room.

"What the hell just happened?" Mike asked.

"The same thing that always happens with Nathan," Serge said. "Too much bloody drama. I told you it would end up like this. Come on. We're leaving."

And Simon obviously didn't have a lot of choice in the matter. He got up and followed Serge out of the room, reminding him that they "should have just gone to Biarritz."

"Wait, I'm coming with you," Debbie said, slugging back her own wine and tottering out of the room after Serge and Simon. "Nice to meet you," she said, almost apologetically to Archie. "But if you've got any sense, love, you'll run for the hills."

Russell noticed that she tucked one of the champagne bottles under her arm as she left.

"Well, bugger me," said Patty. "And I thought my family was dysfunctional!"

Joe shook his head, topping up his own glass as one of the waiters emptied the broken glass into the bin. There was no sign of the waiter who'd dropped everything in the first place, and the others looked pretty grumpy about being left to clear up the mess.

The sounds of arguments, cajoling and slamming of bedroom doors filled the house from upstairs.

"I'm going for a fag," Patty announced. "Who's coming?"

"I'm going to clean up this mess," Russell said, examining the blood-soaked napkin in his hand and testing his nose gently.

"I'll give you a hand," Freddie said.

With a glance back at the forlorn looking Archie, and a nod to Russell, Joe and Mike followed Patty out of the dining room.

"Are you okay?" Freddie asked Archie.

Archie sighed heavily.

"Yeah," he said. "I just need a moment to get my head around it."

Freddie obviously took the hint and hustled Russell out of the room as Archie hung his head, papers in hand.

"WELL, YOU DIDN'T TELL me *that* was going to happen," Russell said, as he and Freddie squeezed through the door into the downstairs bathroom.

"I warned you he was going to do something big," Freddie said. "But I didn't know what. I didn't draw up those papers. He knew I would have told him not to do it. I mean, he hardly knows the guy."

"It looked like it came as a bit of a shock to Archie, too," Russell said, splashing water on his face to wipe away the blood.

"Are you okay?" Freddie asked, handing him a towel.

"He's got a solid elbow on him. I'll give the kid that much."

Russell looked at himself in the mirror, drying his face on the towel. The blood still stained his shirt, but at least his face looked okay. He tested the bridge of his nose with thumb and forefinger, winced a little and smiled at Freddie.

"Nothing broken," he said.

"You're so butch," Freddie laughed, and kissed him.

"I suppose we'd better go and see what's going on," Russell said.

"Oh, I don't know," Freddie said, locking the door. "I think they all need a little while to calm down, don't you?"

IT WASN'T JUST THE COLD air hitting them as they stepped out into the courtyard garden that made Joe catch his breath—sparkling fairy lights formed a canopy over the whole terrace, twinkling like multi-coloured stars.

Steam rose from a hot tub off to the left, which had obviously been primed for the guests to retire to after dinner. Another reason to be grateful, perhaps, that the festivities seemed to have drawn to a halt with the whole proposal debacle. Joe wasn't a fan of the communal hot tub.

"Will you look at the state of that," Patty said, crossing to the hot tub and running a hand through the water. "Nice. What d'you think lads? Time for a dip?"

"Maybe later," Joe said. "Let's see how this drama plays out first, shall we?"

Another door slammed upstairs. More yelling followed.

"Oh, don't mind that lot," Patty said. "They're always doing this. I've never been to a do of Nathan's that didn't have some major blow out in the middle of it. It's like a bleeding pantomime. They'll all be down in a while acting like nothing's happened, you watch. Best thing to do is just get on with the party and wait for them to catch up."

She lit a cigarette and offered one to Joe and Mike.

"Ta," Joe said.

"I reckon it still beats Christmas at home hands down," said Mike, and Joe had to agree.

Christmas in Soho was a far cry from his small home town, where his parents would probably be slumped on the sofa right now watching soap operas while his two sisters bickered in the kitchen and their kids ran riot around the house.

His family had invited him back for the season, of course—they did their best to at least pretend they accepted him, but he had declined, saying that he had a party to go to with his boyfriend. He could hear the mixture of relief and concern in his mother's voice as she'd said: "Oh, that sounds nice, dear."

She hadn't asked when, or if, they'd be meeting this boyfriend of his. She'd simply told him to be careful, as she always did, and had hung up. *Happy Christmas to you too, Mum.*

The chef came out into the garden with a glass of wine in his hand.

"Alright, Giuseppe?" Patty asked. "Good tucker in the end."

"Delighted you approved," Giuseppe said sarcastically. "Pavlova's ruined though."

He leaned back against the side of the hot tub and took the cigarette from Patty.

"Cheers, love," he said. "What a palaver, huh?"

"I swear, it's the last time I'm doing one of these."

"Yeah, right," Patty said. "I'll believe that when I see it."

Mike took Joe's hand.

"Come on," he said. Leaving the other two at the hot tub, he led Joe over to a darker corner at the back of the courtyard, with overhanging creepers and a small bench. Joe gave a little shiver, and Mike put his arms around him, pulling him into a warm embrace.

"I wanted to tell you how happy I am," Mike said, pulling back to look Joe in the eyes.

"Don't you go getting soppy on me, officer," Joe teased. "And you'd better not pull out any contracts of your own."

"Don't worry, I couldn't afford the lawyers," Mike replied. "But I mean it."

He sat down on a small metal bench, still holding Joe's hand, and Joe sat beside him. Joe would ordinarily have felt this was all moving into serious territory too fast, but there was something so genuine and sincere about Mike, that he felt completely comfortable with it. He squeezed his hand and leaned his head on Mike's shoulder.

"Don't tell anyone," Joe said. "But I'm pretty happy too."

He felt Mike's cheek wrinkle into a grin, pressed against the top of his head, and smiled himself. They were only a few meters from the others, but this little space felt entirely private. A secret little hidey-hole off to the side of the courtyard, away from the arguments still raging upstairs, and the dwindling party noise downstairs, where they could just enjoy each other.

They heard Patty and Giuseppe head back indoors, complaining about the cold, and then they were alone. Taking the opportunity, Joe leaned in for a kiss, losing himself in his new boyfriend while the sounds of fighting from within the house gradually quietened down to be replaced by the sound of the Pet Shop Boys ironically singing about being left to their own devices.

RUSSELL LEFT THE DOWNSTAIRS bathroom with Freddie in tow and a slightly smug grin on his face. This was shaping up to be a much better party than he had thought it would be.

"Sounds like things have settled down a bit, at least," Freddie said, nodding towards the now quiet upstairs.

He was right; the house was quiet and still. The arguments and door slamming of earlier had gone. As they passed through the kitchen, they found Patty and Giuseppe sharing a pavlova with two spoons.

"Alright, lads?" Patty asked, holding up a loaded spoon. "Wanna try?"

"No thanks," said Russell. "Where is everyone?"

"Shouting, sulking or snogging, basically," Patty said. "Joe and his fella are in the garden, if you're looking for them. I was about to go for another fag, but I got distracted by Pepe's meringues."

Russell grinned at the weak innuendo, grabbed a couple of glasses of wine and led Freddie out into the garden. They found Joe and Mike coming back across the courtyard looking concerned.

"You okay?" Russell asked.

"We just heard something from over there," said Joe. "It didn't sound good."

Russell and Freddie followed them both into the darkest corner of the courtyard. As his eyes adjusted to the darkness, Russell saw a shape on the ground in the corner of the courtyard. It looked like a sack of rubble, but there was something odd about it.

Staring for a moment, he realised that there was a shoe. His heart sank as he realised that the shoe was attached to a leg. Surely no one could be drunk enough yet to have passed out in the freezing courtyard?

"What's that?" he asked aloud, but he already knew.

The others gathered around him, peering over his shoulder as though in some kind of danger that he could protect them from.

"Oh Jesus," Mike said. "Is that... Archie?"

"No," Russell said, dropping onto his haunches to look at the young man. "It's one of the waiters."

The waiter who had dropped the tray of glasses was lying face down on the tiled courtyard. Joe bent down closer to him, too, and gave him a little shake.

"Hello, mate? Are you alright?" Joe asked.

But he was not alright. He was very much dead.

PATTY AND GIUSEPPE ARRIVED outside to find Joe and Russell crouched beside the body of one of the waiters. Freddie and Mike stood back slightly, allowing them in.

"Jesus," Patty said. "What's happened to him? Christ, d'you think he's OD'd?"

"I told him to lay off the charlie," Giuseppe muttered.

"He hasn't overdosed," Russell said, bending over the body and looking closer.

"Are you sure?" Patty asked. "Because he looks pretty dead to me."

A pool of blood had collected beside the young man's head, and on closer inspection, Russell could see the open wound on his temple that had probably been the death of him.

Patty turned away, looking queasy as Russell titled the guy's head to one side. From the state of him, it looked as though he'd fallen from the window above.

Russell stood up and stepped back from the body, looking up the building. All of the windows were closed. So how had he fallen? Joe joined him.

"Do you think he fell?" Joe asked.

"Undoubtedly," Russell replied. "But how, if all the windows are closed?"

"What?" Mike asked, looking up.

Russell glanced back at Patty and Giuseppe. Not really wanting them to hear his theory yet, he turned away from them and kept his voice low.

"And take a look at that."

He pointed his toe towards the open gash on the side of the young man's head, just above his temple.

"What am I looking at?" Joe asked, leaning closer.

The kid's head was a mess anyway and there was blood all over his face and neck, but the wound on this side of his head had clearly been inflicted by something heavy and blunt and not the fall from the high window above.

"Looks like he was hit before he fell," Russell said. "Look, he clearly landed face down, all the damage from the fall is on the other side of his face. But this wound is swollen, like he was hit hard from behind."

"You mean somebody killed him?" Joe asked.

"Yes," Russell said, quietly. "I think so."

"Oh God," Mike said.

"Right," Russell said, turning back to the rest of them. "Patty, you go call the police. Tell them we have a dead man here. Fallen from an upstairs window. No need for paramedics."

Patty tottered away, clearly glad of something to do.

"Freddie, you gather everyone who's still here inside, and don't let them out here. Giuseppe, how well did you know this kid?"

Giuseppe looked green.

"Not at all," he stammered. "He works at the restaurant, I shout orders at him. His name's Kevin. I think."

"What about the other staff?" Russell asked. "Would they know him?"

"Sure," Giuseppe said. "Should I bring them out?"

"No," Russell said. "Just get them all together in the kitchen and don't tell them what's happened yet. I'll be in in a moment."

The chef turned and left, wiping his forehead with a tea towel he'd had draped over his shoulder and muttering about a quiet Christmas. Russell walked over to Mike, who looked a little shocked himself as Joe whispered to him urgently.

"You have to," Joe said. "Just think how it'll look if they find you here."

"I know," said Mike. "But I can't just leave. I'm a policeman. I made an oath. Besides, I'm a witness."

"Are you? What did you actually see?"

"Well I..."

"It's not worth it, Mike. Think of your career."

"He's right," Russell said quietly. "It's only ever Skinner who works the Christmas shift, and if he finds you here, it's all over for you."

"But it'll make me look guilty."

"Not if you just sneak out now. Look, and I don't mean this horribly, but everybody inside is far too wrapped up to notice that you've gone, and those of us who would notice are not going to say anything. I'll make sure of it. Trust me."

Mike nodded earnestly. "Thanks Russell," he said, turning back to look at the body.

"But you have to go, *now*. They'll be here any minute."

Mike gave Joe a quick peck on the cheek and headed back indoors.

"You alright?" Russell asked Joe, noticing the stern look that had crossed his face. Joe sighed.

"I just hate that we have to hide it all the time," he said.

Russell put an arm around his shoulder.

"We all hate it," he said. "And it won't be forever. Safer for him all round if he's not here when his colleagues turn up."

"I know," Joe said, but his voice was heavy.

Attitudes had come a long way over the decade, but nowhere near far enough, and especially not in a police force with the likes of Detective Simon Skinner still at the helm.

Russell hated that Mike was still forced to keep his sexuality secret, but they were working on getting rid of Detective Skinner once and for all, and after that, perhaps, he could have both a life and a job.

Besides, they had bigger things to worry about tonight. A murder at a gay celebrity's party, on Christmas Eve. Skinner—and Russell was sure it would be him that turned up—would have a field day.

"Come on," Russell said. "Let's see what we can find out before the fuzz turn up."

3

JOE WALKED OVER TO the dark corner where the young waiter lay. He shivered. It was cold out here. Even though the young man was clearly dead, Joe considered getting a blanket to cover him up. He turned as Russell hurried back from the kitchen clutching a large black-handled torch.

"Found one," Russell said, clicking the torch on and casting a sharp light on the scene. "Poor kid. Surname's Flint, apparently, according to one of his colleagues. Not sure he was much liked though. A slacker and a chancer, they described him as. Course, they don't know he's dead yet."

Joe bent to look at the wound on the side of the waiter's head in the torchlight. As well as the swelling, there was a deep cut there. *Who would do this?* It had to be one of the people inside right now, didn't it?

"What do you think he was doing upstairs?" Joe asked.

"Good question," Russell said, passing the torch over Kevin's body. "One of his colleagues suggested he'd probably been looking for things to nick. Apparently, he has a bit of a reputation for being light-fingered."

"So, someone caught him with his fingers in the cookie jar and smacked him over the head?"

"Sounds a little over-the-top as a reaction, doesn't it?" said Russell, bending down and focussing the torchlight on the young man's hand. "Look here," he said.

Joe peered closer. There was something there, between Kevin's thumb and forefinger. A small piece of paper.

"What is it?" Joe asked.

Russell lifted the man's hand and shone his light on it.

"Looks like a torn off part of a cheque," he said. "Now that's interesting."

"Strange," Joe said, as Russell carefully laid Kevin's hand back on the ground.

They both moved around the body slowly, searching for anything else to give them a clue, but there was nothing more to be found.

"Right," Russell said decisively. "I'm going to go and take a look upstairs, see if I can find out what he was doing up there. You go and talk to the guests. Tell them he fell, but don't mention that he was hit first, we don't want to tip his killer off that we know until we have a little more to go on."

"Got it," Joe said.

They had become a good team over the past few years, and had already solved a handful of murders that the police hadn't been interested in looking at. Russell had been a good detective in the police, but Joe would argue that he'd become a better one since leaving.

They worked well together, and Joe knew Russell trusted him to get secrets out of people without them realising they were giving them up. Perhaps there was some use for that psychology degree of his after all. He followed Russell indoors to gather the other guests feeling like a modern-day Poirot.

RUSSELL PASSED THROUGH the kitchen with a nod to Giuseppe, who was now sitting up on one of the work surfaces, surrounded by his waiting staff. Given that one of their own had just died, Russell thought they all looked more bored than concerned.

"How's everyone holding up?" Russell asked.

One of the lads murmured something about wanting to go home.

"We're alright," Giuseppe said. "What happened, do you think?"

"We're trying to figure that out," Russell replied. "The police will be here any minute. They'll probably want to talk to all of you about Kevin."

There was much tutting and sighing, but no one said any more. Kevin was obviously not that popular among the waiters.

"Do any of you know when he went upstairs? Or why?" Russell asked, pausing in the doorway on his way to the stairs.

He couldn't remember which of the waiters had made the offhand comment that Kevin was probably casing the place for something to nick, but they weren't saying it again. This time, there was a lot of shaking of heads and shrugging, but none of them volunteered an answer. Russell decided he'd come back to them later, and go and see for himself before the police got here.

He could hear raised, bickering voices in the front room, and the sound of Freddie's usually calm voice snapping at Nathan to calm down. He smiled, taking the stairs quickly—Nathan would be furious that this had happened at his party.

Russell dreaded to imagine the newspaper headlines. *The Sun* was only too keen to point out the depravity inherent in the gay lifestyle at every opportunity, so a young man killed in a drug-fuelled gay orgy at a fancy celebrity house would probably be the way they'd spin it.

It struck him, as he headed up the stairs, that Nathan may need to start thinking about other career options. It was unlikely the BBC would keep him on that Saturday evening slot after this scandal broke.

He found Patty standing outside the bathroom on the first floor, knocking on the door.

"Oh come on, Grace," she called through the closed door. "Just open up. It's important."

She turned to Russell as he passed, hands thrown up in a plea for assistance.

"What do I tell her?" Patty whispered urgently.

Russell stepped up and did his best policeman's knock on the door.

"Grace, open up," he said, as though he had some kind of warrant and would break the door down if she didn't comply. "There's been an accident. The police are on their way. And I need everyone downstairs by the time they get here."

Patty looked impressed. "Get you," she mouthed.

The sound of the toilet flushing, followed by an over-dramatic clearing of the throat, a running tap, a pause, and Grace opened the door.

"What kind of accident?" she asked, with an air of disinterest.

"One of the waiters is dead," Russell said flatly, watching for a reaction.

"I'm not surprised, darling," she drawled, the alcohol hanging on her breath. "The amount of blow that lot have been doing all night. It'd be enough to see anyone off."

Patty looked at her aghast.

"So what's the problem?" Grace asked, ignoring her. "You need a grown up to come and sort out the mess?"

It hadn't seemed possible for Patty's jaw to drop any lower, but it did. Russell patted her arm as Grace bustled past importantly.

"Just go downstairs with the others," Russell said to Grace. "And when the police do get here, try not to mention the drugs."

"Why the hell have you called the police?" Grace asked incredulously. "We could have handled this. We've dealt with worse."

"A man is dead, Grace," Russell said, in his calmest voice. "And while I may no longer be a serving officer of the law, I still respect it. *We* will not be *handling* anything. Now, downstairs, and have a think if there's anything you need to tell the cops when they get here. Given you were upstairs at the time the young man fell, maybe you heard something? Saw something?"

The way he left the last question hanging, as though the next would be "Did something?" had Grace scuttling off with Patty following after her with an appreciative wink over her shoulder. Russell turned to the upstairs corridor and began his search for answers.

JOE'S EXCITEMENT FOR HIS role as detective faded almost as soon as he walked into the front room. Freddie had so far only managed to gather Nathan and Armand, who were currently scowling at each other sullenly from opposite sides of the room with Freddie standing between them like a referee in a boxing match.

"Where are the others?" Joe asked, as Freddie approached.

"Patty's gone to find Grace," Freddie replied, looking harassed, but keeping his voice low. "Apparently she's locked herself in the upstairs bathroom and is refusing to come out."

"Does she know what's happened?" Joe asked.

"God knows," Freddie said, leaning in closer and whispering the next part. "It's all I can do to stop these two killing each other too."

The door flew open and Grace strode in followed by a tottering Patty.

39

"What's going on?" Grace demanded. "Your squat little friend upstairs tells me someone's carked it."

"Jesus," said Armand. "Show some respect."

"Oh please," Grace sneered. "Friend of yours, was he? I'm sorry I can't get all teary-eyed over a waiter taking too much coke that didn't belong to him in the first place and falling out of a window."

"Oh just sit down, Grace," Nathan said with a curtness that gave Grace pause.

"Well, I mean..." she huffed as she sat beside Nathan and patted his knee. "Oh look, everything will be alright. It's not our fault, is it? We'll just tell them he must have brought his own supply of drugs. He was obviously up to no good anyway. He had no business being up there. They'll see it's not your fault."

Nathan and Freddie both looked like they were about to protest.

"Wait. Has anyone got rid of the rest of the drugs from the kitchen?" Patty asked. This was a clearly more pressing question.

"What?" Nathan asked.

"Well, we've called the pigs, haven't we?" Patty said, as though explaining to a group of idiots. "They'll be here any minute and, if I'm not mistaken, there's enough china through there—all laid out on pretty plates like a bleeding tasting menu—to kill an army. So good luck persuading them the waiter brought his own."

"She's right," Nathan said, standing up urgently, his eyes wild. "We need to flush it."

"Bollocks to that," Patty said. "We just need to hide it. Trust me. If they don't find it, they're not going to go looking. They've got enough to deal with."

With a broad smile to show how simple it was, she turned to the door.

"Don't worry. I'll sort it," she said dramatically, as she flounced out.

Joe caught her grin on the way out. Patty was a demon for cocaine, but very rarely had the money to feed her tastes. The supply she'd clear up from tonight would keep her for a few weeks, at least.

"So where is he then?" Grace asked. "The dead boy?"

"In the courtyard," Freddie replied.

"He fell from a window," Joe added, gauging her reaction.

The smallest hint of a raised eyebrow, a plastered smile. There was something about the way Grace smiled said she was enjoying this a little too much. She loved drama—that much was clear.

"Oh, well that *is* unfortunate. And what was he doing poking around upstairs?"

"We don't know," Freddie said.

Nathan stood up and crossed anxiously to the window, looking out, fingers drumming against his legs.

"Where were you, Grace?" Joe asked. "About half an hour ago?"

Grace laughed like she was at a comedy gig, going as far as to slap her thigh.

"Oh, please!" she said. "I was in the bathroom, darling. Waiting for an apology from my husband for his ghastly behaviour."

"*Ex*-husband," Armand muttered, and Nathan stood up and began pacing again.

"Why don't you ask *Armand* where he was?" Grace trilled. "He was ferreting around up there too, weren't you? What exactly were *you* up to?"

"Nothing," Armand snapped. "I was packing my things to leave, remember?"

"And, not a moment too soon, if you ask me," Grace snarled.

"Just stop it, both of you," Nathan said, and they both huffed but shut up.

The door opened and Archie walked in, a bottle of wine in hand. He looked ashen. Nathan stopped pacing and turned to him but, Joe noticed, didn't move to console him.

"You alright?" Joe asked.

Archie nodded, said nothing. He crossed the room, took a clean glass from the ridiculous reindeer trolley and filled it almost to the brim with wine. When he sat down, he stared at the floor.

"Did you know him well?" Joe asked, sitting down beside Archie.

"No," Archie said sullenly, without looking up. "We did a couple of shifts together, but I barely knew him."

"Huh," Joe said, sounding confused.

Archie looked at him suspiciously.

"What's that supposed to mean?"

41

"Nothing," Joe said. "It's just that the two of you seemed to know each other well enough earlier. I saw you arguing."

Archie snorted derisively.

"We weren't arguing," he said. "I was just telling him to keep his hands to himself."

"Why?"

"Because the one thing I *do* know about him is that he's a sneaky little thief, and I didn't want him helping himself to any mementoes tonight."

"Done that before, had he?"

"He was already on a final warning at the restaurant when *I* worked there," Archie said. "It's a miracle he's still there. Can't help himself. He's lifted watches, wallets, you name it. Light fingers, see? No wonder he agreed to work Christmas Eve for a private client. "

"You think that's what he was doing upstairs?" Joe asked.

"I have no doubt," Archie replied, taking another big gulp of his wine.

He seemed both shocked and nervous. If he didn't know the guy that well, Joe wondered, and nothing had actually been stolen, why was he reacting this badly?

"We had a deal." Wasn't that what Kevin had said when Archie'd grabbed his wrist.

"Shouldn't we be doing something?" Nathan said suddenly, interrupting Joe's train of thought.

"Like what?" Freddie asked. "The best thing you can do is calm down, sober up, and prepare to explain yourself to the police."

"Why would *I* need to explain myself?" Nathan asked defensively. "It's got nothing to do with *me*."

"Because, Nathan," Freddie said. "This is *your* house. *Your* party. And a man *you* hired has died falling from one of *your* windows. It's got everything to do with you."

Grace and Armand stepped to Nathan's defence immediately, both insisting that Nathan had nothing to do with the waiter's death.

"I'm not saying he did," Freddie said. "But they're going to question all of you at some point tonight. So why don't you all sit down and have a think about what you're going to say because, right now, they could take any and all of you in, and there'd be very little I could do to stop them."

"What the hell are you talking about?" Nathan said. "You're my lawyer. You can stop them doing anything."

"Not this," Freddie said.

"But it was an accident," Grace said. "You said so yourself. He fell from the window."

"We can't say for sure he wasn't pushed," Joe said, standing up. He didn't want Freddie telling them they knew he'd been hit first. "We can't be sure that it wasn't deliberate."

Grace laughed explosively. No one else did.

"You can't be serious," she said. "Why on earth would any of us want to kill a bloody waiter?"

"And that's exactly the question the police will want you to answer," Joe said. "So we may as well run through it now."

Grace snorted but said no more.

"Grace," Joe continued. "You were in the bathroom you say? Can anyone confirm that?"

Heads shook all round the room.

"Nathan, how about you? You were upstairs trying to persuade Armand to stay?"

"Huh," Nathan huffed. "I knocked on his door, but he wouldn't let me in. So I went to my own bedroom, across the hall, to wait for him to come out. This isn't the first time he's packed his bags in a huff."

"I'm still be leaving," Armand said.

"So what you're saying," Freddie said. "Is that all three of you were upstairs at the time the young man fell, and none of you can vouch for each other. You can see how that might look."

"Well, what about Archie?" Grace spat his name as though it was poison.

"What about me?" Archie asked, finally looking up.

"I heard your voice, upstairs, while I was in the bathroom," she said. "Who were you fighting with?"

"You're a liar," Archie said, standing up suddenly, wine splashing from his glass as he did. "I was down here the whole time."

"But you knew him, didn't you? I mean, this time last month you *were* him. As good as. What's wrong? Was he trying to muscle in on your patch?"

"Drop it Grace," Nathan said.

"No," Archie replied, standing up. "She's right. This time last month I was *just* a waiter. But then I met Nathan. And everything changed."

Nathan smiled, though it was tinged with sadness.

"And we can all change, can't we? We can all move on from where we started out. Just like Nathan did."

Nathan turned to him quickly, looking tense, eyes wide.

"Of course we can all move on," he said. "And I suggest we do just that. Archie is here now, and that's what's important to me. Not where he came from, or what he was doing when we met. You of all people should know that, Grace."

Grace huffed but said no more. Joe made a mental note to find out what she had been doing when she and Nathan had met, just to ease his curiosity.

Nathan crossed over to Archie and took his hand, getting him to sit down again.

"I'm sorry," he said, quietly. "This must be a shock."

Archie shrugged. Nathan held Archie's hand up to kiss it, but stopped, looking quizzically at his palm.

"Are you okay?" he asked. "Are you hurt?"

Archie took his hand back and studied it. Then he laughed.

"It's nothing," he said. "Just some red wine."

But Joe saw the slightly guilty way he wiped his hand on his trousers, nonetheless. He exchanged a glance with Freddie, seeing that he had noticed it too.

"Can I have a quiet word?" Armand asked Joe surreptitiously, indicating that he would prefer to do it outside the room.

Joe looked to Freddie again, who nodded, so he followed Armand out into the corridor.

MEANWHILE, UPSTAIRS, Russell peered through the doors on the right-hand side or the corridor, trying to figure out which one overlooked the bit of the courtyard Kevin had landed in.

In a bedroom just past the landing he saw an open suitcase, half packed and then abandoned. This must be Armand's room.

Sure enough, the picture on the nightstand—lit by a small side lamp—was of Armand and Nathan together somewhere cold and snowy, dressed head to toe in ski gear, beaming for the camera. They would still have been a couple in that picture, Russell guessed, seeing how much younger they both looked.

Armand's wardrobe hung open, hangers stripped in anger, and clothes roughly pushed into the open suitcase—a half-hearted attempt at packing by a man who wanted to be stopped, pleaded with. Had Nathan been in here with him when Kevin fell to his death? He'd followed Armand upstairs to stop him leaving, certainly. So that put both of them in the right place to be the killer, but they would easily provide each other's alibis if they were together. Russell crossed to the window and peered down directly on to the hot tub. This wasn't the right room. He moved on.

Outside the study, he noticed that one of the statues on Nathan's award shelf had been moved. The display had been so neat and organised before, the missing statue stood out like a gap in a smile.

The door to the study was ajar, so Russell pushed it open and stepped in, looking over his shoulder and feeling like a sneak. A standard lamp in the corner had been knocked over but the light was still on, casting a dim, yellowish light across the floor. The leather armchair in front of the bookshelves had been knocked over too, and papers had been scattered from an upturned in-tray on the desk.

A painting on the wall hung at a strange angle. The window was closed, but the curtains were open. Russell crossed the room and looked down. This was where Kevin had fallen from. And from the small smear of blood on the carpet, this was also where he had been hit.

The lamp light was too dim to see clearly by, so Russell switched his torch back on and peered at the smudge on the carpet. A solid stain of what looked like blood. How had that got on the carpet unless Kevin had lain there for a while.

He stood up again and examined the window. The handle was the kind which needed to be lifted to engage the locks. And it was locked. So someone had deliberately shut it after Kevin fell.

Russell turned his attention to the papers on the floor, which included the contract Nathan had presented Archie with at dinner, a receipt for seven thousand pounds in cash for the sale of an original sculpture to a buyer from Germany, some payments slips for water and electricity bills that had been torn off, filled in and now had cheques attached to them with paperclips. Russell looked through all of the cheques to see if any was missing a corner, but they were all intact.

He stood up and moved behind the big desk in the corner, looking for the chequebook they'd come from. He found it in the long drawer at the front of the desk, but it gave up no other clues. There with stubs with 'Gas', 'Water', and 'Elec.' written on them, but the last stub was frustratingly blank. He would have to ask Nathan who he wrote that cheque for.

The picture on the wall caught his eye again—hanging at an angle, as though it had been knocked. It showed an old pastoral scene—a farmer, shotgun on his shoulder and dog at his heels, walking down a misty path with a pheasant rising in flight. It seemed completely out of keeping with Nathan's style, even in this rather old-fashioned study.

As Russell reached to straighten it, he realised it hung a little too proud of the wall. Leaning closer, he saw that the picture covered a wall safe. And the safe was open.

He eased the painting out on its hidden hinges and opened the safe further. On the bottom shelf were several tightly bound piles of twenty-pound notes. Probably the seven thousand pounds of cash mentioned on the receipt he'd found.

Ignoring the cash for now, he looked on the shelf above, to find a neatly printed and bound manuscript. It was the final draft of Nathan's Autobiography—You Don't Know Me.

The book was due out in the New Year, and Russell dreaded to think of the sycophantic name-dropping that would be contained within its Perma-tan stained covers. He lifted the manuscript out and flicked open the first couple of pages, reading that well-worn tale of Nathan's journey from relative poverty to the celebrity superstar he was today. Russell rolled his eyes and put the manuscript back on the shelf—he'd be forced to read it when it came out anyway. It could wait.

Underneath the manuscript, he found a loose bundle of photocopied newspaper articles and a handful of old photographs. Russell lifted the photographs and studied them.

A black-and-white, wrinkled-edged print showed a young boy, shorts pulled up way too high with braces, school tie hanging slightly skew, his little cap at a jaunty angle on his head. He stood on the steps of a normal looking semi-detached that could have been anywhere in 1950s suburbia, sandwiched between a man and a woman. The boy was clearly Nathan—that cheesy grin was recognisable anywhere. The parents looked detached and distant, standing either side of the child with no attempt at a smile and a safe, no-touching, distance between them all. The mother had her left arm in a sling, the father leaned on a walking stick.

On the back in faded handwriting, was the caption: "First day at school. 1954." Nathan was the only one who looked happy. The parents looked like they couldn't care less.

No wonder he never talks about home, Russell thought, flicking through the rest of the photos. They showed a life about as far removed as you could get from the glamorous one Nathan had built for himself here in Soho. A solitary boy, captured only in a handful of key life moments.

In one, a teenage Nathan, looking gaunt and haunted, stood beside a different woman with an infant swaddled in her arms. Her tight lips and her fixed, angry glare at the camera suggested she wasn't too happy having the picture taken.

Russell turned the photograph over to find the words "Nathan, Auntie Kay and Bubba, 1963. Moving in!". The first attempt at writing the names had been crossed out, with Nathan's name now written above the scribble. The handwriting was different, but the boy in the picture was unquestionably the same—older, and with no hint of the earlier smile, but it was definitely Nathan.

Russell wondered if these pictures would feature in the book when it was published. It was strange to see Nathan as the awkward-looking child he once was, somehow it had always felt like he'd arrived in Soho fully formed and larger than life.

Russell put the pictures back in the safe and lifted the bundle of papers out. Headline after headline of photocopied newspapers from the early 1960s talked of the suicide of a local councillor. Henry Mawson.

Russell had never heard of him and didn't recognise the pictures used in the news stories. Apparently, he had taken his own life after killing his wife. There was speculation in one of the later articles that she had found out about his secret life as a closet homosexual and he had lashed out when she confronted him. This suspicion, however, was only mentioned in one of the tabloids and there seemed to be little substance to it. *Poor guy, if it was true.* Maybe the book would be more interesting than he'd thought.

The photocopies looked fairly new. Russell wondered if they were part of the research for Nathan's book, though he'd had never known Nathan get passionate about any gay rights issues apart from his own right to party.

He flicked to the next article, but didn't have time to read it as he heard the doorbell sound below. That would be the police. They shouldn't find him poking around in here.

He tucked everything back in the safe and pushed the door closed without letting the catch engage. He returned the picture to its place in front of the safe and straightened it up. No one would ever know he'd been there.

RUSSELL QUIETLY PULLED the study door closed and hurried downstairs to find Freddie heading for the front door.

"Alright?" he asked, urgently.

Freddie gave him a nod. "They're all set to blame each other for this," he said, sourly. "Looks like I may have a long night ahead."

Russell gave his shoulder a squeeze and waited at the bottom of the stairs as Freddie opened the door to two bored-looking police officers, badges waving lazily.

Christmas Eve in Soho was a notoriously troublesome night for the police and reports of people passed out drunk at parties would have been ten to the dozen. Hopefully Patty had been clear with them that he was definitely dead, but even then, he probably wouldn't be their first accidental death of the evening.

One of the officers recognised Russell straight away, and the curl of his lip reminded Russell that he had been one of the more venomous once Russell's sexuality had been exposed to his colleagues.

"Mills," Russell said, flat and dismissive.

"Mr Dixon," the cop said, closing the door. "I would say it was a surprise to see you here, but I'd be lying. You seem to turn up like a bad penny whenever there's trouble."

PC Mills looked around him with obvious distaste, as though the house itself was somehow contagious.

"Who is the owner of the property?" Mills asked.

"Nathan Bentley," Freddie said. "He's through there. I'm his lawyer. Freddie Gillespie."

"I see," said Mills, raising an eyebrow. "Well, *you* got here quickly didn't you?"

The intonation was clear. Freddie didn't rise to it.

"I was already here," Freddie said. "We were having dinner."

"And what exactly's happened?" the other officer asked.

Russell didn't recognise him, but he was a big lad and, despite the winter temperatures, he had a sheen of sweat on his brow. His blazer was open to reveal a stained uniform shirt that was struggling to hold his belly in.

"Well, we don't know, do we?" Freddie said, tersely. "That's why we called you lot."

"There's no need to be snippy, Sir," Mills said, eyeing Freddie suspiciously. "I'm only trying to do my job."

Chance'd be a fine thing.

"Don't you think it would be a good idea to secure the body, first, officer?" Russell stepped in. "You know how important forensics can be these days. You don't want people trampling all over your crime scene, do you?"

Freddie raised an eyebrow, as though to say: "Like you've just been doing?" Russell replied with an almost imperceptible shrug.

"So, it's definitely a body then?" the larger officer asked, as though he'd been hoping to find the victim now revived and feeling a bit the worse for wear.

"I think I've seen enough bodies in my time to know," Russell said, and Freddie gave him a gentle nudge to warn him to keep his tongue.

"I'm sure you have," PC Mills said, with a look of disgust. "Very well. Lead the way."

Russell heard him whisper some comment about "not letting him get behind me" to his colleague and they both sniggered.

"Have a little respect, officers," Russell snapped. "A man has lost his life here. People are upset."

He knew it would make no difference to the way they treated everybody here, but he felt he had to say something. Imagine if poor Mike had stayed. Imagine this being the way his colleagues found out that he was gay.

"Well, I might have known it'd be something to do with *you*," Detective Simon Skinner's snivelling voice stopped Russell in his tracks and caused the two uniformed officers to bump into the back of him.

"Ah, Detective Skinner," Russell said, turning around to greet him, all fake charm and sarcasm. "How good of you to finally join us. I was just about to show your colleagues the crime scene. Would you care to tag along?"

Skinner scowled, and Russell saw Freddie turn away to hide his own snigger. He shouldn't wind the guy up, especially not in the circumstances, but he couldn't help himself.

"You," Skinner barked at PC Mills. "Stay here and start interviewing... witnesses. FatLad, you're with me."

The other uniformed policeman didn't seem too pleased with his nickname, but was happy at least to be chosen as Skinner's wingman. Russell realised that the core team working with Skinner to cover the Christmas period must all be a similar type to the snivelling detective himself—single, lazy and probably corrupt.

Feeling annoyed by them all, he turned and continued down the hallway, not waiting for Skinner. FatLad waited, though, and Russell was already at the door to the garden when they caught up.

"He's out here," Russell said. "We found him after he'd fallen."

"And who is the victim?" Skinner asked.

"He was a waiter. Kevin Flint."

"You had waiters?" Skinner asked, incredulously.

"*I* didn't," Russell replied. "Our host did."

Skinner looked blank.

"Nathan Bentley," Mills said, checking his notes.

"The TV presenter?" His tone of voice said Skinner was clearly not a fan.

"Correct," said Russell.

He saw the twitch of a sneer on Skinner's lip.

"So, what exactly were *you* doing here tonight?" Skinner asked, the emphasis on the word 'you' suggesting this wasn't the sort of place he'd have expected to find the likes of Russell.

"I was having dinner with a group of friends. It's Christmas Eve. It's what normal people do."

"*You're* friends with Nathan Bentley?"

"I'm friends with a lot of people," Russell said. "Unlike you."

"At least *my* friends don't go around killing each other," Skinner sniped.

"Neither do mine," Russell responded.

"Russ." It was Freddie's calm voice, standing in the door to the garden. "Why don't you let the Detective get on with his job?"

He held out his arm to escort Russell back inside.

"We'll be waiting in the front room, Detective. With the other *guests*. If you have any questions, I'll be happy for you to direct them through me."

There was no deference in the way Freddie spoke to Skinner, and Russell knew he was right—standing there exchanging unpleasantries wasn't going to help anyone.

Besides, he should try, at least, to have a word with everyone who had been upstairs when Kevin was killed, before Skinner started throwing his typically wild accusations around.

Only this time, Russell thought, *they may not be too wild.* Any of the people in the house right now—apart from Patty, Freddie, Joe, and Russell himself—could have killed Nathan. And no doubt Skinner would find a way to make the evidence fit whoever he needed it to, once he'd decided who the guilty party was.

He wondered how Joe was getting on talking to the others downstairs. Had he got any closer to figuring out what had happened to Kevin?

JOE AND ARMAND WERE HUDDLED into one of the alcoves off the new kitchen extension, speaking in whispers. Joe had already clocked Detective Skinner being led past by Russell and Freddie, but he'd managed to keep Armand on track of the confession he'd just made.

"You paid him to come here tonight? To cause trouble?" Joe asked, taking in what Armand had just told him.

Armand hung his head in shame.

"I'm not proud of it," he said, quietly. "But I mean, look at him. Archie's barely twenty-five, and Nathan's acting like it's love's young dream. It's pathetic."

"Because of the age gap? But Nathan's only forty, isn't he? It's hardly the end of the world."

"It's not just the age," Armand said, exasperated. "It's everything. He's just some boy from a small, backwater town, trying to get what he can take. I've seen his kind before. He doesn't love Nathan."

Joe felt himself bristling. Armand's judgement of Archie seemed a little harsh. Joe, too, had been a kid from a backwater town, arriving in London in his early twenties, wide-eyed and eager. It seemed like a lifetime away now and, sure, he'd changed a lot since settling in Soho, but he would always be a smalltown boy.

"So you paid Kevin to come here and try to break them up? How was that going to work?"

"Please don't tell Nathan," Armand whined. "Oh God! This is all my fault!"

"Calm down," Joe said. "Look, he works at Giuseppe's restaurant anyway, right? So, it's not completely out of the question that he'd be here tonight. Who else knows that you paid him?"

"No one."

"So why are you telling me?" Joe asked.

"Because I paid him with one of Nathan's cheques and the police will probably find it on him now, and blame Nathan."

Joe thought of the torn corner of a cheque they'd found in Kevin's fingers and wondered where the rest of it was now.

"What happened?" Joe asked, sensing there was more to come.

"He said it wasn't enough anymore. He said he knew things about Nathan and he would tell all unless we paid up."

"What did he know?" Joe asked.

"Private things," Armand said, shutting down the enquiry.

He looked at Joe, and Joe waited.

"He wouldn't let it go. So, I hit him. I only meant to scare him off."

"Hold on," Joe said, trying to understand the deluge of information Armand was dumping on him. "You killed Kevin?"

"No, I just hit him. He was fine. Well, he wasn't fine. But he was breathing. I checked. I'd just knocked him out. I didn't mean to. I had to protect Nathan. I went for help. When I came back, he was gone."

"You think he fell out of the window on his own?" Joe asked.

It was plausible, after all. Waking up, discombobulated, losing his balance and tumbling out of the window.

"He must have," Armand said. "I swear, he was on the floor when I left the room."

Joe shook his head.

"Right. Take me back to the beginning. Why was he even up here?" Joe asked.

Armand's shoulders slumped. He sighed.

"As soon as Nathan made his big declaration, I knew I'd made a mistake."

Joe let him speak. Armand's hand was shaking, but he seemed relieved to be unburdening himself.

"He followed me upstairs when I left the party. He thought it was all going to end soon, and he wanted his money. So, I wrote him a cheque and told him to go."

"But…" Joe prompted.

"But he refused. Said he was onto something here, and he could get a lot more than I was offering him."

"What did he mean by that?"

"I don't know. He kept saying that he knew who Nathan was. I don't know what he meant. I mean, we all know who Nathan is." Armand looked desperate. "I tried to tell him to go, but he walked straight into Nathan's study like he knew exactly where to go, and he walked right up to the safe. It was already open."

"So, he knew where to look?" Joe asked.

Either Kevin had been there before, or someone had told him where to go.

"It was as though he'd been here before."

"What's in the safe?" Joe asked.

"Cash," Armand said. "And documents. Nathan's private papers. He *never* leaves it open."

"And you didn't want Kevin stealing what was inside," Joe prompted. "So you hit him?"

"With the bloody BAFTA," Armand wailed.

"We're going to have to tell the police," Joe said. "You know that, don't you?"

Armand nodded, resigned.

"I didn't mean for him to die," he said. "I hit him, and then I panicked—I went for help. But I couldn't bring myself to tell Nathan what I'd done."

He heaved a great big, snotty sob.

"I paid that guy to try and ruin their relationship," he said, choking on the words.

Joe patted his shoulder, not really sure he should be standing here consoling Kevin's killer while the police were pouring over his body outside as they spoke.

"And Nathan's the only one I could've asked to help me. So, I had to come back to fix it myself. But he was already gone."

Joe suspected Armand was telling the truth, but he also knew that it wouldn't stop Skinner arresting him.

"It's my fault, isn't it?"

Armand flung himself desperately into Joe's arms.

"It's looking that way, Armand, yes," Joe said. "But listen, if you explain what happened like you have to me, I'm sure the police will see that you didn't mean it. It was an accident. You weren't even there when he fell."

"What a mess."

Joe couldn't disagree with him there.

"WHAT'S HAPPENING?" Nathan asked as Freddie herded Russell into the front room. "Are the police here?"

"Yes," Freddie said. "So, it would be a good idea if you lot just shut up and sat down for a moment. Throwing accusations at each other within earshot is not helping anything, is it? We could hear you from out there."

"Freddie's right," Russell said. "They won't need any excuses to arrest any one of you, so try your best to stay calm."

"But this is ridiculous," Grace protested. "We're just guests. We shouldn't have to stay"

"You're suspects," Freddie said. "All of you, unless any one of you can come up with a witness to where you were when Kevin fell from that window."

Nathan sagged back into his seat beside Archie. They all looked up as Joe came back into the room with Armand in tow, red faced and wet eyed.

"What have you two been up to?" Grace said, suspiciously.

"I need to talk to you," Joe said, taking Russell's hand and pulling him straight back out into the corridor.

"WHAT'S GOING ON?" Russell asked, looking over his shoulder to make sure they weren't being overheard by PC Mills or the larger chap who was now busy interviewing Giuseppe and the waiters, taking meticulous—but painfully slow—notes.

"It was Armand," Joe said. *No time to beat around the bush.*

"What?" Russell exclaimed, and then dropped to a whisper again. "What?"

"It's a bit of a long story. But Armand has just admitted hitting Kevin with Nathan's BAFTA award."

"Bloody hell," Russell said.

"I know," Joe agreed. "Problem is, he says he left him on the floor and went to get help, then chickened out of telling Nathan why he'd hit him and came back. But Kevin was already gone by then, so Armand assumed he hadn't been as badly hurt as he'd thought, and had done a runner while he still could."

"Bloody hell," said Russell again.

"What do we do?" Joe asked.

"Well, I mean… he has to tell that lot," Russell nodded towards the garden where Skinner was still examining the body.

"I know," Joe said. "And he will."

"Why did he do it?" Russell asked.

"He says he paid the guy to stir things up between Nathan and Archie. Kevin was a friend of Archie's from the restaurant. Anyway, apparently the kid refused the money—said he knew Nathan's secret and threatened to tell all. Armand hit him to shut him up, but then realised he have to tell Nathan what he'd done."

"Sure, but…"

55

"Look, Armand said he was still breathing when he left him to go and get help and when he got back Kevin was gone. Do you think he could have woken up and just stumbled out of the window?"

"No," Russell said, definitively.

"But…"

"Joe, the window was closed, remember? So, unless he closed it behind him on the way out, which seems impossible, it looks like Armand's not been telling the whole truth."

"But why tell me anything at all, then?" Joe asked. "It's not like we had any idea what had happened, was it? Why would he tell me most of the story, but not the bit where he threw him out the window?"

Russell paced away from him to the bottom of the stairs and back again, looking over Joe's shoulder to the garden door, where Skinner was just coming back in.

"Because *he* didn't throw him out of the window," Russell whispered. "Someone else did."

"But who?"

"I don't know. Shh."

DETECTIVE SIMON SKINNER strode into the front room with the confidence of a man who knew exactly what had happened that evening and who was to blame.

"Nathan Bentley?" he asked, looking around all of them as though he didn't even know who the celebrity presenter was.

Joe and Russell sidled back into the room, their conversation unfinished, but both keen to see what would unfold.

"That's me," Nathan said defiantly, dropping Archie's hand and standing up.

"Nathan Bentley, I'm arresting you on suspicion of the murder of Kevin Flint…"

The uproar that followed from Nathan's nearest and dearest drowned out the rest of Skinner's spiel. Mills and the FatLad ignored the protests and stepped in, slapping the cuffs roughly on Nathan's wrists, enjoying the opportunity to manhandle a celebrity.

"On what grounds?" Freddie thundered.

Skinner stopped dead and looked Freddie up and down. Resentment coupled with delight that they were, yet again, at loggerheads. Nathan wasn't the first of Freddie's clients Skinner had falsely arrested, and on top of that Skinner had tried to catch him out with exactly the same sting that had seen Russell lose his job.

"You're his lawyer, I suppose?" Skinner said, smiling disingenuously.

"Correct," Freddie said. "Can you tell my client the grounds for his arrest?"

"I have it on good authority from the victim's colleagues, that he had been seen having some sort of argument with Mr Bentley earlier in the evening." Skinner said. "Apparently, it looked personal."

"That's nonsense," Grace said. "We've never seen that boy before, have we, my love?"

Russell saw the frown of confusion cross Skinner's face.

"Shut up, Grace," Nathan said.

"Nathan?" Archie asked the question just with his name. *Did you sleep with him?*

Nathan shook his head.

"It's not what you think."

"Don't say any more, Nathan," Freddie warned.

Archie stood up and tried to run out of the room, but Skinner stuck out an arm and stopped him.

"Not so fast, lad," he said. "Where d'you think you're going?"

"Get off me," Archie said, pushing him out of the way.

Skinner was quick as a shot. Archie's arm was up behind his back and he was screaming in pain.

"Take this one in too," Skinner said, thrusting him towards Mills, who let go of Nathan and caught Archie in both hands. "Trying to flee the scene."

"Now hang on a minute," Russell said. "Neither of these men had anything to do with it."

"And how would you know that?" Skinner sneered. "Something you want to tell me?"

Russell looked at Armand, who could barely scrape his gaze from the floor. He brought his eyes up to meet Joe's. Joe nodded his encouragement.

"It was me," Armand, said quietly. "I hit him."

If the earlier outrage had been enough to drown out Skinner's caution, what came now went through the roof. Even Grace looked like she was going to jump to Armand's defence, before clearly realising that would obviously get her arrested too, the way this was going.

"Take him away boys," Skinner said.

Mills and his large companion began releasing the cuffs on Nathan's wrists.

"No, no," Skinner said, realising what they were doing. "Take them too. And anyone else who fancies a go."

Russell stepped between them and Armand.

"Don't be an idiot, man," Russell said to Skinner, unable to keep the anger from his voice. "You can't arrest everyone. This is ridiculous."

He had been this man's superior once, and Joe knew he hadn't rated his talents back then. Everything Skinner had done since getting Russell suspended from the force had seemed to focus only on targeting the various misfits in the Soho community that Russell and Joe had grown to love. It was as though he had some personal vendetta against anyone that ever came into contact with Russell.

"We've got a dead body outside," Skinner snarled. "In case you forgot. I should arrest all of you."

The threat made. Russell couldn't resist. He wasn't going to be able to help any of them from the outside anyway, he needed to know what had happened between Nathan and Kevin, and Archie and Kevin, and the only way he could find out was by talking to them.

"Then you'll have to arrest me too," he said, blocking the door so that they couldn't get past.

"Really, Mr Dixon?" Skinner always made a point of stressing the "Mister", reminding Russell that he was no longer a detective. "And what did *you* have to do with it?"

Russell stared at him defiantly.

"As much as any of these three did," Russell said. "Why don't you just try doing your job *properly*, for once?"

"Very well," Skinner said. "Arrest this man too will you boys."

"Oi, get off him you arsewipe!"

This time it was Patty's turn to have a go, coming out of the kitchen having clearly hidden some of the cocaine up her nose. She strode towards Skinner—as much as a drag queen on a rising high *could* stride in those heels—finger raised like an old schoolmistress about to give him a telling off.

"And arrest...*that* too, would you?"

The disdain in Skinner's voice as he refused to give Patty her pronoun made her lunge for him. Mills grabbed her just before she could do too much damage, but she did manage to rake a nail across Skinner's cheek, instantly drawing blood.

"I'll arrest the lot of you if I have to," Skinner shouted, dabbing at his cheek nervously.

"I hope you don't catch something, love." Patty sneered, right up in his face as she was roughly marched past with her hands now being cuffed behind her back.

"I think I broke a nail," she said in passing to an anxious looking Freddie.

"You're making a mistake, Skinner," Freddie said.

"Oh really?" Skinner smirked. "Prove it."

"He's right. You shouldn't do it like this, boss."

They all looked up, surprised to find Mike filling the frame of the front door. Still not in uniform, but he'd obviously been home to change from his party clothes.

"What are you doing here?" Skinner spat, echoing Joe's internal question.

"I heard the call, and I wasn't far away, Sir," he said. "I thought I'd see if you needed a hand."

Nathan looked like he was about to say something, but Freddie stepped in quickly before his client could reveal that the young officer had also been one of the guests there tonight.

"If you arrest these men," Freddie said. "I'll make sure you lose your badge."

"Oh," Skinner laughed. "What? Like you've been trying to do for the past six months without any luck. You forget which one of us is on the inside."

"Not forever," Freddie snarled.

"Right, you," Skinner said, turning his attention back to Mike. "Give me a hand getting this lot down to the station."

With that, he turned and stalked out of the front door, leaving his minions to do the dirty work of herding the suspects out of the house.

"What the hell are you doing here?" Russell asked quietly as he was shepherded towards the front door.

"I figured I'd be more help here than at home," Mike whispered. He was probably right. They would need all the help they could get with Skinner's men tonight, especially once he got them all down to the station.

The larger of the two other policemen was still trying to wrestle Patty out of the door. Mike did his best to block their path.

"Out of the way, officer, please," Skinner called back. "Help the FatLad with …" he waved a dismissive hand in Patty's direction.

"Would it not be better, sir, to question these people here? The nick's already pretty full."

Russell saw what he was trying to do—once they got to the station, they would all be split up and there was no telling what Skinner's lads would do to them to get a confession. Certainly, Nathan wouldn't cope well with any kind of rough treatment. He was far too precious for dirty cells and open plan toilet facilities.

"I'll thank you to do as you're told," Skinner said, stepping right up to Mike, chest to chest. Mike held his ground.

"Yes, Sir. But why are you arresting all of them, Sir? Surely only one could have done it?"

The disingenuous tone skimmed straight over Skinner's head.

"Leave it Mike," Joe said. "He's not worth it."

Skinner cocked his head, smirking again.

"Oh, *Mike* is it?"

Russell cringed. *Oh Joe! What have you done?*

"Friend of yours, officer?"

Mike flushed, stammered, came up with nothing. He wasn't going to deny Joe, at least. But it was all out now.

"I should have known," Skinner said, curling his lip as though he'd just chewed on a lemon. "I don't think we'll be needing *your* assistance tonight. I'll send a couple of real men to deal with the coroner and the corpse. You can consider yourself suspended, pending further enquiry. No officer on my team consorts with these kinds of perverts and reprobates."

And with that Skinner turned and followed the two officers shuffling Russell, Nathan, Archie, Armand and Patty all into the back of the waiting police van.

Hands on hips, Skinner watched as they were bundled inside. With Joe, Mike and Freddie standing in the doorway, they were driven off in a wail of unnecessary sirens and wheel spin, flanked by Skinner's squad car.

"I'm so sorry, Mike…" Joe began.

"Doesn't matter," Mike said, forcing a smile. But it clearly did.

FREDDIE TURNED BACK, closing the door behind him in a show of calm, though Joe could see that he was anything but. Joe took Mike's hand, feeling him still trembling. He felt terrible for outing him like that. What a stupid thing to have done. He was surprised when Mike turned to him, squeezed his hand reassuringly and smiled a tight smile.

"I need to talk to the DCI," Mike said, quietly.

"It's Christmas Eve," Freddie said. "I doubt he'll thank you for interrupting his family time."

"I think he would want to know who Skinner's just arrested, and why," Mike said with a dark smile.

"What's going on, Mike?" Joe asked. He recognised that look and it usually meant Mike was up to something.

"I've been feeding him reports on Skinner's behaviour. I went to see him when we started going out. I told him about me being gay, I said I was friends with Russell, and I also told him I was scared of what Skinner and his mates would do if they found out."

"Wow," Freddie said. "That was brave. Well done."

"It wasn't easy, but he was actually great about it. Russell had told me the Chief had been as sympathetic as he could have been when his own situation arose, and the force can't afford too many more scandals on this front. So I sort of made it clear that if I was hounded out like Russell had been, I would go public with my experiences on the force."

"Why didn't you say something earlier?" Joe asked. "Why did you argue when we told you to leave?"

"Because you were right. It would have done me no good them finding me here when they arrived, but also I needed to go home and get my kit," he said, waving a small Dictaphone. "I've been recording all the little snipes, the barbed comments, the insults. If you hadn't tipped him off, I could have been in the car with him now, and the things he'd have said would've been gold. I'm sure of it."

"I'm sorry," Joe said. "I wish you'd told me."

"You'd have only told me not to risk it, wouldn't you?"

"Usually, yes, but if you have the boss's backing and it means you might stop Skinner once and for all, I'd have helped. Hell, I'd even have put myself on the line for it and got arrested just to help you."

"Well, in that case, I'm glad I didn't tell you. He may have treated Russell appallingly, but you should see how he treats the gays that aren't in the police force. He's come close to killing a kid with one of his beatings."

"Jesus," Freddie said. "How does he still have a job?"

"Because no one on the inside will grass him up, and no one on the receiving end will file a complaint because they know they'll be shut down. It's awful."

"Speaking of which," Freddie said. "I need to get down there, pronto. The mood Russell was in he could kick off at any point, and I can't imagine either Nathan nor Armand dealing well with the cells."

"You think you can get them out?"

"Everyone apart from Armand, I reckon," Freddie said. "You can't beat an outright confession."

"Except he didn't kill him," Joe said.

"But he said he did," Freddie replied, looking confused.

"He said he hit him," Joe corrected. "He found him trying to steal from the safe in the study, hit him, left him on the floor and went for help."

"So?" Mike said. "What? He just fell out the window?"

"Well, there's the catch," Joe said. "The window was closed when we found him."

"Maybe one of them saw it open as they passed, and pulled it closed." Mike said, ever the rationalist.

"Or maybe the killer closed it after they pushed Archie out the window. We'll have to wait for the coroner, of course, but Russell was fairly sure he wouldn't have recovered from that initial head wound quickly enough to stand up, let alone open the window and walk out."

"But he would have recovered?" Freddie asked. "If he hadn't fallen out of the window?"

"Again, that's for the coroner to say," said Joe. "But Russell seemed to think so. It looks like someone found him and tipped him out of the window while he was still unconscious."

"God, why?"

"I don't know," Joe said. "But Armand also told me that he dropped the award he'd used to hit Kevin straight away and left it in the study. Yet when Russell went into the room, there was no sign of it."

"So where is it?" Mike asked.

"Well, you're the cop," Joe said, with a smile. "Why not see if you can find it?"

RUSSELL HAD DONE MORE than enough Christmas Eve shifts in his time to know what a state the holding cells down at the station would be like tonight. He hadn't been wrong. The main cells were full of people already processed and there for the night, leaving only the pen they used to keep offenders in while they were waiting for more cell space to open up or interviews to be conducted.

This was a good thing, Russell thought. The idea of any of them being alone in a cell with any of Skinner's goons was chilling. Better to be out here with the rest of the rabble. At least there'd be witnesses to any assaults.

The pen was an open cell, crammed full of drunkards and miscreants, with Russell, Nathan, Archie, Armand and Patty now among their number. Nowhere near as romantic as The Pogues would have had it— the was no police choir for starters—but the cell was certainly filled with scumbags and maggots and, if the toothless tramp in the corner was to be believed, cheap lousy faggots.

A quick "Shut yer pie hole" from Patty—still head to toe glamour— had silenced any commentary from the old tramp on their arrival. She may be a pretty thing, but there was no doubting she could have that stiletto off and in your eye before you could ask her how much she charged.

Speaking of which—a couple of prostitutes that Russell recognised from the block were sitting together in the other corner, probably grateful to be off the streets for the night in those skimpy outfits. One had a thick lip and a trail of blood on her top while the other had a look of utter boredom on her face.

They shuffled to make room for the newcomers, but only Russell sat down. He saw the appalled look of horror on Nathan's face that he was being forced to share close quarters with the tramps and vagabonds, whores and hedonists of Soho.

Russell didn't mind, they were probably all equally innocent of whatever they'd been charged with tonight anyway. That's how it always was on Christmas Eve—get them off the streets and deal with them in the morning.

"Alright Trish?" Russell said as he sat down beside her with a weary sigh.

"Oh, alright detective?" Trish replied, after peering at him for a moment, her broad grin revealing her bad teeth. She was the one without the bloody lip. "I didn't recognise you on the wrong side of the bars."

"Not a detective any more, Trish," said Russell.

"Well, no shit love," Trish smiled. "This is hardly a social club, is it?"

"Oh, I don't know," said Russell. "Christmas Eve in the drunk tank, and all that."

"Don't you start," Trish said. "Bloody Christmas. Makes everyone think they're entitled to a freebie."

"Get into a bit of trouble, did you?"

"Not me," Trish said proudly. "Bunch of lads thought our Janet here owed them a free kiss under the mistletoe. Didn't like it so much when she said no. Good job I was there, wasn't it, Jan?"

Janet barely raised her head for the nod. Her lips was cut as well as swollen and she would have a nice black eye in the morning. She was lucky, Russell thought. Good old Trish was always getting herself arrested wading in to protect her friends. She loved a good fight, but her fierce loyalty for the girls on the street went beyond the rough and tumble of Soho life. They were like her children, and she wouldn't think twice about castrating anyone that tried to hurt them.

"Yeah, saved her bloody neck, I did," Trish continued, "and this is the thanks I get."

"I said thanks," Janet mumbled through her swollen lip.

"Not you, love," said Trish, patting her hand. "Those divots out there, arresting an honest woman just for helping them do their job. Anyway, enough about me. What happened to you then? I thought I hadn't seen you around. Just figured you'd finally got a comfy desk job. So how did you go from top brass to brassic and in here with the rest of us?"

She turned to face Russell full on. He was not going to get out of this interrogation. The first time she'd seen him since he'd left the force, and it had to be on a night like tonight.

"It's a long story," Russell admitted. "Safe to say, I didn't always see eye to eye with my colleagues."

"I'm not surprised," said Trish, raising her voice as the duty sergeant put down the phone and looked up. "Bunch of wankers!"

She waved the appropriate hand gesture at him, and Russell smiled. She wasn't wrong, for the most part.

"What they bring you in for then?" Trish asked, obviously enjoying her new-found friendship.

"A friend of ours died earlier," Russell said, quietly, keeping his voice low enough that only Trish could hear. He didn't want to upset either Nathan or Archie again.

"Murder?" she whispered, thankfully sensing his need for discretion. "Bloody hell fire."

She leaned back, appraising him for a moment, before looking at Nathan and Archie deep in their conversation, Armand crouched on a bench in a deep malaise and Patty at the bars adjusting her boobs and trying to cajole the desk sergeant into letting her wait on the outside.

"Wait," she said, cautiously, leaning away further. "You didn't...?"

"Oh God, no!" Russell shook his head vigorously.

"But one of *them* did, right?"

She looked wide-eyed with interest.

"Who knows?" Russell said. "Maybe he just fell."

She looked at him for a moment, before her face creased into a big grin.

"Oh," she said. "That kind of party, was it? I have to say, detective, I never had you pegged for substance abuse."

"I am not a detective," Russell reminded her, "And you are right about the substances."

"So, why did you get nicked then?" she asked.

"Detective Skinner was the arresting officer," Russell said, and by the way Trish rolled her eyes, he knew she understood what he meant.

"That bastard," she said. "You know he nearly killed our Candice with that beating he gave her. She still can't walk right, and that's nothing to do with the op."

"Candice?" Russell asked. The name was distantly familiar.

"You'll have known her as Carl in your time," Trisha said. "She finished transitioning last year. Skinny bitch. Beauty spot just here." She tapped her cheek just under her right eye.

"Oh yeah," Russell said, remembering. "Candice? I thought she'd settled on Carla?"

"Nah, she said it wasn't glamorous enough, besides, people just kept on shortening it to Carl, so she changed it to Candice. Candy to her friends. Fair enough. She deserved to get as far away from her old name as she wanted. Especially with *her* parents."

Trisha sighed and leaned back against the wall, stretching her neck until it clicked.

"She had a boyfriend and everything, you know? She'd properly cleaned up her act. She'd even stopped being on the game. But that weaselly little dickwad recognised her. He stitched her up, arrested her and then beat her so bad in the cells that she couldn't see. All that money on her face, and then he goes and smashes it up anyway. Bastard."

"Jesus," Russell said. "Did she report it?"

Trish laughed bitterly. "What would be the point in that?"

"Bring her to see me, will you? In the Red Lion. We have to stop him. This can't go on."

"If you're buying, love, count me in. You really think you can do something about him?"

"Oh," Russell said, smiling. "I *know* I can. Better yet, we can all do it together."

"I always liked you," Trish said, smiling back at him and patting his knee maternally. "Force could do with a few more like you."

"Hello?" Patty called angrily through the bars. "Some of us need to pee in here."

"Tie a knot in it, mate" the duty sergeant said tersely, turning his back on the pen.

"I've got your number, fella," Patty shouted. "This is a violation of my human rights."

"What's up with old Tinkerbell over there?" Trisha asked.

"Patty? Oh, she just likes winding people up. She's alright. Besides, I think she's supposed to be an ice queen."

"Huh. And isn't he that fella off the telly?" asked Trish, nodding exaggeratedly towards Nathan.

"Yes," Russell said.

Even if Nathan got released without charge—which wasn't looking likely with Skinner in charge—this would do his career hideous damage. The TV viewing public had tolerated his open sexuality because he was funny and he hosted inane and family friendly shows.

Once it got out that a young man had been murdered at a party he'd hosted, the tabloid press would have a field day. Either way, Nathan was probably about to find the Great British public far less accommodating.

Looking at Nathan, standing alone in the corner, head bowed in muttered conversation with Armand, not protesting his innocence or bemoaning his wrongful detainment like Archie and Patty were, Russell figured that the TV star had already guessed as much.

"And this lot are all mates of yours?" Trisha sounded both impressed and incredulous. "I wouldn't have thought you had it in you. How the hell did you ever work with *that* twat?"

He knew she was talking about Skinner, even without following her gaze to see him stride up to the duty sergeant and mutter something to him. The guy looked uncomfortable until Skinner disappeared again. Russell wasn't surprised. He may wield some power, but Skinner wasn't particularly well liked among his co-workers.

"I avoided him most of the time," Russell admitted.

"Must have been one hell of a party. Someone was murdered you say?"

"Shh," Russell warned, glancing at Nathan. "It's sensitive."

"Murder usually is, love. So, what happened?"

"Patricia McCarthy!" the duty sergeant called out.

"Sorry, love," she said apologetically to Russell, standing up. Her tone had changed by the time she snarled her "Yeah?" at the duty sergeant.

"Your brief's here. We're ready for you."

A young kid in uniform that Russell didn't recognise opened the pen door for her to step out. He must be very newly qualified to pull this shift. He couldn't even make eye contact with Trisha, who was one of the easiest people to get along with that Russell had ever met.

"Sit tight, Jan," Trisha called over her shoulder as she followed the young officer. "We'll be out of here in no time."

Russell liked her confidence. The door had barely closed when Nathan slipped into the gap that Trisha had left.

"What the hell are we going to do?" he asked, urgently.

"Don't worry," Russell said. "This is all just bluster. Freddie will be here in a moment and we'll all be out."

"All?" Nathan asked incredulously. "Didn't you hear Armie? He said he hit him.

"Hmm," Russell said. "I did hear that. But I don't think that he killed him. What was he doing up in your study, Nathan?"

"How should I know?"

"Armand said the safe was already open. Did you leave it open? Because he's sure it's only the two of you with the code, and he knows he didn't leave it open."

"Well, he's lied about everything else, hasn't he?" Nathan said.

"Don't be stupid," Russell snapped. "He was trying to protect you."

"He just told me he paid that waiter to try and get between me and Archie. Can you believe it? How is that protecting me?"

"He loves you Nathan," Russell said.

Russell didn't know why he was defending Armand, other than because he felt sorry for the guy and hated seeing how manipulated he was by Nathan's ebb and flow approach to their relationship.

"Yeah, well that's always been his problem—he has never been able to accept that I've moved on."

"He only hit the kid over the head to stop him finding out your secrets."

Russell turned to look at him with such a frightened expression it made Russell recoil slightly.

"I saw what was in the safe, Nathan. "The photos of you, the money, your manuscript. Armand wanted to protect you. He knew the kid was a thief."

"You shouldn't have been looking in there," Nathan snapped.

"I was trying to find out what happened," Russell said.

"Nonsense. You were snooping. Just like everyone else. What did you think? That the killer had left a confession in the safe?"

"No, but I thought I might find the rest of the cheque that had been torn out of his hands. Or a clue as to what he'd been looking for in that safe. Why was it open, Nathan?"

"I don't know!" Nathan was quick to anger. God help him when Skinner started in on him.

"Who else knows the combination?"

"No one," Nathan said, but Russell could already see that wasn't true.

"Could anyone have seen it without you realising?"

Nathan looked across at Armand, and then at Archie. He knew. Russell knew. Nathan's shoulders slumped.

"Wait here," Russell said, but he knew he wouldn't get long alone with Archie before Nathan flipped.

JOE OPENED THE DOOR to find another disgruntled looking policeman standing in front of Harry Palin, the forensic officer—a man Joe knew had been one of Russell's few friends on the force. The policeman held his badge out.

"PC Riley," he said. "And you are?"

"Joe Stone. Come in."

Harry Palin followed the officer in, introducing himself more politely. He also ushered in a young woman who seemed to be carrying the bulk of the forensic equipment.

"This is Claire Goldman, my assistant. So, what have we got?"

Joe smiled his greeting as he closed the front door.

"Young guy called Kevin Flint," Joe said, leading them towards the kitchen and courtyard. "Looks like he fell from the window, but he was hit before he fell, with one of the host's television awards, by all accounts."

"Very impressive," Harry said, admiringly. "Are you sure you need me here? How did you figure all this out?"

Joe grinned.

"Our host's assistant has already admitted to hitting him, but denies throwing him out of the window."

"Bloody hell," Harry said.

"How long are we going to have to hang around here?" Giuseppe asked as they filed through the kitchen where he and his waiters were still waiting. Grace had joined them now, having been unable to sit alone in the front room. She was leaning against the counter in the corner, a cigarette dangling from her mouth and a champagne glass in her hand.

"Until I've interviewed everyone," PC Riley said curtly.

"Why don't you make a start on that then officer, I'm sure Claire and I will be fine on our own with the body."

PC Riley actually seemed a little disappointed to be dismissed, but he hung back, taking out his notepad and pen.

"Since you're so keen to go," he said to Giuseppe. "Why don't I start with you? Name?"

"I've already told your colleagues everything," Giuseppe complained.

Joe opened the door to the courtyard and stepped out, holding the door open for the others to pass. He saw the look of disdain for PC Riley that passed between the two of them and smiled.

"You're Russell's friend, aren't you?" Harry asked as the door closed.

"Yes," Joe said, smiling.

"I thought I recognised you."

Harry had been the forensic officer in charge of a case Joe and Russell had solved last year involving the death of an A-list Pop group's manager.

"How's Russ doing?" Harry asked.

"He's good," Joe replied. "Same old Russell. He was here earlier but managed to get himself arrested."

Harry chortled.

"Skinner by any chance?"

"Who else?"

"What a fool," Harry said. "Well, I hope he gets out soon, because he still owes me a drink."

As they set to work on the crime scene, Joe stood back and watched them, fascinated. The last time he'd seen Harry, the guy had offered him a job. He wondered whether it was too late to retrain? He did have a good eye for detail, but science had never been his strong point.

They hadn't been out there long when Mike stuck his head out of an upstairs window. He was in the room next to the study.

"Joe! Come and look at this," he said. "Oh, hello, Dr Palin. You'd better come too."

Harry left Claire examining the body and followed Joe back into the house. They didn't linger in the kitchen, where PC Riley seemed to be working his way through the same series of questions with the other waiters. They all looked bored and resentful.

They took the stairs quickly, Harry panting a little as they reached the top. Mike was standing in the corridor, outside the master bedroom.

"What is it?" Joe asked.

"I found the award," Mike said. "In here. Don't worry, I haven't moved it."

"Good lad," Harry smiled.

The followed Mike into the master bedroom, and peered down into the dark leather holdall nestled just inside the door. Sure enough, the unmistakable gold mask of a BAFTA award was partly covered by some clothes.

"It's Archie's bag," Mike said, pointing to the initials embossed into the leather.

"Oh God," Joe said.

"Who is Archie?" Harry asked.

"This is Nathan Bentley's house," Joe explained. "Archie is his new boyfriend. There was a bit of friction earlier when Nathan proposed to Archie. The whole party went into melt down. That was just before Kevin died."

"Proposed?" Harry asked, looking confused.

"Well, as good as," Mike said. "He'd drawn a contract up giving Archie the equivalent of spousal rights."

"And this Archie turned him down?"

"He didn't get the chance," Joe said. "It all kicked off with Nathan's ex-wife and his assistant. The whole thing descended into a screaming match and they all went off to different parts of the house in a sulk."

"And the assistant, Armand was it? He was the one who hit this kid."

"So he says," Joe said. "But he swore that Kevin was breathing when he left him in the study. He had decided to go and get help, but had then chickened out of admitting what he'd done. So, he'd hidden in his room instead."

"Do you think he slipped the weapon into Archie's bag?"

"Why would he? And why admit hitting him but not killing him? He swears he dropped the award after Kevin hit the floor. He also swears he left him there. And I think I believe him."

"So, someone else came in and moved the statue, and helped young Kevin out of the window?" Harry asked.

"Well, the window was closed when Russell went into the study to see what had happened. And no one else is admitting to closing it. So I think poor Armand might be about to take the fall for the whole thing."

"What about Archie? Is he the kind to have turfed an unconscious waiter out of the window?"

"Well, he did know Kevin," Joe said. "And there seemed to be a bit of tension between them. Perhaps there was something deeper going on there."

"We're going to have to let the police know we've found the potential murder weapon," Harry said. "If they've got people in custody already, this could affect their statements."

"I'll go," Mike said.

"Are you sure?" Joe asked.

"As good an excuse as any to get in there and see what Skinner's up to."

Joe gave Mike a slightly cautionary glance. He knew Harry Palin was an ally, with little time for Detective Skinner, but he didn't think too many people should know what Mike had been doing for the boss. Just in case. Harry hadn't seemed to notice.

"I'll get it processed, bagged up and sealed, you can take it in as evidence," said Harry decisively.

ARCHIE LOOKED UP as Russell sat beside him. He looked like a broken man. His leg was jittering and his fingers drummed repetitively on his knees. Dark rings hung under his red rimmed eyes. Either this was a horrible come down, or he was hiding something. Probably both.

"How're you holding up? Russell asked him.

Archie shrugged and shook his head. *Not good.*

"Tell me about Kevin, Archie."

Archie studied his hands. He was going to need coaxing.

"Well, you took your time," Patty said loudly, and Russell looked up to see a harassed looking Freddie checking in at the desk. He approached the bars, and Russell gave him a look that he hoped said "Give me a minute…"

No need to ask, though—Nathan was up and at the bars, immediately demanding information as soon as he saw Freddie approaching.

"You knew him more than you're letting on, didn't you?" Russell asked, quietly, while everyone else was distracted with Freddie.

Archie nodded. Russell waited.

"We've worked scams together for years," Archie said. "Since we were in sixth form."

"Scams?"

"Con jobs," Archie said. It was all going to come out now. "It started when we were kids."

"You've been running a con on Nathan?"

"No! No. Well…" Archie shook his head again. "In the beginning I thought we could make a score, but that was before I got talking to Nathan properly."

"Go on."

"Well, it's obvious, isn't it? I mean, he's a rich celebrity with a fragile ego. You could see straight off the bat he just wanted someone to fancy him. And when you're getting the champagne and caviar lifestyle, it wouldn't be hard to pretend for a while, would it?"

Russell felt another pang of sympathy for Nathan.

"So, you played him?" Russell said. "And very well, by all accounts. That contract he presented you with pretty much gives you the world."

"I didn't know he was going to do that, I swear," Archie said. "And I wasn't playing him, actually. Like I said, as soon as I got to know him, I called the con off. You can believe me or not, it doesn't really matter now, but we got talking and I realised he was just a normal bloke, underneath it all. Then I realised he was from our manor, out East. He was from the next village originally, but he did is teens in our town. You don't know what it's like to find someone who grew up where you did, and made it out and made it big. Especially not someone who's gay. You know?"

As it turned out, Russell did know.

"As I said to you earlier," Russell reminded him. "We all come from somewhere."

73

Archie sighed.

"I've messed it up, haven't I?" he said.

Russell didn't see the need to answer.

"I never knew Kev was going to pitch up as a waiter. As soon as Nate and I got serious, I told him the con was off. I gave him a grand—most of my savings—and I told him to drop it. Then he turns up tonight, pretending it's just a waiting job. And I knew he was up to something. I've known him all my life. I know when he's up to something. I was scared he was going to tell Nate who I really am."

Was he confessing to killing the kid? Russell was confused. He was sure that Armand was telling the truth when he said he'd been the one to hit him. Had Archie found his prone body in front of the safe, Nathan's cheque in his hand? Had he been the one to push Kevin out of the window?

"So, what happened?" Russell asked. "You found him unconscious on the floor and thought you'd finish him off for good?"

"What? No! He was one of my best mates."

Russell waited.

"He said he knew something about Nathan," Archie said. "Something big. He wanted to see how much he could get to stay quiet."

"What did he know?" Russell asked, already suspecting part of it.

"He wouldn't say. But…"

Russell waited again, sensing that this could be key to figuring out what had happened to Kevin. Archie looked at him.

"I'd figured out what the code for the safe was, and I knew there was a stack of cash in it. I told him I'd leave it open and he could help himself and go, and that would be the end of it. I didn't know that Armand would catch him, or react the way he did. But I was downstairs the whole time, I swear it. I didn't kill him."

There was a disturbance out at the front desk and Russell looked up to see Mike talking to the duty sergeant. He looked like he'd been running. Freddie turned away from Nathan at the bars and Russell got up to join them. This looked important.

Having spoken to the guy on the desk, Mike hurried over to them. The bars meant they couldn't keep Nathan, Armand or Patty out of earshot

"We found where the statue was stashed," Mike said, looking from Freddie to Russell. Nathan and Armand were also at the bars. Only Archie didn't move.

"Well?" Nathan asked.

"In Archie's holdall, in the master bedroom."

Archie dropped his head into his hands. Nathan turned on him. Armand looked completely confused.

"What did you do?" Nathan roared, lunging for Archie's throat.

Patty was the only one quick enough to step in and stop him strangling the kid. Russell was shortly behind, pulling Nathan back while Archie protested his innocence.

There was a brief moment where Armand and Archie stood side by side, with Nathan being held back from both of them.

"I hope you're proud of yourselves," Nathan said, with a bitterness that Russell for once thought was justified. "You were all supposed to be on my side."

"Archie Mitchell?"

It was Skinner, calling him up to be interviewed, of course. The desk sergeant had already called through the new evidence Mike had brought in, and Skinner would have seen a shoe-in for an easy conviction.

As he waited for the sergeant to open the gate to the pen and let Archie out, Skinner clocked Mike talking to Freddie and Russell.

"What are you doing here?" he asked, his voice more aggressive than necessary. The speed he approached with also spoke of a barely contained rage. Mike squared his shoulders. Freddie put an arm out to stop Skinner reaching him.

"New evidence was found at the house, Sir, as you know. I was still there. I volunteered to bring it in."

Russell admired how calm Mike had remained—he must know what damage to his career this would be doing.

"I'll re-phrase," Skinner said, slowly, through clenched teeth. "What are you *still* doing here?"

"I work here, Sir," Mike beamed.

Russell got the sense he was deliberately winding his superior up. He noticed that Mike nudged Freddie gently aside, clearing the way to Skinner. What was he playing at?

"Not for much longer, you hairy poof," Skinner snapped.

"I'm sorry, Sir?" Mike said, innocently. "What was that you just said?"

Skinner stepped up to him, face right in Mike's.

"You heard me," he snarled. "We don't like shirt-lifters on this team. Ask your mate, here."

His nod towards Russell made Freddie clearly bristle. Again, Russell noticed Mike nudge Freddie's hand to keep him back. He was definitely up to something.

Mike leaned in to Skinner and whispered something into his ear that none of the rest of them heard. Russell didn't need to hear. He'd seen Skinner's face change like that before, and it never ended well.

Sure enough, Skinner took a step back and swung, spinning Mike almost off his feet as the punch connected with his jaw. Freddie immediately tried to stop Skinner, but was pushed back against the bars as Skinner swooped in to land another punch.

Mike went down to howls of protest from those both in and out of the cells. Skinner moved in again, foot raised, but only managed to get one kick in before Mike's hand shot in the air, a black plastic Dictaphone held high for Skinner to see.

Skinner tried to grab it, but this time Freddie managed to pull him back, pushing him hard against the bars of the pen.

"You have just assaulted a police officer—a subordinate—in front of multiple witnesses," Freddie pointed out, finally giving Skinner pause to think about what he'd just done.

Mike stood up, dusting himself down and gingerly testing his jaw where the punches had landed. He clicked off the Dictaphone dramatically right by Skinner's face.

"Touch a nerve there, did I, Sir?" he asked, facetiously. "You know, you only had to ask…"

Before Skinner could go for him again, Mike turned and headed down the corridor to the station offices, waving the Dictaphone over his shoulder.

Skinner turned to the sergeant who still had Archie by the arm.

"Well come on then," he hollered. "We haven't got all day."

Freddie turned back to Russell with a look of bemused confusion. Russell grinned back.

"What was that?"

"I think our boy Mike is just about to put another nail in Skinner's coffin."

"I bloody hope so," Freddie said.

"Right, well, I don't see how any of this helps me," Nathan said, bitterly. "How quickly do you think you can get me out of here?"

"Shouldn't be long," Freddie said. "They haven't really got grounds to hold you."

Nathan slumped against the bars.

"Not unless Archie tells them what he knows," he sighed.

"What are you talking about?" Freddie said, looking worried.

"I thought I could trust him," Nathan said. "I honestly thought he was the one."

"Okay," Russell said. "Putting that aside, does he know something that can incriminate you?"

"I don't know. But if he was closer to that kid than he was letting on, then yes."

"Tell me," Freddie said.

"I suppose it's all going to come out now anyway," Nathan said, turning to Russell with a look of abject resignation. "Even *you* said you saw the papers in my safe."

"Your autobiography?" Russell was confused.

"No, the bundle of papers that arrived in the post earlier in the week. The newspaper articles, family photos, all the stuff you saw. They were sent by that waiter. Kevin."

"What?" Freddie asked. "What papers?"

Nathan sighed deeply.

"Yes. Apparently, he and Archie were mates from school. When we got together, and Kevin challenged him about going with an older guy, Archie happened to mention that I had spent a bit of my childhood in the same town, and good old Kevin asked his parents if they knew that I was a local boy."

"So?" Freddie asked, still playing catch up. "Why is that such a bad thing?"

"Because his parents, apparently, got the old scrap book out and filled him in on all the sordid details of my childhood."

"I'm sorry Nathan," said Freddie, still looking confused. "You're going to have to spell it out for me."

Russell's mind was whirring—those photographs, the copies of the newspapers… the happy young boy going to school on his first day, the unhappy teen standing outside with a different woman, and her new baby. What had the caption said? *Moving in.* Russell remembered the first version of the name had been crossed out, and Nathan written above it. And then there were the articles, photocopied from the newspapers. The gay councillor who killed his wife, then killed himself.

"That was you? They were your parents?" Russell blurted.

Nathan swallowed hard and nodded.

"What *is* going on?" Freddie asked, getting increasingly annoyed.

"When I was fourteen," Nathan said, keeping his voice low, between the three of them. "My father, who had always been an abusive alcoholic, killed my mother, and then he killed himself. It was in all of the papers."

"What?" Freddie spluttered. "How did I not know this?"

"Because I never thought it would come out," Nathan said, even quieter. "The problem is, I think it is all going to come out now. The real truth, that is. I mean, it's true that he killed my mother, but he didn't kill himself."

"Nathan…"

"No, wait, I have to say this."

They both waited.

"He was a drunk. He'd always been quick to temper and even quicker with his fists. The night he killed my mum… it was the night I came out to them. To her. She said she'd tell him. Said I should go out and when I came back, she'd have made him see that everything was fine. But when I got back, he had beaten her to death."

"Jesus, Nathan," Freddie whispered.

"I couldn't help myself," Nathan said. "I loved her so much, and she was all I had. She understood me."

"What happened?" Russell asked.

"He was already paralytic," said Nathan. "So, I fixed him another whisky, but I laced it with every tablet mum had ever needed to stay sane. There were enough sleeping pills in that glass to bring down a lion. I gave it to him, told him to drink up and said everything would be fine. And then I went out for an hour. When I came back, he was dead. So, I called the police."

"But why did they say *he* was gay in the tabloids?"

"Because, at one point, when I was being interviewed, I suggested that he'd always been unhappy, that he'd been hiding his sexuality, and that my mum had once caught him with the plumber."

"Why?"

"Because I was angry. Because he used *my* coming out to kill my beautiful mother and I wanted to ruin any reputation he thought he had, even though he was already dead."

"And no one ever suspected you?"

"Of course they did—his family especially. But there was no proof, no witnesses, and I was just a kid."

"So, what happened?"

"I was fifteen. They sent me to live with his sister, Auntie Kay. She was certain he hadn't killed himself. She always suspected me. I always denied it. She blamed me anyway. I stayed a year, and then moved to London as soon as I was old enough. Because of the whole scandal, they'd already changed my name to Nathan when they'd been forced to move house because of all the publicity. I didn't want to change it again, so it stuck. I picked the surname from the first car I saw when I came out of the Tube at Piccadilly—a Bentley. I remember thinking that it was a sign. I thought 'one day that will be mine'."

"That's terrible, Nathan, but given that no one really knows, I still don't see what it has to do with Kevin," Freddie said.

"Really?" Nathan looked at him incredulously. "He was trying to blackmail me. He had got the whole story from his parents. My Auntie Kay is his mother. He's the baby in the photograph. He thought it was about time there was some payback for the family."

"So you killed him?" Freddie asked.

"No," Nathan said. "I was angry, but I told him to leave. I said I was going to call the police. I left to go and call them. I won't be threatened in my own home, especially not by anyone from that family!"

"You would have risked letting him tell everyone about your past?"

"When the package came earlier in the week, I knew it was going to come out anyway. I made the decision to ride it out. They couldn't prove it then, and they won't prove anything now. Besides, I would tell my own version in my autobiography and the scandal would only help boost sales."

"That's a hell of a risk, Nathan. What if they'd gone to the tabloids?"

"I almost assumed they would, and I couldn't do anything to stop them. All I could think of was to tell my side of the story. The abusive father, the beatings, the booze. Who wouldn't see my side?"

"Did Archie know all this?" Russell asked.

Nathan shook his head.

"No. Only Grace and Armand know the truth, and they'd never do anything to hurt me."

"The police just found the statue used to hit him in Archie's holdall. How did it get there?" Russell asked.

"Well, I don't know, do I?" Nathan snapped before looking at both of them beseechingly. Russell felt like he was telling the truth about that at least.

Russell looked across the cell to where Armand was sitting alone, head in hands, awaiting his certain fate. Had he stashed the award in Archie's bag to frame him and get him out of Nathan's life? But if so, why would he have confessed to hitting Kevin in the first place? Why not just let Archie take the blame for the whole thing?

Looking back at Nathan, it suddenly made sense. He turned to Freddie, leading him along the bars away from Nathan.

"How quickly can you get me out of here?"

"We'll have to wait until Skinner's interviewed you," Freddie replied.

"That's too long," Russell said. "Go and find Mike, he'll be with the DCI upstairs, they'll let you through if you say you're here to see him. You're going to have to persuade the DCI to let me go."

"What's going on?" Freddie asked.

"I think I know what happened, but there's something I need to check first, and I can't do it from in here."

"YOU THINK ARCHIE tossed his mate out the window? Harry Palin asked, as he and Joe looked around the study.

"God knows," Joe said. "I was pretty sure he was downstairs the whole time, but there was so much going on. I think 'mate' might be pushing it a bit, though. I mean, they didn't look too friendly earlier in the evening. It looked like they had history."

"Enough to kill him?"

Harry was busy dusting the window catch for prints, while Claire, his assistant, was scouring the floor for clues, camera slung over her shoulder. Every now and then she'd pull it round and snap a few shots of something interesting. Thorough and methodical.

"Who knows," Joe said, peering round the side of the picture to find the safe behind it pushed to.

"But," Joe said, as he eased the safe open, knowing that he was snooping. "Why would he hide the statue in his own bag? I mean, he finds the body and the statue, hauls the body out of the window, and then hides the statue in his own bag? Who would be that stupid?"

Harry shrugged. "You'd be surprised."

"*And* he wasn't the one who hit Kevin, we already know that much, so why would he risk incriminating himself, and leaving his bag open for all to see. It seems a little staged to me."

"So, the guy who confessed to hitting him. Armand, was it? Who is he again?"

"Nathan's assistant and former lover. He would basically do anything for Nathan."

"And he insists he didn't finish the job?"

Claire was on her hands and knees, shining a torch under the desk. She laid the torch on the floor and reached under the desk, squirming to get to what she'd found.

"I think he would have told me while he was busy confessing all," Joe said, lifting out the sheaf of photocopied papers and discovering the bundles of twenty-pound notes lying beneath.

"Jesus," he said. "Look at all this cash."

Harry joined him in front of the safe.

"How the other half live, huh?"

"This is where Armand found him," Joe said. "He said he thought Kevin was stealing from Nathan. But none of this looks like it's been moved. Only these papers."

He handed the sheets to Harry, and peered over his shoulder as the forensic officer leafed through them all.

"I wonder who this guy was?"

Claire shuffled further under the desk, arm outstretched.

"Aha," she said triumphantly.

"Ah, look," Joe said, lifting out the huge ream of papers that was Nathan's autobiography. "Maybe this was what he was after."

"God, I bet that's got some dirty little secrets in it," Harry said, smiling.

"This would be worth a fortune if it got out before publication date, wouldn't it?" Joe asked.

"Look," said Claire, holding up something small and pink.

"What've you got?"

"A fingernail, a falsie."

She held it out for Harry to see, before reaching for an evidence bag to put it in. Joe craned to see too. Hot pink. He'd seen that before.

"Hmm," Joe said. "That's interesting."

"What is it?" Harry looked at him.

"I know whose that is."

JOE WALKED INTO THE KITCHEN to find Giuseppe and his remaining waiters piling the last of their now clean pots and pans.

PC Riley was in the corner talking to Grace, with his notepad resting on his knee and a plate of food in his hand. When he saw Harry following Joe into the room, he stood up suddenly, trying to hide the glass of wine he was obviously halfway through.

In the process of standing up, he dropped his plate, tipping some of the food into Grace's lap. She in turn stood up, brushing the pastries and salad from her dress.

"Clever lad," Harry said quietly to Joe.

As she fussed at her dress, Grace's hot pink nails were clear to see. One missing on her index finger.

"Grace Bentley?" Harry asked. "I wonder if I might have a word?"

"I've already said everything I have to say to your colleague here," she said dismissively, with a saccharine smile for PC Riley.

"Nice nails," Joe said. "Shame you've lost one."

"The glue's just not strong enough, dear," she said, sitting back down and picking up her wine glass with a flourish and a derisive look at her remaining fake nails.

"Especially not when you're trying to lift a grown man out of a top floor window on your own," Joe said.

Now Grace spluttered her own wine all over PC Riley. They'd make a great slapstick double act.

"How dare you?" she bellowed.

Harry held up the evidence bag, her missing nail clear for all to see.

She stood up, as though about to lunge for the evidence, but Harry passed it back over his shoulder to Claire, and she wasn't going to let anyone near it.

In a move worthy of Cagney and Lacey, Grace reached into her clutch bag and pulled out a small pistol. It looked like a water pistol—it was so small, but by the way both Harry and PC Riley recoiled, it was real enough.

Giuseppe raised a defensive frying pan, gathering his remaining waiters behind him like young chicks.

"Take it easy, Grace," Joe said, stepping out from behind Harry.

Harry tried to hold him back, but Joe was one of the only people in the room who even vaguely knew Grace, and he was good at talking to people.

Grace levelled the gun at his chest.

"Get back," she said.

"Why did you do it?" Joe asked.

"I don't know what you're talking about," she said.

"So why are you waving a gun around?" asked Joe, stepping forward again.

Grace looked at the gun in her hand as though it was a surprise to see it there. It didn't help that she'd been on the champagne all night. Her lipstick was smeared, her mascara clumping. The way her hand shook made Joe worry that she might just pull the trigger if pushed too hard.

Suddenly the front door burst open, and Nathan strode in, followed by Russell and Mike, with Patty bringing up the rear.

"Grace Bentley," Nathan hollered, striding into the kitchen. "What the hell have you done?"

"You figured it out then," Russell whispered to Joe as Grace swung the gun casually around the assembled group.

"Stay back, Nathan," Joe said. And when Nathan saw the gun, he did.

"Put it down, Grace," Russell said. "It's over."

Grace's lip wobbled. Her hand wobbled. Everybody took a step back.

"Why did you do it?" Nathan asked.

She turned the gun on him.

"To protect you, you idiot. What did you think I was going to do? Just leave that boy lying on the floor for the police to find. In your office, clutching your cheque, with your bloody award at his side? They'd have hung you out to dry."

"But you *killed* him, Grace. What did you think we were going to do? Just wrap him up and put him out with the bins?"

"No, *you* killed him. And then you just left him lying there for all to see. So I had to clean up after you, as usual."

"What are you talking about? It was Armand who hit him, and he was not dead, he was unconscious, until you threw him from the window."

Grace faltered, gun dropping slightly. Joe noticed Mike edging closer. He hoped he wasn't going to try anything rash—the woman was unhinged.

"But I heard you arguing," she protested. "I heard a scuffle, and when I went to look, he was lying there. He looked dead."

"Put the gun down, Grace," Mike warned, edging closer again.

"Stay back," she said, levelling the gun at him. "Don't you come near me."

"It's over, Grace," Russell said. "Whether they arrest you tonight or tomorrow, they are going to arrest you. You killed that man."

"But I did it for you, darling," she whined, turning to Nathan beseechingly.

Mike took the opportunity to lunge for the gun while she was distracted, grabbing it with one hand as he circled his other arm around her shoulders.

The gun fired, and they all ducked. With a ping and a glassy clatter, the cherubic ice sculpture was removed of his member.

Gun secured, Mike handed it to Russell who placed it far away on the kitchen counter.

"Grace Bentley, I'm arresting you for the murder of Kevin Flint…" Mike began, and Grace's wailing moan drowned out the rest of his caution.

PC Riley finally stepped up and helped Mike restrain her, as Nathan slumped back into the armchair in the corner.

Joe felt a little sorry for him—his nearest and dearest had all thought they were protecting him, and now, aside from landing themselves in particularly hot water, they had also all but guaranteed his reputation would be ruined forever.

WITH GRACE DISPATCHED in a squad car, Harry Palin stood beside Joe on the pavement watched the body bag being loaded into the back of the van. Doors slammed, Claire gave him a nod and climbed aboard. Harry looked across at Joe.

"That offer's still open you know?" he said, with a wry smile. "I could do with a bright mind on the team."

"I told you," Joe said. "I'm no good at science."

"The science I can teach," Harry said. "It's the rest of the package that I struggle to find. At least think about it."

"I will," Joe said. And he meant it.

Harry headed for the van, and Joe went back inside to join the others. Patty handed Nathan a shot of vodka, while Giuseppe and the waiters finally filed out with quiet goodbyes and solemn faces.

Joe gave Mike a quick squeeze, standing back to look at the fresh bruise that had bloomed across his face.

"And what happened to you?"

"Skinner," Mike began.

"I'm going to kill him," Joe said angrily.

"Oh, I think he's suffering enough right now," Mike smiled. "I think the boss may be giving him his P45 for Christmas."

"What exactly did you say to him to get him to hit you?" Russell asked. Mike smiled.

"I told him I was going to screw him like he'd never been screwed before."

They all laughed.

"What?" Mike said, all fake innocence. "It wasn't a lie, was it?"

4.

THE RED LION was officially closed for Christmas day but, inside, the jukebox was playing all the Christmas classics and the party spirit was high.

"Pass the spuds," Patty said, stretching her hand out over the table towards Russell.

The whole gang were there, gathered around a long table in the middle of the bar. Ron and his beloved Jean had pushed the boat out with Christmas dinner and all the trimmings. Russell, Freddie, Joe and Mike had provided the crackers and silly hats, and Patty had revealed the haul of booze and drugs she'd liberated from poor Nathan's house.

In the end, they'd left Nathan drowning his sorrows, alone—probably for the first time in years. His two closest friends and confidantes had both thought they were protecting him when, in fact, they had made everything worse.

His lover, Archie, had lied to him about his past and about his motives, and having revealed himself to be little more than a con artist, he had been left to answer some of the police's questions about his and Kevin's previous exploits.

Rather stoically, Nathan had suggested he needed to rewrite the ending of his autobiography to get all of this out in the open. Kevin's parents—Nathan's uncle and aunt—would doubtless be making their allegations about his past very public once they found out where their son had been when he'd been killed. That toxic family would continue to haunt poor Nathan for the rest of his life.

Russell smiled at Joe across the table. It may not be as glamorous as Nathan's place, but at least this was home. Friends, good food, and laughter. Looking around the table at all of them, he realised that this was better than any family he'd ever known.

"Happy Christmas, everyone," Russell said, raising his glass.

The returning toast was loud, raucous and full of love.

BEFORE YOU GO

Dear Reader,

Thank you for my Soho Noir series. I do hope you enjoyed it.

If you did, please leave a review in the place you bought the book from or on Goodreads, or Amazon.

Reviews help authors like me to make more sales, and break through the barriers to get our work seen. It's the best gift you can possibly give.

Thanks again for reading.

Yours,
T.S. Hunter

ABOUT THE AUTHOR

Claiming to be at least half-Welsh, T.S. Hunter lived in South Wales for much of his latter teens, moving to London as soon as confidence and finances allowed. He never looked back.

He has variously been a teacher, a cocktail waiter, a podium dancer and a removal man, but his passion for writing has been the only constant.

He's a confident and engaging speaker and guest, who is as passionate about writing and storytelling as he is about promoting mainstream LGBT fiction.

He now lives with his husband in the country, and is active on social media as @TSHunter5.